❧ PRAISE FOR *The Doors You Mark Are Your Own* ❧

"*The Doors You Mark Are Your Own* is a dystopian masterpiece."

—KYLE MINOR, AUTHOR OF *Praying Drunk*
AND *In the Devil's Territory*

"*The Doors You Mark Are Your Own* is one of those intriguing,
compelling books that defy description, or, the impact is a reflection
of keen imagination, surprises, a new vision, but yet one that is rock-
ribbed intriguing. All I can say is that you should read this and
enjoy it, since it is a rare thing, a very rare thing indeed, when
something new comes into the world."

—CRAIG NOVA, AUTHOR OF *Wetware* AND *The Good Son*

"*The Doors You Mark Are Your Own* is an expansive tale of good
and evil, of friendship and loyalty, of fear and courage. A literary
dystopia that is both an elegant and engrossing read."

—DAMIEN ANGELICA WALTERS, AUTHOR OF *Sing Me Your Scars*

"A richly imagined post-apocalyptic Russia."

—*BOOKLIST*

"*The Doors You Mark Are Your Own* is a stunning and ambitious
literary speculative fiction novel that should be read by all who enjoy
reading well written fiction, because it's one of the best, biggest
and most literary novels of its kind. It's an unforgettable vision of a
dystopian and post-apocalyptic world that is ravaged by a horrible
disease and social unrest."

—*RISINGSHADOW*

THE D

OORS

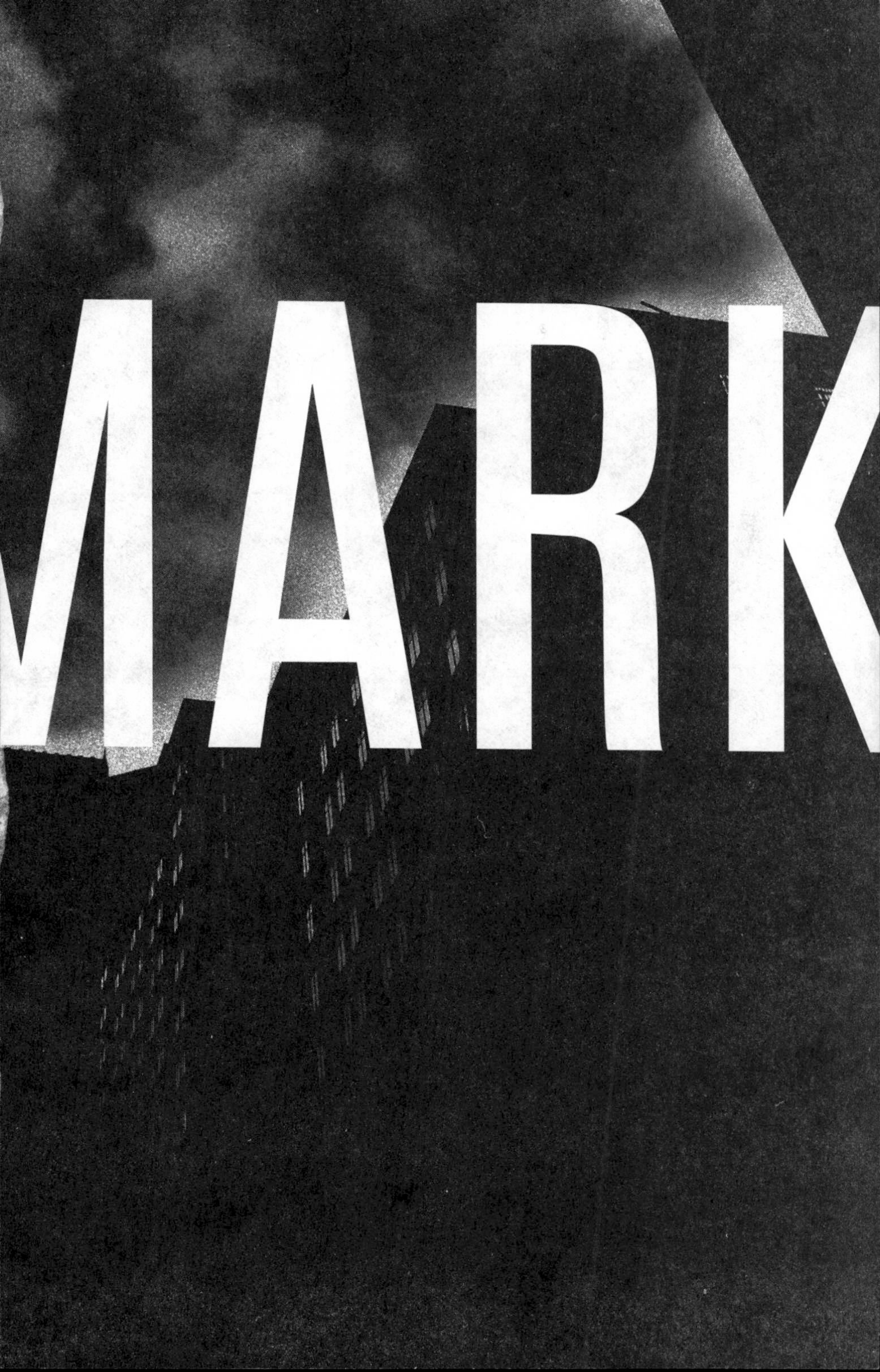
MARK

YOUR

OWN

A JOSHUA CITY NOVEL

ALEKSANDR TUVIM

TRANSLATED BY OKLA ELLIOTT
AND RAUL CLEMENT

PUBLISHED BY DARK HOUSE PRESS, AN IMPRINT OF CURBSIDE SPLENDOR
PUBLISHING, INC., CHICAGO, ILLINOIS IN 2015.

FIRST EDITION
COPYRIGHT © 2015 BY OKLA ELLIOTT AND RAUL CLEMENT
LIBRARY OF CONGRESS CONTROL NUMBER: 2015935630

ISBN 978-1-940430-20-1
EDITED BY JACOB KNABB
COVER ART BY GEORGE C. CATRONIS
JOSHUA CITY LOGO BY LUKE SPOONER
BAIKAL REGION MAP BY GABRIEL HURIER
BOOK DESIGN BY ALBAN FISCHER

MANUFACTURED IN THE UNITED STATES OF AMERICA.

WWW.THEDARKHOUSEPRESS.COM
WWW.CURBSIDESPLENDOR.COM

"The writer is the engineer of the human soul."

—BEFORE-TIME SAYING, SOURCE UNKNOWN

The Baikal Region

Larki Island

Baikal Sea

Mountains

Joshua City

Baikyong-do

al-Khuzir

New Kolyma

Kihl Mihnor

Gaal-Inhoff
Prison Outpost

R Uda

Baikalingrad

Ulan-Ude

R Selenga

Kazhstan

LIST OF PRINCIPLE CHARACTERS

Nikolas Kovalski—medikal skolar at Joshua University; our hero

Adrian Talbot—medikal skolar at Joshua University on skolarship; Nikolas's roommate, friend, and intellectual antipode

Doktor Brandt—professor at Joshua University; Nikolas's research advisor; a fool with shameful coattails

Elias Kreutzer—legal skolar at Joshua University; smarter and better than Nikolas likes to admit

Mouse/Naomi Huvsky—comparative philology skolar at Joshua University; "Mouse" becomes the worst misnomer in Joshuan history (just you wait, Esteemed Reader)

Sarah Vilosopov—engineering skolar at Joshua University; one of the first women admitted to the engineering program

Endre Talisin Pinyak III—engineering skolar at Joshua University; ticket inspektor for the Joshua City Rail System

Alarik Schedrin—steelworker; heavy drinker; master quilter

Katyana Steingart—masked prostitute from the city of Baikalingrad; her future and the future of Joshua City are tied in important ways

Yung-jin/Yu—sociolinguistics skolar at Joshua University; émigré from Baikyong-do; twin brother of Yi-Jun/Yi

Yi-jun/Yi—sociolinguistics skolar at Joshua University; émigré from Baikyong-do; twin brother of Yung-jin/Yu

Neil Martin—successful Silverville film direktor

Vivian Scott—famous Silverville aktress; star of many films by Neil Martin; wife of Abraham Kocznik

Abraham Kocznik—Joshua City's foremost engineer; husband of Vivian Scott

Lydia Kocznik—daughter of Abraham and Vivian

Jürgen Moritz—engineer at Ministrie of Technology; Abraham Kocznik's closest friend and frequent collaborator

Ariah Prusakova—patient in New Kolyma Laborers Hospital

Marcik Kovalski—private in Baikal Guard; brother of Nikolas; writes to his mother daily; (oh, there's more . . .)

Fredrik Vore—private in Baikal Guard; Marcik's friend and bunkmate; his talents for warfare are only matched by his love for taffy

Samir Hosani—artillery gunner in Baikal Guard; émigré from Kahzstan

Yosef Parlov/Yoyo—artillery gunner in Baikal Guard; (you know the type—large, lovable, loyal)

Mayor William Adams—mayor of Joshua City; self-proclaimed owner of a grand destiny

Pierre Kabot—personal aide to Mayor Adams

Hannah Kaplani—ambassador from Baikalingrad; ally to the great and illustrious Mayor Adams

The Tongue—ambassador from Baikyong-do; unimpressed by Mayor Adams; speaks every known language without flaw

Ambassador Kalukar—ambassador from Ulan-Ude; a solid man, supporting his culture and his Khan with all of his being

The Great Khan—the leader of Ulan-Ude, hallowed be his name; a killer of many enemies; his skin-trophies are spectacular

Uferth—"I am the greatest warrior and the greatest lover the Seven Cities have ever known. The Great Khan himself praises me and offers me his ale-maids!"

Anwym Laikan—influential psychoanalyst; some consider her the greatest genius to have ever lived, some consider her a charlatan

Slug—"Slug love!"

Olgar Fakuth—kommandant-warden of Gaal-Inhoff Prison Outpost

Oberlieutenant Lotar/Face—second-in-kommand to Olgar Fakuth

Messenger—band of nomadic mercenaries; referred to as "Messenger" both in singular and plural; from the legendary eighth city; no one has seen Messenger defeated in battle

A NOTE ON THE TRANSLATION

The DIFFICULTIES in translating this novel (or novel-history, as its author Aleksandr Tuvim calls it) were manifold. To begin with, Tuvim wrote the bulk of it in Slovnik—the lingua franca (or lingua joshua, if you will) of the Seven Cities and their environs. We were able to decode the language through analysis of component parts, our knowledge of other Slavik languages, general principles guiding the evolution of languages, and a little help from linguist friends (particularly Kristofer Higgins and Patricia McLloyd) here at the recently rebuilt University of Illinois.

But the usual difficulties of translating a dead language were not our only obstacles. In addition to Slovnik, Tuvim employs several other languages—most notably Ularik, the language of Ulan-Ude, but also Kazhmiri from the south and Hangul from the east. The same process of decoding applied to these languages.

Additionally, among the many cultures that converged on the Baikal region, there were ethnic groups from Before-Time Europe and Before-Time Asia, as well as others. During the era of Tuvim's story, it had become fashionable among the elite of Joshua City to take on names from these dead cultures. This is seen most clearly in the adoption (by motion-film stars and politicians mostly) of Anglo and Teutonic names: Neil Martin, General Malcolm Schmidt (though he had his own different reasons), and Vivian Scott. Combine this with the Before-Time origins *of names such as Abraham Kocznik and Adrian Talbot, and you have a picture of just how onerous a process this translation was.*

In the end, we decided it was not enough to decipher Tuvim's seminal work from the comfort of our akademic confines. While there is a small body of skolarly research on Baikal in the current Federated States of America, it is often speculative, as primary sources are hard to come by. As the reader will know, post-Calamity reconstruction took longer in our part of the world, and it was not until recently, historically speaking, that an adequate archival system was reestablished. For these reasons, as well as personal ones best not delved into here, we elected to visit Baikal ourselves, hoping to track down key original documents and to gain a firsthand sense of the culture and language. The region of Baikal and its language families have undergone notable changes since Tuvim wrote this work of Joshuan novel-history and the one that follows it, The Engineer of Souls. Nevertheless, many useful traces remain.

We'll spare the reader the bulk of our travails as we journeyed to Joshua City (or what is left of it). Our personal narrative is not relevant here. It is worth noting, however, that intercontinental travel being what it is in this day and age, our research was limited by concerns of budget and time. You no doubt have heard legends about the ease with which our ancestors travelled before The Great Calamity—zipping along in aeroplanes nearly as large as ocean liners or driving down well-paved superways. Hearing these tales, we felt a twinge of professional jealousy, not because of the personal discomfort we would have been spared, but because of all the additional research we could have done. The Librarie of the Sun is still standing in Al-Khuzir, but sadly we were never able to grace its doors. And once we arrived in Joshua City, we found a political, social, and religious climate that none of our reading had prepared us for—but that, as they say, is a story for a different time. Perhaps we will set it in print someday.

A final note: as with any work of translation, an exact rendering is impossible. We've elected to translate chiefly into New High American, this being the default language of literature in our country. However, sometimes we have opted for the more casual New Middle American, hoping to mimic the differences in levels of formality in Tuvim's own writing, as he attempts to channel the language and thoughts of characters from all strata of his society.

Given these, our best efforts, we hope that what emerges is a reasonably clear interpretation of Tuvim's work. It is our sincere wish that as the Federated States of America rebuild their other institutions of higher learning, this text will be taught as a cautionary tale, historical artifact, and literary work of the highest artistry.

—O.E. & R.C.

A PROLOGUE OF SORTS

(OR HOW THIS MOSTLY TRUE HISTORY CAME TO BE WRITTEN)

UNTIL TWO YEARS AGO, I had never met General Schmidt, though he has had perhaps more impact on my life than anyone else. He has taken away my life several times and returned it to me in various states of disrepair. The first time was the mock execution. For a few moments on a beautiful spring morning, I thought I would be put to death by a firing squad. The Guardsmen led us handcuffed and ankle-bound through a courtyard and lined us up along a sun-bleached wall. They even went so far as to raise their rifles and train them on us. We emitted little squeaks of fear and louder pleas for mercy, and many of us soiled our prison uniforms.

Then came the last-minute "reprieve"—I put the word in quotes because it had been planned all along. Why would they do such a thing? To put the fear of God in us, they said, though I saw no god in that sunny courtyard, experienced no conversion under the gun. In a sense, that first time my life was given back to me was an illusion, since they had never planned on taking it; but they could have, and I came to peace with being dead as I pressed my back against that rough rock wall, and so I do count it.

The second time my life was given back to me was after I had spent ten years in a work camp watching my fellow Joshuans drop dead from harsh labor and hunger. Only when I was old and harmless did Schmidt grant me amnesty. (Do not confuse amnesty with amnesia, Esteemed Reader. I have forgotten nothing.) Freeing me would be seen as an act of mercy, not one of weakness. How else to explain Schmidt's unexpected softening?

I was offered my former position as head of the Akademie of the Literary Arts, a position I declined, having no desire to dirty my hands with the smut of institutional affiliation. All this is not to say I had suffered any *correction* in my way of thinking; I had merely decided to be more prudent. I took a little room above a butcher shop with its own in-house eatery. Some afternoons I walked my old bones down the rickety staircase for a sandwich of tough and tasteless corned beef, but mostly I stayed in the room and wrote—pages upon pages I intended to show to no one. If they were distributed, it would be after my death.

And, for unknowable reasons, my writing now took the form of poetry exclusively—very free, without self-consciousness—unlike my earlier structured and polemical writings, writings that led to my being sent off to the camps in the first place.

One morning, the landlady came to the door. Though I could not see her face because of the porcelain mask she wore, I could tell by the way she clutched the door jamb that something was wrong. She was one of the few émigrés from Baikalingrad left in the city. One used to see masked men and women in the street, running fish shops and bakeries, and even in high levels of government. But that was under the previous regime.

I had been looking over my recent poems, had them sprawled over my desk to assess the full spread of things. I wasn't thinking of putting together a new book, though without realizing it, the poems were taking such a shape.

When the landlady knocked on my door, I was thinking wistfully back to the appearance of my first novel, all the adoration and acclaim that was poured upon my youthful head. Perhaps I had been too young, only twenty-five years old, to be granted such prominence. Perhaps that early rise to fame was the dramatic prelude to my eventual fall and my current pathetic state.

"Mr. Tuvim, sir," she said. "There are some men . . . "

Before she could finish, two Baikal Guardsmen in full combat gear strode into the room. They began knocking things about. I looked at the papers on my desk. So they had finally come. In a way, it was a relief; I had lived in fear of going back to the camps since my release. I had told myself that if they sent me back, I would commit suicide, an act I disapprove of in the young because it lacks a sense of proportion: we are dead for an eternity; whatever we suffer is only momentary. But I had maybe ten more decrepit years to live. I hoped to spend them in some small comfort. If they were not going to allow me that, I might as well get started with oblivion.

But my papers did not interest them. They checked drawers, tossed the mattress, rummaged through my closet.

"All clear?" asked one Guardsman.

"Clear," answered the other.

Satisfied, they left the room. A moment later, General Schmidt entered.

Of course I recognized him. His face was in *The Joshua Harbinger* almost every morning for some reason or another. One day, he will no doubt be immortalized on our currency. That moment might come sooner than later; I did not expect him, a military man nearly twenty years younger than I am, to look so haggard and near death. I had heard that horrible things had happened to him as a prisoner of war and later during the uprising he led against his brother—more horrible than anything that happened to me, to be truthful—but I assumed the details were exaggerated (or outright falsified) for propaganda purposes. Nothing enthralls the masses more than a battered war hero.

He lowered himself with difficulty into the chair. He smiled. It wasn't the arrogant smile you might expect. There was a sadness to it. A fatigue. He clutched an official-looking sheaf of papers to his chest.

"To think I was so afraid of you," he said, loading his voice up with fraternity and benign warmth.

I felt a rush of empathy for this thwarted lion. But I checked myself. Despite his physical frailness, he could still hurt me.

"I want to let you know it wasn't personal," he said.

He must have registered my confusion. He explained, "I believed at the time that the expectations of the citizenry should be carefully managed. We were living in a time of great want."

Some of us were, I thought.

"And afterward . . . afterward, I was too busy holding everything together," Schmidt said. "For that I apologize."

He rearranged his documents, putting them in neater order.

"I have a proposal," Schmidt continued. "I know you have little reason to trust me. And even less to do me any favors. But I think this might interest you."

He reached with visible pain into his jacket pocket and pulled out a packet of cigarettes.

"May I?" It was not quite a question.

I abhor cigarette smoke. It reminds me of the camps, where so much emphasis was placed on this useless indulgence—a way to stay sane, I suppose. But I'd seen more knife fights break out over cigarettes than bread. Cowardly rabbit that I'd become, I nodded for Schmidt to light up.

As he smoked, he moved the pages on the table around, finally picking up one of my poems. He read through it slowly, pursing his lips in concentration. At last, he set the poem down.

"Nice to see you are still writing," he said.

"It's just something I do," I said. "I've shown no one."

He pushed my comment aside with a slow wave of his hand. "That's the purpose of my visit, in fact," he said. "I want you to write a history of Joshua City."

I should have seen something like this coming, especially after I had turned down the Akademie position. It was yet another assertion of his dominance over me. I would be made his propagandist. Was there any way to refuse?

"I will give you full access to our archives, of course."

"The Joshua University Librarie?" No offer could have been more useless.

Schmidt snorted. "What can be found there? I mean the archives at the Ministrie of Intelligence. And the Ministries of Defense, Justice, and Technology. All the ministries, in fact. *My* archives."

He thrust his sheaf of papers at me. "Here. A sample."

※ ※ ※

Ministrie of Intelligence, Intelligence Report–19 October:

- Intelligence Officer ███████ has successfully infiltrated inner circle of Akademie of the Literary Arts and established himself as co-conspirator

- I.O. ██████ has provided substantial proof, both through eye-witness testimony and in document form, of distribution of pamphlet of seditious and inflammatory nature on the subject of "water-rights." He has given evidence of ███████████████████████ ██████████████████, including but not limited to ███████████ ███████████

- ███████ has detailed organizational structure to conspiratorial circle, with Aleksandr Tuvim, chairperson of Akademie of Literary Arts and author of several previous documents falling under the scrutiny of Ministrie of Intelligence Article 7-A, as head or "leader" of circle. ██████████████████████████████████ ██████████████████████████████████████ ██████████████████████████████████████ ███████████

- ███████ has further indicated his belief that Aleksandr Tuvim is the author, both in content and wording, of the aforementioned seditious pamphlet

Conclusions:

- After careful review of the evidence presented by I.O. ████████, a specially appointed ██ ████████████████████████████ has concluded that the acts of this circle qualify as treasonous and are subject to appropriate sanctions
- These sanctions will vary in degree in accordance to level of involvement in conspiracy, Aleksandr Tuvim being established as the head of conspiracy

※ ※ ※

Despite the betrayal of ████████[1] our essential mission had succeeded. The pamphlet was distributed widely, and I like to believe it had its small role in the mass uprisings that followed. I never learned who ████████ was. I could not imagine that any of them would do such a thing—still cannot imagine it—but clearly one of them had. I know I should forgive him; so many years have passed, and besides, who knows what circumstances drove him to his actions? But I cannot. In some ways, his crimes against me were worse than Schmidt's, those closest to you having the deepest power to wound.

"You understand that we had to take certain...precautions," Schmidt said.

"Will similar precautions be taken with this history you want me to write? Will my work be subject to..." pausing and looking at the redacted document for effect, "ministrie approval?"

"They're not all like that," he said.

He had not answered my question, but I didn't press the matter. I flipped the page and stopped.

"These are real?"

"Yes, those are the journals of Nikolas Kovalski," he said.

---

[1] Translators' Note: During our research in the Baikal region, we combed the archives as thoroughly as our talents allowed, but we were unable to determine who the informant was.

"Unedited?"

"Untouched," he said, and his spine stiffened with soldierly pride, as if his honor were staked on this and this alone. "Let us say . . . for sentimental reasons."

The journal pages were handwritten in small precise script.

※ ※ ※

22 of September

Drinking blackroot at The Samovar, thinking of work and the future. The future of my work, such as it is . . . ventricle rhythm . . . bacterial spread in nekrotic lesions . . . Blood. I need to think more about blood . . . As Doktor Brandt likes to say: blood is the water in the earth of the body . . . (A poetic phrasing he no doubt borrowed from someone with a more literary bent.)

※ ※ ※

This was from when Nikolas Kovalski was still a medikal student. I flipped forward several pages.

※ ※ ※

The Guardsmen led me through the holding facility, my arms behind my back. I took in everything: the loose chain of keys around a guard's belt; the locking mechanism of the doors; the number and types of prisoners. I used the methods of observation Messenger had taught me. Many of the prisoners appeared healthy and strong. One even looked at me hopefully, as if asking me to free him so he could join our cause. I added him to my mental inventory. I was learning much of use for later.

They pushed me into a holding cell. The door slammed shut. High-wattage bulbs were trained at my eyes. The Guardsmen moved in on me, their implied violence a precursor to their questions.

Half an hour later, I was numb to the pain. No, that's not quite right. I had retreated into that deep place, the place that Messenger had shown me. Pain was a mere theory, something someone was feeling somewhere, not me here and now. As they struck me with stones wrapped in wet cloth, I repeated my situational mantra.

"Schmidt," I said. This was the mantra I had chosen for the occasion. It would keep me on my task.

They approached with the live wires. I decided again to let them do it, finding a yet deeper place. How far would I let them go? How much could I endure? Part of me was curious where my limits lay. I knew I was not anywhere near the level of Messenger, but I felt a pervasive calm, did not fear these men in the least. I went even deeper.

"Schm-idt," I managed, as my body convulsed.

※ ※ ※

I set down the pages and willed myself to meet the gaze of this still powerful man. Perhaps he was serious after all? Perhaps this wasn't some elaborate trap?

"But not just this," Schmidt said. "I want the whole history. The true history. Joshua City as it used to be."

He extended his hand, signaling the meeting was over. His handshake was powerful.

"You are the writer," he said. "You will make shape and meaning of it. But it won't be *my* story. It will be all of ours."

And with that, our deal was done.

CHAPTER ONE

QUESTIONS AND ANSWERS

1.

THAT MORNING, at an unnaturally early hour, Nikolas Kovalski's new roommate called to say he would be arriving by the five o'eve train. He spoke so softly Nikolas could barely hear him on the dormitory house telefone.

"I don't have many things," he said, as though he were committing some terrible imposition by needing a place to live.

Nikolas couldn't fall back to sleep, so he went to The Samovar. He had just purchased his medikal texts for the semester and wanted to familiarize himself with the material. As Nikolas entered the teahouse, he saw a municipal information-paper pinned to the announcement board.

MAYOR ADAMS—TITUS HALL, 7 O'EVE, 24 OF SEPTEMBER

MAYOR ADAMS TO ADDRESS THE STATE OF JOSHUA CITY, HIS TIME

AT JOSHUA UNIVERSITY, AND SUNDRY MATTERS

QUESTION AND ANSWER SESSION TO FOLLOW

FREE ADMISSION

Nikolas knew all about the state of Joshua City, thank you very much. He ripped the paper off the wall. The teahouse was nearly empty, most of the skolars having not arrived on campus yet. In the back, two young university skolars hunched seriously over a wooden board, deep in a game of Seven Cities.

Nikolas and his brother Marcik used to play the game as children. Though Marcik often cheated, sometimes even putting "dead soldiers" back on the board, he invariably lost. One time he threw a tantrum, flinging the pieces across the room. A small rectangular section representing Joshua City's Outer Wall struck Nikolas in the face and he decided to let Marcik win for once.

He left the flank of his army open for three turns before Marcik finally noticed. Nikolas had almost lost the willpower and kindness to lose when Marcik made the devastating attack from which Nikolas would not be able to recover, even if he had wanted to.

"I can't believe you were so stupid," Marcik said. "There are girl-children who would make better soldiers than you."

"You played well, brother. Good win."

"Let's go again. I've figured out how to beat you now."

Marcik's gloating was insufferable, and Nikolas wanted to crush him in the next game. But if he did that, then what was the purpose of allowing him to win in the first place? Nikolas refused to play another game, which Marcik took as an act of cowardice, an ultimate admission of defeat.

At his favorite corner table in The Samovar, Nikolas made an orderly stack of his books and looked around for familiar faces. He wouldn't have admitted it to anyone, but it was good to be back. Even the bad art on the walls—done in the style of Baikyong-do, or some first year art skolar's approximation of it—was a comfort. One piece, on the wall beside his table, was fairly compelling. Carved in wood, and colored in with delicate shades of lavender, frosted mint, and seashell, it showed a frothy sea, waves higher than any on Baikal, a half-naked woman locked in the many snakelike arms of a vast sea creature. The woman was being ravished—or, to put it more crudely, raped. The picture appealed to some perverse part of Nikolas; he liked that anyone who looked in his direction would also have to take in such a scene.

He ordered a samovar of blackroot tea from the new girl at the counter. Blackroot tea was good for concentrating the mind, especially useful when he studied or wrote in his journal. The girl held out her hand. She had long ropy braids with snakeskin woven into them in the Ulani style, though judging by her accent, she was a native Joshuan. He gave her the money. She counted it and shook her head.

"One dram more."

Nikolas rummaged in his empty pocket. "I didn't realize you'd raised the price."

"New price starting this semester." Her hand was still open. "It's the water shortage."

"All right then," he said, "look at it this way. You read *The Joshua Harbinger*, don't you? Why is there a water shortage?"

"Because the water has been tainted?" Her voice lifted at the end, as if he had asked a trick question.

"And that causes the nekrosis, right? So what if someone could cure that nekrosis? The water wouldn't be tainted anymore then, would it? It would be pure-baikal."

"I guess so," she said.

"And then we wouldn't have to go to war. Isn't that so? And if we didn't have to go to war, lives would be saved. So that would make the person who cured the nekrosis a kind of hero." He paused to let his words sink in. "I'm saying that you could be a hero."

"I don't follow." She was smiling just a touch now.

"See my books over there?" he said. "I'm working on a cure for nekrosis. I need blackroot tea to think. Therefore, by giving me more water you increase my chances of saving the lives of thousands."

She blew air out from between her pierced lips. "If it's that important to you, I'll give you the old price, but don't try selling me some herd-shit story about heroes and saving thousands of lives."

Back at his table, Nikolas sipped his hard-won tea. He opened a textbook, *Experimental Kardiology*. He usually loved this beginning-of-the-semester process of delving into new material, but now he looked at the diagrams of hearts with mounting impatience. He read on, as the book explained the history of heart surgery and the advancements in the field.

"Kardiologists at Joshua Hospital performed the first successful triple bypass surgery recently. But in some more advanced cases, a bypass is not enough. Then the only thing that will keep a patient alive is a donor heart. Though a successful heart transplant has yet to be done, the hope is that such procedures will one day become commonplace."

Nikolas shut the book. It wasn't that he had no interest in kardiology, just that it was secondary to his real interest: nekrosis. He hadn't precisely lied to the girl at the counter—he still planned to study nekrosis, one way or another—but it seemed like it might be more difficult than he first thought.

※ ※ ※

The instructor of Experimental Kardiology was Doktor Brandt. Since Nikolas's arrival at Joshua University, Brandt had been his benefactor and mentor. He had been supportive, enthusiastic even, about Nikolas's nekrosis research. He had even helped arrange a summer fellowship to visit the infirmaries of Joshua City and study nekrotic patients. Brandt had hinted that the summer fellowship might lead to more permanent funding. But when they reconvened at the beginning of the semester Brandt informed him that there would be no more money for nekrosis research. They would be moving on to experimental kardiology.

"So, they didn't want anything to do with nekrosis," Nikolas surmised. "I imagine it's become politically messy."

"Oh, I doubt it had anything to do with that," Brandt said. "With the war an inevitability, there's only so much funding to go around. In these times they tend to focus on the more essential projects. And there are great breakthroughs to be made, ones that might save lives, Nikolas. Just imagine. We could perform the first live heart transplant."

But whose lives would be saved? The poor? No, a transplant would cost a fortune. And there would be a waiting list for viable patients—

and it wouldn't be the poor who had friends powerful enough to move them to the top of that list.

Meanwhile, nekrosis cases would continue to mount in the areas of the city with inadequate filtration—in other words, the poorest distrikts. Of course the filtering systems in the rich distrikts of Joshua City had been upgraded immediately. Nikolas had not heard of one case of nekrosis in Silverville.

"And your work in nekrosis can add to your contributions here," Brandt continued. "Your newfound expertise in hematology due to your work with nekrosis will of course prove invaluable when dealing with heart patients."

Brandt shuffled some papers about. Nikolas lingered, hoping still.

"I look forward to seeing you on the first day of class, Nikolas. You elevate the level of discourse wherever you go."

Realizing he had been dismissed, Nikolas rose slowly and left with a quiet *thank you*.

※ ※ ※

The girl was wiping glasses now. Nikolas opened his journal, trying to seem profound, as he assumed women preferred. He thumbed the smooth blue leather of the journal he had spent too much money on. He wrote meaningful things, and kept writing even after it stopped having meaning.

The girl came over to his table. She leaned against the back of the chair opposite his and wound one of the snakeskin braids around her finger, let it fall.

"I see an inconsistency, however," she said. "In your theory from earlier."

"What's that?"

"By taking water at a cheaper price, aren't you part of the problem? Aren't you pushing us toward the very war you're trying to stop?"

"Hmmm..." Nikolas drummed the tip of his pen against his teeth, playing at deep contemplation. "What's your name?"

"Leni."

"A very good point, Leni. And a good name." Her shirt seemed to have lost a button or two. "Have you heard of the utility principle, Leni?"

"I imagine you'll instruct me."

"The utility principle says that small wrongs are justifiable in the service of the greater good. I'm only thinking about the greater good here." He gave a little smile, letting her know he only half-believed what he was saying.

"So noble."

"Oh, I'm capable of *any number* of small wrongs," Nikolas said with a wink in his voice.

"Well, good luck with your research," Leni said and went back to her work.

※ ※ ※

A few hours later, still reading *Experimental Kardiology*, Nikolas wondered if perhaps she were not right. Did he live his life a little too conveniently, believing one way and acting another? He couldn't concentrate. It wasn't just that every time he looked up she was watching him, her eyes darting away from his slyly, and it wasn't just the knowledge of her dormitory telefone number on a folded slip of paper in his pocket. He decided to pack it in for the day, get well and drunk.

As he gathered his books, the crumpled municipal information-paper fluttered to the floor. He should throw it in the waste bin where it belonged. But as he bent down to retrieve the paper, he had a different thought.

24 of September. Less than a month from now.

Question and answer session to follow.

He could think of a few questions worth asking.

※ ※ ※

From the Journals of Nikolas Kovalski:

28 of August

How much can I learn here? Working for Brandt could be good for me. But do I want kardiology to be my focus? Am I changing my interests to please him? No. Not really. As he pointed out, don't all these issues interconnect? But still . . .

Nekrosis is clearly the most pressing issue.

Query: Is nekrosis caused microbially or chemically?

Query: Is nekrosis the same disease called "flesh-rot" in the *Book of the Before-Time*?

I'd always believed flesh-rot to be, like so much of that compendium of nonsense, mere mythology. However, the similarities seem too striking to dismiss—that is, if the descriptions from that book are to be believed. And don't most historical skolars agree that some of the book is rooted in fact? If so, why has the disease been dormant for so many generations?

Query: Is this possibly a new strain?

If so, what if one could get access to the old strain? Would that prove fruitful for finding a cure? But so little is known about generational mutation in microbes that even if the old strain were found, it would still be a monumental undertaking to develop a vaccine.

But Brandt is probably right. I should not focus on a problem for which there is no funding or political traction—though why do anything else?

And look at that girl over there. A girl I hope thinks of me as an object of desire. Aren't we all objects, made more beautiful by our actions?

Speaking of actions, what I am doing is meaningful. Will be. Must be. I will find a way.

2.

BY THE TIME Adrian Talbot arrived at Joshua University, carrying a worn-out suitcase, Nikolas was already back in his dormitory room, engaged in one of his favorite activities—pacing in front of the window, looking down on the courtyard, and judging the passers-by. This was especially pleasant at the start of a new semester. A clueless couple walked beneath him, easy specimens. The boy would join the Barons Club and the girl would try out for the Dames of Joshua City but would be rejected; and their love would not survive this social gap. Too obvious. What about that young man there? His brow was weighted down with confusion, a good sign. Anyone who walks with a confused look on his face is thinking. Across the courtyard several students tossed a ball amongst themselves in a game Nikolas did not recognize. Were they happy? Nikolas half-hoped they were not.

At first sight, he did not think much of Adrian, though he knew immediately that he was seeing his new roommate. At least he would be an improvement over the one from last year. Tom Astor had been the typical Joshua University student, brash and pampered, intent on advancing through the ranks of a ministrie as fast as possible. And due to Tom's family connections, which he liked to remind Nikolas of at every opportunity, he would have a solid start. Nikolas was unsurprised when Tom told him he had requested a change of rooms. He was going to live in the Delta-Vasser Club, a prestigious society made up of the sons of ministers, water-barons, and university provosts. ("You understand, I'm sure," Tom said. "These people can help me. You have to play the part.") But anyone could tell Adrian was a skolarship student. It was not just his clothing, but also the unsure way he stood on the steps of William Adams Hall—a building named after the father of the current mayor, who had been one of the richest men in Joshuan history. Adrian was pale and thin, with shoulders that caved beneath his peacoat. He struggled to carry his suitcase up the steps.

Semya, the concierge of the dormitory, an honorably egalitarian man, rushed out to help Adrian. He grabbed the suitcase and led Adrian inside.

※　※　※

The concierge took Adrian's suitcase into a dark back room. The casualness with which he did this let Adrian know that it was a routine procedure, but nonetheless, Adrian was nervous to see all his worldly possessions taken from him. That bag contained everything important to him—everything he had brought from St. Ignatius's Home for Boys—and should it go missing, he could not afford to replace it. He had no one to turn to, he knew, but he also knew that this did not entitle him to any special treatment. The matter out of his hands, Adrian waited for the concierge to return to the sign-in desk.

"Don't worry about your bag," the concierge said. "We check every bag for contraband."

"Oh, I would never do anything like that," Adrian said.

"Calm down, calm down. I'm certain we have nothing to worry about from you."

Adrian followed the concierge upstairs, passing identical doors with noteboards bearing innocuous greetings, until he stopped in front of a door reading:

ATTENTION ALL: SPARE ME YOUR EMPTY DISPLAYS OF

NEIGHBORLINESS. PEDDLE YOUR FLIMSY OFFERINGS ELSEWHERE.

The letters were large and angry, as if their author had hoped to make the paper bleed.

"That's just Nikolas's way," the concierge said. "I'm sure you'll get along wonderfully."

The concierge knocked—no answer. He turned the knob and the door swung open. Nikolas was sitting on his bed, reading an enormous book. He did not bother to look up.

"I'll bring your bag up presently," the concierge said. "Be nice to this one," he said to Nikolas and walked back down the hallway.

"I'm Adrian."

"Shut the door, please."

※ ※ ※

Nikolas continued looking at his experimental kardiology book, processing some third of the words he read, letting Adrian know he was not worthy of attention. He enjoyed Adrian's thumbing of the worn wooden beads on his necklace. After perhaps ten minutes of this, Semya brought up Adrian's bag.

Adrian opened his suitcase and painstakingly organized his possessions, trying not to offend his new roommate. He had a few undershirts, a single bar of soap, some shapeless long underwear, and a book in brown leather. He set the book reverently in the center of his desk and enjoyed the official neatness of his display. He removed a set of rosary beads and a metal statue of a praying man. He set the statue on the desk beside the book and pulled from his pocket a half-burned candle, placing it in a hole in the statue's head. From his other pocket, he pulled a book of matches, and lit the candle.

"What are you doing?" Nikolas said.

"Sorry?"

"Didn't they tell you that matches are contraband?"

"They are? I guess they didn't check my pockets."

Nikolas scratched his goatee, which he had worked to cultivate, giving him an air of seriousness. "I won't report you, but on two conditions."

"And what would those be?"

"First, you keep that religious nonsense away from me." He stood up and set his book down.

"And the second?"

"You give me one of those matches. I need a cigarette."

Nikolas lit his cigarette and watched this new creature's sedulous enterprises, placing each of his belongings in just the right spots. When Adrian had at last finished with all his tiresome fussiness, he pulled out a pillbox and took a small yellow pill along with a larger blue one. He swallowed these down with a dainty sip of water, and looked over his shoulder to where Nikolas was staring at him.

"I won't find you dead in the bathroom some morning, will I?" Nikolas asked.

"Only God knows our fate."

Nikolas did not notice that Adrian had already broken the first term of their arrangement.

3.

HIGH ABOVE The Train Hub, a meeting was underway.

If you can call it a meeting, Mayor Adams thought. It had started pleasantly enough, with the usual exchange of gifts and prosperity-greetings. There had been that business at the door where the ambassador from Larki Island refused to give up his ancestral axe—it would be a grave offense to his family, he protested—but Mayor Adams was able to persuade him that it would remain in respectful hands. And then the ambassador from Al-Khuzir had insisted on a prayer mat, and insisted that it face toward the Evening Lands, which his religion held in holy regard. What was wrong with a chair, Adams wondered, especially one upholstered with fine Ulani goat-leather? And the Evening Lands were likely nothing but ruins now. But Mayor Adams accommodated the man; this day was too important to quibble over mythology.

Despite Mayor Adams's best efforts, however, the proceedings had swiftly degenerated into an argument worthy of children. Mayor Adams sat behind his desk of Larki oak. Joshua City was in panorama behind him. The greatest of the Seven Cities. He watched and listened as ambassadors from the Lesser Six bickered among themselves. He would be doing them a favor if he finally succeeded in uniting them all under the banner of Joshua City, with him as the hegemon over the entire region. But he was getting ahead of himself . . .

"You would fight over water," Zoba, the ambassador from Kazhstan, said. "You would let our thirst own us."

Kazhstan was far to the south, on the limestone flats. Its people took pride in their rugged, sparse existence. They thought that those who lived near easy water were soft.

"Go eat dust," the ambassador from Larki Island said, the words issuing from his enormous red beard. "You rock-dwellers make me ill."

Through this all, the ambassador to Al-Khuzir kneeled on his prayer mat in silence, facing west. The ambassador to Baikalingrad, Hanna Kaplani, was here as well. She had the composure of tempered steel and a nuanced mind Mayor Adams admired. And she was not mired in superstition like the others here. Yes, she wore the porcelain mask of her people, but she had told Mayor Adams privately that this was mere political theatre, a concession to the religious customs and beliefs of her society. In the things that mattered, she was unfailingly practical, if not downright savvy. And he knew he could count on Baikalingrad for support, which further warmed him to her virtues.

Behind her mask, she was silent now, playing the same game Adams was.

Pierre came in. "The ambassador to Baikyong-do."

Pierre had been Mayor Adams's personal aide since Adams was a lowly city kouncilman. Mayor Adams gave him a questioning look. Pierre nodded. This was not good.

The Tongue. A mild rustling preceded his entourage. The Tongue entered in a bright swirl of fabrics, his posture stiff with dignity. Behind him came his androgynous Voicemaids, holding up the train of his robes. It was rumored that half of the Voicemaids were female and half male, but you could not tell them apart; the Tongue chose them specifically for this feature, and for their lovely voices. Mayor Adams stood and bowed. If he had learned one thing in his years as mayor, it was how to play the role of diplomat, no matter how much it might chafe. The Tongue bowed as well and his Voicemaids rustled his train, making high-pitched ululations with their throats.

"We are honored to have you," Mayor Adams said. "I hope you don't mind that we've begun. We weren't sure of your presence."

The Tongue greeted each ambassador in their native language, his accent flawless in each. Though Mayor Adams did not understand every word, he recognized these as the traditional prosperity-greetings of the Seven Cities.

Finally getting around to Mayor Adams, "May your days be pure-baikal."

The Voicemaids lifted the elaborate fabric of the Tongue's robes, and he lowered himself fussily into his appointed seat. He was a small man, his tiny wizened face dwarfed by elaborate headdress. The other ambassadors had left off arguing for now, taken up with The Tongue's display.

At the door, there was a commotion. A man dressed entirely in black was trying to come into the room. Mayor Adams put his finger on the alarm beneath his desk. If he pressed it, the hall would soon be swarming with Baikal Guardsmen. Not that that would help.

"My envoy," the Tongue said.

"Let him in," Mayor Adams said, determined not to let his apprehension show.

Two Guardsmen searched the robed man, disarming him of several knives and a vial of something no doubt poisonous or explosive. The true weapon was the man himself though. He crossed the room to stand behind the Tongue and his Voicemaids, his movements reminiscent of the musculature of underwater creatures. Adams hardly wanted to think the name: *Messenger.* A band of nomadic assassins of legendary prowess, Messenger answered to nobody except the highest bidder. Sometimes not even that was enough. How had the Tongue won such an ally?

One thing's certain. He's brought him here to intimidate me. The Tongue may have preached peace and unity, but when you got down to it, he might have been the most devious man in the room.

"There are serious matters that have caused me to bring you here," Mayor Adams said, his voice heavy with officiousness and circumstance. He surveyed the room, looking each of the ambassadors in the eye, hoping to establish control of the situation and to let all the ambassadors know they were truly important to the proceedings at hand. He even forced himself to look toward Messenger, though he did not quite manage direct eye contact.

"Those gathered for peaceful discourse make much wisdom, but those gathered to divide the price of blood make much folly," the Tongue said.

Mayor Adams offered a tolerant smile in the absurd man's direction and went on with his planned comments. "Tensions are high, and I hope we can come to a peaceful agreement over resources, which are scarce for all of us," he said and looked at Zoba, letting him know he felt his people's suffering and admired their courage in the barren desert lands they so prided themselves on, then looking to the Larki Island ambassador, as if to say that his comparative abundance of water did not make him invulnerable to shortages.

"Division will be our undoing," the Tongue said. "Without water there are no clouds. And without clouds no rain, and without rain no water. Unity is life."

The maids ululated. They rustled his garments.

"The Tongue speaks!" they cried in unison in Hangul, the common language of Baikyong-do. Mayor Adams knew just enough of that language to understand them. "Listen and hear!"

"Unity?" the ambassador from Larki Island grumbled. He had one mode of speech. "The gods of Baikal can damn your precious unity. We were fine without it until now, and we'll be fine without it until the end of the Now-Time."

Gruffness aside, he had a point. The Larki Islanders were self-sufficient on their northern island, fortressed in so that no one would dare attack them. To do so, you would have to cross the water. And if you did, there would be a fleet of ships waiting for you. And the Ministrie of Intelligence had informed Mayor Adams that the Larki Islanders had ships that could travel underwater. That was like—like having trains that could go underwater. *What I could do with underwater trains.*

"You say that now," said the ambassador to Al-Khuzir. Until this point he had not spoken, had just kneeled on his prayer mat. "Your water is still untainted."

"Yes," Mayor Adams said, deciding it was time he got the meeting back on track. "No thanks to the efforts of Ulan-Ude."

"But how do we know it's them?" the ambassador to Larki Island asked.

"We know," Hanna said.

Well-timed, thought Mayor Adams. *You are a formidable woman indeed.* He let the notion of marrying her float idly through his mind, then allowed it to disintegrate of its own accord.

"So you say," said Larki Island. "Pardon me if I don't want to go to war over your vague suspicions."

"For once we agree," said the ambassador to Al-Khuzir. "Al-Khuzir will back Ulan-Ude on this. What possible motive would they have? The water-tainting is a problem for all of us."

"They have the best source of untainted water now," Hanna said.

"And what good will that do them with an army at their gates?" Al-Khuzir responded. "Six armies, if we would listen to your friend here."

Perhaps Ulan-Ude is counting on our inaction. What made me think I could get these children to agree to anything?

"And this is precisely why we must not be slaves to our thirst," the ambassador to Kazhstan said. "As even your own *Book of the Before-Time* tells us, our sins are the architects of our demise. Joshua City—all of you in fact—live in a state of water-decadence, and this has not gone unnoticed by the gods. There is some version of the prophecy in each of the Seven Religions. When we are found deserving, as those who were destroyed by The Great Calamity were, the gods will visit the same punishment on us again."

"Suspicion is a shadow," the Tongue said. "It takes the shape of he who casts it."

"The Tongue speaks!"

Mayor Adams rubbed his forehead. This was going nowhere. And after this he had a meeting with the Minister of Aesthetics. They wanted to implement a new set of standards and practices for the Silverville film industry. He wasn't sure what came after that. Pierre would know. And still the bickering continued.

From his spot in the corner, Messenger watched.

"Honorable ambassadors," Mayor Adams said, standing abruptly. "I thank you for your time. We'll be in contact."

※ ※ ※

After they were gone, Mayor Adams stood in front of the window and looked out over his city. From the base of The Train Hub, rail lines extended outward, spider-like, spanning Joshua City from sea-wall to desert-wall. The Hub was the head of the city, and he the head of the head. He had not expected much from this meeting. Perhaps one more ally. It was not a total loss, however; he now knew how tenuous his situation was. Joshua City would have to conduct the war, at least at first, on its own.

Mayor Adams walked to the back of his office and opened the twin engraved doors of The Special Closet. He peered into the obscurity.

"It's worse than I thought," Mayor Adams said.

Is that so, my dear? came the three-voiced response from the silky dark. *Nothing you can't manage, we hope.*

"I will manage."

Good. We can't have your destiny thwarted with trifles, the Oracles said.

"What should I do?" Mayor Adams asked. "Without the support of at least one more of the Lesser Six, my position will be considerably more precarious."

As the poison spreads, so spreads your power.

Mayor Adams shut the closet doors, took two pain pills, and called for Pierre to send in the Minister of Aesthetics.

4.

THE SECRET LIFE OF MAYOR ADAMS
(OR THE LESSONS THAT MADE HIM WHO HE IS TODAY)

The Lesson of the Father:

On a glorious morning in mid-April, Joshua City having been washed clean with recent rain, William Adams, future mayor, was born at a robust nine pounds and eight ounces, his skin ruddy with the vigor of grand destiny. William Sr., the most successful water-baron in Joshua City, was in particularly high spirits because the rain would increase his already considerable fortune. Later, on the ride home, he even held the baby.

"This is an important day, isn't it, Little William?"

Mayor Adams, who was already Mayor Adams before he became Mayor Adams, performed his first act of rebellion by promptly urinating in his father's lap. William Sr. cursed and tossed Mayor Adams to his mother who, though exhausted from a prolonged childbirth, caught him—what can only be called providentially—just before he broke on the limousine floor.

In the following years, the Adams mansion was filled with sound: the clinking of brandy glasses as William Sr. brokered larger and larger deals; the daily bustle of servants; workers building extra wings on the house and then, when William Sr. had become the richest man in Joshua City, an indoor pool. But the loudest sound of all was the crying. From the nursery, Mayor Adams's cries for his mother; and from behind the closed door of the librarie, where his mother spent most of her time, the crying of an unhappy wife.

The swimming pool was housed in an enormous wing of glass. When Mayor Adams was eight years old, after countless legal setbacks which, thanks to William Sr.'s money and influence, were not insurmountable, the pool was finally completed. William Sr. showed Mayor Adams the finished product with pride. Mayor Adams marveled at the blue jewel of the water, the way the light struck it through the glass and did a skittery dance he couldn't quite follow.

"You will be the heir to all of this," William Sr. said. "Everything I build."

Mayor Adams took on the confident wide-legged stance of his father.

"But you'll have to learn certain lessons, just as I did." He rested a hand on Mayor Adams's back.

The water hit Mayor Adams in the face. Flailing, the glass above him, and the light blinding him, he took a mouthful of water as he tried to call to his father. His father stood colossally distant.

"What I've done to you is unfair," his father said. Mayor Adams quieted his splashing, trying just to keep his head above water now, more to hear his father's words than to be able to breathe. "You can't swim. But practically no one in Joshua City can. And that's the point. To fulfill your destiny, you will need powers no else has."

Mayor Adams gathered up an animal willpower with a human hatred and decided not to drown. He looked up toward his father, but the image he saw through the wavering fluid was a three-headed woman, each face distorted in dark grimaces. They beckoned him upward. Arms chopping toward the pool wall, he reached the grainy stone, but couldn't grab the lip of the pool wall. He clawed at the stone and tore off a fingernail. He clawed again, doing damage that the doktor would later say had fractured three fingers, finally reaching his hand over the edge. He pulled himself out.

His clothes heavy with water, he looked at his father, who did not seem so colossal now.

"You've made me very proud, son."

That was when Mayor Adams knew he would kill him.

The Lesson of the Mother:

On a lovely perfect day in mid-April, made peaceful by the recent rain, Josephina Adams struggled through seven hours of labor to give birth to the one joy in her married life. She clutched little William to her breast and looked at her husband, her hair stringy and her face moist with exhaustion.

"Can we leave now?" William Sr. asked the doktor.

"If your wife feels ready."

She kissed little William on the forehead, and with a dreamy look in her eyes, speaking to herself and her new son, said, "After the storm comes peace."

The first years with the mother were all warm milk and favorite blanket. But, at three, when the first flickerings of consciousness introduced themselves, the mother walked in with the red on her face again. And her eye-water. He cried more and she tickled his belly the way he liked.

When he was eight years old, he walked into the house dripping water everywhere. His mother tried to help him out of his soaked clothes.

"I can do it," he said, struggling to make his fractured fingers do the simple task.

She brought him dry clothes, a towel, and called the doktor. This was the doktor who had come before, but always for the mother.

"No, not me," she said, directing him to the boy.

"Is this becoming a problem?" the doktor asked.

※　※　※

She did it in full view of all the servants. "You desert thug," she screamed.

She slapped him with real force. Mayor Adams had never seen his father cringe. His father stood there, trying to seem unstunned.

"You can do anything you want to me," she said, "but if you touch my son again, I will kill you."

The Oracles had told him he would learn this lesson three times. This was the second.

※　※　※

At thirteen, he sat on the edge of the tub while his mother bathed. Bubbles spilled out of the bath and circled up into the air. She liked his company at times like these, when his father wasn't around. But she usually wasn't so quiet.

"Pass me the razor."

He wondered if she would slit her wrist. Would he stop her or would he just watch? But she dipped the razor into the bathwater to wet it.

He had never thought of his mother as a woman before. One slick leg emerged and she shaved the bubbles down.

The sound of the door slapping against the wall behind him. The voice of his father: "What are you two doing?" And the *plop* of the razor falling into the water. His father grabbed him and tugged him to his feet. Mayor Adams resisted, pulled against his father's strength. His mother's hand was a fish swimming the bathwater for its hook, the razor. He stared at his father, who had paused, taking his new son in with a kind of fear. A yelp from his mother, and the water went pink with mother's-blood. Mayor Adams charged his father, swinging his impotent fists wildly, hitting hard muscle and unbreaking bone. His father let himself be hit, feeling his power renewed with each helpless impact. And then one stray swing landed in his father's groin, and he grunted in actual pain. Mayor Adams stopped, looked up at his father's face, smiled at the grimace he saw there.

He was weightless off his feet and then came the hollow-solid crack of skull on porcelain. His mother was out of the water, holding the razor, blood in streams down her beautiful arm, and then the world blurred into the distance, into nothingness.

The Lesson of the Self:

It was a promise to himself, his promise, and it was what he was beholden to. Hadn't it begun one fine April, after the rains had blessed Joshua City? Mayor Adams knew it wasn't true, but he liked to think that the rain had brought him to cleanse the world of its filth. He did not yet know he was Mayor Adams, though he was. This final lesson would show him his true promise; it would make him what he was to become.

No one spoke of The Lesson of the Mother, in those terms or any. He was sent to the best technical institutes and the most expensive tutors were hired to instruct him during his holidays at home. In the years that followed, few would think of Mayor Adams as an intelligent man, especially today, but he was the brightest of students, as quick with mathematics as he was with foreign languages and rhetoric. Many would praise his moving speeches, but few would know he had written them himself. He suffered many setbacks at his father's hands, but as his favorite quote from the *Book of Before-Time* runs: *Almost every genius is familiar with a stumbling existence as one stage in his development, a feeling of hatred, revenge, and rebellion against everything that is and no longer becomes . . . an incomplete ego—the form in which every leader pre-exists.*

Mayor Adams learned this and many other lessons at his prestigious technical institute. Some were lessons his father would have condoned. But he also learned how to float above, untouchable and untouching. When he returned home on his second winter break, his father was locked in his study with work. Who knew what he worked on besides the business of work itself? His mother wandered, a woman without meaning now that her son had left, only the occasional bruise her husband gave her to remind her she was alive. Mayor Adams saw all this without surprise, without even anger now. It was time. And remembering his first lesson, he knew what to do. After all, what had he taken all those chemistry classes for?

He brought his father a glass of water. Hunched over the large oak table, his father looked tired and old. But that didn't matter.

"I thought you could use a drink," he said. "You work so hard."

His expensive spectacles, designed to look expensive, slipped down his nose, not unkindly. "Why thank you, son."

The water's shadow, with its core of sun, wobbled on the table. Would his father ever take a drink of his future? Both of their futures filled that glass.

"You know, you're growing into a fine young man, William. But I hope you are learning the importance of water to this family. The very essence of all life is held in this fluid."

He lifted his glass to punctuate his point. He swirled the contents. Mayor Adams's chest tightened.

"There are creatures in the Baikal Sea that are 99% water. Think of that. Were it not for that one percent, they would be exactly the same as the contents of this glass here. Amazing. And you, you are 60% water. Your blood is 92% water."

Mayor Adams knew all this. He also knew the meaning of blood, whether from a razor in the bathtub or from the other lesson that could not be unlearned. He would carry on his father's legacy, but it would not make his father immortal.

"Your future floats on its surface," his father said.

"I know it does. You have taught me that before."

"I have. But I don't think you appreciate this fact, not in its fullness."

"I do, father. Believe me, I do."

His father drank, a large self-satisfied gulp as he always did. Mayor Adams had not skimped on his assassin's purchase; the poison was incredibly strong and undetectable by normal forensic procedures. His father slapped his chest and then the table, knocking previously important papers to the shiny marble floor. The water spread over the hard smooth surface, glistening beautifully.

With a voice that mimicked real panic, Mayor Adams screamed out, "Mother! Mother! Something's wrong with father. Quick!"

His father fell to the floor, gasping. He looked at Mayor Adams, who peered down with no discernible emotion. If there were words to say, he did not say them. Their eyes met and everything was known. His father slithered like a broken lizard toward the northwest corner of the house, where oblivion awaited him.

5.

IF NIKOLAS was entertaining doubts about the merits of kardiology, they doubled when he learned that his new roommate planned to make it his focus. They walked to class together that first day—not because Nikolas wanted to, but because he couldn't see any way around it. Adrian would likely get lost if he tried to make it there on his own.

"So, why kardiology?" Nikolas asked.

"It's an interesting question" Adrian said, all boyish eagerness. "I'm not sure I know myself. But if I had to make an answer, I guess I'd argue that the heart is the engine of the body. Of course, we now know that feelings and thoughts all originate in the brain, but we still can't help but use the heart as a metaphor for love, for passion, for all the things we care about."

"Don't you think that's a bit, I don't know . . . *romantic*?"

"Maybe," Adrian said. "But I think it's more than that. I'm interested in the science, first and foremost. However, I find that thinking about our, how shall I say it, *poetic relationship* to the heart gives a metaphorical lift to my study of it."

"Do we really want a doktor thinking in metaphors, though? I mean, he has your life in his hands. He should be focused on the surgery."

"You don't think it's possible to do both at once?" Adrian asked, somewhat rhetorically but also deferring to Nikolas's greater experience and knowledge.

Nikolas, sensing Adrian's deference, replied as thoughtfully as possible, temporarily suspending all his prejudices (an ability of his Adrian would come to admire), "I suppose if a doktor could maintain total focus, then the metaphorical lift, as you so aptly put it, would not necessarily be a bad thing. In fact, if it strengthened his conviction and attentiveness, then I'd even be in favor of it. For me, it's all about the end results. The metaphysics are less important than the practical effects, so I ultimately don't give a baikal-damn about the metaphysics."

(This was not, of course, strictly true. Nikolas often became annoyed despite himself with metaphysical positions he found incorrect or absurd, even when they were harmless or inconsequential. But he knew this was a bad tendency of his, one he was constantly trying to rid himself of.)

"I suppose for me, they are inseperable," Adrian replied. "Metaphysics and ethics."

They arrived at the medikal sciences building and ascended the great stone stairs. It was a building that Nikolas had spent most of the last year in. He knew every inch of it—the carvings on certain desks, which windows opened and which did not, where the most private water-closet was located. Despite his newfound reservations, he still felt a sense of pride and belonging here.

They entered the main instructional building, and a few short turns led them to the Experimental Kardiology laboratory. Nikolas opened the door and took stock of his surroundings. A few skolars, already situated at their large seatless laboratory tables, looked up. Some nodded at Nikolas, recognizing him from last year. Most were new faces, however, bland and dull.

It's one class, he told himself. *It commits you to nothing. Just do the work and see where it leads. It might even prove interesting.*

Predictably, Adrian walked to the lab table Nikolas had selected, assuming that they would be partners simply because they knew each other's names. There was something equal parts pathetic and touching in the way Adrian began unpacking his skolarly utensils.

While the other skolars were still arriving, Doktor Brandt walked around from table to table, greeting the students and wishing them well on a new semester.

He lingered at Nikolas's table.

"Nikolas," he said. "I'm glad you decided to enroll. I trust you'll remember the goals we discussed."

"Of course, Doktor Brandt."

%. %. %.

Adrian unpacked his notebooks and pencils. Hard to believe it was just a month ago he had stood in the stationary aisle of the printing shop. There were leather-bound journals, heavy-threaded clothbound cases, holding-tablets engraved with scenes from Joshuan lore, and paper of every imaginable color and design. At first he didn't dare touch anything. Then he picked up the most beautiful journal: the spine was made out of a dark rich wood and the leather cover had no adornments. Its paper was etched with faint golden lines. Then he saw the price—eight drams—and set it back on the shelf and went in search of more affordable items.

In the back of the store was a large metal letterpress. The floor around it was stained with powdered ink detritus. It was amazing that such a clunky machine was the vehicle for so much eloquent language. There was a box of metal letters beside the press; Adrian wondered what they felt like. The printwright approached Adrian, wiping his thick fingers on his apron. Thin-rimmed glasses rested primly on his large nose.

He saw the St. Ignatius rosary around Adrian's neck and asked, "Are you the boy they've sent to pick up Father Samarov's Sunday pamphlets?"

"I am from St. Ignatius's School, but no, I'm not here to pick up anything."

"My mistake then. What can I help you with?"

"I am off to university next month and need notebooks."

"Follow me," the printwright said. He led him to a different aisle. "You boys come in every year. You'll find what you need here."

Adrian looked at these other notebooks: they had flimsy binding and looked like they might fall apart. He chose the least offensive one.

Now, setting his things neatly on the table in the classroom, he took a look around at his fellow skolars. He wrote the date at the top of the page. Surrounded by the seriousness of medikal studies, he felt an unexpected generosity toward his cheap notebook which would be filled with so much lofty knowledge.

%%%

That first day, Doktor Brandt explained the goals of the course. They would simulate the conditions and technical process of a heart transplant, using corpses as models. The corpses would have to be fresh enough that the heart valves had not begun to deteriorate. When asked where the corpses came from, Doktor Brandt explained that the Joshua City prison system had a program that allowed prisoners to donate their bodies for medikal research. The families received a small sum of money in return for their contribution to science.

Adrian felt sadness for the families holding a few hundred drams, the sum their loved ones were now worth. Nikolas tried to imagine a similar program for heads of ministries and kouncil members and grew angry at a world in which that was unthinkable.

%%%

The third week of the course, when the medikal skolars entered the Experimental Kardiology laboratory, there were corpses lying on the examining tables with ice-boxes containing human hearts beside them. Nikolas and Adrian went to their table and looked down at the naked corpse of a woman, neither young nor old. The pallid veiny breasts sagged to either side of the sternum. She had a thick thatch of hair. Adrian busied himself with organizing their surgical instruments and pulling the rubber gloves over his slightly shaking fingers.

Doktor Brandt called the room to attention. "The procedure we will perform today is as difficult as it is unprecedented," he said, pacing behind his lectern. "The left posterior portion of the recipient's atrium must remain in place. The donor's left atrium will be sewn onto the recipient's left atrium. The right atrium is sewn onto the superior and inferior vena cava, a particularly delicate maneuver in the surgical arts. All the measurements must be exact."

When he was told that the corpses were those of prisoners, Nikolas had assumed they would all be male. *We rarely think of criminals as female.* But it was more than that. *Medikal science assumes that the human body is male*, Nikolas thought. *But death has no gender. And physical differences persist after death, even if social ones do not.*

The initial steps of the surgery were simple enough, so Nikolas allowed Adrian to do them, though he watched closely as his partner sawed into the ribcage, exposing the chest cavity. Adrian executed the procedure neatly. He made a neat slice with his scalpel and peeled back the pericardium. The corpse was splayed, the open flaps of its torso like the wings of a flightless bird. The skin was loose and fatty and the heart they were supposed to remove was surprisingly small: a wet red-gray fist. The woman's face, which Nikolas had barely allowed himself to notice, seemed to smile welcomingly.

"Skolars, you're looking at the organ that gives life. I invite you to imagine that the body is a Baikal Guardsman wounded in defense of Joshua City. He is your recipient. The donor is beyond hope, though his heart is still healthy. The task before you is to transplant the possibility of life."

Brandt's words were poetic, but Nikolas didn't need poetry. All that mattered was the result. Nikolas severed the recipient's pulmonary artery and moved to the aorta. There was too much blood in the cavity. Nikolas motioned and Adrian dabbed it away. The aortic incision complete, Nikolas moved to the superior vena cava.

"Don't cut there," Adrian said.

Nikolas waited for an explanation.

"See the deterioration of the vascular wall?"

Nikolas saw the uncharacteristic grain. Adrian was right. This woman must have suffered from a heart condition; that was likely what killed her. Sutures would not hold in such deteriorated flesh—not that it would matter to this corpse, but to a living patient it would mean death.

"Let's cut three centimeters down and trim the donor heart to match," Adrian said.

Nikolas completed the removal of the recipient's heart and expertly trimmed the donor's vena cava. Despite his keen observation, Adrian did not yet have Nikolas's skill with the scalpel. Doktor Brandt went around the room examining everyone's work, saving Nikolas for last. Nikolas and Adrian stepped back to allow him a clearer view.

Brandt's face turned from pleased to disconcerted. "Skolar Kovalski, it seems your incision on the superior vena cava is at least a centimeter off, maybe more."

Nikolas pointed out the deteriorated flesh and explained the consequences for a living patient. "Since that's the eventual goal of this experiment, I assumed you would condone this action."

Brandt smiled. "Very good, Nikolas."

※ ※ ※

Until now Adrian had felt like an imposter among his fellow skolars. Yes, he had read widely and had done well on the entrance exams. But what was that compared to performing his first operation? How could he hope to impress in the prestigious environment of Joshua University?

But as Brandt continued his rounds, Adrian allowed himself to imagine that the corpse on the table was a living patient and he had just performed the first successful heart transplant.

Adrian looked up at Nikolas and smiled. "We did it."

"Yes, well ..." Nikolas said. "That was quick thinking on your part."

6.

ON SATURDAY, 24 of September, the night Mayor Adams was scheduled to speak at Titus Hall, Nikolas bounded up the stairs to the dormitory and into the room he shared with Adrian. He had been out drinking with friends, carousing and discussing politics. On the way home, giddy with drink and the cold fall air, he had taken it into his head to run a little. Now his face was flushed in the close heat of the room.

Adrian was sitting on his bed, alone as usual. Every time Nikolas came back to the room, there Adrian was, alone and studying. In Nikolas's current state, he felt a warmth for this sad solitary figure already dressed for bed at six o'eve on a Saturday night.

"Oh, hello," Adrian said as he came in.

"Another exciting week's-end, I see," Nikolas said.

Adrian shut his book. "I thought I should get ahead. It's my first semester and I don't know how difficult it will prove."

Nikolas had pulled on his coat, but he lingered in the doorway. Adrian coughed and picked up his book again.

"Listen," Nikolas said. "There's a thing. Over at the lecture hall. Mayor Adams is speaking."

"Yes," Adrian said, setting down his book gratefully. "I saw an announcement for that."

(In fact, Adrian had seen the municipal information-paper Nikolas had brought home on the day they met. It had been lying on Nikolas's desk for a week. He wanted to go, but didn't want to get in Nikolas's way.)

"Why don't you come along?"

%% %% %%

On the walk over to the lecture hall, Adrian remarked that it was interesting the event should be held in Titus Hall, which was named after the former mayor. Titus and Adams had clashed many times, both during the election, which some said had been rigged in Adams's favor, and after. Titus had criticized Adams's foreign policy and his cavalier management of the city's water reserves.[2] Adrian recited all this in a skolarly tone, aware that Nikolas probably knew it already—any informed Joshuan did—and yet he blathered on, nervous at being on his first public outing since arriving at university.

"Mere theatre," Nikolas said, "so that Adams can show that there are no hard feelings. Never mind that those hard feelings were manufactured to begin with. These politicians are all the same. They belong to the same private resorts. I bet they even frequent the same prostitutes."

Was Nikolas trying to shock him with such a cynical comment? He let it go, not wanting to think ill of his new friend.

A crowd was gathered outside Titus Hall, waving handmade picket signs. Their tone ranged from the tame and practical *Give the Baikal Treaty a Chance* to the more emphatic *No Blood for Water*.

A young man with the herd-tattoos of Ulan-Ude crawling up his neck was arguing with the Baikal Guardsman at the entrance to the lecture hall. Though Adrian had no way of being sure, he guessed that the protestor was not actually Ulani. Such tattoos had come into fashion

---

[2]Author's Note: "He grew up water-rich," Titus says in the 22 of August issue of *The Joshua Harbinger* I have sitting on my desk, not a month before Adams's speech described here. "Only those of us who have known thirst truly fear it."

He goes on to talk about his experiences in The Great War. Adams did not fight in the war, while Titus served with distinction, achieving the rank of admiral. During the vicious and hard-fought election campaign, Titus criticized Adams for taking extra university classes instead of enlisting. Adams meanwhile argued that his classes in water management and his subsequent success as a water-baron would provide the practical knowledge that the city needed.

"We are done with the age of warriors. Now we need a businessman."

To which Titus replied that if he had inherited his father's business, he too might have chosen to stay home.

On a side note, it is fascinating to read this article and remember how tolerant the political climate was in those times.

in the last few years in Joshua City. The people of Ulan-Ude prided themselves on being herdsmen—of cattle, yaks, and sheep; of goats, reindeer, and snow-horses; of desert elk and even the goitered gazelle worshipped by the Kazhstani in the south. The Ulani region, abundant in river water and diverse in terrain—foothills, rocky mountain passes, lush valleys, and high arid plateaus—was perfect for raising all types of livestock. The Ulani people sold the milk and steaks of their animals to Joshuans, who, tired of eating the fish of the Baikal Sea every day, paid exorbitant prices for this more exotic fare. The hides of the yaks were made into leather, the wool of the sheep woven into blankets and clothing, the horns of the reindeer prized for decorative purposes.

So important was this livestock to the Ulani economy, and so great was their worship of the herds themselves, that they refused to brand the livestock, instead tattooing themselves to indicate how many heads of livestock they owned and of what type. These tattoos were purposefully conspicuous: on the forearms, the neck, and even—for the more prosperous owners who had exhausted all other available skin—the face. In Joshua City, it had become fashionable among a certain subset of the youth to mimic these herd-tattoos, usually with no interest in plausibility; the number of livestock claimed would be absurd, or the proportions would border on the nonsensical—twelve yaks, four sheep, two hundred twenty-five oxen, one reindeer. Because the tattoos were written in the Ulani language, these fashionable Joshuans often didn't know the claims their own flesh was making.

"You're free to stay out here," the armed Guardsman said to the tattooed protestor. "But I can't have you causing trouble in there."

"I have a right to go in."

After being patted down, Adrian and Nikolas were allowed inside.

"Shouldn't we have helped him?" Adrian said.

"People like that just want attention. He's much happier now than if they had let him in." Nikolas knew he only halfway believed this, but for some reason the protestor annoyed him just now.

The lecture hall, a vast amphitheatre-like structure, was crowded with skolars, professors, ministers, and common Joshuans. There were even a few Silverville celebrities. You could recognize them by the press gathered around, the flash bulbs going off, the hangers-on with pen and paper in hand, hoping for an autograf. There was the great Dame Neville, the famous patroness of the arts, with her bouffant of silver-white hair. And there was the playwright Umberto Lemkin, with an adoring young aktress on each arm. Most recently he had authored a five-act opus about Adams's rise to fame. It had met with much critical, if not popular, success.

Nikolas spotted some skolars he knew at the back of the auditorium, gave a wave, and proceeded toward them. Adrian would have liked to sit, but he followed Nikolas. There were four of them—three young men and a girl dressed in too many layers. By far the most striking of the young men was a pale blonde student dressed all in black. His hair was so fine you could see his pink scalp beneath and his eyebrows were nonexistent. Above his tight leather jacket, a scarf was tossed jauntily around his neck. He smoked a long cigarette, ignoring the *No Smoking* sign. The young man was telling a story, an amused sneer on his face, but he broke off at Nikolas's approach.

"Fair Nik," he said and shook Nikolas's hand with ironic playfulness, as though greeting a high dignitary from a far-off land.

"This is Elias," Nikolas said to Adrian. "He runs the Progressive Skolars for a Better Baikal. Elias, this is Adrian, my roommate."

"Oh," Adrian said. "That's very impressive."

Elias gave a sharp quick laugh, almost a bark.

"Did I say something wrong?" Adrian asked, looking to Nikolas.

"You'll have to forgive Elias," Nikolas said. "It's just that our meetings mostly consist of the five of us slumming it at a workers' tavern, mingling with the masses, and getting stumbling drunk. You should come to our next meeting. We meet every Saturday. Met today, in fact. But we had to cut it short for this display of pomp and circumstance."

"I'd like that," Adrian said, though he couldn't help notice Elias's disapproval. "What do you study, Elias?"

Elias stubbed out his cigarette on the shining tile of the auditorium floor. "Toxicology. Its effects on the Joshuan psyche."

The girl snorted laughter and covered her mouth. Her eyes were wide and green; she had a tiny squashed nose. "He means he gets drunk and shows up to lectures. He's a law student. I'm Naomi, by the way. People call me Mouse."

"And I'm an ineffectual . . . I mean an *intellectual,*" Elias said.

Adrian listened to Nikolas and his friends banter, adding nothing more to the conversation. The room filled. The crush of bodies made Adrian somewhat lightheaded. Finally, the lights dimmed and the cacophony reduced to a diffuse murmur. The Dean of Joshua University, Hippolyte Andrews, wandered out on stage, blinked into the lights, and thumped the microphone. It issued a shrill feedback. The Dean laughed nervously. He was not a man with much taste for public speaking. The joke went that the Dean's signature had made more public appearances than he had.

"Good evening," Dean Andrews said.

"Good evening," most of them replied dutifully, though there was a good deal of jolly sarcasm in the way Elias and his friends said it.

"I guess I'll get right down to business then," Dean Andrews said. "Not many gatherings like this are worthy of the importance given to them. And I am sure many of you young skolars don't see why tonight should be any different. But I assure you it is."

Adrian found Dean Andrews charming. Sincere even. As he listened, a light trickle of sweat beaded down his back. He would have liked to hang up his jacket, but he was afraid it would be stolen. It was his only one, and he could not afford another. Dean Andrews was describing the accomplishments of the Adams administration and extolling the mayor's personal virtues.

"And in these times, with the troubles we face today, I can think of no one else I would trust more as the konduktor for this train of state," Dean Andrews said and surveyed the audience, letting his words sink in. "We are very privileged to have with us tonight my close personal friend, a great benefactor to this university, and the finest leader Joshua City has ever had...Mayor William Adams!"

※ ※ ※

The lights glared as Mayor Adams stepped onto the stage. He couldn't see the audience. It wouldn't have mattered though. He was not nervous; he had not been nervous since the Lessons. He saw the audience as a unified mass, a single entity called History. He bent over the microfone and addressed himself to History. His entire existence had been leading up to this. Every event had conspired so that this one might happen, an imbricated series of causes. He had created these people by creating this moment. His Being emerged from this moment, and this moment revealed the fullness of itself through his Being. He was the conduit for the hub-Being of Joshua City, knotting all the threads of history and destiny together in beautiful inevitability.

※ ※ ※

Mayor Adams was shorter than Adrian had expected, but there was a palpable vitality to him. His suit fit perfectly, like those impossible models in magazine advertisements. There was something unreal in his composure. Adrian was too far away to see Adams's face clearly, but he had seen it often enough in newspapers: his cheeks dimpled, his jaw square, his eyes darkly attentive. It was not hard to see that he had once been very handsome and that he still was in that ageless way certain distinguished men were. He was more...*present* than anyone else in the room. Adrian wondered what that quality was. Nikolas had it too. Even Elias to an extent. The two of them were whispering to each other, ignoring the commotion all around them with a confidence that suggested they were the only two people in the world.

"I see many young people in the audience tonight," Mayor Adams said. "That's good. It fills me with great hope for Joshua City's future."

He waited for more applause. The audience complied.

"But even the oldest of us does not remember the Before-Time. Well, maybe Minister Lancaster."

Laughter. The minister in question stood on feeble legs and took a playful bow.

"Sure, we've all heard the stories. But have we really listened? Have we learned?"

Mayor Adams glanced at his speech on the podium. But he did not turn the pages. The next part was from the *Book of the Before-Time*. He had practiced the rhythms, imagining it as a piece of music where tempo and emphasis were everything. Any halfwit could say the words. What is that quality that separates mere noise from a masterpiece? Or even a competent symphony from a masterpiece? Knowing the notes, the way they might support each other, might please the listener's ear— but these are not enough. Something more is needed. It must carry the force of nature, must leap through the gravity behind the notes, must have the tirelessness of the true believer.

※ ※ ※

Adams was now quoting from the *Book of the Before-Time* and his adoring crowd was drinking it up like pure-baikal water. Elias said something in a sarcastic tone; Nikolas nodded without fully hearing him. Nikolas was as familiar with the book as anyone; his mother was an old believer. Every Sunday morning, she had dragged Nikolas and Marcik to St. Bartholomew. Or rather, it was Nikolas she had dragged. Marcik had gone willingly. Had it been up to Nikolas, he would have spent the time in the Joshua Public Librarie, reading tales of adventure and texts on the natural sciences.

Mayor Adams droned on.

"In the Before-Time, the great book tells us, there was water in abundant supply, the soil rich as chocolate. Rivers cut cool ravines through the world, and the Baikal Sea was more than twice its current volume. But then came The Great Calamity."

A sound of exaggerated woe went through the room.

He must have planted people throughout the audience to start up these supposedly spontaneous reactions, Nikolas thought.

"The water went bad," Adams continued, "spreading plague even as it used to spread life. People died by the thousands; whole nations were wiped from the Earth. Crops wilted in the fields. And so we, our ancestors, came from cities and countries far and wide, places whose names we've forgotten, looking for that good water. They wandered in the desert for months, these seven lost tribes. And just when it seemed they could walk no more, that they would surely die out there on those treeless plains, fate was kind to them. They settled on the banks of the vast freshwater sea, the greatest the world has ever seen. And the tribes began to multiply. And the wondrous things kept springing."

Mayor Adams paused for emphasis but raised his hand, holding back the audience's reaction.

"Soon the Seven Tribes built the Seven Cities. We entered the After-Time. And it was a good time. A peaceful time. But, as always, men became greedy. Then The Great War came and many lives were lost— fathers and husbands, brothers and sons, wives and daughters. But out of it came something good. The Baikal Treaty. The Seven Cities came together and vowed to work as one. So long as one of us has clean water, we agreed, none shall go thirsty. This treaty has held until today. And the Seven remained unbroken.

"But now the water has gone bad again. And the rotting-sickness mentioned in the great book is upon us again. And standing here before you, in these dark and troubling times, I am forced to wonder: Did we truly survive? Or was it that we were never tested?"

To Nikolas's amazement, even some of his friends were listening now, half-rapt by what Mayor Adams was saying, their ironic postures deflated. Couldn't they see through his suave veneer? This man had no philosophy, only a shiny rhetoric. At least Elias did not seem taken in. Sure, the Mayor's all-too-natural confidence was charming; everyone loves a man fully himself. But the purpose our charms serve is the measure of us.

"Because now, at the moment of our greatest need, the Unity crumbles. The Treaty is forgotten," Mayor Adams said. "This threatens our hard-won peace."

Here was the crescendo. He drummed his fist against the podium, hammering the notes of his performance.

"But I cannot . . . " His fist hit the podium. "I will not . . . " He struck it again. ". . . stand by as Joshua City goes thirsty."

The crowd went into a paroxysm of applause.

※ ※ ※

Nikolas and his friends pushed their way to the front of the lecture hall. Again, Adrian followed. It was hotter up here. People jostled in the aisles, trying to make themselves heard. Adrian hoped the question-and-answer session would not be long.

Nikolas listened as Mayor Adams answered the first question. Wasn't there something a little scripted in the way the engineering skolar, who looked just a few years too old, asked the question about improvements to safety mechanisms on the Joshua City rail lines? And didn't Mayor Adams's "I'm glad you asked" come a little too quickly? *Great*, Nikolas thought, *another question about trains.*

Even the more interesting questions were phrased in a leading way.

"How would you respond to those who say there is no proof of Ulan-Ude's involvement in the, um, recent health issues?" said a young man who claimed to be a medikal skolar.

"Well, to them I'd say that we have ample evidence of Ulan-Ude's involvement. Now, much of that evidence has not been released to the public for security reasons. However, rest assured that it will be made public at the time it is safe to do so. For right now, it should be noted that Ulan-Ude has had every opportunity to refute these charges. There has been a total breakdown in diplomacy."

Nikolas lifted his hand. But just then one of Adams's men, dressed in the desert-browns and water-blues of the Baikal Guard, came out onto the stage and whispered something in Mayor Adams's ear. Adams nodded and turned a face of exaggerated disappointment toward the crowd.

"Ladies and Gentlemen," he said, "I deeply apologize, but we'll have to cut this portion of the evening short. I've just been reminded I've got a city to run."

There was mild laughter and then more applause as Adams walked off, waving to the crowd. But below that, a few boos. "Coward!" someone yelled. Elias and the others were by the exits, smoking. Adrian was right behind him. He looked pale and feverish.

"Come on," Nikolas said. "Maybe he'll talk to me outside."

※ ※ ※

The cool night air made Adrian feel a little better. There was a rope-line leading from the rear exit of Titus Hall to Adams's idling motorcade. Armed Baikal Guardsmen stood at regular intervals, thumbing their weapons and looking nervously at the protestors. The protestors had doubled in number, and their shouting filled the air. Elias and the others, feigning boredom, had headed off to find *defiling fluids*, as Elias phrased it. Adrian had to admit his relief at their departure.

"WE DON'T WANT YOUR SENSELESS SLAUGHTER! WE WON'T DRINK YOUR BLOODY WATER!"

Someone pounded a tribal drum from Ulan-Ude.

"WE DON'T WANT YOUR SENSELESS SLAUGHTER! WE WON'T DRINK YOUR BLOODY WATER!"

Closer to the rope itself, the crowd went perhaps five meters deep of admirers waiting to shake Adams's hand or get him to sign something. There was press, too, with motion-image kameras trained on the double doors of the exit.

"I'll never get close enough," Nikolas said.

Nearby, at the edge of the commons, there was a fountain. Seven medium-sized statues, one for each of the Seven Cities, encircled a stone basin in the shape of the Baikal Sea. Like the other fountains on campus, it had long since been shut off. Nikolas hopped up on the fountain's edge.

Nikolas's shadow stretched against the dying horizon. A tingle went over Adrian. He was filled by the water not in the fountains. Nikolas seemed like a gasoline bomb waiting for its fuse to be lit.

The doors swung open and Adams stepped out, surrounded by a dozen bodyguards and advisors. Adrian only caught glimpses through the crowd. Nikolas was a dark statue now. Mayor Adams stopped to talk to Dame Neville. She extended one gloved hand and he bent to kiss it. The playwright, Umberto Lemkin, said something to Mayor Adams and the Mayor laughed perfunctorily. He slapped Lemkin on the back and squeezed his shoulder before moving on.

Mayor Adams paused to take a foto with some skolars. The flashes turned the statues into bright gargoyles.

※ ※ ※

From his perch on the fountain, Nikolas saw the faces in the crowd, saw Adams's entourage. Nikolas felt afloat on the seething mass. He was not in control; there were forces that pushed him toward some inevitable crisis. But what was the crisis? It was taking a life of its own in the voices of the protestors, in the very design of the streets and buildings. Mayor Adams was close now—his ugly grinning mouth, his too-white teeth.

Nikolas pulled a loose chunk of rock from the fountain. It was dense desert brick with a severe heft. Nikolas looked to the protestors, questioning the pulse of their protest. Nikolas cocked his arm back and threw the jagged rock with all his strength.

※ ※ ※

Adrian staggered. The lights flashed and the rock traced a comet's arc. Something smelled wrong. *Burnt fish? Formaldehyde from the lab?* The comet rolled in the exploding sky, all the stars falling as it went up. The stars were snakes snowing down. He couldn't feel his arm. The drumming grew more frenzied, speeding the flow of his blood.

※ ※ ※

The rock struck one of the Guardsmen in the face with a misty red spray. He stumbled into the rope and dragged it down.

The Guardsmen took a defensive formation around Adams and hurried him to his car.

Nikolas took up the protestors' chant.

"WE DON'T WANT YOUR SENSELESS SLAUGHTER! WE WON'T DRINK YOUR BLOODY WATER!"

The others chanted with more fervor. Many more joined in, swept up by the violence of the words.

※ ※ ※

Mayor Adams was inside the limousine now and Vanya, good old Vanya, shifted into gear. Adams had not seen what happened. One minute he was addressing a charming young lady and the next he was being pushed rudely forward by his men.

"Did you see it, Vanya?"

"No, sir," he said. "I think something was thrown, sir."

"What do they want from me?"

Usually, when Mayor Adams asked questions like this, Vanya would pretend to consider for a moment and then give the kind of non-answer he knew his employer wanted to hear. But the riotous protestors were throwing themselves into the limousine, rocking it side to side. Vanya eased the car forward and the protestors surrounded them.

※ ※ ※

Adrian fell. Nikolas pushed his way through the crowd past people running in the opposite direction. A picket sign struck him in the face.

Adrian lay on the ground, twitching. Spittle gathered in the corners of his mouth, his eyes fluttering unnaturally. The riot Nikolas had started went on behind him, but that didn't matter now. He kneeled beside Adrian, sunk in the calm of his training. He checked Adrian's vitals.

A Guardsman grabbed his shoulder. "What is going on here?"

"He had a seizure," Nikolas said. "Don't worry. I'm a medikal skolar."

"Good work, citizen," the Guardsman said, moving on.

※ ※ ※

They had completely engulfed the car and were pounding on the hood. Someone hopped on the roof and the metal crumpled. The wooden stake of a picket sign stabbed at the window in three sharp thrusts. The glass didn't break, but thin lightning shot across its surface.

"Sir?" Vanya asked.

"Just get us out of here," Adams said.

Vanya had never disobeyed an order. A protestor fell beneath the limousine. He hit the brakes. But he had to get Mayor Adams to safety. He hit the gas again. The front wheels rose slowly and there was a scraping along the bottom. Another protestor jumped in front and he drove on. Another bump. Another scraping. The street was clear up ahead if they could make it that far.

※ ※ ※

Adrian woke up in his own bed. Nikolas was flipping through a thick book and listening to the radio.

"...gave a rousing speech at Joshua University today, but events took a nasty turn..."

Nikolas lowered the volume on the radio. As always after a seizure, a darkness was with Adrian; it would not pass for a day or more. It was like some creature coming over the horizon, too big to see in its entirety. "Some will call this an affliction," Father Samarov told him the first time it happened at the orphanage. "But in truth it is a special providence. It will bring you closer to God." But Adrian had never seen God during a fit, nor in the aftermath.

He sat up and nearly collapsed at the blade of pain between his eyes. "Did I...?"

Nikolas nodded.

"I made tea. I nearly had to strangle the concierge for some water."

"There are some pills," Adrian said and motioned toward the drawer where he kept them.

"I already gave you some," Nikolas said. "I hope I was right to do so. I started reading about . . . your condition. I know a little, but I've never treated someone."

Nikolas picked up the book, which Adrian recognized as his own neurology textbook, and snapped it shut.

"You wouldn't believe how useless it was. All this knowledge, and it's of no avail at the most important moments."

"Thank you."

Adrian took a sip of tea. The warmth radiated through him. His hands shook, but he managed not to drop the cup. Nikolas's eyes wandered to the radio.

"*. . . three injured, and rumors of at least one dead . . .*"

"Will you be all right?" Nikolas asked.

Adrian hesitated. How could he explain that this was the worst part? The attacks were nothing compared to it.

"I'm fine. This isn't the first time."

Adrian wondered how Nikolas had gotten him to their room. *He must have carried me like a helpless child across campus.*

"Why didn't you tell me?" Nikolas asked.

"I didn't want to you to think I was weak."

Nikolas gave him the same look of well-intentioned sympathy Adrian had seen since his condition first manifested when he was eight years old. It was frustrating to be the object of another's pity, but at least it was better than the disgust that was always on his uncle's face.

Adrian had only scattered memories of his parents. There were no fotografs, so the image of their faces had faded. But he did remember certain things. And he had his favorites. The feeling of his mother's wool sweater on his cheek, the smell of horse manure from the stables where his father worked. But he also remembered the beatings his uncle had administered—with anything available, a wooden spoon if they were in the kitchen, his bare hand, or his studded leather belt when he really wanted to do damage. When Adrian had his first seizure, his uncle thought he was faking to avoid being beaten again.

"I don't think you're weak," Nikolas said. "I imagine it takes a special kind of strength to live with something like that. I wouldn't presume to understand it, of course."

Adrian sat up straighter, ignoring the pain.

"You threw something, didn't you? Sometimes, right before one happens, I imagine things."

"Never mind that," Nikolas said as his attention drifted back to the radio.

They sat in brief silence. On the radio, the volume low but audible, a voice described the events with calm authority. There was now confirmation, the radio-lady said, that three agitators had died in the course of their organized disruption of Mayor Adams's speech.

"... no official statement from the mayor's office. Joshua Intelligence agents are still looking into the matter..."

Nikolas stood and walked absently toward the radio, his face slack, so consumed with what he had heard that he no longer noticed Adrian. Nikolas stopped in front of the radio, staring. His hands clenched slowly.

Adrian asked, "What does that mean?"

Nikolas paced the room twice.

"It means that our lives don't matter. It means the truth doesn't matter."

Nikolas's boots stalked the floor, his strides barely contained by the small room. He stopped again in front of the radio.

"That's not how it happened," Nikolas said.

※ ※ ※

Though Nikolas had not seen the car run over the protestors, he was right, of course. At this time in Joshua City there were many kinds of knowledge. There were the things you knew but did not want to admit you knew, things you saw briefly and then chose to look away from. Then there were the things you knew you knew. The known knowns, as it were. From Brandt, Nikolas knew power shaped his ability to perform his duties; medikal science, which ought to be about the preservation of life, no matter how weak, would be twisted by politics to serve the powerful. And he knew he was playing along for his own selfish good. Now he knew something else. Knowledge, or apparent knowledge, does not have to be true, and so you have knowledge of a thing you don't truly know. But when you've heard it on the radio, you think you know it, even if it's not true knowledge. The lure of the radio-lady. The lure of the trains. The lure of the slick rhetoric you know is not knowledge, but the opposite of knowledge. An unknown known. The lie you believe. But what Nikolas knew he needed to know were the unknown unknowns— the things he had previously not even known he needed to know.

Nikolas ended his exercise in tortured reasoning and turned off the radio.

CHAPTER TWO

BROTHERS IN ARMS

1.

SUCH A GOOD BIG BROTHER. Marcik bent over the puddle, sieve in hand, pail at his muddy feet. Had he not been aware of Sergeant Volfgang shouting him forward, the droplets leaping from the ground would have reminded him of the oversized rain boots his mother had given him as a child, the ones he lied about and said fit perfectly. The world was stingy with its rain, which makes any reasonable person wonder what virtue there is in the way the world supplies itself. Why isn't everything provided to us? The obvious answer is that life derives value from adversity ... but why? Is a cactus clinging to a bare rock-wall truer than a man gorging on hors d'oeuvres he doesn't even want?

Fredrik Vore, his fiery-orange hair hanging like the fur of a wet dog, was several meters ahead of Marcik, sliding the pail along and draining his sieve in one continuous motion. Marcik thought of another soldierly task he had struggled with at first: draining the rain tarps, their weighty udders of accumulated water sagging and shifting beneath his hands, and then funneling the water into the troughs. He tried to guide their fluid weight toward the reservoirs unsuccessfully, and eventually, despite his panic and feeling of hopelessness, he mastered the task.

And yet he felt he would not be able to do the same thing here. There are dexterous minds, those that quickly absorb the gist of a task, and then there are those that learn slowly. Is slower learning a more nuanced learning? Perhaps. Or maybe it is just clumsiness, nervousness, ineptitude. In the end, there are probably just as many ways of learning as there are people, and though the generous-minded or idealistic among us refuse to say so, not all people are equal.

But there are those who have it worse, Marcik's mother had written. He could not quite get it, this fluid motion. It was three separate actions, made more difficult by the cumbersome contraption of the sieve and the sergeant's jeering voice. *Doesn't he know he's making it worse, watching me like that?* Marcik's water-pruned hands fumbled at the long wooden handles of the sieve.

"Soak it up, you nekrotic scabs!" Sergeant Volfgang said.

Marcik sped his pace, scooting his pail forward with the instep of his foot like Fredrik. The pail tilted and Marcik let go of one side of the sieve. He grabbed at it, trying to catch its draining contents. Half the pooled mud slid down his pants' leg, and the other half dumped into the pail. He looked down at the water he had ruined.

The sergeant called Fredrik back. Fredrik trudged with his pail back across the field and put himself to the task of cleaning up one more mess Marcik had made.

"Private Vore" the sergeant said. "Soak up Private Kovalski's parts." The others nearby laughed as the sergeant had meant them to.

Fredrik lifted Marcik's pail and redrained it through his sieve into his own bucket. Marcik put his hands on the sieve to steady it, knowing he was annoying Fredrik further, getting in his way more than helping.

"I have the task in hand, Private Kovalski," Fredrik said, falling back on their rank to hide his anger.

As Fredrik bent over the pail, he grimaced, and Marcik noticed the deepening of the pocks in his cheeks, the rot of his teeth, the white specks on his gums.

※ ※ ※

Later that night, Private Marcik Kovalski sat on his bunk with a candle balanced in his lap. Someone had pushed a table to the center of the room and there was a card game with cigarettes and rations as the wagers. A fan whirred rattlingly, sending its breeze over him at irregular intervals. Someone was listening to the radio on the other side of the barracks. Someone else was humming along to the tune of the popular song "The Single Bed."

Marcik paid none of this any mind. He held his mother's letter to one side so that he wouldn't get wax drippings on it. The light was poor, but he liked the way the candle shone through the paper, making the words seem to extend off the page. It was the third time he had read the letter; he practically had it memorized.

%% %% %%

Dear Marcik,

I doubt you have time to read letters from your poor old mother. But the house feels so empty since you've been gone. This is the first time in my life I've lived alone. I met your father while still a girl and then after he passed there was always you and Nikolas around the house. My two little men! You make me so proud. Do you ever talk to him? I know you have had your disagreements, but he will always be your brother, and it's not right for you to go on fighting. Family is all we have in the world.

I make it sound worse than it is. There are still the customers for my seamstressing, mostly neighborhood women who bring me the hard jobs that they cannot handle themselves. Not so many anymore. There is not much money to throw around. Many of their boys have joined the Guard like you, and sometimes their husbands have too. It is our duty of course to support our city, but with them goes their jobs. I sometimes think that most of the work these women bring me is out of pity.

But there I go, feeling sorry for myself. Just the other day a servant girl came to the little booth I run at the market. She was there from a rich lady, a minister's wife, imagine that! She needed a new gown for one of those high society parties. How she had heard about me, I can't imagine. The girl seemed shocked when I quoted her the price. I suppose she expected me to give her an inflated quote like everyone else, knowing her mistress was rich. No doubt Nikolas would say I should have. You know how he always spoke of rich people. I am just not made that way, I guess.

※ ※ ※

More people were gathering around the radio. There was quiet chatter among them, but Marcik tried to ignore it. They stood tightly together, their backs to him. One Guardsman slapped his friend on the shoulder and laughed a happy laugh. Marcik turned back to his letter.

※ ※ ※

But there are those who have it worse: Mrs. Ang has a son with the skin-rot and she cannot afford to have a doktor in. Maybe Nikolas can take a look at the boy if he ever comes home. If you get a day off maybe you could visit him? I've sent him letters but he probably doesn't have the time to write back. The work of a medikal skolar must be very demanding.

By the way, I am working on a fotograf collection. I am arranging the pictures in order, and I've just gotten to the time Nikolas was born. You are three years old and holding him in your arms. Such a good big brother. What happened between you two? I can't help but blame myself. I don't mean to hurt you. But Nik was always so much stronger. I never meant to play favorites, and in a way, I have always loved you more. But just look what he's done, and just think of what he will do.

Your choice, which I support of course, to join the Baikal Guard worries me. I trust you in every way—but are you ready for this?

Still, these fotos give me comfort: it's like having the house filled again with people and the happiness of past times. I hope to see you soon, my little snow-horse, and then everything will be like those days again.

Love,

Mama

※ ※ ※

"Marcik?" It was Fredrik. As usual he was chewing on a rope of taffy. He pulled at the candy with a disgusting smacking sound.

Marcik folded the letter quickly but carefully, making sure to follow the creases, and put it back in its envelope. Then he opened the cigar box beside him on the bed. It was full of similar letters, all in the same pale blue envelopes. Under the letters, in a cloth bag, was the letter opener he had used, gently slicing the envelopes open with such care they looked untouched. If anyone ever found the letter opener they might confiscate it; anything that could be used as a weapon had to be regulation. Marcik snapped the box shut.

"What is it? Can't you see I'm reading?"

"You're always reading one, aren't you?" He adopted a high-pitched motherly tone. "Your Mommy Dearest misses you so very very much. I hope you have someone to tuck you in and sing to you like I always did. Should I send you some of Mommy's special sugar-cake? A million hugs and kisses for my special little boy—"

Marcik knew Fredrik meant no harm, but still the words stung. Before he could manage a proper retort, a commotion rose from the radio-crowd.

"What are those idiots on about?" Fredrik asked.

"No idea."

Fredrik hopped down from his bunk athletically. "Let's go find out."

Marcik slid the cigar box under his mattress, and got up to join him. Fredrik shouldered their way in.

"*. . . ongoing investigation. Ulani agents suspected of . . .*"

"What's happening?" Fredrik asked.

"We're going to stomp some Ulanis into the sand is what's happening."

"Joshua City-style. They're going to get run off the tracks," another said.

They all seemed so self-satisfied and eager, even Fredrik. One of them shoved another playfully and sent him bouncing into Marcik. Marcik stumbled back, outside the circle again.

"You goatfucker!" the first Guardsman-in-training said to his friend. "Now we're going to see some real action."

Marcik looked back to his bunk where his letters were stashed and wondered if he was ready for war.

2.

From the Journals of Nikolas Kovalksi:

I WAS EIGHT, Marcik ten. Father had left mysteriously one evening, never to return, and it was just the three of us now—Mother, Marcik, and I. Marcik and I shared a small pallet. We breathed each other's air, guessed each other's thoughts, and stepped gingerly over each other's boots and moods. At times it was comforting, but mostly it was stifling. I was the younger brother—and I knew even then that I was the braver, the stronger, the smarter; Marcik's being two years older afforded him the official title *man of the house*, but it was an open secret who could be depended on for things that mattered. When Mother needed something from the market, I had to accompany Marcik, because she trusted me to get it right. But it was Marcik who carried the money and did the purchasing.

"It makes him feel older," Mother said.

I didn't bother to argue. Let him have his illusions, I reasoned.

And it was I who had to hold Marcik when there was thunder on the horizon, its rumble vibrating our thin walls—but next morning he was all orders-given and orders-obeyed, a natural Guardsman before he ever became one.

One evening, as Mother was serving up the boiled cabbage whose smell I loathed, Marcik burst in, nearly ripping the door from its rotted hinges. He had a leaflet and was waving it like a captured flag. For a minute, I thought it might be an exam from primary school. I felt a twinge of annoyance: there were already ten or twelve such exams plastering the walls—Satisfactories mostly. My Outstandings were received with a perfunctory pat on the head and shoved in a drawer. I was preparing my mind for my future in university studies, while he was still engaged in boyish games. I watched Mother to see if she would scold him for being late.

"Karnival's coming," Marcik said. "May we go, mama? May we?"

"Let me see." I grabbed for the leaflet, but he ducked behind the sewing table. My elbow sent a spool of thread unraveling across the floor. Mother bent and gathered it up without complaint. She stood between us and laid her hand on Marcik's shoulder. He grinned at me.

"I'm afraid that's impossible," she said.

He pouted. "But it's only half a dram."

"Unless..." She turned to me. "I know you were saving for that watch, Nikolas."

"Compass," I corrected.

I had been planning to slip away one night—past the Guardsmen standing watch at the borders of Joshua City, where trenches had already been dug for the Outer Wall—to see what was left of this hell-swept planet.

"It would mean so much to him."

She gave me her adult look, the one that said: *Humor him. For me.* Marcik studied a crack in the ceiling. He wanted to say something, but knew it would not be to his advantage. I swallowed and nodded yes.

"What do you say to your brother, Marcik?"

"Thank you," he mumbled.

"Look him in the eye."

"Thank you, Nikolas."

His glance slid off me with an oily quickness, and he went to the bedroom looking for all the world as if he had been punished. Mother squeezed my hand and smiled at me.

The following morning, we were off in our Sunday best. The karnival was ten blocks away in an overgrown field. The ticket-taker seemed unsurprised to see boys our age, though I did detect a strange carnivorous glint in his one good eye when I asked directions to the Puppet Palace. The other eye was made of glass, a milky thing that wandered in its dark socket. Marcik stared dry-mouthed and refused to give him the ticket until I pinched his arm. He hit me and I elbowed him off.

Marcik wanted to try out the firing range, so we did that, taking aim at targets no bigger than teaspoons. He could barely shoulder the rifle. We were out another quarter-dram, and for our troubles we were awarded a second-rate inkstand. Then he wanted to see the Mermaid

Lady, who turned out to be an ordinary, not even pretty, woman in a sequin dress with papier-mâché fins.

"Let's play," Marcik said, pointing to a bright red tent with a large slick table with slits cut in either end; the goal was to sink all seven black pucks, and the player who sank more won the game. The pucks represented the Seven Cities, and so reminded me of the time I let him win at the Seven Cities board game and why I had promised myself never play such games with Marcik again.

I told him we were going to the Puppet Palace instead. I expected him to argue, but he simply shrugged. Then at the door to the Puppet Palace, he hesitated. The grinning maw of the Puppeteer hung over an archway draped with strings, so that it seemed we might become aktors in the grisly drama ourselves.

"Don't be a baby," I said.

Now that we were here, I was determined to enjoy myself. We had spent over half the money I had saved that summer, and the puppet show had been the chief attraction for me when I saw the leaflet. I silenced Mother's voice in my head.

"It was you who wanted to come to this stupid karnival," I reminded Marcik.

I pushed him down a shadowy corridor into a crowded musty room. Rows of rickety chairs were set up before a box-frame stage. The light was dim but not menacing, and the Puppet-Box was unimposing. I prepared to be bored. The lights dropped off and a cavernous voice filled the stands.

"Ladies and Gentlemen!" the announcer began. "Creatures big and small! What you are about to witness will shock and amaze, horrify and thrill! It is not for the faint of heart. Those without courage are advised to leave."

Marcik gripped the arms of his chair. The lights dimmed further and a red glow emanated from the cracks between the floorboards of the stage. A cool track of nerves ran along my arms and back. The sensation was pleasant—this mild fear I knew to be unattended by actual danger. The question of why people would pay for this sort of entertainment struck me briefly. It didn't come to me in those terms, of course, but now I marvel at the price people are willing to pay to be scared, to be reminded of their imminent and perhaps horrific deaths. They are frightened of the truth, but still they want to experience it. (This is what, if I understand the theory correctly, Doktor Laikan means by *limit-desires*. Even as we recoil from the inescapable realness of violence and pain and death, we are likewise drawn to it and desire it—though, to be honest, I can rarely make full sense of her writings.)

The Puppet Master appeared, a stooped figure in a robe and pointed black hood like an executioner's mask. He addressed the audience in a hiss, his mantis-like head swiveling in its hood. Marcik was halfway out of his seat, looking back toward the exit.

"Sit down," I whispered. "I'm not leaving."

Marcik hunkered back in his seat.

"It is said by races older than ours," the Puppet Master was intoning, "races who possess a knowledge beyond the reach of our feeble science, that the Puppet Master may control more than what lies at the end of his strings . . . that he may, in his tugging manipulations, touch something in the very soul—a Puppet soul within us all—and in doing so wield absolute control."

I allowed myself a glance to Marcik and enjoyed his palpable terror. It served him right, acting like my better. Some man of the house he was. Couldn't even watch a puppet show without pissing himself.

The Puppet Master ripped off the hood. It was the ticket-taker from earlier. The eye had been removed and all that was left was the socket. He stared directly at us, and there was a dizzy moment when I felt I would be sucked down that blind hole. His head swiveled on to other audience members, but the image of that meaty absence was seared in my imagination.

"Does he tug at you?" the Puppet Master asked.

Marcik made a sad little spasm at the sound of his voice. I put my hand on his arm to reassure him, though I ought to have let him suffer alone. He recoiled and made for the exit. He stumbled out, trying to retain some composure. I considered following him, already envisioning the real dangers outside. At the same time, I was pleased in a way I didn't want to admit to myself. It was the pleasure of seeing everything go according to plan—as if I had known Marcik would bolt and I would have the slow joy of being alone with the Puppet show, as if I had known he might be kidnapped or lost in the karnival forever when I didn't go out after him. I forced the image of Mother from my head and watched the Puppet Master manipulate his puppets into a wonderful play.

About half an hour later, I found Marcik sitting on a discarded plank of wood, just outside the entrance to the Puppet Palace. He was no longer crying, but his face was streaked and his eyes puffy. When he saw me, he came lunging in a fury of snivels and balled fists. We fell back against a tent post, and something metal scraped down the side of my face. Eventually he tired of hitting me. He wiped his nose. He looked at the gash down my face and at the blood I could feel warm and wet on my cheek and neck. I looked back in perfect calm. His tears had proven who was who between us.

"I hate you," he said. "I'll always hate you."

He kicked me one last time and then ran off, into that confusion of blinkering lights and whirring contraptions. I stood and brushed myself off, wondering how I would to explain all of this to Mother.

3.

THE TRAIN-DOGS were out in alarming numbers. There weren't so many of them close to Joshua University, but as the train rolled deep into New Jerusalem, Nikolas and Adrian saw them wandering the station platforms, waiting for the trains to stop and the doors to open so they could board. Mangy black terriers; woeful yellow hounds; enormous huskies with mismatched blue and black eyes; Baikal water-dogs too far inland; proud wolfish laikas; the grinning jackal hybrids—no matter the breed, they all had one thing in common: a feral desperation. Their ribs pressed against once shiny coats, now covered in dirt and dried blood from alley fights.

Adrian tried to remember if there had been so many the last time he came this way. At first, the train-dogs were a harmless curiosity. Joshuans on their way to work found them soothing and offered scraps from their lunches; children petted them or chased them from car to car; one zoologist had even authored a monograf on the migratory patterns of canines in urban settings. But in recent months, their numbers had grown, and there were reports of attacks now and then as more feral dogs joined the packs.

Adrian eyed the train-dogs warily, thinking how much things had changed since he had last taken this route several months ago.

"I grew up in a neighborhood like this," Nikolas said.

It was a Saturday several weeks after the protest and they were heading to a meeting with Elias, Mouse, and the others—the Progressive Skolars for a Better Baikal, as they called themselves. After the events of Mayor Adams's speech, it had taken some coaxing by Nikolas to get Adrian to come out with him again. But eventually Adrian had given in, enjoying as he did the frank and sometimes heated political discussions he and Nikolas had. Besides, he knew it would be good to start socializing.

"So did I."

"If I ever wake up screaming in the middle of the night," Nikolas said with amused bitterness, "it's because I've been dreaming of my childhood."

As he often did when he remembered his childhood, Nikolas unconsciously touched the scar on his cheek that Marcik had given him that night at the karnival.

※ ※ ※

Adrian thought about his own childhood. After his father left, his mother became a ghost of her former self. She moved through the shadowy rooms of their house in a shapeless gray nightgown, fingering at the rosary beads around her neck. She did not seem to want a relationship with anyone, least of all him, but when Sunday came around, she put on her best clothes and made her way down to St. Cyrill's to kneel in the pews until her knees were sore and she could barely walk back.

His mother had no means of supporting them, and so his father's brother moved into the house. Adrian did not recall anyone asking him to do that, but he acted as if Adrian and his mother were an insufferable burden, one last gift from his failure of a brother. After a few weeks, he began sharing Adrian's mother's bed. Adrian did not believe his mother loved his uncle; in fact, she seemed hardly more aware of him than she did of Adrian.

And shortly after exercising his privileges with Adrian's mother, his uncle began *disciplining* him. At first, it would be to-bed-without-dinner or sit-yourself-in-that-corner, but it grew worse. His mother never lifted a finger to stop his uncle, and even made excuses. He resented her for that, though he knew he should not.

One day he came home from primary school and his mother greeted him at the door. The fire of life burned in her eyes. Her cheeks were flushed and her entire body seemed to radiate heat.

"Mother," he said, "are you sick?"

She squeezed his hand.

"I prayed today and I've seen the way. I've been asking and asking what to do and finally he's showed me."

"Who, mother?"

"Why ... Him, of course."

Adrian was afraid of her then. This possession did not seem holy, but rather its opposite. Still, he was only eight years old. What did he know? Besides, he was grateful that his mother was speaking to him. That night, he slept uneasily, and in the morning when he went to wake his mother for breakfast, he found her hanging by a rope. His uncle was not at home, having taken an extra shift at the slaughterhouse, and Adrian didn't know what to do. Should he try to get her down? But how? A boy, small and weak as he was, had no options.

And so she hung there for hours. Adrian could not recall how long his mother hung there, lightly penduluming and growing ev-ermore bloated and blue-skinned. He stumbled into the corner and pressed himself against the wall and slid down the wall into a crouched-scared-animal position. The light from the window was a sharp sliver that shifted across the hardwood floor as the day passed and the sun made its steady journey across the sky. It seemed to move faster then more slowly then faster again. He would not let the sliver of light touch her, he told himself. Before that happened he would cut her down. But the light shone on her old yellow stocking, the hole in the toe there, a bit of hard sharp toenail sticking through. It crept up her legs, the veins like tiny blue wires, and still he did nothing. His mother stank worse than anything he had ever smelled, worse than the public dump near their house, where all the households in their neigh-borhood dumped their rotting food, soiled paper, and other trash. Her eyes bulged and Adrian tried not to look at them but they stared right at him and he felt he had to meet their gaze or else he was denying his mother in some obscure way. When the windows went dark, he began crying in full-body heaves, sucking air into his scrawny chest and drip-ping snot down his face.

He may have blacked out more than once. He prayed and prayed to God to bring his mother back, closing his eyes and mouthing the words in a reverent whisper, but every time he opened his eyes again, there she was, hanging in her nightgown, eyes bulging inhumanly.

Finally, his uncle came home and cut her down like a slab of meat at the slaughterhouse. When he sawed through the final bit of rope, her body dropped with a ghoulish lurch, and his uncle caught her awk-wardly under her arms. Her rosary beads broke and scattered across the floor. Adrian's uncle looked at him accusingly but said nothing.

After his mother's death, his uncle's violence grew worse. Even though his mother had not intervened on Adrian's behalf, her absence seemed to give his uncle further license to do as he would with Adri-an. There was no longer a watchful presence, however passive, to hold him back. Adrian would not have to endure this for long, however. Two months later, Adrian had his first epileptic fit. His uncle did not understand Adrian's disease.

"I won't suffer a defective to live under my roof," his uncle said, claiming ownership of Adrian's house. "In a better society, we'd put weaklings like you out in the desert to die."

As soon as his uncle could get the paperwork settled, Adrian was sent off to the orphanage.

※ ※ ※

At St. Ignatius's Home for Boys, there was the shadow from the stained glass window—the way it crept across the floor in the darkened dormitory room at night. He knew it was the image of the Harbinger, which was plainly visible by day, but at night it became a long-toothed monster. He prayed harder during the day to make up for these sinful thoughts. The other boys teased him. They preferred to spend as little time as possible in the damp cold rectory, instead playing cornerball and swinging on the trapeze bars. But he liked the smell of the rectory, the quiet there. It reminded him of his mother.

※ ※ ※

As Nikolas and Adrian neared their destination, the people changed with the scenery. At first the train was crowded with skolars, but they got off at the motion-image theatre or in the garment distrikt of Printz-Påhlsson or at the last strip of university taverns. As the train moved through the neighborhood of Baikyong-shi, the high-end businesses were replaced with plankwood stalls selling fermented burdock root and pickled pigs' feet. Kiosks sold threadbare rugs in a haze of lilac incense. Then they moved into the workers' distrikt of Brecht-Altgard where the faktories expelled a thicker, less pleasant smoke. It coated the streets and the windows of butcher shops and the tombs in the churchyards. Now the people on the train were bored or tired or desperate-looking. A drunk with a broken nose chugged from a bottle in a bag. His feet were shoeless and black and caked with mud. A washerwoman held her two children protectively. Adrian waved at the little boy, but he buried his head in his mother's coat.

The train-dogs stretched out on the benches and curled up on the floor. Hadn't they begun to eat the flesh of the nekrotic dead? Adrian wasn't sure he believed that. Even so, they did not exactly look friendly—as likely to bite your fingers off as lick them.

The train stopped in front of an iron foundry and a group of workers boarded. They were large men with arms like twisted rope. They paid the dogs no more mind than the passengers. They slapped each other on the back and made ribald jokes. One man put two fingers up to his mouth and stuck his tongue between them, making a lizardy licking motion. Adrian wanted to turn away from this crudity, but who was he to judge these men? They worked hard, laughed, drank together, and at the end of the day went home to their families and a hot meal.

The men exited the train with a fraternal ruckus.

"I grew up around men like them," Nikolas said. "Strange to have strayed so far from one's past."

He looked out the window absently.

"Yes, I know," Adrian said, "but you could see it as a good thing, a kind of progress."

"Oh, I wouldn't trade places with them. I've certainly gained many things, but there's also been something lost. And in a way I never left their world."

The New Jerusalem platform was all sagging plywood and ugly gray concrete. The walls were painted with stick-figure drawings and outsized anatomy. *Mair Adamz fuks his mother*, someone had scrawled in angry red letters. *And she likes it*, a different more literate author had written underneath. Even the sky seemed grayer here. There would be rain, which in Joshua City was always welcome, but somehow Adrian doubted it would bring much optimism in these parts.

A man wrapped in bandages stumbled toward them. Adrian smelled the stink of rotten flesh.

"Brother," the man said. Only part of his face was visible, where the bandages had come off to reveal wet pink skin.

The man fell to his knees, almost in an attitude of worship. Nikolas bent over him and put a hand on his head.

"Yes, brother," he said. "Tell us how we can help."

"Brother," the man said. Now he collapsed. Bloody drool trickled from his mouth onto the train platform.

"Adrian," Nikolas said. "Help me."

Adrian forced himself forward. He had seen many nekrotics at St. Ignatius's, but seeing one and touching his ulcerated skin were different things altogether. But what sort of doktor would he make if he couldn't do even this? They lifted the man under his arms and got him to his feet. They walked him, step by step, down the stairs of the train platform to St. Leocadia Avenue. They approached an old woman in her sabbath garments; she recoiled and scurried off, crossing herself all the while. Other pedestrians gave them a wide berth and avoided eye contact.

"What should we do?" Adrian said.

The man was coughing violently now.

"There's an infirmary around here," Nikolas said. "I came here once for my research but I can't quite..." Nikolas looked left, then right. "I believe it's down that way."

They dragged the man around a corner, past a grocery with fly-swarmed vegetables. The owner came out and yelled at them in the language of Baikyong-do, lilting nasal sounds Adrian didn't understand, though their intent was obvious. *Get that nekrotic away from my store.*

"Are you sure it's this way?" Adrian asked.

Nikolas kept moving. The man muttered as they dragged him, a steady stream of nonsense interrupted by fits of coughing. In addition to the rot, he reeked of urine and liquor. They saw the sign, a pink cross ringed in blue. *St. Leocadia Infirmary.* In the entryway, a man slumped in a wheelchair. He was so still that Adrian wasn't sure he was alive;

then he wheezed and his breathing apparatus contracted, expanded. A woman behind the front desk looked up with vacant eyes until she saw the wet sticky bandages on the man's face.

"Not in here," she said, waving them out the door.

"This man is very sick," Nikolas said.

"I can see that," she said. "Take him around back. Didn't you see the signs?"

They dragged the man out into the street again. There was a small sign with an arrow pointing down an alley: *Nekrosis Ward.* The alley was littered with old broken gurneys, waste cans stuffed with dirty bandages, used syringes. One of the train-dogs had a bandage in its mouth and was tossing it back and forth. Nikolas shooed the dog away as he passed, and it ran behind an overturned crate.

The nekrosis ward was lined with small cots, patients in various states of decay. The stench was unbelievable. There didn't seem to be a check-in desk, nor any staff in sight.

"This can't be right," Nikolas said. "Where are the doktors?"

From the next room over came a moan of agony.

"We can't just leave him here," Adrian said.

"There's a free bed."

They dragged the nekrotic to a cot by the window. The same ugly gray light fell through the crosshatched bars to show a mattress stained with blood and something fouler, yellow-green in color. Nikolas placed the man on the floor and pulled the sheet off the mattress.

"We need a fresh sheet," Nikolas said.

Adrian moved through the ward, stepping over bodies, trying his best to ignore the pleas for help. He tried several doors and found them locked. He went down a light-flickering hallway. At the hallway's end, he turned another knob and a door swung open. A supply closet. Brooms, mops. Cleaning supplies. And a pile of dirty linen. He grabbed a bottle of bleach and soaked a sheet with it. When it was done he rung it out as best he could. If the bleach got in the man's wounds it would sting terribly, but it would also disinfect them.

When he returned, Nikolas was flipping the mattress with the aid of a large muscular man. His hair was long, coarse, and woven through with snakeskin in the Ulani style.

"There you are, my friend," the man said to Adrian. The man slapped him on the back warmly, as though they had known each other for years. "You have the sheet? Good."

"You don't have something cleaner?" Adrian asked, handing him the wadded rag.

The man shook his head. "Too many sick. Not enough sheets."

They put the sheet on the mattress and the man told them of the infirmary's troubles. He spoke with an accent but knew common Slovnik well enough. The other patients refused to be housed with the nekrotics so they had been moved to their own ward. Even some of the doktors and nurses refused to treat them, despite the fact that a healthy person had little to fear.

"We are alone here," the man said. "With so many. It is good to find ones who care."

When they were done, the man shook their hands, nearly crushing Adrian's in his giant paw. "You are medikal skolars, yes? You will tell the word? Tell what it is like here?"

Adrian and Nikolas assured him they would. They took one last look at the man they had saved—for now at least—and stepped out into the street.

"It wasn't like that when I was here just a few months ago," Nikolas said. "It was bad, but at least functional."

Adrian said nothing, leaving Nikolas to his brooding as they walked the dilapidated streets.

※ ※ ※

The place had no name, so people called it The Nameless Tavern. Underneath a tin awning, propped up by wooden poles of different lengths, the door stood open. Somehow that did not make it look any more inviting. The floor was covered with sawdust—"To soak up the spilled drinks," Nikolas explained to Adrian as they stepped inside. "And various other fluids, unfortunately."

A few tired broken-looking customers sat at the bar. One looked up at Adrian and Nikolas then went back to staring into the mystery of his drink. It was still the lunch hour; his drunken slump suggested this man was unemployed. Adrian read the papers and listened to the radio: he knew how few jobs there were. Many Joshuans blamed it on the immigrants, but of course there had also been immigrants back when jobs were plentiful.

The war will solve all our woes soon enough, as Adrian had often heard Nikolas say.

Elias and his friends were in a gloomy back corner. He stood to greet Nikolas and Adrian, swayed a little, caught himself on the back of a chair. He grinned, proud of his drunken state.

"Fair Nik," he said. "Have you come to save us with lively debate?"

"You've wasted no time, I see."

By way of apology, Elias held up his open hands. "You were late," he said. "You've brought your roommate. I'm sorry. I forget your name."

"It's Adrian," Nikolas said.

"It's all right," Adrian assured them both. "Hello again."

Mouse, the girl he had met at the protest, smiled and scrunched her nose at Adrian. "Hi, Adrian," she said. Adrian couldn't tell if she was making fun of him. Around Nikolas's friends, he often felt as though he were missing some inside joke.

Elias's other friend had thick black-framed glasses and a severe look. His wiry black hair stood high on an acne-scarred forehead. He nodded at Adrian but didn't introduce himself.

"That's Peytr," Elias said, stubbing out his cigarette and immediately lighting another. "He doesn't talk. He maintains that words are for the bourgeois."

"I see," Adrian said, not seeing at all.

Elias clapped his hands together. "Drinks?" he offered. "I had Dmitri bring the bottle. We could practice moderation, but why deny our essential nature?" He smiled, pleased with his witticism.

He went around the table, filling their glasses from an unlabeled bottle of clear liquor.

"None for me, thanks," Adrian said.

"Are you sure?" Elias tilted the bottle invitingly. "This stuff can fuel a train engine."

Elias studied him, and Adrian prepared himself for some subtle barb. Instead, Elias shrugged. "More for me," he said.

%% %% %%

Over the next half hour, Adrian watched and listened to the revelry at the table. Each drink was followed by an exaggerated grimace, a wiping of the mouth with a shirtsleeve, a dramatic slamming of the glass on the table. Playing master of ceremonies, Elias promptly refilled their glasses. Nikolas drank with the rest of them but didn't engage in their joviality. Cigarette smoke hovered in a fog, making Adrian mildly nauseous. At one point, a woman entered the tavern. She wore the mask of the Faceless Prophet of Baikalingrad. The cheeks of her mask were painted with a delicate pink blush. Around the eyeholes of the mask, eyelashes had been painted on as well. She moved quickly and purposefully through the room; clearly she had been here before. All the men in the tavern, and even Mouse, noticed her. Though you couldn't see her face, you could tell she was beautiful. She was dressed in form-fitting black: black pants that emphasized her long shapely legs; a tight black sweater. But it wasn't just her body that made her beautiful. It was the way she walked, her defiant go-ahead-and-test-me posture.

The masked people of Baikalingrad wore masks to honor the Faceless Prophet, Adrian knew. The Faceless Prophet had not actually been faceless but horribly burned in a refinery accident. By covering the face, his teachings went, superficial judgments were removed and souls could communicate unhindered by corporeal distractions. But now, watching this woman disappear up a stairway in the back of the room, Adrian wondered if there wasn't an unintended consequence to the masks. Isn't there something more intriguing, more erotic even, about what we cannot see? The guiles of imagination tempt more thoroughly than vulgar reality.

(If imagination is more powerful than reality, reality can nevertheless intrude upon the imaginary—*and wasn't that woman as much reality as imagined possibility?*—by the insistent nature of its concrete presence. Isn't beauty the perfect confluence of the imagined and the real?)

After the woman had disappeared, it took a little while even for Elias to recapture the smooth flow of his rhetoric, the nonchalant bandying-about of lofty ideas. The question turned to how best to communicate their goals to the proletariat.

"Maybe we should have, I don't know, a seminar or something," Mouse suggested. "Like this meeting, only bigger."

Elias agreed but took it one step further.

"We've got to take the message to them. To their faktories. To their homes. We've got to teach them what's good for them," he opined, loud enough for anyone in the tavern to hear, including the very working class patrons he was talking about. "They lack our tools of discernment. They can't see the shape of the machine from inside the machine."

"Isn't this all a little ... I don't know ... presumptuous?" Adrian asked. It was his first contribution to the conversation. Everyone turned toward him.

"How so?" Elias asked.

Mouse gave Adrian a sympathetic smile. Peytr continued to scowl silently. From behind his cigarette, Nikolas projected a casual curiosity. Adrian felt he must say something significant.

"You talk about them as if they were children ... or a different species," Adrian said. "But they aren't. They're people, just like you and me. And some are older than us, wiser. They've done things we never will. Hard things ... "

Elias began to object, but Adrian was warming to his subject. "All their lives they've been told what to do. *Work this job you don't want to work, pay these taxes. Fight this war for us.* Why should they listen to us? We would be just one more voice telling them what to do."

Elias smiled. "I hardly think our message is the same one Mayor Adams gives them."

"But that's the point!" Adrian said, losing his composure, and aware that he sounded a little hysterical. "No messages. We should *listen*. Treat them like individuals . . . not some massed group to be bent to our own ends."

"And how will that lead to real change? Many of them are more conservative than Adams himself, more backwards in their thinking," Elias said.

Elias crossed his arms and waited in a posture of triumph. Peytr nodded vigorously in agreement with Elias.

"Adrian is right, though," Nikolas said. "In a way, at least."

He spoke softly, but he commanded their attention. They waited for him to go on. He took a long drag from his cigarette.

"They won't listen to us. There isn't a common language between us. And they can sense when someone feels superior to them," he said, looking at Elias. "But they do need education. Education—proper and right-thinking education—is the only solution. The problem being this: How to deliver this education effectively. And how to be educated ourselves in the process, because as Adrian says, they have much to teach us."

Everyone, Elias included, listened.

"Take today, for example. On the way over, Adrian and I realized something about ourselves." He looked to Adrian, though Adrian was not sure what they had realized. "Tell them, Adrian."

As best he could, Adrian described the man with nekrosis, the infirmary, the orderly who had helped them. Adrian tried to convey the horror of the place, made sure to emphasize how compassionate Nikolas had been while leaving out his own moment of weakness.

"Better a gunshot to the head," Elias said when Adrian finished. "Leaving him there was a death sentence."

"Adrian told the story well," Nikolas said, pouring himself another drink. "But that's not the entirety of it. There is much to learn by seeing the horrors of how our city treats the least among us. But we can't forget our roots, what we've learned by our rising up." Here Nikolas paused, sipped judiciously. "And I realized that we have to stay true to our passions, to what we really believe." The table reverberated with pounding cups.

Adrian knew what Nikolas meant by this—that he had been forced to quit his research on nekrosis, and that he blamed himself for acquiescing. Adrian also knew the others only thought they understood.

"There are those who were born in places like this who found their way out of such dark ignorance and blind need," Nikolas continued.

"There are the exceptions, of course," Elias retorted. "But most of them are brutes content in their brutishness. Our words won't work with them. They only care about clinging to their meager scraps. They'll step on the backs of their brothers if it means an extra dram, another liter of this stuff right here." He raised the empty bottle. "And if one of them tries to improve his situation, the others will drag him right back down."

He's right, Adrian thought. *I've seen it among the other boys at St. Ignatius. But what made Nikolas and me different?*

"So what do you propose then?" Nikolas asked, conceding some ground to Elias. "How would you enlist their support?"

Elias smiled enigmatically. "I wouldn't enlist it at all. I would demand it."

Perhaps it was the alcohol, perhaps it was Elias's fickle nature, but he did not notice his reversal of position.

4.

SERGEANT VOLFGANG called the Guardsmen-in-training to attention. "Present yourselves, you water-louts!"

Marcik and his fellow kadets lined up in perfect rows and straightened their spines with soldierly pride. It was striking how much they had improved over these last several weeks. Most of these boys had arrived padded in baby fat and city softness. Now they were lean muscle, dense with violent potential. Even Marcik had lost weight; his arms and shoulders were more defined; his stomach flat and his legs taut. He had no illusions that he was ready for the battlefield, but he was not the same water-weak Joshuan he had been on his arrival.

"Today we are doing another war game," Sergeant Volfgang said. He looked his troops over, deciding who would act as kommanding officer for each fire-team.

Marcik lowered his eyes slightly, like some poor pupil who hadn't done his homework and didn't want to be called on by teacher. Each kadet had to play the role of kommander at least once, and those who showed promise would be chosen repeatedly to prepare them for leadership roles. Marcik knew his time would come, but he dreaded it and wanted to put it off as long as possible.

"Private Kovalski," Sergeant Volfgang said, "You'll be kommander of the defending team."

Marcik winced.

"Private Kovalski, is there a problem?"

He did not answer.

"Private Kovalski!" Sergeant Volfgang screamed. "Do you have a problem with my order? Are you soft as your mother's cunt?"

"No, sir," Marcik managed.

"No, sir—what?"

"No, sir, I do not have a problem with your order, sir."

"And no, sir, what else?"

Marcik hardened himself and said, "No, sir, I am not as soft as my mother's cunt, sir."

"That's excellent to hear, Private," Sergeant Volfgang said. "Now, who should be the kommander of the attacking forces? How about your bunk-buddy Private Vore?"

Last week, Fredrik had been kommander of a fire-team. He had done very well, Sergeant Volfgang had said, though not brilliantly. "But you have real potential. You'll have more chances to prove yourself. You might have what it takes to be an officer one day."

Fredrik had glowed with pride all day, and Marcik was proud for him as well, his best friend (perhaps his only friend) among the kadets.

And now Marcik would have to compete against him. There was no way he could win.

"And to make things interesting," Sergeant Volfgang said, "we're going to add two new aspects to the game today. First off, the attacking team will have twice as many troops, and secondly, both teams will know the exact starting positions of each other's units."

The rules of the war game were simple enough. The players were armed with NLPs (non-lethal projectiles) and dolly-guns. If an NLP hit within five meters of you, you were dead. You then tossed a red flag in the air. And if you were hit by the red paint from the dolly-guns, you were also dead, and so you tossed up a red flag. If you were surrounded and had no hope of survival, you could toss a white flag. The flags had lead ballasts sewn into the lining, so they would go high enough for the opposing team to know you were dead and for Sergeant Volfgang, from his judge's perch, to see. Both teams were given maps of the battlefield, though usually only one or two positions would be revealed; the rest of the map would be mere terrain.

But today, all positions would be known. *Just to see me humiliated*, Marcik thought. Having the positions out in the open would be of greater advantage to the attacking team, since Fredrik had double the manpower. Marcik's jaw cramped and his throat tightened, but he stifled his frustration and prepared to take his beating like the true Baikal Guardsman he hoped to become.

The kadets were divided into the two teams, each given their allotment of armaments, their red and white flags, and a crudely drawn map of the battlefield, replete with hills and trees and troop locations. No need to waste the effort printing up nice maps for these games, Sergeant Volfgang reasoned, and so he simply scratched out rudimentary ones on loose sheets of paper. Marcik's kadets stood in a semicircle around him, awaiting orders. Marcik stared at the map.

"Sir?" one kadet asked, his voice full of mock reverence for Marcik's authority.

"Marcik?" another asked, unable to play along but worried for his fellow kadet, who was clearly terrified at finding himself in the position of kommander.

With one last glance at the map, Marcik said, "Well, let's get to it. Nothing gained by wasting time."

Something about the tone of his own voice gave Marcik a modicum of courage. Strange how that can work; conjuring courage from nowhere; just by sounding courageous you trick yourself into being courageous. Maybe that's all courage is. *Let's get on with it.* He wanted the slaughter and humiliation over with; he wanted the whole filthy and unfair world over with.

The two teams took their positions and waited for Sergeant Volfgang's signal—a single gunshot—to begin the exercise. After what felt like an interminable amount of time but was actually mere minutes, the gunshot burst through the air, its echo seeming to linger long after it was gone.

At first there was no motion. Marcik knew he needed to move his troops from their initial defensive positions. Should he send out a strike team? That might disorient Fredrik, but it might also spread Marcik's own defenses too thin. No, he would just reposition and hope to surprise the attacking kadets as they entered his field of fire.

"Private Stark, take your men and secure position 2-A," Marcik said, jabbing his finger into the map, indicating the new position. "And hit them hard if they come through those trees. They shouldn't be able to see you. If we're lucky."

"Yes, sir," Private Stark said.

Marcik felt stronger for having made such a decisive move. It won't pull me out of the water, but it might make the loss less embarrassing.

Still there was no movement. What is he doing? It was possible Fredrik was being kind and giving Marcik time to prepare. As a friend, he might be tempted to do that. Or he might be repositioning for an unorthodox attack. It would be good for Fredrik to win two weeks in a row; that might guarantee him a spot on the shortlist for officer training. Yes, it would be best to assume Fredrik was going to try to win a decisive victory.

Marcik ordered another unit to move twenty meters southwest and a third unit to move forty meters due west. He couldn't totally reposition everyone, but by moving these three units, he had created a triangular shooting field, a nice defense against a frontal attack. Maybe Fredrik would be sloppy, given his advantage in numbers.

Three kadets came skulking through the copse, and Marcik gave the signal. Just as he had planned, they were pinned down immediately and mock-killed. Three red flags flew through the air in a high neat arc. Elated at his plan's success, Marcik wondered what to do next. How should he press his advantage? It was suspicious that there were only three men in Fredrik's frontal attack. That was likely a diversion, perhaps designed to make Marcik show his own strategy, which is precisely what he had done. But three enemy combatants down was three fewer men Fredrik had. Maybe this won't be a total embarrassment, Marcik thought again.

But that advantage was pure illusion. Now the real fighting would begin. Fredrik sent kadets to flank two points of Marcik's defensive triangle. Marcik saw their movements but couldn't see a way out of the danger. Then Fredrik made his bolder move—an NLP scudded through the sky, fell through the tree-canopy, and landed ten meters away from the third point of Marcik's triangle. Ten meters; that meant they were still alive. But not for long. The other men were moving in.

Then it came to him. Just like when he was a boy and cheated at Seven Cities against his brother Nikolas, putting dead soldiers back on the board. But in reverse. Instead of pretending dead soldiers were alive, he would pretend live ones were dead, and then bring them back into play.

"Throw your red flags in the air," Marcik whispered to the men near him.

"But . . . we're not dead, sir."

"Of course you're not, but if they think you are, then they will focus on the others and then you can make a surprise attack," Marcik said.

He quickly outlined his plan to his ghost-troop. They would lie in waiting until Fredrik's troops had gone by and then attack from the rear.

Marcik would lead an attack from the opposite direction to draw their attention. Sergeant Volfgang would be observing from the judgment tower. He would know the NLP had landed a safe distance away. Would he allow this tactic? *Who cares? I've got to do something.*

Fredrik's troops marched forward, seeing that they were unthreatened from the south vector, where Marcik's dead men were alive and waiting. Marcik motioned for three kadets to join him for an attack from the northwest, hoping to draw the enemy's attentions there, thus making them fatally vulnerable to his surprise attack. As he ran at full pace, the three men following him, Marcik felt the thrill of certainty. This was the right move; he knew it deep in his blood, in an instinctual place more capable of knowledge than mere intellect. This was animal knowledge; nothing they could teach you at Joshua University, where children quibbled over meaningless disputes and chased twittering girls. This was the certainty of torn meat. This was real.

Marcik looked over his shoulder and saw a cluster of NLPs arcing toward him and his men, but he calculated they would miss by a good twenty meters. Should he have two men pretend to be killed? Having another ghost-troop could be useful. No. Stick with the plan. And so they kept running until they reached a position northwest of the advancing force. He gave the signal and he and his men fired their dolly-guns and launched NLPs fast and hard, attempting to create the illusion of a force large enough to warrant a full-on attack. Marcik hoped that Fredrik could not resist dealing a crippling blow. Marcik and his men kept up their attack. They were even causing some minor damage, judging by the few red flags tossed into the air. Hopefully those losses would incite Fredrik to carelessness. *Come on, you bastard,* Marcik thought, forgetting Fredrik was his friend. *Come on.*

The enemy troops began marching in unison toward Marcik's position. It had worked. Now he just had to survive until his ghost-troop accomplished their mission. He motioned for the three men with him to scatter apart, taking positions behind trees to better defend themselves and to fire against the incoming enemy. Shortly before Fredrik's forces overtook Marcik's position, the ghost-troop emerged from the bushes behind them and opened fire, "killing" over half of Fredrik's troops before they could react. Marcik and his three men rushed into the enemy's ranks and fired, "killing" even more.

"Surrender or die," Marcik screamed, still firing.

A few more men were eliminated, their chests spattered with the red-paint of death, before Fredrik tossed the white flag in the air.

Marcik had won.

The kadets on the opposing team looked around, murmuring in anger and confusion. Why had Fredrik surrendered? Those kadets couldn't attack; they were dead. Then they heard the horn blow that signaled the end of the war game. All the kadets on both fire-teams froze in their current position, as was the rule. Sergeant Volfgang would give a lecture on the exact positions of the kadets at the end of the contest. He would discuss how they had gotten there and why the winning team had won. Or at least that was the custom. No one knew what would happen this time. Nothing like this had ever happened.

"Interesting turn of events," Sergeant Volfgang said, almost philosophically.

"But he cheated," one of the kadets on Fredrik's team complained.

Marcik looked to Fredrik to see what he thought. He didn't want his friend to think he had cheated. But more than that, he wanted to be declared the winner.

"What Private Kovalski did is unorthodox," Sergeant Volfgang said. He pulled out his packet of tobacco and slowly rolled a cigarette, considering what he should say and enjoying the anxiety his silence produced in the kadets. "But unorthodox tactics often win the day. The question is this: Could he have pulled such a move in a real-life situation?"

"No way," said someone. Marcik refused to turn to see who it was.

"Why not?" said another.

Sergeant Volfgang struck a match and lit his cigarette.

"I am inclined to think this would be, under certain circumstances, possible," Sergeant Volfgang said. "And more importantly, Private Kovalski played with the rules in such a way as to make a difficult situation manageable."

Marcik suppressed a smile.

"I therefore declare Private Kovalski and his fire-team the winners."

Fredrik approached Marcik, his expression inscrutable. Marcik's smile left his face and all the joy of victory was drained from him for a brief moment. Fredrik stood there, saying nothing. Marcik considered apologizing, but that would be an insult. Fredrik looked him over and finally extended his hand. Marcik clasped Fredrik's hand in a brotherly fashion.

"Congratulations," Fredrik said somberly, and then switched his voice to playful jabbing, "You can write your mother and tell her how well you're doing here."

5.

IT'S THAT SAD HOUR of early evening. Nikolas is in that liquid state of drunkenness where everything is felt in its immediacy, everything exists in the eternal present. He and Adrian have moved to the bar. Elias and the others left some time ago, defeated by Nikolas's stamina and Adrian's sobriety. Nikolas jabs the air and orates to Adrian. He's in a good place, his ideas urgent and his mood lucid. Being drunk allows him to really think. It strips the rage and the sense of futility and suffuses everything with a warm romantic-tragic glow. Time is a remiss passenger.

"You know something?" he's saying. "I'm glad they're gone. They talk a lot—well, Elias anyway—but they're not serious. Not like us. Elias is so filled with hatred for everything. And Mouse is a not much more than a little girl. Peytr—don't get me started on that bit of ridiculousness. I bet you could lock all three of them in a room for a week and they wouldn't solve a simple problem you or I could dispatch in ten minutes. They approach things already knowing what they'll find. They're not scientists. They don't have our brain."

Wan October light gives the open tavern door a meaningful yellow glow. The street sounds are louder now; working Joshuans on the way home for the evening. A woman yells something from an upstairs window. Cooking smells, curried meat of some sort. Immigrant food. Adrian sits stiff on his bar stool, too polite to say he wants to go home, but also too much in the thrall of Nikolas's attention. He recognizes Nikolas's flattery for what it is but is also helpless not to be flattered. *Our brain.* They are a team now. Brothers of a sort.

"If you dislike them so much," Adrian wonders, "why do you come to these meetings?"

"They amuse me at times," Nikolas says. "And anyway, what other choices have I got? I mean, Brandt . . . The thing is I'm looking for someone, anyone, who cares. Who doesn't want to see things continue as they are. I'm looking for . . . I don't know. It sounds silly when I say it this way, but I'm looking for Truth."

Truth. Capitalized.

"I'm also looking for the water-closet," Nikolas says, self-consciously lightening the mood. "I'll be right back."

He stands and puts both palms flat on the bar, testing his drunkenness. A drinker's maxim: you don't know how drunk you are until you stand. He walks to the back of the tavern. The water-closet has no lock—just a swinging half-door on loose hinges. The room is illuminated by a psychotically flickering bulb. The floor is sticky with urine. The toilet has no seat.

Nikolas urinates lustfully, bracing himself with one hand against the wall. The wall is covered with scrawled messages. There are the usual vulgar offerings—*Call Inga for a good time*, followed by a telefone number—and assertions about sexual practices—*Melina does it Ulani style*. The whole city is scrawled with such puerile filth these days. He closes his eyes to it and enjoys the dizzy swimming blackness of his mind.

On his way back to the bar, he stops to look at Adrian. He is meticulously shredding a bar-napkin, setting the strips of napkin in some order. Nikolas pauses and takes in his friend. This is the mystery of the Other. And more mysterious precisely because he knows him so well, lives with him, sees him at his daily rituals. Observing him from this distance brings the mystery starkly back. What is the pattern Adrian is creating there? Seems so familiar. Nikolas sees him suddenly as a different person, which of course he always is.

He sits down beside Adrian. The pattern becomes clear. Adrian was recreating the stitches they had used to sew in the corpse's heart during their Experimental Kardiology lab. He was still working on the problem. Nikolas feels a rush of affection for this intimate stranger.

"What are you doing there?"

Adrian sweeps his project off the bar and into his hand, crumples it into a ball of mere paper. "Nothing."

Nikolas lets the lie go past. *Let him have his privacy. Everything is exactly how it should be.* Nikolas scans the room; the empty chairs are perfect; Dmitri with his calm, efficient gestures is perfect; existence in all its dubious glory is perfect. And there she is, the Woman with the Porcelain Mask. She's come back. She has stopped at the bar and is talking to Dmitri. She's never stopped before.

Nikolas has seen her every Saturday since they started these meetings and she always goes up the stairs for an hour or two, comes back down, walks straight out the door. But this time, a drink.

Dmitri sets a shot glass for her. He waves off her money. She downs the drink in one tilt of the head, getting it through the small mouth-hole in her mask without spilling a drop—a practiced gesture; Nikolas realizes he has never considered how people from Baikalingrad drink. She raises her finger for another. This time Dmitri lets her pay.

"How is he?" Dmitri asks her.

"The same," she says. "He has good days and bad days."

Her voice sounds like a regular woman's voice, maybe a little muted by the mask. This surprises Nikolas. What was he expecting? A choir of angels?

"And today?" Dmitri asks.

"Good," she says. "Well, mostly. He confuses me with my mother."

Dmitri nods. He continues to wipe down glasses. "It's a hard thing, I think. To see a parent grow old."

"Yes, it is hard. Even though he's only my stepfather."

Nikolas has spun fully on his stool to take in the conversation. He leans forward with a voyeuristic slouch. From behind her mask, it's hard for Nikolas to know if she notices him.

"Your stepfather?" Nikolas says suddenly.

The woman stiffens. She has some history with men, views them as objects of careful negotiation.

"Let me rephrase that. May your face remain faceless, good lady," Nikolas says, using the prosperity-greeting of Baikalingrad, and waves his hand around in the air with an and-so-forth gesture, like a prince at court. He is in playfully ironic mode now, a technique that serves him well with the kind of women he knows.

"Does your stepfather share your . . . beliefs?"

"First of all, you don't know anything about my beliefs," she says. "And if you are going to use our greeting, mean it. You're wondering about my mask. But do you ever ask yourself about yours? All of you university skolars come into this place for a taste of real life. And you think if you show a bit of interest in us, we'll fawn over you."

Adrian jumps in, "We only ask because we're both interested. In The Faceless Prophet in particular . . . and understanding belief systems in general."

"Yes," Nikolas echoes. "That's precisely it. We want to understand everything." He flings up his arms all-encompassingly. "Everything in this whole besotted world."

"You say you want to understand." She finishes off the last of her drink and slides the glass across the counter toward Dmitri. He catches it with practiced familiarity, reestablishing the proper alliances. "Then you'll understand, I'm sure, why I'm not about to tell you my life story."

She slaps a bill on the counter.

"That's for you," she says and nods a goodbye to Dmitri.

Nikolas and Adrian watch her go.

"That, gentlemen, is Katyana." Dmitri takes the bill, and folding it almost lovingly, tucks it into his shirt pocket. "She's not someone for you to mess about with."

CHAPTER THREE

THE BRIGHT HEARTS
OF SILVERVILLE

1.

A ZOMBIE[3] WALKS with outstretched arms toward a woman wearing a lotus-white Baikyong-do-style dress. The woman steps back, her legs failing her. Her soundless mouth opens in horror. As the zombie marches forward, the woman's fingers creep back on the operating table. They find a stethoscope, fumble it aside, find a large rubber eyedropper and dismiss that too, finally grasping the gleaming length of a scalpel. She tries to pick it up, drops it. The zombie is closing in. Will she find her weapon in time?

※ ※ ※

Neil Martin flipped a switch and there came a *slap-tap, slap-tap, slap-tap* of the loose film running out its reel. Abraham wondered vaguely how to innovate projektors; perhaps film itself could be replaced. The lights of Neil's palatial sitting room shone down—soft white bulbs em-

---

[3]Translators' Note: The Slovnik word *smerch-mensch* literally means *dead-man* (or even more accurately *dead-human*), though the New High American equivalent of the idea is, of course, *zombie*. This, however, is perhaps an error on our part. We assume, given the evidence, that Joshuans learned the concept from old film reels from the former United States film industry. However, as all cultural concepts do when traversing cultures, they change. It is almost impossible to imagine that their plague of nekrosis did not shape their usage of the zombie concept. To return to the older term, therefore, elides the changes Joshuan culture made.

bedded in a ceiling whose curves reminded Abraham of the undulat-
ing belly of an Al-Khuziri sun-dancer. The guests applauded with more
enthusiasm than Abraham could muster. He let his hands fall lightly
together. As the merry party noises began, Vivian asked how he liked
the film.

He didn't want to admit he had no idea what the title meant. *Potlatch*. A strange word, vaguely suggestive of Ulani tribal practices and
cooking utensils all at once. And he never knew what to say at these
pre-screenings. Being too complimentary seemed false, but real criticism was not allowed either. You have to find that unnoticed detail to
praise, or perhaps you ironically adopt the voice of a critic you know
they dislike, thereby delivering to them a negative review that is actually
a form of validation.

"I felt like the close-up on her hand was a microcosm of the entire
scene," Abraham said. "There was something about her fingers...I
don't know, insectile maybe...It made her seem as inhuman as the
zombie."

Finishing his little speech left Abraham embarrassed and depleted,
but Vivian kissed him with some affection before mingling with the
other guests. He tried to look calmly philosophical as he surveyed the
room—the elegantly dressed would-be starlets (so much like Vivian
when she was starting out), the bowls of fat happy grapes from Baikalingrad, golden stacks of gourmet bread, Ulani ox-steaks in mushroom
sauce (weren't Ulani meats contraband these days?), and the white-suit-
ed waiters gliding effortlessly through the crowd. He noticed, in an obscure corner, the glint of a small bit of glass. He recognized it as one of
his. He had made such advancements of late in the miniaturization of
kameras. It was a bit disturbing to see one here. But surely there was a
good reason for it. And by contract he was prohibited from telling anyone about the whereabouts or uses of his surveillance devices. He put it
out of his mind, filled a small plate of food and nibbled absently, trying
his best to seem natural.

Vivian grabbed a glass of champagne from a passing waiter's tray, gracing Neil's hired help with a pat on the shoulder. Downing half of the glass, she made herself part of Neil's circle. She laughed; Abraham could hear it from across the room. Neil was a famous wit, all right.

With his drink and a half-eaten plate of food, Abraham drifted across the room. As he passed, he caught snippets of conversations. He couldn't distinguish the voices, who was saying what. How could this be recorded usefully? Which sonic rules would determine this device? The pitch and volume of the voices would have to be taken into account. And the distances between them. But the human ear does this without effort. Two people walked away, still talking. That would make it more difficult. You have to be able to track the voices even as they move. A new idea, a new invention, came to him. He would have to tell Jürgen about it at the Ministrie on Monday. Jürgen had lately expressed some reservations about the work they were doing, but he would be excited about this. He was still a scientist, after all.

※ ※ ※

"Did you hear about Alphonse Cvaldi?"

"You mean the big one? Who always played a Larki Islander?"

"Rumor is he *was* a Larki Islander, just changed his name so no one would guess it. But that's not what I wanted to say. He's disappeared."

"Ha. Probably gone off on another of his famous romps. He'll be found passed out in a ditch covered in his own vomit."

"Maybe."

"You're not suggesting . . . "

"No, of course not."

※ ※ ※

"Have you tried the grilled octopus?"

"None for me, thanks. Tentacles make me shudder."

"That's just because they remind you of a certain other appendage."

※ ※ ※

"He enlisted in the Baikal Guard, the stupid child."

"Probably thought it was the brave and noble thing to do."

"Nonsense. He just wanted to get even with me."

"In fact, it *is* brave and noble. These young men risk their lives to preserve ours."

"That's all well and fine when it's not my Walter. He's a very delicate boy, you know. He wet the bed until he was twelve."

"What are you going to do?"

"I don't know. I'm just distraught."

"You know my husband's brother's wife had a son with a similar situation. She paid someone to have it fixed."

"Fixed?"

"Well, what they do, you see, is they pay someone else . . . I'd better not say too much. I'll give you her telefone number."

※ ※ ※

"What was she thinking? Wearing that?"

"She's beautiful. She can wear whatever she wants."

"But look at her date's haircut. He looks like a harassed pelican."

"Indeed! That is unforgivable. I would never allow myself to be seen with him."

※ ※ ※

"It was awful, I tell you, just awful."

"You were there? At the university?"

"Front and center. I saw it when it started. Absolute chaos."

"Did you see who—pardon me—did you see who cast the first stone, so to speak?"

"I see you know your *Book of the Before-Time*."

"It's a good thing more people weren't hurt."

"Truly a miracle."

※ ※ ※

Abraham was not the only one at the party who was thinking about surveillance. A man had been standing in one corner of the room for most of the evening. No one had seen him arrive, and the few who noticed him at all mostly ignored him. He wore a nondescript gray uniform as unremarkable as his expressionless face. He didn't move. He didn't speak to anyone, and if someone seemed about to engage him in conversation, he waved them off. He didn't eat. He hardly even seemed to breathe. No one knew who he was or why he was there.

Abraham, with nothing to do but observe, wondered if he might be a municipal agent. Should he say something to Neil after all? First the kamera, now this. But agents from various ministries were common enough at these parties; and besides, no one was doing anything wrong. Sure, there were drugs, but the people using them confined themselves to backrooms and water-closets. And there were some off-color remarks, but anyone could tell they were in good fun. The best thing in this situation, he knew, was to do nothing. Show that you have nothing to fear, and they will stop looking.

Neil had also noticed the man. It frustrated him, but he hid it under a mask of high-wattage charm. Who did they think he was, that he should have to tolerate such an insult? *Don't let them get to you.* But he was becoming angry now. He could grab the man by the lapels and throw him out the door, though that would be uncouth and no doubt ruin the mood of the party. *No. Enjoy yourself.*

Neil sauntered showily to the bar to refill his drink. He tapped a young aktress (who might have real talent) on the shoulder, kissed her on the cheek.

"Don't give me a paltry pour, my man," he said to the barkeep. "It is my party after all."

"Mr. Martin," the aktress began, encouraged by his touch, "are there any openings..." Over her shoulder, Neil looked at the mysterious man, hearing nothing she said.

The man waited for the moment when he could speak to Neil Martin alone. There was unpleasant business to be conducted, but Neil

Martin was still an important personage, with his hands in all the right pockets. It was best to treat the matter discreetly.

At university, the man had studied film himself. He had hoped to become a direktor like Neil Martin, but it just hadn't worked out. Had he lacked the guts, the perseverance? Or maybe he was just plain untalented. But he knew his Joshuan film history. And he knew how crass and uninteresting Martin's films were.

Still, Martin could prove useful; no reason to damage the man's reputation. Discretion above all. Discretion and prudence. That had always been his philosophy.

※ ※ ※

Abraham took a seat on a plush backless sofa of a stained-red hue. Its availability, but also its absurdity as an object of furniture, was what drew him to it. What was it about fashionable objects—and, he supposed, people too—that they had to exhibit a perverse inutility? Abraham could imagine someone arguing that being fashionable brought you useful accoutrements. And if he was perfectly honest, weren't certain features of his trains designed not for their function but for their aesthetic flair? But these things were mere pleasantries, enjoyable of course, but not essential. Wasn't this what attracted him to science? To create new utility, to make something useful. His trains had made the lives of Joshuans more functional; his surveillance would make them safer. It was a modest arrogance he felt; the modesty of the lonely inventor. He would invent these things, but they would have a life of their own.

Take the people at this party for example. They were simply propagating their egos. The only way they would succeed was to get enough people to agree they were important. But science doesn't work like that. Abraham did not care that much about fame. He wanted to be known, sure, but he served The Idea, whichever one happened upon him. In science, there is such a thing as compelling evidence. He had to change his position based on new findings, even if they weren't his own. No artist would accept such a model. The only thing that was worthwhile to them was their own art, or the art *they* admired. They were more like priests in that regard. Artists and writers as secular priests was an idea that pleased Abraham; he wondered if anyone had written about that. Probably.

A woman he thought he recognized as an extra in the film—what was one more corpse on the pile?—sat heavily beside him on the sofa. Somehow her hand remembered her body's natural elegance and she didn't spill the drink. She rested her weight on one slender arm, eased toward him, the strap of her sapphire evening gown slipping from her shoulder.

With a teasing finger, she pushed the strap back up. "Sorry, I always get so silly at these parties."

Abraham smiled helplessly.

"So what are you doing here anyway?" she asked.

"My wife's in the film so I have to be here."

"Oh, which one of the girls is she?"

"Vivian Scott."

The woman dropped her innocent-girl act she likely put on at all of these events. "You're Abraham Kocznik?" she asked with sober admiration.

"I'm afraid so," he quipped.

"Well, I'm Tonya." She looked around the party. "Let me find my husband. He's going to want to meet you. Chaim!"

Chaim was suddenly there—a balding man with frazzled hair and a suit he had obviously outgrown during married life.

"Chaim," the woman said. "This is Abraham Kocznik."

The man looked at him more closely. His face brightened. "Sir," he said, "What an honor to meet such a great Joshuan."

"Chaim is Neil's cinematografer, you know," Tonya said.

"I didn't know that," Abraham said, "but I was just remarking to my wife about the excellent cinematografy."

"Of course, you're the one who designed the kameras I use," Chaim said.

Abraham laughed. "That's a bit of an exaggeration. I merely designed the housing mechanism for the film itself."

"Without which the film wouldn't turn and none of this . . . " Chaim gestured toward the room behind him, ". . . would be possible."

"But that's all for nothing without men like yourself." Abraham squeezed the man's arm in a show of brotherly solidarity. "I've always said that those of us who make and run machines are the ones who make the world as people know it."

"We should drink to this," Tonya said.

She raised her glass and her husband followed. Abraham raised his long-empty glass and made a sheepish toasting gesture.

"That won't do," Chaim said. "I'll get us all another round."

He leapt to his feet more agilely than his frame suggested was possible.

"The way machines work fascinates Chaim, any machines," Tonya said after a moment of silence. "I think it's their perfect comprehensibility that he loves so much." How strikingly different she was now that she had dropped the twittering aktress pose Abraham assumed was practically necessary for these young women in Silverville.

"I suppose that is part of any engineer's or scientist's interest in machines. They are trustworthy in their mechanical logic."

"I understand that," Tonya said, "but I have always preferred the messiness of human psychology more. I guess that's why I'm an aktress and he's what he is."

Chaim was back with the drinks. They toasted properly and Chaim asked Abraham if it would be all right if he introduced him to his assistants. "They are going to want to meet you."

※ ※ ※

Twenty minutes later, Abraham was holding forth to a small semicircle of eager listeners on the technical issues of various voltages. "Well, until I could develop a working solid-state rectifier, I couldn't use a 20-kilo-volt alternating current as I wanted. And with voltage that high, there is the danger of a worker or passenger somehow touching a live wire and being killed instantly, so we had to put safety mechanisms in place as well."

"So you're always thinking of the people when you design something?" someone asked.

"Not exactly. But if the city's infrastructure is working well, then my trains are doing their job. I've focused on new inventions the past few years."

Chaim, eager, nearly begged, "What are you working on these days?"

"That," Abraham said, "is classified. I wish I could tell you. Quite interesting, but you know how these municipal contracts go."

Even as he spoke, Abraham was aware of the larger gathering around Neil Martin. He couldn't find Vivian among them. He wanted her to see him as these people saw him.

﹪ ﹪ ﹪

A Baikal-fusion septet, combining the musical styles and instruments of all seven cities, had been playing this whole time. Now Neil said something to the percussionist, a man with the herd-tattoos of Ulan-Ude who was seated behind an array of sheepskin tribal drums, woodblocks, and brass gongs. (Unlike the Joshuans who wore Ulani clothing and tattooed themselves in a faux Ulani style for reasons of fashion or political statement, this man actually was Ulani. The prudent thing for Neil to do would have been to fire him months ago.) The bassist, playing a hollowed-out Kazhstani gourd-bass, blew notes across the open mouth of his instrument to begin a steady walking line. Neil picked a microfone off the surface of the Larki pipe-organ, twirled it once, caught it, and walked casually from end to end of the room.

Looking over his shoulder, Neil gave a signal to the rest of the band, and broke out in the smoothest, purest voice Abraham had ever heard:

> *I've been walking these seven cities,*
> *Begging for a drink,*
> *Anything for this unholy thirst.*

Abraham could have sworn he knew this song. Maybe Vivian had even played it for him once.

> *I've been watching you,*
> *Begging for a drink,*
> *But I want you begging me first.*

Neil got down on his knees in front of the organist, pretending to beg.

> *I've been thirsty for you*
> *For forty days and nights,*

Neil weaved his way through the crowd, drawing out his syllables. The people stood immobile as statues. He grabbed a bald man and kissed his shiny pate, and moved on before the man could smile. The band watched for his cue, the way he slowed down the tempo with a dip of his shoulders. He leaned his head back, with the microfone held over his mouth as he prepared to launch into the coda.

> *And you're thirsty for me too,*
> *And you know . . . yeah you know, it's going to be all right.*

Here Neil began to seriously croon, his whole body taken up with song.

> *Oh, oh, oh, you know it's going to be all right,*

He punctuated each *Oh* with a pushing-away-from-himself of all things that didn't matter. He pointed to the band, who took this opportunity to show their skills. Beginning with the organist, they improvised in four-measure breaks. The flautist, playing a reed flute from Baikyong-do, did a series of trills so fast you could hardly see his fingers.

The sun-harpist picked sharply and precisely at the strings of his sickle-shaped instrument from Al-Khuzir. The drummer threw his head back in joyful hilarity at the sheer creative exaltation of it. Then there was a brief slowing in tempo, building up with a series of open-palm drum hits, and then the cathartic release of the song's final lines, repeated over and over, until near collapse:

> *In this city of waters,*
> *You know it's going to be all right!*

> *In this city of waters,*
> *You know it's going to be all right!*

The crowd was unable to contain their wild applause at this, Neil's second brilliant performance of the evening.

Abraham was saying, "But the thing about train wheels is that metal on metal runs faster, but that added speed also causes extra risks..."

But Chaim wasn't listening to him anymore, taken up in Neil's performance like all of the guests were.

Abraham suddenly wanted more to drink. A lot more.

%% %% %%

"A man asked me today..." Neil said into the microfone.

He wiped the sweat from his forehead and tossed the handkerchief into the crowd like a bouquet of flowers.

"...he asked me how I could continue to engage in the...in the *frivolity* of filmmaking, with the war happening. You know what I told him?"

In unison, his audience shook their heads.

"Nothing. Absolutely nothing. Why should I answer a question like that?" Neil said and purveyed the room. "Somebody get me some water."

A glass appeared. Neil took a luxurious sip. "That's the stuff. Worth fighting for."

Neil stepped off the stage. He carried the glass of water across the room, bumping into guests without regard, spilling not a drop. He lifted the glass, a toast to no one. He stopped in front of the gray-uniformed man in the corner. Those partygoers who had not noticed the man before were plenty aware of him now. In fact, hadn't they had the sensation of being watched throughout the party?

With agonizing slowness, Neil raised the glass and tipped it over the man's head. It ran through his hair and down the shoulders of his jacket. The man flinched, just barely, but otherwise maintained his composure.

The cup empty, Neil balanced it on the man's head like a silly toy hat.

The band had gone silent.

"Thank you for attending my party," Neil said.

※ ※ ※

But sometimes discretion will not do. The subject has to be put down. He needs to remember who holds the whip.

I am the whip, the man thought. *And I serve the hand of the whip.*

He walked to the water-closet and looked at himself in the mirror. He looked like a wet puppy. But he could take any manner of insult. It was not him, but the hand, who lashed back. With a washcloth, he dried his head thoroughly. His suit jacket was still wet, but that too would dry.

The man walked outside. He lit a cigarette. In the driveway was a vehicle with darkened windows. Inside sat two Guardsmen. They had been advised to await his signal. He held the cigarette away from his body, trying to keep its vile smoke off his clothes. He did not smoke the cigarette, but merely let it burn its orange way down.

The doors of the car opened and the two Guardsmen stepped out. The man in the gray uniform went back inside. From the sitting room came the sound of the band starting back up.

※ ※ ※

"Do another, Neil!" someone shouted.

"We love you!"

"Yes," another voice shouted. "One more song, Neil!"

"Oh, I couldn't possibly," Neil said, playing to the crowd. He turned back to the band. "Should we?"

He brought the band members together. He told them secrets the crowd wanted to hear.

The trumpeter raised his Baikalingrad-style trumpet—its mouthpiece specially designed to be played through the narrow slit of his porcelain mask—and lifted the party in one high golden blast. The drummer did fancy hand-tricks everyone loved. They forgot his braided hair. They forgot his tattooed skin. They forgot everything but the thrill of the tribe.

But the gray-uniformed man was back. He looked over his shoulder with casual confidence. A Guardsman entered. Another.

Abraham fingered his ministrie badge. Neil had gone too far.

An excited, voyeuristic murmur rippled the crowd. The Guardsmen approached. Neil watched them, amusement fading.

"What's this?" he asked.

Then, directing his words at the partygoers, "What have I done this time? I know my singing's not that great, but surely it can't be that bad?"

He laughed at the Guardsmen. He laughed at the world, the whole ridiculous ordeal of it.

Abraham admired Neil's composure.

The man in the gray uniform stepped forward. "Neil Martin," he said. "On behalf of the Ministrie of Aesthetics, under article 1474-A, effective immediately, I have been charged with the confiscation of all extant copies of *Potlatch*."

Neil set his microfone gently on the stage. He breathed in and out twice. This was more than mere frustration.

"So you're back?" he asked the man.

"Yes, I am."

"Does this job keep you interested?"

The man stared at him.

"Does it keep you well-fed and fat?"

"You brought this on yourself, Mr. Martin. I was willing to do this discreetly. You were impudent."

"You brought this to me. You came to *my* house and imposed *your* new rules."

"I do not make the rules, Mr. Martin," the man said, nodding a go-ahead to his Guardsmen. "I am a servant of Joshua City. We are all servants of the city, and it would do you well to keep that in mind."

The two Guardsmen rolled the film projektor out of the room. The partygoers lingered. They looked to the door and then back to the scene before them. Some of them even were concerned about Neil Martin the man. But surely nothing could happen to a figure of his stature, could it? They were conflicted; they wanted a good story for their friends, but they didn't want to be caught in a scandal.

"This is absurd," Neil said. He motioned for the guests to stay. "This will all be sorted out."

A woman in a sparkly dress pulled on her coat apologetically. A man peeked at his watch and, pretending to have just remembered some pressing appointment, slipped out the door. Someone coughed.

In embarrassed increments, the party thinned.

Vivian looked at Abraham from across the room. *Do something.*

The Guardsmen came back inside.

A glass display case stood in a corner of the room. It was full of awards Neil had won—a dagger-shaped crystal for Best Film, a man on a pedestal for Lifetime Achievement, and so on. Also in the case were several reels of his previous films sheathed in gray canisters. They all had the dates and the name of the film on them.

"Take those."

"What are you doing?" Neil said. "There's nothing you want in there."

"Mr. Martin," the man said. "I refer you again to article 1474-A."

"What should we do with these?" one of the Guardsmen said.

The man smiled for the first time. It was a thin, malicious smile and it transformed his whole face. The guests still left at the party would remember that smile for a long time.

"Destroy them," the man said to his Guardsmen and they set to stomping the delicate cultural awards beneath their heavy leather boots. *Do something.*

2.

ONE MORNING, three days after Neil's party, there was a knock at the door of the Kocznik-Scott household. Agnieszka opened it like the dutiful servant she was. An agent in a gray uniform and two Guardsmen stood there in all their officiousness.

"May we speak to the master of the house?" the man in the gray uniform asked.

"Can I help you?" Abraham asked, coming down the stairs.

"Mr. Kocznik, is your wife here?"

With a sinking feeling, Abraham recognized the man from Neil's party. What was he doing here?

"Yes," Abraham said, clearing the distance between them and offering his hand. "She's in her room, but I can call her down."

The man shook his hand firmly. "Sorry I did not get a chance to formally introduce myself the other night. Herman Koestler."

"Pleased to meet you," Abraham said, pulling his hand back. "What business do you have with Vivian?"

"Is there somewhere we can talk?" the man asked. "We have a sensitive matter to discuss."

Abraham called over his shoulder for Vivian to come down, but she was already standing on the staircase. She had none of her usual make-up on. He turned back to the men at the door, not wanting to meet her eyes. They had argued earlier, and Abraham wondered absurdly if Mr. Koestler could sense the domestic tension in the house.

"This way," Agnieszka said, leading them toward the den.

※ ※ ※

Oh god, the advertisement-poster, Vivian thought. But there was no way to take it down now. She should have done it the minute they returned from the party. She had never imagined they would show up here. *How much do they know?*

Agnieszka seated them so that Vivian's and Abraham's various awards were visible behind them, the way Vivian had ordered her always to do when they had guests. Everyone should see their accomplishments. Abraham would never have thought to suggest such a thing. Now Vivian regretted it. The advertisement-poster for *Potlatch* was on full display.

"You mentioned a delicate matter?" Abraham said.

"Would anyone like a beverage? Tea or vodka?" Vivian asked.

"Tea would be nice," Herman said.

"Agnieszka," Vivian said.

"Five teas then?"

"Yes."

Abraham put his hand in Vivian's. "Agent Koestler?"

"Yes, I imagine you are eager to know why I am here."

"We are," Abraham said.

"As you know, Ms. Scott, your associate Neil Martin is under some scrutiny."

Vivian clenched Abraham's hand more tightly. "Yes, an unfortunate affair."

"*Unfortunate* is one word for it."

Vivian straightened her dress and shifted in her seat.

"What does this have to do with us?" Abraham said.

"That depends entirely on you."

How much trouble is Neil in? Vivian wondered. *They usually forgive him his eccentricity.*

Agnieszka was back with a pot of tea and five cups.

Herman took a connoisseur's sip. "This is Baikyong-do jade, I presume."

"Yes, it is," Vivian said. "You have discerning taste, sir."

"This is a fine house you have." He took another sip, swallowed it slowly.

"We've been reviewing the careers of various Silverville direktors and aktors," Agent Koestler continued, "and we're finding some disturbing patterns. Particularly with your associate Mr. Martin."

"We're a good Joshuan family," Abraham said. He realized they were here to threaten Vivian. He wanted to perform his husbandly duty to protect her. "And you know my position."

"Yes, sir, we do. And that is part of why this visit has been conducted the way it has."

"Why are you here then?" Vivian asked.

"We have an offer for you," Agent Koestler said. "May I pour myself another tea?"

He helped himself to the tea, then produced a package from beneath his jacket. It was a film script. He explained that it would be used to boost the morale of the Baikal Guardsmen on the front. It would be a short film, made in only weeks, and the payment would be large. And, he suggested, any association with unsavory parties would be forgotten.

"And I understand you have no current projects in Silverville. It would be a shame for such a talent as you, Ms. Scott, not to grace the screen again."

"Who are the other aktors? Who is the direktor? To make a film is much harder than you might know. Technicians, kameramen, and so forth are all needed."

"We've taken care of all that," Agent Koestler said. "All we need now is you."

Vivian set the nib of the pen on the government document. She did not want to sign this, but what was the alternative? She did not in fact have a current project; what was Neil's future?; what effect would her refusal have on Abraham's career or Lydia's enrollment at Sister Nadya's?; and more aktors were being blacklisted every day... This was what she told herself to justify a choiceless choice. Her hand scrawled her signature on page after bureaucratic page.

Abraham watched helplessly as Vivian signed. It was her choice after all. And if it might help those poor young Guardsmen. But he disliked the implication of what might happen if she refused.

※ ※ ※

HE TALKED to Jürgen about it the next day at work. Jürgen Moritz and Abraham had been friends since university, but they had drifted apart after Abraham and Vivian were married. It was Jürgen who had convinced him to take this job designing surveillance equipment for the Ministrie of Technology, and part of the allure of the position had been a chance to work with his old friend again.

"It all felt so . . . coercive," Abraham said, sitting at his large work-table in the center of the room. "I never thought they would show up in our home. Neil—you know how Neil can be. Did I tell you they had kameras installed in his house?"

"It doesn't surprise me," Jürgen said quickly. He returned to fiddling with knobs on a vast bank of komputational systems that lined the walls. He held a headset to his ear. "Damn. Still interference." He turned to Abraham and gave him a searching look. "Does Neil know about the kameras?"

"I don't know. Why? I thought you didn't like Neil."

Jürgen shrugged. "Everybody has secrets. How's Vivian through all this?"

"You know her. We haven't even talked about it. She claims it's for the best, that she needs the work. And maybe she's right. I mean, what's the harm in a little motion-film to make the Guardsmen feel good?"

"But?"

"I get the feeling she blames me for it."

"Listen to this." He handed Abraham the headset. "Does that sound better to you?"

Abraham listened to the crackle of voices—innocuous conversation coming from the foyer of the Ministrie itself. They had been instructed to test all of their devices on a one-hundred-square-meter space of public real estate. All the important surveillance footage was kept in a room with restricted access. He and Jürgen both had the authorization to enter this room, but they had to log all their activity while in the room. Abraham personally had no interest in listening in on the conversations of strangers.

Abraham handed the headset back to Jürgen. "I can't tell. What do the frequencies look like?"

"Still spiking all over the place. But it's an improvement. If we could compress the sound somehow?"

"Yes," Abraham said. "That might do it."

※ ※ ※

For the next half hour, they worked in companionable silence. It was good to be beside his friend. It was good to be working. Four years ago, he had completed what would likely be his life's great project—the implementation of the new multiple-unit diesel engine in Joshua City's trains. The double-engine and the use of diesel fuel instead of coal had made the trains more efficient, more lightweight, faster. And it had made him famous. But after the new rail lines were installed, after a schedule of inspektions had been finalized, after the inaugural test run, after the public appearances, the speeches and banquets, the radio spots and interviews with newspapers and magazines, Abraham found himself temporarily unemployed. For a few months, he slept in late, did not bother with social engagements, even ignored basic hygiene many days.

Then he hated his sloth. Himself. He started new projects. There were sketches and diagrams all over his study. But they amounted to nothing. Tinkering. Boy-dreams.

At just that moment, when it seemed he couldn't possibly continue this way any longer—if not for his own sake, then for Vivian's and Lydia's... what kind of example was he setting for his daughter?—Jürgen called. There was a position open. And they could use someone with Abraham's expertise.

"It's interesting work," Jürgen said. "And important too. You'll be keeping the city safe."

That had been more than a year ago, and lately Jürgen had switched his stance on the nature of their work. Abraham couldn't account for the change. They were doing the same job they had always done, weren't they? Yes, it was a bit disconcerting to see their kameras in unexpected places. And yes, what had happened at Neil's party was unsettling. But that was Neil. If you weren't doing anything wrong, if you were a good citizen, what was there to fear? Yet after the visit from Mr. Koestler, Abraham didn't know what to think. He turned back to the simple clean comforts of his work.

※ ※ ※

"I think that's done it," Abraham said. "Maybe some sort of dust filter? Something sheer that wouldn't muffle the sound. But we can figure that out tomorrow."

"So listen," Jürgen said. "Do you want to get a drink? Like old times?"

Abraham glanced at his watch, aware the gesture was a transparent one. "Normally, I'd love to. But Vivian starts work on the film tonight. Accelerated production schedule and so forth. Someone has got to watch Lydia."

"Some other time then," Jürgen said. "But Abraham—"

Abraham paused in the doorway to the lab, his coat and hat in hand.

"I wouldn't hold myself responsible. Vivian probably just feels guilty."

"You mean about the film?"

"Yes. The film," Jürgen said. "Anyway, tell Lydia Uncle Jürgen says *hello*."

"Are you coming now?"

"No," Jürgen said. "I think I'll stay and work a little more. Working late—just one more privilege of the bachelor life."

Abraham shut the door, leaving Jürgen alone in the lab. As he walked down the long, nondescript halls of the Ministrie, he thought that yes, he did have a family waiting for him at home, and how lucky he was for that.

CHAPTER FOUR

DECISIONS

1.

NIKOLAS DIDN'T KNOW why he was still conducting the experiment. It was for an inessential class taught by a substandard professor. But he disliked leaving a task unfinished, and the results, while minor, might provide some insight into how the animal brain processed information.

When he released several flies into the glass cages containing frogs, their tongues shot out at the flies' motion. But when he placed several recently killed flies—which would be perfectly edible for the frogs— they ignored the black lumps as though they were mere pebbles. They would lie there and starve to death, an abundance of food all around them. He tried not to make too many metaphors about the workers of Joshua City.

Nikolas concluded that the frogs had no understanding of nutrition as such; they had evolved over millennia to react to a specific type of motion, a motion that just happened to be shared by precisely those species of flying insects the frogs survived on. Could they somehow be trained to recognize the dead flies as sustenance as well? Unlikely, given their rudimentary brain structures and lack of neurological complexity. But more evolved species could be conditioned to see the nutriment they needed, even if it was camouflaged or offered in a form they were unaccustomed to.

How much of this behavior was learned and how much inborn? The debate raged on, and sentimentality about the specialness of the human species clouded people's opinions when it came that most important of animals.

Nikolas released more live flies in one cage, then looked at those cages that contained the starving frogs. The slow pulse of their breathing was unimaginably sad.

He moved to another experiment he was working on, this one for his own edification and interest. In the course of his research on nekrosis, he became interested in angiogenesis—the growth of blood vessels, which only happens in wounded flesh among adults. He had read an article on angiogenesis in cancerous tumors. The author speculated that since blood vessels grow in these tumors, which is how they get the nutrients they need for their aberrant growth, if a way to prevent angiogenesis could be found, tumors could be, in effect, starved. To date, no such method had been developed, but it was a promising line of thought—and one that was just as promising in reverse. What uses might stimulating angiogenesis have? The deteriorated organs of the nekrotic patient might be compelled to heal, if artificial angiogenesis could be induced. And of course, Doktor Brandt's precious heart transplants might benefit from such an advance in medikal science.

Having nearly forgotten his thriving and dying frogs, Nikolas began the vivisection of a pig. The organs and blood vessels of pigs were remarkably similar to those of humans, and thus what instigated or hindered angiogenesis in a pig would most likely do the same in humans. Nikolas had bolted the pig to the table and had an IV feeding a vitamin solution into the animal. Panicked muffled noises penetrated the leather muzzle he had placed over the pig's snout. He had isolated the nutrient compounds found in greatest prevalence in the newly formed vessels around injured flesh and concocted a solution that had hundreds of times more such nutrients than usually found in the body. Now, he just had to observe as the pig's flesh tried to heal itself to know whether his theory was correct.

But even if I am correct, then what? Can I convince Brandt that this is a path worth following? What am I doing here?

Nikolas pressed his scalpel into the pig's abdomen, the angled blade puncturing the skin and slicing into the soft flesh. Blood welled up and the pig let out a raspy squeal. Its hind hooves kicked at the table. Nikolas pressed the scalpel down hard. He grabbed the two flaps of severed flesh and peeled them back to reveal the wet bulbous sac of intestines and kidneys beneath.

What am I doing here?

2.

From the Journals of Nikolas Kovalski:

14 of November

"I wonder," Brandt said, with no preamble, "what is it you hope to accomplish here at university?"

Brandt was sitting on the edge of his desk in an attitude of casual fraternity. The laboratory had emptied and the building itself had already gone quiet with end-of-the-semester sadness.

"To make a difference, I suppose," I said. "Isn't that what medikal science is about? Saving lives?"

"Yes, yes," Brandt said. "And that's noble enough. But you shouldn't get mired in idealism. I've seen many promising skolars in my years, Nikolas. But none as promising as you. It would be a great tragedy—for me personally, for you, but most of all for the future of Joshuan medikal science—if we were to lose you."

"I'm still here."

"In body perhaps—sometimes, at least. But in spirit? You'll pass this class. In fact, you'll get high marks. And I imagine the story will be the same in your other classes. This is easy for you, am I right? But for those of us for whom it comes easy, there is a greater responsibility. A duty to rise above the average."

"I have my . . . doubts. About kardiology, sir."

"What's to doubt?"

"I just question whether it's the right path for me."

Brandt frowned. "This is still about...your previous studies? I thought we'd made that clear. To continue that course would be irresponsible at best, reckless at worst. You wouldn't want to jeopardize your career with any sort of radical agenda. You're here to practice the medikal sciences, not politics."

"Heart transplants seem so *specialized*. There's more good to be done elsewhere."

"Politics again. Why is one dying man's life more valuable than another's if the issue is not political? Remember that first day, when you corrected me in front of the class? About the incision? You saw clearly what I could not. You thought beyond mere procedure."

That was not how it had happened, but I did not tell him that. He was not talking to who he believed he was talking to; or rather, I was not who I had been.

"Some of us don't get to choose, Nikolas. We are called. Culled, even." Brandt smiled dryly at this last bit of wordplay.

3.

ADRIAN SAT at his desk, flipping through cards with kardiology terms. Nikolas was out, as he was more and more of late. Adrian worried about him. His friend carried such a dark cargo. Adrian went back to quizzing himself on medikal terms.

It was near midnight when the door to their dormitory room opened and Nikolas stepped in heavy-booted, closing the door behind him without his usual conviction. He dragged his chair out with a sharp screech and dropped into a defeated slouch. Adrian watched, saying nothing. Nikolas opened one of the books on his desk briskly. He turned the pages, searching for something. He turned further pages, not finding it.

Adrian could smell the vodka from his side of the room.

"What are you staring at?" Nikolas said and slammed his book shut.

"Nothing. I'm sorry."

Nikolas pulled his chair around with another piercing screech. He slumped, elbows on his thighs, and rested his chin in his hands in a posture of weary confession.

"You know what I did today?"

Adrian held his face carefully neutral.

"I cut a live pig's organs out," Nikolas said. "All in the name of knowledge."

Adrian sat in interested silence.

"Then I met with Brandt . . ."

"And how did that go?"

"Horribly."

Here Nikolas reached down to the bottom drawer of his desk and grabbed a bottle of vodka, took a small drink then another.

"Drink with me."

Nikolas offered the bottle. Adrian hesitated. He had never consumed alcohol before, not that his religion explicitly forbade it, but it seemed spiritually weak to indulge in such an escape from God's reality. And it might be dangerous, given his condition, though no definitive studies on the matter had been published.

"You're going to need something to mix it with."

Nikolas jumped up with something like happiness. He pulled out a carton of fruit concentrate. He mixed a small portion of vodka into a glass and loaded it up with concentrate.

"Here," Nikolas said, "this should be good for you."

With both hands firmly around the curve of the glass, Adrian took a tentative sip, nearly gagged, swallowed it down dutifully. "Tastes good."

"You know what I love about you, Adrian?" Nikolas said. "You are incapable of telling a good lie."

Adrian drank again.

Nikolas considered Adrian abstractly. "And that's because of your fundamental kindness. No, follow me for a minute. You don't want to lie to anyone, because you find that unkind. But if it is unkind to tell the truth, you will lie. That's why you are so bad at it."

"But you consider yourself a good liar?"

"Yes," Nikolas said, "better than I would wish to be."

Nikolas tilted the bottle back, squinted painfully. He stood abruptly and nearly fell onto his bookshelf, propped himself against the wall. He ran his fingers across the spines of his books. His fingers slid disinterestedly along medikal texts and stopped on a gray spine with red lettering. *The Ethics of Being*. He pulled the book out and turned it in his hands abstractly.

It was by Aleksandr Tuvim, municipal poet laureate of Joshua City. Adrian knew this was Nikolas's favorite writer. When Nikolas got drunk, he would read to Adrian from one of his books, pronouncing each sentence as though it were the only truth in the universe.[4] It sometimes became annoying, the way he would read the same passage over and over, as though by repeating it, it gained further significance. And he would give commentary, nearly always the same, every time he read those passages. There was something endearing about Nikolas being so committed to another person's words and thoughts; he usually gave his own thinking perfect priority; but also, he needed so badly, in these drunken moments, for Adrian to like what he was reading to him, as though by Adrian's approval these words would mean the entire world had acquiesced to Nikolas's position. Adrian always listened.

Nikolas flipped through the pages of the book, searching for a passage. "Here it is," Nikolas said. "Paradoxically, the only ethics of Being must be based on lived life, yet the primary enemy of any complete ethics is the closing off of the fullness of Being by our limited experiences—that is to say, it is our lived life that . . . " Nikolas put the book back on the shelf. "Even this bores me now."

---

[4]Author's Note: As previously mentioned, much of this novel-history is derived from actual documents. This scene in particular is based on the journals of Nikolas Kovalski, and these journals are unexpurgated, I might remind you. Were the author looking to put false praise in the mouths of others, this would be a very different type of book. At the same time, however, I can't help but admit a shiver of pride the first time I read that Nikolas esteemed my work so highly. An author should love his characters; he never dreams of being loved by them.

"Why do you say that?"

"What do you really want to be doing, Adrian? I mean, if you could do anything in the world?"

"Honestly? Exactly what I am doing."

"Which is?" Nikolas took a casual sip from his bottle.

Adrian lifted his cup to his mouth. "Learning medikal sciences for the purpose of helping people."

Nikolas waved a drunken hand with bemused contempt.

Adrian asked, "You don't think we're helping people?"

"And is this what you have always wanted to do?" Nikolas asked, ignoring Adrian's question.

"When I was younger, at the boys school, I spent some time thinking I would become a priest," Adrian admitted, "but for several years now, I have known this was my path."

"I don't mean to be indelicate, but did it have anything to do with your . . . condition?"

"Yes, it certainly does," Adrian said. "A priest, a particularly kind one, told me that I was special because of my seizures, that it would bring me closer to God. And in a way it did."

Nikolas waved the vodka bottle in the air, inviting Adrian to carry on.

"While I never saw the face of God as some believe people with my condition do, I think this was God's way of guiding me to where I am today. To helping others. I think I might be able to understand the sufferings of a patient better. It's not just the disease I will be treating, but the person suffering from it."

"Like you've suffered?"

"Exactly," Adrian said. "I know you don't approve of religious ideas like that."

"Forget about all that. I'm bored by myself too. That is old ossified thought, not new thinking."

Adrian had never seen Nikolas like this. If anything, his friend usually exhibited an excess of confidence. Not knowing what to say, he drank more and felt the skin on along his arms pulse with warmth.

"I don't think I can keep doing this," Nikolas said.

"So, what would you do if *you* could do anything? You're the best medikal skolar here."

"I'm not entirely sure why I picked medikal sciences. It seemed like a good option at the time."

Nikolas had scored highly on all the standardized tests. This had allowed him a choice between engineering or medikal sciences, law or psycholinguistics, anything really. And he would have received an equivalent university fellowship no matter which field he chose.

"But I believe there is a reason for everything we do," Adrian said. "You picked nekrosis your first semester."

"I think you and I just see the world differently," Nikolas said. "And we conduct our business in it differently."

"How so?"

"Of course, I am exaggerating the differences here, but I think you fundamentally see each case individually, thinking how you might help someone on that given day. And I don't deny the merit in helping people. But my reason for studying here was not to become a custodian of minor differences in thought. I came here to understand the world in order to change it."

"That's not true, and you know it," Adrian said, made bold by the vodka Nikolas had been feeding him. "What about the nekrotic we helped?"

"Oh, I was performing being me there. What was the nekrotic's name? What was the name of the man who worked there?"

"I think their names were Levi and Ahkbaar," Adrian said. "Is that right?"

"I don't know, and I don't care," Nikolas said. "See? And that is precisely the difference between us."

"So you forgot some names . . ." Adrian said. He was getting drunk now.

"But you remember . . ."

". . . not always, and I am just as arrogant as you!"

"Then you think I'm arrogant?"

"You've said so yourself . . . "

Nikolas fell against his desk, offered Adrian more from his bottle, saw it was empty, pulled another from his bottom drawer. It occurred to Adrian that Nikolas was performing *now*. Was he really so drunk as to fall into things? Was he so uncaring? This was how Nikolas liked to view himself. He had shown his true commitment at the nekrosis ward. Now he was acting. It was a bright warm thought in Adrian's clouded mind. He almost told Nikolas, but he was losing his words.

"I admire you," Nikolas said.

"You know . . . "

"Yes, yes . . . "

Adrian stumbled forward. They hugged and Adrian spilled half of his drink down Nikolas's back.

"That's fine," Nikolas said. "That's fine."

"I said it . . . before . . . you'll change what a doktor is."

They went on like this for hours, lifting each other up with predictions of grand destiny. Adrian stumbled about the room, knocking books to the floor, laughing at the oddity of his clumsiness. Nikolas played the corrupting older sibling, offering Adrian more and more drinks. Their anxieties disintegrated by alcohol, they made the usual lofty pronouncements friends do in this state. Though they exaggerated—about the providence of their initial meeting, about the hugeness of their abilities—there was an anchor of truth to every excess. Nikolas wondered whether Adrian might not be more intelligent than he, perhaps the first time he had this thought about any person; Adrian wondered whether Nikolas might not be more moral. Nikolas enjoyed being Adrian's guide through this new drunken vulnerability. The evening ended with Adrian vomiting and Nikolas standing over him, drinking one more, but in careful watch over his friend.

4.

NIKOLAS TURNED THE PAGES of his biochemistry textbook, skimming the key terms, wondering what would be on the final exam, which was just a few weeks away now. Class was scheduled to begin in five minutes. His fellow skolars filled the room. They sat in their self-assigned seats, the same ones they had randomly chosen on the first day. *Why are we such slaves to routine? Are we incapable of accepting our own freedom?* He looked back to the textbook, flipped to the middle, and found that the material there was remedial in comparison to the research he had done the previous summer. Why had he bothered with this class at all?

"Hey, Nikolas," Dulcina, a redheaded girl, said. Her mind was deft, and she might make a fine researcher one day.

"How are your studies going?"

"Very well, I think. It would be nice to get a fellowship to work with one of the professors . . . "

Was she flirting with him? She was nearly as beautiful as she was bright, but what was she after?

"It must be nice to work with Doktor Brandt the way you do."

So that was it, she wanted a better position at the university; everyone at Joshua University was after something. The chatter of the room, now full, grated on his nerves. He was perhaps being unfair to her. She was making conversation, nothing more.

"What kind of research do you want to do?" he asked.

She launched into what Nikolas knew would be an overlong explanation of her current project—how many times had he subjected some poor soul to such a barrage of scientific fervor?—but Doktor Zoradi entered and called the class to attention.

Dulcina broke off with a pinched smile, then added, "Perhaps we can meet at The Samovar someday."

"Yes," Nikolas managed. "I'm often there." It sounded almost cruel, the subtle refusal to make a date of it, to relegate it to happenstance that they might run into each other instead of making a fixed time that would shape one's week like a stitch shapes a length of cloth.

Doktor Zoradi began his lecture. Nikolas wondered what was wrong with him. Dulcina was precisely the sort of girl he should be lavishing with attention.

The formulae swirled meaninglessly across the page. He slammed the textbook shut, gathered his things hastily in his arms, and left the room by the rear door.

Outside, he breathed the good Joshuan air and let the empty weight of the classroom behind him float from his mind. From some hidden depth, the certainty came that he would never return to the class—or any other class for that matter.

5.

ADRIAN RETURNED FROM CLASS to find Nikolas with his suitcase open on the bed. He did not have to ask where Nikolas was going. He decided he wouldn't try to dissuade him, though he worried about the irreparable choice his friend was making. If Nikolas left now, he wouldn't finish his current coursework, guaranteeing that he would be unable to return to Joshua University—or at least certainly not with any funding. All of those failing marks would never go away, and no amount of future good performance could erase them.

Adrian rubbed his head absently. It still hurt from their revelry of the night before. Did people actually enjoy this feeling? No, of course not. They enjoyed what he had felt previous night, right up until the end when he became sick. He had managed to drag himself to his one class today—a somewhat dull seminar called Research Methodologies and Practices, which was required for all first-year skolars in the sciences.

He flopped down on his own bed. "So you're leaving me."

"Look, Adrian," Nikolas said, "I want you to know that this has nothing to do with you."

"I know that."

"In fact, if it weren't for you, I might have left sooner. No, I mean it. You were the one bright spot in this otherwise wasted semester."

"I understand. And the feeling is mutual."

Nikolas grabbed a piece of paper off his desk. "I've written down my home address. My mother's address. I won't be there much. But I know where you are and I want to stay in touch. You've been important to me, and I expect you to factor in to whatever I do in the future."

Adrian took the paper. "What *will* you do now?"

"I don't know."

Nikolas fastened the clasp on his bag. There were still clothes hanging in his closet, books on his desk. He looked at them with mild regret.

"You can have these."

"Where will you go?" Adrian asked.

"My mother's home for the night. And tomorrow anywhere I want. This is a good thing. Trust me." Nikolas looked at the clock on the desk. "I have twenty minutes. Walk me down to the train station?"

Adrian readily agreed despite his aching head. The walk was a short one and the train was on time (it was always on time when you wanted it to be late; always late when you needed it to be on time). They made further promises to keep in communication. They embraced. And for a long time after, Adrian would remember his friend's gesture of good-bye—a casual two-fingered wave from the brim of his imaginary hat, almost a salute, a gesture both nonchalant and charmingly self-mocking. Somehow that gesture said everything about Nikolas, capturing his personality the way a Silverville aktor could capture the essence of a character in a single frame. This moment would come back to Adrian at the oddest times—months later, in mountain passes as he kept fearful watch for marauding banditii, in a remote desert hospital as he tended to the woman he would come to love, in the gardens of a vast estate as he watched the sun set over the Baikal Sea—and whatever the circumstances, he found the image an unlikely comfort.

CHAPTER FIVE

THE PAST AND FUTURE

1.

S ITTING AT HIS DESK in the Ministrie of Ministries, Mayor Adams read the letter again. It was the end of a long day, just before the holiday. The building was nearly empty. He had many loyal workers, he knew, and they worked hard. But he insisted on working harder. Greatness wants to inspire greatness. Of course, Pierre was the last to leave, and Mayor Adams nearly had to order him to go home. Despite the holiday, Pierre was eager to put in a full day's work. *I wonder if he enjoyed the gift I sent him?* Mayor Adams thought. A suit from perhaps the most expensive and sought-after tailor in the entire city. He stopped thinking about it and returned to the letter.

He couldn't believe that anyone would have such temerity. Didn't people understand he had a government to run? And there was a war on. There was danger from all sides, and if he had to exercise extra vigilance to keep his city safe, wasn't that a small price?

What irony. Abraham Kocznik defending Neil Martin. *Kocznik should be thanking me.* Besides, Mayor Adams had seen Neil Martin's films—crass entertainment, nothing more. If anything, none of his films even deserved to exist.

※ ※ ※

Dear Mr. Adams,

As you know, I am the husband of the aktress Vivian Scott. For years now, thanks to the open treatment of the arts by your administration, she has been able to make her films unimpeded. In doing so—if you'll permit a little husbandly bias—she has provided no small amount of pleasure to the Joshuan people. My wife is not a political person; she is an aktress. The films are not in any way political. She was, therefore, shocked to learn that there was something in the newest film that the Ministrie of Aesthetics found unacceptable.

I also know Neil Martin personally. I can safely say that his feelings on politics are the same. While there was an unfortunate scene at the pre-screening, I think that stemmed more from embarrassment than anything else. Neil is a proud man—to a fault, to be sure—but I think some amount of ego is necessary to make an artistic product, which is, after all, just that: a product. Something for public consumption. He is opening himself up to judgment by critics and by his audiences. If they don't buy tickets, he doesn't make money. I am sure you, in your position of public visibility, can understand what it is like to be scrutinized. If you handle it better than he does, it's because you are particularly suited to a career in politics. Artists, on the other hand, tend to be excessively temperamental.

I fear I've strayed off topic. I merely wanted to inform you of the character of these two people. I assure you they had nothing but the best intentions, and if there is something in the film you found objectionable, it was accidental. They are dutiful Joshuan citizens. They pay taxes; they abide by the law. For what it's worth, I'd like to add that I too have worked hard to make Joshua City a better place—as I'm sure you're aware. This is not to revel in my accomplishments, but to suggest that I do not write to you lightly.

I would appreciate it if there were some way to resolve this matter without anyone sacrificing a year of hard work. If I write to you with some frankness, it's because I respect and admire you as a man of intellect and discernment. I hope I've said nothing to offend.

May Your Days Be Pure-Baikal,

Abraham Kocznik

※ ※ ※

Mayor Adams folded the letter and put it back in the envelope. He considered what to do. Abraham Kocznik was, if not necessary, then at least useful for Mayor Adams's plans. For one thing, he was idolized by the train-loving Joshuan people. For another, he was a brilliant technological mind. The best in the Seven Cities, some claimed. One ought not waste a valuable municipal resource. *I could just ignore the letter*, Adams thought. *But would that be a sign of weakness? No, showing mercy is the privilege of the powerful.*

Besides, he hadn't even seen the film. He did not, in his exhaustive duties, have time to deal with every film slated for release. And so he trusted his Ministers of Aesthetics and Information, their subministers, their cabinets and panels of advisors, and their clerks, secretaries, and researchers. As much as he liked to think he had absolute knowledge and control, he had to admit human limits. Mistakes were made.

He dimly recalled having signed off on the order to block release of the film. That was weeks ago, and it was one of a dozen papers he had signed that day. He wouldn't have noticed at all if it had not been a film by Neil Martin—the first by that direktor to come under the purview of the new aesthetic standards. There was some question, it seemed, about a scene where a zombie epidemic—*ridiculous drivel!*—was blamed on the government. Normally, the scene would have just been excised from the film, but the advisory board had dug a little deeper and they were now suspicious that the whole film might be a metaphor, or worse yet, an allegory. Those idiots in Aesthetics often worried about meaningless distinctions, but in this case they might have a point. So in his duties as Minister of Ministries, he had signed off on the order to block it. What was one film more or less?

So, now... He couldn't ignore Kocznik's request. He could just flatly deny it, let him know who was in charge here, or he could accept it. But what if they could make use of each other? Sometimes a firm hand was required, sometimes a subtle one.

Kocznik's technological prowess could be put to use in many arenas. But the letter stood before him odious and offensive. Mayor Adams paced his office. His anger rising. He grabbed his cigarettes. He had been cutting back, but he deserved one now. As the smoke rolled its meandering way around the room, he saw the door. Behind it were The Oracles. He wondered if this was a large enough problem to bother them. No. He decided they were too important to waste on this. He should be able to handle this on his own. But he kept staring at the door.

You-need-us-now.

2.

A FEW HOLIDAYS had occurred while Adrian had been at university, but they had all been short, a day or two without classes at most, and many of the skolars had remained on campus. More importantly, Nikolas had stayed—and so life continued in its usual manner. But now their room was empty; technically it was no longer *their* room even, but because Nikolas had dropped out with only a few weeks left in the semester, Adrian had not been assigned a new roommate. He was still waiting to hear back from the housing committee about the spring semester—whether he would be assigned a roommate, and if not whether he would be allowed to stay on in this room or have to move to a single room. When he looked out the window, all he saw was the dry gray façade of the fountain, the empty walkways, the frozen grass of the commons. How would he survive two weeks of winter holiday? He closed his book, unable to study. He checked his pockets and found several drams worth of change. Enough for a sandwich and tea at The Samovar.

He shivered as he walked. He passed St. Varenukha's and decided to go inside. He walked up the steps to the chapel and pulled on the massive red oak doors. They were locked. He pulled at them again. He went around the side and put his face up to the tiny window. Only darkness. Even the priest had gone home. He supposed clergymen had mothers and fathers as well, brothers and sisters, cousins and uncles. He was the only one alone.

He could go to St. Ignatius's Homes for Boys, of course. Father Samarov would regale him with stories of the new students, everything that had happened since he had been gone. But he could not go back so soon—not after he had worked so hard to feel he belonged here. That would be admitting defeat.

The Samovar was also locked. Adrian checked his watch. It was scarcely past four o'eve. Everything was deserted. He sat on the brick sill beside the door and tried to figure out where to go, what to do.

The door opened. The girl with snakeskin braids stuck her head out.

"May I help you?" she said.

"Oh, no," Adrian said. "I was just trying to decide where to go."

"Well, you can't sit there."

"I know. I'm very sorry."

She squinted at him. "You're Nikolas's friend, aren't you?"

"Yes," Adrian said. "We're roommates. Or were. He . . ."

She opened the door.

"It's going to take me at least an hour to clean up," she said. "You're welcome to come inside."

"I wouldn't want to impose."

"And I wouldn't have offered if you were."

Adrian entered the empty teahouse. A blast of warm, almost stifling air. All the chairs were upside down on tables. She gestured for him to sit. Adrian took down a chair from Nikolas's favorite table. It was where they always sat when they came here, though the obscene painting above the table made Adrian uncomfortable. Now he decided he didn't mind so much; the discomfort he felt because of the painting was offset by the comfort of habit. The girl went behind the counter.

"Would you like some tea?" she called out to him.

"If it's not too much trouble."

"Don't be so polite," she said. "It's not an attractive quality."

"Sorry."

She came out in front of the counter. "You know something? I've got a better idea. Do you like schnapps?"

"Yes," he lied.

He hadn't had a drink since that time with Nikolas in their room. Had it really only been a couple of weeks? And after the way he felt when he woke up the next morning, he wasn't exactly eager to try it again, though Leni's easy air made him want to be more free himself.

"I've got peppermint and berry. Which do you prefer?"

"I don't know. Either, I guess."

"Peppermint schnapps it is, then."

She disappeared behind the counter. In a minute, she came back carrying a bottle. With a mock-flourish, she displayed the label to him like a waiter at a fine restaurant. He read the flowing script there, something about a distillery in Baikalingrad.

"It's not the best we have," she said. "Grigori would kill me if I took one of those."

Adrian mumbled something.

"Don't worry," she said. "I'll just tell him I dropped it."

She opened the bottle and took a long swallow. She passed it to him. "I hope you don't mind drinking straight from the bottle. The last thing I need is more dishes."

Adrian drank casually, the way he imagined Nikolas would. He liked it better than the vodka, which wasn't saying much.

"Not bad, right?" the girl asked.

"What is your name?"

"Leni," she said.

She grabbed the bottle from him, their fingers touching lightly.

3.

From the Journals of Nikolas Kovalski:

18 of December

I should have expected him to be there. Why wouldn't he be? Still, I was surprised when I saw Marcik sitting in the low light of our childhood kitchen. He looked too big for the chair. In the blue and gold of his

Guardsman fatigues, his muscles bulged. Was this the brother I had grown up with? And was he starting to grow a mustache, too?

"Nikolas," he said.

"Marcik," I said. I set my bags on the floor. "How goes the warmongering?"

"You don't waste any time, do you?"

"Boys!" Mother said, shuffling by us to stir a pot. "I don't want you fighting. St. Nikolas's Day is almost here. Marcik, it's nearly your brother's name-day. And Nikolas, you should be more charitable."

It was like she did it deliberately to taunt me. She knew my impatience with religious matters, and yet she refused to accept it. She seemed to think it was a temporary condition that could be alleviated with enough motherly guilt. Marcik sat calmly in his chair. There was something more confident, more adult in him now.

"How long is your leave?" I asked.

"Just through tomorrow," he said. "Our kompany leaves for the Provinces the day after."

"So you'll be celebrating the holidays in the desert," Mother said.

"I am a Baikal Guardsman now, Mother."

"Yes, I know," Mother said. "And we're all very proud of you." She looked at me, asking my approval—which I could not give.

"It's a pity they wouldn't let you stay longer," I said.

"Some of us have more important things to do than dally at Joshua University," Marcik said.

I let that go without responding. Mother sampled the soup and added more salt. She was always over-salting everything, I remembered now. Last year, the one time I'd come home, I'd told her it was bad for her blood pressure. She'd given me such a wounded look I never mentioned it again.

"My boys," she said. "Together again. Just the way it should be. I'm making my special borscht. Your favorite."

I gave Marcik a secret smile; Mother was always saying this or that was our favorite. Marcik surprised me now: he looked at Mother, then at me, and rolled his eyes. It was as though we were children again and she was forcing her favorite dishes on us, pretending we loved them too.

I wished suddenly that things were different for Marcik and me, that I wasn't so hard in my thinking sometimes. Just as quickly, I thought about him out there in the desert, getting shot in the gut for no good reason, and the old frustration returned. How could people be so blind, so unconsidered in their beliefs?

We ate. It was more pleasant than I had expected. Marcik talked incessantly about his new status as Guardsman. He had been inducted the week before, the final step in his training. These people were not like me, but they were mine, bound to me by blood. What is Mother to me anymore? Why must I feel this? I prefer elective affinities. The friends I have chosen mean more to me. And they should, I think.

Marcik chewed complacently. Mother beamed at both of us. I pushed my plate aside.

"I'm going to lie down and read," I said.

4.

IT WAS JUST PAST five o'eve and already completely dark when Leni locked the door of The Samovar behind them. Adrian's eyes involuntarily followed the curve of her hips as she bent to pick up her bag. Another bottle of schnapps poked out of the top of the bag; they had finished the first one while she swept the floor of the shop, counted the money in the register, took out the garbage, and cleaned out various contraptions for brewing tea.

She turned and smiled at him. "You ready?"

She took his arm and they walked across the empty campus. She smelled good, not doused in perfume like so many girls around here, but earthy, a slight hint of healthy natural sweat. He noticed he was not shivering and wondered if that was the alcohol or having a girl holding his arm. Was this how Nikolas felt when he had been with Leni? Of course, Nikolas didn't think such things were a sin—which was what made him comfortable with it. The thought was too complicated to follow right now. There were stars shining down through the leafless trees.

They passed the turn for his dormitory.

"Where are we going?" he asked.

They crossed the road to the Institute of Fine Arts. He had never been over here, though the girls who studied at the Institute and their supposed lasciviousness were a common topic of vulgar talk among his fellow medikal skolars. They stopped in front of a building, covered in dried ivy and in need of repair.

"Wait here," she said and went inside.

After a few moments, she poked her head out of a side door, looked around, and then waved him up with an urgent motion. As soon as he set foot inside the door, she grabbed his arm and pulled him along. They hustled up the stairs, the schnapps in Adrian's stomach sloshing, a sour taste rising in his throat. They went down a cold hallway with high ceilings and exposed beams.

She unlocked a door and they were in a disorganized but cozy room. Clothing was piled in mounds on the floor. In the place of curtains, the windows were draped with sheer colorful fabric. Leni flopped down on her bed, the blankets lifting in a swirl around her.

"Adrian, Adrian," she said. She said it with a sigh; she said it like music. "What do we do now?"

"I don't know."

"I do. More drink." She spun away from him, rolling over on her stomach, and pulled the bottle out of her purse. She drank with visible pleasure and handed it to him.

"I'd better not."

She pushed the bottle to his lips and tilted it. The schnapps went into his mouth and down his chin. He swallowed and wiped his face.

"All right. I surrender," he said.

He looked for a place to sit. There was only one chair. On it rested a lamp with a green shade and multicolored glass beads that refracted the light into a lively rainbow. She patted the bed beside her. He sat and passed the bottle back. She unlaced her boots, kicked them thuddingly to the floor. Her stockings were pale pink, yellow on the toes.

She rose slowly from the bed and went to the fonograf. She put on a record and lowered the needle. The music gave a scratchy start and then began. It was a soft intimate tune—all smoky horns and the pitter-pat of drums. She danced swayingly to it, looking over her shoulder at him.

"You've got a lot of books," he said.

On the windowsill were stacks and stacks of well-thumbed books. There were also books on the floor and fanned over the surface of a desk.

She noticed where his eyes had gone.

"I have a horrible confession to make," she said. "I'm a literature student."

"Poetry?" Adrian guessed, judging by the slimness of many of the volumes.

"It gets worse, doesn't it?"

"You shouldn't apologize for what you love," Adrian said. "Poetry is noble, I think. Poets are like historians of hub-thought."

"*Historians of hub-thought.* That's nice. I'll have to remember that when my father comes to visit," she said. "And that's exactly how Laikan has theorized language. It's the vehicle for the collective thoughts of a culture, and even of the things we never allow ourselves to think. Language can reveal those things, she says."

"But poetic language, right?"

"Yes, yes. She says that regular everyday language can even cover up what we really think and feel. It's poetic language that—what's the term she uses?—*discloses* how we exist."

"What does that mean?" Adrian asked, confused and excited by what she was saying.

"Well . . ." she began and looked to the ceiling as though her thoughts rested there, "in everyday language, we tend to think that our words match up with or link into things in the world. But that's not right, Laikan says. When I offer you a drink, for example," she said and passed him the bottle, "the word *drink* has to do with the alcohol, but it means much more about our situation, about our existence in this precise moment."

Adrian took a small sip, then a larger one. He tried to understand the meaning behind the meaning of her words. He was aware all the time of Nikolas's unseen presence in the room, as if he were in disguise as the lamp in the green chair. Nikolas was what they had in common, was what had brought them together. He tried to drink and act in a way that he thought Nikolas would approve of—or rather, as Nikolas might in the presence of a woman.

She hopped up on the bed and, kneeling, leaning forward, read the spines on the windowsill. She finally pulled one down.

"Want to hear my favorite?" she said. "Do you know Aleksandr Tuvim?"

"Of course."

Odd that she should mention Tuvim, given that he was Nikolas's favorite writer. Or perhaps not odd at all, Adrian thought; perhaps it was only natural that they should both like this author.

She read to him, from a poem he recognized as one of Tuvim's most famous.[5] He had to memorize it in the literature class at Saint Ignatius's. He leaned back, propping himself on his extended arms, and closed his eyes. The words washed over him.

Impure-Baikal

I.
You, green rotting dock of summer.
When I think of you, I think water
Warm and stagnant.

---

[5] Author's Note: I must confess that I am still somewhat baffled by this poem's popularity. I do not consider it my best work. At first this bothered me, and I wanted to protest when I was asked to read it in public, or I wanted to disown it when I was asked about it in interviews. How could such a simple and unambitious theme have caught on? In the end, though, I accepted and even became grateful for the poem's popularity. It allowed me a certain authority; people listened to what I had to say, which is all a writer can ask for.

I think mud. Forgive me,
These are not ugly thoughts.

I do not want you perfect,
I do not want pure-baikal.
Life is not these things.
Why should its variegated beauty be?

I want this swirling mud of cosmos,
This universe, perfect in its imperfect *is*.

The poem went on from there, moving from love to politics to meta-physics, all with this same idea—the existential perfection of imperfec-tion. But Leni stopped reading. Her fingers touched Adrian's chin and he opened his eyes.

She looked at him sadly. "You're not like Nikolas, you know."

"Should I be?" he asked.

"Nikolas would never listen to poetry. I imagine he thinks it's frivo-lous or a waste of time or whatever."

He should defend his friend. He could tell her how much Nikolas loved this very author she had read with such passion. How well did she know Nikolas, really? But there was the memory-feeling of her hand on his face, and he coveted all her affections just now.

"Nikolas can be a little . . . severe," he said. "We come from similar backgrounds. And his experience changed the way he interacts with the world. Everything to him is a conflict. And coming from that back-ground, I can understand. I've felt bitter myself at times."

"He makes the people around him feel small."

"Yes," he said. "He does that, doesn't he?"

Adrian's eyes drifted across the charming clutter of Leni's room, and he wondered if this was true. Was it Nikolas who made him feel small? Whose fault was that? He looked back at Leni and noticed again how beautiful she was.

She slapped him hard across the cheek.

Adrian pressed his hand to his face.

"What was that for?"

"You should have heard the way he talked about you when we were together," Leni said. "He barely knew you then. But he went on and on. 'My new roommate is brilliant,' he said. 'He might even end up a better doktor than me. And I know he's a better person.' He pointed you out to me one time when you came into The Samovar. That's how I knew who you were. Now here you are, shrinking him—and all to get a shot at me, a girl you didn't even notice until tonight."

"You said those things first," Adrian protested.

She arched her back in exasperated defiance. "That's different," she said. "You're his friend."

"You're right," Adrian said. "I never drink. I'm not supposed to on account of my condition. This only the second time . . . " He stood quickly. The room tilted. He steadied himself on the lone chair. The lamp wobbled but did not fall. "I should go now."

"I didn't say you had to leave."

"But then . . . " he trailed off drunkenly.

"Come here."

She pulled him to her on the bed, and he lay gratefully beside her. Adrian's hand found glad purchase on Leni's hip. He stopped thinking and let happen what would.

5.

From the Journals of Nikolas Kovalski:

19 of December

This morning, Mother shook me awake at some ungodly hour—but aren't all hours ungodly? (A little joke at Adrian's expense, though he is not here to read it. It's strange. I only lived with him a few months, and yet I find myself arguing with him in my mind, as though he were there with me.)

"We're opening the gifts," she said. "Marcik has to leave today."

This was the first I had heard of gifts. I rinsed my mouth and went out to the cramped room with the sewing machine, the dining table, a shabby couch, a work desk, and all the unimportant accoutrements of this house. This was the only room big enough to be of any use, and so Mother had crammed her entire life in here. Now it was even more crowded than usual: on the floor was a stack of wrapped boxes. Had they hidden these boxes and brought them down this morning, as if to surprise me with Saint Nikolas's magical visitation? Marcik was sitting at the foot of the pile in his pajamas, just as if he were eight years old again. I've been experiencing the claustrophobic sensation of time folding back on itself since I arrived.

"You look like hell," Marcik said. "Out drinking again?"

I shook my head, though in fact he was right. At nearly one o'morn, unable to sleep any more, I had slipped out to the local tavern. A piss-hole worse than The Nameless Tavern, but it did the trick. I came back in as quietly as possible, but I bumped against something trying to maneuver through this room in the dark. Mother stood there in her nightgown like a ghost. She said nothing. And to her credit, she didn't mention it now.

Mother had prepared a breakfast of cured ham, poached eggs, and potato cakes with butter. Marcik came to the table and filled his plate. All I could eat was a piece of toast, which I dipped in the dark gravy she had prepared.

"No one told me we were doing gifts," I said.

"That's because we knew you wouldn't get us anything," Marcik said.

"We're just happy you're here," Mother said.

Marcik insisted that Mother open the first gift. It was a shiny new cooking pan. She looked like she might weep.

"If I'd known, I would have waited to cook breakfast," she said.

"Well, I had some back pay saved up," Marcik said. He looked at me. "Open one of yours."

To spite him, I opened one from Mother. It was a scarf—hand-knit and full of vibrant yellows and purples and greens. This was how she made her scant income these days, making and repairing clothing for her neighbors.

"I thought since it's getting colder . . ." Mother said shyly.

I knew I would never wear it. "It's terrific, Mother," I lied. I put it around my neck.

Marcik opened one of Mother's gifts—an ornate pen and stationary.

"So you can write me every day from the front."

Marcik hugged her with a warmth I wished I could muster.

"It's perfect," he said. "And you know I will write you."

Now I was up again. *To Nikolas*, the label said. *From Marcik and Mother.* The box was surprisingly heavy.

"We pitched in on this one together," Marcik said, dropping his earlier antagonism.

I tore the wrapping carefully at the seams and discovered a leather-bound edition of *Bellefleur's Encyklopedia of Medikal Science*. This book cost over one hundred drams. I had thought of buying one for myself since I had matriculated at Joshua University. It must have put them out tremendously. And it was likely Marcik who had contributed the bulk of cost.

"You shouldn't have," I stammered. Yes, I stammered. "I've wanted this for some time now."

Mother beamed. Marcik had a plain look of pleasure on his face.

"My big brother, who will be a great man one day, deserves only the best."

I almost admitted it to them right there, almost told them the truth of who I had become, that I was no longer the brilliant medikal skolar they were so proud of, but rather a cast-about drunkard.

"Thank you two so much. Truly, thank you."

If I still had the ability to, I would have cried just then.

6.

ADRIAN WOKE the next morning in Leni's bed. He was in his underwear, at least. Thank God for that. Leni slept naked beside him, half out of the blankets despite the cold of the room. He glanced at her goose-fleshed breasts, his head pounding and his throat raked dry. He grabbed his coat from the chair.

"Are you leaving?" Leni said, rolling over and stretching.

"No, I was just . . . well, I don't have to. I just thought . . . "

She sat up, smacked her lips against the taste of last night's schnapps. She made no attempt to cover herself.

"It's all right, Adrian. I am a grown woman. I do what I want."

"So should we . . . I mean . . . do you have the number of my dormitory fone? Did I even tell you where I live?"

She snorted. "Why, so we can meet for tea?"

Adrian said nothing, taking in the absurdity of the situation.

"Please," she said. "Go. I give you permission."

Not knowing what to say, Adrian left in sheepish silence.

Adrian stumbled from the room, down the hall, and into the bright morning. He wanted nothing more than to curl up and die. He had never felt so empty—well, almost never. It was like the dark wave that folded over him after one of his seizures. The universe had been hollowed out, drained of any color or meaning.

He walked quickly to the chapel. This time the doors were unlocked. Inside all was shadows and quiet. His footsteps echoed on the stones of the church floor. What little light came in was colored by the giant stained-glass windows depicting scenes of the Before-Time saints. Here the Harbinger turned wine into water, which he used to quench the thirst of a dying man; there the Saint of the Burning Heart felt the radiant hand of the Almighty rip open his chest.

At the front of the altar was a statue of the Harbinger just before he was beheaded. Despite the blade hanging above his neck, the Harbinger looked off to one side, a distant beatific smile on his face. It was the expression of the perfect man. Adrian knelt. He composed his own prayer on the spot.

My Lord and Harbinger, he thought, mouthing the words. *I believed I was good. But I see now that was a kind of pride. Or maybe covetousness. I coveted the notion of my own goodness. I have judged others, my Lord. I judged them even as I told myself I was pitying them. But pity is a form of judgment. "Judge not." How many times have I heard this? And*

yet I never understood until now. I am just like them, my Lord. Worse,
because they accept what they are, while I take pride in my difference.
Teach me. Teach me how to be good. In the spirit that moves along the
water, Amen.

He kneeled there, in the radiance of the Harbinger's image, emptying his head of all thoughts of the night before, divorcing himself from
himself. He kneeled until his legs hurt, and then he kneeled yet longer.

※ ※ ※

Back in the dormitory, he took a hot bath. He lay in bed and sipped
tea. The way his head felt, he worried a seizure might be coming
on. He lay there, trying not to move, not to upset his system. Now
that he was a medikal skolar, he thought of his seizures differently,
conceived of them as flow of blood, sugar levels, and hydration. No
one quite knew what caused them, but they had to be caused by
something.

After several hours, he rose, pulled on his pants and jacket, and
headed out.

He found himself outside of The Samovar again. A few students
were inside, stragglers like himself. Nowhere to go. There was no sign
of Leni. Through the window he saw a young man behind the counter
reading a book. Of course she wouldn't be working today. Hadn't she
told him that last night? And what did he want from her anyway?

"Do you have a minute?" a small woman with coppery spiked
hair asked.

Wanting to fulfill the promise of his prayer, he said, "Of course I do."
He now had time for all humanity.

"Hi, Adrian" she said.

"Hello?" Was this Mouse? She looked so different. She wore a thick
jacket and had dark makeup under her eyes.

In her hand, she held a stack of pamphlets.

"Would you like some information on how to make a difference?"

"In what way?"

She looked down at the pamphlets. "It might seem silly to you. Elias says it is, but I'm recruiting people to go work at this desert hospital. A hospital at a work camp, actually. They're criminally understaffed—excuse the pun, ha-ha."

"That doesn't sound silly at all."

Encouraged, Mouse went on. "We enjoy such privilege here in Joshua City, and our privilege is built on the exploitation of others. I think it's time we give something back."

"I agree," Adrian said.

"And they really need medikal skolars. Others can do a lot, but it's the medikal skolars and engineering skolars we most need."

"I'll take one."

※ ※ ※

And so Leni Castorp changed the lives of both Adrian Talbot and Nikolas Kovalski without any of them realizing it. Adrian never told Nikolas of his meeting with Leni, too ashamed of his behavior at first, and later having more important things to think about. And Nikolas, fancying himself independent of thought and action, would scarcely have credited a harmless flirtation as life-changing.

Whatever the case, it's natural to want to make something of this coincidence: the role that a young woman played in the lives of two of the most important Joshuans, especially given all that happened later. Maybe it does mean something. That depends on your point of view. Some, like Adrian, might see it as an act of God. Nikolas, no doubt, would have found it momentarily unsettling but ultimately uninteresting in the way that coincidence always is—the universe like the proverbial one thousand monkeys with one thousand typewriters who eventually write the dramas of Umberto Lemkin. Some would argue it would take fewer than that, judging by the quality of the man's work. Myself, I don't like to disparage other artists. We all did what we thought we must in those troubling times. But still, whatever your metaphysical explanation of Leni's role in the story of Joshua City—be it providence or happenstance—it is worth noting and remembering, for she will return in future events and play a less obscure role in the unfolding of the tragicomedy that is history.

7.

From the Journals of Nikolas Kovalski:

20 of December

The house is empty. Mother must be out shopping. This is how her day is divided now—cook breakfast, shop, cook lunch, clean the house, cook dinner, maybe a little radio or organizing of her fotos and letters, then bed. How do people live this way? And yet many do. It's not enough for me. Does that make me better or worse?

I went down to The Nameless Tavern again. No one was there. I drank a drink I didn't want, or didn't want to want. Turned around. Came back.

Marcik was gone when I returned. We didn't say a proper good-bye, not that he'll mind. He's shipping out tomorrow—is that the term they use? What a strange world. He's off to kill strangers for reasons he doesn't understand. And the Joshuan government is paying him to do it. In a way I envy him his clear path. What outlet do I have for all my self-righteous rage? I used to have my studies; now I'm reduced to impotent discussions at the bar.

I talk and talk but nothing ever changes...Words...

8.

THE MAIL WOULD COME right up to the front lines, they told him. Marcik wondered about the person who had that job—was he a Guardsman or just a regular postman conscripted by the duties of wartime? What a miserable job. All the dangers of soldiery without any of the glory. He imagined being shot in the back with a full sack of mail—love letters sealed with a lipstick kiss, care packages full of home-baked treats, and who knew what other kind of comfort? He didn't know whether he felt sadder for the fallen postman or for the undelivered mail. There is something tragic about an unopened envelope.

He put his own envelope, opened so many times, back in the cigar box. He set the box on the center of the bed. He wouldn't need that now. It was a sentimental indulgence. A sign of weakness. He hoisted his Guardsman-issued pack and began following the others, his brothers-in-arms now, out of the barracks.

He was about halfway to the door of the barracks when he turned around. He sprinted back to his bunk—or as much of a sprint as he could manage with a thirty-kilo bag on his back. He grabbed the cigar box and shoved it into the bag. He had to jam it inside, so full was the bag with rations, ammunition, and medikal supplies. Finally, and only with great effort, he managed to pull the drawstring shut. He was the last person in the barracks. He dashed outside just in time to see the others lining up in formation. He took his place beside Fredrik, his chest heaving and the bag like a sack of cement tugging him down.

"At last," Fredrik whispered, using the side of his mouth in the way soldiers learn to do. "Volfgang is going to let you have it."

Marcik had seldom seen the whole kompany lined up like this. The platoons, groups of fifty, generally trained individually, sometimes even splitting up into squads of a dozen or less. Now there were nearly two hundred men standing shoulder to shoulder, backs straight despite the heavy packs, chins thrust up and out—the C-Kompany of the 5th Battalion, 12th Regiment of the Baikal Guard. They were just one of many, and Marcik was just one speck among them.

Fortunately, Volfgang had more important things on his mind than Marcik's tardiness. Volfgang stood at attention with the other officers, no longer the sole arbiter of Marcik's fate. Behind the platoon leaders were the squad leaders—sergeants and kolonels—and behind them the non-commissioned officers. In front of them all was Major Schmidt, a man Marcik had rarely seen since his induction ceremony.

The major stepped forward. He was a surprisingly young man for his rank. There was nothing noteworthy about his appearance: plain face, brown hair, a build no more impressive than Marcik's own.

"Men of the C-Kompany," Major Schmidt said. "My fellow Guardsmen. At ease."

Developed through years of field combat, Schmidt's voice carried without him having to shout. The men relaxed, but not too much. Their platoon leaders and their squad leaders, their real masters, were still watching and could punish them later for the slightest infraction—a nervous titter, a whispered joke.

"I won't speak for long," the major said. "What good are words on a day like today? You are, most of you, going into battle for the first time. You have had as much training as we can give you, and you may even make good soldiers yet. Well, some of you."

He paused, but his tone was so flat, no one could tell if they were supposed to laugh. He went on.

"But all your training is theoretical. We try to simulate true combat as best we can, but the truth is that you can't simulate real bullets, real danger. The best we can hope for is that when the bullets do come, your training kicks in. This, as I'm sure your officers have explained, is the point of all the repetition. It may have seemed cruel at the time, but we hoped to get the training deep down in you, at the level of instinct. We can't know how well it worked until you're tested. But I'm looking at you today, and I'm seeing your young fresh faces—some eager, some afraid...yes, it's all right to be afraid. In fact, I'd be afraid if you weren't...And I believe, looking at you, that many of you will surprise us, will surprise yourselves. There is a great man for every moment. Why not be that man?"

This time his pause was filled with the expected clapping and *hut-hut!* of soldierly approval.

"Good luck," he concluded. "We leave on the hour."

CHAPTER SIX

THE NOVEL AS SURVEILLANCE

1.

A BRAHAM FELT the lift of personal accomplishment each time he approached The Hub. *His* trains, traversing Joshua City from sea-wall to desert-wall. Never mind that as a member of Silverville's elite, he no longer rode the train. Never mind that the trains had existed well before him—and that all he had done was improve their engines and rails. Never mind that The Hub dated back to the Before-Time, a reconstructed edifice that had been used, it was believed, as some sort of large-scale power source. Never mind any of that. It all bore the stamp of his innovations, and the people of Joshua City had taken to calling them *the Kocznik trains.*

His driver, Cesar, drove him to the gated entrance to Ministrie of Technology. There were thirteen Ministries: identical onion-domed structures that encircled The Hub. The Ministrie buildings were differentiated by the color of their corkscrewing spires, the Ministrie of Technology being yellow and green. In the vast smooth black dome above The Hub was the Ministrie of Ministries. It watched over them all.

Abraham showed his Ministrie pass to the Guardsman at the gatehouse and he was ushered through. Cesar pulled the car up to entrance of the building and Abraham got out, thinking of his current project and the work he hoped to finish that day. The Ministrie never gave him deadlines, allowing him wide berth for his research. This had been a worry at first. Would they understand the trial-and-error process that was necessary? But they had understood—or at least accepted—his demands, and his laboratory had shown the desired results.

At the entrance, he showed his pass again and removed the contents of his pockets to be radiation-scanned. His belongings were returned to him, and he continued down the hallway, wondering vaguely whether finer holes in a mini-microfone would decrease unwanted static. He arrived at an inner doorway and raised his arms, like he did every morning, to be searched for weapons or other contraband.

"How are you today, Mr. Kocznik?" the Guardsman asked.

"Doing well, Mikah. And yourself?"

"The daughter was ill this morning, but her mother is with her now, so all is well."

Mikah finished checking Abraham and punched in the code to open the door to the series of laboratories, but just as Abraham was about to wish Mikah a good day and say that he hoped his daughter felt better soon, an alarm sounded.

Mikah set his hand lightly on Abraham's shoulder. "Sir, just a moment please."

"What's going on?" Abraham asked.

"I'm not sure, but I need you to stand over there," Mikah said, closing the door to the laboratories.

Other Guardsmen were gathering workers at the Ministrie against the wall where Mikah had sent Abraham. Questioning murmurs could be heard under the alarm's insistent howl.

After nearly half an hour of this, the alarm stopped. A collective relief went through the gathered workers. "Thank the Seven Prophets!" someone said.

A Guardsman Abraham did not recognize approached them and said, "Which of you is Abraham Kocznik?"

Abraham stepped forward. "I am Kocznik."

"Come with me please, sir."

※ ※ ※

Abraham was led to the office of the Minister of Technology.

"What's going on?" Abraham asked, growing concerned.

"Please sit down," the Minister said. "There has been a serious security breach."

Abraham did as he was told and waited for the Minister to explain.

"Do you know the whereabouts of your colleague Jürgen Moritz?"

"He should be in the laboratory. He tends to arrive very early."

"He is not here today," the Minister said. "Where else might he be?"

"Has something happened with Jürgen?"

A large cache of logbooks and several reels of both audio and video surveillance had gone missing, the Minister explained. These were very sensitive materials, he said, without divulging their exact contents.

"And you think Jürgen is responsible?" Abraham asked, indignant.

"There are only five people who have clearance. You are one of them. And here you are. I am one. And the others are likewise accounted for."

Leaving only Jürgen.

"He would never do anything of the sort," Abraham said, but even as he spoke the words, he remembered the reservations Jürgen had recently expressed about the possible uses of their technology.

※ ※ ※

The Ministrie of Technology closed for the day after all the workers had been questioned. Abraham telefoned Cesar to pick him up. On his way home, he sat in the front seat instead of the back so that he could more easily listen to the radio. He was rarely on the road at this time. How patternized his life had become.

He tuned in to Joshua City radio, first:

"Breaking news: A high-ranking official in the Ministrie of Technology is wanted for crimes of treason. We have the exclusive here."

Abraham turned to Radio Free Joshua, a small radio station with deliberately limited broadcast range. Mayor Adams allowed them to broadcast their "alternative content" as proof of his democratic spirit. If Cesar wondered about Abraham's fiddling with the radio dial, he gave no indication of it; he played to perfection his role as the discreet hired help of a rich man.

"... *surveillance of the most famous in Silverville. The highest levels of the government. And even common Joshuans. You, listeners. If this information is accurate, the depth of municipal surveillance is truly frightening."*

Here, they played a snippet of an innocuous meeting between a film producer and a prostitute.

"But this is more than a titillating matter. Jürgen Moritz, one of the developers of the technology has given us permission to divulge his identity, at great risk to himself, because, as he wrote in his letter to us 'The implications of this are far-reaching and concern everyone in Joshua City. If I want transparency, then I will be the first to offer it. I hope Mayor Adams will do the same.'"

Abraham listened as the powerbrokers of Joshua City said unforgiveable things, admitted to transgressions and corruption. Then the radio went silent. A burst of static.

"Breaking news: A high-ranking official in the Ministrie of Technology is wanted for crimes of treason. We have the exclusive here."

He turned the dial and heard the same official report again and again on every station.

2.

MARCIK'S KOMPANY had been marching for twelve days. The men were growing restless. More than one fight had broken out—always over something trivial, such as who received the larger piece of bread or the better sleeping arrangements. Marcik's boots chafed him and in the evening he winced as he removed his socks. He didn't mind not being shot at, but this limbo was a kind of torture, neither the idyll of peace nor the violent chaos of war. Anticipation, extended long enough, amounts to dread. Even Fredrik did not say much. He stared out at the frosty horizon, his fingers touching his rifle, his jaw hard-set.

There were only four trucks, not enough to carry all of them. Two of the trucks were loaded with supplies, hundred-liter barrels of water, medikal kits, ammunition, rations. The other two carried passengers. Each of these trucks had fifteen seats, mostly reserved for officers of the rank of lieutenant or higher. That left eighteen spots for enlisted Guardsmen. These spots were assigned in shifts. Roughly every ten days, each enlisted man was allowed to ride in the back of a truck. For that day, he was the envy of the kompany. The next day, he became an ordinary Guardsman again.

The only advantage of walking was that it kept you warm. On the rare occasions they came across a well, they had to chip away ice to refill their canteens. Doing anything that required taking off your gloves was torture. They tested the water with a special instrument to determine whether it contained the pathogen that caused nekrosis. It was unlikely this far from the city, but it was better to be safe. If the water was contaminated, they had to drink the limited supply on the trucks.

When it was Marcik's day to ride in the truck, he climbed in and found that every seat was taken. The other Guardsmen looked at him: *Sorry, brother, you're too late.*

Marcik resigned himself to walking. Though his feet hurt terribly, it was not worth fighting over.

One of the Guardsmen lumbered from his seat. His name was Yosef, but everyone called him Yoyo. A hulking beast, all gristly blubber and raw strength. His arms were as big around as Marcik's legs. His face was an enormous block with a great jutting forehead. He had big soft lips in a mouth that hung open slackly.

"You can have my seat. I am too big."

"Are you sure?"

"I like to walk." He slapped Marcik on the back with joyful force.

※ ※ ※

At dusk, they approached a small town.

"Thank the Seven," one of the officers said.

His name was Cantor and he had replaced Volfgang as the leader of Marcik's unit. Volfgang had stayed in Joshua City to train more Guardsmen. Sergeant Cantor was firm but fair.

"The major has something special planned for you boys tonight. A little treat to raise your spirits."

They were still safely within Joshuan territory, which meant no hostiles but also a continuation of their limbo. But they would at least sleep indoors tonight. That was something.

At a gate made of spiked wooden posts, a sentryman waved them inside. The town was alive with lights and merriment. Children played with sparkle-sticks. On the upper floors of a tavern women in undergarments leaned out to whistle at the passing Guardsmen. The men in the truck hollered back. The Guardsmen on foot stroked their rifle barrels lewdly and pumped their hips in sexual pantomime. Yoyo, walking behind the truck, took it all in with wondering eyes.

※ ※ ※

Once settled, the men were allowed a few hours of respite. They spent their wages on drink—spiced wine and root liquor—and on gambling or dalliances with willing women.

Later that night, the kompany was gathered in a drafty single-room building lined with chairs. Many of them were drunk and a few had brought their dates with them. The wind whistled through the loose boards, but it was still warmer than outside. The men warmed themselves with their drink and their companions.

Marcik found himself in one of the better seats toward the front of the room. Yoyo sat beside him. Marcik looked around for Fredrik, trying to save him a seat, but he did not spot him.

Another Guardsman came hurrying up.

"Move over," he said to Yoyo.

The Guardsman was Yoyo's best friend, Samir. He was a small, skinny boy with a smashed-in nose. He was from Kazhstan but had come to Joshua City when he was just twelve—as he was quick to tell anyone who would listen, being fond of talk and something of a braggart. He had fled that water-poor region and left his family behind, finding work in a market and joining the Baikal Guard when he was of age (or possibly a little before, Marcik speculated—lying about one's age was common). In training drills, he was quick as a desert-hare, performing with ruthless efficiency.

Yoyo slid over, wedging Marcik between him and the arm of the bench. Kaptain Nguyen came forward to address them. Nguyen was Major Schmidt's second-in-kommand; he executed most of the major's daily orders. That he had managed to advance so high despite his Baikyong-do origins was a testament to his military acumen, but also to his fierce loyalty to the chain of kommand.

"Guardsmen," Kaptain Nguyen said, "the major has asked me to address you. He knows how rough this march has been on you. He knows how eager you are to see a little action."

Grumbles and shouts. One voice: *Baikal-true!*

"He also knows that in normal circumstances, you would have celebrated Saint Nikolas's Day with your families. But we are all out here together, enlisted men and officers alike."

Marcik's kompany had spent Saint Nikolas's Day marching. It was the same as any other day, though the walk seemed a little longer, their bags heavier, their boots tighter. Still, the night ended well. After making camp, the men stayed up late to talk and drink and play cards. The usual lights-out was not enforced. Fredrik shared his flask with Marcik. They swapped stories. Marcik talked about his uneasy relationship with his brother.

"He doesn't respect the Guard," he said.

"My family is the opposite," Fredrik said. "My father was an officer. His father was an officer. If I'm anything less, I won't be able to show my face to them again."

"My father was a Guardsman too," Marcik said. "But I hardly remember him."

Now, Kaptain Nguyen informed them, "As a reward for your patience, and hopefully to remind you of why you're out here—the enormity and honor of your task, as the major would say—we've got a film for you. And food. Plenty of it. Good food. And drink. Which a few of you seem to have already indulged in." Komradely laughter went through the room; Kaptain Nguyen smiled at his own joke, letting them all know he was one of them. "You'll find plates on the table at the back. Please help yourselves, and we'll start the film shortly."

The Guardsmen all stood and sang the refrain of "The Glory of the Baikal Guard," some more competently and some more drunkenly than others. *The water sparkles brightly! And we guard the city nightly!*

The men pushed toward the table.

"In an orderly fashion, Guardsmen," Nguyen instructed playfully.

After they were seated with great hunks of roasted ox in pig-fat gravy, buttered rolls, and even lemon cake for dessert, the film started. A film projektor stood in the aisle between the chairs. It cast its sheet of flickering light out onto the white wall at the other end of the room. The wall was pocked and the image dim, but Marcik and his fellow Guardsmen watched with the gratitude of men denied easy pleasure for too long.

The film started.

※ ※ ※

A domestic scene, a family eating dinner. The father, in his conservative brown suit, tie loosened, every bit the mid-level municipal bureaucrat. The children are prim and proper—the boy's hair combed stiffly to his forehead, the girl with pigtails and a pleated dress.

※ ※ ※

But the Guardsmen weren't interested in the husband or the children.

※ ※ ※

The wife asks her husband if he would like more water. She faces the kamera.

※ ※ ※

"Is that . . . ?" Samir whispered.

"Very beautiful," Yoyo said.

No, not beautiful, Marcik thought. *Perfect.* Marcik had been a devotee of Vivian Scott since an early film, *The Night Walks*. He remembered the day he first saw it: he and Nikolas sneaking into the cinema; the way he distracted the boy at the refreshment bar while Nikolas stole them truffles; the cold dark of the theatre, the dream-shimmer of the images, the comfort of knowing his brother was beside him. But mostly he remembered Vivian Scott, rising star of Silverville—freckled shoulders, long gloves, the knowing curve of her smile.

She was intoxicating, but also dangerous—like one of those spiders that ate the heads of their lovers. Or so he imagined her now. Then, he had worshipped her as a symbol of a world he would never know—a world of witty banter, of women in white gloves, of champagne parties and perfect entitlement. While he and Nikolas had to steal candies, the children of the other world rode in shiny autos and gorged on whatever foods they wanted.

※ ※ ※

Now, displayed on the pocked wall, Vivian Scott fills her husband's glass with icy-cold water.

How does the viewer know the temperature of the water onscreen? Something in the way it splashes, almost in slow-motion into the glass. As she pours, she bends forward, and her breasts strain at the buttons of her dress. The dress is cut a bit too low to be modest. She looks once again at the kamera. That famous slyly tilted smile.

"Thank you, dear," the husband says.

"I hope it freshens you up," she says, caressing her husband's cheek before sitting back down.

※ ※ ※

The Guardsmen ignored the silliness of the line, hooting and stamping their feet. Someone gave a low whistle.

Samir leaned forward in his seat. "Talk about something to come home to," he said.

"Very beautiful," Yoyo said.

※ ※ ※

The father rises and addresses the kamera directly.

"At the end of a long day of performing my municipal duties, there's nothing I like more than to come home to a hot meal and a glass of fresh clean water." Here he sips from the glass and smacks his lips.

"Mmm . . . Pure-baikal."

※ ※ ※

The Guardsmen booed, caring little for this interruption.

※ ※ ※

The husband pauses dramatically. "But what if that water was poisoned?" He throws the glass on the floor and it shatters. "There are those who would threaten our security, our very way of life. They would shatter it like glass."

Cut to: *Another sound of glass breaking*. Dark-bearded men wearing the grotesque pelts of dead animals—an exaggerated representation of Ulani warriors—stream through the windows and doors of the house. They snatch up the children, ignoring their kicking and screaming. A particularly vicious-looking one grabs Vivian Scott by her waist. She struggles and her dress rips tantalizingly.

The husband, oblivious to the action behind him, continues: "And so I say to you, brave men of the Baikal Guard, remember what you are fighting for."

"And for whom," Vivian Scott says, unnaturally calm, as she is dragged off-screen, presumably to be raped.

Black screen. Stark, gothic script: *If you don't protect our way of life, who will?*

We see a shot of an empty and ruined dining room, food uneaten on the table.

⁒ ⁒ ⁒

"Shit on a snow-bear," Samir said, when the lights came up. "Doesn't seem fair, does it?"

Marcik waited for Samir to elaborate. Even before Samir spoke, Yoyo was nodding enthusiastic agreement.

"A waste of such a beautiful woman. Those Ulani can't tell the difference between a woman and horseflesh."

Marcik didn't know how to respond. He didn't want to be seen as soft. He was still searching for an answer that would please Samir when Fredrik came up.

"And what about you goiter-drinkers?" Fredrik said. "I hear you'd rather fuck a rock."

Samir jumped up from his seat. He stretched to his full height, pushing his chest into Fredrik's. Fredrik stared Samir down; he was the taller man by a head. Fredrik, remembering his hand-to-hand combat training, set two fingers on Samir's sternum.

"Do you remember what they taught us? About leverage?"

Fredrik pushed at a downward angle and Samir fell back into his seat. Yoyo stood with his massive fist clenched. Marcik knew that even as good a fighter as Fredrik was, he was no match for Yoyo's intimidating size.

Samir motioned for Yoyo to sit.

Across the room, Sergeant Cantor sipped berry-liquor and talked with Kaptain Nguyen.

3.

VIVIAN WAS OUT for the evening. Abraham oversaw Agnieszka as she put Lydia to bed. He was glad to know she was happily tucked in.

He poured himself a drink and wandered around his private study. He didn't feel the usual need to solve any particular problem. He moved the parts of what he knew was a failed invention back and forth across the table. He took another drink. He picked up the spidery insides of a control panel. He let it fall back to the table. One day it might revolutionize information distribution. But he had no idea how to make it work and didn't even want to consider that idea just now. He went back to the kitchen and poured another drink.

A branch rattled against the kitchen window. Would it be a stormy night? It had been drizzling all day. Abraham loved storms. The house felt empty with Vivian gone and the others asleep. He thought to turn on the radio. But it would be filled with the same sterilized broadcasts as earlier. He decided instead on the fonograf.

The branch rattled more loudly. He went to look out the window, to enjoy the coming storm. He leaned close and nearly spilled his drink when he saw Jürgen's spectral face on the other side of the glass.

※ ※ ※

Jürgen stood wet and haggard in the doorway.

"What are you doing here?" Abraham said. "You're all over the radio."

"I need your help."

"What have you done?"

"I've got to get out of the city. Let me in."

Abraham led Jürgen to the kitchen and handed him a towel.

As Jürgen dried his hair, he nodded at the open bottle of liquor on the counter. "Can you spare a drink?" he asked.

"What are you doing here?" Abraham repeated.

"It wasn't supposed to happen this fast," Jürgen said. "I should have been gone by now."

He was supposed to be on the karavan that left this morning, Jürgen explained. But he had underestimated the extent of internal oversight at the Ministrie. By the time he handed off the materials to his contact at Radio Free Joshua, they already knew. He was unable to make it past the checkpoints, and there wasn't another karavan for two days.

"I need to hide out here until then," he said. "I've paid a man who promised he can get me a new Outer Province travel pass."

"That's impossible," Abraham said. "It's not possible for you to stay here."

"Where's Vivian?" Jürgen asked suddenly.

"She's at a meeting with Neil."

A look Abraham couldn't read passed across Jürgen's face.

"What is it?"

"Never mind. You've got to help me."

"You can't stay here," Abraham said. "Lydia's upstairs. But there might be something I can do."

⁒ ⁒ ⁒

In his study, Abraham showed Jürgen a new device he had been working on. "This might be able to help you." It would blur the image of the kameras. Using this device, Jürgen could make his way out of the city without being seen.

"Does it work?"

"It should," Abraham said, "if my calculations are correct. I haven't tested it."

"I'm dead if it doesn't."

"You're going to need food too," Abraham said. "Do you have any money?"

Jürgen nodded that he did, then noticed an incomplete experimental circuit board on Abraham's work table. "You're still working on this after all these years?"

Abraham looked at the circuit board, not yet processing his friend's words. What did this have to do with anything right now?

"Yes . . . sometimes," Abraham said. "But that doesn't matter now. We need to hurry."

In the kitchen, Abraham shoved items of food into a bag and handed it to Jürgen.

"I'm sorry I couldn't do more for you."

"You've done more than you should have," Jürgen said.

They stood awkwardly there, in the harsh light of the kitchen, looking at each other. Then Jürgen embraced him and said, "Thank you, old friend."

4.

As MARCIK'S KOMPANY neared the river, one of the advance scouts came hurrying back to tell Sergeant Cantor that enemy troops had been spotted.

"Just over that rise there," Marcik heard him say from his vantage point behind the passenger truck. "Maybe twenty, twenty-five of them. We should take them easy."

"Any cover?"

"A few trees, sir, not much else."

"Anywhere else they could be hiding?"

Marcik remembered what they had been taught about the enemy in tactical training. Ulani soldiers loved to lay in ambush. Sometimes they hid all together, sometimes they sent out a few decoy troops to draw you in.

"No, sir. Well, not that I saw."

"Are you absolutely sure? Men's lives depend on this, Private."

"Yes, sir."

Marcik couldn't tell whether this Guardsman, a young pimpled kid he didn't know by name, was confirming that he was "absolutely sure" or whether he was merely agreeing with Cantor. But it seemed their lives were to be staked on it either way. They moved forward, stopping just before the ridgeline to organize their offensive.

The plan was simple. They would split into three units. One would attack from the front, one from the left flank and one from the right. Some men—the officers over the rank of sergeant, who were too valuable to be risked, and two units of men—would remain behind with the trucks and additional weapons in case a second wave was needed. *Let me be in the second wave,* Marcik thought. He had known this moment would come, and yet he still felt unprepared.

He was assigned to the left flank. Not so safe as staying behind, not so bad as the frontal attack. *You can do this. Remember your training.* He tried to think of his small successes there—when he had finally mastered loading his rifle quickly, when he first hit the center of the target, and most importantly when he won the battle simulation. He had led men to victory. He glanced surreptitiously over to Fredrik who, as part of his platoon, would be in the left flank with him. As Fredrik listened to Cantor say a few last encouraging words, his face was the picture of calm and focus. Marcik remembered something Fredrik had said to him once, about his calm place, and he realized that he had not found his own calm place yet. He cast about desperately for it and realized he already had it: the letters. Why else had he gone back for them? At the time he thought it was weakness. It reassured him now to think it was actually a form of strength.

They moved into position and crawled over the lip of the hill. Marcik was three ranks back—he was still scared enough to be thankful of that—and from his vantage, he saw one of the men wave them forward. They all bunched together. Sergeant Katz, given temporary kommand of this platoon, told them to await his signal. He lifted his hand in the air. Out of the corner of his eye, Marcik saw the frontal offensive stand and dash over the hill. There was a flurry of sharp gunshots. Sergeant Katz lowered his hand—the signal. Then they were in it.

※ ※ ※

It happened so fast Marcik would have trouble reconstructing it later. He felt the weight of the pack on his back, and the hard kick of the rifle in his hands as he fired it once, twice, three times. He saw the Ulani soldiers ahead of him, in a thin spread. He sensed bullets whizzing by him, but whether they were far or close he did not know. A man near him went down, clutching his leg. Marcik reloaded, his hands shaky with adrenaline but his mind a perfectly razored point. He stood and fired again. Again. An Ulani soldier's head exploded and he fell in a heap. Marcik didn't have time to wonder whether it had been his shot. Later, he would assure himself it had been, and would even describe to Fredrik the sensation of his first kill.

Then he was firing at nothing. It was over. Three Ulani soldiers stood back to back to back as Guardsmen approached them from all sides. The Ulanis had not yet lowered the guns, but they did not seem about to shoot either. The barrels of the guns pointed down at the ground, half-defensive and half-forgotten. The Guardsmen moved in.

"Throw down your weapons," Sergeant Katz shouted at them. "You'll be treated fairly."

Did they understand what he was saying? These men were ragged, bearded. They looked like they had been sleeping outside for months.

One of the Ulani soldiers raised his gun and the Guardsmen cocked their weapons, ready to fire. Quickly, before any of the Guardsmen could act, he put the barrel of the gun in his mouth and squeezed the trigger. Blood and brains flew out the back of his head in a splattering mush. He collapsed. Quick as the first, the second soldier did the same. The third soldier caught Marcik's eye, his look terrified and defiant. He pulled the trigger and was gone.

Afterward, Katz stood over the bodies, wiping the blood from his glasses. He kicked one of the bodies with the tip of his boot.

"Bastards always do it," he said to no one in particular. "They have this idea that surrender is shameful. Probably smart, though. We can't make them give up information this way."

※ ※ ※

As they marched on toward the river, Marcik thought about what he had seen. That moment of total self-sacrifice, of self-annihilation, stuck in his memory more than anything from the battle itself. The fighting had been a blur, while the Ulani soldiers' killing themselves had happened in slow motion. He felt himself to be that last soldier—could taste the metal of the barrel in his mouth, feel that flicker of indecision before the trigger squeeze. At the same time, it all seemed so stupid, pointless. Which was it, barbaric or brave? Or was it both?

Stop thinking about it. He had made it through his first battle alive. *Breathe the night air, Guardsman. March in time with your brothers.*

5.

THERE WAS A GOAT in the palace hall. It hopped and bleated, its spindly legs driving its hooves into the dirt floor. Two men dressed in thick leather armor stood on top of a table the length of the room. They stamped their feet on the heavy unfinished wood and snorted like bulls. The crowd drummed their fists against the wooden walls, lightly at first, swelling to an almost unbearable crescendo. Simultaneously, with no apparent cue, they broke off and let out a joyful growl.

The men charged at each other and collided meatily. They fell on the table and rolled onto the floor. One man pinned the other, chest heaving. They separated and clapped each other on the back. They jumped back onto the table and the fist-drumming began again.

The Tongue had been forced to leave his Voicemaids at the palace gate. If you could call it a palace. Traversing the muddy path from the gate to the palace entrance, lifting his train in an ineffectual attempt to keep it clean—so unaccustomed was he to carrying his own clothing—he reminded himself that the Ulani word for *palace* literally meant *gathering-hall.* And it did, minimally, qualify as that.

He looked around for the ambassador. Or anyone to acknowledge his presence. An ale-sodden man staggered toward him, his beard dripping with saliva and unwashed revelry.

"Honored guest!" he said. "Honored . . . sir!"

He offered The Tongue a sloshing bronze goblet. The Tongue accepted the offering. He raised the goblet and intoned in flawless Ulani, "May your thousand-thousand herds stampede across the sky."

"A thousand-thousand to you too, sir," the man slurred and stumbled into a happy embrace, spilling half his drink down The Tongue's back.

The man turned to the gathering-hall and belted, "A thousand-thousand to our guest!"

"A THOUSAND-THOUSAND!" the crowd shouted. And louder, "A THOUSAND-THOUSAND!"

Just when The Tongue thought he couldn't take another second of their infernal shouting and stamping, the ambassador appeared. He put his hand on the drunkard's shoulder and said, "Uferth, I saw some bright ale-maidens yonder, and they were bemoaning your absence."

Looking in the direction the ambassador had indicated, the man said, "I shall not deny them my choicest bits." And galloping off, slapping his thighs, he screamed, "Uferth!"

"May your thousand-thousand," Ambassador Kalukar said.

"And yours as well, Kalukar," The Tongue returned.

"I trust your travels were not too unpleasant," Kalukar said. "I apologize for the meanness of my people. They have good hearts, but they are not used to such illustrious visitors."

"May we speak in private?"

"Yes, of course. But first let me show you something that might interest you. You should know the wealth of my city before you enter into a compact with us."

The Tongue steeled himself and followed.

Kalukar insisted on showing The Tongue the palace. And given the famously violent pride of the Ulani culture, it would be not merely impolitic but perhaps even fatal to refuse. The Tongue had met Kalukar many times, but always in other cities. The din of the crowd died behind them as he followed Kalukar up a staircase.

Kalukar led him onto a wooden platform of loose planks jutting out over the rocky meadow far below. The wind whipped at The Tongue's robes. He hung back.

Kalukar put his hand on The Tongue's shoulder. "Come forward, my good friend," he said. "There is nothing to fear."

The Tongue followed Kalukar reluctantly. A few meters from the edge, the wind bellowed and roared. It grabbed The Tongue's train and ribboned it over the edge. For a sickening moment he thought he might be pulled along with it. *What a beautiful death.* A fluttering butterfly death. The Larki Islanders would call it *lufft-erdrinken*, which meant air-drowning. And wasn't that exactly how it would be, that slow parachuting drift down to oblivion?

"Look at our Kahn's wealth," Kalukar said. "Uncountable oxen graze below. And surrounded by mountains no army dares penetrate."

Kalukar stepped closer to the edge, peeking with mild interest over the sheer drop. The Tongue resisted the urge to pull him back.

"But that is not the only wealth you're interested in," Kalukar said. "Come."

Kalukar led him back into the relative safety of the palace. The Tongue followed him down an undecorated hall. Kalukar took a key from around his neck and opened a massive but unremarkable door. The Tongue was surprised to see the gleam and throttle of modern machinery and a line of capable technicians assembling rifles as good as anything made in Baikyong-do.

"Our enemies underestimate us," Kalukar said. "They think us barbaric."

An assembly worker stamped and locked a rifle barrel into place. He set it on a rack beside hundreds of others.

"There is more to show," Kalukar said, closing the door behind him, moving on.

He rushed The Tongue along a series of winding hallways and ever-thinner staircases. Finally, when The Tongue was short of breath, Kalukar stopped before a round ornate door.

"We are not merely herdsmen and warriors," Kalukar said, "We understand the finer pleasures in life."

He opened the door on a smoky den with women in various states of relaxed undress. Seeing Kalukar, they swirled to attention. Two of the women danced languidly forward, their movements in perfect synchronization, eager to please any master. They rubbed against The Tongue. A translucent silk scarf spilled over his shoulder. In all the important places, The Tongue felt nothing.

"Is there need?" they asked.

"Not for me," Kalukar said. "For our guest perhaps?"

The Tongue controlled his revulsion at this vulgar display and said, simply, "No."

Though Kalukar had used the word "barbaric" first—a word The Tongue despised, being a citizen of the world, as all his people were—looking at these women so well trained in their enslavement, he had to admit the word, like all words, had its place.

"In that case, allow us to continue your tour."

Kalukar led The Tongue down a further corridor and through a large door covered with metal war insignia. The Tongue stopped at the doorway. Kalukar walked into the center of open room and opened his arms as though extending a generous offer. On the wall opposite The Tongue, a human skull with mummified skin stretched back in perpetual surprise was mounted on the tip of a war-pike. Hanging from the ceiling, just above where Kalukar stood, a wind-chime of femurs and jawbones and ribs rattled ghostily.

"What is this place?" The Tongue asked.

"Have we frightened the noble ambassador?" Kalukar laughed. "Don't worry, my friend, this room is only for the bones of our enemies. And for those who betray us."

The Tongue walked around the grotesque gallery and took it all in as though he were a connoisseur of human remnants. He had been thinking it, without fully realizing it, since he had arrived: *The Ulanis share much in common with our own Savage Ones.* Except the denizens of Baikyong-do were civilized enough to exile those who acted in such a manner to The Kolony. The Tongue had been taken on a tour of The Kolony when he completed his indoctrination for The Kouncil of The Enlightened—a tour not unlike the one he was now suffering.

He completed his survey of the room. "Are you ready to conduct the business for which I was summoned?"

"But we must feast first! Ulanis never do business on an empty stomach. As our saying goes, 'Fruits for the belly yield fruits of the mind.'"

※ ※ ※

They found their winding way back to the Gathering-Hall, where The Tongue was seated between two ale-maidens Kalukar indicated were considered the most attractive by Ulani standards. The men had become drunker and were now tearing chunks of boar meat from two freshly slain animals steaming on the table. A large copper plate was set before The Tongue with a bloody flank and roasted potatoes piled high enough to feed three.

"Drink, ambassador?" one of the ale-maidens said and filled his oversized copper cup without waiting for his response.

Over the years, on various diplomatic occasions, The Tongue had been forced to eat meat as part of ritual meals, something it would be politically counterproductive to refuse. In Baikyong-do, he observed a strict vegetarian diet, as all of The Enlightened did. It had been a year since he had been forced to swallow down murdered flesh. But this alliance was as important, if not more important, than any he had established in his long career. He cut a small sliver of the dead creature free, slowly raised it to his mouth, and chewed it dutifully. Nearly gagging, he took a drink of the ale to cover the corpse-taste. He cut a larger piece.

"The best meat in the Seven Cities!" a man across from him said and tore free a dripping maw's worth of the roast.

The Tongue managed a nod and swallowed another piece. He drank again.

"And he likes my ale even more," the woman to his right said as she refilled his cup.

It was a game of patience. The Tongue knew Kalukar's tactic well. He would pick the precise time of their meeting, preferably after The

Tongue had gotten tired and perhaps a little drunk. There was nothing to be done. Let Kalukar think he was in charge; it would only make the negotiations easier when they came. It is simpler to manipulate a man who suffers under the illusion that he has the advantage.

Across the room Kalukar tilted back cup after cup. Various fights, mostly good-natured, broke out around the gathering-hall. Another boar was slaughtered and prepared. There was much spilled ale. Maidens in half-dress. Music rang brokenly from ill-tuned instruments. The Tongue finished as much of his meal as he felt necessary. But they would not let up on the ale, and so he drank and drank.

The night withered on.

Tired from his travels, blurry with ale, and ill from the boar meat, The Tongue felt himself beginning to drift, but through strength of discipline, he sat rigidly and willed his eyes wide open.

Finally, at a late hour, the room emptied and ale-maidens began clearing the table. Kalukar made his majestically uninterested way to The Tongue's place at the table. He wondered if Kalukar meant to delay their negotiations until the next day.

"Are you still fit for our business?" Kalukar said. "Or do you need to rest?"

"I am ready as ever," The Tongue said, forcing his voice straight and clear.

※ ※ ※

Again Kalukar took him through a never-ending maze of staircases and corridors, ending at a small door with two guards. At Kalukar's approach the guards opened the door.

A blast of hot air rushed over him as they entered. The only light in the room was from a fire in a stone fireplace. Wood popped, and The Tongue blinked as his eyes adjusted to the dry hot air and the shadowy dark. On a large bed, a figure was propped against a mound of pillows.

"Great Kahn," Kalukar said, "allow me to introduce the ambassador from Baikyong-do."

The figure leaned forward. He was shrunken and frail, a thin wiry beard hanging loosely from his chin. He raised a palsied hand in greeting.

This was the Great Kahn?

"Welcome," the Kahn whispered.

"It is an honor to be in the house of the Great Kahn," The Tongue said, "to see your vast and thriving herds. Long may their hooves trample your enemies."

"And may the voice of Baikyong-do illuminate the world," Kalukar said, answering for the Kahn. "But let us delay no longer."

They sat at a table placed beside the Kahn's bed, presumably for meetings like this one. The Tongue nearly tripped on his robes as he took his seat. The hot air and the nauseous weight of his meal made his stomach roil. He laid his hands flat on the table, steadying himself.

"What the Kahn offers is simple," Kalukar said. "He offers the bravest warriors in the Seven Cities, our full arsenal, and an unfaltering dedication to see Joshua City fall."

"Baikyong-do is a peaceful city," The Tongue said. "As you know, the founding of our city was particularly bloody and brutal. Since then, we have sworn ourselves to nonviolence. We have never waged war on a neighbor."

"Pretty words, but what can you offer the Kahn?"

The Kouncil of The Enlightened had debated through many sessions about whether to ally themselves with these people. Look at them. And look at him now—his ceremonial train caked in mud, his body defiled with meat, the ale rising acidly in his throat. But the Kouncil had decided that the Joshuan ambitions were a threat to the Unity of the Seven. Any price must be paid.

"Mainly, we can offer advanced technology and strategic advice," the Tongue said. "But we're also willing to lend our not insubstantial wealth."

Kalukar looked at the Kahn on his pillows. The Kahn nodded almost imperceptibly.

"The Kahn accepts your offers," Kalukar said. "But he worries that it will be our men who bleed and die."

"Do not fear, Kalukar," The Tongue responded. "We have ones who will fight."

%   %   %

Out in the hall, the meeting over and the compact sealed, Kalukar led The Tongue to his quarters.

"He may seem weak," Kalukar said in a low voice. "But over half of the kills in our trophy room were by his hand."

The Tongue had noted the weakness of their leader, and that Kalukar was probably in charge—protecting him, even. The Tongue knew from his studies of Ulani culture that when a leader became weak, the foremost warrior would come forward and challenge him for his rule. Why had Kalukar not done so?

"He is a wise and powerful man," The Tongue said.

"But enough of that. Here are your quarters," Kalukar said. "Someone will wake you in the morning."

6.

IT WAS ELEVEN O'MORN and Nikolas stood outside the locked door of The Nameless Tavern, waiting for Dmitri to open. Dmitri never opened on time. And why should he? Nikolas would be his only customer for the next hour or so until the lunchtime drunks came in. And Nikolas suspected Dmitri had other, more substantial sources of income.

Suddenly dizzy, Nikolas rested his head against the metal grate barring the door. The cool metal pressed against his face with a pleasant solidity. He had never been so tired. He was sleeping around the corner, in some old woman's flophouse. His mattress was stained with what looked like blood and the springs poked into his back. From the other rooms, beds squeaked night and day—women and men, even children, selling themselves to pay the weekly rent. There were frequent shouting matches in the halls. This is what Joshua City had come to. He was disgusted with himself and his surroundings.

Most of all, though, he was hungry. He had never realized how hard it is to sleep on an empty stomach. Even in childhood, despite their poverty, he had been well-fed. His mother had seen to that, skimping on clothing and whatever else to make sure her boys had nutritious meals. He could always go crawling back home. His mother would take him in, no questions asked. But no; he simply would not do that.

The lock turned and the door opened. Nikolas jerked awake from his reverie. Dmitri frowned and unlocked the grate as well. Nikolas followed him into that dingy familiar room. Dmitri positioned himself behind the bar. He crossed his arms, waiting for Nikolas to order, not dismissive but not exactly welcoming. Nikolas ordered a vodka. He tossed it back, ordered another. He dug in his pocket and came up with just enough change. He had some bread and dried meat back in his room, so he wouldn't starve tonight. And tomorrow was tomorrow. The second vodka he nursed, feeling better by the minute. The alcohol didn't solve his problems so much as dissolve them. His mind clearer, he took stock of his present condition.

Had he made a huge mistake? He met with Elias and the others almost every day; they would be in later this afternoon. He and Elias had been making plans. To organize. To gain new members. To really make this a *movement*, instead of their former intellectual dithering. Still, a movement needed money. He needed money. Elias was all too happy to wield his petty power by ordering everyone drinks at their meetings, and he tipped lavishly, so Dmitri was inclined to stand Nikolas a free drink from time to time, knowing he brought such excellent business— but Nikolas could tell Dmitri disapproved of his spending so much time here, even if it was good for his wallet.

A few lunchtime drinkers arrived. Old drunk Tibor slumped at the other end of the bar, thankfully well away from Nikolas; the old man smelled like moldy clothes, urine, and sloshed drink. Tibor lived off some sort of military stipend, compensation for a leg wounded in The Great War, though his problems seemed to be more with his trauma-damaged mind than his leg.

"Do you need someone to work here?" Nikolas asked as Dmitri passed by.

"I suppose I could pay you in vodka?" Dmitri said.

Nikolas set down his glass. "Another."

Dmitri poured another drink. He waited for Nikolas to pay.

"Listen," Nikolas said. "I'm a bit short."

"Two drams."

"Elias will be here shortly."

"And what does that have to do with anything?" Dmitri asked, knowing full well what Nikolas meant.

"I've spent hundreds and hundreds of drams in here."

"So does Tibor," Dmitri said. "You don't see me giving him free drinks."

Tibor perked up at the mention of his name. His veiny red nose twitched. When he saw that his services were no longer needed, he went back to staring into his drink.

"I don't want free drinks," Nikolas said. "I want a tab."

Dmitri shrugged, apparently not in one of his generous moods.

"What ever happened to trust?" Nikolas asked, his voice rising.

"I like you, Nikolas. But I can't condone this." Dmitri said. "And don't take that tone with me, or I'll have to ask you to leave."

"All right," Nikolas said. He held up his hands in a gesture of peace. "I'm sorry. You've always been decent to me."

"I'll buy his drink," a female voice said from over Nikolas's shoulder.

"Katyana," Dmitri said. "You'd spend your money on this lowlife?" There was almost a note of endearment on that last word.

"I like lowlifes," Katyana said, sliding onto a stool next to Nikolas. Then more quietly, almost to herself, "They might be the only people I like."

Dmitri poured two drinks.

Nikolas raised his glass to Katyana. "May your days be pure-baikal."

"And yours."

She performed the casual miracle of drinking through her mask. When they were done, she ordered another round. Wanting to offer something of his own, Nikolas produced a crumpled packet of rolling tobacco and papers. He could no longer afford machine-rolled cigarettes. Soon his tobacco would be gone as well. He rolled a cigarette, but Katyana refused it. He put it in his mouth and lit it.

"I've been hoping we could talk again," Nikolas said.

"Yes? And why might that be?"

What an advantage concealment gives her, he reflected. The face is the visual seat of personality; it is how we understand a person; it is what we imagine when we try to remember them. He had no way to read her on this most basic level.

"I sense in us a kind of...communion." Nikolas said. "I know, I know...That sounds like some sort of...But it's not. Well, it is. But it's not just that."

"I'm not that easy to offend," Katyana said. "Another drink?"

"Where do you get all this money?"

Katyana turned to him on the bar stool so that her legs were practically touching his thigh. She folded her hands on her knees. "I think you know."

"I don't want to presume. Anyway, it's none of my business."

"And yet you asked."

"I'm not judging you."

"Of course you are," she said. "Everyone does. It's all right. I judge myself. I tell myself that there's no other way. How can a woman make money in Joshua City? It's either sell her body or live off her husband."

"All too true."

"It's just something I tell myself. It doesn't make it less self-serving."

"Similar to what I said earlier," Nikolas said. "About the sense of communion. A mere self-serving truth. Well, not mere."

"So we're both utterly self-interested."

"I told you we had something in common," Nikolas said.

"A communion. Between kindred souls."

"I don't like that word."

"Communion?"

"No. *Souls.*"

The tavern door swung open. A huge man with the powerful arms of a steelworker stood in the doorway. Nikolas was relieved to see it was no one he knew. He wanted this moment to last.

He felt he needed to raise the stakes or he would lose her interest. He had always assumed women of her caliber required a constant performance.

"Do you ever take that off?" he asked her, meaning her mask. "Sorry if that's a terrible question. You've made me drunk."

"I don't think you're as drunk as you claim," she said. "Anyway, do you mean with clients? Never."

"Don't they ask?"

"Most want it on," she said. She pushed herself to her feet. "It's been nice talking with you. I was feeling out of sorts, but now I think I am feeling a bit better. I really should go upstairs though."

"Thank you again."

She slid a ten-dram note his way. "Enjoy yourself."

She walked off, no doubt aware that he was watching. What did she do up there anyway? Did she meet one of her regulars? Or was that her base of operations, so to speak?

He decided then and there to fall recklessly in love with her.

7.

ONE EVENING, several days after Jürgen's visit, Abraham was in his study. He had had a particularly empty day at work and was tinkering aimlessly with various half-finished projects on his desk. All that week, he had been thinking of Jürgen, whether he had made it out of the city. Would he ever see his friend again? If he made it out safely, he could never return, and if they caught him . . . he didn't let himself think about that. He should have done more. He wanted an opportunity to change his cowardly disengagement from his friend's situation. He set aside a hopeless device intended to cool the air in buildings during the summer months. Abraham hated sweltering days and had started this project out of self-interest, but of course there would be sizable commercial possibilities for it as well. But he couldn't figure out how to do much more than suck the moisture out of the air; cooling it was a conundrum. Perhaps there was some chemical whose properties lowered the kinetic force of the molecules in the air. Perhaps...

He poured a small drink and returned to his desk. Thinking again of Jürgen and their collaborative efforts in years past, he picked up the experimental circuit board. If he could perfect this, then his long-term dream of electric trains could be realized. He turned the circuit board over, and something blocky and gray fell to the desk. It was a video-kartridge. Jürgen must have hidden it here when Abraham wasn't looking. He turned the gray plastic thing around in his hand. He wasn't sure he wanted to know what was on it, but he knew he would watch it. He put it in his video-projektor and sat down.

At first he couldn't tell he was seeing Neil Martin's mansion. A woman walks flirtatiously across the room in a Baikyong-do silk dress. Then Neil steps into the kamera's view.

"I've paid you well," Neil says, "and I want a good show."

"You'll get one, sir, and much more," the woman says in a voice uncannily like Vivian's. (And didn't that dress resemble the one Vivian wore to high-class dinners?)

She steps close to Neil and grabs his tie, walks her way back with it, lets it drop. Her hand goes to her side and pulls teasingly at the sash holding up her dress.

"How badly do you want it?" she asks, with exaggerated sultriness.

Neil puts his hand to his crotch and rubs up and down. "You can come here and feel how badly."

The woman lets the sash drop to the floor but holds the dress loosely on arms crossed over her chest in faux-modesty.

"Should I show you?" Neil asks.

They step toward each other and her face comes squarely into the kamera's view. (*It* is *her*, Abraham thought, and the whole world collapsed in on his chest.) They embrace and the dress slides down Vivian's body. She undoes Neil's belt and pants, goes to her knees, and looks up at Neil. "May I?"

※ ※ ※

An hour later, after Abraham had watched the entire video-kartridge twice and was midway through a third viewing, there was a knock at the door and he leapt to the video-projektor and turned it off.

"Mr. Kocznik, dinner is ready," Agnieszka announced through the door.

※ ※ ※

Abraham sat down at the dining room table, where Vivian and Lydia were already seated.

"...and then Mrs. Janusk said my painting was the best," Lydia was saying.

Abraham placed his napkin in his lap and lined his silverware up in perfect parallel lines.

"Of course it was, Lydia," Vivian said. "My daughter is so talented."

Agnieszka brought in a tray with sweetmeats and a savory soup. Vivian served Lydia and petted her back lovingly.

"Did you hear, Abe? Our daughter is going to be a famous artist."

"Maman, these are just my early works. I'm mostly interested in the shapes of things right now."

"I am just glad you are enjoying your time at Sister Nadya's. Remember how you fussed?"

Lydia stabbed a sweetmeat with her fork and chewed it loudly.

"You're awfully quiet, Abe," Vivian said.

"What? Oh, just thinking about a troubling matter at work."

"You mean Jürgen?"

"Yes," Abraham said. "It has to do with Jürgen."

She reached across the table and set her hand lightly on his. He forced himself not to recoil. He stared blankly at her hand, that beautiful object with no connection to him.

8.

THE NOVEL AS SURVEILLANCE: AN INTERLUDE

IT HAS OCCURRED to me more than once that the novel itself is a form of surveillance. It monitors, it invades, it shows us things we would never otherwise see—the private chambers of our lives.

But there is no such thing as total surveillance, even in a novel. In life, there are always unseen moments, without kameras or listeners. We cannot steal the contents of the human mind, cannot access the innermost feelings. Though the novel can do this—and it does—it is also an incomplete surveillance. It only gives the impression of omniscience and absolute continuity.

The surveillance enacted by the Adams administration was limited by the technology and by the inability to sort and make meaning of it all. Even if Abraham Kocznik had designed the perfect recording device, discreet enough to be hidden in any location but powerful enough to monitor the most private conversations, there would still have been the trouble of listening to it all, of knowing what to listen to. And even if you knew what to listen to, you would have to make sense of it. Is it important what the butcher says to his favorite customer? Maybe, if the butcher has wrapped a choice loin with paper containing a coded message. Should we plant a listening device in the florist's bouquet? Should we eavesdrop on the confession booth? Will we hear tawdry sins or state secrets?

Here is where the novel has an advantage. It can shape and choose its surveillance. It can show us the thoughts and motivations even its characters don't recognize. The novel chooses its surveillance in the service of this thing called story.

But in choosing moments to include, it omits others. For the purposes of narrative, we novelists often move quickly through the subterranean shifts, slowing for the moments that have a significant impact. We make a scene, as one novelist friend so neatly explained it, employing that colloquial phrase generally reserved to describe a child throwing a tantrum. "Don't make a scene," a mother might say in public, meaning, "Don't draw attention to us and embarrass me." But when novelists use scene instead of summary, we want to draw attention. This thing matters, we are saying. But who's to say all the subterranean shifts don't have a larger impact than any single moment? People don't change all at once, after all, and even though circumstances sometimes do, there are always reverberations and aftershocks.

Over the next few months, nothing happened that we need examine at length. But that is not to say that nothing happened. We know that Nikolas left Joshua University, that he now spent his time at The Nameless Tavern. In the afternoons, he was joined by his komrades, as he had begun calling them. We have already met many of them. There was Elias, whose deep pockets and easy extravagance kept the alcohol flowing and the conversation loose and interesting. There was Peytr, still silent. One day he did not show up for one of these informal meetings and no one knew why.[6] Some talk was made of tracking him down, but it emerged that no one, not even Elias, knew where he lived. And so that was the end of Peytr, for our purposes anyway. Mouse, well, we have already seen some of the changes time and political conviction wrought on her. One day, she showed up to a meeting arm in arm with another girl with short hair, the muscled chest of a man, and a piercing through her nose.

"This is Sara," she declared. "We're lovers," she added and kissed the girl roughly.

Others joined the movement, others left. Still more showed up for a meeting or two and fell away. They drank. And Nikolas talked and talk-

---

[6]Author's Note: In my researches for this novel-history, I have come to suspect that Peytr was in fact an agent of the Ministrie of Information, a man named Karl Bindeman. There is a certain report this Karl Bindeman wrote in which he requested re-assignment to a more promising task. "These young skolars are eager to talk, but there is little danger of real action here in my professional opinion." If I am right that this was Peytr, then the irony will not escape my readers. Had he stayed on a mere few months longer, the revolution might not have happened at all, and you would not be reading this.

ed. He hardly knew what he was saying, but he spoke with a diffuse urgency and people listened. Sometimes it was not just the Progressive Students for a Better Baikal but the whole tavern that gathered around their dark little corner. He knew he should be careful with his words, but he didn't care. They had all heard the reports about surveillance; there could be kameras even here; that old drunk Tibor might very well be a covert agent.

Dmitri unhappily took this risk for the extra business it brought him. As the meetings grew, the tavern sometimes filling to near capacity with Nikolas's hangers-on, Dmitri took to closing early, telling angry customers that there was a private party. Nikolas might be careless, but Dmitri took this precaution on his behalf. And on his own.

※ ※ ※

(Let us look in on our friend Nikolas, Esteemed Reader.)

"That's a common objection I keep hearing," Nikolas responded. "An argument against true social change. You tell the students to leave their cloistered and artificial life. You tell the workers to throw their bodies on the gears of the machine. You tell them to halt a production mechanism which benefits the owners and not the ones responsible for that production. But what then? That's what they ask. Where will I work? How will I survive? Well, I ask you . . . Is mere survival the goal?"

A large man with a beard approached the table from the bar, grabbing a chair without stopping, carrying it as easily in one hand as if it were a child's toy. By his dress and demeanor, this was no Joshua University skolar. He placed the chair at the outer edge of the circle and turned it around backward, then lowered himself onto its creaking frame. Nikolas wondered if it would collapse beneath his bulk. For the past few weeks, this man had been sitting at the bar alone, staring across at them. At first Nikolas had worried that he might be one of these agents, but if so why did he allow the meetings to go on? Why had he not reported Nikolas to his superiors?

"But a man must survive first," the man said. "What does a dead man care for social justice?"

"You are right, my friend," Nikolas said. "But if we could ensure survival on our own terms? I'm talking about a place where everything is shared and work is done toward a common goal."

"If such a place existed, I would not fear losing my job."

"And where do you work, komrade? I am Nikolas, by the way."

His name was Alarik, he said. He worked at the steelworks. The work was hard even for a man like him, the pay was meager, and the hours were long. "My wife works too. We hardly see each other."

"Yes, yes," Nikolas said. "This is what I mean."

Katyana arrived. She came up to the table and stood just behind Nikolas. Here was true surveillance. She saw inside him—inside his heart. And yes, he knew that the heart was not the seat of emotions. He and Adrian had discussed that once, on the night they saw Mayor Adams's speech. That had been . . . how many months ago? He remembered it vividly. It was the night this had first started, whatever it was. With Katyana watching, he had to get it right. He had to speak the true-baikal.

He addressed Alarik and the rest of the crowd, but his words were for her. He thought of where she had just been, what she had been doing. He slept in her room now when she wasn't using it for business, willing himself not to think of the human fluids, those that belonged to him and her—and those that belonged to others.

"Listen, komrades," Nikolas said. "Let us band together. Let us rise above mere survival—above those sordid things we do to survive, things that make us feel lesser. Things that make us feel ashamed of our lives. Without dignity, what are we but beasts? I say, there is a way. And I say it should start now."

※ ※ ※

(And how has Adrian faired in Nikolas's absence?)

Adrian had not been assigned a new roommate. He had the room entirely to himself, which suited his tendency toward solitary thought.

He enjoyed reading his textbooks in bed or making notes at his desk without interruption. But he kept the room much as Nikolas had organized it, out of a strange respect for his departed friend, and when he lighted his votive candles, he even missed Nikolas's scolding him.

At the laboratory, Doktor Brandt lavished him with compliments and had even arranged a generous research assistantship for Adrian, praise and money that had been intended for Nikolas. But the work went well. They made progress with heart transplants. Come evening, reeling from the pressure and excitement of the long day's work, he thought of Leni and prayed for forgiveness.

Throughout all this, the application Mouse had given him—to spend the summer working at the Laborers Hospital in the Outer Provinces—lay forgotten on his desk.

%% %% %%

(And because the irony pleases me in this meditation on the novel as surveillance, let us spy on the man who made Joshua City's real-world surveillance possible.)

Abraham did not tell Vivian what he had seen on the surveillance footage. In the way of cuckolded husbands everywhere, he found an excuse for an argument in every domestic activity. If Lydia was five minutes late in the morning, he blamed Vivian. If there was something misplaced in the den, he blamed Vivian. If she poured a drink in the evening, he subtly reminded her that she drank too much, that it was bad for her. And in the way of the guilty everywhere, Vivian took it all, knowing she deserved whatever punishment she received.

(Esteemed Reader, I daresay we have all played—or will one day play—Vivian's role in this, and Abraham's as well. I beg you to feel compassion for these two sad well-meaning people.)

Abraham knew one thing: he loved his wife and did not want their marriage to end.

One night, Abraham tossed a series of pamphlets on their bed. Vivian set aside her drink and picked them up. They advertised a couples' retreat designed by the famous Doktor Laikan. It was the sort of thing Neil would make jokes about. The sort of thing she found ridiculous.

"Do you really want to do this?"

"We both can admit there have been problems."

And indeed, there were. If this was what Abraham wanted, then she would do it. And there was Lydia to consider.

And so they made the decision to save their marriage.

※ ※ ※

(When we last saw Marcik, he had gotten his first taste of battle and survived. That's more than some can say. Over the next few months, he was shot at, bombed, and ambushed more than he could count. He was always exhausted and frequently confused. He got to know his fellow Guardsmen better, sharing stories of home—though Marcik was still more inclined to listen than to talk. If he couldn't join in their bravado, he nevertheless learned to laugh at their crude jokes and to nod in the right places. And he gained a respect for them, the kind of respect that risking your life with someone will create. The bullets were aimed at them as much as him, and the knowledge that any day could be some-one's last made you listen a little more closely. Even Samir had noticed the change.)

"I've got to say, Kovalski," Samir said as they stood beside each other in the dinner line, fresh off a minor skirmish, "you showed balls out there. How many confirmed kills did you have?"

"I'm not sure," Marcik lied. "I wasn't counting."

Three. I shot and killed three Ulani soldiers. The first had been through the gut and he had slumped over, looking surprised that any-one would do such a thing. The second was nearly fifty meters distant and fell without drama. The third charged at him, rifle raised, and Marcik shot him right through the face. He wasn't wearing a helmet and his head exploded. Something warm landed on Marcik's shirt.

"Well, good job," Samir said. He patted Marcik on the back. "If I didn't know any better, I'd say you had some Kazhstani in you."

(In effect, Marcik was becoming a true Guardsman. Plunging through the fire so many times and emerging unharmed had the effect of making him less afraid of the flames. I'm reminded of when Abraham Kocznik's new high-speed trains were first introduced in Joshua City. Initially, the passengers were terrified. They could not believe that the trains wouldn't simply fly off the rails. But after riding them a dozen times, and having nothing of the sort happen, they began to believe in their own immunity from disaster. Marcik did not go quite this far—he maintained a healthy respect for the enemy—but he was able to sleep more soundly. In the end, constant terror is as monotonous as any emotion. It's not just the subterranean shifts that change us; it's time, the plodding march of it. Most days, nothing happens. But all that nothing adds up to something enormous—life—in fact, the most enormous thing there is.)

CHAPTER SEVEN

THE COST OF BATTLE

1.

T HEY HAD BEEN FOLLOWING the river for months. The land was flat and empty and the river flowed wide and slow and brown with mud. Marcik had never seen a river before. He didn't know what he had expected. Odd that it should make such a difference, the shape a body of water took.

It was early spring now, and along the riverbank life was in fertile abundance. The grass grew thick and sharp. Insects buzzed—drunk fat flies and long-nosed bloodsuckers that devoured you in the night. The Guardsmen slept in tents with nets, but even that wasn't enough. Like the other Guardsmen, Marcik kept his socks on, sweating. Still, he woke in the middle of the night with welts he could not stop scratching. One night, Samir heard him tossing and turning.

"Hey, Kovalski," he said. "Stop your scratching."

Marcik, in his annoyance and discomfort, nearly told Samir to go drown.

"You want to get rid of those bites?"

"Of course."

"There's this plant out by the river," he said. "It's got these thick leaves with a thorn. You bust it open and rub the juice on your skin. It'll soothe the itches. Plus, the bloodsuckers hate the taste."

"Really?" Marcik said. "It's not poisoned or something? I don't see you using it."

Samir leaned forward. The moonlight through the skein of the tent illuminated his face. "The blood-suckers don't like me. But lots of people use it."

"How do you know this?"

"Our people know many useful things. We don't just drink goiters. By the way, sorry I fought with your friend that other time."

Marcik had to think for a second to even understand what Samir was talking about. He remembered the non-incident with Fredrik. "That was months ago."

Someone in the tent cleared his throat. "Shut your mouths, you two."

About an hour later, the itching was too much to take. Marcik lifted the tent flap and went down to the water. He knelt among the rushes, looking for the plant Samir had described. He saw it, a green shrub less than half a meter high. He broke off a couple of leaves.

There was a violent rustling and a big white bird took off from a hidden nest, its feathers glowing whitely angelic in the moonlight. He watched it go and then snapped one of the leaves in half, feeling as though he were performing an ancient rite. The juice in the leaf was cool and scented like springtime. He rubbed it into the skin of his arms. It was sticky, but otherwise not bad. He rolled up his pants and coated his legs until the hair there was wetly plastered. Then he washed his palms and returned to the tent.

In the morning, his bite-welts were gone. He approached Samir as they were breaking camp.

"Hey," Marcik said. "That plant of yours really worked."

"Of course it did," Samir said. He pulled the drawstring on his rucksack with the self-satisfied look of someone who has been proven right.

Samir hopped into the back of the truck in that nimble-quick way of his. It was his turn to ride. He squeezed in beside the other Guardsmen who had the privilege of riding for the day.

"Maybe you've got some sense after all, Kovalski," Samir said. "I don't care what they say."

Fredrik came up behind Marcik and tossed his bag in the back of the truck. It was his day to ride too.

"Kind words are only worth as much as the person saying them," Fredrik said to no one in particular, as he climbed into the truck.

Marcik watched them sitting across from each other and hoped they could get along. He wanted everyone to get along. It was easier that way. Of course he knew there were enemy soldiers out there, and of course he knew it was his duty to kill or subdue them; despite his fear, he was even eager to fulfill that duty; it gave him a sense of purpose he had never had before. Still, he didn't like confrontation and preferred to keep it to the battlefield.

The trucks moved forward and Marcik fell in line, easing into the rhythm of another long day's march.

※ ※ ※

The river thinned and narrowed, eventually diminishing to a trickle—seepage from a cracked gray bed. At its narrowest point, they came upon a village. Dirt hovels, starved cattle munching on dead grass. Why had anyone built a village here? These people were caught in between two armies. Marcik's kompany had been marching from the west, laying claim to all the settlements and choice riverbank in their path. And in the east was their regiment, which they would soon join, thank the Seven, and beyond that, the mountains and the armies of Ulan-Ude. War. Real war, not just the skirmishes he had encountered thus far.

The villagers watched them arrive. They did not seem surprised by the presence of Guardsmen, only cautiously sullen. A farmer looked up from his wilted crops, his hoe dropping unattended in the sandy soil. A three-legged dog limped toward them, begging food. A young woman came out of a shack, lifted her shirt, scratched her flea-bitten belly. The skin of her face was peeling away. Nekrosis. A horse swatted fat bluebottles with its tail. A man stood in the door of his house, a hunting rifle propped against his hip. He was chewing something, blackroot no doubt, and as they passed he spit a dark glob in the dirt. Down by the river a young girl was hunched over, washing her long black hair. She was pretty in a simple way—dark eyebrows, tanned skin. Then she did something surprising: she smiled. At him? Marcik smiled back, but she had already returned to her work.

In what passed for the town square, there was a single tree, surprisingly leafy given the surroundings. Maybe its roots had found some untapped source reservoir far below the surface? *Life is resourceful, isn't it? Finding ways to survive in the harshest of circumstances*, Marcik mused.

A boy dropped from the branches of the tree. He dug a rock from the dry earth, cocked it behind his head, and flung it impotently at the Guardsmen. A few of them looked disinterestedly at where the rock had landed, several meters from them.

%% %% %%

Marcik needed to piss. He opened the tent flap sleepily and wandered out into the cool night. It must have been very late; the village was completely silent. A fat moon hung over the village square. There were dim lights and the hum of a generator from a nearby barnlike structure, the largest building in the village. That was where the officers were sleeping. They had requisitioned the barn and installed it with a generator for lighting and communications. The enlisted men slept in tents along the riverbank, lined up in their usual neat rows.

He relieved himself behind a shed. When he was done, he began back toward his tent. He heard a sharp noise like laughter. Stopping, looking around, he noticed a dirt path. Coming to full wakefulness, he followed the noise.

He looked through the door of a hut. A woman was splayed out on a table, her arms pinned by a large man at the head of the table. Another smaller man was at her feet and was pushing her dress up. His pants were around his ankles. There was only a single gas lantern in the hut and the shadows cast angled darkness across the faces of the men.

"Cover her mouth," the small man said.

"Why, Samir?" the large man said. It was Yoyo.

"Just do what I say and then it will be your turn."

Samir thrust into the woman. She twisted her hips, trying to buck him off, a scream muffled by the giant hand over her mouth. Marcik stepped forward, his shadow falling into the doorway. He looked out into the dark village for support. Physically, he was no match for Yoyo. Even Samir could probably take him.

"What are you doing?" Marcik said.

Samir turned to him, still pumping. "You're going to have to wait your turn."

As trained, Marcik never left his tent without his sidearm. He considered pulling it out now, but what Guardsman would pull his weapon on another Guardsman?

The woman looked at Marcik, thinking she was saved.

Marcik stood decisionless. He should stop this. "Please, stop," he said.

"Get out of here, Guardsman!" Samir said.

Marcik stood a second longer, not looking at the woman's frantic terrified eyes. He tried to forget the image of Samir's bare skinny legs, the tail of his Guardsman's shirt hanging over his ass.

He turned and trudged back to his tent, the muffled screams still pleading in his ears. It took him hours to get to sleep.

※ ※ ※

The next morning, camp was fully broken and the trucks had started rolling out of the village when a group of armed men stepped into the road to block their path. The konvoy stopped.

"We wish to have a word with your major," one of the men shouted.

He was older, bearded, with strong broad shoulders. Likely he was the leader of the village, or maybe just the man with best grasp of the common Slovnik.

The door to the second truck swung open and Kaptain Nguyen stepped out.

"I speak for Major Schmidt," he said. "What's the problem here?"

"We invited you to our village. We shared our hospitality," the man said. "And your men repay us by raping one of our women."

Near Marcik, Guardsmen grumbled in anger.

"That's a serious accusation," Nguyen said. "Do you have any proof?"

"Lilica," he said. "Show yourself."

The young girl stepped out from behind the men. She looked down at the ground, but she was not able to conceal her battered face.

"Two of your men forced themselves on her," the villager said to Kaptain Nguyen.

And then in a muted voice, he spoke to the girl in the provincial tongue—that mangy mix of Ulani and common Slovnik. The girl lifted her finger and pointed at Samir and then at Yoyo.

Nguyen turned to the two Guardsmen. "Artillery Gunners Parlov and Hosani," he said. "Please step forward."

Yosef Parlov and Samir Hosani took a step out of formation.

"Is this true? Did you force yourself upon this woman?"

She's just a girl, Marcik thought.

"No, sir," Samir said, looking straight ahead, a model of soldierly comportment, "I've never seen this woman."

"You lie!" the girl yelled.

The man beside her put a hand on her arm, restraining her.

"And you, Parlov?" Nguyen said. "How do you reply?"

Yoyo looked at Samir, then at Nguyen, and then at the girl. "We were only having some fun," he said. "Samir, you said we were only having fun."

"Shut up, Yoyo," Samir said.

"Hosani," Nguyen said. "Your stories don't seem to match."

"I admit it, sir," Samir said.

"You see?" the villager said. His men took a step forward, intending to take Samir into custody.

"I admit that we had some fun with the girl," Samir continued. "But no one forced her. She invited us."

The villager grabbed the girl by the arm, pulling her roughly forward. He squeezed her face in his hand and turned it to the left and right, displaying her bruises.

"A woman does not look like that after a little fun," he said.

One by one, the villagers raised their guns. The Guardsmen at the front of the line raised their own in response. *It will be a massacre. We outnumber them ten to one. Say something, you coward. Tell what you saw.*

"Lower your weapons, men," Nguyen barked. "I'll not have a bloodbath today."

The Guardsmen lowered their weapons. Slowly and with much reluctance, the villagers did the same.

"Can anyone corroborate this?" Nguyen asked, looking first to the villagers and then to his Guardsmen.

Here Samir gave Marcik a look. Their eyes locked briefly, and Marcik turned his eyes to the ground, saying nothing.

"I have the only important witness right here," the village leader said.

"Without any eyewitness testimony, it's her word against the word of my men," Nguyen said. "You understand I can't simply turn them over to you on the strength of that?"

"We demand justice," the villager said.

"And you'll get it," Nguyen said, "but through the proper channels. A thorough investigation will be conducted the moment we meet up with the rest of our regiment. I promise you that. Until then, what does getting all of your men killed gain you?"

The village leader nodded to his men. They stepped back, creating just enough space for the trucks to drive through. As Marcik passed on foot, he looked at each man in turn. He almost wished the village leader would do something, both to punish him for his cowardice and as a release for his anger and guilt. As Samir and Yoyo passed through the crowd ahead, the girl stepped forward. She spat. It struck Samir on the cheek. He flinched slightly but stared straight ahead and continued marching.

Then the villagers were behind them, and soon the village itself, and Marcik's kompany marched along the banks of the feeble river, eastward to Ulan-Ude and war.

As the Guardsmen progressed across the landscape, Samir slowly moved his way up to Marcik. "Thank you, friend," he said. "I won't forget it."

※ ※ ※

A few days after they left the village, Marcik pulled Fredrik aside during their evening meal and told him what he had seen. They were in a half-dead pasture underneath a scant copse of trees. Two long boards had been propped on barrels of water to form a table. For chairs, the men used boxes, packs, whatever they could find.

Fredrik nodded after Marcik finished, so unsurprised that Marcik wondered if he had understood. "I knew he was lying," Fredrik said. "And of course he forced that big dumb friend of his into it."

"What should I do?"

"Nothing."

"That's your advice? Nothing? What would you do?"

"You could talk to Cantor about it. He's a fair man."

"I have to do something," Marcik said. "Just look at him over there. He knows he got away with it."

Samir was dipping a biscuit into a kind of hominy gruel, chewing at the bread complacently, his elbows up on the table. A bit of slop ran down his chin and he wiped it with the back of his hand. Another Guardsman pulled up a crate beside him and said something in passing. Samir muttered a response between bites, and the other Guardsman laughed.

"You could always kill him," Fredrik said. "But I'm guessing you're not ready for that."

It was difficult to tell how serious Fredrik was being.

"Maybe I'll talk to Cantor."

※ ※ ※

He had an opportunity later that night. Sergeant Cantor was making his rounds, confirming everyone was where they were supposed to be and that their camp was running smoothly.

"Sir," Marcik said. "A word?"

"What do you have, Guardsman?" Cantor said, without breaking his stride or looking at Marcik.

"I was actually, um, hoping for somewhere more private."

Cantor stopped and squinted at Marcik. "Kovalski, is it? Come into my tent."

Cantor lifted the tent flap and they went inside. The tent was twice the size issued to regular Guardsmen. The cot was more like a bed, with real pillows. This was the reward of a career in the military—of being tested in battle and performing well. Marcik tried to picture himself in such a position. Cantor waited for Marcik to speak, a slight amused smile working across his lips. This close, Marcik noticed the lines under his eyes, the lack of sleep that goes with being in a position of kommand. If there were benefits to being a leader of men, there were also counterbalancing weights to be borne.

"The girl, sir," Marcik blurted out. "Back in the village. I think she might have been telling the truth."

Cantor nodded and motioned for Marcik to continue. Marcik told Cantor what he had seen. Cantor seemed even less surprised than Fredrik.

"Thank you for coming to me, Private," he said when Marcik had finished. "I will take this into account when presenting the case to the review panel."

"You mean you'll tell them what I saw?"

"Did I say that?"

"Sir?"

"Let me tell you how this works," Cantor said. "If I tell them what you saw, you'll have to testify. Do you understand what that would mean for you? If you testify against a fellow Guardsman, you'll be a pariah. You'll never advance a single rank. Is that what you want?"

"No, sir."

"Good," Cantor said. "Because I think you have ability. Does it surprise you to hear me say that? I heard about your stunt back in training. Very ingenious. And you've handled yourself well in combat so far. I know you don't think of yourself as much of a Guardsman. But I was like you at your age. These overconfident boys, they're always the first ones to get killed. It could be that your . . . ethical dilemma . . . will take care of itself. But if you can't live with your conscience, I understand that too. Respect it, even. However, something tells me you can. It's part of being a Guardsman."

"Thank you, sir."

Cantor smiled again. "For what?"

Marcik wasn't sure what he was thanking him for precisely. "For your forthrightness, I suppose."

"It's a tough situation. Now go and get some sleep."

"Yes, sir."

"Dismissed."

2.

AT THE DESIGNATED HOUR, Nikolas and the others gathered in The Nameless Tavern. The meeting was small today, its purpose to discuss the progress they had made in setting up a kommune. To that end, only the most trusted members of the movement had been invited: Elias, Mouse, Sara, and Alarik; Endre, a ticket-inspektor on the Silverville train line; and the Baikyong-doan twins, Yu and Yi. Their actual names were Yung-Jin and Yi-Jun, but they had shortened them for ease of pronunciation when they arrived in Joshua City.

Nikolas started the meeting by asking for a general update.

"Has anyone found us a place to live?" he asked, when no one was quick to supply information. "No? What about funds?"

This was a source of anxiety for him. He had just come from Katya's apartment. How long could he continue to live off her before she would start to resent him for it? And how far could the movement go without some sort of kapital? He had committed a few petty thefts, once stealing a church collection plate and another time robbing a florist he knew didn't own a lockbox. He hadn't minded the first robbery so much—taking money from an institution that keeps the people in a superstitious slumber—but the second had made him sick to his stomach. The florist was an honest man and a poor one (as honest men usually are), the type of person he was supposed to be helping, not stealing from. Fortunately, he had an idea of where they could get money from someone who could afford it.

"I can fund part of it, as you know," Elias said. "But the cost of such an endeavor will be huge."

"Fine. What else?"

"I've found a few more members for our group," Elias said. "Possible ones anyhow. My hope is that some of them will have money. Maybe even a lead on a place we can live. There's a lot of discontent in the rank-and-file of law skolars. The government does what it wants, irrespective of the law. It's in the pocket of the water-barons and the war machine and the mining business. And then of course there's corruption within the counselors-of-law as well. If you're from the right family, you've got a nice little position waiting for you. If not, you might as well burn your degree."

"It is this way everywhere," Yu said.

His words were slow and precise; he came from a culture which used language sparingly, regarding words as having near-mystical power.

"In sociolinguistics, there are few prospects for the skolarship students such as us," his brother added. "Especially when you are from one of the *Lesser Six*."

"Try being a woman in engineering," Sara said.

"But are they serious?" Nikolas said. "These recruits, I mean. I don't want any more hangers-on. This isn't some social club."

"Who's a hanger-on?" Endre said. "I'm ready to do what it takes. I don't want to go to a work camp, is all."

Endre was right to be frightened—he wouldn't last a month in a work camp. His skinny arms hung skeletally in his ticket-inspektor's uniform; his eyes squinted from behind thick eyeglasses; his anemic pallor suggested some vague chronic ailment.

"The risk to you is minimal," Nikolas said. "And I meant in general. This group lacks focus."

"And what have you done?" Elias asked.

"I'll tell you what," Nikolas said, "I'll show you how serious I am. Endre, you work Saturday, don't you?"

"I am done at seven." It was part apology and part refusal of whatever Nikolas was about to ask.

"Can you get us to Jardin Prospekt?"

"That's past Checkpoint 4," Endre said. "Normally, you need residency cards to go there."

"Can you do it or not?"

"I guess I could get a few visitors' passes, maybe."

Visitors' passes were for all those who wished to travel past Checkpoints 3 or 4 but did not have residency cards for those areas. The usual procedure was to apply for a day-pass at the Ministrie of Transport; but Endre would have access to stacks of the things.

"Good. We'll go around nine."

"Are you taking us to a cocktail party?" Elias said.

Uneasy laughter around the table. Nikolas ignored it.

"We're going to tear down one of those bourgeois facades you love to go on about," Nikolas said. Then to the rest of the group, "I trust you all are in?"

None of them said anything. Elias put out his cigarette in the ashtray, twisting and mashing it. When he was done, he looked at Nikolas without blinking. At last, he nodded. Alarik grumbled affirmation. The twins glanced at each other wordlessly.

"Yes," Yu said.

"We will attend your outing," Yi added.

"You can count on me," Mouse said, her voice clipped and cold, filled with steely purpose.

Sara said, "Me too."

That left only Endre.

"All right. All right," he said. "I'll do it. Just don't be late. And wear something decent. You don't want to attract attention. And try to be sober."

3.

AS THEY NEARED the river's source, the land began to rise. Yesterday they had caught the first distant peaks of mountains, capped with white in the blue haze. In the valley between two of those peaks, where the Uda and Selenga rivers met, was the city of Ulan-Ude. About forty kilometers outside of the city, Marcik's kompany would meet up with the full regiment. The air here was clear, the land dry and treeless, and as they topped each progressively higher ridge, they had a view that seemed just a few kilometers but was in reality perhaps fifty or more. They could not yet see the regimental camp which, consisting of more than four thousand Guardsmen and their officers, should resemble a small city. Still, according to the maps that Marcik studied almost religiously (determined to be the solid Guardsman that Cantor seemed to think he was), they could not have been more than a few days' march off.

On the second day after they saw the mountains, the land began to close in on them. As the terrain grew hillier, their caution increased. Advance scouts were sent ahead at every rise or bend in the road. Sometimes the kompany proceeded at a near-crawl. The trucks rolled down the hills in neutral, a fuel-saving technique, but also a means of proceeding more slowly and quietly. The men made nervous jokes as they marched.

In a narrow pass with a stream of snowmelt, they made camp for the night. Marcik tried to sleep, but every snapping branch or the rustle of some rodent went through him like a shot. He knew there were half a dozen men keeping watch at strategic points around the perimeter of the camp. But what could even a dozen men do against a surprise attack?

They were woken an hour earlier than usual. Marcik sat up in his tent, grabbing for his rifle. *Something's wrong.* He stepped out into the pale purple dawn.

The kompany was lining up in orderly rows. No sign of the enemy. After a seemingly interminable amount of time that was probably less than ten minutes, Major Schmidt came out of the officers' tent.

"Guardsmen," he said. "Sorry to have interrupted your sleep. Our advanced scouts have returned from their morning recognizance. They report a camp of some one hundred Ulani soldiers in a valley up ahead. The number is larger than we would like. But we cannot move forward without engaging them. And right now we're fortunate to have the element of surprise on our side. Like all of you would be if we had not woken you, they are mostly still asleep. If we move fast we can catch them that way. Your platoon sergeants will fill you in on the details."

Two to one, Marcik thought. *Not bad.* Granted, the biggest deployment they had encountered so far had been perhaps forty men. And even there, they had not escaped without casualties. A guardsman named Danielovski had been killed almost immediately. Another named Jopek had been shot through the leg, shattering the bone. The leg had been saved, but he would likely never walk normally again. *It will be worse this time.* But his fellow Guardsmen showed no fear and he wouldn't either.

※ ※ ※

The position of the Ulani camp created both advantages and disadvantages for the Guardsmen. The approach was narrow, which meant that the Ulanis would have difficulty making an escape. However, it also meant that Marcik's kompany could only approach from the west as opposed to from all directions simultaneously. Ideally, they would have staged a rear attack to prevent retreat, but the terrain was impassible except by going through the Ulani camp. This mitigated somewhat the advantage of the Guard's superior numbers.

"We'll knock out as many as we can with the long-range artillery," Sergeant Cantor told Marcik's platoon. "Once we've hit them with one good set of volleys, we will send in the first wave of infantry. Support units will be dispatched as deemed necessary. And please, try not to shoot the Guardsmen in front of you."

"Sir?" a Guardsman raised his hand.

"Yes, private?"

"Will we be in the first wave?" The eagerness in his voice begged to be met with an affirmative answer.

"We will be, in fact. It should be plenty dangerous for the thrill-seekers among you. But remember the proverb from the *Book of the Before-Time*: 'Sometimes the worst thing God can do is grant your prayers.' And that's true no matter which of the Seven Gods you believe in."

Marcik went with the other Guardsmen to unpack the long-range artillery. Ten grenadiers were given their grenade launchers and belts equipped with a dozen grenades each. Several Guardsmen took down a mortar from the back of a truck, struggling with its weight. They finally dropped the enormous object on the ground, kicking up a cloud of dust. It sat there on its steel base, its long barrel stabbing upward, waiting to be loaded with explosives.

"Artillery Gunners Parlov and Hosani," Cantor called out.

Yoyo and Samir stepped forward.

"Are you ready?"

Yoyo nodded, looking straight ahead, chin held high—the very image of soldierly comportment.

"Yes, sir!" Samir said.

"Then man your positions."

Yoyo went behind the mortar. He loaded the first shell into its chamber, a task it would have taken two or three other men working in tandem to accomplish, yet he did it with no visible strain. He positioned the mortar barrel at a 45-degree angle and stepped aside. Samir made the finer adjustments using the mortar's sighting mechanism. He put his fist straight up in the air to indicate all was at the ready.

"Formation," ordered Cantor, and twenty Guardsmen went into the Titus formation. The grenadiers moved to the front and checked and loaded their grenade launchers. The riflemen fell in to the side and just behind them. Marcik followed Fredrik, who gave him an encouraging nod.

Marcik's hands were sweat-slippery on the rifle's grip. At least he was not a grenadier. The grenadiers would be in the vanguard, running exposed to get within firing range. The riflemen, whose weapons had a longer range, would be on either flank and well behind them, laying down suppressing fire. Marcik's whole body shook from adrenaline and anticipation.

"Fire!" Cantor yelled.

Samir pulled a lever and the mortar recoiled to life. A whistle and a trail of smoke went through the air, and seconds later, a boom echoed through the valley. The shell had hit the periphery of the Ulani camp. Yoyo quickly loaded another shell into the mortar, and Samir adjusted his aim. His fist went up again; and again Cantor ordered him to fire. Another whistle and smoke-trail; another explosion, this time in the center of the Ulani camp. Marcik watched as Ulanis ran frantically about, grabbing their weapons and seeking cover. Yoyo and Samir did their load-and-fire routine three more times before Cantor gave the signal for the first wave of Guardsmen to rush the valley.

Fredrik turned to Marcik and said, "We've got this."

Marcik ran along with the other Guardsmen, his legs scissoring and his feet gliding him forward. He was no longer shaking now; the heft of his rifle was reassuring, the certainty and speed of their assault exhilarating. There was Ulani fire now, and the riflemen returned fire. The grenadiers ran on, waiting for their moment. One, then two grenadiers fell. Marcik pulled his trigger several times. Fredrik beside him fired less frequently, but with what Marcik knew would be with greater deadliness.

They ran and fired, and time stopped having meaning. Ahead of him, the grenadiers hunkered down and began their rain of grenade-fire upon the enemy. The explosions echoed deafeningly through the valley.

The air in the Ulani camp was filled with exploding dirt and rock. Marcik kept running, kept firing his rifle. When the smoke and dirt cleared, he saw an Ulani soldier, his body severed at the waist, entrails roping loosely from his abdomen. The man crawled weakly toward nowhere.

The grenadiers fired another round, and more explosions rang out through the valley. Marcik and the other riflemen advanced into the camp, inspecting the carnage all around. A few wounded Ulani soldiers were the only ones alive; a burning tent-flap waved in an indifferent breeze; the earth was pocked from the mortars and grenades.

They had done it.

Fredrik and Marcik stood there looking at each other. "See, I told you."

It had ended so quickly, Marcik was almost disappointed. At this rate, the war would be over tomorrow. He was still fairly vibrating with excitement.

Cantor sent a flare up, letting the second wave of Guardsmen know there was no need for reinforcements.

"Pick through what's left," he ordered. "There might be something of use here we didn't pulverize." The muscles of his face twitched toward a smile.

The Guardsmen sifted through the debris, occasionally patting each other on the back or making a joke about the weakness of Ulani men.

% % %

Fredrik was tossing a ration-bag toward Marcik when a frightening metallic noise came over the ridge. A horn? And another sound, like that of a stampeding herd. Birds flew up from the thin tree coverage. Dozens of men—they weren't dressed in uniforms of any sort, not even the less formal uniforms of the Ulanis—came over the ridge. In unison they let out a war cry that only distantly sounded human. The mountain air was frozen cold and blue between Marcik and this berserk trammel of men. They were halfway down the ridge before the Guardsmen could react.

"Harbinger save us," Cantor said. "The Savage Ones."

Cantor had never seen them except in fotos from his days in officer training. They were the outcasts of Baikyong-do, and they earned their name by their deeds. Even at this distance, Cantor could see their grotesque patchwork clothing, their knotted hair decorated with twigs and animal bones, their faces smeared with filth. The Savage Ones were armed haphazardly—some carrying merely a cudgel or a curved blade, others with automatic rifles of Baikyong-doan design.

"Fall back!" Cantor ordered, and the Guardsmen under his kommand, who had heard nothing more than rumors of The Savage Ones, grew more afraid at hearing the fear in his voice.

The Savage Ones charged down the hill, those with rifles firing them. The Guardsmen scattered helplessly under the echoing spray.

Beside Marcik, Fredrik slumped to the ground, motionless. Guardsmen ran in every direction.

"Fall back, I said!" Cantor screamed and tried to funnel his troops out of valley.

Marcik wanted to help Fredrik, but he forced himself to raise his rifle and return fire.

"Grenadiers!" Cantor said, and a paltry few fired in the direction of their attackers, killing several but not slowing their advance.

The second wave of Guardsmen arrived, having been ordered in at the sound of new gunfire. Marcik made his way to Fredrik's body and turned it over. His uniform was soaked down the chest with blood and his eyes stared wetly from his skull. *Where is the bullet?* He lifted Fredrik beneath the arms, and dragged his awkward weight behind a rock. Some part of him knew Fredrik was dead, but he couldn't leave him there. The second wave of Guardsmen rushed in all around him, firing at the endless stream of Savage Ones. The Savage Ones sent a chaotic but deadly burst back, maneuvering closer for man-to-man combat. By the time they engaged the Guardsmen with knife and sword and bayonet, they had killed or wounded over half of them with their rifle-fire. Marcik left Fredrik slumped against the rock and rejoined the fight. Men were falling all around him. Twenty meters off, a Guardsman was lifted on a Savage One's pike and flung aside like a limp rabbit. The Savage Ones attacked indiscriminately. Marcik watched in horror as a Savage One moved without pause from decapitating one Guardsman to opening the guts of another.

Cantor scrambled enough of his men together to effect a retreat. Marcik chased after them. Then, in the direction of the base-camp, explosions plumed skyward.

※ ※ ※

Major Schmidt had to make a decision. He surveyed the situation through a pair of telescopic lenses. The Guardsmen in the valley were surrounded, greatly outnumbered, trapped with no hope of escape. Sending more men in would only mean more men dead. He had been forced to leave men behind before, but it didn't make it any less difficult.

"Load up the trucks and let's pull out," he said to his officers.

The officers climbed in to the passenger truck and the enlisted Guardsmen lined up behind them. They moved slowly back down the road.

A few meters from the officers' truck, Major Schmidt watched as Private Dekar climbed in behind the wheel; he was a Guardsman like all those Schmidt had just left behind to die. But before this war was over he would have to make many such decisions.

There was a movement in the air farther down the road, though Major Schmidt did not recognize it as a rocket until the last fraction of a second. He went for the ground. It struck the truck dead on. The truck split open in a tear of metal and fire, killing Dekar and the officers in the back instantly.

Major Schmidt lay on the ground, ears echoing nothing loudly; somewhere unimaginably far away, his leg throbbed around the sharp pinch of metal stabbing into it; someone screamed something he couldn't understand in Ulani; noises like underwater explosions were everywhere; he tried to stand but fell on his face in the dirt.

※ ※ ※

There was no way out. Marcik fired wildly in all directions. He had never been so efficient, never operated so quickly. But The Savage Ones kept coming. All around him Guardsmen dropped. A Savage One charged into the middle of a clearing, swinging an axe with wild force. The axe wedged itself in a fallen Guardsman's shoulder and the Savage One stepped on his neck to pull it free. He swung the axe again, with more fury than sense, accidentally severing the arm of another Savage One. Unbothered at having maimed a fellow soldier, he pushed the man into the dirt and waded into further battle.

Marcik reloaded, fired. Reloaded, fired. Up ahead, Cantor clutched his arm and fell to one knee. *I should...* But then a blade cut Cantor's head clean off. Marcik fired at the Savage One who had done it, screaming wildly. He fired again. Everything was noise, smoke, and fury.

%. %. %.

The officer's truck lay in a mangled mess on its side. Ulani soldiers swarmed in on the Guardsmen behind the truck. The Ulani trap now came to its lethal completion. The few surviving officers would later damn their idiotic incompetence for falling for what was known as the Ambusher's Gambit. Set up a target for ambush, and then ambush the ambushers.

%. %. %.

Marcik was able to fire his weapon twice before he was overtaken. The Savage One kicked him in the leg and something popped in his knee. Before Marcik hit the ground the attacker's barbed club struck his wrist, knocking his rifle free. He yanked Marcik up by his uniform, smiled at him through his hideous mask of wrinkled skin, and with the joyful snarl of a dog snapping at a scrap of meat slammed his forehead against Marcik's own.

Then there was blackness.

※ ※ ※

His head hurt. His feet dragged through the dirt. He was being carried. Where was he?

There was smoke down in the valley; there was an overturned skeleton of a truck in flames; blood soaked warmly into his uniform. How badly was he injured? With his head still ringing with the sharp crack of The Savage One's forehead against his own, Marcik struggled to stay afloat on a swimming confusion.

"Good. You are awake now," an Ulani soldier said.

Marcik fumbled for his sidearm. There was nothing there.

"Did you think we would leave that for you? Climb up."

4.

NIKOLAS AND THE OTHERS crouched in the bushes outside Brandt's mansion. It was after dark, but there were no lights on inside. Good. Nikolas had heard the rumors about Brandt's nightlife and hoped he would be doing whatever it was he did at the taverns and dancehalls. Had he been home, Nikolas would have settled for smashing a window or two, pissing on Brandt's doorstep, overturning one those absurdly ornate flowerpots.

"Follow me."

They made their way to the back of the house as quietly as a group of eight, many of them half-drunk, can. Brandt had a modest garden patio, a little stone path, some well-trimmed shrubs, several wrought-iron chairs. Nikolas jiggled the handle of the back door. Locked. He tried a window. Mouse lifted a brick, ready to smash the glass of the window, but Nikolas motioned Alarik forward. He nodded at the door.

Alarik gave a casual kick and the door flew open, banging against the wall.

Nikolas entered and turned on the light. They were in a spotless kitchen with great gleaming counters. It looked as though it had never been used. Beyond, through an arched double-doorway, was a dining area Nikolas had seen once during the second semester of last year. It was there that Brandt first told Nikolas about the summer fellowship he had recommended him for.

Nikolas already knew something about the background of each of the people with him, but even if he had not, he would have been able to guess at it by their reactions to their surroundings. Elias, accustomed to such opulence, made no reaction. Endre, who was the son of a low-level government worker, was more appreciative. There was Mouse who had changed so much her moniker had become more ironic than accurate. She was a real success, turning from meek hanger-on to toughened komrade. He knew less about her lover, but she seemed devoted to Mouse and equally tough. Alarik, the laborer son of laborers, looked around with confused admiration. Yu and Yi were always hard to read, their expressions inscrutable in their twinned foreignness. Nikolas wondered what advantage he might gain by having two citizens of Baikyong-do in the group.

Elias found the liquor cabinet and lined up a row of crystal snifters—glasses was an insufficient word to describe them—and was pouring them all drinks.

"Come on," Nikolas said. He emptied a snifter in one quick motion and grabbed another one.

Nikolas headed through the dining room. When Elias didn't follow, Nikolas said, "I said come on. Bring the bottle."

Elias took a connoisseur's sip of his drink, grabbed the bottle, and followed Nikolas with no apparent hurry.

"What about the servants?" Endre whispered.

Nikolas remembered having met Lénárd, Brandt's personal driver. He had been a good man, Nikolas thought, and felt momentary embarrassment at the idea of Lénárd finding him like this.

"Don't worry about it," Nikolas said.

If Brandt were not home, then his driver would be with him. Of course, there very well might be others. They would have to take that chance.

Straight ahead was the sitting room, and to the right, down a long hallway, a study or librarie. Nikolas remembered a stairway in the foyer, ascending to a second story he had never seen. If there were valuables in the house, that's where they would be. Their sale would help fund this movement, whatever it was.

But first he had something important to see.

After a couple of false turns, he found the study. He flicked the light switch and an enormous chandelier cast its many-armed light over the room. There were shelves and shelves of books. There were paintings on the walls, meticulously hung, like in a gallery. *He probably hired some art student to arrange them just so.* Nikolas ignored them, as he ignored Elias and the others behind him.

"Is this it then?" Elias said. "We're here to look at art?"

"Some of you should go upstairs," Nikolas said. "I'm sure there are things we can use up there."

"Things we can use?" Elias questioned. "Why are we even here, Nikolas? What are we looking for?"

No one moved. They stood bunched in the hallway outside the door, waiting to see what he would do.

Nikolas stood riveted before a particular painting. It depicted the famous scene from the *Book of the Before-Time* where the Harbinger is beheaded for delivering warnings of the coming Great Calamity. Most paintings of this scene showed the Harbinger right before he was beheaded, the blade above his neck abstracted and the smile on his face beatific and unafraid. But in this painting, the Harbinger's head was already severed. The Harbinger's body was still held upright by the executioner's scaffold, his severed head lay on the finely elaborated grass, and a bit of spinal column protruded from bloodied stump of his neck; the executioner himself stood bent and forlorn at his deed.

※ ※ ※

Nikolas had first seen this painting during one of the better nights of his life. Brandt had invited him to dinner; Nikolas, being a first-year skolar eager to make a good impression on a man of Brandt's influence, accepted eagerly. Midway through the meal, Brandt mentioned the summer fellowship as casually as someone might mention the weather.

"It's not much, of course," Brandt said, "but I suspect it will lead to more permanent funding."

"For nekrosis research?"

"The summer funding is for nekrosis. As for the next semester, we'll have to see. It would no doubt strengthen your case ... But here, have another glass. Let us celebrate."

They ate their breaded cutlets and drank their wine. When Brandt had grown merry and flushed in the face, he took Nikolas around to see his prize possessions. First and foremost was his study. He showed Nikolas his rare medikal texts with subdued pride, dismissing their importance even while boasting about their value. With each acquisition he showed Nikolas, it was as though he were saying, *All this can be yours, too. That is, if you listen to me.*

Nikolas found himself drawn to a particular painting. Brandt came up and stood close behind Nikolas, and they admired the painting together.

"Do you like it?" Brandt asked. "It cost me no small effort to purchase it, you know. The original owner did not want to sell."

"I'm not sure that *like* is the word," Nikolas said. Something about the painting—its marriage of religious content and medikally precise detail—taunted him.

"Then you feel as I do," Brandt said. He put his hand on Nikolas's shoulder. "We're outsiders, you know. Both of us."

The wine was going to Nikolas's head. In those days, he was a much less experienced drinker. "If you'll excuse me, I need the water-closet," he said.

He left Brandt there, alone in his study, thinking whatever mysterious thoughts men of influence think. Later, Lénárd drove Nikolas home, and the next time Nikolas saw Brandt he was relieved to learn that he had not ruined anything with his drunkenness. In fact, Brandt seemed to feel the dinner was a total success.

"We'll have to do it again soon," he said. "I think this will prove a very fruitful relationship for both of us."

※ ※ ※

Now, Nikolas took a knife from his pocket, lifted it and brought it down in a swift arc, slashing the canvas; he slashed again and again; the crescent-shaped wound in the center of painting widened; it gaped. He knew he should take the painting and sell it, but his sudden rage would not listen to reason. Jagged flaps of canvas hung down, and still Nikolas slashed. He slashed left and right wildly now, creating a patternless network of X's across the painting's face. Soon the canvas was mere ribbons, but he continued slashing.

5.

BRANDT LEFT The Sub Rosa[7] by the side entrance, which was the only real entrance; the front door led to a boring little tavern meant to throw off the authorities who might take a dim view of the patrons' activities. He looked both ways down the narrow alley, making sure that no one saw him. Reassured, he let the door swing shut behind him. Brandt hurried down the alley toward the deserted street where Lénárd was waiting with the car. Lénárd was the only one who knew about Brandt's excursions, but if he had any idea what went on between the men at clubs like this he knew better than to say anything. Not even so much as a raised eyebrow, good old Lénárd.

Brandt heard footsteps behind him but kept walking.

"Professor," a high-pitched voice called after him. "Please. I only want to talk."

Brandt turned around in a fury. "What do you want?"

---

[7] Translators' Note: A reader might object here that the use of the Before-Time Latin phrase *sub rosa* or its equivalent is not likely, or even possible, in Slovnik—and the reader would be right. In the process of translation, compromises are made. In some cases, we have elected to convey the intended meaning rather than merely preserve the literal.

The man—boyish in appearance, with slim narrow hips and a face a razor had never touched—seemed taken aback by Brandt's anger. He fumbled for something to say. "Leaving so soon?" he asked finally.

"What does it look like?"

The man approached Brandt. He straightened Brandt's tie and smoothed what was left of his hair. At first, Brandt let it happen, closing his eyes ever so slightly as he gave in to the urge. Coming to his senses, he pushed the man away.

"Not here," Brandt said. "It could ruin me."

"Poor professor," the man said, trying to smooth Brandt's hair again. "He can't be himself."

"I told you to stop it." Brandt swatted the man's hand away. "And stop calling me that. I'm a doktor."

"Doktor then." The man held his hand to his heart. "I'm sick, Doktor. Won't you examine me?"

"I'm leaving now," Brandt said.

He turned and left the man standing in the alley.

"See you next week, Professor?" the man called out after him.

At the end of the alley, just around the corner, in the shadowed awning of a building, Brandt's car was parked. Lénárd unlocked the doors and Brandt slipped inside.

"Home, sir?" Lénárd asked.

"Yes," Brandt replied, "home."

6.

NIKOLAS STEPPED back and watched the chaos he had unleashed. The others had taken their cue from him. Alarik overturned a bookcase, sending the books fanning across the floor. Sara pulled down her pants and squatted over the books, letting loose a stream of urine. It pained a part of Nikolas to see works of literature and science defaced this way. Mouse smashed glass figurines with a fireplace poker. Endre restricted himself to pulling paintings meekly from the wall, unable to join in the nihilistic fervor. He stacked the paintings in a neat pile and stepped on them ineffectually.

Elias walked two fingers along the length of the mantle, knocking off crystal vases and porcelain dolls one by one. He seemed almost bored. He had a crystal snifter filled with baikal-expensive liqueur and drank from it with ironic superiority. He raised an eyebrow at Nikolas. Nikolas shrugged. This was not what he had intended—at least he didn't think so. But he also had no desire to stop it.

"I am the destroyer of worlds!" Endre screamed, jumping onto the pile of paintings.

His foot struck the frame of one painting and the pile went sliding. He fell back, struggled to keep his footing, then sprawled on the floor among the piss-soaked books. Elias did not even try to stifle his laughter as Endre scuttled to his feet and looked down at the pile of wet books with disgust and embarrassment.

Mouse approached the pile with the poker raised.

"Give it here," Nikolas said, yanking the poker from Mouse's hand.

He plunged the poker into the stack of paintings, brought it back up. A painting of a train traversing a fertile plain was skewered and lurched pendulously on the poker. No such train-line or landscape existed—not since the Before-Time anyway. It was one of those utopian dreams Mayor Adams used to distract the people. Nikolas stomped on the painting and pulled the poker free.

He noticed a painting of Mayor Adams, crudely done, his face more handsome than in life. Picturing Brandt's little red face, he brought the poker down. Someone overturned the coffee table. Seated on the rug, Yu and Yi were tearing out pages of books, tossing them up in the air, letting them fall like leaves, giddy with the transgression of their sworn duty as Baikyong-doans to preserve written knowledge.

"Someone's coming," Elias said, still leaning against his wall, and emptied his drink.

※ ※ ※

Brandt entered his home, still disturbed by his encounter outside the nightclub. He would have to be more careful. A man in his position could not afford to have his indiscretions known. Especially in today's political climate. They wouldn't send him to a work camp, but you could be sure his funding requests would become more difficult. He would be relegated to worse and worse teaching appointments. All the subtle ways to destroy a career. Taken up with these thoughts, he did not notice the light in the back room. He did not hear the noises upstairs.

It was not until Elias came bouncing down the stairs that he realized he was not alone and safe in his home.

"Well, hello there, good Doktor!"

"Who are you?" Brandt asked. Then, more forcefully, "What are you doing here?"

"Don't be scared, distinguished sir," Elias said. "Nikolas brought us. We're all friends here."

More of the group came crowding down. Nikolas lagged at the back, playing at nonchalance.

"Nikolas, what is all this?"

"I'm sorry, Doktor Brandt," Nikolas said, with something like real pity in his voice, "I wish you had not shown up."

"Why shouldn't I? It's my baikal-be-damned home!"

"Oh, look, Nikolas," Elias said, "your hero is angry at you. Whatever shall you do now?"

"Shut up, Elias."

Nikolas stepped off the final stair as the others surrounded Brandt. There was no way out of this. Brandt could notify the authorities. He looked to Elias, who was dancing back and forth on his toes like a wrestler preparing to engage.

"I am truly sorry for this," Nikolas said and rushed forth and punched Brandt with all his force. He felt something small give in his hand but hit Brandt again, sending him all the way to the floor this time. "Alarik."

Without hesitation, Alarik swept forward and sent his boot that had made such short work of the door into Brandt's ribs.

Nikolas's hand throbbed in the distance. His past with Brandt throbbed in a different distance.

"Again."

Alarik kicked Brandt again, lifting half his body off the ground, and stepped back, stood at attention.

"You know," Nikolas began, "some say that the machine is broken. What do you think, Doktor Brandt? I think it's just the opposite. The machine works all too well. And that is precisely the problem. Cog upon cog, belt pulling and piston pumping, water wetting every motion." Nikolas paced back and forth, gaining confidence as he spoke; he liked what he was saying. "I think it's time someone broke the machine. The bad parts anyway. And Doktor Brandt, you are the worst."

At this, he pulled the knife from his pocket and lunged down to stab. The broken bone in his hand caused the knife to slip slightly, and he cut himself. On the second stab, Brandt's and his own blood made the knife slippery, and he cut himself more, but he stabbed again. He grabbed the knife with his other hand and slashed at Brandt without aiming, hitting him in the neck and forehead and cheek.

He stumbled back, suddenly aware of what he had done but had not decided to do, just done, and a terror filled him. He was completely present and his action made his past and his future disappear for a long hollow second.

He saw the blood on his hand and on Brandt's body and clothes. A tremble went through his legs and stomach, and for a moment he was in danger of collapsing or vomiting. He composed himself. For Elias. And all the others. An eerie businesslike calm came over Nikolas. How would they react? Horror pressed Endre to the farthest wall. He stared at Nikolas unseeing. Yu and Yi shared flat smiles of fascination. Elias assessed the situation in much the same way Nikolas was, cold and wondering. Alarik slapped Mouse on the back in a komradely fashion. "It's begun," he said and looked to Nikolas with satisfaction.

Alarik's pronouncement and the truth of it sent a fissure through the tension, and several of them began stamping around like Ulani goats, belting out cries of revolutionary glee, ecstatic in their transgression.

Nikolas looked to Elias only to find Elias was also inspecting him. They nodded at each other knowingly. *It's begun.*

CHAPTER ONE

DEPARTURES

1.

THE MORNING ADRIAN LEFT Joshua City for the Outer Provinces, there was no sunrise. The sky changed in shades of darkness
from nighttime shadow to dull morning gray. A rare mist hung in
the air, wetting his hair and clothing. He felt a finality now that he
was out of the city. The road stretched into the desert like a scroll he
couldn't decipher. The towering walls of the ravine were sepulchral,
and the sky was crowded with blackbirds flying northwest—the direction the karavan had come from. Watching their blade-like wings,
Adrian wanted to fly back with them, to reenter through the Joshua
City Customs and Regulations checkpoint, to crawl whimpering back
into his dormitory apartment and admit that he was not brave enough
to complete this task, that he did not have the existential courage necessary to uphold his abstract convictions. But the karavan went on,
and Adrian could not stop it and was happy he could not stop it. His
situation was as pleasant as it was frightening; the fear was integral to
the pleasure. He was traveling into the Outer Provinces where men
died every day—from all the dangers one expects, and from many
unexpected ones. And with new skirmishes with the Ulanis being reported daily, it seemed only a matter of time before war engulfed this
region as well.

But he was answering a call greater than himself by volunteering at the New Kolyma Laborers Hospital, and this call, Adrian believed, was the highest duty he could fulfill.

Even as a young boy, Adrian had been fascinated with the Outer Provinces. Father Samarov read to the boys at St. Ignatius's from *The Joshua Harbinger* about events in the Lesser Six, and Adrian imagined himself as one of the banditii—an outlaw, but pure at heart—aiding in the overthrow of an unjust city. Odd, Adrian now thought, that he wanted to go to these outposts to help the citizens, not as a marauder, but as a doktor. Odder still how wrong he had been about what the journey would entail.

He was given the cushioned passenger seat in the truck. He had wanted to protest that he did not need such special treatment, but since claustrophobic situations tended to bring on his seizures, the cramped space in the back of the truck was not an option. Behind him, sitting along wooden benches bolted to the frame of the truck bed, were other travelers. Some were prospektors, others were journalists stuck with Outer Province duty, and there were people visiting exiled relatives. There were no Baikal Guardsmen, however; they had their own personnel karavans to ship them off to battle.

Heinrich, the driver, stared blankly at the pocked road before them. He was a large man, barrel-chested and thick-armed, seemingly built of nothing but gristle. He wore ratty military fatigues with the insignia torn off. He had a hat of a sort Adrian had never seen—with flaps to cover his ears or shield his eyes (to protect against sandstorms in the desert?).

"How long have you been driving this route?" Adrian asked.

"Six years." His voice was not overly terse, nor was it inviting. He had the accent of a Larki Islander. Heinrich rolled his window down and spit out a pulpy wad of blackroot. "And you? What business do you have out here with the laborers and murderers?"

※ ※ ※

Adrian knew he would be asked this question often. And he had thought hard about the answer. Why *was* he doing this? It came down, he believed, to everything that had happened to him in the previous akademic year. He had met Nikolas, discovered he not only belonged at Joshua University but could excel there, and then been left to fend for himself. When Nikolas quit university, Doktor Brandt took Adrian on as his research assistant. Things were headed in the right direction, akademically at least, but then Brandt was killed. Adrian still didn't understand how such a thing could happen. He spent the rest of the semester in a shocked daze. His funding had already been assured, but he had no guidance and little purpose.

One day, with only two months left in the semester, Adrian returned to his room and tossed his books on his bed. He sat down at his desk, exhausted in more ways than one. He stared out the open window at the university commons. It was spring and everything was in colorful bloom. Two skolars walked hand in hand. The boy said something and the girl laughed, shoved him. He tripped and fell over in playful exaggeration, went sprawling in the grass. He sat up, laughing now too, then hopped to his feet. Elsewhere, skolars tossed a thin diskus back and forth. One serious young man sat on a bench, reading.

A breeze came in the window. A piece of paper fluttered on his desk. It was the form that Mouse had given him—for an internship at New Kolyma Laborers Hospital in the Outer Provinces. How many months ago was that? He had forgotten all about it. He looked at the deadline to fill out the form. It was just two days away. He took this as a sign, not that he needed one.

But how to explain any of this to a total stranger?

※ ※ ※

"To help," Adrian said. "If I can."

"That's plenty noble."

Adrian wondered if Heinrich was mocking him.

※ ※ ※

Much to Adrian's surprise, among the passengers was also a family—a woman, her husband, and their two children. One was a boy, about nine years old, Adrian guessed. The other was a baby, not yet a year old and still in need of its mother's milk. The woman was thin and frail-looking, with pale freckled skin. She wore a kerchief around her head, leaving only a few strands of her red hair visible. Her hands, bony and delicate, were endlessly busy with something—rocking the baby; slapping her older rambunctious boy lightly, without real anger; preparing a meager meal from the supplies she carried in a shoulder bag she never removed. Her husband by contrast was dark, solidly built, and silent. He barely moved except to whisper what seemed to be words of admonishment in his wife's ear. He looked Al-Khuziri, Adrian thought and felt a rush of admiration for him. The Al-Khuziri were known for their fierceness in combat and their devoutness in religion, and while Adrian had little use for the former trait, the latter warmed his heart toward this family. Perhaps he would have an opportunity to speak with them and learn more about their traditions and language.

"He's going into what they call *elective exile*," Heinrich said. "Going to New Kolyma, like you. Well, not quite like you. He'll be working the mines to pay off his debts back in Joshua City."

"And his family?"

"Came along with him," Heinrich said. "There's a kolony for wives and children outside the mining camp."

"What's her name?" Adrian asked.

Heinrich looked at him with suspicion. "Yves. And her husband's name is Jarir, in case you're curious about him as well."

Adrian blushed at the implications of Heinrich's subtle rebuke.

※　※　※

The rest of that first day, Heinrich and Adrian said nothing more to each other. Adrian watched the landscape rattle by. The sparse vegetation was otherworldly, the rocks pale-gray and purple-tinged, the sky enormous and blue. He thought about the hospital. He had seen fotografs—straw mattresses, filthy hallways, as many diseases spreading as were cured. But now, with the new military wing of the hospital being built, there was hope the facilities would be adequate. *How sad that it takes a war to obtain funding for a hospital,* he reflected.

At one point, the road passed over some beams of broken steel half-buried in the earth. They stretched into the endless desert distance.

"Are those . . . ?" Adrian asked.

"Railroad tracks, yes," Heinrich answered. "Used to be there was a train that went out this way. Only no one knows when, or where it was going. A Before-Time relic, they say."

Adrian remembered a passage from the *Book of the Before-Time* that described something called the Transbaikal Railroad. This must be the vestiges of it. What must it have been like to live in the Before-Time, when resources were so abundant, the world so easily traversable, and everyone so prosperous?

The karavan stopped just before sundown. Adrian was eager to be out of the truck. His back hurt and his legs were numb. Stretching his muscles, Adrian took in the vibrant chaos of people setting up folding tables and pulling rations from their bags, sentries checking their weapons and picking their posts. The workers of the karavan—the drivers, guards, cooks, mechanics—had formed a community, and this community had been in place a long time now. Adrian imagined future travelers like himself in similar karavans, spread out across the desert like a repeating line through time.

"Here, lad," Heinrich said, and handed Adrian a small shovel.

Adrian took the shovel obediently and stared at it, not wanting to ask why Heinrich had given it to him. Was it a gift? Some desert ritual?

"Everyone pulls his weight around here," Heinrich said. "I need you to dig us three fire pits, about two feet deep and four feet wide. Spread them out about ten meters apart. All around the camp. People will be needing them to build cooking fires later, and we'll want them to keep our asses from freezing solid as Larki steel."

Adrian nodded and smiled, happy to play a useful role for the karavan.

※ ※ ※

The following morning, Heinrich laughed as Adrian dragged himself into the cab of the truck with his blistered hands and aching muscles. He tried not to wince as he settled himself into the seat.

"Been a while since you've done a day's labor, eh, Doktor?"

Adrian shifted, trying to find a more comfortable position, and winced again. "I'll manage."

Heinrich frowned with pleasure. "Yes, lad, I suspect you will."

※ ※ ※

The second night, Adrian lay on his back atop his thin bedroll. The sky was impossibly crowded with stars. In Joshua City, the lights bounced off the pollution from the trains and faktories, creating a haze which drowned out all but the brightest stars. But out here, Adrian could see every stellar speck against the blacker black of the universe. The soreness in his muscles did not diminish his enjoyment of the night's beauty. If anything, it added to the charm; that the world should contain such infinite joy and struggle made it all the more worthy of awe. His body was real in a way it hadn't felt since he was a child struggling to keep up in schoolyard games.

"Good eve," Heinrich said. "Mind a bit of company?"

"Please," Adrian said, sitting up and offering part of his bedroll as a seat.

"Oh, it's no bother," Heinrich said and sat in the sand.

"I was thinking what a beautiful night it is."

Heinrich looked up at the sky as if he had never noticed it before. "Indeed it is."

Ashamed at having said something so childish, Adrian said, "But I imagine you came here for more important reasons than to talk about the weather."

"That I did," Heinrich said. He rubbed his scruff of beard and Adrian could almost hear him make a mental note to shave the following morning. "I don't want to scare you, but there might be trouble."

Adrian looked around for malignant signs, but the night's beauty persisted.

"They like to hit you on the second night, when you've still got all your supplies and you're city-weak."

"I see," said Adrian and felt embarrassment at the word city-weak. He was that indeed. A whole life of living in Joshua City.

"Here, take this." Heinrich handed Adrian a large knife that gleamed with light from the campfire.

"Who are *they*? And why do I need *this*?"

"The banditii. And, son, you hope they don't come tonight."

"I'm not a fighter," Adrian said.

"That much is obvious," Heinrich said without a hint of malice. "But even a saint'll kill banditii to save the karavan."

And as easy as that, Adrian had been inducted into Heinrich's makeshift tribe. Heinrich patted his new soldier on the back and stood. "Try and get some sleep."

"I will," Adrian promised.

But Heinrich was not listening. A lone figure was coming over the hill toward the camp.

"Is everything all right?" Adrian asked. His hands shook and the knife seemed absurd in his grasp.

"It might be," Heinrich said. "Now it just might be."

2.

MARCIK'S CELLMATE, Tozhin, was the same age as Marcik but the skin on his neck was wrinkled and sagging, and he was pale as if suffering from a fever. Tozhin had endured malnutrition since his capture half a year ago. Marcik had only been in the camp for a little over a month and already he weighed five kilograms less than when he had been captured. The thought of becoming like Tozhin, or of watching him get frailer and frailer like some sort of mirror into his own future, was terrifying. Whenever Marcik looked at Tozhin, he didn't see a fellow prisoner or a brave Guardsman who had defended Joshua City with honor—no, he saw the inevitable time when his own skin would hang loose and his hair would be lighter and his blood would run sluggish in his veins,

pumped by a heart no longer filled with the pride of living and soldiering, but instead crushed under the daily and hourly stone of his imprisonment. It made him dislike Tozhin, and not liking Tozhin made him
feel guilty, considering all that he had done to help Marcik adjust—as
much as anyone could adjust—to the hell he had been cast into.

Tozhin had been a medik in the Guard. His job had been to set
bones and stanch wounds as best he could. From his own admission,
he wasn't a particularly talented medik, more a glorified nurse (though
many a battle has been lost for want of a decent nurse). He was sufficient to most minor needs, which made him useful if not essential to
the Joshuan forces. To Marcik's good fortune, Tozhin was better than
he claimed, having earned several badges for field procedures and basic
surgeries. When Marcik arrived at the prison, his injuries were not fatal, but without Tozhin's steady hands to set his broken leg, and without
his constant care to keep the wounds from the Savage One's barbed
club clean—well, Marcik didn't want to think what shape he would be
in now.

"Don't tell anyone I did this," Tozhin said the first time he administered to Marcik.

"Why not?"

"The Ulanis need doktoring just like we do. When they had me
in one of their interrogation cells, I lied and said our medik had been
killed. Of course, they beat me until they believed what I was saying, but
I never let on as to how I might help them." He smiled wide, showing
his missing teeth.

"They did that?"

"Makes it hard to eat. But it was worth it." Tozhin eyed Marcik carefully. "You're not the collaborating type, are you?"

"Me?" Marcik said, mustering all the outrage he could. "I'll never
give those bastards anything."

"You say that now, and maybe you even mean it. But wait until the
pain starts."

A different kind of pain had already started for Tozhin. That afternoon Marcik sat watching Tozhin sleep—almost peaceful for once—and tried to estimate where the Joshuan forces would be by now, though he knew there was no way to predict the outcome of so many months' skirmishes and recalculations, retreats and advances, reformations and new deployments. But what was he to do with his time? They were not allowed books or games or entertainment of any sort. The only way he could tell it was afternoon was by a sharp sliver of light that made its way down the wall as the hour drew later. Midday passed with its hot rays, and then it was almost dusk. And so, watching Tozhin sleep and wishing mightily for some distraction from his gray prison walls, Marcik had nearly dozed off when the door to their cell crashed open and a rifle butt came down on his jaw.

※ ※ ※

He awoke in a room with a caged light bulb on the table before him, its cord running across the floor to a wall outlet. The bulb was glaringly bright yet somehow failed to illuminate the room. That, or his vision was still blurry from the blow. He moved his jaw to see if it was broken, found that it wasn't, and blinked several times to accustom his eyes to the odd lighting.

"Private Kovalski." It wasn't a question, but neither was it merely a statement. A man of medium build and wiry muscles leaned against the wall. There was something in his face, a professional calm, that made Marcik relax a little.

"Yes?" Marcik answered.

"Good," the man said. "I am sorry for the way my guards treated you earlier. I hope you'll believe me when I say to you that I ordered them only to bring you to this interview. I did not intend for them to harm you."

"Thank you," Marcik said and hated the peasant in his voice, thanking this man who was his captor—and for what? For having not been the man who nearly broke his skull? A dizziness came over him that made the world seem unreal, and gave him a brief sensation of sinking through the floor, but it left him as quickly as it had come on. *I might have a concussion.*

"I hope we can be friends," the man said. "I am Kommandant Olgar Fakuth. But, please, call me Olgar." Olgar smiled, raising small wrinkles on skin tanned and weathered from his mountain home in Ulan-Ude.

He must have been in his late thirties, Marcik could tell from the wrinkles, but when he wasn't smiling, the man looked barely out of university. He spoke Slovnik almost perfectly; most of these herd-fuckers mangled every other word they said, but this Olgar had nearly no accent and was completely comfortable speaking it, which further relaxed Marcik—though he knew this simply meant the man was more dangerous than the others. Idiots can hit you with a rifle butt, but intelligent men can do much worse.

Unlike most Ulani males, Olgar didn't have the usual tribal tattoos indicating herd ownership—at least not visible tattoos, anyway—and he didn't wear the leather armor or decorative animal skins his fellow Ulani soldiers did. Marcik didn't know what to make of all this, but he filed it away.

"Do you smoke?" Olgar asked and offered a cigarette which Marcik took perhaps too eagerly. Olgar lit Marcik's cigarette and continued, "So, Mr. Kovalski, you were picked up . . . "

". . . captured, you mean."

"If you like," Olgar said and shrugged as if the distinction were of no consequence in a conversation among friends. "You were captured along with half a dozen Joshuan invaders. One of them was Major Malcolm Schmidt."

※　※　※

Half a dozen. Marcik let the number sink in. In the dazed bloody aftermath of the battle, as he was shoved into the back of a military transport vehicle, he only knew that most of his kompany was dead. He remembered tripping as he climbed into the truck, falling on his ass right into the mud, and someone laughing at him. For all he knew it was his own laughter. He remembered the rucksack being taken from his back, its contents dumped unceremoniously on the ground: water, food, ammunition, but also the cigar box with all his mother's letters. *At least let me keep those.* But a boot kicked him hard and he fell again.

A long and bumpy ride. When he was not sleeping, he was staring at the opposite wall of the truck. He was wedged in between barrels of water and crates of food and other supplies—all of it once belonging to the Baikal Guard. Across from him were two Guardsmen, one badly injured and moaning. The other was Major Schmidt. Marcik's hopes sunk on seeing him. If Schmidt had been captured, then their whole kompany had been overtaken. Who would come to rescue them?

Speaking in rapid fluent-sounding Ulani, Major Schmidt addressed the enemy soldier in the back of the truck. He gestured at the barrels of water, at the wounded Guardsman.

The Ulani soldier shook his head. Major Schmidt muttered something. The soldier continued to shake his head. Major Schmidt reached over and patted the wounded Guardsman's hand. The Guardsman smiled back weakly.

"And how are you holding up, Private?" Major Schmidt asked Marcik.

"I'm all right," Marcik said, though his leg and head were throbbing. "Thank you, sir."

"You'd think they could spare a little water. We're surrounded by the stuff." Major Schmidt shook his head. "Not that it would make much difference now."

The Ulani soldier gestured angrily with his gun, speaking in Slovnik, "Quiet. No more talk."

The wounded Guardsman moaned and clutched at his side, where his uniform was soaked through with blood. Major Schmidt said nothing. Marcik said nothing. By the time they arrived at the prison, the Guardsman—who like so many others Marcik had never known properly—was dead.

※ ※ ※

"Major Schmidt's wounds are beyond the powers of our healer-scientists," Olgar said with no trace of emotion. "I thought you should know. I felt it was my duty to tell you myself—soldier to soldier. He is not yet dead, but he is in terrible suffering and, though he may continue on for a while, there is little hope of a recovery or his long-term survival."

Major Schmidt dying. Marcik was surprised to find how much his hopes had rested on the man. And if this prison could kill him, it could kill anyone. Schmidt had been young for a major. In the truck, Marcik had noticed a slight gash in Major Schmidt's leg, a trickle of blood running down his thigh. Shrapnel? But it had not appeared serious; Marcik's wounds had been equal if not worse. Still, if not properly treated even a minor wound could become infected. Tozhin could treat him, Marcik thought suddenly. But then he remembered Tozhin's words. *You're not the collaborator type, are you?* No, he was not. And he wouldn't ask that of Tozhin either. Tozhin might save Schmidt's life, if he was allowed to treat him at all. But it was just as likely that he would be beaten for not supplying the information earlier, and then forced to treat the Ulani guards while Schmidt slowly died.

Schmidt dying; the Guardsman in the truck dead. *So few of us left.* But might this not be an attempt by Olgar to crush his morale? Even the number—*half a dozen*—could not be believed. He had seen only a few of his fellow Guardsmen since his arrival. If others were indeed still alive, they were being kept in separate cell blocks.

"Thank you for telling me," Marcik said. "I am glad to see there is honor among your people."

"There is much honor among us," Olgar said. The light quiver in his voice softened Marcik's disposition toward him. "That will be all for today. And I hope you can forgive my men. War is ugly and soldiers sometimes perform their duties over-zealously."

Olgar tapped on the door and two guards entered and motioned for Marcik to rise. They both avoided eye contact with Olgar; their fear of him was palpable, and Marcik took pleasure in their discomfort.

Back in his cell, Marcik lay on his straw mattress and stared at the cement ceiling, trying to organize his thoughts. Tozhin groaned in the corner, rolled over, went back to sleep. Why had they brought Marcik into the interrogation room? What did they want from him? Merely to frighten him, most likely, at least for now. But sooner or later, they would want something. He swore that when the time came, he would not give it to them.

3.

ADRIAN SLEPT FITFULLY, worrying about the banditii and wondering who the newcomer was. More importantly, why was Heinrich so taken with the man? He had seen the two of them talking by the fire, Heinrich saying something and the hooded fellow—he wore a black robe like some sort of sinister priest—nodding wordlessly. What did Heinrich mean that things might be all right now that he had arrived? Despite the robe, it was impossible not to notice the man's composure: it was in the way he stood, at ease but alert; it was in the way he limited himself to just the necessary gestures. He must have been a soldier at some point. A mercenary? Adrian disliked the idea of mercenaries. To fight and kill was wrong, but to do so for one's city, to protect one's family and way of life, was at least somewhat defensible; but to fight for private gain, to kill for money—that was pure evil.

He wondered what Nikolas would think of that. They had never discussed mercenaries. He supposed Nikolas would have asked one of his annoying, though astute, questions: *Who has hired the mercenary and what is the outcome of the mercenary's efforts?* Nikolas would no doubt have argued that the mere act of selling one's services was ethically neutral; the outcome is what must be judged.

Let's take for example, Nikolas's voice said in Adrian's reverie, *a nunnery in need of defense. The nuns are incapable themselves. They hire mercenaries to defend their works and deeds. Could you condemn that act, Adrian, or are you so unbending in your dogma as to never see the human use of inhumane acts?*

Sure, Adrian thought, *in the example you give, I'd have to allow it. But, and here's the point, how often do mercenaries get hired for such noble tasks? Do they ever? I doubt either of us can recall a time in history when they were hired to protect children instead of kill them, and more nuns have been raped by mercenaries (likely offered as part of their payment) than have been protected.*

It seems your problem is not then with mercenaries, Nikolas continued, *but rather with the people who have the money to hire them. Your problem is one of class struggle. But if I could raise enough money to hire mercenaries to kill those who exploit young girls in the houses of flesh, or those who use the mayor's office not to represent the people of Joshua City but rather the militaristic and corporate interests who enslave us, I certainly would. And what's more, I'd be morally right to do so.*

Adrian let the imagined argument trail off, the voice of his friend floating out of his mind, and pondered, vaguely, whether murder was ever morally justified. In their debates, Nikolas almost always won, using one variation or another of the utilitarian argument on him—that reducing the bad and increasing the good, by any means necessary, was justified. But Adrian couldn't help wondering whether the means justified the ends just as much as the ends justified the means. How can the two be so neatly separated? The basic premises were undeniable, that more good and less bad in the world was desirable, but Adrian could not accept that even small evils could ever be good, or that there were degrees of debasement. Adrian's thoughts went on in this fashion until he slipped back into an unrestful sleep. A few hours later, when the noise of Heinrich organizing the karavan woke him, Adrian felt he had hardly slept at all.

※ ※ ※

The karavan rolled on into the desert, every curve and shrub-smattered hill taking them farther from familiar land, into a place he seemed to know from dreams or some form of hub-thought. It was an ancient world out here, both better and worse for being largely untouched by human influence—brutal yet rawly beautiful. *This is why Saint Dartok said all wise-men must go forth into the desert to gain divine wisdom,* Adrian thought.

They began to rise and the air turned colder. They traveled into a bracing wind, like fish swimming against the stream to their place of death, or perhaps rebirth; yes, there was life in this wind, a smell of grassy distance and cleanness. Several kilometers in front of them rose snowy mountain passes. He remembered the first time it had snowed at the orphanage. He had watched out the window until Sister Amelia, the harshest of the nuns, made him lie back down. He complied but could still see the falling snowflakes through a sliver of window above and adjacent to his bed. He watched well into the night, with quick-blooded excitement much like he felt now. The next morning he was dismayed to see men from the Municipal Waterworks outside the orphanage with giant vacuum machines, scooping up the white mounds to be purified as potable water.

Heinrich must have noticed his amazement. "Them mountains— the Kihl Mihnor Peaks, they're called—stand in the way of where you're going," he said. "You'll be seeing enough of them soon."

"You mean we have to cross over them?"

"Hope you brought something warm to dress yourself in."

Adrian thought about the contents of his bag; he had been advised by the internship materials to plan for unexpectedly cold weather in the desert at night. Already this proved to be sound advice. The nights were so chilling that he always woke a little sorer than when he had gone to bed.

"Will we be in the mountains long?"

"Not if I can help it," Heinrich said. "The mountains are lousy with banditii. A wise man runs from danger," he said, and nodding toward the back, in a softer voice he added, "even with our new passenger."

Adrian looked back into the karavan where Heinrich had set up the stranger. He had thrown back his hood, and for the first time Adrian saw his face. It was, in its way, handsome—scruffy and square, with dark eyes; but there was something a little worn, a little uneasy, a little stricken even, that made Adrian avoid eye contact.

"Is he . . ." He debated how to say it. It was a word he had only heard in whispers or bawdily violent films from Silverville—so much so that he often wondered whether it was not all a myth: ". . . a Messenger?"

Heinrich gave him a brutal look, dropping all pretense of civilization from his face. "What are you doing?" he said in a hiss. "Aiming to get us killed?"

Adrian shrank back in his seat, half-expecting a blow that never came.

%% %% %%

The rest of the afternoon, Adrian watched the driver out of the corner of his eye, the way he worked the blackroot in his tense jaw, and was relieved to see him gradually relax. Still, he felt it best not to say anything for now: Heinrich reminded Adrian of a caged animal—seemingly harmless, but liable to lash out if provoked.

But Adrian couldn't stop thinking about the man behind him. He was positive now that his guess had been right; he was no ordinary mercenary. Adrian had heard the rumors—*the best fighters on the planet, unstoppable gods of violence*—and to judge the man, these rumors were more than the talk of foolish children.

%% %% %%

Later that evening, he was warming himself by the fire when the man approached him. He gave a curt nod and Adrian nodded back, unsure of what to say. The flames of the fire jumped and crackled, pieces of burning tinder catching the wind and taking flight into the starry air.

He removed his hood. "You've been asking questions."

"I meant no offense," Adrian apologized. "I just wanted to know what a Messenger is."

The man studied him. Then he smiled, a slow and knowing smile. "What do you want to know?"

Adrian divined something of the casual assassin about the man. He could kill without remorse, likely had many times in the past and would again in the future. But there was something more about him as well—

something noble, regal even. Adrian began to understand Heinrich's relief at this man's arrival. It was all but impossible to imagine him lying on the ground in defeat.

"What do you want to know about the Brotherhood of Messenger?"

Suddenly Adrian couldn't bring himself to ask. "It's none of my concern," he said. "I apologize again ... Truly sorry ... I should be getting to bed."

Adrian began walking back to his tent, but the man's hard voice stopped him. He was scarcely more than a shadow in the light of the campfire.

"Adrian," he said. "It is Adrian, isn't it?"

"Yes."

"It's Messenger," he said.

"What?"

"Not *a* Messenger, not *the* Messenger," he said. "One Messenger. Two Messenger. We don't distinguish ourselves the same as others do. Messenger wouldn't have been angry that you asked about us—that's natural. But next time remember: it's just *Messenger*."

Messenger walked away without another word.

4.

EACH DAY THE ZEKS—as the prisoners were called—were allowed a half hour of exercise outside. The prison yard was a fenced-in area about thirty meters in each direction. There was not much in the yard besides some dirt and rocks, a few straggling weeds. The prisoners either stood in small groups or walked laps around the yard; occasionally they created weights from chunks of cement, which the guards allowed indifferently. But the guards watched the zeks closely to make sure they didn't get too close to the fence or congregate in overly large numbers. There were only two guards, and the thirty zeks allowed outside at a time could have easily overtaken them had they banded together. However, such an alliance seemed unlikely. As paltry as it was, the prisoners looked forward to their half hour in the yard as though it were a release order. Their captors used this fact to great effect. It was useful punishment to deny the half hour to individual prisoners, but what proved even more useful was to punish an entire cell block by denying that luxurious half hour due to the actions of one zek. This led to immediate ostracizing, and occasionally the zek in question was beaten by his fellow inmates. Marcik had seen one disobedient zek's face pulped beyond recognition—and not by the guards. It was another zek, encouraged by the whistles and shouts of his caged cohorts. The guards didn't exactly let it happen, but they didn't stop it until after the damage was done. The attacker was punished, of course, though not severely. His victim was carried unconscious to the infirmary.

Marcik had to give it to these Ulani bastards; they knew their ugly business well. By singling out certain zeks for greater torture and others for special treatment, they prevented any serious solidarity from emerging among them. Even the name they were given, *zeks*, kept them from admitting what they were. They were prisoners being held against inter-municipal treaties. And the zeks—even Marcik himself had taken to using the term—had internalized the language of their captors, calling themselves by the slur. Indeed, the Ulani guards knew their ugly business well.

Because Marcik did not know anyone in his cell block besides Tozhin, who was now too weak to come outside, he kept to himself in the prison yard. In the southeast corner, if you craned your neck just a bit, you could see between buildings into the wide desert. Sun-heated rocks and purplish thistle spread out for uncountable kilometers. The desert's lack of vegetation, which might have under other circumstances seemed boring or barren, represented a majestic freedom. Just one quick slip past the guards, a nimble climb over the fence, and a man could disappear forever, become a ghost of his prison self.

Every day, Marcik crossed the yard to this spot where he would stand sullen and captivated, taking in the scene. He wondered if others had noticed it. He never had anyone join him in this particular corner of the yard. And he dared not linger too long in the same spot, for fear that the guards would get suspicious. Nor did he dare mention it to anyone—not even Tozhin—out of fear that the guards would get wind of this pleasure of his and use it as leverage against him. Thus even his greatest joy become an element of his torture; its mere existence gave rise to the fear that it would be taken away, and that fear gave rise to his unwillingness to share it with others, increasing his already substantial loneliness. Maybe the guards didn't need to worry about the idle chatter in the prison yard; it was so hard to trust anyone that there was little danger of zeks conspiring.

But other zeks had made alliances. One of the larger groups congregated around a tall, heavily muscled zek named Karkov. There was something heartening and frightening about the handsome pocked wreckage of his face. A Guardsman of middle rank, he had been captured and brought to this prison several months before Marcik's arrival. During that time, due to his strength and total lack of fear, he had become what was called an *oberzek*, one of the prisoners chosen to aid in the daily running of the prison, for extra rations and other special treatments of course. Even the guards seemed to like him—or at least to respect him more than the other prisoners. And as far as oberzeks went, Marcik had to admit that Kharkov was a good one, not needlessly cruel as many of them were.

Marcik had considered joining his group but could never find the proper excuse. And Kharkov was not a man you wanted to bother unnecessarily.

※ ※ ※

But the worst part of prison life wasn't the way the zeks were pitted against each other. Nor was it being caged like an animal, nor the meager soup they ate, nor even the interrogation sessions that were getting more violent with each passing day. No, none of that. It was the latrine. Marcik's captors had set up a long metal trough, used for both urination and defecation. Men lined up without privacy or courtesy and stood or squatted over the trough's metal lip. They were taken in small groups, three times a day. The cells were equipped with simple metal buckets that could be dumped into the trough when latrine-call came around. The waste built up as the men relieved themselves and emptied their buckets. To conserve water, the trough was only flushed out once or twice a day; a rush of water would wash all of it down the trough and into a large hole, about two meters wide, and the sewage would make its way through an aluminum tunnel and out of the prison.

Every time Marcik stood or squatted before that trough, he felt all human dignity leave him. The men beside him became mere beasts squeezing out the waste of their bodies. If he knew the men sent to the latrine with him, he took pains not to look any of them in the eye. And they did the same. Somehow, under such circumstances, acknowledging the squatting animal beside you as a person was all but impossible. And this was the final reason why the latrine was the worst part of his imprisonment. The stench, the gut-stripping vileness of the place, yes, that was horrible, but a million times worse was the reduction of men to beasts.

He wanted out of this place so badly. His entire existence raged against his situation, but that rage made him feel all the more impotent. He tried to calm himself, knowing that keeping his sanity and maybe getting out of this prison required a cool head, a cold heart. He breathed out deeply and closed his eyes.

I am going to kill you, he thought, with no one particular in mind.

※ ※ ※

Meanwhile, Tozhin was not doing well. He sweated; his teeth chattered; he moaned like an unhappy specter in his sleep. He could barely keep down his food. Marcik spooned the thin gruel into his mouth and Tozhin thanked him with a touch of his clammy hand on Marcik's arm. He tried to speak, but Marcik hushed him. He gave Tozhin his own thin blanket and spent the night shivering with his arms tucked into the sleeves of his prison uniform.

When the guard brought them breakfast, Marcik banged on the cell door and shouted through the slot. "There's a sick man in here. He needs help."

The guard pushed the tray through the slot, banged the slot shut, and left without a word.

In the afternoon, when it came time to go to the yard, Marcik pointed at Tozhin, crumpled like a rag on the cell's floor.

"Please. I think he's dying."

"Do you want to go outside or not?" the guard said.

Marcik had to admit that, yes, he did want to go outside. He wanted that very much. He looked regretfully at Tozhin. If the guards wouldn't listen to him, what could he do? He would try again when they led him back to the cell.

⁓ ⁓ ⁓

That night Tozhin died. Marcik kicked the door of the cell. He yelled until his voice was hoarse. He cursed his captors, called them every name he could think of. He did not care if they beat him, so long as they came. The dark became a wan glow, became dawn, became morning. Two trays of food came through the slot in the door.

"There's a dead man in here," Marcik said, his voice weak from screaming and lack of sleep.

The slot banged closed. Minutes passed. Marcik ate his own food and set to devouring the extra tray of food, hating himself but unable to stop.

The metal on metal rasp of a bolt being slid back: the door opened. Two guards strode in. One shoved Marcik against the wall. Marcik was able to turn his head enough to see the other guard checking Tozhin's pulse. A third guard entered with a gurney. They loaded Tozhin onto the gurney while the other guard watched Marcik. They tossed a sheet over the corpse—that's what it was now—and carried it from the cell. The bolts clanked shut and Marcik was alone.

⁒ ⁒ ⁒

But not for long. After their half hour in the yard later that day, another prisoner was led to Marcik's cell and thrust inside.

Marcik had noticed him in the yard before. Like Marcik, he kept to himself, but nonetheless he radiated an intelligence that made him stand out from the other civilian prisoners—because it was obvious from his physique and demeanor he was a civilian. He was a thin man with a shuffling walk and a squinty way of looking at his surroundings. He had a pair of glasses, hopelessly broken—by the guards, no doubt—which he kept in the pocket of his loose-hanging prison shirt. He would occasionally lift the glasses to his face to see something, pinching the frames to keep the cracked lenses from falling out. Despite his outward frailties, he maintained a quiet dignity any Guardsman could admire.

Now he walked the cell slowly, examining the cracks in the walls, the tiny barred window, the dirty pallets on the floor, as if these objects might reveal some crucial detail. He touched Tozhin's pallet with his foot.

"I suppose this is where I'll be sleeping," he said. "On a dead man's pallet."

"How did you . . . ?"

"It doesn't take much deduction to figure out. You've been here for more than a month. I've seen you in the yard. And suddenly you get a new cellmate?"

"What happened to yours?"

The man shrugged. "Same as you. The guards."

"How do you know I didn't kill mine?"

"I suppose anything's possible, within the laws of physics of course," the man said. "Still, you don't strike me as the type. I see you in the prison yard, looking out on that little stretch of freedom. You don't want to kill anyone."

Marcik was both thrilled and dismayed that someone knew about his secret spot in the yard.

"What do I want, then?"

The man sat on Tozhin's pallet.

"Same thing I want. Only I think it's best not to say it out loud. By the way," he added, waving his hand in a casually dismissive gesture, "I'm Jürgen Moritz. I always forget that part."

5.

THEY WERE GOING to make the mountain pass today, Heinrich explained to Adrian over their midday meal of stale oat-bread and flavorless tea, and it would not be wise to be caught there after dark. The banditii preferred the mountain trails. On these thin and treacherous paths, the karavan was utterly exposed. As they ascended, the juniper and sage of the desert plain gave way to firs and elms, and Adrian was surprised to hear moving water in the distance.

"Snowmelt, my boy," Heinrich said. "Them mountains trap the moisture from the clouds. Ring 'em like a washrag."

Adrian looked up at the sky, which was indeed clouded over, but they were crisp clouds and flat, not entirely unpolluted, but nothing like the ones that scudded above Joshua City. Farther up the trail, fog rolled between the low piney branches. It was amazing to think that in Joshua City there was water rationing due to the nekrosis contamination, yet here there was such unspoiled bounty.

"I know people who would kill for this."

Heinrich grinned. "Ay," he said. "I know some who have."

Adrian gave him his curious skolar's look.

"The banditii," Heinrich explained. "They make camp around these parts."

Heinrich had mentioned the banditii several times, and Adrian was beginning to think that he enjoyed watching him squirm.

"I hear you talked to Hank," Heinrich said.

"Hank?"

Heinrich nodded toward the back, where the Messenger—no, where *Messenger*—appeared to be sleeping. The way his arm gripped something (a knife? a gun?) under his robe, however, told Adrian he was very

much awake. He wondered if the man ever slept: he had been staring at
the fire when Adrian left him the night before, and he was staring at it
the next morning when Adrian woke.

"Not his given name, mind ya," Heinrich said. "They don't have
names. They give 'em up when they join. Hank's just what I call him—
but don't you go telling him that."

"Of course not."

The murmur of the water became a steady hum, and finally, a roar.
They rounded a corner and a white frigid-looking river spilled into
view, crashing between rocky banks. There was a bridge in the road before them, a narrow rickety-looking thing of waterlogged wood. Whole
navies of fish swam beneath the clear blue-white water. The light from
the immense sky above this juncture between desert and mountain
was glareless and gave every object God's own justice. Adrian wished
suddenly he were a motion-image artist and that he might capture this
most unlikely of locations. If only they would use their art for this, Adrian thought, maybe mankind would be in a better state. Maybe if someone could show Joshuans this kind overwhelming beauty and—Adrian searched for the right word—this *majesty*, they might call off the
hounds of war and seek a peaceful solution. Perhaps . . . but then again,
some souls are encased in obsidian and will not be penetrated except
by an obsidian spear.

Heinrich kept looking in his mirror. "You have what I gave you?"

Adrian started to pull out the knife, eager to give it back, but Heinrich shook his head.

"Just you be ready," he said. He nodded toward the cab of the truck,
where Messenger sat. "He will be, too," he said, "yet he's only one man.
And the bridge is perfect for an ambush."

They nosed up onto the bridge. As it took their weight, the boards
creaked and sagged, so that Adrian was more worried about plunging
into the gulf than banditii in the forest. He had always been a coward
when it came to heights; even sitting on a balcony could put him in a
spinning terror. Worse yet, though, was watching others tempt fate. He

clenched his hands into sweaty fists, fingernails digging into the skin on his palms. He looked back to the cab, at the tense faces there, and Yves met his eyes and smiled reassuringly. She held her youngest on her lap; though she rocked and sang to her, the baby continued its red-faced howling. *He'll protect you*, Adrian thought, hoping that she would somehow get the message.

The car bucked and Adrian was thrown against the passenger door. They were halfway across the bridge, at the most dangerous point. But when he looked over, Heinrich was grinning. "Thought the banditii had got us, did ya?"

"Will it take our weight?"

"I've passed over this bridge many times," Heinrich said. "Today won't be the day she gives."

They rolled on, one painstaking meter at a time. Underneath the wheels, old wood groaned precariously. The truck lurched again and for a sick second, they were falling. There were a few cries from the back of the truck. When the bridge stopped swaying, Adrian leaned out of the window and looked toward the back of the truck. Just behind the back tire, a board hung split and swinging by a frayed cable. It swung back and forth, once, twice—with the patient regularity of a pendulum—and then fell into the river, where it was swallowed.

"Them boards break all the time," Heinrich said. "Someone will fix it."

They were nearly at the other shore of this abyss when something came crashing through the underbrush just beyond the bridge's edge. Heinrich stopped the truck and threw it into reverse, ready to recross the bridge backwards. He grabbed his pistol from under his seat. Adrian fumbled for his knife, but his sweaty fingers could not undo the latch of the sheath.

Heinrich relaxed. At the edge of the woods, standing mesmerized by the karavan, was a thin and haggard-looking mountain goat. It watched them curiously for a moment, then lowered its head to nibble some grass. Heinrich laughed from deep in his belly.

"He's a dangerous fellow, a'right."

Adrian let go of the knife, which had never made it out of its sheath.

The truck eased onto firm ground, and after the rest had made it across, Heinrich pulled to a stop. "We'll make camp here," he called out to the people in the back.

※ ※ ※

A while later, Adrian sat warming a can of beans over a puny fire. It was cold up here, and the wind cut at hard angles, fanning the flames, but also nearly putting them out. Even Heinrich had struggled to light a fire in these conditions. Adrian rubbed his hands together and held them over the bits of burning cedar and pine needles, but there wasn't much heat. To think that people lived, and maybe even flourished, up here. What was that quote from the *Book of the Before-Time*? Adrian had learned it in a class at St. Ignatius's and still loved it to this day. He searched his mind for the exact phrasing, wanting for some reason to get it completely right. *A human is a creature that can by dint of its ever-mutable soul grow accustomed to any circumstance.* Yes, that was it—and how true it was.

Beside the truck, Yves nursed her baby, whom she had wrapped in her own coat. Her shirt was thin and partially unbuttoned for nursing, and Adrian could tell by her huddled rocking that she was cold. Her husband was setting up his family's tent; the family tended to keep to themselves, not sharing in the dancing, game playing, or the casual conversation that took place at night. Even Heinrich mostly stayed out of their way—whether from courtesy or for some other reason, it was difficult to say. Jarir went about the construction of the tent silently, making sure its entrance faced west in the Al-Khuziri way. The Al-Khuziri called themselves the People of the Sun; at set intervals throughout the day, they prayed toward the west, facing toward what they called the Evening Lands—those fabled lands to the west many believed no longer existed, having been destroyed in The Great Calamity. Al-Khuziri temples had specially designed windows that used sunlight to spell out the name of their god on the temple floor; this name was otherwise never to be uttered or written by human hand. In their houses, they hung curtains that imitated the effect of the temple windows. Jarir now hung one of these multicolored and beautifully woven curtains on his family's tent.

Adrian took off his jacket and brought it to the woman.

"Here," he said. "You need it more than I do."

She looked to her husband, who was coming out of their tent.

"I can't accept that."

"Nonsense," Adrian said. "I want you to have it."

Jarir approached them with quick steps. He grabbed the jacket out of Adrian's hands. He slapped his wife lightly in the face. Then he turned to Adrian. "You have no business with my wife."

"But she is cold. Can't you see that?"

"My property is not your concern."

Property. Adrian looked into Jarir's unblinking eyes. "She's holding your child, for God's sake."

"I warn you, it is best for you to leave us be," Jarir said as he reached his hand behind his back.

Adrian remembered the knife Heinrich had given him and took two steps back, pulling it awkwardly free from its sheath. His opponent bent his knees and assumed the stance of a knowing fighter. A small curved blade was in his hand, though Adrian hadn't seen him pull it out. Adrian's own weapon was more than twice the size, but Jarir showed no fear. If anything, he seemed as bemused as he was angry. Adrian's leg shook from adrenaline and fear. What was he thinking to have drawn a weapon? Why had he been so rude to this stranger? He took another step back.

By now a small group of karavan members were gathering around, and at first Adrian thought they would intervene, but they just watched, as if they were at a motion-image theatre enthralled by the newest product of Silverville.

Jarir took a small cautious step toward Adrian, then a larger one. Adrian thrust his knife out in the air before him, slashed a few wild diagonals, and moved back, though he was running out of room; the crowd had circled around them, containing them like an arena. They wanted this fight to happen, needed it in some primal way, which scared Adrian almost as much as Jarir's graceful maneuvering. Even Heinrich did not interfere, though he wasn't cheering them on like the others.

Adrian was certain he was going to die and wanted to fall on the ground and simply cry, but he forced himself to stay standing. He deserved this for being so stupid. Coming out to the desert was a mistake, a decision made by a naive child. And confronting this man about his wife was equally stupid. He hated himself for throwing his life away, hated the ease with which he had preached sacrifice. This is what sacrifice comes to, death, and he did not want to die. He slashed the air again and bent his legs, trying to mimic Jarir's fighting stance. He grew angry with this man and the irreversible absurdity of the situation they were in, which gave him a sudden strength. Jarir noticed the difference and slowed his approach, though he was still coming.

Adrian heard chatter behind him and to the left, but he dared not turn to see what the commotion was about. If he did, he knew, he would be dead. Jarir's face tensed, and Adrian braced himself for the plunge of metal into his flesh. Then he heard the sound of bone breaking and a heavy thump, but he felt no pain and hadn't seen Jarir move.

"Traveler, unless you want to make your children orphans, you will apologize now and walk away."

It was Messenger, and on the ground at his feet was the corpse of the wiry goat they had passed earlier; its spine was broken, twisting the creature at an unnatural angle. He expected Messenger to have a weapon in hand, but he was standing calmly, unarmed, merely staring at Jarir, whose face was twisted up with indecision.

"This offer will not be repeated."

Jarir put his blade away.

"I am sorry to you, sir," he muttered to Adrian. He must have seen Messenger glaring at him, because his tone suddenly became more contrite. "I pray to the Evening Lands that your heart is generous enough to forgive me."

Adrian couldn't speak, so he nodded affirmation and made his lips turn up in something resembling a smile, and Jarir bowed to him, then to Messenger, and returned to his cooking, trying to pretend nothing had happened.

Messenger looked to Adrian and nodded as if communicating weighty knowledge, but Adrian didn't understand anything that had happened. He stared dumbly as Messenger grabbed the goat's front two ankles in one large hand and slung the poor dead beast over his shoulder and walked toward a cooking fire on the other side of camp. The ribs of the goat showed through its meager flesh and Adrian felt sad for such a creature to have to live as it had, out here in the unwelcoming desert, and then for it to die to nourish the likes of him and Jarir and the other members of the karavan, who were still murmuring as they filed away from what was nearly the scene of his murder.

6.

OVER THE NEXT SEVERAL DAYS, Marcik learned more about his cellmate. Jürgen was reluctant to talk about his past, and Marcik supposed he understood. He tried not to pry overmuch. But some things came up on their own. Early one morning, the guards took Jürgen out of his cell. When he came back, he wasn't wearing the new bruises Marcik had expected, but there were spots of brown muck on his prisoner's uniform and he stank horribly.

"They had me repairing their sewage pump," Jürgen said. "In my old life, I was an engineer."

Marcik nodded.

"I'm surprised you haven't heard of me," Jürgen said. "But I suppose with the war..."

"Yes," Marcik said. "We didn't get much news from Joshua City."

"Anyway, that part of my life is done. These days I only make the occasional simple repair. At first I tried to refuse. But you know what happens when you refuse them something they want." He tapped meaningfully on the broken glasses he carried in his pocket. "Finally, I decided, *What's the point*? Am I gaining anyone anything by refusing to fix one of their supply trucks? Also, I've learned a lot of valuable things by playing along."

"How so?"

"Well, you see, I may have picked up a bit of Ulani here and there," Jürgen said coyly. "Only they don't know that. You'd be surprised the kind of things they'll say if they think you can't understand them."

"Like what?"

"Oh, it's mostly pointless chatter. Bickering, talk about their wives back home. Who's the best herdsman. But I've also heard details about the quantities of shipments and where they keep certain supplies, how the war is going, who is killing whom. Which brings me to another point: how many guards have you counted in the yard?"

"I haven't been counting."

"And why not?" Jürgen asked, as if scolding a child. "All right, what you need to do, and I'll do it as well, is begin taking note of every guard, no matter how insignificant, and let's ascertain the number we are dealing with. Based on little things I've overheard, I think they keep us separated because there are many more of us than there are of them. If we could find a way to band together, we could overtake them easily."

Marcik nodded. Maybe the enemy was stretched so thin this facility was dangerously understaffed. He let himself hope. *They likely need most of their able-bodied men for their war effort*, he thought. And seeing so few men between him and Olgar was reassuring. Just having a plan of action, a strategy, a soldier's task of determining how many guards there were, lifted Marcik's spirits immeasurably; but it was necessary to appear beaten, hopeless.

After that talk, life went back to its boring and occasionally brutal ways. They did not discuss their plan any further, if you could call it a plan. It was prison life and nothing more. There was only the half hour of exercise to look forward to. And the daydreams of prisoners should not be considered plans for a real escape but rather an escape into possibility.

%% %% %%

A few days later, on his way back from his half hour in the yard, Marcik was escorted into the interrogation room where he had met with Olgar. He was not permitted to return to his cell first, nor was he permitted to use the latrine before entering the room, though given the vileness of the latrine, this did not at first seem like a punishment.

"Kommandant Olgar will decide where you will go and when," said a smallish man whose face was pocked with what Marcik assumed were shrapnel scars. There were dozens of cuts ranging from half a centimeter to the full length of his cheek. Along his arms were the herd-tattoos of the Ulani people, but many of them were rendered illegible by heavy burn scars. The zeks called him Face. Marcik had never heard his real name spoken.

"Yes, sir," Marcik said, making a show of his willingness to cooperate. Face was known for his outbursts, which often included beating the zeks so badly it took weeks to recover; or maybe he would deny an insubordinate man dinner for a full week, which could prove to be a death sentence. Despite not being a large man, he was intimidating, and you knew within seconds of encountering him that he was a connoisseur of pain, an enthusiast for violence. It was rumored that Face had decorated his sleeping quarters with the skin and bones of the men he had killed in battle. Marcik did not want to know what other methods of torture lurked inside Face's mind; his outer ugliness seemed like a pale manifestation of his inner cruelty.

As Face shoved him into the interrogation room, Marcik heard a loud sharp noise like a bugle calling reveille from deep within the compound. He had never heard it before and wondered what it might be. Something in its high tinny sound made him feel it couldn't be good. He imagined his fellow zeks lined up for a degrading inspektion or something worse. Marcik had this image in mind when the door opened and Olgar marched in.

Normally Olgar was an unhurried man. He took his time with everything, careful and observant in even the minutest of tasks. But not today. In two long strides, he was beside Marcik, his hand moving so fast Marcik barely saw it before it slammed into the side of his head. Marcik thought he was going to black out, Olgar had hit him so hard. He looked up, foggy with pain and surprise. He had known all along that Olgar was likely the most menacing of the Ulanis here, but he never expected direct violence from him. That would be left to others.

Marcik also knew this change in demeanor, while partially staged and meant to increase his misery, was borne from panic on Olgar's part. Something was happening. He needed something, and he was being pressured to get it in less time than he had previously been allotted. Marcik didn't know what kind of attitude to take—submissive or dignified? Each had its advantages and dangers, but he was so thrown by Olgar's sudden violence and by the pain and fear that now filled him that he sat, looking dumbly at his tormenter and rubbing his head.

"Is there another Joshuan regiment on the way to this region, Private Kovalski?"

"I don't know," Marcik said. "They don't entrust privates with military tactics."

Olgar punched him squarely and powerfully in the mouth. Blood ran from Marcik's split lip.

"What are you made of?" Olgar said, his voice a barely constrained scream.

Marcik let the blood accumulate in his mouth, tasting its mineral warmth, and then spat onto the floor. He knew it was a bad idea—reckless at best—to antagonize a man who held so much power over him. But he thought of Tozhin and he could not help himself; he felt that surge of anger and he gave into it.

"Where are your tattoos?" he asked.

"I will ask the questions here."

"Your herd-tattoos," Marcik continued. "Where are they? Don't you own any cattle?"

Olgar grabbed Marcik's wrist. He slammed Marcik's arm down on the table.

"Answer me," he said. "Are there more Guardsmen on the way?"

Olgar seized one of Marcik's fingers and yanked it up and back. The bone bent backwards with a dry complex crunch. Marcik bit down on his tongue to stifle a moan of pain.

"No sheep either?" Marcik said. "Who do you fuck when you get lonely?"

Olgar snapped another finger up and back. The pain was neither less nor more than the first time.

"Is that why you're here?" Marcik said. "Too poor to be the big chieftain back home?"

"Answer me."

Olgar broke another finger. The pain seared through Marcik's mangled hand. *I can take this*, he realized.

He stared into Olgar's eyes and waited for a further crunch of bone.

Olgar released his wrist. Marcik let his hand lie on the table.

"You're an interesting man, Mr. Kovalski," Olgar said.

"I could say the same for you," Marcik managed to say.

"I apologize if I've hurt you too badly," Olgar said. "I'll have you taken back to your cell now."

It was not until he was back in his cell that Marcik realized he had never given Olgar his answer. It was a pathetic victory, to be sure. And one that had cost him in pain. Nevertheless, he smiled a dim smile as he clutched his poorly bandaged hand. He did not realize it, but it was the first time he had smiled since his capture.

※ ※ ※

Olgar Fakuth, kommandant-warden of Gaal-Inhoff Prison Outpost, stormed down the hall. Oberlieutenant Lotar, his second-in-kommand, whom all the zeks called Face, followed Fakuth at a respectable distance. It was best not to get too close when he was angry like this. Olgar was not quick to anger. Among the Ulani guards at the prison, he was something of an oddity. It wasn't just that he lacked the tattoos typical of their people, or that he kept the walls of his sleeping quarters free of the skins of his enemies. It was his cold and calculating manner. When Olgar became angry, there was a purpose behind it, which made him all the more deadly.

And he had every right to be angry. One of their guards had been killed that morning during the attempted escape by a zek, a piece of Kazhstani scum named Samir Hosani. Lotar had taken it upon himself to beat the prisoner within an inch of his life, but that had not brought back the dead guard. Sublieutenant Gudrik had been a brave herdsman, and Lotar had liked him as much as he was capable of liking anyone. Lotar had wanted to kill the zek immediately, but Kommandant Fakuth said they needed to make an example of him instead.

"I want our men together right now," Fakuth said now.

"Yes, Kommandant." That would leave the prison dangerously un-guarded for however long this meeting took. But Lotar knew better than to question an order.

Lotar went to the latrines and to the prison yard and to the various spots in the halls of the prison where their guards were positioned. He instructed the other guards to take all prisoners back to their cells. Last-ly, he went to the armory, where he found First Ensign Ingvar asleep at his watch.

He slapped Ingvar in the back of the head. "Rise, First Ensign."

Ignvar leapt to his feet and saluted. "I was . . . "

"Derelict in your duties? And after everything that happened this morning? Come on. The Kommandant wants to meet with us."

Ingvar straightened his uniform and scuttled after Lotar.

When they were all assembled, Kommandant Fakuth addressed them. "As you know, Sublieutenant Gudrik was killed this morning. This is unacceptable. A prisoner was allowed to not only escape the yard but to fashion a knife with which to stab Gudrik. Where did he get the metal from? It does not matter. The point is that we've not been vigilant enough in our watch over these prisoners."

Ingvar stiffened uncomfortably and stood a little straighter. He wouldn't be sleeping on the job again, Lotar knew that. Not if he valued his physical wellbeing.

"Kommandant?" one of the men, another Ensign named Ottar, asked. "Will we be receiving someone to replace Gudrik?"

"I've written to the brigade-general. He *might* send a man, if we're lucky."

"We don't have enough men as it is."

Lotar winced. Ottar had balls as big as an ox, but roughly the common sense of one too.

However, Fakuth surprised him. He simply sighed and perched himself on a desk in the room.

"I'm aware of that," he said. "Believe me. And I've written over and over requesting more men. The response is always the same. *We cannot spare any men at this time.* It's a difficult situation and perhaps it will be remedied when an alliance with Al-Khuzir is finalized. Until that time, we must make do with what we have. And the way we do that is to be more vigilant. As always, I welcome your ideas for how best to employ the resources we do have."

※ ※ ※

Indicating Marcik's hand, Jürgen said, "What happened there?"

"I didn't tell them what they wanted."

"Is that all?"

A fleeting smile of pride went across Marcik's face. "I might have offended his Ulani pride." Despite the pain, his smile grew larger.

"That was foolish," Jürgen said. "There is no utility in antagonizing them."

"But there is use in collaborating with the enemy," Marcik shot back, "as you know all too well."

Jürgen's face clenched, but he simply lay down on this bunk, saying nothing for the rest of the evening.

Marcik massaged his hand through the simple bandages the Ulanis had wrapped his broken fingers in. He played his words to Olgar over and over, savoring them more each time.

7.

AFTER THEIR CONFLICT, Adrian tried to stay out of Jarir's path and ignored his family. They reached the highest point of the mountains without much difficulty and they passed over and began their descent. The land opened out before them and a vast rolling steppe stretched out into an incalculable distance, the sky brittle and clear and the horizon showing the curve of the earth. Again, Adrian was stunned by the immensity of existence, and he thought that coming all this way had been worth it. If he was fated to die out here, at least he would die having seen something outside of Joshua City, which is more than many could say. Heinrich also seemed, if not overawed at the landscape's beauty, at least grateful to be leaving the mountains.

"See them red hills up ahead, lad?"

Adrian squinted, but his eyes were not as keen as Heinrich's. The man seemed to have no physical weakness, and not for the first time, Adrian cursed his own frail body. "I think so," Adrian lied.

"That's New Kolyma," Heinrich said. "Your stop."

"And you? Will you travel much farther?"

"Just a mite more," he said. He chuckled a little. "After I drop your new friend and his family off and get you to your destination, we'll be heading all the way to the blackroot fields of Baikyong-do for some of the best product Joshua City has ever seen."

Adrian didn't let himself judge Heinrich for this. Instead, he glanced back to Jarir and Yves. The baby was crying and she stroked its forehead. Jarir was holding his wife's free hand.

"He's no friend of mine," Adrian said.

Adrian had never allowed himself to feel much anger, and now he was surprised and a little dismayed to find that a part of him liked the sensation. What other emotions had he shut off out of a need to see himself as good? *But that man is an animal,* Adrian told himself, enjoying the uncharitable thought.

That night the woman's baby began crying as Adrian was just about to drift off to sleep. The high-pitched bell of her voice woke Adrian completely. They should not have brought an infant along with them. Out here? What kind of parents would do such a thing? It was unfair to all of them, the baby and everyone else in the karavan. Adrian reprimanded himself for thinking this way. He rolled over and breathed out deeply, trying to ignore the hot cries of the baby. He laid his arm over his exposed ear, but to no effect. He hummed the Day of Joshua hymn, recited verses from the *Book of the Before-Time*; but finally he sat up and looked into the distance where a million stars were dusting the sky. He tried to identify as many constellations by name as he could, but they never looked like what they were supposed to. As a child, his favorite had been the Harbinger. There it was.

The image of a kneeling man at a scaffold. The Harbinger was about to be beheaded. The image had always possesed a very specific meaning for Adrian: we must suffer, even die, to save the world. Finding the constellation calmed him to the core of his being, as though it were an old friend and a guide into his new life. But suddenly he wasn't sure. What if he had chosen the wrong idea to give his life to? It was so difficult to know what God wanted; He kept so maddeningly silent about everything.

But there were some, like his old classmate Alyosha Prelevski, who seemed to have a direct link with God.

※ ※ ※

It wasn't until Adrian had graduated from primary at Saint Ignatius's that he met Alyosha. He had very few friends in primary school and even fewer now. It was lunchtime and all the boys were crowded noisily in the dining hall. The clattering of trays and silverware, the shrieks and laughter—all of the bustle you would expect from a roomful of young boys—filled Adrian with anxiety. The doktor had said too much stress might bring on another seizure. Adrian sat in his lonely corner, imagining himself on the floor convulsing and flopping like an electrocuted fish. He squeezed his eyes tightly shut, as though that could stop him from seeing what was in his mind. He opened his eyes again and forced himself to eat the food on his plate.

A boy Adrian didn't recognize plopped his tray opposite Adrian's and sat down.

"Hello," he said vibrantly. "My name's Alyosha. What's yours?"

Hesitantly, "Adrian."

"Well, we all need friends, Adrian, and I'm here to be yours."

Adrian looked around, waiting for some joke or betrayal, but this boy seemed sincere. He was smiling, showing his crooked teeth and healthy-pink gums. Liveliness and concern fairly beamed from him. Alyosha. Adrian liked the name, thought it was beautiful but also chose to see providence at work in the fact that it began with an "A" like his own name did. Adrian and Alyosha. Friends.

"My mother abandoned me," Alyosha said in an unabashed matter-of-fact tone. "She was addicted to crystal-black, one of the worst drugs around, imported from Baikyong-do. She turned to prostitution to pay for her habit. She had to give me up. Devils plagued her. God forgives her though. I know He does. And so, I do too." He paused and gave another beatific smile, unburdened by guilt or blame. "What brings you here, Adrian?"

"I guess . . . I don't . . . " Adrian wished for the same openness Alyosha had shown, but he was embarrassed to admit his mother had killed herself. That was one of the worst sins a person could commit, and he didn't want this bright angelic boy to think of his mother as a sinner.

"You don't have to say if you don't want to," Alyosha said with real pain on his face. "I am sorry I asked."

"No . . . it's all right," Adrian said. "I guess my mother abandoned me too. But not that way."

Alyosha titled his head like a curious and loyal puppy.

"She killed herself. She said God told her to," Adrian said. "Do you think He told her to do that?" He was on the verge of tears, his voice cracking through the last words.

"God would never bring evil into the world," Alyosha said. "That is the result of men or devils. If God did tell your mother to kill herself, it was for a good reason. And if it was not for a good reason, then God did not tell her to do it."

"What good reason could there be for that?"

"We have met, haven't we?" Alyosha said. "And we will become great friends and do great things. If it was God's will that your mother die that way, then perhaps we meant to make the good come of it."

Adrian felt the first twinge of happiness since he had found his mother swaying slowly, a dead pendulum in the center of time. He had a friend. He felt destiny swelling all around him.

The two boys ate the rest of their meal in silence. A pact of sorts had been formed in Adrian's mind. They would become inseparable and share everything. They would understand holiness together. They would be brothers in the Lord and brothers in every shared deed.

(We might speculate, Esteemed Reader, that this was the beginning of Adrian's lifelong need for a companion with whom to share his most profound convictions and projects. But of course such deep-seated psychological compulsions do not have one distinct origin; and so let us put speculation aside and return to the facts we do know . . .)

※ ※ ※

In the following weeks, Adrian and Alyosha became nearly inseparable, just as Adrian had wished. They did their homework together, Adrian helping his new friend with mathematics and natural science—something he seemed to have an inborn aptitude for—and Alyosha explaining the finer points of theology from the *Book of the Before-Time*. Adrian was better at theology than most students in their level, but no one was as sophisticated as Alyosha. He understood the text on an analytic level, and here Adrian could nearly match him, but he also made intuitive leaps from thought to thought and insight to insight in a way that at first seemed almost absurd, but upon further reflection became brilliant. Adrian and a few other students noticed that even the nuns and priests in charge of their education were often confounded and then captivated by his *theses*—for that was what they were, theses, not mere opinions or tossed-off answers designed to impress his instructors; they were his working-through of the great mysteries of existence and the Truth hidden in the *Book of the Before-Time*.

One afternoon, several months into their friendship, Alyosha sat in a sandbox meant for the younger boys, tracing and erasing words with his forefinger. A small group gathered around him, curious at what he was drawing. More boys came, and even some teachers. They were drawn to him like iron filament to a magnet, but he continued etching words in the sand, more interested in what he might communicate to the ground than the tumult growing around him.

He looked up and said, "Fret not for the words in the sand. All words are in the water before they were in our mouths or fingers; Time and Being do not follow the order of our mortal thinking. What *is* may have happened before what *was*. The water of my utterance may have quenched the thirst of a dead man in the Before-Time. Drink not only the words you hear and speak, but also those words that will be spoken in the past, for those are truly the Words of God."

Alyosha lay down in the sand, and Adrian wondered if he was going to have a seizure like his own, but instead he merely lay there, calm as a breeze off the Baikal Sea.

⁊ ⁊ ⁊

Alyosha was a remarkable talent at quoting from the *Book of the Before-Time*, knew practically the entire thing chapter-and-verse. He never quite fit in with the other boys and was more at ease among the priests at the orphanage-school. And he had a nearly supernatural empathy, could almost read a person's mind, one was tempted to believe.

As a reward for having won the orphanage's annual recitation contest, where the boys competed to see who could produce from memory the most passages from the *Book of the Before-Time*, Alyosha was given a beautifully engraved copy of The Book—as the Fathers at the orphanage often called it—and would be allowed to offer a sermon the following Sunday morning. Adrian knew Alyosha was by far the best at reciting from The Book and that he deserved to win. And he was proud of his friend, happy that his talent and dedication had been recognized.

Alyosha received the Book from Father Samarov with a nod and small smile of gratitude. Everyone commented on how beatific he seemed, how unperturbed by his ego at winning. Later that night, Alyosha walked calmly to the bunk of Ditur Szygur, a boy known for trouble-making and ignoring his scripture lessons, and gave him his prize copy of The Book.

"My copy is in fine condition," Alyosha said, "and I've noticed you don't have one."

Ditur raised himself up on one elbow, a sneer prepared, but Alyosha simply stood there, book outheld. The other boys were barely breathing, expecting Ditur to jump out of bed and pummel Alyosha. Ditur was bigger than the others and already growing facial hair and muscles. But it was hard to imagine someone hitting Alyosha's face, even as it seemed to ask for it.

Something softened in Ditur's features. He sat all the way up and leaned forward. "Do you mean it?"

"Why would I lie to you, brother?" Alyosha asked. "Lying is no way to spread the Truth."

Ditur took Alyosha's present slowly, tentatively. He gazed down at it in wonder. It was as though no one had ever given the boy anything in kindness in his entire life. He looked back at Alyosha, who set his hand on Ditur's shoulder lightly, blessing him.

"Thank you," Ditur said, his voice a frail whisper.

The air in the bunk-room was so thick with anticipation and silence, that when one of the youngest boys sneezed, it was like a gunshot.

"God bless you," Alyosha said. Then he turned back to Ditur. "Perhaps we can talk some tomorrow. For now, I think I need to rest."

Ditur, and everyone else in the bunk-room, watched as Alyosha made his way back to his bed.

%   %   %

It was four days later when Alyosha gave his sermon. His boyish form was dwarfed by the ceremonial pulpit.

"Faith, we are told," Alyosha began, "is like a rock. Our priests have told us this and they have quoted this verily from the *Book of the Before-Time*. It would be raw foolishness to contradict those words, either by pretending they are not set down in the scriptures or by claiming that faith is not like a rock. Indeed, it is like a rock."

Alyosha paused, and several voices filled up the silence with *Yes, yes* and *Pure-Baikal*.

"Do not offer your pure-baikal assent just yet, brothers. We have repeated this truth a thousand-thousand times, and it becomes truer with every repetition, but our understanding has grown dimmer and dimmer even as the truth of this holy fact has grown. Verily, faith is like a rock, but not in the way we usually mean it. It is solid, yes, but it is also breakable. A single blow from a powerful hammer will shatter it."

He paused again, but this time the silence floated unfilled.

"This is what makes faith the great weakness of much religion. Some new heresy from the engineers and doktors at Joshua University has shattered many a rock of faith. Isn't that so, brothers? Haven't you seen loved ones lose their way by believing in the science of man instead of the Truth of God? I have, and it breaks my heart. It breaks my heart as surely as their faith was broken by the blunt hammer of mortal knowing."

He paced back and forth, building up momentum into his speech. Everyone was standing. Adrian didn't remember when he had risen from his pew.

"And so I am here to tell you that the *Book of the Before-Time* was giving us a warning, not a comfort, when it instructed us that faith is like a rock. It was telling us to refuse faith for its fragility. It was telling us to have divine hope, for hope is like sand and can take any blow from any hammer man devises. It can reshape to the situation. It can absorb water by the Baikal Sea, or it can sit dry for centuries in the desert."

Adrian listened to his friend preach, barely able to take his eyes away.

"And so I say to you, brothers, have your hope be like the sand and eschew the rock of faith."

It started as murmurs. Alyosha stood silent and unmoving behind the pulpit, his eyes closed. He was done with his sermon as abruptly as he had begun. The congregation looked to each other, then to the priests, for the proper reaction. Even the priests were at a loss. From somewhere in the back of the church a call of *pure-baikal* came forth, and then another, and Adrian heard himself saying it too.

※ ※ ※

After some time spent ruminating on this and the day's events, Adrian yawned widely. He was suddenly very tired, so tired in fact, he considered sleeping right where he was, but the thought of banditii slitting his throat in the night made him stand and find his way back to his bedroll. He tugged his boots off and was asleep the moment his head touched his pillow.

8.

IT WAS BEFORE REVEILLE, the sun a gray thought in the distant dark, when the guards swung the door to Marcik's cell open with a mind-rattling crash. In his confusion, he tried to get out of bed and to attention, but his feet were tangled in the sheet and his eyes burned from the hard light stabbing in from the corridor, and then more brightly from above. Jürgen didn't move and the guards didn't make him. It was Marcik they wanted. In his confusion, Marcik thought that maybe Jürgen was dead and instead of sorrow he felt jealousy. Jürgen would get to sleep a few hours longer because he was dead; Marcik recognized the absurdity of the half-asleep thought and forced himself to fuller wakefulness.

"Up, you desert-roach!"

Marcik's eyes still hadn't adjusted. "Yes, sir."

If he could have seen himself, he would have laughed—his hair jutting this way and that, his underwear uneven on his hips, his face like that of a boy recently woken from a nightmare.

Marcik tugged on his prisoner's uniform, a procedure made both difficult and painful by his broken fingers. The guards stared impatiently. He was marched down the corridor toward the interrogation room. What could Olgar want with him at this hour? But as they approached the room and Marcik began veering toward what he assumed was his destination, the guard behind him struck his shoulder with a baton.

In the courtyard, some two dozen prisoners were lined up. Marcik's shoulder still pulsed painfully. He joined the line of prisoners without looking at them. He stood dumb and rubbing his shoulder, all his disorientation leaving him in the pre-dawn cold. There were more guards out here and some of them had guns.

Olgar stood with strict posture in front of the zeks. "Prisoner Hosani, step forward please," he said with no agitation, no malice, nothing but professional necessity. For the first (though not the last) time, Marcik wondered whether Olgar weren't a sociopath by the clinical definition.

A zek stepped into the dim light of one of the courtyard's few electric lamps.

Samir. Marcik had not seen him since he and Yoyo had loaded up the mortar before the vanguard, Marcik among them, had charged into the valley. He had assumed Samir was dead.

Olgar ordered Samir to remove his shirt and trousers. Marcik felt growing discomfort as Samir stripped to his undergarments. His back was scored with dozens of long wounds, fresh and raw-looking. Knife? Whip? Clearly, he had not fared any better than Marcik.

"Everything," Olgar said, motioning absently toward Samir's remaining clothing.

Samir stood naked and shivering. His hands went to his genitals.

"Hands behind your head."

A guard moved forward with his gun ready, and Samir quickly put his hands behind his head.

"Kneel."

Samir kneeled, his head titled forward. The guard lifted his gun.

They're going to shoot him.

"You are accused of an attempted escape," Olgar said. "And you killed an Ulani. Do you admit your crimes, zek?"

Samir's mouth tightened into the silence of a stone. The stoic straight line of his lips refused Olgar's desire for confession or blubbered pleading.

"Proceed," Olgar said to one of his men and stepped away from Samir.

The pale morning light glinted weakly off the quartz dust in the sand on the other side of the prison's fence. The guard fired his gun and the echo deafened the prison yard. When Marcik opened his eyes, Samir was still there, still alive.

The guard brought the butt of the gun down on Samir's face. Samir fell over into the dirt. The guard smashed his face again, then kicked his ribs repeatedly. Samir clutched his genitals, protecting them from the blows, but like a good Guardsman he did not cry out. The guard kicked Samir's hands aside and stomped powerfully down on his groin, but Samir, so far gone now, only twitched slightly.

The beating did not stop until Samir was left unconscious and bloody in the yard. He hardly looked human any more, but a few weak bubbles of blood rose and fell on Samir's nostrils, letting Marcik know he was still alive, at least for the moment. He had seen many men die in recent months, and though he had no special affection for Samir, Marcik felt a wave of nausea go over him, from the base of his skull down into his stomach, and he thought he might vomit. The nausea passed, leaving in its place a hopeless dread.

We're all going to die here.

"And that is what will happen to the rest of you if you disobey prison rules," Olgar said.

The guards lifted Samir up and carried him off like so much meat.

9.

THAT MORNING, as the trucks of the karavan groaned into motion, Adrian was in a better mood—or at least his doubt had turned into curiosity. He looked on as Heinrich shifted the truck low, high, low to navigate the changes in terrain. He admired Heinrich's confidence, how he utterly inhabited himself. If Heinrich ever doubted himself or his path, he would never show it, which in a way meant he could never truly doubt himself; to have enough poise to hide his fear and doubt from unwanted detection was proof that he controlled those unmanning emotions, not the other way around.

Their journey was almost over, and Adrian realized he hardly knew the man despite the many hours they had spent squeezed together in the cab of the truck. Just a few more days would bring them to the hospital, and after that, they would go their separate ways.

The hospital: he could almost visualize it now—like an oasis in the red desert, but an oasis-in-negative, housing the sick and dying. There would be the laborers who had been injured in the mines or the refineries. There was a ward of nekrosis cases. And of course now there would be the wounded Guardsmen to treat as well. He recalled a film he had seen about medikal officers in the Baikal Guard. A scene of a young doktor sawing a leg off a corpse as a military surgeon screamed at him and held a timer in his hand had particularly affected Adrian. Some of these operations would have to be conducted under the least favorable of conditions and with only minutes left before the Guardsman died.

Adrian pushed the image of dead body parts from his mind and tried to focus on what he considered his true calling as a doktor.

"I must warn you," the Direktor of Hospital Operations had said the one time Adrian spoke with him on the telefone, "you may find the situation a bit more primitive out here in the desert than you're accustomed to."

"That's perfect," Adrian had said and felt a bit of shame at the eagerness in his voice, as though he were almost happy to find suffering in the world to alleviate.

"What do you mean?"

"I just want to be somewhere where I'm truly needed."

"There's little room for idealism out here, Mr. Talbot."

"Yes, sir," Adrian said. "I'll see you in a few weeks."

Those weeks had seemed like they would never pass: there was his coursework, which all seemed so pointless with Brandt dead, and of course the never-ending bureaucratic requirements—background checks required for anyone requesting an extended stay in the Outer Provinces; vaccinations of various sorts; and paperwork to ensure he would receive university credit for his work at the hospital. But the time had passed, as time does, and Adrian was almost at his journey's end. He was saddened by the idea that he might never see Heinrich again. He almost certainly would never see any of the other passengers, would never know what fates awaited them.

One day he would return to Joshua City, and there was a chance, slim though it was, that Heinrich would be karavan leader on that trip as well; he might even find a way to arrange his travel plans such that he would see Heinrich again. The others, however, would cease to exist for him as thoroughly as if they had never met.

Adrian was mulling over these melancholy thoughts and trying to imagine what the hospital would look like as the karavan descended from the mountains and they were enveloped by the cool winds of the plain, rising up off the river he could faintly see in the distance. A large number of people were gathered along the river's edge, all dressed in black it seemed, but they were too far in the distance for him to see what they were doing. He considered asking Heinrich who those people were but let the question drift away in his consciousness.

The road widened and turned to smooth tamped dirt; it was clear that civilization was not far off, and this was confirmed as they rolled over a small rise and saw a settlement in the distance. It had wood walls with spiked posts—like a crude and scaled-down version of the Outer Wall that surrounded Joshua City. At the gate a sentry slid back a hatch to reveal a tough long-mustached face. Heinrich handed over some papers and gestured to the cab. The sentry walked to the back of the truck and opened the rear-flap. Adrian heard voices as official documents and travel permissions were inspected.

After several minutes, the gate opened. Adrian looked around with curiosity: as humble an outpost as it was, it was the first town they had seen in weeks. The streets were silent and haunted-feeling. The faces that Adrian did see, from darkened windows and dirty thresholds, were haggard and stared at him with a combination of suspicion and a kind of muted plea. A boy tumbled an old half-shredded tire down the street in something that might have passed for play. In the square, a woman washed clothes from a tap that spit water at irregular intervals. She hummed to herself, a thready half-broken lament. She checked her laundry basket, as if making sure no would steal it, every few seconds. Adrian wondered how horrible it must be to do laundry in constant fear like that. And then he noticed the bulge of her stomach and guessed her at five months pregnant; his heart leaped out toward her, dreading what treatment she would get from a doktor in an impoverished outpost like this—if there was a doktor at all, that was. He wondered if there was some way to convince her to allow him to examine her, but something about her furtive harassed-animal demeanor let him know there was likely no way she would trust him enough to allow such an examination.

"What is this place?" Adrian asked.

Heinrich said the name of the town and Adrian recognized it as the place where two or three of their passengers were scheduled to get off. He looked back into the cab at Yoram, a silent young man with a boyish face and a wet upper lip. As he clutched his bag and stared out at his new home, he looked even more nervous and pale than usual. Adrian had not talked to Yoram much—nothing beyond the mumbled pleasantries of campfire meals—but from the ragged leather of his bursting suitcase, and what little he had heard, he knew the young man to be quite poor, probably from a background similar to his own. He wore the dazed and blinded look of a creature who had lived all his life underground and had just now come into the sunlight. Adrian could guess the rest: with whatever paltry sum the boy had managed to save, he had bought passage on this karavan in hopes of striking it rich. He had heard there were mining jobs to be had out here, Adrian knew, just as he knew there were hundreds like him every year who came out for similar work. They had romantic dreams of travel and were ore-greedy.

From the looks of things, Yoram had arrived too late. Whatever prosperity this particular settlement once enjoyed had been sucked dry. The place was not long for this world; the smartest and most successful among its inhabitants had already moved on. He would have to find the next outpost—surely not too far away, perhaps fifty or a hundred kilometers—if he was to attain his dream.

For some time, there had been a rattling noise in the distance—a little like wind-chimes. Adrian had paid it no mind, nor had the other members of their party, having enough to take in already. Now the noise swelled, and with it a kind of ghostly wailing. The woman at the well set aside her laundry and cocked her head. A Guardsman rounded a corner followed by a procession of stooped forms. At first it wasn't clear to Adrian what he was looking at; prisoners clearly, but they had something on their heads—cages? The objects looked like heavier, dingier rusted bird cages. His mind would not settle on what he was seeing. Yes, all the prisoners had something like a giant nightmarish bird cage on their heads, from which frightened faces peered out.

The rattling he had heard was the sound of chains, attaching the prisoners' necks to the cages, rattling the bars as they walked. Occasionally one would stagger and the rest would howl, as if in sympathy, though their mouths never seemed to move. A soldier behind the group kept them in line with the threat of his machine-rifle. As they approached the well, the pregnant woman checked her laundry basket.

"Who are they?" Adrian asked.

"Prisoners," Heinrich said. "Thieves mostly. When there's little to be had, folks will do almost anything."

Among the dozen or so people in the procession, nearly half were women. There was one boy of perhaps sixteen.

"And why are they wearing those . . . those things?"

Heinrich said, "Out here there's no punishment like public punishment. It's—how would you say?—a badge of shame."

As the prisoners passed, they stared at the karavan with blank expressions. The woman at the well reached into her laundry basket and pulled out something long and gleaming—a sickle. She charged at the closest prisoner, and before the Guardsmen could raise their guns, she was on top of the man, beating the bars of the cage with her weapon.

"You murdered him," she screamed. Her voice was as much animal as woman, her pain palpable to Adrian even at this distance.

She swung the sickle repeatedly, and the man held his arms up defensively. The sickle ripped into his flesh, tearing chunks of skin and meat from the underside of his forearms. Blood was smeared on his chest and had spattered onto the woman's dirty blue dress. She swung at his gut, trying to rip him open, and he tripped over one of the dislodged bricks of the well and fell to the ground. The cage on his head banged against the dirt and twisted at an unnatural angle. He lay in the dust, not moving. The woman screamed again as she swung the sickle, sticking it into his exposed back. Over half of the sickle's metal crescent was pocketed inside the man's back. Adrian was amazed at her strength. As she was trying to dislodge her weapon from the dead man's back, presumably to strike him again, a Guardsman yelled at her to stop, but she ignored him. He stepped directly in front of her and ordered her to stop again. She nearly had the sickle out of the man's back; it seemed stuck on a bony something, perhaps a rib.

"Stop now, citizen!" the Guardsman screamed, unsure and angry and scared.

He lifted his rifle as if to shoot her but did not pull the trigger. She got the sickle free and looked at the Guardsman, then back to the dead man at her feet, as if deciding at whom to swing. The Guardsman flipped his rifle around and brought the butt of it down on the woman's face so hard her cheek bone collapsed and skin tore away, letting forth a gush of blood. She slumped to the ground and convulsed and cried in confused anguish. The Guardsman stood over her, unable to move, visibly shaken by what he had done. Another Guardsman arrived and kicked the woman hard in the back.

"Someone stop him," Adrian said, looking at Heinrich and then back toward Messenger. "He'll kill her baby."

The Guardsman kicked and kicked her, again and again, until finally the first Guardsman came out of his daze and motioned for his companion to stop, pushing him back lightly. Heinrich looked on gravely, but he did nothing. Messenger removed a weaponless hand from under his robe. Heinrich put the truck into gear. In the rearview mirror, the Guardsmen lifted the body of the woman and carried her somewhere out of view.

※ ※ ※

That night, as Adrian was trying to sleep, he thought he heard a noise. He sat up on his bedroll and stared out at the dark knotty underbrush. He could not get the images of the day out his mind. They returned again and again in a disjointed narrative. The woman falling on her belly. The dust settling. The Guardsman's stricken face. Reluctant water sputtering from the tap. He wrapped his coat around himself. They were on the plain and the wind, unhindered by buildings or rocks, whipped across the campsite. Odd that it should be colder here than even in the mountains.

On the other side of the campsite, the baby cried softly. He should check on Jarir and Yves, make sure their child was all right. He was so wrapped up in his thoughts and emotions, he didn't hear the footsteps until they were just behind him in the dark.

"Who's there?" he half-yelped.

"It is Messenger," Messenger said, stepping into the last of the firelight.

He sat beside Adrian. His face was illuminated in eerie yellow for a brief moment. Smoke curled sinuously in the cold air.

"He won't make it through the night," he said.

"Who?"

"The child."

"You mean she." Adrian corrected. "It's a girl."

"She won't make it through the night."

"She's that bad?"

The stamping of boots and a few gruff throat clearings indicated Heinrich's approach. He lit a match, touched the nimble flame to the blackroot in his pipe. Then he pulled out a flask but Messenger waved it off.

"You know it's against our code, Heinrich," Messenger said.

Adrian took interest in this refusal, feeling kinship with Messenger, remembering his night with Leni, remembering the things he had done and said.

Heinrich grinned and took a sip. It was the first time that Adrian had heard Messenger call anyone by name. For a moment, Adrian felt privileged to be sitting beside these two, then the baby cried again, interrupting.

"He says she'll die tonight," Adrian said to Heinrich. "Is that true?"

Heinrich glanced at Messenger. "You're the doktor, lad. You tell me."

Indeed, he was the doktor here. Why was he shirking his God-given duties? He gathered his willpower and stood. He dusted off his hands and blew on them for warmth. Messenger and Heinrich watched him with quiet interest. Adrian went to the truck for his medikal supplies. He finally found his bag, wedged between two heavy suitcases. When he opened it he cut his finger on a sliver of broken glass. Half his bottles were smashed. He carried the bag back to the fire and dropped it on the ground.

"Well, the supplies I need are destroyed," he said. "But if we go now we can make it to town and back."

"Impossible," Heinrich said, "It would put the whole karavan in danger."

"She'll die then," Adrian said. "That little girl will die."

"Aye," Heinrich said.

Adrian turned to Messenger. "And you? You won't do anything?"

"There are larger concerns here."

Adrian turned to Heinrich and held out his hand. "Give me the keys."

"And what would you do?" Heinrich asked. "Drive alone for four hours through this terrain? At night? You'll have your throat slit or end up in a ditch freezing to death."

"So be it. It's better than doing nothing."

"Can you even drive a truck?"

"I'll learn," Adrian said. "It can't be that difficult."

"Jarir wouldn't lift a finger for you," Messenger said.

"That doesn't matter. It's part of *my* code. You of all people should understand." Before Messenger could reply, he turned to Heinrich. "So you won't give me the keys and you won't come with me?"

Heinrich shook his head.

"Fine. All right." Adrian grabbed his bag and gathered together what few supplies were still usable.

⁊ ⁊ ⁊

At Jarir's tent, the curtain was open, revealing Jarir's back as he leaned over Yves who held the infant desperately against her mothering form. Adrian coughed to get Jarir's attention. Jarir saw Adrian and began to pull the curtain shut, but Adrian caught some of the fabric with his hand.

"My wife is sleeping," Jarir said.

Over Jarir's shoulder, Adrian could see Yves rocking the baby back and forth.

"No, she's not. And your child is very sick."

"I will take care of it."

Adrian tried a different approach. "Listen," he said. "I didn't mean to offend you before. And I don't mean to question your ability to handle your child now."

Jarir tensed.

"I'm a trained doktor," Adrian said. Jarir glared at him. "You'd go to a sun-priest if you needed spiritual advice," Adrian said. "Wouldn't you?"

Jarir looked at his wife, and Yves nodded shyly. He stepped aside, which Adrian saw cost him a great effort. Inside the tent it was damp and hot, filled with the stink of illness and vomit.

"Leave that open," Adrian said, indicating the tent flap.

Adrian pulled what remained of his instruments and medikaments from the bag—his stethoscope, a small vial of antibiotics, a thermometer. He shook the thermometer to settle the mercury, though it was clear the child was feverish. Her cheeks were bright red and her forehead shiny. She cried in gasps. Adrian considered the possibility of a bronchial infection or, worse yet, pneumonia.

He turned to the boy who was sitting wide-eyed on an adjacent bedroll. "What's your name?"

"Amir," the boy said.

"Amir," Adrian said, thinking. "That means general, right?"

The boy nodded.

"Well, if you're a general you must be very brave," Adrian said. "Do you think you're brave enough to go out into the dark night, down to the river? Your sister needs water for us to boil."

"I should go," Jarir said.

"I need you to light a fire," Adrian said.

After the boy left, he held out his arms and spoke to Yves in a low soothing voice. "I'm going to have to take her now."

"Please be careful," she said.

"Don't worry," Adrian said.

As Jarir stoked the ever-growing flame, he watched the exchange. His son ran back in with a sloshing pot. Adrian put the water over the flame and they waited. Adrian placed a rag over the little girl's head and held her face near, but not over, the boiling water. He wafted the steam in her direction. She tried to twist away, avoiding the heat. Adrian held her in place. She howled but breathed the steam in nonetheless.

"This will hopefully clear her airways," Adrian explained.

He read the thermometer. It was not encouraging: forty degrees centigrade, well above normal. Too much higher and she would suffer irreparable brain damage—if she was lucky enough to survive. All his medikal training—the hundreds of hours of lab work, class preparation, and reading case studies—had come down to this. He was terrified but also thrilled. He felt like some fine-tuned and perfectly functioning machine built for just this purpose. With the full spectrum of antibiotics, all would have been fine, but most of them had drained out of the smashed bottles onto the truck's dirty floor. He only had the one small vial, enough to combat the infection but likely not enough to entirely kill it.

But he couldn't think like that: the word *if*, as Brandt used to say, was the physician's most useless tool. He must focus on the materials he did have, not on what he might do if he had others. Surely there would be something he could make work.

He remembered having seen knapweed growing all around their campsite, its brittle white-downed stalks swaying ungamely in the breeze coming down from the mountains. Goats would eat it if they were desperate, but it remained largely untouched due to its bitter taste. But if boiled, it was the active ingredient in a rudimentary remedy for fever. Of course, he had been taught at Joshua University to distrust such remedies—the wisdom being that they worked more by wishful thinking than by any curative effect—but he had always secretly believed that there was some truth to their medikal powers. Perhaps the knapweed mixture with the dosage of antibiotics he still had would work.

Besides, he had no choice.

"Do you know what knapweed looks like?"

The boy shook his head. *Of course not*, Adrian thought. *He's a city dweller.* Adrian himself would not have known had he not seen images of it in textbooks and samples in botany class. He described the plant to Amir and the boy ran off to fetch some.

There was a long agonizing moment where Adrian had nothing to do but rock the little girl back and forth and study her flushed face, the thin flax-colored hair plastered to her head. *Fontanelle*, he thought, remembering the word for the soft spots on a baby's skull that allowed it to pass through its mother's birth canal. It would not calcify over for another year, he thought, remembering this detail from his exams on childbirthing. But what good was any of his knowledge if he couldn't save this girl here tonight?

"She's going to be just fine," he said without conviction and to no one in particular.

Amir returned with the knapweed and Adrian picked the rose and sea-blue flowers off one by one and dropped them in the still-steaming water. In about ten minutes, the water would be infused and would turn a kind of oily rainbow color. Or so he had read—not having tried it, he had no idea what to expect.

Jarir watched with interest and, it seemed, a begrudging respect. "My people do this, too."

When the concoction was ready, he poured some of it in a clay drinking cup he had asked Yves to wash out for him. He swirled it around, letting it cool to the point where it would be drinkable, but not so much that it lost its throat-opening effect.

"I'm going to need you to open her mouth," Adrian said to Yves, thinking it would be better and easier with her help, "and I need you to hold it open no matter how she struggles."

Yves nodded and began easing the baby's lips apart, but not enough for Adrian to pour the liquid down her throat without spilling it.

"You'll have to be more forceful than that," he said.

"Let me," said Jarir, seeing Adrian struggling not to spill the knap-weed brew.

Adrian nodded and Jarir squeezed between her upper and lower jaw so that the girl's mouth opened. Adrian briefly admired how Jarir had known exactly how much force to use—enough to get the desired effect, but not so much he hurt her—and he thought it showed a deeper knowledge of his girl child than he would have suspected, or than the man himself would have likely admitted. Adrian tilted the cup and prayed that she would drink the noxious-smelling concoction.

She spit more than half of it back up. He stuck his finger in the cup and brought it to his own lips. The moment it hit his tongue, he gagged; it was an uncontrollable reflex. He smiled weakly.

"I don't suppose you have any honey?"

Both parents shook their heads.

"Go ask Heinrich for his flask," Adrian said to the boy. "Tell him it's for me."

The boy came back in a minute, having accomplished what Adrian hoped would be his last errand for the night. He handed Adrian the dented tin flask and Adrian unscrewed the lid to smell the contents inside. It was cognac, thankfully: a dark liquor was better for the purpose because of its sweeter taste. He poured the dark sweet fluid into the cup.

"My religion doesn't allow it."

"Surely your religion will make an exception in this case?" Adrian said.

"Even a drop of that poison will jeopardize her eternal soul."

Adrian looked to Jarir's wife; she opened her mouth to say something and then thought better of it. The child cried again and Adrian lost all patience.

"Do you want your child to live?" Adrian did not wait for a response. "Then you will do exactly as I say."

He lifted the cup to the girl's lips again.

"Let him do it, Jarir," Yves said.

Jarir looked at Adrian, then Yves, then his boy, then back to Adrian who held the baby while awaiting his decision. Jarir nodded.

With some difficulty, Adrian poured the drink down the little girl's throat. She resisted at first but eventually swallowed with a scrunched-up expression. He then administered the antibiotics and gave her one more mouthful of the knapweed brew.

He gave the baby back to her mother and they all sat together in the dense sweaty silence of the tent, listening to the desert crickets rubbing their strange legs together. Somewhere someone laughed, unaware of the drama going on in this tent. The little girl's fist uncurled, showing a palm, moist and soft. Her lifeline, if such things are to be believed, indicated that she would survive not just that night, but many years to come.

"What is her name?" In the chaos and fear of the night, Adrian had not thought to ask this simple question.

"Anya," Jarir said.

"That's lovely," Adrian said, "It's not Al-Khuziri, is it?"

"We named her after her grandmother," Jarir said. "My wife's mother."

"Look, she's sleeping now. That's a good sign."

They knelt side by side by side—Yves, Jarir, and Adrian—looking down at the sleeping girl. *Anya.* Adrian admired the curve of her cheek; she had her mother's thin graceful eyebrows; he imagined the way her face—and the shape of her personality—would emerge from all that soft clay. Just the way the fontanelle would harden to protect the brain inside her head, she would emerge stronger from this, even if she never remembered it.

"I can leave you now," he said. "All of you need your sleep."

"Stay," Jarir said.

Adrian kept a wordless vigil with the husband and wife (the boy, sensing the danger over, had fallen quickly to sleep) throughout the night. Through the opening of the tent, the sky was visible. It turned from black to gray to the whitish blue of morning, the stars sinking into the light like pebbles into an endless ocean—no, not quite that, but the sky was filled with watery light which subsumed the stars, though Adrian knew those same stars would re-emerge tomorrow and the next night and the next, but for now he felt he had crossed over into something, that he had survived more than just a single night.

He shook Jarir's hand and made his way out into the day just in time to see the others rising from their beds. He looked reflexively to Heinrich's quarters and saw that he was already fully dressed and sitting on a stool outside. Their eyes met; Heinrich tilted his head questioningly; Adrian nodded, and Heinrich smiled, stood, stretched, and walked toward the breakfast fire. It occurred to Adrian that Heinrich had sat there all night, keeping his own private vigil.

CHAPTER TWO

DARK THINGS RISING

1.

IN THE WEEKS following Samir's attempted escape, the zeks were put on half-rations. Their exercise time in the yard was reduced to fifteen minutes. This was both good and bad. On the one hand, it made it more difficult for Marcik and Jürgen to recruit men to their cause. On the other hand, the zeks had grown restless. Angry, even. Angry men are more likely to take risks. Marcik and Jürgen walked their usual path around the yard.

"Where is he?" Jürgen asked.

※ ※ ※

"We must act on this," Jürgen had said to Marcik the previous night in their cell. "We must make their own strategies work against them."

"Yes. But how?"

"Who do we know here? Who can we trust?"

Marcik thought about it. "No one."

"Not even this Samir? He seemed eager enough to escape."

"No . . ." He had not told Jürgen yet about his history with Samir.

"And Schmidt is dying, you said. So we need to find a hub."

"A hub?"

"You know. Someone around whom others congregate. We merely need enough men to execute the first stages of the plan. Once we unlock the doors, the rest will take care of itself. But we need to act quickly, to take advantage of the mood this Samir of yours has created."

"I think I know just the man," Marcik said.

※ ※ ※

Kharkov entered the yard with his zeks.

"How do we approach him?" Marcik asked.

"It has to be you," Jürgen said. "He won't trust a civilian."

Marcik strode over to Kharkov with less hesitation than he felt. "I need to talk you."

One of the zeks stepped forward, but Kharkov held up a restraining hand. He looked Marcik up and down appraisingly. Marcik had rehearsed this moment in his mind—how should he handle himself? Should he approach the matter sidelong, standing in the circle of zeks and waiting for his moment? Should he make idle talk at first? Should he be humble? Subservient? In the end, he decided on the direct approach. A man like Kharkov would respect that, he felt. Marcik hoped he was right.

Kharkov nodded at the other zeks. "Leave us."

The zeks dispersed, grumbling vague dissent. When Marcik and Kharkov were alone, Kharkov took a pack of toothpicks from his pocket. Where did he get those? He shook two from the pack and offered one to Marcik. Marcik declined and Kharkov shrugged.

"I'm trying to quit smoking," Kharkov said. "These help."

He chewed on his toothpick calmly, in full view of the guards. As if they weren't a potential weapon. As if you couldn't poke a guard's eye out with one quick jab.

"Say your piece," Kharkov said.

As quickly as he could, Marcik explained what he and Jürgen had noticed about the shortage of guards. The fear they had detected in Olgar's behavior. "We outnumber them twenty to one. Maybe more. If we could just get a set of keys . . ."

Kharkov took the toothpick from his mouth and spit in the dirt.

"If."

Marcik couldn't understand the man's hesitance. Didn't he want to escape? Was he secretly a coward? Or was he just in so deep with the guards that he felt he had too much to lose? None of these were things he would say, of course. If Kharkov himself didn't beat Marcik bloody for it, there were a dozen men who would. And the guards would let it happen.

"What you're offering me is mere information. Information I already have."

Marcik blinked stupidly.

"You think I haven't noticed the number of guards?" Kharkov said. "Come back to me when you have a plan."

Marcik nodded.

"Thank you for your time."

He walked off, somewhat discouraged. Had he been wrong to pin his hopes on an oberzek? A man who would collaborate in such a way— could he be trusted? Would he feel he had too much to lose in risking escape? Yet if Marcik and Jürgen wanted men on their side, Kharkov was their best hope.

%% %% %%

Marcik recounted the conversation to Jürgen. When he was finished, Jürgen nodded.

"Good."

"Good? He told me wasn't interested."

"No, he didn't. He said to come back with a plan. And he was right. We don't have one. But he didn't outright rebuff you. We need to think about it, get our details straight. Then we'll make our real pitch. This was just first contact."

"First contact," Marcik repeated mechanically.

Meanwhile, the guards had signaled that their exercise time was up. Kharkov, in his duties as oberzek, went around the yard, rounding the prisoners up and pushing them into rank and file. When he got to Marcik, he said nothing. But was it Marcik's imagination or was the guiding hand on his back a little less rough than usual?

2.

IN DEFENSE OF WATER-RIGHTS: A POLEMIC

[pamphlet distributed widely to Joshuan homes, businesses, and official buildings; author unknown]

What is that substance most indispensible to life? Ask the Joshuan people this question and without hesitation they will answer, "Water." No matter their political leanings, religious beliefs, income, or level of education, the answer will be the same. Water. First we must drink, then we must eat. And the food we eat cannot be grown without water. And without water there is no one to grow it.

After the people have quenched their thirst, after they have fed their bellies, we can talk about justice and freedom and poetry and the sciences and the arts. After they have sipped of the pure-baikal, only then can they look to the cosmos and wonder what it all means. Why are we here? Why do we thirst? Until then, these are arid interrogations.

It follows, then, that water is the most inalienable of human rights. During The Great Calamity, when the water was tainted and in short supply, the Seven Tribes migrated to the shores of the Baikal Sea and founded new cities so that the people might drink freely. But over time, greed showed its ugly face. Men devised schemes to own that thing that should never be owned—water, and with it, life itself. The Legion of Water-Barons was established. These men amassed huge wealth by determining who got to drink and when. And their sons inherited that wealth, having done nothing to deserve it besides being born the children of greed.

And now the water is tainted again. A second calamity is upon us. And once again, those who own the unownable decide our fate. They decide who should receive clean water and who should not. They shower their wealthy and powerful friends with yet more wealth, allowing the

poor to thirst and sicken. But surely there is enough for all? The Bai-
kal Sea is large. More purification plants must be built. More efficient
means of water distribution must be designed. But most importantly:
we must share in the process and share in the wealth. Every Joshuan
citizen, and in fact all citizens of the Baikal region, should possess the
water equally. Water-rights must become a tenet of our constitutions
and our inter-municipal treaties, as widely accepted as laws against
murder and theft. For water-theft is the most heinous theft of all: it is
the theft of life itself.

3.

THE NIGHT MESSENGER came to Nikolas, the sky was a stark black canvas. Not even the moon was visible. Clouds thick as oil-smoke crowded
out all the celestial lights. Nikolas was reading by candlelight, smoking
a cigarette, lazily pondering the rights of humans and the duties of the
revolutionary. Was there a list of ethical Oughts (capitalized and eternal)? Or were there in-the-moment oughts (lower-case and situational)? He wasn't even trying to answer these questions. He was allowing
the feel of their mystery to wash over his consciousness, seeking the
vague shapes of answers, not the answers themselves. Later, he would
scold himself for giving over to cheap sentimentality, the pleasant sense
of importance and depth he felt at times like these, but he wasn't yet
criticizing himself or his sensations; he was enjoying them. He took
a flavorful drag from his cigarette and watched smoke ghost its way
through the candlelight. The world was so flush with meaning. *It's not*
that there is no meaning or no substance in the world, as our pathetic
nihilists would have it, Nikolas thought. *It's that the world is too replete*
with meanings and substance. We can't handle such a surfeit of Being, so
we take refuge in the idea that the world is empty.

Earlier that evening, he had been at another meeting of The Underground. He couldn't say they were making no progress, but things were
moving too slowly for his taste. At least they had named specific issues
they planned to solve at the meeting; not the diffuse nonsense that usu-

ally ensued. And there were many new possible members, which was heartening. But had they accomplished anything? Would they ever find a way to accomplish something?

※ ※ ※

They gathered in the room Elias had found. (He had his uses.) Elias called it The Pump Room, but Nikolas didn't like that. It was an accurate description, to be sure: you could hear the millions of gallons of water and waste pumping through the labyrinthine network of pipes. Thin pipes ran across the ceiling, rusted metal ones snaked down the walls, and thick trunks squatted in the middle of the floor. But there were huge expanses of empty space. There were recesses in the walls where the permanent members had made rudimentary homes—some of them like squatter's dwellings, some of them elaborated with domestic love. They had taken to calling these living spaces *domiciles*, a word too grand perhaps for their quality, but it was evidence of a kind of pride of place, and Nikolas knew that to be a good thing. The breadth of their exaggeration matched the depth of their newfound love for The Underground.

And this was why a crude name like The Pump Room couldn't capture what they had created here. There was something grander, more powerful happening. Nikolas and Katya had made a domicile of their own, once a large maintenance closet of some sort. What it lacked in luxury, it made up for in intimacy. In one corner, they had set up a box frame and a simple mattress. There was a lamp, a small table, and an old office desk from a faktory. It was everything they needed, and more importantly, it put them in the heart of The Underground. (Yes, that's what Nikolas preferred to call it, The Underground. It meant both the room and the movement.)

Now the permanent members started coming out of their domiciles. Some members emerged from under the stairs, some from behind a gnarl of pipes that gave them a modicum of privacy. A curtain hand-woven in Baikyong-do style was swept back by a large powerful hand; a heavily muscled man with an enviable beard lumbered out. His petite partner jumped out and landed on her dainty feet. (Everyone assumed she had woven the curtain, but Nikolas had watched Alarik fumble painstakingly over it for weeks. He had gathered up threads from who-knew-where and had woven them together with his hands that seemed unsuited for such delicate work.)

Nikolas watched all this from the half-open door of his and Katya's domicile. The first of the above-ground members spilled into the room, Elias at their head. Most of them Nikolas recognized, but there were many new faces.

Nikolas and Katya finally joined the others. All their eyes were on Nikolas. He leaned over and patted the shoulder of a young recruit. He hoisted himself onto one of the thicker pipes and called the meeting to order.

"When I look around this room," Nikolas said, "I see our numbers are growing. Which is good. Because this meeting is about recruitment and infiltration. All of you have done excellent work, especially Komrade Elias, who brought so many of you here tonight."

One of the possible inductees stood out. He was not of university age, but he didn't seem like a laborer either. His face had an ageless quality. Nikolas got the sense that this man noticed everything, took in every detail of everyone's movement. Was he an informant? Did Adams already know about The Underground? He couldn't settle the matter now, but Nikolas made a mental note to strike up casual conversation with him later. If there were already informants among them, something had to be done. It might even work to their advantage. He could feed Adams false information, if he knew for sure this man was in municipal employ.

Now that the meeting had begun, murmurs died down around the room, and the last of the attendees found a place to sit or stand, and yet Nikolas did not speak further. *Wait until they are entirely silent.* Almost by instinct he knew to do this. Several seconds dragged on, then several more. The light noise of sludge flowing through a distant pipe was all he could hear when he finally decided to carry on. As he looked around the room, making sure he had everyone's undivided attention, he saw the annoyance on Elias's face and knew that if he had waited even a second longer, Elias would have made some comment to break the thrall he had the room under. Nikolas recalled the way Mayor Adams manipulated an audience and was uncomfortable at the thought.

"It is practically a maxim of revolutionary thought that you cannot win the revolution unless you first win the people. They are where the revolution must start and they must be the primary weapon of the revolution." He paused to let his words sink in. "But how do we win the people? There are several tactics available to us, of course. And we've even begun implementing some of them. Komrade Alarik has been organizing his fellow workers at the steelworks."

He motioned for Alarik to step forward.

"Brothers of The Underground," Alarik said, his voice quavering mildly from nervousness. "As Nikolas said, we have only begun, but I feel we've laid sturdy tracks. We're making them aware of the dissatisfied slumber they languish in. But it's too early yet to fully awaken them." He paced back and forth a bit, staring at the ground as though his next words lay somewhere at his feet. "But how are we doing this?" He continued, unconsciously echoing Nikolas. "First off, we compiled statistics on how much profit the steelworks makes per hour, comparing that to what the workers receive for that hour of labor. The numbers are—as you all know, komrades—alarming. The workers have been filled with fairy tales about how this city works, but numbers cannot lie the way the faktory bosses and our politicians do. Steel does not lie, and they know their steel. And so, secondly, we have compiled a list of facts about the possible uses of steel and how the powers use it. These uses—as you all know, komrades—are not always in the interest of the workers who produce it. They ride the trains, but who truly profits from them? And of course weapons for Mayor Adams's war machine."

Alarik paused, wondering where to go next, waiting for Nikolas's approval.

"And tell them about the strike efforts, Alarik," Nikolas said.

"Yes, of course. That's the thing. The most important thing, even. We are teaching them that in the," he searched for the phrase, "economic exchange of labor and capital, they are half of that exchange, and the more important half, because without the workers' sweat, all the bosses have is just a pile of useless drams."

Alarik seemed amazed to hear so many words in his own voice.

"Thank you, komrade. That was very instructive," Nikolas said. "And we have others doing good works around the city as well." He looked to Nawaz, an immigrant from Kazhstan (Kazhstanis made such excellent revolutionaries, given their culture of self-denial; and there was so much a member of The Underground had to learn to live without). "You have the floor, komrade."

Nawaz had been working in Silverville, running the small machinery and building stage sets when Nikolas had found him. Nawaz had moved to Joshua City to escape the ascetic culture of Kazhstan. He loved films, all of them. But after several months in Silverville he grew disgusted with the decadence, and learning how the illusions of film were made ruined them for him. He was poised to quit his job and return to Kazhstan, though that place held no allure for him either, when he met Nikolas at a workers tavern one drunken evening. Throughout the course of their conversation, Nikolas had convinced him to stay on at his job, but for a different purpose.

Nawaz explained to the members of The Underground how he was learning the communications technology that would be essential to the revolution. People often forgot that the majority of radio broadcasts also originated from Silverville, not just films. Nearly every sort of media in Joshua City had its center in Silverville, Nawaz informed them, and whoever controls the media can manufacture political and social acquiescence. He concluded by detailing his next moves and the difficulties to recruitment in such an affluent part of society.

Nikolas called forth other members of The Underground. Mikhail had a brother in the Ministrie of Water Resources and was pilfering documents when possible. Endre was a ticket-inspektor on the train line running into The Hills. (This had already proven useful, hadn't it?) And there were others in various positions ranging from the meatpacking industry to the elaborate fisheries along the Baikal Sea to simple market vendors. They had members in all ranks of society. When they were done with their presentations, Nikolas hopped off of his perch.

"But as I have said, every voice from the people must be heard. And you, komrades, are the people as well. I would like to hear any thoughts you might have—either about what you have heard or any direction you might like to see our efforts take."

Nikolas stood silently and raised his hands as if to receive an offering. A few vague murmurs began in the back of the room. He hoped Elias might begin the discussion by describing his efforts among the law skolars at Joshua University; Nikolas had grown particularly interested in that. But Elias sat quietly, though looking around with real eagerness.

A member whose name Nikolas could not recall stepped forward. "Well," he began, "I've been working on something."

"Go ahead," Nikolas said.

"You were saying the other day that every idea has its symbol."

Nikolas nodded vaguely.

"Well, I guess I think you were right about that," the man continued. "I am, you might remember, an art student. My professors tell me I have some talent, but I am not interested in their ideas of art. I want to see art have real use, real social value."

Nikolas nodded again, encouragingly.

"So, anyway, I made these and thought everyone might like to see them. I would be happy to make changes as well, if the group decides that's what's best."

He held up three squares of artboard, on which he had drawn designs Nikolas could not quite make out at that distance. He looked to Elias, who was seated close to the eager art student.

Elias stood. "Let me take a look."

Elias flipped through the designs. He looked up at Nikolas briefly.

"Good work, komrade," Elias said. "Indeed, we should all see these and make a democratic decision about our symbol."

He passed the designs around the room. There were more murmurs.

Elias had played this well, if in fact it was a play on his part. Nikolas had to stand impotently as the designs made their way around the room. He could not react to them, but standing there doing nothing was not exactly the attitude of a leader. Katya raised her hand slightly, palm forward, indicating that he simply wait.

The designs finally made their way to Nikolas. The first one had a large circle with seven red stars inside it and a dark scythe slicing through it all. The second one showed three robed female figures, each with seven stars around their heads like halos. These were The Three Sisters from the *Book of the Before-Time*. The Three Sisters were said to be the forerunners of a new perfect age in Baikal. The third was simpler, more abstract. A circle with seven lines crossing through like spokes in a wheel.

"But what does a scythe have to do with Joshua City?" someone objected.

"Exactly. It should be a railroad spike being hammered through the top."

"Maybe even with a worker's hand swinging the hammer!"

"That's silly. That would be too complicated. And how are we going to put that on walls and pamphlets?"

Nikolas kept himself silent, hoping something useful might come of the debate. He flipped absently through the other designs. They were quite good, he had to admit. So much talent in this group.

"And the other drawing," a particularly venomous voice said, "with that religious imagery. Do we really want to associate the freedom of mankind with the very thing that has kept it enslaved?"

Nikolas certainly had a distaste for religion; the person had a point; but that might have been the most beautifully rendered of the designs. And weren't there possible liberating uses for religion even? The people love their religion. It could be used to bring them to the movement, and then one only had to repurpose their beliefs.

This debate was growing wearisome, however. Debate was healthy, but this was becoming mere quibbling.

"Perhaps we're focusing overmuch on the specifics," Nikolas said. "What we need to recognize is our komrade's talent and commitment."

The art student, who had shrunk back into his seat, now beamed at Nikolas's praise.

The ageless man Nikolas had noticed earlier was gone now, though he hadn't seen him leave. This was doubly disturbing—Nikolas prided himself on his powers of observation, and this further increased the possibility that the man was an informant. How much vital information had been shared that evening? Luckily, everything had been kept vague, as was the protocol, but it would be inconvenient if Mayor Adams knew even the outlines of Nikolas's plans. He needed to know who had brought the man in. Had his background been properly investigated?

"These are all important issues," Nikolas said distractedly. "And ones we'll examine further at our next meeting. For now, however, we should enjoy each other's company."

It had become an unspoken tradition at the end of their meetings to drink and revel, play music and dance, anything to break the bourgeois codes that bound them. Nikolas poured a tall vodka and rested his hand on Katya's back, as two young men and a girl stripped down to their undergarments and began cavorting in the middle of the room. A small group in a corner passed around a bottle of wine and began a lively debate. A happy-looking man not yet old enough to grow a full beard plucked the strings of a balalaika with something approaching professional skill. Elias walked over to where Nikolas and Katya were standing. Drums and metal jangles slowly joined in with the balalaika, making it impossible for anyone to hear their conversation.

"I notice you did not ask for my progress report," Elias said.

"And I noticed you didn't offer one," Nikolas responded.

"There are some matters better kept between the three of us," Katya said.

Nikolas did not yet broach the subject of the possible informant.

"I have to say things are going well," Elias said, "but I am not sure I should continue at my current task."

"And why is that?"

"Like you, I want to drop out and dedicate myself full-time to the cause."

Nikolas paused. "You can devote yourself full-time, if you wish, but I believe strongly that your particular skills are best put to use where you currently are. We could think of other things for you to do as well. If that's it—that you want to be doing more."

Elias had no immediate retort, and so he poured himself a drink as strong as Nikolas's. Their friendship had formed from many long nights of drink and discussion, very much like this one. Though many things had changed.

"Pure-baikal to you," Elias said and raised his glass to Nikolas. "And to you, Katya."

The three komrades touched glasses and took brief stock of each other.

"Did you ever think to see us at such a juncture, Elias?" Nikolas said, gesturing with his drink at the room, now filled with pandemonium.

Elias shook his head in disbelief. "Remember Peytr?"

Nikolas mouthed silent words in faux rage, imitating their former compatriot. They both laughed unguardedly.

"Which one was that?" Katya asked.

This was another thing that had changed. Katya was now so central to his life and to the movement.

"He was the one who refused to speak," Nikolas said.

"What an idiot. As though shutting oneself up could change what other people say," Elias said.

They took sips of their drinks, searching for something more to say.

"Did you see that man who was here earlier?" Nikolas asked Elias.

"Which man?"

"The one who said nothing and slipped out unnoticed," Nikolas said. "Unnoticed to me at least," he added, a reprimand to himself.

"Yes, I did see him," Elias said. "A curious sort. Did you invite him?"

"I was going to ask you the same thing."

"Do you think it's a problem?" Elias asked.

"I sincerely hope not."

※ ※ ※

After a few hours, Nikolas left the others to their revelry. He grabbed his journal and started up the staircase to the outside world. Katya was talking to Elias, but she noticed Nikolas. She nodded to him, knowing where he was going, and giving him a sort of permission.

He walked the dark alleyways of Joshua City, heading to a place no one else but Katya knew about. The alleys narrowed until he had to turn his shoulders a bit to squeeze through. He finally arrived at the fire-escape. He pulled himself up in one fluid motion, pushed off the rough brick wall, his foot slipping drunkenly, then got clean purchase on the rungs, and climbed his way to the roof.

Seated in his spot, he placed his journal on his lap and looked out across the dark horizon. The vodka coursed pleasantly in his blood. Everything seemed so rich and full of meaning when he was drunk. He rolled a cigarette and took in the lights of Joshua City. Several kilometers to the east, the domed curve of the Hub stood out majestically against the surrounding buildings. He thought briefly again of the art student's drawings and decided that among the arts, perhaps architecture was at once the grandest and most functional. Who could look at that structure and not feel a sense of awe at the powers of the human mind? And even the buildings in the New Style; they were also sublime as mountains. *Just think of what this city could be.*

He turned suddenly, hearing a footstep. It was the ageless man from the meeting. How had he gotten up here without Nikolas's having heard him? Nikolas fumbled in his rucksack for the large knife he had recently taken to carrying and pushed himself to his feet.

The man moved; Nikolas did not feel the knife being taken from his hand; it was simply on the ground at his feet.

"You will not be needing that tonight, friend."

Nikolas cast about in his mind for something to do, but he instinctively felt his helplessness. But there was no reason to worry either. If this man wanted him dead, he would be.

"Listen closely," the man said. "We have heard and believed so long . . . and after all our searching . . . this is the moment we knew would come." Here the man paused and seemed not entirely in control of himself. "Are you the Harbinger?"

※ ※ ※

Katya sat on the bed reading *A Woman's History of Larki Island*. Nikolas couldn't see her face, of course, but her posture was one of perfect concentration. How lucky he was. How proud he was to share his life and his city's historic times with her. She gave a small wave and went back to her book.

"How did the party end?" he asked. "There were a few people left when I came in."

"Did you know that the engineer of Larki Island's first underwater train was a woman?"

"No, I didn't," Nikolas said. He looked her over, this amazing woman he loved and admired and would miss, "but I am not surprised."

"Of course, in that backwards society, she was not allowed to publish her research, so it had to be under her husband's name." She set the book down. "There is so much we must fix in this broken world."

"Yes," Nikolas said. "I agree."

"What's wrong?"

"I have something I have to tell you."

Katya stood from the bed, worried now.

"What is it, Nikolas?"

"I don't really understand it myself."

"We have always talked openly. Don't let anything change that."

What must she be thinking? That I fucked some girl? But he had to admit the scene was going that way.

"No," Nikolas said. "Nothing can ever break our bond."

He told her about the man he had met on the roof, who he knew now was Messenger. He told her what Messenger had said about his destiny, how grand it might be. He told her he would have to go away. He didn't know how long.

"He thinks I might be someone... someone special," Nikolas said. "But I don't understand any of it yet."

"How do you even know you can trust this person?"

"I just know I can. I can't explain to you, but I do," Nikolas said. "He could have killed me, Katya."

"And that is supposed to increase our trust?"

"This has to happen," Nikolas said, no bending in his voice. "And I am going to need you to play your part while I'm gone. This is all for the revolution."

Her white mask tilted toward the floor.

"Katya, this is good for us."

She turned away from him, her shoulder keeping him out. She grabbed her book and touched the pages without looking at them. He stepped forward but did not touch that shoulder.

"Fine. But you're asking me to trust a man I have never met."

"You've met me. Would I ask this if I weren't sure?"

"What do you need me to do?"

"Elias will run the day-to-day operations."

"All right. What else?"

"Alarik will know about this. You and Alarik. If anything happens you don't like, tell him. He's loyal."

"I know Alarik. Of course I can trust him."

She set her book down and held her hand out to him. He pulled her toward him, lifted the edge of her mask, kissed her lightly on the mouth.

"I will learn so much from this man," Nikolas said. "You didn't see how he moved..."

"I said it was fine, Nikolas. Stop apologizing."

"We are going to accomplish so many things."

"When do you have to leave?"

"He is waiting for me now. Outside. I have to go, but you know I love you."

"Yes, of course I do."

※ ※ ※

Messenger and Nikolas walked out of the city and into the desert. At the Outer Wall, Messenger produced official papers for himself and Nikolas. The papers were stamped with Mayor Adams's personal seal, making the Guardsmen at the gate treat Messenger with a deference Nikolas had rarely seen. And Messenger's own overwhelming presence added to the Guardsmen's obsequious attitude. Most of the other travelers were held up for hours, but Nikolas and Messenger were through in minutes.

Once in the desert, they continued walking north for several hours. Messenger said nothing, and Nikolas got the sense he should remain silent as well. Messenger was not a man to be disturbed by idle chatter. This was Nikolas's first time in the desert, the first time seeing that barren beauty. The desert silence was perhaps what struck him most.

Civilization was, of course, a byproduct of the need to escape this barrenness and the harsh lack of resources. Early humans huddled together near water. They built their primitive shelters to protect them from the elements. And as their technology rose above the simple task of mere survival, they built more elaborate structures. Cities formed. And after the Calamity that ended the Before-Time, they huddled together again. All of that was obvious enough, boring even in its obviousness. But wasn't there something more? Something about the void of the desert that required us to fill our cities up with noise? The erudite chatter of the lecture hall was born from a fear of that silence. He had never admitted it to himself until now, but he loved that chatter, even at its most annoying. The reward of civilization was safety and knowledge and belonging.

It was uncannily quiet out here. Nikolas wanted desperately to talk to someone about these ideas. He considered asking Messenger, who must know about other civilizations, what his opinion on the matter was. He wished that Katya was with him. But no. If he was going to earn Messenger's training, he must learn control.

When night came, Messenger laid out his blanket and dug a small hole in the sand. He lined the hole with flat rocks he had picked up throughout the day. He ordered Nikolas to gather dry wood and brush from around their campsite. Nikolas disliked being told what to do, but he did it anyway.

When he returned with the kindling, Messenger broke it into smaller parts and filled the rock-lined hole. He pulled out some loose paper and a container of matches. He lit a fire inside the hole. Smoke trickled out, but the light was invisible unless you were standing directly over the hole. Nikolas recognized that this was part of the point of digging the hole.

Messenger unwrapped a packet containing a dry dough and another packet with salted meat. He tore chunks from the meat and buried them deeply into the dough. He placed this meat-filled dough on a broad flat rock set just inside the mouth of the hole. Messenger had constructed a primitive oven, Nikolas realized. He smelled the baking bread and felt his stomach clench with hunger.

They ate in silence. Nikolas had perhaps never gone this many waking hours without speaking. During those first few hours, his mind had raced, as though he were having a conversation. He even imagined an interlocutor. But now, the constant internal chatter had ceased, and his mind was freed to truly take in the world. It was strangely calming; his head felt clear; he understood what mystics must feel after long hours of meditation. Perhaps it is simply clearing the mind of the need to communicate every thought one happens upon that leads to the sensation of wisdom. Was this part of Messenger's lesson?

4.

NEEDING A PLAN to bring to Kharkov, Marcik spent his days and nights analyzing his surroundings for possible weaknesses. He stared at the keyhole on his cell door; he shook the door uselessly. He raged against the brute fact of imprisonment. At Jürgen's prompting, he began counting the number of guards on each detail. He counted the number of steps it took to reach the yard from his cell. He counted the number of able-bodied zeks. Who among them would be strong enough to fight? He wondered about the height of the fence (how many seconds would it take to scale it?) and about how many men Kharkov would bring with him. How many guards or oberzeks could he take down? The man seemed possessed of a violence that could decimate half the prison if he put his mind to it. How to enlist his support?

But Kharkov was not here right now. And Jürgen was not here either. Marcik had been chosen, along with five other zeks, to reinforce a flimsy portion of the fence with a small brick barrier. The other zeks were from his cell block. And he knew the oberzek who would supervise the day's labor. Oberzek Wikolo was known for a cruelty that often matched and occasionally exceeded that of the Ulani guards. Not all oberzeks took to the job so eagerly as Wikolo; most were just trying to get an extra bit of food or more time in the yard. But Wikolo was known for whimsical brutality. He exercised his power by not bothering to have a reason for his outbursts of cruelty.[8] A strange name, Wikolo. Rumor had it that his mother was half-Ulani, but there was no way to verify this. He had grayish blue eyes, a sallow complexion, and a small dimpled chin. He was always clean shaven (no doubt having received barber privileges as part of his payment), though a

---

[8] Author's Note: During my own time spent in a labor camp, I learned that those who ought to be in solidarity with each other, those who ought to feel some kind of fellowship, could not be counted on for any more kindness than our oppressors. Privilege and power are sought at every level in a prison camp, and those who gobbled the smallest crumbs which had dropped from higher levels cherished them all the more for their smallness. Some of the worst beatings I received were not by the guards, but by my fellow inmates who enjoyed their petty satraps.

beard would have suited him, would have created the appearance of a stronger jaw.

"See those bricks and that trough of cement?" Wikolo asked and the zeks nodded dully that they did. "Get started carrying the bricks, set them carefully, and cement them together. If you do your job right, I might be able to convince our Ulani friends to get each of you an extra bowl of stew tonight." The zeks' faces brightened at the prospect. "But only if you do exactly as I say."

A short distance away, an Ulani guard sat, tapping out a disinterested éclat with his baton. There was something reminiscent of the famous Ulani drumming in the idle noise he made.

The zeks set themselves to their task, Marcik included. It was dull but ultimately easy work. You carried three or four bricks over, and using a small beveled spade, dug a wet lump of the cement from the trough. Then you pasted the bricks together. For the first hour this procedure went on uninterrupted and with ease, but slowly the bricks grew heavier, your legs wearied of the back-and-forth and your arms grew tired of carrying even a few bricks. And the task was made more difficult for Marcik due to his fingers which had not yet healed completely.

An emaciated zek, known by the nickname of Lizard, dropped his armload of bricks. When they hit the ground, one of the bricks shattered.

Wikolo first looked over his shoulder at the Ulani guard, who watched with some interest. The guard continued tapping his rhythm. Wikolo kicked Lizard hard in the stomach as he bent over to pick up his error.

"You make a mistake like that again," Wikolo said, "and I'll see to it you miss three days' rations."

Marcik moved to help Lizard with his task, but Wikolo put himself between them, breathing in Marcik's face with moist intimate menace. His bird-of-prey eyes pierced Marcik's own stare, sending him back to work.

It was a special kind of torture to be this close to possible escape. There was only one guard; if the zeks joined together, they could overtake him. But then what? Nothing. Or they could rush through the weak point in the fence. But then what? Nothing. So Marcik worked like a good zek and swallowed down the bile of his helplessness.

They worked for another two hours. In the midst of their effort, so as not to look at Wikolo with the hatred he felt, Marcik took to observing the buildings in this part of the compound he had never seen. You could almost reach this area from the yard, but not quite. What was worse, there was a stench of sewage everywhere, coming from a large pipe that spit out the human waste flushed from the latrines. Despite all his talks with Jürgen about the possibility of escape, Marcik felt a total despair. *If our own are working against us . . .*

The zeks worked on and on, creating an impenetrable wall, closing themselves further in by their own efforts. And Wikolo watched them work, his hands on his hips, a self-satisfied look on his face as the sun drained away behind him.

※ ※ ※

His body sore and his hands blistered, Marcik lay in his cell, trying not to think of his situation, though that was part of the horror of being a prisoner: you could never escape the blunt fact of your imprisonment. You ceased being yourself in many ways, or what you used to be was overwritten by that one cruel word, *zek*. Instead, he thought of Wikolo. He imagined picking up one of the bricks they had been made to carry and smashing Wikolo's face repeatedly—that short sweet moment of blood victory before he was shot in the back. But even that would be a welcome release.

"Any ideas?" Jürgen asked, surprising Marcik. He had believed Jürgen was asleep, and for a moment he almost forgot he wasn't alone in the cell.

Marcik shook his head. "There is that weak section of the fence. But I'm not sure how that will help. Especially now that we've repaired it."

"But where there's one weak section, there are likely a dozen others."

"Yes, but . . ." Marcik frowned in the dim light of his cell. There was some connection he couldn't quite make. He kept coming back to the fence, Wikolo's smirking face.

"Get some sleep," Jürgen said. "We'll figure it out tomorrow."

※ ※ ※

Marcik sat up in the dark. "Jürgen," he whispered. "Wake up."

When there was no response, he went over and touched Jürgen's shoulder. Jürgen sat up with a jolt. Recognizing Marcik, the terror left his face. Marcik wondered not for the first time what horrors Jürgen had been forced to endure before Marcik had arrived at the prison. Or out in the desert before that. One day, Marcik would demand Jürgen tell him his story. However, right now there were more important things to talk about. Far more important.

"What is it?" Jürgen asked. "Is something happening?"

"No," Marcik said. He smiled. "Not yet."

As Marcik told Jürgen what he had realized about the latrine, that it emptied out just outside the fence and that a man could crawl his way to freedom if he was willing to get dirty enough, Jürgen grew more and more excited.

"This is perfect," he said, when Marcik had finished.

"It's still not a plan, though."

"No, but it is. I didn't think it was important until now, but there's an armory not fifty meters from there. I saw it one day when they took me to repair the sewage pump. There are all the guns we could ever need inside."

"All we would need would be a key. We can get that from one of the guards. Surely, they all have one."

"We'd need one more thing," Jürgen said.

"What's that?"

"Someone to crawl through the tunnel."

※ ※ ※

They took the plan to Kharkov the next day. This time Jürgen joined Marcik and they both told Kharkov what they had observed.

"And who is going to go down there?" Kharkov asked.

That was the question. They had no idea how narrow the tunnel between the latrine and the outdoors would be. There was the horrifying possibility of becoming stuck. And if you had to turn around and go back, the punishment at the hands of the guards would be severe.

"I'll do it," Marcik said.

Kharkov showed surprise, the first time Jürgen recalled seeing that particular emotion on the oberzek's face.

Marcik shrugged it off. "What's the worst they can do? Another beating? I can handle another beating."

Jürgen thought that in this case the guards—even Kommandant Fakuth—might make an exception to their usual practice and beat Marcik to death. And he knew that Marcik knew that to be true as well, but he was putting on a brave face; it was a calculated bluff aimed at selling their plan to Kharkov. This was a bit of improvisation on Marcik's part. Jürgen and he had not discussed this when rehearsing what they would say at this meeting.

Jürgen replayed the affectless tone in which Marcik had just discussed being beaten. This man had changed a great deal in their time together. You could have almost mistaken him for an overgrown boy when they first met. Now, he seemed resolute as desert rock. But then four months in this place would change any man—though not necessarily for the better. Marcik still did not understand his natural charisma, nor did he fully grasp the strength and willpower he held within himself, though Jürgen was certain that with a little guidance and a little luck, Marcik would become a truly great man. Nothing in Marcik's manner betrayed nervousness or fear or apprehension. He was utterly in his body and in the situation that life had thrust upon him. Indeed, Jürgen had picked the right man.

"All right," Kharkov said. "My men will be ready."

5.

THE NEXT TIME Olgar had Marcik brought to the interrogation room, it was a brief though terrifying visit.

"I regret to inform you," Olgar said, without a trace of regret in his voice, "that Major Schmidt's suffering has come to an end. He is dead."

Marcik had nearly forgotten about Schmidt. What sort of Guardsman forgets his fellow Joshuans so easily? A wave of guilt went through his guts; then that emotion was replaced with pure fear. *Olgar has been torturing him all this time. The shrapnel wound was a flimsy cover and I knew it. Why was I so willing to lie to myself?* A different kind of guilt came at the thought of how easily he had succumbed to the narkotic effect of Olgar's lies.

"I am sorry to hear that," Marcik said. "May I request that my men and I who knew him have the opportunity to hold vigil over his body and offer him a proper burial?"

Olgar looked at him slyly. "That will not be possible. We have already buried him."

Unbidden, images of Major Schmidt's beaten and mutilated body came to Marcik.

"I thank you for that. And for informing me." Marcik paused, trying to read something in Olgar's face, but got nothing. "At least he isn't suffering anymore."

"A mercy indeed."

※ ※ ※

"They killed Major Schmidt," Marcik said. He jumped up and grabbed the water pipe that ran across the ceiling of the cell. He chinned himself up. He had been doing kalisthenics in his cell each night, keeping himself limber and taut. He had grown lean from the exercise and from the ration sizes, but he was keen, alert, and, admittedly, hungry, but like a predator.

"That is unfortunate," Jürgen said. "For the obvious reasons." There was a look on Jürgen's face that Marcik couldn't quite read. "Does this change your willingness to go through with the plan?"

Marcik remembered his brazen words to Kharkov. He had proven he could handle a beating, but was he willing to give up his life?

Marcik dangled from the pipe loosely, then pulled himself up again. Holding that position, he looked over his shoulder at Jürgen and said, "Of course not. I would rather die trying to escape than rotting away like Tozhin did."

Jürgen sat silently, chewing his lower lip in concentration. Marcik dropped down and went to the floor for more kalisthenics. After a moment, "Well, what are you thinking over there?"

Jürgen hesitated. "There might be an upside to this, loathsome as it is to think such a thing,"

"What do you mean?"

Marcik continued his exercises. He enjoyed the strain in the fibers of his muscles, enjoyed the idea of becoming stronger.

"If we're going to break out of here and rejoin the Joshuan forces, we're going to need a leader."

"Obviously, but Schmidt would have been the most logical choice."

"You are correct, my friend. You are entirely correct," Jürgen said. "Schmidt is exactly the right choice to lead us."

The smile on Jürgen's face made Marcik uncomfortable.

CHAPTER THREE

THE MAKING OF A MAN

1.

T HE LAST DAYS of Adrian's journey passed without event. They loaded up at dawn and drove until sundown. Progress depended on the state of the roads and how long it took them to find a suitable campsite. They passed through small towns, some as blighted as the first, others in the swell of prosperity or just setting up. This was oil country and derricks bobbed like thirsty birds on the horizon. Around each settlement there might be a full-fledged village with taverns and hotels. Sometimes there were just a few tents, if the site was new and people were still unsure of its yield. But whatever the state of the settlement, it was always surrounded by an air of tenuousness, as if the desert wind might blow it away at any moment.

With each town they passed, more passengers left the karavan. Many had come out here seeking their fortune, but it was hard to believe they would find it. The desert looked like a dry maw ready to eat up any life that entered it. All of the passengers had their reasons for making this journey. Maybe they were just tired of the same few hundred square kilometers of Joshua City, those high walls almost blocking out the sun. Or maybe they had left something or someone behind. Things they would rather forget. As the passengers departed, Adrian found himself wishing he had taken more time to get to know their names and stories. A wonderful book could be made of their testimonies. The remaining travelers, however, were only too happy for the extra leg room. Soon, there were no more than five or six in the back of each truck.

When the karavan arrived at the work camp in New Kolyma, Adrian watched as Jarir and Yves said their goodbyes. The sun glinted off the sand behind them. Jarir leaned toward her, wanting to kiss her, Adrian assumed, but restrained himself. Yves held the baby. Jarir ran his hand along the little girl's forehead lightly and moved even closer, still not embracing Yves. Yves tilted her head forward and pressed her lips against Jarir's. Adrian thought he should look away but couldn't. Jarir gave himself over to the kiss in a way Adrian would not have expected. Before he was led off by Guardsmen to his prisoner quarters, Jarir turned and noticed Adrian. He nodded to him with quiet masculine respect.

I will likely never see them again, even though they will be so close by.

They arrived at the hospital a little over an hour later. Heinrich's jaw loosened as though he were about to say something, but instead he offered his hand. Adrian took it with komradely pleasure.

"You do pure-baikal here, lad." Heinrich said. "And take care yourself."

"You do the same, Heinrich." He continued to squeeze Heinrich's hand. "And we will see each other again. I promise."

"Don't go making promises you cannot be sure of keeping."

"You aren't planning to stop running karavans, are you?" Adrian said, already knowing the answer. If he knew one thing about his new friend, it was that he loved these karavan journeys more than anything in the Seven Cities. "And I intend to return home. We'll see each other again. You can count on that, Heinrich."

"In that case, I look forward to it," Heinrich said amiably. "Well, off with you then."

※ ※ ※

Adrian entered the hospital administrative offices, though that term seemed too grand for the small desk behind which sat a middle-aged woman performing bureaucratic tasks with neither enthusiasm nor disdain. It was not resentment he read on her face. Resignation, maybe, or something sadder. On the far side of the room, there was a door with a large semi-opaque white window. The garish lettering on the door identified this as the *Direktor's Office*. If they still cared enough to declare their positions, then they had not completely given up on their duties, Adrian reasoned.

He gave his papers to the sekretary.

"Came out here all the way from Joshua City, did you?"

"Yes, ma'am, I did."

"No need for such formality. Call me Marsela."

"Thank you, Marsela. I am Adrian."

Marsela tapped the papers he had handed her. "I see that." It was a good-humored little joke, and Adrian felt a fondness for this woman who could find the wherewithal to make friendly jokes out here at the end of the world. Adrian was ashamed for having thought her drab or resigned. He sensed that she had suffered a great loss at some time, probably several years previously, and of a severity he did not want to contemplate. The mixture of weight and levity in her eyes, coupled with his intimation of her tragic history, made her all the more likeable.

"Head on back to the Direktor's office. He should be able to meet with you now." Something in the way she emphasized *should* gave Adrian the impression she was not particularly impressed with the Direktor. Adrian took note of this; for some reason, he immediately trusted this woman's judgment.

"Thank you, Marsela. It was a pleasure meeting you."

"Let me know if you need anything," Marsela said. "We're all out here together, after all."

Adrian knocked tentatively on Direktor Spargo's door, and when he got no response, he knocked again, this time with more determination. Papers rustled and a chair squeaked. Footsteps. Adrian straightened his spine and let out a breath, releasing all the tension he could. The door opened and a tall man, maybe forty years old, stood looking Adrian up and down, like one might do with livestock.

"Adrian Talbot, I presume?"

"Yes, sir."

"Come on in, then," Direktor Spargo said. "Let's get the paperwork out of the way and get you settled in. You must be exhausted from your trip."

"I suppose I am," Adrian said apologetically.

Direktor Spargo's office was neat and sparse. One shelf of medikal texts ran along the east wall; a small metal pen-holder, engraved with the Healer's Oath, sat beside a stack of carefully arranged papers; no art on the walls, only Direktor Spargo's medikal diploma from Joshua University.

"We received your proof of student preparedness. Your professors are quite impressed with you," Direktor Spargo said. "Much more so than any of mine were of me."

"Thank you, sir," Adrian said, though Direktor Spargo's tone had kept any compliment out of his words.

He stood in the middle of the room, not having been offered a chair. As the Direktor flipped through his papers—keeping Adrian waiting on purpose perhaps?—he talked offhandedly about the situation at the hospital.

"You've caught us in a bit of a transitional time," he said. "There's the war, and as you know we've had to devote an entire wing over to treating the Guardsmen. But I must admit it's good to have an active relationship with the Guard. The Outer Provinces are a dangerous place. You've got the work camp and the banditii and now the war itself. It's nice to have a little institutional support."

It was all a little too casual for Adrian's taste, but he tried to keep an open mind about this man. *Who knows what difficulties and setbacks he's endured out here, especially since Mayor Adams declared the hospital part of the war effort?*

Direktor Spargo handed Adrian a dossier.

"If you would fill this out by the end of the week," he said. "Marsela will answer any questions that might arise."

Adrian lingered, waiting to be dismissed. Spargo looked up at him, as if surprised he was still there. He returned to his papers.

"Sir?" Adrian said. "If someone could just show me to my quarters . . . "

"Marsela will take care of that," Spargo said, without looking up.

※ ※ ※

In his room, Adrian looked around perfunctorily, barely noticing the size of his new living space. He stuck his head under the faucet and closed his eyes, letting cold water run over his face and down his neck. *At least they have running water in the rooms.* He lifted his head and turned off the faucet. The nerves along the skin of his back vibrated with the chill of the water, as droplets scudded down his spine. Coming out here had been a mistake. What was he thinking?

He steeled himself, or at least went through the motions of steeling himself—straightening his back, looking at himself sternly in the mirror—against the very real horrors he knew he would have to endure in his months here. He thought of Heinrich and Messenger and of the desert and mountains he had just passed through. He prayed for renewed strength and hoped God would grant it.

2.

A SQUEAL OF METAL on metal cut through the staff's quarters. Adrian had slept fitfully, plagued by dreams he could not remember, though a foul mood was left in their wake. He sat up and his bed gave out an ugly metallic moan. He surveyed his room and wondered again whether this hadn't all been a mistake. What had he been thinking? Why should he be worthy of such sacrifice? Wasn't it pride of the highest order to make oneself a martyr for a cause? Wasn't there a twinge of desire to be like the healer-prophets from the *Book of the Before-Time* in his decision to come here?

Adrian shook his head to clear it of such thoughts and willed himself out of bed, though sleep tugged at him, enticing him back into its restful unworried darkness. The shock of the ice-cold floor on his feet rejuvenated him. He washed and dressed. Fully awake now, he saw everything in its run-down existence. *This is home* came unbidden to his mind. He was both terrified and soothed by the thought.

% % %

His first day at the hospital was all blunder and confusion. He was shoved from person to person, each showing him some portion of what his responsibilities would be in such a jumbled and rapid way he forgot half of what he had been told by midday. He followed doktors with their clipboards, nurses with their solutions to be administered, nuns with their wimples billowing as they marched sternly from ward to ward offering prayers and ablutions to the dying sinners. He tried not to get in the way, and yet he was more than once shoved aside by some nurse or doktor needing to access a cabinet of supplies or enter a room with a dying patient.

"Why are you in here?" one nurse said to him as he looked in on a scene he did not quite understand. A body was draped head-to-foot in a white sheet. Had someone died? But they were all standing around, acting as if nothing had happened. He slipped out of the door and tried to find somewhere else to be.

There was a commotion in the corridor. Shouting. A gurney came around the corner, pushed by two attendants, shaking on its rickety wheels. The patient was a man of indeterminate age, his wrist chained to the metal bar of the gurney. Two armed Guardsmen followed. This man was a prisoner, Adrian realized. He had known that there would be prisoners from the Laborers Kolony in the hospital, but he hadn't considered the practical reality of the situation.

The prisoner turned his head in Adrian's direction. Half of his face was gone, the jaw hanging loose, the tongue leaping about in an attempt at speech. *He's trying to scream*, Adrian realized. The tongue wriggled and slithered in the wet ridges of the exposed throat; a saliva-coated burbling sound was all that came out. The man's eyes rolled back and he lifted his arms in the air, clutched at nothing, his whole body contracting in pain.

% % %

Adrian shuffled through the day's duties. He tried to regain the strength that had filled him that morning—so long ago now. This was all suddenly too much. On the journey out here, he had the hospital to look forward to, and the daily changes in scenery kept his anxiety mostly at bay. And what fear he did experience—on the bridge, during the knife fight with Jarir—was also positively charged with excitement. But now that he had arrived, the sheer fact of it all came crashing down on him like boulders from the mountains he had so recently travelled through. He would be here for months. In his panic, his heart beat thunderously, and he could feel the blood rushing in his veins; he took several deep breaths and swallowed one of his pills with a small glass of water, hoping to ward off a seizure.

Marsela was still at her desk when Adrian entered the office.

"What is it?" she asked. "Adrian, was it?"

"Is there a way to..." Adrian didn't want to ask, but he had to. "When is the next karavan back?"

She continued with her paperwork. She squinted at something, crossed something else out, clicked the pen against her teeth. "Not for several days."

"Can I get on it?"

"Are you sure?" Marsela asked.

Adrian didn't consider it at all. "Yes. I think I've made a mistake coming out here."

She set aside her papers and looked up at him for the first time. "This happens to most new people out here. It's hard, but if you really want to go home, I can arrange it."

"Please."

"I'll tell you what. Come back to me in five days. If you still want to leave, your passage will be arranged."

※ ※ ※

Toward the end of his second day of training, Adrian was asked to take part in an operation. Had an *entire* day already passed? Had it been *only* one day? Both possibilities struck Adrian as improbable. He was exhausted from the day's work, as well as the previous day's, and his lack of sleep.

"Mr. Talbot? Come with me," a doktor of Al-Khuziri origin said to him.

Adrian had already forgotten the doktor's name in the rush of information and activity. He struggled vaguely to remember it as he followed the man into the operating room. It was cleanly kept, but the equipment was rudimentary at best. It was not the dilapidated infirmary he and Nikolas had visited, but it was a far cry from the facilities at Joshua University.

"This ought to be a simple enough procedure," the doktor said, "and Direktor Spargo thought it best if you began assisting with some of these operations. Soon enough, you'll be doing them on your own."

There were bone-saws and a syringe with a disturbingly long needle. There were ointments and bags of fluids that could be administered intravenously.

"Yes, sir. Of course. That makes sense."

Adrian felt he should say something more but didn't know what.

"What were your specialties at Joshua University?"

"Kardiology, mostly experimental. Hematology, particularly blood antigen systems, as well as paraproteins such as the Apitz Agent. And I am working toward a third-area certificate in rheumatology with particular emphasis on soft bone tissues and their influence on auto-immune disorders." Hearing himself say it all, Adrian was amazed he had come so far. Less than a year ago, he wouldn't have even known what most those words meant, much less have been able to offer competent service in such fields.

"So that means you're going to be mostly useless for today's procedure," said Dr. Abuawad—*Abuawad!* the name suddenly came back to him.

Adrian was stung by the casual dismissal of his talents. He knew, of course, that not every doktor could prove useful in every situation, but hearing his limitations so bluntly stated hurt. His exhaustion settled in more deeply; every ligament tingled with the effort of movement. He closed his eyes, inhaled, and summoned all of his willpower.

"What is the operation?"

"Nothing complicated, but nonetheless very difficult," Dr. Abuawad said. "An advanced nekrosis patient. We are amputating his leg."

Two orderlies wheeled in the patient. The man's skin had the paleness of infection. He sweated heavily. He was no more than a year or two older than Adrian.

"Place him here," Doktor Abuawad said, indicating the operating table.

The orderlies set him carefully on the table. He grimaced at the movement. The nekrotic leg was wrapped in yellowed bandages. A sickly red seeped through.

"Remove the bandages, please," Doktor Abuawad ordered Adrian. "Use this."

He handed him a bottle.

Adrian lifted the leg by the heel gingerly and unraveled the first layers of cloth. He checked the patient for pain. "How are you doing?"

The man smiled bravely.

"This is going to hurt a bit," Adrian said.

He squirted solution from the bottle to wet the bandage, hesitated a moment, then pulled it off. The man clenched his teeth and slapped at Adrian's thigh.

"It will be over soon," Adrian said.

He peeled back the final layer of gauze and was hit in the face with the most putrid smell he had ever encountered. He kept a stoic face, resisting the urge to vomit. The unnaturally swollen tissue oozed a thick yellow seepage.

"Wash and disinfect it," Doktor Abuawad said.

Adrian took a swab and squirted it with more solution. With every sterilizing dab and swipe, the man grimaced more.

"What's your name?" Adrian asked, and scraped more nekrotic mess from the man's leg. He set aside one soaked piece of cotton.

"Patrik. It was my grandfather's name."

He grimaced again.

Taking the man's hand, Adrian said, "My name is Adrian."

"We have to begin," Doktor Abuawad said. "I am going to administer an anesthetic now."

"Am I going to live?"

"Doktor Abuawad is an excellent surgeon. You can trust him."

Doktor Abuawad picked up the syringe from the table. He shoved the long thick needle into the nekrotic leg, pushing past the meaty resistance. He pulled it out, re-sterilized the needle, and filled the syringe with another solution. He plunged it into the meat again. When he was done, he wiped the syringe off and set it down on a cloth on the table. He surveyed his instruments, selecting the appropriate one—a large gleaming bone saw.

"Shall we begin?" he said to Adrian.

※ ※ ※

Even though every muscle slumped toward much-needed sleep, and though there was an ache in all his joints from walking the hospital halls, helping patients from wheelchairs into their beds, and carrying supplies from one ward to another, Adrian could not fall asleep. The young man's moans and drowsy screams as Dr. Abuawad sawed into his leg reverberated in Adrian's mind like the death cries of some deranged animal. They had drugged the young man heavily, but even in his half-conscious state, he cried out with each grinding cut of the saw. Working on corpses had been one thing, but living bodies was quite another.

Adrian forced himself to think of what he had learned; that was the point, after all, to coming out here to the desert on this internship. What right did he have to close his mind to new knowledge when so many back home in Joshua City would need him in the future? To say nothing of those who needed him here. He had observed as Dr. Abuawad, after completing the amputation, pushed the flesh of the man's thigh back several centimeters, exposing a length of his femur. Dr. Abuawad then sawed off that bit of bone as well and carefully massaged the muscle around it, finally sewing degradable stitches into the red and agitated lump.

"This way, the flesh can heal over the bone and thus protect it," Dr. Abuawad had explained. "Early amputations did not use this technique and so the bone was often exposed and vulnerable. Also, it was harder to get a clean suture of the muscle tissue, thus allowing for various infections, often leading to the patient's death due to the blood becoming septic."

It made sense, but Adrian had never studied the procedure and had not given it any thought. An elegant solution, if you could apply the word elegant to something so brutishly raw. And the sick wet sound of pushing his thigh muscle up to expose the femur . . . for a long hollow second, Adrian closed his eyes and floated there in the spaceless dark. He searched his memory, and the operating room came back to him in its clean-medikal and messy-human detail.

He opened his eyes and continued his previous train of thought.

Brutishly raw, yes, but a simple and effective solution to the problem of permanent bone exposure or infection, neither of which, of course, could be allowed. Who had been the first doktor to think of it? There must have been a first. *Whoever he was, he was a genius.* And with that thought, Adrian lapsed into sleep.

3.

AFTER A WEEK of walking in the silent desert, venturing out to where no roads reached, Messenger pointed to a small mountain range and said to Nikolas, "That is where we are headed."

Nikolas felt more relief than he dared show. These long days of walking in the arid heat had taken their toll on him, but he could not afford to seem weak in front of Messenger.

"Looks like we will make it there around dusk," Nikolas said matter-of-factly.

"Yes," Messenger said. "If we keep up the pace."

Hours later, they were standing in front of a mountain's dark-gray rockwall. It was a steep unmarked surface. For a moment, Nikolas thought Messenger meant for them to climb it, and he was filled with dread at the prospect of such an effort.

Messenger leaned his face forward and let out an unsettling sound. It was not quite the high-pitched grunt of a Baikal crane nor the mammalian screech of a desert bat, yet it had elements of both. He made the mysterious sound again, and a slab of rock ground noisily open along an unseen track, revealing a dark tunnel carved straight through the mountain.

He took two torches from inside the tunnel, lit them, and handed one to Nikolas.

"Come," Messenger said, "we are nearly there."

A few nimble steps down the tunnel, Messenger leaned into a small enclave in the wall filled with ancient striations and let out his grunt-screech. The slab-door closed their path behind them.

Twenty minutes later, they emerged into something resembling a courtyard—that is, if the belly of a dead volcano filled with myriad plant life, a captive jungle in miniature, could be said to have a courtyard. A large stone basin was at the center, raised two meters off the ground. A pool of water with a lushly flowing fountain filled the basin. A single star floated in the water. Nikolas looked overhead and saw the desert star through an opening in the mountaintop.

He felt the thrill and awe of a child seeing his first sunset. No, that was not correct. Children are innocently unaware that they should be awed by sunsets or oceanic horizons. It takes an adult mind aware of its own eventual termination to fully appreciate the splendor of existence.

"Come," Messenger ordered again, "there is much to show you and much to prepare for our time here."

Nikolas followed Messenger, taking in as much of his surroundings as his overwhelmed senses could manage.

There were several huts of desert brick, each identical in size and design. Messenger and Nikolas were the only people here as far as Nikolas could tell, but they shared one hut. Messenger installed Nikolas on the second floor and took for himself a small cot on the ground floor. Nikolas had not realized how tired he was or how much he missed the luxury of even so modest a bed as the one in this room until he lay down. Sleep was an instantaneous oblivion.

※ ※ ※

Training began immediately after a breakfast of eggs, raw vegetables, and unleavened bread. Messenger quietly and methodically set up targets for Nikolas: this target half-obscured by leaves, this one more heavily grounded, this one easy to see and lightly planted; another one set such that Nikolas would have to take it in the right order if he intended to finish the exercise in the allotted time (*a mere seven seconds*). As Messenger went about his business, Nikolas had an urge for a cigarette, but he was terribly anxious of disturbing Messenger by striking a match. That little flare of noise seemed so vulgar just now. But he knew he would need steady hands for the task. *But if I am scared to light a match, how can I hope to have the courage to set Joshua City on fire?* Nikolas almost laughed out loud at how ridiculous his thought sounded; so melodramatic and false.

Nikolas lit his cigarette, looking out of the corner of his eye toward Messenger. Messenger went on undisturbed. *He didn't even notice, you little rabbit!* He took a long redolent drag from his cigarette and, leaning his head back, let a large cloud of satisfying smoke into the air above him. His nerves calmed and he felt focused. He could get it this time. He had made countless attempts in the past twelve hours, coming closer and closer to hitting all the targets within the allotted time, but something always went wrong. He missed one too many times and ran out of lead balls. Or he hit all the targets but went in the wrong order for optimal efficiency, and thus did not make it in time. Something always went wrong. *But not this time.*

Messenger approached, and Nikolas waited to hear his usual instructions. There was a hardness about Messenger that Nikolas admired. *If only I had ten men like him to add to my current cadres, we would overtake Joshua City within days.* He brought the cigarette to his lips and prepared for the pleasant intake of smoke; he barely saw Messenger's hand move and began just the faintest of dodges; a loud slap rang through his skull and a brief flicker of blackness went through him, but he stayed conscious and upright.

"What was that?" he asked, assuming what he knew was a useless defensive stance. If Messenger wanted him dead, he would be dead. He tasted the faint metallic fact of blood in his mouth and his tongue unconsciously probed a wide split in his lower lip.

Messenger stared at him for a moment, taking in his pupil. He looked toward Nikolas's cigarette which had fallen on the ground.

"Those will make you weak. We will not waste our secrets on someone determined to be weak."

"You could have just told me to put it out."

Messenger slapped him again, harder this time. Nikolas almost fell to the ground but managed to get a hand beneath himself and push himself back up. His eyes were watering from the force of the blow and the skin on his cheek pulsed with a warm pain, but he refused to look away. There was no sense in fighting back, but he could at least show Messenger he was no coward.

"Now, on the count of three, begin your target obstacle."

Nikolas had forgotten all about the targets, hadn't felt the pendulous pull of the lead balls in the bags at his sides, but now they were all he felt.

"...three. Go!"

And Nikolas ran, pumped his legs hard, cleared his mind of panic and anger. He slid his hand into the satchel on his hip, let his fingers curl loosely around one of the lead balls. He chose the order of his targets—second on left, first on right, third on left... His first throw hit its mark; he spun, slid his left hand into the satchel on his left hip; second throw was perfect center hit (Nikolas smiled slightly at the pleasure of a sure strike); spun again, opposite direction, pivoting on the toes of his left foot, and knocked down another target (*barely hit that one*—the smile replaced with a grimace of concentration) and continued his spin, lunged forward and took down the last one on the right, leaving only the first on the left, now several meters behind him; he leapt, turned in the air, let the last of the lead balls fly, and almost as if in the slow-action shots from a bad Silverville film, the ball traveled toward its target as Nikolas fell to the ground. He blinked as the wind went out of his lungs. He opened his eyes. The target was down. He looked to Messenger, who was standing there holding his timepiece, and was rewarded with the closest thing to a smile he had ever seen on that inscrutable face.

Nikolas leaned his head against the grassy earth and closed his eyes and willed the tension and anxiety out of his body, the way Messenger had taught him. He also tried to feel nothing more than a mild tingle of accomplishment, not outright pride. Pride was a useless emotion, and a dangerous one; on that point, he agreed with those silly priests. He wondered what Messenger had in store for him next.

%% %% %%

Messenger showed Nikolas how to mix volcanic ash and water to make desert brick. Nikolas poured the volcanic mud into interlocked wooden frames and set them in the sun to bake. When the mud dried to brick, Nikolas unfastened the wooden frames and set the bricks upright on the table, as Messenger instructed. Messenger shattered three of the four bricks with his fists.

"Now watch." Messenger torqued his body, cocking his fist back beside his ribs. "Power must go through your hips, around your spine, and to a focal point behind the brick, where your fist must be."

He uncoiled his wound-up body and volcanic debris littered the air.

Nikolas made more bricks and Messenger shattered them all. Nikolas made more bricks.

"Do you understand?" Messenger asked.

"I think so."

Nikolas mimicked Messenger's movements, twisting his body in the same way, putting his cocked fist at the same level. He imagined his fist on the other side of the brick. He hesitated, then swung.

Crouching on the ground, holding his bloody hand, he heard the brick fall over on the table.

"Your motions were identical," Messenger said.

"Yes . . ."

"And that is why you failed. Every man who is capable is capable in his own way."

Over the next few days, Nikolas spent hours knocking over the bricks and bloodied both of his hands. Messenger watched from a distance, occasionally stopping Nikolas and directing him to other exercises, particularly those designed to perfect balance.

"As you learn the shattering art of breaking rocks, which will prepare you for breaking the bones of your enemies, you should also learn the subtle skill of balance in all situations."

Nikolas was made to walk across thinner and thinner poles set up over the water-basin. Then he was made to juggle the lead balls from his target exercise as he performed his balancing exercises. Then Messenger began tossing more balls at him for Nikolas to integrate into his juggling pattern. Nikolas felt like a karnival monkey—a very wet karnival monkey, due to his falls into the basin—but there was also a pleasure in performing the ever-increasing intricacies of Messenger's exercises. And since he continued to fail to shatter the volcanic rock, his success at these exercises gave him a respite from the sensation of failure.

One night, Nikolas came back to his hut for his dinner and bed. But the door was locked. He hadn't seen Messenger for most of the day; that morning, he had been instructed to continue his exercises on his own. But Messenger must be in the cabin now. The only way to lock the door was from the inside. Nikolas pounded on the door for long minutes and demanded to be let in. He pounded the door longer.

He walked back to the table and stood the bricks upright again. He let his hands dangle beside him, releasing them of all purpose. He set his right foot behind him, turned his front foot just so, and lifted his right fist to head level. He brought it down and through. The brick didn't explode the way it did for Messenger, but it collapsed in three separate pieces. Nikolas rubbed his hand in quiet awe. Both of his hands ached, but it was the pain of accomplishment.

This time the door of the hut was open.

※ ※ ※

Nikolas's training went by faster than he could have predicted. Every day was filled from dawn to dusk with the learning of some new skill, exercises to make him stronger and more nimble, and an hour of meditation at the end of the day, during which he was instructed to both remember the lessons of the day and to forget them. In the manner foreign language students at Joshua University are at first required to memorize the rules of grammar, and then later expected to stop thinking about the rules, but rather to use them naturally, Nikolas was expected to internalize all he learned. "You must make it part of you the way your blood is part of you," Messenger instructed. A moment's gap between thought and action in real combat could mean death.

There was a crash just meters away, and Nikolas shot upright in bed. He scanned the room, but the darkness was all but impenetrable; ghostly gray outlines of the small chest-of-drawers and the bookshelf were partially visible on the other side of the room. Then the room was filled with blinding light; in the searing brightness, Nikolas saw two men with wooden clubs. He rolled and planted his feet on the floor, placing the bed between him and his assailants. He stood there completely naked. He was filled with a brief-desperate wish to have his pants and shoes on; he had never felt so vulnerable in his life.

Who could these men be? No one knew Nikolas was here except Messenger.

"Nikolas Kovalski?"

Nikolas did not answer. He blinked, his eyes adjusting to the light, the startling flare of its surprise receding.

"We have a message from Mayor Adams," the first man said as he made his way around the bed. "Give up now, and this beating will be the only price you pay for your defiance."

The man lunged. The few seconds Nikolas had bought himself by forcing them to go around the bed along with the adrenaline pumping through his system brought him fully to his senses. His eyes were still adjusting to the light, but he could see well enough. And this man moved slower than cold honey. Nikolas caught the man's wrist midswing and with a deft wrestler's twist flipped him over his back, sending him crashing into the wall. He thought he heard the crunching collapse of the man's shoulder when he hit, but he didn't want to take any chances. Nikolas kicked him beneath the jaw, shattering several teeth and knocking the man unconscious.

He spun around and stared at the second man, who was now coming toward him. Nikolas bent quickly and grabbed the first man's club and took a defensive stance. In the moment before the man attacked, Nikolas felt the full exposure of his nakedness. He had almost forgotten as he dealt with the first attack, but now, given this brief pause in the fighting, he became aware of the absurd vulnerability of his exposed genitals, his shoeless feet, and the skin along his back. He shut the thought out and focused on his assailant's approach.

The man swung, and Nikolas sidestepped. On the man's backswing, Nikolas brought his own club down on the man's fingers, causing him to drop his club. Nikolas kicked him in the groin and smashed his club into the man's face, flattening his nose to a crooked red mess. A sharp left jab to the man's temple and he was down. Nikolas looked around the room for further danger. Messenger stood in the doorway.

"Are we under some kind of attack?" Nikolas asked.

He set the club on his bed and fumbled around for his clothes.

"You are nearly ready, Nikolas," Messenger said.

"Nearly ready?" Nikolas asked, stepping into his underwear. "Nearly ready for what?"

Messenger ignored his question. "It is not that you dispatched two armed men, and without a weapon of your own, though that is pleasing. It is that you did so under such difficult circumstances. Most men cannot bring themselves to action so suddenly after being brutally awakened. And until one has done it, it is nearly impossible to imagine how difficult it is to fight entirely naked."

Nikolas began to understand. "You sent these men?"

"Yes," Messenger said without apology. "They were the final test of your preparedness."

"So, what they said about Mayor Adams having...?"

"Mere theatre, to make the exercise more real for you. That is something men of this sort might one day say to you, Nikolas. It is good for you to hear now."

Nikolas pulled his trousers on and looked at Messenger in wonder. "And what if they had succeeded in killing me?"

"Finish dressing," Messenger said. "And come down to breakfast. This was only the first exercise you must complete today." He nodded his head toward the men at Nikolas's feet. "A medik will be sent for them."

When Messenger was gone, Nikolas felt both anger and gratitude. These men really might have hurt him. This was no mere exercise. If he had not performed well, he would be lying battered and bloody on the floor right now. Messenger had put him in real danger. But he had performed well. Better than that; his form had approached perfection. For that, he was grateful; for that, he had Messenger to thank. *Nearly ready.* What else was left for him to learn, what other tests did Messenger have planned for him?

4.

AFTER THOSE FIRST few days, Adrian's time at the hospital went somewhat more smoothly, at least in part because the staff largely began ignoring him, assuming his brief introduction to hospital procedure should be enough for him to join the normal flow of traffic.

As Adrian stood in the courtyard, not quite ready to sit down for his lunch, a rattling squawk pierced the air just above his head, giving him such a start he nearly dropped his tray of food. It was a stark-black raven perched on the molding of the hospital wall. It let out another squawk, seemingly directed at Adrian. He stared at the carrion bird and marveled at its sleek beauty. He had never seen a raven this close up before. In the sky, at a distance, sure, but never this close—perhaps a mere two meters away.

"In the dark water," the raven said in a cracked sing-song, "drowns the dark father."

Adrian took a step back, awed and a bit terrified of the talking bird.

"That's Shosho," a girl at a nearby table said, and again Adrian was startled and nearly dropped his tray. Damn his nerves. Why couldn't he be more like Heinrich? He gathered himself.

"Shosho? It has a name?"

"He," she said. "He's a he. Used to belong to a patient from Al-Khuzir who was here for a while."

"Why didn't he take his pet with him when he left?" Adrian asked.

The girl looked at him until he understood.

"So who takes care of him now?"

"We all toss him a crumb of bread when we have it to spare," the girl said.

"Ask it. Ask it," crooned the bird. "The answer is a casket."

"Charming creature," Adrian said and smiled what he thought was a humorful and ironic smile in the direction of the bird.

"My name is Ariah," the girl said. "Care to join me?"

They ate in silence. Adrian paid more attention to the procedure of forking turnips into his mouth than was necessary as he tried to think of something appropriate to say. Ariah reached over and grabbed Adrian's sandwich.

"This looks good."

She took a large bite, but as she leaned over again to set it back on his tray, she dropped it to the ground. They stared at the sprawled lump of bread and meat. Shosho swooped down, planted atop the sandwich, flapped his wings noisily, and flew away with an enormous slice of bread.

Ariah pushed her tray toward Adrian. "Here, you can have some of mine."

※ ※ ※

From that day on, Adrian ate his lunch in the courtyard with Ariah. They talked of many things. Adrian told her about his journey to the hospital; he described Heinrich and Messenger and the collapsing bridge and the people with cages on their heads. He left out the part about almost fighting Jarir, because it made him seem petty and cowardly. He briefly considered telling her how he saved the baby, but if he was going to leave the less flattering part of the story out, he should omit the part that made him look good. It was only fair, he reasoned.

She wanted to know all about Joshua City. She missed it so much sometimes, she said. He told her about Brandt being murdered, and she said how sorry she was. He told her about the protest, leaving out the part about his seizure. It was not that he was ashamed of his epilepsy; it was simply that in this place of death and suffering, his own illness seemed trivial.

"We hear so few reports out here," she said. "But they all make it sound so awful. Is it really so bad there?"

Adrian thought hard about this. "Yes, and no. I have a friend, or maybe I should say I *had* a friend . . . Anyway, he dropped out of Joshua University because he thought that he couldn't possibly make any changes working within the system."

"And what do you think?"

"I still have some faith," he said. "I'm out here, after all."

"But you're not in Joshua City."

"No," he said. "I guess I'm not. What about you? How did you end up out here?"

"I came with my husband."

"I see," Adrian said cautiously, remembering Yves and Jarir.

Looking down at the ground, swinging her legs back and forth on the bench, she said, "He died a while ago. Before I got sick. In a mining accident."

Now it was Adrian's turn to express his condolences.

"It's all right," she said. "So much has happened since then. It hardly seems real sometimes."

Shosho came squawking up beside them. Ariah held out her hand and the bird pecked at a few crumbs there. He cocked his head curiously as if waiting for her to continue. For once, the bird had nothing to say.

"My husband wasn't a prisoner, like some of the men are, paying off their debt to society by working in the mines," Ariah said. "He was a trained technician, called one of the best in the trade at repairing broken equipment—which is really important this far out from Joshua City. It takes weeks to get a replacement, but if you can repair it on site, you can keep working right away." Her voice was filled with loving pride at the memory of her husband.

"What made you two want to live out here?" Adrian asked, suppressing a note of jealousy he could feel rising through him.

"Bogdon was incredibly excited when he received word that he had gotten the position ... "

※ ※ ※

Bogdon was incredibly excited when he received word that he had gotten the position. He was worried that Ariah might not like it in the Outer Provinces, but he promised himself he would do everything in his power to make her happy. And he just had to take this opportunity. He imagined himself welding a crane-arm in place, the harsh desert wind blowing in his face, miners depending on him to get it done right. He had been raised in the Outer Provinces, not more than seventy kilometers from where they would be living. Some people found the harsh environment too much to handle, but he loved it. And hoped Ariah might learn to love it as well.

Ariah, for her part, dreamed of being a journalist. However, she had not made much progress in that profession which privileged men so much over women. She needed something to set herself apart from her male colleagues; a female journalist needed to be twice as smart, to write twice as well, and have access to information others did not. When Bogdon told her about the position, she immediately began envisioning the book she would write about it. *My Year in the Outer Provinces* or *New Kolyma Stories* or *Scenes from a Laborers Kolony*. She had any number of working titles. She knew in some part of her mind she was rationalizing; Bogdon had his heart set on the job and she had no choice but to make the most of it. Still, she managed to talk herself into a growing enthusiasm.

Soon after her arrival, she discovered how misguided her fantasies had been. New Kolyma was dusty, dry, empty—less a city than a smattering of buildings. She had expected something along these lines, but she had not sufficiently imagined just how little there would be for her to do. The men did not want women down in the mines or on the building sites where her husband worked. The wives of the free workers bored her. They spent their days gathered in the one little supply shop in town, gossiping about life in the camp. They knitted and cooked and waited for their husbands to return home. The wives of the prisoners were more interesting, but they rejected her as an outsider, a woman married to the enemy. There was a tavern and more than once she was tempted to go there. But the only women there were prostitutes or old widows.

She read a lot, though soon her supply of books ran out as well. She wrote in her journals, still not entirely given up on the idea she might make a book out of her experiences. She stared out the window at the unsympathetic horizon and waited for Bogdon—no different from the other wives she so disdained. And in the evening, when he did return, they fought. The conversations were always the same. This was not the life she wanted, she told him. He replied that he had less than six months remaining on his initial contract. When that was done, maybe . . . But maybe wasn't good enough for her. Speaking of maybes, maybe she would take the next karavan back to Joshua City. He outright rejected that idea. The karavans were too dangerous. They must travel together.

"How very modern and enlightened of you," she mocked.

But some part of her knew he was right. You never saw a woman alone in the karavans—and there were good practical reasons for that.

Bogdon understood her position. And he wanted her to be happy. He did. But she had to understand that this was what he knew how to do. And this was where the work was. There were other larger mining camps. Maybe one of those would suit her more? If they moved back to Joshua City, his opportunities would be greatly reduced. Still, that was what they would do if they could reach no other compromise. Just give him a few months. Maybe in that time she would change her mind?

But then her symptoms began, and all of their discussions on the matter were moot.

%% %% %%

On her first visit to the Laborers Hospital, the doktor administered a series of tests. She had been feeling weak and sleeping ten or twelve hours a day.

"Your tests show that you might be suffering from mild anemia," the doktor said, flipping the pages of the report. "What is your diet like?"

"Nothing unusual, I would say. The same as anyone else out here."

"Well, I am going to prescribe a vitamin supplement. You need more iron, but it might be something else as well. We'll run some more tests, if that doesn't work."

Ariah was heartened that it might be such a simple solution.

"But there might also be another explanation," the doktor ventured. "Do you find your life here . . . satisfying?"

Ariah recalled the arguments with Bogdon, her long days without activity. "I am slowly growing accustomed to being here."

"Many wives of workers suffer from boredom, which can lead to a depressive state. It might not be a physical issue at all."

"But I have real symptoms."

"Yes," the doktor said, "but psychological problems often manifest physically."

Ariah wondered if this was true. Was it all in her mind? But no, she felt how she felt.

"We'll start with the vitamins for now. Come back in a few weeks, and we'll see how you're doing."

※ ※ ※

But her condition did not improve. It worsened, in fact. She was subjected to a series of ineffective and progressively more invasive tests. She became weaker and weaker. Finally, the doktors determined that her kidneys were not processing toxins as they should. Her blood was becoming toxic, which, they explained, meant that it could not transmit nutrients sufficiently. She and Bogdon discussed returning to Joshua City again, this time under a different mood.

"When my contract is fulfilled," Bogdon said, "we'll go back. I talked to my foreman, and there might be a possibility for me there. But even if not, we're going back."

Bogdon cooked their meals now, following the suggestions of the doktors to the letter. And he ate with her, the same things she had to eat. Bogdon was more loving than ever before.

The blood-filtration treatments the doktors administered and the new diet had their intended effect. She grew stronger and slept less; and her marriage was at its best point since they had left Joshua City. She had resumed control of her house. One day, when she was cleaning and preparing dinner—a surprise for Bogdon—a man came to their door.

She skipped across the room. The man's clothes were covered in dark dust and his face was drained of color. She recognized him. He was one of Bogdon's friends at the mine, Kurt.

"Ariah?" Kurt said.

She knew it was something horrible. "Yes."

"May I come in?"

Ariah stepped aside, her legs barely obeying.

He walked into the center of the room, looked to the floor she had just cleaned to a shine. He straightened himself.

"There was an accident at the mine today," he said. "The drilling machine had broken down. I was moved to a different section of the mine. I was there earlier. But . . . what am I saying? Anyway, Bogdon was called down to repair the machine. He's the best we have, you know. And he was called down there, and I was sent to another section. It collapsed. They're saying the drilling had weakened the supports."

"What happened?"

"I'm sorry," Kurt said. "He was, he was killed in the collapse. Along with about a dozen other men."

Ariah found a chair and slumped into it, her new strength now stolen.

※ ※ ※

"After that, I just didn't have the will to fight," Ariah said. "I kept telling myself I'd take the next karavan back to Joshua City. But a week passed and then another. It was the middle of January. Winter is always difficult for me, but this time it was worse, and it seemed like it would never end. I slept and slept. I missed one of my blood-filtration treatments. I might have died like that, alone in the little cabin where Bogdon and I used to live, if one of my neighbors hadn't been concerned. Lucette, the wife of a free worker. I think she came by to bring some sort of pastry—one of those condolence cakes people are always baking you when someone dies. I had half a dozen of them sitting in my kitchen untouched. Anyway, I'm not sure exactly why Lucette was there or how she got in. I was half-gone at that point. She ran and got her son, she told me later—she must have told me the story twenty times—and together they carried me to the Laborers Hospital. The doktor said if I'd gone without treatment for even another day, I would have died. So it was one of the women I had so disliked who ended up saving my life."

Ariah paused, lightly chewing on her lip, lost in thought. "You know, it's funny. This is the first time I've really talked about all of this. It feels good, I think, to share it." She smiled. "And you're a very good listener."

"You listened to me too," Adrian said.

"Yes, but most people are only waiting for their turn to speak," she said. "And the kinds of things I've been through make them uncomfortable. I can feel the pity dripping off of them."

Adrian thought about the way people treated him when they found out he was an epileptic—as though they were handling some very fragile piece of pottery while walking on a slick floor. He still hadn't told her about his condition. Maybe this was the time to do so? To show her he could relate on more than a patient-doktor level?

"You want to hear the worst thing?" she said.

"Only if you want to tell me."

She leaned in with a mischievous confidentiality. "I still don't like her. Even though she saved my life. She's just so impossibly . . . boring."

Ariah forced a bit of laughter at herself and leaned back, her cheeks flushed with defiance, waiting for Adrian's response. She seemed to expect him to be offended. He didn't know what his own reaction was, until he found himself laughing. There was something so refreshingly honest about her words. And she laughed along with him, this time without having to force herself—there in the courtyard, dowsed in summer sun. It was good to laugh. He had not done enough of that lately.

% % %

As their friendship progressed, Adrian learned everything he could about Ariah's condition and treatment. He read her case file, telling himself she was just another patient at the hospital; it was his duty to be informed about the medikal history of all his patients. Of course, she wasn't technically his patient. But understanding her case couldn't hurt, could it? Besides, she had already volunteered much of this information. He was simply filling in the details.

Her condition was in a troubling stasis. Provided she continued to receive frequent blood-filtration treatments, she could live for many years. However, all the treatments could hope to do was slow the deterioration of her kidneys, not totally alleviate it. Eventually, she would need a new kidney. A transplant would have to be performed in Joshua City, and it would be inordinately expensive. If Brandt was still alive, Adrian might have been able to beg him to use his influence and have her placed with an experimental team of doktors and medikal skolars. This happened rarely, but it did happen; a poor patient who needed experimental treatment that was too costly for their finances could volunteer to have their procedure be part of the curriculum at Joshua University. Adrian worried over the ethics of such a program, but at least it got the patient the required treatment and medikal science was forwarded. Perhaps he could write a letter to the renal specialist, just to see if there was a slot available. It was a dangerous procedure, and only a small number of successful operations had taken place thus far—but there had been successes; the procedures for kidney transplants were a decade, maybe two, ahead of those for heart transplants. Adrian suddenly wished he had taken experimental nephrology; if he had done that, he might have helped further the medikal science that could save Ariah's life.

He wanted a normal healthy life for her; he wanted that for all his patients, of course. If only... but that was a useless thought. He reminded himself that Ariah was not the only patient at the Laborers Hospital. He must remain impartial. He must make sure his attentions were given *everywhere* they were needed. It was disgraceful how neglected the hospital had been. Even with the militarization of the facilities, things had only slightly improved, and largely in the areas that serviced the military patients. Adrian considered writing an exposé on the situation, but he didn't have much faith in his writerly abilities and even less in the efficacy of such a piece. And that brought him back again to Ariah, the aspiring journalist. With his medikal knowledge and her writing experience, they could author an excellent collaborative book...

And so his thoughts went on and on in this manner, getting nowhere, always returning to the same impossible ground.

5.

"MESSENGER CONSIDERS the use of firearms cowardly, but given the proliferation of cowards in the world, it would be impractical to ignore such weapons."

Nikolas understood Messenger's point about firearms being the coward's weapon of choice, but he was practical and knew the revolution would need many armed men, men who could use their weapons efficiently and fatally.

"First we will focus on handguns and the sniper rifle. Ultimately, all other firearms are simply variations on these two types. Once you know the basics of these, you can improve your skills with them on your own, and you will be able to transfer those skills to other types of firearms with little difficulty."

They spent the next several days going over every part of various handguns and two types of sniper rifle. Messenger made Nikolas disassemble and reassemble each gun many times, showed him techniques for cleaning each piece and repairing minor damages. Nikolas was made to fire from a stationary position, using both his right and left hand; he was made to fire during a slow approach on his target; he was made to run, turn, and fire. Every variation of possible combat was simulated. With the sniper rifle, he was assigned targets at a greater and greater distance and of a smaller and smaller size. Messenger was an expert in these weapons he claimed to detest, and he was, as in everything, the perfect instructor.

Messenger kept up Nikolas's daily regimen of kalisthenics, and in the mornings they did an hour of hand-to-hand combat training. Otherwise, their entire efforts were focused on training Nikolas in mastering the mechanized ease of murder firearms allow. Even as Messenger's distaste for these weapons became ever more palpable, Nikolas found himself attracted to their brutal efficiency, the fine accuracy of their engineering. Their potential uses for The Underground and their sheer scientific wonder blended to work a powerful charm on Nikolas. And he improved even faster than Messenger had predicted. Between his natural aptitude and Messenger's excellent tutelage, Nikolas was, if not a professional marksman, a highly competent one—and, more importantly, Messenger had taught proper technique and a series of exercises to continue improving his abilities. Nikolas knew he didn't need to be as good as Messenger with firearms, or at anything for that matter; he only needed to be able to teach his komrades how to defend themselves and, when the time came, how to attack.

※ ※ ※

On a day like any other, Messenger stopped Nikolas in the middle of one of these marksmanship exercises. "Enough," he said.

Nikolas waited with a clenched stomach for Messenger to berate him. He had grown accustomed to Messenger's constant criticisms; however that didn't make them any less painful. He almost preferred it when Messenger slapped him; the coldly precise wording of Messenger's critiques sliced to the core of Nikolas's psyche, where he housed the most fragile portions of his ego. The good news was that they had been happening less and less frequently.

But Messenger simply nodded. "Pack your things," he said.

"Are we going somewhere?" Nikolas remembered his first walk through the desert and dreaded the idea of another similar journey.

"*We* are not going anywhere," Messenger said. "You, however, are going home."

Messenger walked off, clearly considering the conversation done. Nikolas trailed after him. "Home?"

"You have learned much," Messenger said without turning. "You are not at the level of Messenger. Nor will you ever be."

Nikolas was more hurt than he would have expected at this blunt dismissal of his abilities, even though he knew it to be true.

"But," Messenger continued, "that was not the goal here. We have instructed you on our principles. And now you can practice them yourself. More importantly, you can pass them onto others—in whatever bastardized form you wish."

Nikolas ignored this final jab. They were nearly back to the hut where Nikolas would gather his scant belongings and leave.

"So that's it? I'm done?"

Messenger stopped, turned, placed his hand on Nikolas's shoulder. It was the first time he had touched Nikolas in such a komradely way.

"There is one last thing. Come."

Nikolas followed Messenger into a room where several needles and a large bottle of ink were laid out. Messenger grabbed Nikolas's left arm and stretched it out straight in front of him, palm upward. Nikolas wondered what last punishment or humiliation was in store; he knew he would accept it gratefully.

"You are going to receive the Messenger tattoo," Messenger said. "This is the highest honor we can convey upon you. Now, keep your arm steady in this exact position. If you falter, you do not deserve it."

Messenger began outlining a row of black rectangular bars on Nikolas's upper forearm. There would be eight bars in total, Messenger explained, one for each of the eight cities.

"*Eight* cities?" Nikolas asked.

Messenger paused in his preparation. "Yes. The current Seven plus the fallen city of Messenger. This tattoo is to remind us of all we have lost and what keeps us united. But understand, this does not mean you are of us."

"I understand," Nikolas said and braced himself as Messenger lowered the needle.

Messenger dipped the needle into the bottle of ink and stabbed it into Nikolas's arm. The dully persistent yet sharply discrete pain was mesmerizing. Nikolas had never understood the attraction some found in getting those Ulani-style tattoos so popular in Joshua City until recently. But now, under the needle, he had an intimation of their appeal. This kind of pain could be addictive. And the added effort of keeping his arm perfectly still and straight in front of him as Messenger worked made the experience yet more intense and invigorating.

An hour later, Nikolas's arm threatened to shake. Another hour, and it was lightly trembling, but Messenger ignored his discomfort and stabbed and stabbed the black ink in. The burn in the muscles of his arm matched the burn of the needle. He imagined Katya seeing this, seeing him.

"Remember your mantra."

Nikolas went to the place Messenger had taught him. The next two hours were made more bearable.

When the tattoo was done, Messenger smeared a liniment on Nikolas's raw flesh and wrapped it with a wet cloth from a boiling pot of water.

"Messenger will be watching your progress with great interest."

"Why are you doing this?"

"The Harbinger," Messenger said, echoing his words from the night they had met. "Now go."

6.

DIREKTOR SPARGO had summoned Adrian to his office. A nurse was sent to the station he was assigned to for the day and interrupted his work—administering small dosages of antibiotics to the nekrotic patients intravenously—to hand him a note from Spargo. *Please report to my office at 14:30. Spargo.* No other information, and so Adrian had no idea what Spargo wanted to speak to him about as he knocked on the Direktor's door.

"Direktor Spargo?"

"Ah, Adrian, come in." Spargo indicated the chair in front of his desk cheerfully and unnecessarily (there was no other place to sit).

"Thank you," Adrian said and took his seat.

"How are you getting along here, young man?" Spargo asked, but without much interest. This was an empty question, not the real reason he had brought Adrian here.

Adrian answered anyway, despite knowing his answer didn't really matter. "Fine. Dr. Abuawad has been very helpful. And I am feeling more comfortable and at home with each passing day."

"Good, good," Spargo said and scratched at his slightly unshaven face. Adrian felt sympathy for the man, not knowing what had caused him to miss shaving for the past day or two. "There is a small matter I wanted to discuss with you."

"Yes, sir?"

"We don't have strict rules about fraternizing with the patients," Spargo began, looking Adrian in the eye like some benevolent inquisitor, "given the situation out here. The isolation we all feel, I mean. It is perhaps inevitable that—how should I put it?—*relations* will emerge, either between staff members or even between staff and patients."

Adrian's skin was suddenly hot and it felt as if all of his blood had rushed to his face. *Does he know that I've looked at her file?*

"It has come to my attention that you and a certain Ariah Prusakova have become close over the past few weeks," Spargo said. "Have I heard correctly?"

"Yes," Adrian said quietly, guiltily. "That is true, sir."

"Don't be so crestfallen, my boy. As I say, we have no *strict* policy on the matter."

Spargo was silent for torturous seconds. Adrian dangled by a precarious thread. He fidgeted like a schoolboy under Spargo's calm administrative gaze. Then, suddenly angry with himself and the situation, he straightened his back and forced himself to sit still.

"What would you suggest I do, sir?"

"I would just ask that you keep it discreet. The other patients mustn't get the idea that you are playing favorites, perhaps giving our Ariah extra medikaments or more exact treatment of any sort."

"That's reasonable."

"Mind you, I don't care if you are giving her special treatment," Spargo said, and then added with a wink in his voice, "so long as she's earning it."

Adrian blushed all over again and said nothing.

"That will be all," Spargo said. "You may return to your station."

Adrian left the Direktor's office, any sympathy he had felt for Spargo having vanished. He was lewd and, Adrian now understood, derived pleasure from lording his petty reserve of power over others.

And it wasn't as if Adrian had truly done anything wrong, he told himself.

%. %. %.

One morning a few days later, Adrian was refilling the saline solution bags. It was something that needed to be done, but normally the nurses performed this task. He set another bag in the cooling-cabinet. He had some time between scheduled surgeries and was avoiding seeing patients; he had seen enough abscesses, rotten limbs, screaming patients in their private states of dying. He filled another bag. Another. He spent two hours at this soothingly mundane task. He saw there were only a few empty bags left; he would have to return to real work soon. It was then that the crackle of the intercommunications system came thinly through the room.

"*Medikal skolar or doktor requested. Medikal skolar or doktor requested. Room 317. Urgent.*"

Adrian recognized the number. Ariah. He left the saline bags on the table.

%. %. %.

Three nurses surrounded her bed, and Ariah was cursing them, kicking them off.

"Get an opiate syringe," one nurse said to another.

The syringe was produced and stabbed deeply into Ariah's thigh. She lurched forward, swiped at the nurse's arm, then sunk back onto the pillows.

Adrian stepped forward and in his most official voice asked, "Have you checked blood-toxicity levels?"

Annoyed, "We haven't had time yet, sir. As you can see, she's non-cooperative."

"You're here . . . " Ariah said and grabbed at the air, a weak brightness on her face.

There was a stench in the room. The sheets of Ariah's bed were soaked in fluids that could be feces or blood or both.

"How long has she been like this?" Adrian asked.

He leaned over Ariah. Her face was covered in sweat. There were crystalline shimmers along her cheeks. He recalled that patients with renal failure sweated out the toxins normally expulsed via urine. *Her condition must be advancing.*

"Only about twenty minutes," a nurse behind him said.

Adrian checked Ariah's pulse. It was pounding. High blood pressure was a symptom of renal fatigue, but it was perhaps the least of her concerns now. And the sedative the nurses gave her ought to solve that problem—for the moment at least.

Ariah's eyes were glassy now from the opiates. "I'm so proud of you for coming out here."

She let her hand slide lovingly down the front of his medikal coat.

Adrian felt a pang of pride at her words. He pushed it out of his mind and ordered one of the nurses to bring the blood-filtration machine.

"She needs emergency blood-filtration." Then, to Ariah, "I'm going to make this all right."

One of the nurses left the room in a hurry.

"You've been so good to me," Ariah said, her words drifting.

Adrian took her hand in his and squeezed. He was going to save her.

"When we came out here . . . " Ariah began.

"Save your strength."

He wetted a cloth and wiped her forehead.

"When we first . . . " Ariah began again, taking up her thought from before. "I was angry with you. I never admitted it."

The nurse and a medikal assistant entered the room with the blood-filtration machine. Adrian turned from Ariah's bed and plugged the machine in.

"Ariah, I am going to start the procedure," Adrian said. "Is that fine with you?"

"I trust you."

He slid the first needle into her left arm and hooked its tube into the machine. He slid the second needle into her right arm and hooked it into the machine. He checked the pump mechanism before turning it on. The whir went low and high, pumping and filtering.

"You went down there every day. I couldn't have . . . The mines are so deep out here and the people . . . Then when you died . . . But I loved you and still love you. It makes me happy to live here with you, Bogdon."

Adrian went on with the procedure, trying to ignore her opiate-laden words.

With a loud noise her bowels emptied onto the bed beneath her. Her eyes went lucid.

"I'm so embarrassed for you to see me like this."

And this time, Adrian was certain she was speaking to him.

※ ※ ※

Fifteen minutes later, in a surgery preparatory room on the other side of the hospital, Adrian washed his hands and arms thoroughly. *These are Ariah's fluids*, he realized. *I'm disinfecting myself of her.* He washed his face with cold water. He had run here directly from her room; the surgery he was about to perform had been scheduled for a week. He shouldn't have responded to the call on the intercommunications system, but he hadn't had time to think. It was Ariah, after all.

But he had done everything correctly. He had navigated his authority with the nurses well; he had diagnosed the situation accurately and swiftly; he had hooked up the machine properly on the first try. *I saved her life.* He must remember that. That was the important thing. Still, his reaction had been odd. Inappropriate, even. When he thought her words were intended for him, he had felt a thrill of happiness despite the danger she was in. And what a disappointment—was it jealousy?—when he realized she thought she was speaking to her dead husband.

Adrian ended his ponderings. He was about to perform surgery on a man's eye and needed his full concentration. Doktor Abuawad had entered the preparatory room and was washing his hands. He dried them carefully on a towel and nodded to Adrian.

"Let's go," he said, and Adrian followed him into the surgery room.

As Adrian began the initial stages of the procedure, Doktor Abuawad observed from a close distance, ready, Adrian imagined, to take over if necessary. Adrian injected the patient with general anesthetic and counted backwards from ten with him until he fell into unconsciousness. Adrian then carefully peeled the left eyelid open and motioned for the nurse to hand him a clamp. He set it in place, holding the patient's eyelid wide.

The patient, an injured Guardsman in his early thirties, had complained of extreme pain, sleeplessness, and an inability to control the movement of his left eye.

"What does that sound like to you, Adrian?" Doktor Abuawad had asked when they scheduled the procedure a week earlier, his voice detached yet somehow expectant, judging yet supportive.

"My first guess would be a torn ocular ligament." When Doktor Abuawad said nothing, Adrian considered further possibilities. "It could also be damaged extra-ocular muscle tissue."

"I think that is the better bet."

"Why do you say that? If I may ask."

In a calm measured voice, "Firstly, what do we know about our patient? His case file says he has suffered from a nervous condition for several months, likely the result of psychological trauma suffered in battle."

Adrian lifted the eye-dropper and let two drops of moisturizing fluid fall onto the patient's exposed eye.

"I have found that the extra-ocular muscles are prone to tears and other injuries in patients who suffer from nervous conditions," Abuawad continued. "They sleep irregularly and their eyes dart about uncontrollably. These two factors lead to extreme fatigue. To tear a ligament, there would need to be some noticeable contusion, or most likely there would be. We're always playing a game of odds in this profession, Adrian. But we make our decisions on what the Al-Khuziri philosopher and mathematician, Ruzil Al-zid, called *an appeal to the best possible explanation.*" He paused to let the idea take root in Adrian's mind. "Am I certain I am right about this diagnosis? Of course not. But given the evidence before me, given my own past experience, and given my fervent hope that we do not have to do the much more invasive and difficult ligament surgery, I am making my appeal to what I think is the best possible explanation for the symptoms exhibited by the patient."

And it seemed Doktor Abuawad was correct. Having carefully peeled back the skin around the eye and pushed the soft globular flesh of the eye itself slightly away from the socket-wall, Adrian lowered the magnifying lens on his headpiece and saw a length of muscle tissue that was dislodged from the eye. He nodded at Doktor Abuawad, confirming their course of action.

Adrian took the degradable sutures and the tiny surgical needle in his hands. He breathed and checked if his hands were shaking. They were not. Not in the least, in fact. He bent over the patient and began the slow and meticulous task of re-attaching the loose extra-ocular muscle to his eye.

※ ※ ※

A little over an hour later, Adrian and Doktor Abuawad were in the post-operation room, filling out reports, as a nurse took the still-sleeping patient to his room for rest. The procedure had been a total success. Adrian stood, went to the sink, and splashed cold water over his face. He dried himself with a scratchy towel that smelled heavily of disinfectant. He had not thought of Ariah during the entire operation, he realized.

"You did well, Adrian," Doktor Abuawad said.

"At first I wasn't sure I would."

"At first?"

"Yes," Adrian said, pondering what he had meant by that qualifier. "At first. But after a few minutes, a calm certainty came over me, and I just did the work. I didn't worry if I would make an error—though of course I took every precaution. I don't mean to say that I was overconfident or careless."

"Of course not. I can't imagine you are even capable of that."

"But even though I took the precautions, I was so totally taken up with my actions that I did not let any conscious worry enter my mind. Or . . . it's not that I didn't let any worry in. It just wasn't there. My entire self was immersed in the necessity of the effort at hand."

Doktor Abuawad smiled. "I know the sensation well. As do many surgeons—the good ones, anyway. A medikal professor of mine once called it the *surgeon's clarity.* I understand soldiers and athletes and even artists talk of similar sensations."

Adrian considered this.

"Yes, I can imagine that."

"Well, enough philosophizing," Doktor Abuawad said. "Let us finish this dreary paperwork and go eat."

Adrian paused, not wanting to engage in something so mundane as paperwork after what he had just experienced—and with thoughts of Ariah finding their way back into his mind—but that was what being a doktor meant. Doing whatever was necessary to keep patients alive and the hospital running smoothly. He sat down to the paperwork before him and forced himself to fill in each bureaucratic slot with the requisite information.

There was still so much to be done—rounds to make and further forms to be completed—before the day would end.

7.

ON THE MORNING they were to enact their plan, Marcik felt an uncanny calm. He imagined that he was already dead. He had died during the attack. Not captured and brought here to rot, but killed; his bones picked free by desert scavengers, his skull smiling at the sky. Free from worldly concerns. It brought him a peculiar peace to think of all this as a postmortem chimera.

Jürgen lay on his dingy bedding, breathing slowly. Marcik knew he was awake, just lying there with his eyes closed. He did not strike Marcik as a man who would lose his nerve, but he had learned in his time out here—first as a Guardsman then as a prisoner—that there was no way to predict how a person would react in a crisis. Cowardice and courage are twin animals, equally eager to take residence in the psyche.

The previous evening they had outlined the last steps of their plan. There was one aspect that Marcik still didn't quite agree with.

"I don't understand why it's necessary."

"Because these are military men," Jürgen patiently explained. "They are accustomed to a certain chain of kommand. Why would they accept orders from a mere private?"

"So I'm just going to steal a man's identity?"

"It's not Schmidt's identity any longer. Dead men have no identity."

Now Marcik rose and began his stretches but decided to forego his usual kalisthenics; he would need all of his strength for today. The dimensions of the cell seemed at once more confining and more open than ever before. He abandoned his stretches and leaned against the cold hard wall.

"Are you ready?" Jürgen asked.

Marcik nodded.

"It's a huge risk, taking this on yourself."

"That's exactly why I'm willing to do it."

Jürgen waited for him to elaborate.

"You want me to be a leader, right?" Marcik said. "Well, a leader wins respect through action. If Kharkov did this, the men would want to follow him. And they'd be right to do so."

"So you're saying it's a selfish act? That's an interesting way of thinking about it."

"Besides," Marcik said with a smile, "that big bastard would never fit through the tunnel anyway."

They sat in silence again.

"What about you?" Marcik asked. "Ready?"

"Me? I've got the easy part. But quiet now. I can hear them coming."

※ ※ ※

"Forward, zek!"

The guard shoved Marcik in the center of his back, sending him rushing forward, half-flailing to stay on his feet. Jürgen was not manhandled in the same way, but he kept his head obsequiously low. On either side of them, the other zeks sat calmly in their cells. *Don't worry, brothers,* Marcik thought. *Soon.* He continued walking forward without looking back at the guard. He took no offense at the guard's bullying rudeness. He did not even see him as the man he had interacted with dozens of times over the past few months. He was now merely an obstacle to Marcik's plan. *No, Major Schmidt's plan.*

"Halt, zek," the guard said when they got to a cell holding two prisoners, both Kharkov's men. The guard unlocked the cell door and motioned threateningly with his baton for them to join Marcik and Jürgen in the corridor. They stood slowly, with a slow confidence, a slowness they would not have dared under different circumstances.

Inside the latrine, the stench was so powerful, Marcik considered abandoning the entire plan. Every part of his organism rejected the idea; even touching that human muck with a finger seemed too much; to slide through it ... Marcik took an unconscious step back and urine splashed on the floor before he could correct himself.

A swift blow from the guard's baton came down on his shoulders. It was a half-hearted blow, not really meant to do damage, but rather to assert authority. Again, Marcik did not think of the guard as a man, or not the particular man he was. He lowered his head, stepped forward, and finished his business. When he was done, he looked sidelong to the other zeks, the first time he had purposely looked another zek in the eye during latrine-call. The first time he had purposely *recognized* them as his fellow men. He nodded. *It is time.*

The two men stepped away from the waste-trough and moved toward the guard, while Marcik pretended to continue urinating.

"On with it," the guard said, looking toward Marcik.

And it was that briefest of glances away from the two men that gave them their opening. They were upon him with reptilian speed and intent. They were on the ground and struggling, the guard swinging his baton as best the cramped space and crowding men would allow, the men desperately hitting the guard anywhere they could, hoping to silence him before the commotion brought reinforcements.

Marcik gave the guard a boot to the face, then another with all his weight and force. Blood ran from the guard's temple. He was still breathing. Should they kill him? *We should kill him. It's the only way.* Jürgen stood impassive. Marcik was in charge now.

"Tie him up and gag him." Marcik saw a supply closet. "Make sure he's bound tight and lock him in there."

Jürgen reached out his hand and Marcik took it.

"Stall them as long as you can," Marcik said.

"Good luck," Jürgen said.

"Just do your part and I'll do mine."

⁂ ⁂ ⁂

Marcik approached the chute at the end of the waste-trough. He took a deep breath and got a lungful of stench. *Nothing compares . . .* He peered into the chute's black space. He would have to press his forearms and thighs against the sides of the chute to control his slide down, until he reached the tunnel system where he could crawl his way to freedom. Or not freedom, but the possibility of freedom—and of capture, torture, death.

※ ※ ※

Jürgen watched Marcik squeeze into the chute, the lower half of his body slipping out of sight. Then he went to the door of the latrine. He looked out into the hall: no guards. Luck was on their side so far.

He hurried toward the main communications room. If he and Marcik had calculated correctly, there would be no guards in this sector of the prison, and he should make it there unobserved. Once there, he would disable the prison's communications system. He would have to act fast—but that shouldn't be too hard; he was already familiar with the communications system from having repaired it before.

That's a lot of shoulds *and* ifs, Jürgen thought. *But that's bound to be true of any plan devised under such circumstances.*

He turned the corner and saw the main communications room not ten meters ahead.

※ ※ ※

Marcik forced himself forward, bile convulsing up from his stomach and filling his mouth with bitter acid. He thought he heard something behind him and stopped, making himself small and silent like a hunted rodent. At first it sounded like metal bouncing on metal, but then the rush of water was clear. The trough was being flushed. *Oh God, no no no.* And then it was upon him. He closed his eyes and cupped his hands over his mouth and nose. It was fast-moving but without too much force. Chunks of feces flowed up the legs of his trousers. His hair was soaked and when the deluge had passed him by, a vile slop was caked over every bit of him. This time more than bile came up.

When he had control of himself again, he moved forward, half-crawling and half-sliding through the tunnel. A hollow pit of fear formed around his now-empty stomach. Why had he thought this would work? He was going to die down here, or he was going to die when he had to crawl back, defeated and shit-smeared. *Shut up. Move forward, Guardsman! Be worthy of your mother city.* And so he slip-crawled forward and forward through the vile plenitude everywhere around him and slathered over him, trying to clear his mind of his surroundings and the terror he felt flowing through every vein.

% % %

The half dozen men under Kharkov's supervision unloaded a food ship-ment—sacks of potatoes, bags of flour, crates of oil. The Ulani guard stood some meters off, his posture casual and unready, unaware of what was going on elsewhere in the prison, unaware that his radio was no longer working.

Kharkov had chosen these men specifically, picking as many as he was allowed for such a simple task. A truck had been pulled inside the prison gates and the men grabbed the crates and sacks from the truck bed and carried them into a storage room stocked with similar supplies. The driver of the truck had gone inside the prison, to receive payment for the shipment.

The zeks worked in a steady efficient rhythm, awaiting Kharkov's signal. It was crucial that he get the timing right. If they moved too early, they would not give Marcik sufficient time to complete his part of the plan. If they moved too late, they would not afford the proper distraction and the men in the latrine would be captured. Everything had to go perfectly. Kharkov had no watch, but from months in prison, he had a highly developed sense of time. He nodded to one of his men, just now unloading an enormous sack of oats—probably a two-person job. The man staggered with the sack and dropped it on the hard dirt. It tore open, spilling the oats everywhere. Kharkov simply stood there, making no move to reprimand the clumsy zek.

The Ulani guard moved forward, shouting something unintelligible at Kharkov. Kharkov watched him approach, calm and measuring. Two men came up behind the guard, unseen.

"What are you doing?" the guard asked, now within hearing dis-tance of Kharkov.

"I'm not yours any longer," Kharkov said.

The guard swung his baton at Kharkov and Kharkov ducked, deflecting the blow with his arm. It hurt; and it would hurt more later. That didn't matter. He caught the guard's arm and twisted. With his other hand, the guard gamely reached for his gun. But it was too late. One of the zeks grabbed him around his neck. Then the other yanked his gun from his belt. The first zek pulled back hard, choking the guard, lifting him off his feet. The guard clawed wildly at the hands on his neck. He kicked at the air. He gasped and sputtered. His face was turning red.

But it's a hard slow thing to choke a man to death. The zek released the guard and he fell into the dirt. The other zek lifted the gun and shot him where he knelt. Brain-mush splattered the dirt and the skin of the zeks. A wet pink string stuck to Kharkov's pants-leg. He flicked it off as casually as if it were a bit of food and not the very essence of a man.

"Give me the gun," he said.

The other zek handed him the weapon without question. Kharkov raised it, slid back the action, and fired twice. In the air.

"That should get their attention."

They hunkered behind the truck to wait the arrival of the Ulani reinforcements. How many would they send? That all depended on how much they knew of what was going on elsewhere.

※ ※ ※

It could not have been more than fifteen minutes, Marcik reckoned, that he had been making his way through the tunnels—though the filth and slow crawling made it seem much longer. The tunnels were simple enough in their layout. That, at least, was a blessing. If he were to get lost down here, he would go mad from the stench long before he died of dehydration or hunger. Just ahead he could see light breaking in on the redolent gloom of the tunnels. *That must be the place.* All he had to do was crawl the several meters left between him and the light.

He reached the mouth of the tunnel and nearly jumped out with a yelp of victory, but he controlled himself. He peeked out slowly. There was the edge of the compound, marked by a dusty road stretching into the desert. And not twenty meters down the road, the armory. A squat building of dull beige concrete, just as Jürgen had described it. He entertained the thought—ever so brief—of simply continuing down the road, to freedom. Just as quickly, the thought was gone. He climbed from the mouth of the tunnel and to his purpose.

At the door to the armory, he methodically tried the keys he had taken off the guard in the latrine. No, not that one. Not that one either. Damn it. He had to hurry.

A movement over his left shoulder. Marcik froze with the keys in his hand. Coming around the corner, zipping up his pants, was a guard. The man fumbled with his baton, snagging it on its loop, finally getting it out.

"What are you doing there?"

He was a small one, thank Baikal. Marcik dropped the useless keys on the ground and raised his hand. At the same time, he propped one foot against the wall of the armory, working his shoe free. As the guard moved forward, Marcik grabbed for the shoe. The guard laughed, thinking perhaps that Marcik meant to beat him with the limp piece of leather. As the guard approached, Marcik threw the shoe at him. The guard ducked it easily and kept approaching. Then he saw the letter opener in Marcik's hand.

It was the one object Marcik had managed to hang onto from the cigar box he carried with him when he left Joshua City; he had known it would come in useful. He had hidden it in his shoe on the way through the latrine, slipping it out just before he threw the shoe at the guard.

The letter-opener was slippery with filth and Marcik was not sure he had it solidly enough to punch its tip though the guard's throat. It had to be the throat, right into the windpipe and then a wide scything pull-back, severing the jugular. Marcik knew this was exactly how it had to be done and had a mystic's certainty that if it were not done precisely in this fashion, he would fail to kill the guard, and the prison break would fail, and he would be killed right here and now.

The guard took a defensive position with his baton in front of him. Marcik took two probing steps forward, and the guard swung wildly to force him back. Marcik easily dodged the blow, though he didn't get the sense the man had even intended on making contact. He simply wanted some distance between him and his strange assailant.

"Help!" the guard yelled, sending a hollow echo bouncing between the buildings. Marcik needed to silence him, and now.

Marcik lunged forward, swatting with his left hand at the baton and jabbing straight and fast with the letter opener into the man's throat. He felt the metal puncture the skin and gristle of the man's throat with an audible pop. He also felt the decorative edge of the letter opener tear the skin between his own thumb and forefinger, but he ignored the pain. He pulled the letter opener out of the man's neck and jabbed it in again. The baton hit him uselessly in the side, taking a little air from him but not slowing him in the least. He jabbed again, this time tearing a wide gash across the side of the man's neck, hitting home. Blood flooded out and the man stumbled, watery noises emerging from his mouth and the puncture-wound in his throat. He tried again to scream for help but only managed a sputter of red. He went to his knees, eyes rolling back in his head. Marcik kicked him squarely in the jaw, sending him flailing back on the ground, unconscious. He would bleed to death quickly, Marcik knew, and he was glad the man would not suffer more than necessary.

Jürgen had been right; he must become Major Schmidt. He looked at the corpse at his feet; he took in a nostril-full of shit and piss and intestinal blood; he picked up the dead man's baton. He was Major Schmidt now.

Major Schmidt removed the keys from the guard's belt. The second one he tried opened the armory. He looked inside, at the wealth of weapons therein. From the back of his shirt, he removed a large canvas sack, stolen by one of the zeks on laundry duty and passed to him when they met in the latrine. He set about the business of loading the sack with as many guns and grenades as he could carry.

※ ※ ※

By the time First Ensign Ottar realized their communication system was down, it was too late. At first, he thought something was wrong with his radio. He had come up with a perfect joke. *Joshuan women are like...* Ingvar would love it. Ottar took his radio from his belt and turned it to the proper channel. Nothing. Not even static. He switched to another channel, also nothing. Maybe it was just a dead battery, but he should go have a look anyway.

He went to the nearest communication station—one of a dozen around the prison—and checked the radio there. Also dead. Now he broke into a run, until he arrived at the main communications room. He pulled out his keys and discovered there was no need. The door was already open a crack.

Inside, he saw a tangle of loose wires hanging out of the main console. Something was terribly wrong. He needed to alert Communications Officer Uthman. If Ottar remembered correctly, this was Uthman's assigned time to take his midday meal. As he started toward the guards' mess hall, he heard gunshots coming from the southeast sector of the compound.

※ ※ ※

Major Schmidt shoved the canvas sack of guns up through the mouth of the chute, into the latrine, and then hoisted himself out after it. His men were waiting. He ordered them to take a rifle and two kartridges of ammunition each. For himself, he claimed a rifle and a handgun and two ammunition kartridges. He looked at the three hand grenades. He would take those as well.

"What do we do now, sir? It sounds like Kharkov's attack has started. A few minutes ago we heard some shots."

There were seven more rifles in the bag. "You two go and give Kharkov support," he said, motioning to two of the Guardsmen.

"Yes, sir," they said and hurried out of the room.

"What about us, sir?" said one of the two remaining Guardsmen.

Never before had he been called *sir* so many times in the space of one minute.

"Grab that," he said, indicating the remaining guns. "We've got some doors to open."

※ ※ ※

Olgar had barricaded the door to the interrogation cell. Fitting that they would have their final encounter here. Major Schmidt, forcing his voice to a pitch of total authority, ordered two zeks to pound the handle with heavy iron pipes, alternating like two destructive pistons. *Clang-clang, clang-clang, clang-clang*, their triumphant music ripped the air. This was all happening. Major Schmidt could hardly believe it. They had won. Or were about to, definitively. He just had to keep Olgar and the other high-ranking Ulani officers from committing honor-suicide, as was their general practice—something he remembered all too well from the one time he saw it up close.

Clang-clang, clang-clang...

When the door finally gave, Major Schmidt stepped forward. There was Olgar. He had his back pressed into the far corner of the room.

"Marcik, I have shown you mercy," Olgar pleaded. "Truly I have. Allow me an honorable Ulani death at my own hand. Or kill me now yourself."

"Call me Major Schmidt," he said. "There is no Marcik Kovalski."

"But I killed Schmidt."

Olgar took a defensive stance. Major Schmidt raised the baton he had taken from the guard and walked casually toward his former torturer.

"You didn't kill him," Major Schmidt said. "You made him. It was another you killed, and I owe you dearly for that. But first, you're going to tell me everything you know about the Ulani plans."

Major Schmidt walked calmly toward his victim, not noticing the dried sewage caked on his face and hands and clothes. He had only one thought in his mind, and that was barely a thought at all.

※ ※ ※

Major Schmidt almost had to respect Olgar. He held out to the end. Broken fingers, a gouged-out eye, fire-heated metal pressed against the soft insides of this thighs. But Face was, if possible, even tougher. Kharkov struck him in the jaw repeatedly, shattering bone and dislodging teeth. Face took the blows without flinching and spit the blood on the ground. Kharkov leaned back, looking at Face with a begrudging soldierly admiration.

"We're going to have to shoot this one," Kharkov said to Major Schmidt.

The communications officer was an entirely different sort. A few swipes with a baton and he gave up everything he knew about the Ulani troop movements. A part of Major Schmidt wished he had begun with this man and left Olgar intact. Another part enjoyed repaying his tormentor.

There were three major conflicts underway, the communications officer told them: one was deep in Ulani territory, too far away for Major Schmidt and the Guardsmen to arrive in time to help; another conflict the Baikal Guard already had well in hand; but there was a third conflict, nearby and hotly contested. The Ulani army had erected a military outpost at the border of Joshuan territory, bridging a main tributary of the Selenga River. A few hundred Guardsmen had seized the outpost and claimed it for their own. But now they were trapped, superior numbers of Ulani troops camped just outside. And now that the Ulanis had allied with Al-Khuzir, yet more troops were likely to be on the way. The siege had been going on for weeks; it was only a matter of time before the Ulanis would breach the walls.

※ ※ ※

The door to Samir's cell swung open. On the floor, Samir lay curled on the pallet. From out in the hall, he heard shouting, gunfire. A man screamed. Something was happening. His body was a battered mess of bruised flesh; he thought some of his ribs might be broken; it hurt so much to breathe. His testicles were swollen sacs of blood; he did not think they would ever work again. The prison doktor had done just enough to keep him alive.

But it was more than the physical strength he lacked. The light came in through the open door, blinding him. He rolled over onto his side, gasping with the effort. *Shut the door*, he thought. *Can't you see I'm trying to sleep?* That was all he wanted to do now. Sleep...and maybe never wake up. That was what he deserved. A deep dreamless endless sleep.

But would his sleep be dreamless? All the horrible things he had done. He had lied, stolen, cheated. And the other thing. Even dragged Yoyo into it with him. Yoyo, that stupid fuck. Got himself killed. He was standing right beside Samir when The Savage Ones came barreling out of the mouth of the valley. No one could say Yoyo hadn't been brave. He even managed to fire one shell, taking out part of a hillside and a few Savage Ones, before they fell on him. It was horrible, and Samir had done nothing to save him. What could he do? But that wasn't an excuse.

His religion, which he had mostly stopped believing in, said that we come back as that which we've done. If so, he would come back as a desert-roach. Or worse.

A shadow blocked out the light. Samir's insides buckled. It was his mortal inquisitor.

"I'm ready," he said, his voice a vermin's wheeze.

The shadow stepped forward. It was Marcik Kovalski. No, not him. A phantom in his shape. It was all so fitting.

"I'm sorry," he said and prepared for a holy reckoning.

※　※　※

Major Schmidt stood in the doorway, looking at the sad quailing piece of flesh on the floor of the cell. Samir Hosani. He had no love for the man, that was true. And he didn't exactly fit the description of *able-bod-*

ied at the moment. He would only be slowing them down. And they would have enough trouble as it was with all the civilian prisoners. Some, like Jürgen, had their skills. Others were mere baggage.

Still, what was the first rule of the Guardsmen? *Never leave a fellow Guardsman behind.* And he was a major now. If he was to lead his people, he must do so by example. Sure, he could simply turn and walk away. The man didn't seem to want his help anyway. Or not in the way Schmidt intended to help him. "Kill me," he kept saying, and Schmidt was tempted to comply. But if Schmidt did that, he wouldn't be able to live with himself—even if no one else ever found out. He walked over to Samir and took him firmly by the collar of his filthy shirt.

"Get up, Guardsman," he said, yanking Samir to his feet.

※ ※ ※

The newly freed zeks, some eighty men in total, gathered in front of the prison. A dozen trucks were lined up, the prison gates open behind them. Major Schmidt, freshly showered and wearing an officer's uniform Jürgen had rescued from items confiscated by the Ulanis, stepped out into the yard, Kharkov and Jürgen at his side. A cheer went up for the three liberators.

Kharkov leapt on the hood of one of the trucks.

"This is Major Schmidt," he shouted. "Some of you may have known him before—or thought you knew him. But now you know him as Major Schmidt."

Major Schmidt looked out in the crowd, meeting the eyes of a few zeks from his cell block, wondering if they would accept him in his new role.

"We have a mission to complete and he is going to lead us in that mission. You can either follow him or stay behind," Kharkov said, waiting for a challenge he knew would not come.

There was a moment of anxious silence, before someone near the back pounded his fist on the metal of a truck and screamed, "Major Schmidt! Major Schmidt," punctuating each scream with another pound of his fist.

The zeks slowly took up the chant. *Major Schmidt! Major Schmidt! Major Schmidt! Major Schmidt! Major Schmidt! Major Schmidt! Major Schmidt!*

※ ※ ※

Condemned to live then. Condemned to live. These words echoed in Samir's swimmy head as he climbed into the back of a waiting truck. He lay down wincingly, curled up again, and closed his eyes. He wouldn't die today. After a few minutes, the karavan pulled out into the desert, the prison shrinking behind it.

8.

AND THERE SHE LAY, with her child's face and woman shapes. It was wrong to think of her in this way. Adrian told himself it was wrong even as he thought it. And so he stayed a bit longer at her bedside to read to her. He had found a collection of fables from Baikyong-do, a nice leather-bound edition with lotus leaves engraved on its cover. He read her the story of a bodivhata, a holy man who had achieved his enlightenment and returned to his village to assist his countrymen in achieving their own. He brought an ox with him, and offered it to the village. One man suggested they slaughter the ox and salt its flesh so they would have food for the winter, but the bodivhata taught the villagers that it would be wiser to keep the ox alive, treat it well, and have it plow their fields so they would have food for many years to come, not just for one winter.

"I love being read to," Ariah said.

Adrian looked up from the book. He wanted to say something to convey how happy he was to be there with her, but there were no words—or at least he had no words. He began a second fable, one about a man stuck alone on a mountaintop. He read to her until she fell asleep. It was good to see her feeling better and resting so deeply.

※ ※ ※

Walking from Ariah's room and down the hospital halls, Adrian could smell the misery of the place. This smell of barely disinfected death, of limb rot, of feces and blood and raw human pain—all of it—but none of it could completely take away his sense of joy.

CHAPTER FOUR

DAY OF JOSHUA

1.

MAYOR ADAMS'S annual Day of Joshua soiree had more than its usual number of attendees. He tried not to glow overmuch at the general chatter and merriment, but very little is more rewarding than throwing an exquisite party.

"Weren't a hundred of them rounded up last week?" one guest, a legal consultant to a massive water purification plant, asked just at the periphery of Adams's hearing.

"No, no. It was over two hundred, I heard."

"Despicable people."

"Of course. Good work by our Guardsmen."

"Aren't these sweetmeats just fabulous?" the legal consultant said, taking a dainty bite.

Adams wandered farther from their conversation and shook hands with two young men of high stock and glowing futures. He wondered casually if he should hate them, whether he should destroy them on principle. He had no intentions of doing so, but the thought pleased him. *The chaos wreaked by the spider upon the fly.* It would be that natural, that easy.

"I hope you enjoy your evening, gentlemen," Mayor Adams said and parted company with the two young men, leaving their futures intact.

On the other side of the room, a short man with grayish skin, a journalist, looked with impotent disdain at the crowd. What would he write about the event? He wasn't sure. These society pieces offered no meat and many risks. Joshua City had changed so much in the past ten years since he began writing for *The Joshua Harbinger*. He found himself talking with a patroness of the arts and a military man of some rank the journalist could not determine. *How can anyone keep track of all those meaningless and petty distinctions?* With men like this in charge, no wonder Joshua City was at war. And over what? Unsubstantiated allegations and mere rumor.

"You're a writer of sorts," the patroness said. "What is your opinion of the state of Joshuan literature?"

"Well," the journalist began, "there haven't been many truly important books lately, but I still think—"

"But of course you admire Umberto Lemkin's work," the patroness said, not really a question. "I funded the last collection of his plays, and everyone just finds them enthralling."

"My wife took me to *The Painted Ostrich* just last week," the military man announced, happy to be able to say something.

"Oh!" the patroness said. "That one is my favorite. And I think the Joshua Theatre Troupe has outdone itself with this most recent production." Then, to the journalist, "Your paper hasn't yet done a review of this most magnificent production. I do hope you plan to, if you consider yourself in the business of covering the events that matter."

"I'm sure someone will be assigned to it," the journalist said.

There was more talk of the State of Poetry, the State of Music, and so forth. As soon as he could politely do so, the journalist extricated himself from the patroness's semicircle of listeners. What was he going to write about this evening that would actually be printed? It hadn't always been this way, but he couldn't remember precisely when things had changed.

He wandered back to the impressive display of food and began loading up a plate with delicacies. In his article, he would have to praise the cuisine of the evening, but without making it seem too extravagant. He could extoll the virtues of the braised sturgeon and perhaps find a nice little bit of faux poetry to describe the puréed duck. At least here he could tell the truth. He planted himself in a corner and enjoyed his food, making eye contact with no one.

2.

From the Journals of Nikolas Kovalski:

IN THE WEEK I have been back from the desert, it has been a pleasure to see how skillfully Katya has managed affairs in my absence. She has even succeeded in growing our numbers in important ways. There are only a dozen or so more new members, but we now have more engineers, a munitions expert, and komrades who practice other useful trades. A judicious way for her to proceed; as good as or better than I might have done myself. But that is not to say that she didn't encounter problems. Though she has not outright accused Elias, I have gathered that he continued his bid for what he considers his rightful place at the head of The Underground.

"Nikolas," he said on my first day back, "so nice to see you've finally returned." There were equal parts dishonesty and reprimand in his words.

"And I am glad to see you have been so helpful to Katya while I was away."

"Everything I do is for the revolution, Nikolas."

I left to make my rounds with our conflict unresolved. Outside, I saw scores of Baikal Guardsmen marking the doors of the infected. And common Joshuan citizens were doing the same, without provocation or reward. When had it escalated so much? I hadn't been in the streets an hour when I saw something so low it turned my stomach.

In the door of a once fine home, three men stood over something ragged and huddled, clapping each other on the back. A black boot swept forward and there was a whimper from the pile of clothes. Then the flash of a knife blade, the snicker-snack of someone bent to dirty cutting work.

"I'll cut his idiot tongue out," said a skinny man on the right.

"No, wait," said another man, large, checking his friend's arm. "I've got something better."

It was the Day of Joshua, and men like these were celebrating what should be a marker of human freedom with thuggish simple-mindedness. The large man unfastened his pants and squatted over the creature's mouth. Down the street, a wagon waited, loaded with tied-up nekrotics. Their faces had gone blank from terror. They did not know their destination—only that it would not be pleasant. The Guardsmen who had rounded them up were a few blocks away, marking doors and taking more prisoners. I might have cut the ropes holding the nekrotics while their captors were occupied. But I couldn't leave these other men to kick the creature to death. I scolded myself even as I was doing it. What right did I have to condemn a dozen people to save one?

I felt a coldness and cleared my mind of hesitation the way Messenger had instructed. And though I knew I shouldn't be, I was eager to confront these men, to test the limits of my new training.

"Stop now," I said.

They looked at me, their fists hanging at their sides. "Who are you?" the large man asked, taking a delighted step forward.

"Before you continue, you might consider the freedom you still enjoy to walk away," I said.

The Messenger Tattoo, scabby and dry, itched beneath my shirtsleeve.

"Sure," their leader said. Behind him the undersized man or ancient child they had been tormenting rose to his feet.

The first blow cracked my temple. My ears rang, but I kicked back. I heard a cry from the smallest of them as I connected with yielding bone. My finger found an eye, worked at popping it. Another blow. I was forced to the ground. Blood ran from my mouth, landed dark and glistening in the mud. Beside the small stain lay a municipal information-paper, one corner caught beneath a chunk of concrete and steel mesh. It announced in garish font: *Day of Joshua Parade! Come one, come all, and celebrate this great city's anniversary!*

I raised my head a few centimeters. The creature was gone—no parting look, no sign of gratitude.

Their leader lifted a brick, wrathful now.

I rushed him, and on the ground my hand found the brick. I raised it and slammed it down against his face; I raised it, slammed it down; raised it, slammed it down—with each blow his face was less human, more meat and dark fluid. Behind me, his friends made their way down the alley, no doubt to their homes, where they would contrive stories to explain their injuries. The man's chest was still moving beneath me, and I wondered if that was a good thing.

The Guardsmen were returning to the nekrotics now.

I ran down the alley, leaving my victim to live, though with the scars of his misdeeds tattooed on his face forever. As I ran, I damned myself for leaving those nekrotics at the mercy of the soldiers, though the joy of violence was still in me.

3.

ON HER WAY to see the old man, Katyana cut through the open-air market to avoid running into Nikolas. As she squeezed down the dirt-floored walkways, she was aware of the stares of the vendors at her masked face. She ignored them; she was used to it. *The old man.* His name was Roman Gregoric, and he was her stepfather; but because Nikolas always referred to him as *the old man*, she had come to think of him that way. Nikolas didn't like her visiting him. He couldn't understand her compulsion, not after what the old man had done to her, the life he had forced her into. Their arguments about it always went the same way.

"You make it sound like I have no will of my own."

"You were a child," Nikolas said.

"I knew what I was doing." The truth was somewhere in between. She had known *and* had no choice.

Nikolas had left The Underground early that morning—to make his "rounds," as he called his scouting of the surrounding neighborhoods for new recruits and potential dangers. This was a task better left to the lieutenants, or even lower-level operatives; but Nikolas's stubbornness and need for control would not allow him to sit back and let others do such work. This was even truer since his return.

"Why are you doing this?" Katya had demanded.

"Why did Messenger choose me if not to be the spearhead?"

"But you're too important," she said. "If we lose you, the revolution is lost."

"That's not entirely true. The revolution is inevitable."

She hated the way what he said was always right, but also missed the point. Of course he knew he was more important for the revolution than others. But there was no way to argue with him when he was like this.

"And what are you going to do today?" he asked. "Going to see him again?"

"Why do you always come back to that?"

"Look, I can't have this conversation right now. There are things that need to be done."

Nikolas was not here in the market with her now, but he was always with her, wasn't he? She worried that one day he wouldn't return, having been arrested or worse. What would she do then? Follow Elias? No, she would return to her previous work; men would pay a high price for a woman from Baikalingrad—something about the mystery of the mask. Some clients had asked, even begged, her to take it off. They offered her hundreds of drams to do so. She always refused; she only took off her mask for Nikolas. According to the Faceless Prophet, you should only be face-naked with your husband or wife. Though they had walked down no aisles, signed no papers, Nikolas was her husband in spirit.

She passed a vendor selling Joshua cakes from a cart. It was the Day of Joshua already, which meant she had been with Nikolas for almost four months. The smell of the cakes made her think of Days of Joshua past, as a little girl, while her mother was still alive. She tried to remember her mother's face but could not. What she did remember was that gut-pinch of excitement as she opened her eyes on the holiday morning. The clouds were soft pinks and purples with the parting dawn; dew still beaded on window panes. She crept down the hallway and into the kitchen, careful to put her feet on the boards she knew didn't creak. She didn't want to wake the old man. He had been living with them for a few years. She checked the names on the gifts to see which were hers. But she did not open them. She saved that for when everyone else woke up. And the best part was knowing that the gifts amounted to only a fraction of the festivities before her: later, there was the Joshua Parade, in which the old man, as a former officer, marched; there was the Kite Festival, with all its pretty fluttering colors; then the neighborhood dance, with wine for the grownups and sparkling cider for the children; and as the last strains of the balalaika faded away, she fell into bed with the cool sheets wrapped around her, a delicious exhaustion in her limbs.

Nikolas would say it was selfish to think this way, that as long as oppression existed, there could be no true Day of Joshua, not one that people such as themselves could celebrate. And of course he was right. But was it a crime to feel pleasure once in a while?

"May I help you, miss?" a vendor asked.

She hurried on through the market, ignoring the outstretched hands of the beggar children. A man selling salted herring stared at her lasciviously. *You could never afford me.* Out in the open avenue, she slowed her walk. If it was easier to breathe here, there were also more Guardsmen. It was not just Nikolas she had hoped to avoid by cutting through the market. They wouldn't know who she was—how could they yet?—but her mask made her an easy target. The Day of Joshua was supposed to be about unity, about the joining of all the Seven Cities under the banner of the one, but with the war, things had gotten ugly. Once a Guardsman had slid his baton through his fist while gyrating his hips in a crude sexual pantomime.

"Hey, dolly," he called. "My little bitty masked doll. You want to play house?"

If Nikolas were there, especially now with his new Messenger training, he would have insisted on what he called *the obvious punishment for an obvious infraction.*

"Look," he would say, "I did not invent consequences."

She turned down a side street ripe with the stink of trash, cat piss, and overcooked cabbage. She went into The Nameless Tavern. She walked through, waving away the cigarette smoke and smoothing down her skirt, as if to keep the place from dirtying her. A few drunks looked up from their tables to watch her pass. They were too abject, too buried under their worthless lives, to whistle or make lewd remarks. She felt sorry for them. She walked on.

She climbed the narrow stairs, stepping over a busted bag of garbage and a sleeping train-dog. It looked pregnant, its belly swollen and pink-nippled.

At the old man's one-room apartment, she paused. Ear to the door, she heard labored breathing inside. She knocked, and when he did not answer, she knocked again. She tested the doorknob. *Unlocked, as usual.* She pushed her way in.

The room was filthy. Mustard-stained plates balanced on the windowsill; newspapers and sweat-darkened undershirts littered the floor. A pair of boots slumped lazily on the writing desk. Beside them sat a glass filled with a yellow-filmy substance she hoped wasn't urine. A cigarette floated in the glass. More cigarettes filled the ashtrays. He wasn't supposed to be smoking—or drinking, for that matter. As she walked forward she kicked something like a piece of dried and shriveled sausage, sent it rolling under the bed.

He was curled up, the blanket pulled to his chin. Beneath the blanket, his chest rose and fell. He eyed her curiously.

"Hello, Daddy," she said.

"Is that you?" His voice was barely a whisper above his toothless gums.

"Yes, Daddy," she said. "It's me."

"You're late."

The clock on the wall hadn't been wound for months, not that that would have helped him. She took it down from its bent nail and tightened the spring.

"It's a mess in here," she said.

"Are you winding my clock? Stop winding my clock."

She put the timepiece on the desk.

He slumped back down. "Doesn't matter. Nothing matters."

"Don't say that," she said. And yet hadn't she believed that until she had joined The Underground?

He sat up. "Where's Rebekka?"

Not this again. Rebekka was her mother's name. She touched his forehead. It was hot and damp.

"You're burning up," she said. "Haven't you been taking your medikaments? Where is the bottle?"

He nodded toward the dresser. The top of it was littered with empty vodka bottles and balled-up socks, a broach attached to a silver chain. She picked up the broach and set it back down just as quickly. It held a fotograf of her mother. She picked it back up and studied the curvature of her mother's mask. This was something Joshuans, even Nikolas, did not understand. Masks were as individual as faces. She slipped the broach in her pocket, hoping he wouldn't notice.

"I can't find it," she said.

"Top drawer," he said, his voice barely above a croak. She fished among the dirty undergarments and her fingers brushed a glass bottle. She unscrewed the cap. It was nearly full. Doktor Mann had come to the room last week, after she found the old man raving and delirious, flailing from side to side. He forced the thermometer under the old man's tongue and stuck a light in his throat. He nodded sagely, as though he had found precisely what he expected.

He handed an amber-colored bottle to Katyana. "Make sure he takes one of these each day."

She promised she would, though the truth was that she had no intention to come by every day. After the doktor left, she turned to the old man and shook the bottle at him. "Are you going to take your pills?

Talking to him tired her to her core. It was not like talking with Nikolas. Time spent with Nikolas wasn't the usual watery time of daily interactions, nor was it the tedious back-and-forth of dealing with the old man; it was thickened time—dense with import, ecstatic with meaning.

She squeezed the old man's cheeks, so that his lips ballooned apart like a fish. She pushed one of the pills down his throat and held it there until he swallowed. Then she put her hands on her lap and gave him her best stern schoolteacher voice. "Why didn't you do what Doktor told you?"

He rolled over and faced the wall. He pulled the blankets up around him again. "You're not Rebekka."

She touched his shoulder and he shook her hand off. She watched his breathing relax. He seemed to be asleep now. *What can I do?* she thought. She put the money she had brought him on the bedside table—not as much as usual, but it was what she had to spare.

She closed the door behind her, shutting him in, and walked down to the street—feeling guilty, but manageably so.

4.

ADRIAN WALKED through the hallways of the hospital, thinking of Ariah, as he caught himself doing more and more lately. He daydreamed of them back in Joshua City, him working as a doktor and her dedicating herself to writing full-time. He imagined newspaper articles with her byline attached; novels with her beautiful face on the cover; her poems being read on the radio. Sometimes he imagined her pregnant, the vital curvature of life growing in her belly. But mostly he imagined them walking through the streets, holding hands, or at the dinner table in the evening, smiling lovingly at each other.

Doktor Abuawad came around the corner.

"Adrian, I was just looking for you. We have a busy schedule today."

Adrian straightened his doktor's coat and composed himself.

"Yes, sir," Adrian said, mock-military. "What's first?"

There were several new patients, three Baikal Guardsmen and two miners who had been caught for over a day in a collapse. The Guardsmen's wounds were superficial, but the hospital's new policy was that they must be treated first.

"Don't worry," Doktor Abuawad said, "this will go quickly."

The first Guardsman had a fragment of a bullet stuck in his shoulder muscle. Adrian tweezed the metal free and poured disinfectant on the open flesh. A quick application of gauze and tape, and the man was sent to a temporary recovery room. The second and third Guardsmen had been near a bomb when it went off and had several pieces of shrapnel in their torso region. Luckily, they had been just far enough away that no major organs were touched. It took some time to find all of the pieces— you didn't want an infection to set in around a missed shard—and then they were sent off as well.

With the miners, it became more complicated. The first one was suffering from a strong cough due to the rock dust he had inhaled, but he would be fine after a few days' rest. Then there was a young boy— seventeen years old at the most—whose arm had been pinned for the entire time the miners were trapped. On the way to the boy's room, Doktor Abuawad predicted less than two days for the boy before all of his organs began failing. While the wound to his arm had not been lethal in itself, the flesh had died and toxins had built up in the crushed area. When they lifted the rock that had crushed his arm, these toxins flooded into his system, poisoning everything. They would give him a strong narkotic, which would reduce the pain and help him sleep. That wouldn't save his life, but it would make his passing less unpleasant.

"Here, this will help," Adrian said, and he injected the narkotic in the boy's good arm.

"Am I going to lose my arm?" the boy asked.

Neither Adrian nor Abuawad said anything. The boy looked back and forth between the two of them, trying to read their silence.

"You should sleep now," Adrian said. "I'll check on you in a few hours."

As the narkotic set in, the boy's eyes drifted in and out of focus.

In the hallway again, Doktor Abuawad said, "You did well back there. Telling him the truth wouldn't have gained anyone anything."

Adrian nodded but didn't respond.

"This next patient has a terminal case of lung cancer," Doktor Abuawad said. "This morning, she attempted suicide."

The woman was old and fragile. Her wrists had been quickly bandaged. Now they would use stitches to fully close the wounds. The procedure was simple enough, but the entire time Adrian did his work under Abuawad's watching eyes, the woman stared at the ceiling as though the goings-on were taking place on some distant planet.

"This stitch might sting somewhat," Adrian said in his warmest voice, but the woman didn't bother to look his way.

Their job done, Adrian patted the woman on the shoulder, and they left the room.

It was barely noon now. How much more of this human suffering would there be?

"It's a sad case," Doktor Abuawad said, sensing Adrian's mood. "But in a way, she has a point."

Adrian turned to him with a questioning look.

"She might have a month or two more than the boy we treated. All we've done is extend her unhappy existence. But that's the job."

They saw a dozen more patients in the following hours, but Adrian continued to think of the old woman. From there it was a logical step to thoughts of his mother. She was always with him, especially in this place of illness. Never before today, though, had he treated someone who reminded him so thoroughly of her.

※ ※ ※

Her funeral had been at St. Cyrill's, her place of worship. Adrian did not remember how he got there, nor who had dressed him in his ill-fitting little-boy's suit. Perhaps a neighbor took him; until Adrian's father left, his mother had been an active member of the community. His uncle came in late, stumbling, his dress shirt untucked. He bowled his way up to the coffin, interrupting the priest's sermon. He looked down at Adrian's mother and began weeping loudly. Someone approached him gently and led him to a seat near the front.

Afterward was the burial. His uncle had paid for a plot in a nearby cemetery. They walked there—Adrian, his uncle, and all these unknown people. In his memory it was raining or at least overcast, the way a funeral should be. The sky should shed its valuable water, giving life to the ground so that the spirit, as it waited to ascend, might not go thirsty. But it had not been raining, he knew—that was just his memory trying to play him false. In an insult to his mother, the sky was sunny and dry. He remembered that and knew it was a true memory because his uncle had leaned against a tree, and Adrian, trying to see what he was doing had squinted into the sun. When his uncle thought no one was looking, he took something out of his pocket and sipped from it. He slumped further down the tree. The coffin was lowered, illuminated by the noonday sun, into the wound carved out of the earth.

As the coffin disappeared, his uncle dashed forward. He grabbed at the chains lowering the coffin.

"No," he said. "You can't."

"She's gone, Semya," someone said.

Someone else, a man—Adrian couldn't remember anything else about him—tried to pull his uncle away from the grave. His uncle shoved the man off. Adrian knew he had to do something. He stepped forward and touched his uncle's shoulder.

"Uncle," he said. "I talked to Mother. She says it's all right. She's happier now."

His uncle looked at him with an absent confusion, but he allowed Adrian to lead him off. He stumbled once and Adrian caught him under the arm, using all the strength in his eight-year-old body to support this lumbering giant.

"She was a good woman," his uncle said. "Why did you kill her?"

"Come on, Uncle," Adrian said. "You'll feel better if you sit down."

His uncle turned suddenly and vomited all over the ground. "I'm sorry," he said, not quite talking to Adrian.

"It's all right, Uncle," Adrian comforted.

※ ※ ※

Toward the end of his rounds, when the sun was cutting sharp angles through the hospital windows, Adrian remembered what day it was. The Day of Joshua. How could he have forgotten? As a child he loved The Day of Joshua Parade, the military demonstrations in honor of the heroes of Joshua City's past, and especially the traditional candies and cakes given to children.

After he had finished his reports, Adrian found himself in the cafeteria kitchen asking if he might use their ovens to make Joshua cakes. He remembered most of the ingredients and improvised the rest. He mixed them into a batter and poured it into one of the available pans. He chose a temperature and slid the pan into the oven.

※ ※ ※

Ariah was sitting up in bed. He poked his head in and knocked on the frame of the open door. Seeing him, she smiled.

"Did you realize it's the Day of Joshua?" he asked her.

"Of course."

"I've brought you something."

He sat down in the chair beside her bed and presented her with the lumpy mess he had concocted.

"It's supposed to be a Joshua cake," Adrian said.

"So you're a doktor, not a chef?" She took the tray from him and set it on her lap. "Knife?"

Apologetically, "I forgot?"

She tore off a piece of cake and lifted it to his mouth. When he was done, she licked her fingers clean.

"Not bad," she declared.

"I saw this woman today..."

"What about her?"

"Nothing," he said. "It was a really long day. Eat your cake."

She plunged her fist into the cake and grabbed a sloppy handful, shoved it into her mouth. Adrian laughed and she laughed too, and with every bit of the cake that fell out of her mouth, he loved her more.

5.

AN ASSISTANT discreetly tapped Mayor Adams on the shoulder and whispered into his ear, causing much stifled commotion among the guests around them. The air was electric with importance; everyone was glad they had come to the party. Mayor Adams made a show of listening to the assistant, knowing that all the eyes in the room were on him.

"There has been an incident," the assistant said. "Nothing too serious, but I thought you should know."

Adams stiffened slightly, annoyed that something might ruin his perfect soiree. He would not let that happen.

"What sort of incident?" Adams said and smiled widely for the onlookers, letting them know there was nothing to worry about.

"It seems a money exchange vehicle was intercepted on its way to the municipal treasury."

"Intercepted?" Mayor Adams said. "Say what you mean, damn it."

"Well, sir," the assistant said. "Hijacked, I suppose."

"How much?"

"Sir?"

"How much of my money did they get?"

"About fifty thousand. Not all in Joshuan currency, though."

Of course not, you idiot. It wouldn't be a money exchange otherwise.

"And the culprits? I take it they haven't been arrested yet?"

"We've sent out notice to the Guard to be on lookout for a group of men carrying municipal money sacks. They left on foot. They shouldn't be hard to spot."

"Unless they're already off the street."

"The culprits would have had a decent head-start. They tied up the driver and the Guardsmen escorting him in the cab of the vehicle. It was quite a while before another Guardsman passed by and they were able to get his attention and have him untie them."

In and of itself, this loss was not a catastrophe. But it was the principle of the thing. There had been reports lately of thefts from various military transports and government supply buildings. He did not like the implication of it: that he couldn't maintain control of his own city. Worse, the Ministrie of Intelligence had given him to understand that the incidents might not be unrelated.

"Do we have a description at least?"

"They were wearing masks, sir. The Guardsmen identified them all as male by their builds and voices."

"So you're telling me that a group of masked men *intercepted*," putting a special sarcastic emphasis on the word, "an armed municipal vehicle in broad daylight, disarmed and tied up two Guardsmen and a driver, and then made off with fifty thousand drams without anyone apprehending them?"

He realized that he was no longer whispering. He smiled at the guests again.

"A mayor's work is never done," he said in a brighter voice. "Now let's have some music, shall we?"

The musicians, a well-trained string ensemble in black-and-white formalwear, began playing a stately waltz. A few of the guests moved to the center of the room to dance. The assistant was still standing beside Adams.

"Well?" Adams said. "If you have nothing useful for me, you're dismissed."

The assistant scurried off, no doubt fearing for his job. *Good. Let him be afraid.* Mayor Adams liked it that way. He turned his attention back to the party. There would be time enough to worry about the rest of it later.

6.

THE DOORS THEY MARKED: AN INTERLUDE

KONRAD'S WIFE, Antonia, had apartment envy. She wouldn't leave Konrad alone about it. Every day he came home tired and sore from the cement faktory, and he wanted nothing more than a plate of steaming sausages and a cold beer. Of course there were rarely sausages, and never a full plate's worth. Usually just a slice or two of dried ham left over from breakfast, a few shriveled parsnips, a heel of bread. And then on top of that he had to listen to Antonia go on about the Xhangzes' apartment.

"Look at this place," she said, gesturing toward their cramped kitchen. "If I only had the Xhangzes' kitchen, I could do some real cooking."

The Xhangzes, a married couple from Baikyong-do, lived in the apartment directly above theirs. They had invited Antonia and Konrad to dinner once. Even Konrad, who didn't care much about where he lived as long as it had a roof, felt a twinge of envy. Their apartment was certainly more spacious. And it had real windows. What was more, they paid the same rent as Konrad and Antonia. The Xhangzes were very polite hosts—serving them dish after dish of their vile fermented root-vegetables and strange meat Konrad thought might be train-dog—but they were also foreigners. What had Mr. Xhangze—whose first name, Kim-il, was suspiciously feminine—done to deserve such an apartment? He worked in the electrical plant, in some sort of supervisory role. But did he work any harder than Konrad? Did he deserve a better apartment?

One particular evening, Konrad came home more frustrated than usual. At the faktory, a small amount of water had ended up in the cement powder, causing it to clump, making it unsuitable for bagging. Konrad, whose job it was to grind the cement after it came out of the kiln, did the proper thing and reported it to his manager. The manager yelled at him, though it was the man up the line working the kiln who should have caught the mistake. In the end, they discovered a small leak in a pipe directly above the kiln—a waste of precious faktory water in addition to ruining the batch of cement powder. Konrad showed the leak to the manager, who had to admit that it was not Konrad's fault. The man working the kiln, a drunkard, was fired. He left threatening legal action. Konrad chuckled at the irony. The man was lucky he wasn't arrested as a saboteur.

So Konrad arrived home wanting little more than to listen to the radio and drink himself to sleep. But there Antonia was with the usual poor fare she called dinner.

"If we only had the apartment upstairs," she said.

"You really want their apartment?" he asked.

She stared at him, uncomprehending. For months, he had simply been nodding his head or giving the occasional grunt of agreement when she went on like this.

"We could always report them," he said.

"Oh, no. I couldn't do that."

"Then stop complaining."

Konrad's dinner safely on the table, Antonia began washing the dishes. She put a plate on the drying rack and sighed, looking out the small window at a paltry view of the building next door.

"What?" he said. "What is it?"

"I suppose maybe . . . if you think it's best . . . "

He had seen the information-papers around town. Everyone had. *A good Joshuan is a vigilant Joshuan.* He told himself he was being a good Joshuan; sure, the Xhangzes hadn't done anything wrong, but these days who could tell? Hadn't Mr. Xhangze climbed a little too high a little too fast? A few blocks away at a street-telefone, he dialed the number on the information-paper and when the anonymous bureaucratic voice picked up, he told them that he had overheard Mr. Xhangze discussing a plan to sabotage the electrical plant.

"You might want to look into his wife as well," Konrad said. "I believe he was talking to her."

"Did you hear anything else? Who is he working for?"

"I don't know. I couldn't hear."

If he said too much more, they might question his motives.

"Thank you for the information, Mr. . . . ?"

He hung up the telefone, his hands shaking with the gravity of what he had just done.

No one came the next day. What was wrong? Had they seen through him? Did they think it was a hoax? He never should have hung up. He could have given them any name. Stupid, stupid. Maybe it was for the best. He really didn't feel so good about it, though Mr. Xhangze surely harbored anti-Joshuan thoughts. They bumped into each other on the way out of the building that morning and Konrad could have sworn Mr. Xhangze gave him a sly little wink. He probably knew someone in a ministrie. How else could he have risen to his supervisory position so quickly?

In the middle of the night, Konrad was woken by a pounding on a door. He sat up in a pitch-dark panic.

"What is it?" his wife said, clutching her nightgown around her. "What is happening?"

The knocking stopped. It wasn't their door. He listened harder. There was the sound of voices, heavy footsteps down the hall. Silence.

Come morning, he crept up the stairs. The door to the Xhangzes' apartment stood open, hanging from its hinges. The door had the red mark on it, that ugly painted scar everyone in Joshua City knew and feared. The landlord came out of the apartment, shaking his head.

"I always thought they were good people," he said. "It just shows you that you can't trust anyone these days."

"Maybe this is not the time," Konrad said, "but didn't you say we could have the apartment if they moved out?"

The landlord looked him from head to foot with knowing contempt. Then he shrugged. He had no time for such moral quibbles. "A promise is a promise."

They moved in the next day.

※ ※ ※

A boy of seven by the name of Alex needed water for his mother. It was just him and his mother in the house since his brother had left to fight in the war. And his mother was very sick. She lay sweating and shivering in the bed. Alex wanted desperately to go to an adult for help, but Alex was alone.

He had to be brave. His brother in the war was very brave and would know what to do. His brother was not here now though. What would his brother do?

"Water," his mother said, her voice barely a whisper.

But he could not bring her the poison water. That was what made her sick. She had told him that back when she was able to speak in clear sentences. Now she passed in and out of waking and said a word or two. Sometimes she reached out to him with a bony hand. Her skin was scaly and soft at the same time. Dry and bubbly. He drew back and hoped she would understand.

"Water."

He went out into the street at dawn looking for the good water. He carried an empty bucket with him. The good water would not be here, where it ran in open gutters in the street. He knew where it would be. Alex knew a lot of things. He knew his mother had the skin-rot and he could tell no one because they would take her. And then he would be alone.

You have to be brave. Like your brother.

An hour later, he was walking back home with a sloshing bucket. The bucket was heavy and it hurt his hand. But he took the back streets even though it made the walk longer. *You have to be careful. Careful and brave.* His mother would drink the good water and it would wash away the bad water and she would be well. He saw the church spire. Past that was the house with the yellow shutters. And past yellow shutters was the crack in the sidewalk that looked like a heart. Past that was home.

"Boy," a voice said.

He saw the black boots before anything. Then the pants of the Guardsman's uniform. The Guardsman smiled down at him.

"Where are you going with all that water?"

"It's mine," he said. "I got it from here."

The Guardsman bent over the bucket without really looking at the contents. "Seems clean," he said. "Pure-baikal."

"Please," Alex said. "It's for my mother."

"And why can't she fetch it herself, boy?"

Alex shrugged. "She sent me to get it."

The Guardsman took the bucket from Alex's hand. He set it gently on the ground. It wasn't heavy to him.

"Let's go see your mother then, shall we?"

% % %

Later that night, a drunk stumbling home leaned heavily against the door of a one-room shack. He needed to rest. Only one moment. He closed his eyes and let his face slump against the cool wood. When he opened his eyes seconds later, he saw the red slashes of paint. He recoiled. The door had been marked.

He hurried off, crossing himself, pitying whoever had lived in such a place.

Meanwhile, Saint Ignatius's Home for Boys had a new admittance. Father Samarov noticed the shy bright-eyed boy at once. It took the good Father a moment to recognize who the boy reminded him of. There was no physical similarity. But maybe a spiritual one.

The boy reminded him of his favorite pupil, Adrian Talbot. He wondered vaguely what had become of Adrian as he settled the new orphan into a room with two others, also recent arrivals.

% % %

Some of those whose doors were marked were truly guilty. Not the Xhangzes, who had the misfortune of possessing something someone else wanted, and not nekrotics like Alex's mother, who had the misfortune of being unwell. But there were those who really *were* harboring thoughts of dissent. I am not speaking of Nikolas and The Underground, but of those who exercised less care in their subversion of deed or thought.

Nicodemus Zbrodneya smashed his brother's head in with a hammer. Afterward he walked out into the street and dropped to his knees. He let the hammer fall to the ground and stared up at the sky, lips moving in silent prayer. When the Guardsmen searched his apartment, they found a basement stockpiled with their own military-grade weapons. Mr. Zbrodneya was actually Lieutenant Zbrodneya. He had fought in The Great War, the war before this war, which had solidified Joshua City's place as the most powerful of the Seven. Lieutenant Zbrodneya believed the city's status was in danger—not from outside, but from within. He thought that Mayor Adams was an imposter, an agent of Ulan-Ude or Al-Khuzir or Kazhstan depending on the whimsy of his paranoia. So he horded weapons and waited and planned. His brother had threatened to report him and so, in a drunken heat, he had solved that particular problem. But his sense of guilt got the best of him.

Guilt, however, can be defined in many ways. Its definition is necessarily flexible; what is legal in one situation and in one society is not in another; when the law changes, the guilty may become innocent and the innocent guilty. And in certain situations, when guilt is the desired outcome, the law can and must be rewritten. It is the prerogative of a municipal leader to declare a state of exception—that is, a state in which the usual laws do not apply and may be ignored for the safety of the city.

A schoolteacher was seized for teaching last year's history books. A banker was heard to make a passing joke that the money he was giving a customer would soon be worthless, once Mayor Adams had new money printed up with his face on it. An engineer named Jürgen Moritz leaked information about covert surveillance; they marked his door, but not before he fled into the desert and was never seen again.

In the fickle world of fashion, a successful artiste was stripped bare and beaten after introducing a new garment-line that cheekily made use of Ulani fighting leather (never mind that snakeskin braids had been in style as recently as last year). A prominent direktor's films were blacklisted, and one night a high-ranking official paid him a visit. The direktor would make a certain film for the Ministrie of Aesthetics, the high-ranking official said. It would be generously funded. What would happen if he were to refuse was implicit. More artists deemed subversive were ending up in the labor camps every day, as both the agent and the famous direktor knew.

What law had they all broken? None but the One Law. This law was ever-changing and infinitely mutable, big or small enough to fit any guilt. And they listened and they listened and they listened. And the Guardsmen went on marking doors.

7.

MAJOR SCHMIDT STOOD just inside his tent, watching the civilians and Guardsmen at their makeshift Day of Joshua feast. The sun was going down over the desert, lending a rich melancholy light to the whole affair. A fire crackled and over it, on a wooden spit, roasted several bony fowls one of the Guardsmen, an expert hunter from Larki Island, had managed to shoot. There was a floury version of Joshua cakes and a small amount of ale for each man—barely more than a half cup's worth. A Guardsman named Gherghi, who had cooked the meals for the guards in the prison, supervised the proceedings, spooning out rations and humbly taking compliments on his cooking. He grumbled about the lack of quality spices, but he had managed to procure a few desert herbs to liven things up somewhat.

It wasn't much, Major Schmidt knew, but his men looked happier than he had seen them since they left the prison. Earlier, in the lead truck of their motley karavan, he and Kharkov had discussed what to do to commemorate the holiday. Kharkov claimed not to be a skilled military strategist, and maybe he wasn't, but he had a real understanding for the needs of a large group. Since they escaped the prison, Major Schmidt had found him invaluable. He had become Schmidt's second-in-kommand when it came to military matters, while Jürgen was his most trusted advisor for everything else.

※ ※ ※

"Can we really afford a celebration?" Major Schmidt had asked. "Our supplies are scarce enough as it is."

"Maybe not," Kharkov said. "But the men need something. A what-would-you-say, *a morale boost*."

It was true. They were weary, sick, hungry, and the civilians were more than a little afraid. So far their luck had been good, marching through Ulani territory as they had been. No doubt word had spread to the Ulani army by now about the prison break. Whether or not there were troops actively looking for them depended on the fighting elsewhere.

Using an Ulani map the Guardsmen had found in the prison head-quarters, Major Schmidt had done his best to steer them as far away from likely sites of battle as possible. That was assuming the map was at all up-to-date, of course. Who knew how far the Ulani front had shifted?

"And it might just be that I have a little surprise," Kharkov said. He grinned. Good humor sat oddly on his weathered face. He reached in a bag at his feet, rummaged through some light weaponry, and brought out a bottle. The liquid inside was a frothy pale gold. "A little ale, courtesy of our Ulani friends. And there's plenty more where that came from."

The Guardsman driving the truck tried to contain his obvious interest in the bottle.

"Make the arrangement as you see fit," Major Schmidt said.

※ ※ ※

Major Schmidt went back into his tent and sat on his cot, sipping at his own glass of ale and looking at the maps again. They were written in Ulani, but Jürgen had already pointed out to him the most import-ant landmarks. If Schmidt's calculations were correct, and if the map was accurate, the military outpost where the besieged Guardsmen were trapped was less than two hundred kilometers southeast. Under ideal conditions, they could reach it in less than a day. But these conditions were far from ideal. Many of his men were in need of medikal attention and along the way there was likely to be heavy fighting. Plus, they had more than a dozen civilians with them—men entirely untrained in combat. They needed... but Major Schmidt wasn't sure what they needed. If he had known that, he wouldn't be staring at this map while the others made merry outside.

He hadn't wanted this. Or had he? *I took it on quickly enough, when the time came.* He thought of something he had read or heard somewhere—was it in a Guardsman's training manual, or was it something one of his superior officers had said, back when he had superior officers? *Every man wants power. Not every man wants what comes with it.* And what came with it? Responsibility, of course, but also loneliness. A distance between you and those you once called friend.

Take this tent for example. An old shabby canvas thing, he hadn't wanted it. It was too hot at night; he would have preferred to sleep in the open desert air with the rest of the men. But Jürgen had been adamant. "You must draw a sharp distinction between yourself and your soldiers" he had said. "It's the only way they'll respect you."

"Sir?"

One of his Guardsmen stood in the door of the tent. Novak, that was his surname. In the prison, Major Schmidt might have called him by his first name, Konstantin.

"Yes, private?" Major Schmidt smiled, to put the young man at ease, "How are you enjoying the festivities? Is that singing I hear?"

"Yes, sir," Novak said. "Sir, Mr. Moritz has found something and he wants you to come look."

8.

From the Journals of Nikolas Kovalski:

I TURNED THE CORNER and was nearly to the entrance to The Underground when I saw a quivering mass on the sidewalk. It was the deformed man-child I'd saved. He looked horrible, forehead split like ripe fruit and the skin of one eyelid ripped and ragged.

"What happened?" I asked, as if I needed an explanation. Those men were riding the wave of patriotic idiocy.

"Where are you from?" I asked. He grinned, revealing sickly pink-and-black gums. His cheeks were rose-colored; his eyes shone with childlike brightness beneath the blood. "Do you speak? Can't you tell me where you live?"

He kneeled in the dirt and with a piece of wire began to draw an elaborate system of boxes and lines. Soon I understood it was a map, charting the streets of the distrikt in beautiful unnecessary detail. When he began in on the trelliswork of the house where I'd found him and his antagonists, I asked him if that was where he had lived.

He pointed backward, over his shoulder, a gesture I determined to mean the past. "Your family used to live there? How many of you?"

He pointed to himself, held up his palm, fingers splayed. Five, including himself. "Where are they?"

Hands behind his back, cuffed, an arm grabbing his neck, tossing him into the back of a wagon.

"Don't you speak? What's your name?"

He stuck out a tongue scored with razor cuts, and let out a saliva-choked grunt. He looked around, saw a storm drain, and reaching down into the urine and the scum, fished out something slick and wriggling. He popped it in his mouth. He grinned, proud as an infant who's just wet himself.

"Slug?" I asked. "Your name is Slug?"

Before I knew what was happening, he had me in a ferocious embrace. He spun me around and set me back on my feet, and when I recovered, I asked him if he would like to see my underground home—if he would like his name to inspire fear instead of scorn. He jerked his head up and down, letting out little happy squeals.

9.

LATER, she would blame herself—her absorption in her uncharitable thoughts as she left the old man. Nikolas would say that was nonsense, that she had done exactly as she should. Whatever the case, Katya did not notice the two Guardsmen at the edge of the market until she was right in front of them. They stood there with their legs spread, slumped in casual arrogance. One had a nasty scar under his eye. That eye watched her as she reentered the market.

She cut down the alley, the Guardsmen following some twenty paces back. At a bread stall, she stopped and pointed to a random loaf, barely hearing the pleasantries of the vendor. She fumbled in her purse for some coins and shoved the loaf in her bag. A Joshua cake would have pleased her more, but this was a more useful purchase.

At the place where she normally turned left, she turned right. Unfortunately, this led her to an open square. A man in a painted dress spun two hoops on sticks. As she passed he lit one of the hoops on fire. Two children clapped delightedly. She tried not to hurry, remembering Nikolas's instructions if she should ever be followed. *Walk normally. Chances are they'll grow bored after a while. If that doesn't work, find a crowded place where you can lose them.*

She hoped the market would provide such a place. But the crowd had thinned since she had last passed through. There was a narrow gap between two stalls. She squeezed down it, and still they followed. In the distance, high over one of the booths, she saw a fluttering.

Like the Day of Joshua itself, the Kite Festival was meant to represent diversity. The vast melting and melding of cultures in Joshua City. The dome of the sky was a clear blue, with just hints of thunderclouds on the horizon. Rain: regarded as a good omen on any day, but especially on the Day of Joshua. In the high-grassed spread of a field, the ornate colorful pageantry of the Kite Festival danced. Big kites, little kites, kites with long tails, kites with wheels, kites like silver arrows, kites requiring a dozen hands to operate, kites as long as parade floats, rainbow-colored kites, solid black wraith-kites, kites like faces with grinning mouths, frightening kites, shy kitten kites, merry prankster kites, kites that swooped and corkscrewed, kites that soared.

Into this twisted menagerie, she entered.

Hundreds of kitesters manipulated their flying objects with deft little string pulls, concentrating on the tiny shifts in wind and the paths of other kites. She cut back and forth, trying to avoid getting tangled in the strings. There were money-prizes to be had, and trophies, for the most beautiful kite, the most creative kite, the kite best exhibiting Joshuan municipal pride. But the biggest prize of all was for the Best Flyer. Nearly a thousand drams! People came from all corners of the city and beyond, from the Outer Provinces, from the other cities, to win this money that could feed a family for months.

"Dram for a tug, miss?"

A kitester offered her his kite string. He wore the many-colored silks of Baikyong-do. His kite floated high above, seemingly without guidance. She could no longer see the Guardsmen. The kite was a flying lizard, its long scarlet tongue extended. With a swooping showmanly turn, the kitester made its body change from yellow and green to red and fiery orange. It was an illusion, its body made up of hundreds of scales, colored differently on each side. As it turned away again, it went back to its original colors.

"No," she said. "No, but thank you."

She hurried on, searching for the Guardsmen. She spotted them, hemmed in by the crowd for now. A homely teenage girl stepped forward with a kite; the Guardsman with the scar on his eye shoved the girl roughly aside. Katya sidestepped a hole in the ground, ducked under a tangle of kite strings, and ended up face to face with a boy of about ten. His kite-hand was nothing but a glistening malformed stump—where had she seen that stump before?—but he clutched his kite with the surety of long experience.

"A pretty-pretty, isn't it?"

He deftly wound the kite string around his stump, making the kite swoop like an eagle after prey. Its gray rag-like shape soared downward.

Just before it hit the ground, he flicked his stump and the kite climbed back up.

"Yes," she said, "very pretty."

"You too, miss. Pretty-pretty mask. Pretty-pretty hair."

With his good hand, he reached out for her hair. She stiffened but did not pull away.

"I know you. You helped my family."

"I hope your family liked the food," she said. "Good luck."

He waved at her as she took off.

Yes, that was where she recognized him from. Distributing food rations. This boy had been in line—despite his dexterity with the kite, he had struggled to hold the ration box. Come to think of it, hadn't the rations been wrapped in gray canvas not unlike the color of his kite?

The Guardsmen were gaining again. Just as they passed the boy, he stuck out his foot and one of the Guardsmen went sprawling. The crowd surrounded him and the boy ran off. The other Guardsman removed his gun and waved it in the air, afraid to do anything for fear of a riot. She was free. She passed a green hillock where families had blankets set up on the ground, eating their picnic lunches and watching the kites. Beyond that was a row of judges' tables, and beyond that, a set of risers with more spectators. A wild cheer went up. She looked back. The boy's gray kite flew into the lonely sky. She ducked behind the risers and spilled out into an alley.

And there they were again.

"Thought you'd got away, did you?" the first Guardsman said. He moved forward. The other Guardsman came in from the opposite side.

"We've had reports of a masked woman seen lifting military supplies."

"*Our* supplies," the other one said.

It was partially true. She had acted as a decoy, talking to a Guardsman, showing interest in him, while members of The Underground stole supplies behind his back. Nikolas hadn't wanted her to do even that. It would be prostituting herself, he said. *I've done worse*, she reminded him. *At least this is for a good reason.*

"There are thousands of us who wear the mask in Joshua City," she said.

"That may be," the Guardsman said, still moving forward. "But we've got you."

"No you don't," Alarik said.

It was over quickly. Alarik brought a length of pipe down on the first Guardsman's arm, and he dropped his baton, crying out. The other Guardsman moved in, fumbling for his weapon. Alarik broke his nose. He staggered back, clutching his bloody face. Alarik dragged Katya down the alley.

"You were following me?" she asked.

"It's my job to keep you safe," Alarik said.

"And who gave you that job? Nikolas? I can look out for myself."

"He doesn't know," Alarik said. "I started while he was gone. You're my sister."

Katya's anger softened. As Alarik tapped the pipe to allow them entrance to The Underground, she felt a surge of gratitude for him. She shared a bed with Nikolas, but Alarik was her closest friend in The Underground. She could talk to him about anything—even concerns about Nikolas himself. And he would listen without judgment. He always knew the right thing to say.

"You also have to keep Nikolas safe," she said. "This has gotten bigger than any of us."

They were gaining the sympathy of the people. But they were also attracting unwanted attention.

"I know that well, sister."

10.

WHAT THE ORACLES OBSERVED was this: Mayor Adams stood glorious among his hangers-on. At his every movement, many tried to follow while others moved out of his path. He was a living magnetic field, attracting and repulsing with equal power, but unlike a mindless magnet, which is as enslaved to iron and iron is to it, Mayor Adams chose which elements he attracted and which he expelled from his sphere of power. The Oracles enjoyed his enjoyment in wielding such power.

What the Oracles observed was this: treachery hidden beneath placated smiles. Treachery in the whispers half-heard in every corner of the room. Treachery in the patient acquiescence of even some of his closest advisors. Like a foul smell slowly filling the room, treachery.

What the Oracles observed was this: his spies wandered, mostly unnoticed, among the guests. They mentally recorded the conversations of the powerful to report to Mayor Adams. The Oracles were especially pleased by the subtlety of Mayor Adams's information gathering.

What the Oracles did not observe (or did they?): Mayor Adams sometimes forgot they existed and gave himself over to the joys of his soiree. Then he would return to them, apologizing with his renewed attention. How could he ever abandon the Oracles, who had never abandoned him?

11.

From the Journals of Nikolas Kovalski:

WHEN SLUG AND I arrived back at The Underground, Katyana was waiting. If she was surprised by my new friend she did not show it. I hid the bloodier side of my face.

"This is Slug," I said. "Our newest member."

With a shy turtle-like twisting of his head, Slug avoided meeting her gaze. I wondered if he was frightened by her mask. I myself scarcely notice it, but I suppose the unfamiliar might find its smooth expressionless surface disconcerting.

"I'm very pleased to meet you," Katyana said.

Slug scampered back and hid behind me. He peeked out, ducked back, peeked out again.

By now some of the live-in members of The Underground had come out from their domiciles. They stood in a cluster, watching us expectantly. I stepped forward into the light to address them.

"Nikolas," Katyana said. "Your face."

"I'm fine."

I pushed her off. Without the others present, I would have enjoyed her doting, but I had my role to keep up.

"Take care that he gets set up properly," I said.

She turned to the others and, in a tone both distracted and authoritative, instructed them to set Slug up with sleeping quarters. When they were gone, she took my hand.

"Come with me," she said.

She led me to our room and set me down on our bed. She opened my medikal bags, found a swab and disinfectant, and began dabbing at the mess of my cheek.

"Does that hurt?"

"Not so much," I said. "They weren't Guardsmen."

"Still, anything could have happened. You must promise to be more careful—if not for my sake, then for our cause."

"I promise," I lied.

I touched her chin, under her mask, sliding up the mask to kiss her. There was a knock on the door.

"Sir?"

Katyana pulled her mask back down. I went to the door; at least our domicile had one. It was a boy I barely remembered, nervous and pimply-faced. Stefan. There were so many now, I thought with a kind of prideful shock.

"What?" I said. "What is it? And you don't have to call me sir. We're all equals here."

"Yes, sir... Nikolas," the boy said. "Elias and the others are back. They have something to show you."

I followed him down the hall and across the main room of The Underground. Elias, Mouse, Sara, Yu and Yi and a few others were gathered at the far end of the room, slapping each other on the back and laughing. Around them on the floor were several large canvas sacks.

"Fair Nik," Elias called out, his pale face unusually flushed. He held a black mask in his hands. "Bear witness to the miracles we have wrought."

He nodded at my escort. "Stefan," Elias said. "Would you do the honors?"

Stefan lifted one of the bags with some difficulty. He fumbled with the clasps but finally got it open and peeked inside. He looked up at Elias hesitantly.

"Go ahead," Elias said. "Dump it on the floor. That's where money deserves to be. On the ground for all."

Stefan lifted the bag and shook it. Stacks and stacks of tightly bound money fell on the floor. They avalanched over each other. When a nice sprawling pile was created, he lifted the second bag.

"That's fine, Stefan," Elias said.

"Where did this come from?" I asked.

"Let's just say that in tomorrow's newspaper you might read a report of a certain money exchange vehicle being hijacked."

I took in the pile of money. There was enough here to fund our efforts for months.

"And whose idea was this?"

"Elias had the idea," Mouse said. "Brilliant, right?"

She wore a machine-rifle over one shoulder. That had also been the bounty of one of our covert operations. I looked at the money again. I was aware of Stefan at my side, waiting for me to react in the way a leader should. This was a good thing, wasn't it? So why wasn't I happy?

"Good job, komrades," I said.

12.

AT THE OUTSKIRTS of their campsite, Jürgen stood at the edge of a hole in the ground. In the hole, two Guardsmen shoveled sand over their shoulders. A shovel struck metal with a resonant clang.

"Careful, careful," Jürgen called out. "Don't damage it."

From the dry hard earth, a large structure protruded. By the curve of it—sleek, like the shell of some alien egg—Major Schmidt got the sense it was something much larger.

"What is it?"

"Something that might prove very useful," Jürgen said.

"What do you mean?"

More Guardsmen were gathering around the hole. They thought this might be one more part of the day's rare merriment.

"Give me a second," Jürgen said. "Wait." He searched his memory. "Does anyone have a copy of the *Book of the Before-Time*?"

"I do, sir," a particularly drunk man said and ran off without being told.

When the man was back, Jürgen ordered him to read the part about the false stars. The man fumbled the pages, not finding the passage.

"It should be just after the story of the false births," Jürgen helped.

"Oh, here it is," the man said.

"Read it for us, Private. Book, chapter, and verse."

"From *The Calamities*, chapter thirty-six, verse seven. Man's hu...b..."

"Hubris," Major Schmidt said.

"...hubris caused him to throw his pride into the sky and make stars that spoke back to Earth. Among the noisy constellations he made, he found his doom. And many of his efforts fell with fire back to Earth. And over the Earth, there were many consequences. The animals and plants changed the way they grew. And verily did their hair, which was beloved by God, fall out like dry weeds; and verily did their flesh grow strange knots, like a sickened tree."

"That's enough, Guardsman."

"Fine," Major Schmidt said, "but what does this have to do with anything?"

"Look, even though the majority of stories in The Book are non-sense, some of them are representative of the facts—as best the writers knew them anyway. I think this, what you're looking at here, is one of the false stars they talk about. If I am right, the material in it is what caused the 'strange knots' The Book talks about."

"And why does that matter?"

"Well, if I am right," Jürgen said, "then the material at this object's core is among the densest materials on the planet. It can be useful for an idea I have."

"What idea is that?"

"I am going to need the hardest blades we've got," Jürgen said. "And you need to get everyone away from the site."

※ ※ ※

Major Schmidt walked back toward his tent, wondering why Jürgen was so insistent that no one but he be in the hole where the false star was. Unable to do anything more about Jürgen, he decided to take Kharkov's advice. He would boost morale. He took three Guardsmen with him and put together several plates of food, a few small cups of the stolen ale. He entered, and the wounded Guardsmen unable to join the festivities all leaned to attention.

"Sirs," Major Schmidt said with a generous smile, "you disappoint me. It is a day of celebration. And here you are, all moping about. One might think you had been wounded in defense of your city."

A bit of laughter.

"Well, I have brought you some food, which I know you want. But more importantly, I have ale for you. Stolen from the goat-fucking Ulanis."

The wounded men laughed again.

Major Schmidt motioned for the Guardsmen with him to distribute the food and ale. The men would enjoy seeing him make the rounds of all the wounded. This was something Kharkov might have told him.

Near the end of shaking hands and congratulating all of his now excited wounded, Major Schmidt saw Samir.

Samir. *How things have changed.*

"Hello, Artillery Gunner Hosani."

"Hello . . . sir."

There were yellow sores on Samir's arms. He was thinner by about two more kilos.

"I hope you are having a good Day of Joshua."

"Considering the state of my body and the state of my soul, I can say, sir, that I am not having a good day."

Major Schmidt motioned for the Guardsmen to give Samir his plate of food and his cup of ale. Samir turned his face back into his pillow.

"Don't give up, Hosani," Major Schmidt said. "You'll survive."

"Unfortunately."

13.

MAYOR ADAMS had given more speeches than he could count. This was just one more. However, each speech had its own requirements; its own cadence, vocabulary, and rhetoric. The occasion mattered—was it a fundraising dinner, was it a patriotic celebration such as this one, or was he campaigning on behalf of some new unpopular law? Who was his audience? If they were skolars, he should appeal to the intellect; if they were common Joshuans, he should appeal to the baser desires—their need to hate, fear, and love in equal measure. In this case, his audience was the elite of Joshua City and he must appeal to their sense of superiority. He must assure them that their positions and wealth were safe.

He felt a momentary twinge of doubt, a hitch in his smile as he stepped forward to address the most powerful people in Joshua City. He craved the reassurance of the Oracles and later, he knew, he would have it. But for now, he did what he always did and matched his words to the needs of the moment.

※ ※ ※

As Mayor Adams finished his speech with a well-sculpted phrase, the patroness let her left hand flutter around her throat and thought, *This is my leader.* She loved him. She loved him. She felt the whole room gather around him. She did not think of sex, but sex was in her mind. She had become slippery drunk and thought of her earlier years, when a party like this would end with a new novelist or ambassador taking her home. She gave a quick glance down her torso, checking her wares. She had stayed thin. She scanned the room. No one had noticed her self-appraisal. Because no one was looking her way? No, earlier in the night, didn't that fine gentleman General—what was his name again? How could she have forgotten that? Too many martinis, must cut back...He had certainly looked her up and down, almost as if inspecting a military recruit, but with something more domestic in mind.

She leaned against the table and recalled how Joshua City had changed over the years, much for the better, she thought. She let her gaze sweep the room, filled as it was with glamorous beauties, famous artists, and the powerful in business and politics. Yes, Joshua City was at a historical zenith just now, and they all had Mayor Adams to thank. She thought vaguely of seducing him; she let the thought drift away like morning mist on the Baikal Sea; she took a slow sip of her champagne, and the fizzy sweetness filled her with a youthful giddiness. Indeed, Joshua City was in a fine state.

CHAPTER FIVE

THE UTILITY PRINCIPLE

1.

SURELY THERE'S SOMETHING else we can do?" Major Schmidt asked. It was half past five o'morn and the rest of the camp was still asleep except for Kharkov and Jürgen, who had joined Major Schmidt for a last-minute strategy session. The desert sunrise came in through the open flap of the tent, casting a pinkish glow over their frowning faces.

Schmidt was mostly speaking to himself. He had gone through every permutation of their options. This was the only way—and they all knew it.

"It really is the closest place to get supplies," Kharkov said.

Schmidt jabbed the map. "Isn't there a town here? And here?"

Jürgen glanced at the map perfunctorily. You didn't have to read the language as he did to see the obvious.

"Those towns are in Ulani territory," he said.

"And we can't afford an engagement with the enemy," Kharkov added. "Not at our current strength."

"It seems like an ugly thing," Major Schmidt said. Then, to Jürgen, "Are you all right with this?"

"What I think doesn't matter."

"Of course it does," Major Schmidt said impatiently. "Why do you think I called you here?"

He was growing tired of Jürgen's constant deference since he had taken the identity of Major Schmidt. Of course, it was a necessary part of the illusion—but here, alone, couldn't he drop the pretense?

Jürgen took out his broken glasses and uselessly cleaned the cracked lenses. He put them back in his pocket.

"All right. I agree. It is an ugly thing. But it's an ugly necessary thing. That's why I say what I think doesn't matter. Neither does what you think. Only the demands of the situation."

"Are you saying that because it's what you truly believe or because you think it's what I want to hear?"

"I'm not appeasing you, if that's what you're worried about. I'm a scientist. For me, there isn't a choice between *versions* of the truth. There's evidence and conclusions drawn from that evidence."

"And what does the evidence tell you?"

"You already know the answer to that."

Kharkov had less compunction about all of this. And that was why he proved so useful: a ruthlessly practical man, not given to idle second-guessing. Major Schmidt knew he must become more like Kharkov. But that didn't mean he had to like requisitioning medikal supplies from one of their own hospitals. *Is this the person I will make myself as Major Schimidt?*

No, he did not enjoy the situation he found himself in, did not enjoy the actions he knew he would take to complete his self-given mission, but he would do whatever was necessary, as he had promised himself and his men. And the hospital would have a military wing; they all did since the war had started. There would be new men to add to his hobbled kompany, the ones healthy enough anyway. As much as he needed supplies, he needed additional troops even more desperately.

"Sound the reveille," Major Schmidt said to Kharkov. "We'd better get moving."

%% %% %%

Kharkov left the tent, but Major Schmidt told Jürgen to wait.

"How is your project coming along?" he asked when they were alone.

"It wasn't without difficulty," Jürgen said. "But we've managed to extract the core. I was right about its density. It took four men just to carry the thing ten meters."

"And you're certain you can construct the device?"

"As certain as anyone can be with unfamiliar technology, sir."

"I need more than platitudes about the fallibility of technology, Jürgen."

"It should work. The mechanisms are all simple enough. Provided they have what we need at the hospital, of course."

"Good," Major Schmidt said. "That's the only thing making me feel halfway decent about all of this."

"A man in your position can't afford the luxury of guilt," Jürgen said. "I suggest you leave that to others."

After Jürgen left the tent, Major Schmidt turned his attention back to the map. It would take two days to get to New Kolyma. And there was no way to predict what supplies the hospital would have. He hoped it would all be worth it.

2.

ADRIAN AND ARIAH lay in her small bed. Ariah brought his hand to her chest, and he fumbled with the buttons on her hospital gown. Earlier that day, he had removed sutures from an intestinal wound. So why were the simple buttons of this gown suddenly impossible to navigate? Finally, he had three buttons undone, and the sallow skin of Ariah's neck and sternum were exposed; her small breasts like soft pears were partially exposed as well; a blue web of veins showed through her thin translucent skin.

"Are you sure about this, Ariah?"

"Yes, of course."

He finished unbuttoning her gown, and again she guided his hand, this time between her legs.

"All right. Is that . . ."

"Uh."

"Are you all right?"

"I'm fine. It feels good."

"It's just you look like you're in pain. And you're not very..."

"It's not anything you're doing. It's my condition. I have trouble..."

"Is there anything I can do? I could..."

"Just go slowly."

"All right."

"Uh."

"This is hurting you. I should stop."

"No, Adrian. I want this. I really do."

"I'm going to stop."

※ ※ ※

"It's strange, you know. My mind wants it. Even my body wants it, on some abstract level. I feel excited right now. To be with you, like this. Here. Feel me." Adrian let her guide his hand. "But then when the moment comes, my body won't do what it's supposed to."

"We don't have to do anything. I like just lying here, talking to you."

"But I *want* to. I told you. I *need* to. I feel like I need this one good thing in my life, just a moment of pleasure before..."

"Don't talk that way."

"This is a hospital," Ariah said brightly. "You must have some kind of lubricant somewhere, right?"

"I told you. We don't have to do anything."

"Quit being so noble. Besides, it's not about what you want. It's about me. The poor little sick girl. Ha."

"I'll look around and see what we have. If that's what you really want."

"It is."

※ ※ ※

"Is that better?"

"It's perfect."

"I could..."

"Be quiet," Ariah said and pulled him against her.

3.

THE NEXT DAY, Adrian and Ariah walked at the outer edges of the hospital's compound, careful not to stray too far from the safety of the Guardsmen stationed there for the protection of the facility. More wounded Guardsmen were being admitted each day and more Guardsmen were assigned to the hospital as sentries as well, giving the place an ever-increasing military atmosphere. But Adrian only vaguely noticed this, given how immersed he was in his emotions for Ariah. Just now, she bent over to touch the soft petals of a blue flower, careful not to let go of Adrian's hand as she did so. Her attentive fingers wrapped warmly in his, her care not to undo their connection as she bent to her lovely gesture of lightly petting the flower—just to test its reality, to feel its existence more fully, innocently curious about the world—her care in this and every matter of their relationship made Adrian unbelievably happy. All he could think about was that happiness, and that was all he wanted to think about right now.

"What is that?" Ariah said with a frown.

In the distance, a plume of dust rose up from the desert road.

The karavan wasn't due to arrive for eight days. "Probably just more wounded Guardsmen."

But as the lead truck in the procession approached, one of the nearby Guardsmen came to attention and asked the man beside him, "Is that an Ulani insignia?"

The second Guardsman squinted and after a moment said, "Yes, I think it is."

Both men raised their rifles.

A second truck emerged from the desert cloud. "Wait," the first Guardsman said, "Isn't that a Joshuan vehicle?"

Ariah squeezed Adrian's hand tighter. "What's going on?"

"I don't know," Adrian said. "Let's go inside."

※ ※ ※

In the courtyard, Spargo spoke with the officer in charge. A half dozen military trucks were parked rudely on the hospital lawn. The hospital staff had gathered around to hear what was being said. Adrian joined them, alone, having insisted that Ariah return to her room.

"Whatever provisions we have are yours, of course," Direktor Spargo said.

"You are a true Joshuan citizen," Major Schmidt said. "I assure you we will take only what we need. The work you are doing here is essential. We wouldn't want to interfere."

With that, the Guardsmen marched inside the hospital and began the process of taking what they needed. Major Schmidt divided his men into groups. He sent one group to the hospital kitchens to procure cooking supplies—bags of oats and oil and flour and rice. Anything that was nonperishable and could travel easily. Another group he sent to the room where all the medikaments were stored. They needed disinfectants, antibiotics, and analgesics. They needed needles and thread to suture wounds. They needed syringes and gauze bandages.

Many of them also needed more immediate medikal attention.

"You there," Schmidt said to Adrian. "What is your name?"

"Adrian Talbot, sir."

"I've got sick and wounded men."

"I will help them however I can."

※ ※ ※

Adrian watched as the Guardsmen stomped through corridors of the hospital, flinging open doors and frightening the patients. He thought about Ariah, alone in her room. He should go to her, make sure she was safe. But Major Schmidt didn't look like a man you refused. Without responding, Adrian grabbed the nearest orderly, a young man by the name of Kantar and together they carried a gurney outside.

"What's happening?" Kantar said.

Kantar was several years older than Adrian but was a volunteer as well. Adrian had seen him with the patients, changing their bedpans and doing other menial duties. Though large and intimidating looking, he was soft-spoken and kind. He had the natural makings of a medikal assistant, Adrian thought.

"I'm not sure," Adrian said. "I think it's best we go along for now."

He and Kantar went around to the open back of one of the trucks. Inside were at least half a dozen wounded. Where to begin?

"Let's start with him," Adrian said, indicating the Guardsman who happened to be closest to the rear of the truck.

The Guardsman groaned as they lifted him onto the gurney. He was not a big man, fortunately—skinny, dark-skinned, with a scarred fever-ish face.

"Where are you taking me?" he whispered.

"This is a hospital," Adrian said. "We're going to see that you get better."

"Just let me die."

Adrian ignored this and assessed the others who would need his attention. They moaned and cried out from the back of the truck. And he could see other trucks, other new patients being unloaded.

"What's your name, Guardsman?" Adrian asked.

"Artillery Gunner Hosani."

"Do you know the first rule of my profession?"

The Guardsman shook his head.

"The practicing physician must offer treatment to the best of his abil-ities and knowledge, using the full resources at his disposal," Adrian said. "If I let you die, I'd be breaking my oath." The man seemed unimpressed. "Besides," he added with a smile, "you're a long way from dying."

The Guardsman closed his eyes and groaned again.

Adrian and Kantar lifted the gurney as gently as possible and carried the first of Adrian's new patients inside.

※ ※ ※

Nearly everything was loaded into the trucks now. The Guardsmen had gathered in the courtyard, their ranks larger now. Though some of the men had stayed on at the hospital, too wounded to be of use in battle, Guardsmen from the hospital's military wing had volunteered to follow Major Schmidt into combat. Some of these men still had visible injuries—an arm in a sling, a patch over an eye—but they looked eager to be off of their backs and fighting again. Major Schmidt felt a burst of gratitude, and maybe a small sense of unworthiness, at having such fine brave men to lead. *Would they follow me if they knew who I really was?* No doubt they would hear about it eventually. At least a quarter of the men from the prison knew his true identity.

Damn it, where was Jürgen? Major Schmidt had sent him off with a group of Guardsmen to find and remove as many of the hospital's heart monitors as possible, leaving at least one for the hospital to use. This was the final piece Jürgen needed for what he called his "artery bomb." Major Schmidt still had only a vague idea what that meant, but apparently it would make use of the "false star" Jürgen had found. The star's core was made of something called uranium, a rare dense metal that when exploded in projectile form would do far more damage than the material of an ordinary bomb. Jürgen assured him that such a bomb could kill dozens of men in one blast. That was just the kind of close-range concealed weapon they needed to help defeat the Ulani troops when they joined up with the regiment.

It amazed Major Schmidt that Jürgen could look at a piece of Before-Time space debris, if indeed it was that, and see a deadly weapon. To Major Schmidt's eyes it had simply looked like a relic of forgotten technology. But his was not a scientific mind. He scolded himself vaguely for having wasted his years of school. *To be able to see the world that way.* Major Schmidt thought of a passage from the *Book of the Before-Time* his mother often quoted. *Each according to his ability.* He wondered what his true ability might be. Perhaps Jürgen was right about this as well. Perhaps he was meant to lead these brave Joshuans to victory.

But he couldn't lead them anywhere until they left this hospital.

Where was Jürgen? He should be back by now. Major Schmidt saw Kharkov across the yard and motioned him over.

"Have you seen Jürgen?"

Kharkov shrugged. "I've been out here."

"You're in charge until I get back. Make sure everything's loaded correctly."

※ ※ ※

Major Schmidt located Jürgen in one of the operating rooms. Direktor Spargo was with him. Schmidt didn't know why Spargo bothered him so much—after all, he had only done what Major Schmidt asked. Was it the alacrity with which he did it, with which he gave up the hospital he was supposed to protect, that disturbed Major Schmidt?

Jürgen had five heart monitors stacked on an operating table—flat gray boxes roughly the size of typewriters. He was hunched over one. Its panel was open and he was examining its interior. As Major Schmidt entered, two Guardsmen passed him, carrying a sixth heart monitor. "Excuse us, sir."

They set the machine beside the others.

"If there's anything else I can do . . . " Direktor Spargo said to Jürgen.

"What's going on here?" Major Schmidt said.

Jürgen looked up, a tiny screwdriver in his hands, noticing Major Schmidt.

"That's quite all right, Direktor. If you could just give the Major and me the room."

"Yes, of course," Direktor Spargo said and excused himself.

To the Guardsmen, Jürgen asked, "Is that all of them?"

"All but the one you asked us to leave, sir. The direktor assured us it's in good working order and that he can radio for more to be brought in on the next karavan."

"Thank you. You can go now."

When the room was empty, Major Schmidt repeated his question. "What's going on here? Why aren't these in the trucks?"

"There's been a change of plans."

Schmidt waited.

"I'm not going with you," Jürgen said.

Major Schmidt blinked. "Of course you are," he said.

"I'm a civilian. I'll stay here with the rest of them."

"But I need you out there."

"Don't worry. I'll build your artery bombs. That's why I asked Spargo for this operating room," he said, and with an ambiguous irony added, "I'm going to perform my own version of surgery here."

"Never mind about the bombs," Major Schmidt said. "Why are you not staying with me?"

Jürgen lifted the casing off one of the heart monitors and pointed to the circuitry beneath. "This is the bulkiest part. The functioning mechanism is actually quite small. If I just remove the body, it will be lightweight and portable."

Major Schmidt honored his deflection and asked, "How long will this take? The trucks are waiting outside."

"I think I can have it done by the morning."

Jürgen tinkered with the heart monitor. He tapped the tiny screwdriver against his teeth, musing, and then returned to work.

"I still don't understand . . ." Major Schmidt began.

"Call it an act of conscience."

"Come with me. We'll return to Joshua City as heroes."

Jürgen set down his tools.

"I'm afraid that's impossible. There's something I haven't told you. I used to work for the Ministrie of Technology, designing surveillance equipment . . ."

※ ※ ※

And Jürgen told Major Schmidt about how he had leaked high-level surveillance documents to a source in the media. How he escaped Joshua City before the authorities could arrest him. How he made his way through the desert without the safety of a karavan. How he was captured by Ulani troops and wound up in their prison. As he spoke, the pieces fell into place for Major Schmidt. He thought about Jürgen's reluctance to share the details of his past—a reticence Major Schmidt had mistaken for an innate privacy and had respected as such. In prison, in war, every man had a right to his past. To his secrets. Sometimes those secrets were the only thing keeping a man alive—ghost companions providing the strength to carry on.

%% %% %%

"I'm sorry I didn't tell you sooner," Jürgen said.

Did he still want Jürgen with him? Did he still trust him with his life? The answer was obvious.

"Whatever you've done," Major Schmidt said, "you've handled yourself bravely. I wouldn't be standing here if it weren't for you."

"I'm an engineer," Jürgen said. "I merely refashioned what was already there."

"There's one other thing I don't understand. If you opposed the government, why did you help me?"

Jürgen thought about that. "I'm a realist. A scientist. I believe in the utility principle. We all act according to a version of it. It simply depends on how extreme our version is. There's individual utility, which some people call self-interest. There's situational utility, which is what you practice, I think. And then there's universal utility, the greatest possible good for the greatest number of people. Follow me for a second: if there was a baby on the train tracks back in Joshua City, and the only way to save it was to derail a train carrying several hundred passengers, would you do it? I would hope not, no matter how ugly the single consequence might be. We have to think like that now. Always, even."

"But surely in a time of war . . . ?"

"More so in a time of war, I would think. Kameras and recording devices on every street corner, in the houses of ordinary citizens? I couldn't countenance that, but I can countenance our decisions here."

"But the surveillance might have stopped Ulani secret agents. We were both in that prison. We saw what they are."

"And that was what caused me to join forces with you. The Joshuan government may not be perfect. But those months in prison stripped away whatever illusions I might have had about the Ulanis. We will be far worse off if they win the war. And that's why I'm building these," a sweeping motion of the table, "but once I'm done, I'm staying here."

"How does that last part fit into your philosophy?"

"If I can mitigate some of the damage we've done here, that too will go toward the greatest possible good."

"The utility principle."

Jürgen brightened at Schmidt's understanding.

"So you're a doktor now?" Major Schmidt said.

"I don't know what I am. But I plan to stay and find out."

Major Schmidt studied the hard line of Jürgen's brow. There was no talking him out of this. And he needed these artery bombs. They might be the difference between a decisive victory and a slaughter. And so, they would stay one more night in this hospital in the middle of nowhere.

"Finish my bombs," Major Schmidt said. "And come get me the second they're ready."

Major Schmidt left to inform his troops of the new plan. He understood Jürgen's decision, and on some level he could respect it. But he could not help feeling that he had lost yet another friend, and at the thought of leading these men into battle without him, he felt more alone than he had in his entire life.

※ ※ ※

The word passed around the hospital that the Guardsmen would be staying the night. There were not enough hospital beds for them all, so they camped out in the halls, sleeping on bedrolls on the floor. Adrian had to step around them as he made his rounds. Using the limited supplies that had not been loaded in the military trucks, he reset broken bones, cleaned open sores, administered antibiotics for a particularly nasty cough, stitched up ragged cuts.

The Guardsman named Hosani kept trying to get out of bed, insisting he was ready to fight. Eventually, Adrian had Kantar hold him down so he could sedate him.

It was nearly midnight when Adrian looked up at the clock. *Ariah.* How could he have forgotten? He went to check on her. Sleeping. Good. He stood in the doorway, looking at her head on the pillows in the moonlight. Her hair unfurled like some strange sea creature. How lucky he was. How *unlucky* he was.

"Adrian?" Her voice, nearly a whisper, in the dark.

"Yes?"

She sat up in bed and flicked on the light. "I dreamed you were here," she said. "And you *were.*"

She held out her hand to him. He approached and took it. She was feverish.

"Maybe you should go back to sleep. We'll do the blood-filtration tomorrow."

She frowned at that. "Again already?"

Ariah hated her treatment, he knew. As sick as she felt now, the treatments left her feeling even worse.

"I'm afraid so."

"That's all right," she said. "I'm just happy it's you doing them."

He kissed her forehead. "Go back to sleep. I love you."

She gripped the back of his neck and pulled his head to hers. They stayed like that for a long moment, foreheads touching.

※ ※ ※

After leaving Ariah, Adrian went to issue his daily report to Doktor Abuawad. In all the confusion, he had not checked in with him all day. He was probably already asleep.

The door to the office was open, light coming from inside. Two

Guardsmen had Abuawad backed up against his desk, their guns drawn. Abuawad had his hands raised.

"What is going on here?" Adrian demanded.

"This doesn't concern you," the smaller of the Guardsmen said. "Go back to your duties."

"What is your name? We can work this out."

"Not that it matters to you, but I am Korporal Vidal. I am a true Joshuan patriot, and the only thing that needs to be worked out is why an enemy of Joshua City would be allowed to treat her Guardsmen."

"I was appointed by the Municipal Office," Doktor Abuawad said. "My contract was signed by the Minister of Health himself. I have no allegiance to my native city."

"We can't trust any Al-Khuziri dust-dog. How many of our Guardsmen have your citymen killed here on the sly?" Korporal Vidal said.

"I was born in Joshua City. I am one of you," Dr. Abuawad said. "My medikal degree is from Joshua University," he added as though that should matter somehow.

"What he says is true," Adrian said.

"Be quiet," the larger assailant said to Adrian. "Are you a sympathizer with the enemy? That would make you just as bad as one of them to my way of thinking." The man gripped his revolver menacingly and Adrian took a step back.

Vidal punched Dr. Abuawad in the face viciously. Dr. Abuawad twirled around from the force and hit the floor. He groaned and seemed barely conscious. He half-lifted himself up, then paused in that crouched position. Vidal kicked him in the stomach, rolling him over onto his back. He kicked again, this time hitting his leg. He pulled his boot back, preparing for another blow, when Adrian leapt forward, but before he could reach Vidal, the other Guardsman clipped him in the back of the head with the butt of his rifle, sending an explosion of white light through Adrian as he fell to the floor. He could feel blood running warmly over his ear and down his neck. He sat up, collapsed, sat up again. The room tilted and he struggled to focus.

Dr. Abuawad lay motionless. The flap of his left ear was hanging on by a stringy redness; both his eyes were swollen shut and puffy with purple bruises. Adrian could see his chest moving slightly. *He's still alive at least.* Adrian tried to think of something he could say or do to end this now, before they killed Dr. Abuawad, but he had said everything he could think of and he had no chance of overpowering the two men. He hated the total helplessness he felt. He prayed to God to save them.

Korporal Vidal planted a foot on either side of Doktor Abuawad and stood there glaring down at him. He spat in Doktor Abuawad's battered face. Then he aimed his rifle down and without hesitation shot Doktor Abuawad once into the chest, causing him to spasm upward and fall back motionless. Then Vidal fired into the center of Doktor Abuawad's forehead, sending a splatter of blood and bone and brains across the room. Vidal holstered his gun and stepped away from his deed. He motioned for his companion to join him on his way out of the operating room.

Korporal Vidal turned back to survey his handiwork one last time.

"Hey, Doktor," he said, completely pleased with himself and proud of his display of power, "consider yourself lucky. Next time you defend an enemy of Joshua City, you might not live to talk about it."

They left Adrian with the corpse of his friend and mentor. He had to get someone. He had to do something. The blood pooled on the floor . . . red sea, red shadow. How could they? They were supposed to serve and protect. *Oh, Dr. Abuawad, I am so sorry.* His mind was white-hot. His scalp tingled and electric nerves scudded down his back.

His palms were wet, and he clenched and unclenched his useless fists . . . then the world wobbled toward an unfeeling blackness, then toward a searing whiteness . . . a seizure was coming on; *not now, no*; but his body convulsed and spittle globbed in the corners of his mouth and his eyes rolled back . . .

⁄⁄ ⁄⁄ ⁄⁄

Slow pulse of light; dazzling blindness, white-blue blindness; the walls and ceiling closed in briefly then were obliterated the white-blue pulse; there was something cold and slick stretching in every direction beneath him; he lay there; the floor stretching cold; the floor; *oh please this time please please*; icy-blue light expanded to every horizon, creating horizons within horizons, making the thereness of Being, then obliterating that too only to make it again against a farther horizon; cold stretching icy blue pulse; *oh please*; where would this plunging end?; there was neither height nor depth but both in one dimension going both ways at once; *oh Lord, appear, oh please this time*, take my hand please; there was nothing to grasp; Adrian had no hands though he reached out with them; dimensions were obliterated in blue-pulsing-white brightness, and Adrian felt a swelling of pity and love for Ariah for that Major Schmidt for Dr. Abuawad for Nikolas Alyosha his mother his uncle everyone; *oh thank you thank you*; this was God; *oh thank you, I see you now.*

%. %. %.

Adrian woke up on the floor of Doktor Abuawad's office.

His face and arms were sticky with what had happened. *Who killed him? Did I?* He put his hand behind him, tried to push himself up. His hand slipped in the congealed mess. He fell and a bone in his back met the hard floor meanly. He turned over, pushed himself up with both arms, managed a leg beneath him. *Red hand. Doktor Abuawad.* He had to . . .

He staggered into the hall. He grabbed an orderly.

"Please," he said. "Inside . . . They shot him."

He stumbled off, unseeing, disturbed a gurney. Wheels rattled. If he could just find his bed. He needed to lie down. So tired . . . he needed . . .

%. %. %.

While Adrian slept, while the orderlies wheeled Abuawad's body to the morgue, while they cleaned the blood from the floor of his office, while

Guardsmen slept on gurneys and tables and in supply closets, Jürgen stripped the heart monitors of their casings. He strapped their circuitry to the uranium cores and wired them with the explosives and a triggering mechanism. He worked through the night and into the dawn. He worked without thought, or rather with this one simple thought: *make it right*. As an ordinary sun crested over an unchanged desert horizon, Jürgen set down his tools.

Now he just had to make sure the men knew how to use them. He would instruct Kharkov, and Kharkov would show the others, those unfortunate volunteers who would do the dirty work of becoming human weapons. He admired those men. They were the utility principle in action. At the same time, it required a special blindness to place honor and duty above one's own life. Or was it vision? Unconsciously echoing the thought, Jürgen held his glasses (now patched with surgical tape) up to his face and examined his work one last time for some critical oversight. He could see none.

His bombs would function despite being inelegant ugly contraptions, but seeing them laid out, a mismatch of spare parts fused together, made the messiness of their dark purpose more than an abstract principle. He took his glasses off again and tried to remember the faces of all the Guardsmen he had met during his time with Major Schmidt. *Which of them will it be?*

※ ※ ※

Kharkov grasped the mechanism of the bombs quickly. *A smart man, a brave man*, Jürgen thought for the hundredth time. Kharkov chewed at his usual toothpick. Jürgen sincerely hoped he would survive the war.

"Did you hear?" Kharkov asked. "About what happened?"

Jürgen tilted his head.

"Some idiots shot a doktor."

Jürgen dimly remembered some commotion in the hospital, noise in the corridor he had ignored while he worked. "Guardsmen?"

"Who else?"

"And I don't suppose anyone's stepped forward to confess?"

Kharkov removed his toothpick and spat in the dirt. "These children. They have no idea of the meaning of war."

Major Schmidt came out of the hospital, rubbing the sleep from his eyes, though doing his best to hide his exhaustion. To look like a leader. He probably hadn't slept—up dealing with this totally avoidable incident.

"He'll need you," Jürgen said to Kharkov.

"I think he'll be fine."

Schmidt joined his companions. They stood in komradely silence, taking stock of nothing in particular. Inside the hospital, lights were coming on. The Guardsmen would be out soon.

"I don't suppose you've changed your mind?" Major Schmidt asked Jürgen.

Jürgen frowned slightly.

Major Schmidt extended his hand. "Good luck to you then."

"And the same to you," Jürgen said, then patted one of his artery bombs with something like regret. "Use these judiciously."

Doors opened and shut, as Guardsmen filed out of the hospital, carrying the last of the supplies; sharp morning light glinted from windows; and there was that unchanging desert horizon again. A man on crutches limped gamely toward the trucks. It was that friend of Major Schmidt's from the prison, the one who'd tried to escape . . . Samir something, Jürgen recalled, already feeling distant from the proceedings.

"Private," Kharkov said, stepping forward. "You're in no condition to leave this hospital."

"Please don't make me stay. I belong with the Guardsmen."

Schmidt nodded. "If he wants to come with us, that's his decision. But I'll not have a man slowing us down."

"I won't, Major," Samir said, placing a respectful emphasis on the title. "Don't worry about me."

Samir hobbled over to the truck and managed to lift himself in.

"You're lucky to have men leaving their sickbeds to fight for you," Jürgen said.

Major Schmidt smiled morosely.

"Luck is for the ill-prepared," Kharkov said. "Come on, Major. We must get going."

※ ※ ※

Adrian lay in his bed, head pounding and throat rasp-dry. He stared up at the ceiling, a cracked dirty concrete caked with some yellow substance. The more he looked at it, the sicker he felt. He turned, hugging his sides. He rolled over, rolled over again. The sheets were tangled around him. He pinwheeled his feet trying to get comfortable. Nothing worked. An image of dark water and a crackled scream—a nightmare? He always had horrible dreams after a seizure. He threw the sheets to the floor.

He sat up abruptly, ignoring the great metallic ripping through his head. *Doktor Abuawad. The Guardsmen. They must be reported.* His mouth tasted like rot, like bitter almond and ash. He pulled on a crumpled pair of pants and his doktor's coat. He left his room without cleaning his teeth or brushing his hair. In this state of disarray, like a half-dressed mental patient, he entered the hall.

Quiet. Empty. *No, they can't be gone already.* Gurneys in the middle of the hall, open doorways, a sense of desolation. He passed a supply closet where medikaments were stored, saw broken bottles on the floor.

The front doors of the hospital stood open, men moving in and out. The trucks were still parked in the yard. He grabbed the arm of a Guardsman.

"Major Schmidt?" he asked.

The Guardsman shook him off with mild annoyance and pointed to the lead truck. The major was climbing inside. Adrian walked out into the painful light.

"Major," he said. "A word. Please."

Already annoyed, "What is it, Doktor?"

Adrian didn't bother to correct him on his form of address. Inside the cab, the driver sat with his hands on the wheel.

"Actually, it's a sensitive matter."

"Anything you have to say to me you can say to Private Petrenko."

How should he begin?

"Two of your men have done something horrible."

Major Schmidt said, "I have been informed. It's a terrible incident."

"You have already taken actions?"

"I assure you I will root out and punish the culprits with utmost severity."

"So they will be court-martialed?" Adrian said. "Will they go to prison?"

"That depends on the evidence."

"I saw them. They shot him in cold blood. It was unprovoked."

"Can you identify the men for me?"

Adrian thought for a moment. One of the men had told him his name. But sometimes after a seizure, he couldn't remember anything that had happened just before. *Not this time. Please.* "Maybe."

"All right, Doktor," Major Schmidt said. "This won't make me popular. But go around to the trucks and have a look. I'll come with you."

※ ※ ※

Who will it be? Major Schmidt thought as he and the young doktor walked up and down the lines of Guardsmen. *Which one of these men, ready to die for me, will I have to arrest?* He remembered the village, how he had done nothing to help that girl, though he had known the truth.

The young doktor moved through the ranks of the Guardsmen, a confused knot in his brow. He looked like he was in pain. Major Schmidt worried he would identify the wrong man; he had heard or read, he couldn't remember where, that eyewitness identification was notoriously unreliable. *Be sure, Doktor. I don't want to imprison someone on a mistake.*

The doktor paused before a korporal named Vidal. The doktor's eyes went to the man's boots, went to his hands, then his face. Major Schmidt tried to remember anything he knew about the Guardsman; they were in prison together, but in separate cell blocks. He seemed an eager and competent soldier, but otherwise, Major Schmidt had to admit he did not know his character. And how many men under his kommand did he truly know? It would be unfortunate to lose one of the few remaining officers.

Vidal accepted the doktor's scrutiny, his hands on his hips and elbows out in a military posture known as the Guardsmen's Diamond.

"We really must get moving, Doktor," Major Schmidt said.

"I'm sorry. Just one more minute. Maybe..."

The doktor shook his head and moved on.

※ ※ ※

Damn you. Why can't I remember? Adrian hated his stupid affliction, his brain that misfired, leaving him scattered and trying to put the pieces back together. All these men, with their close-cropped hair and their Guardsmen's brown and blue. It could have been any one of them.

Adrian shook his head. "I can't remember."

"Well, Doktor. I'm sure you understand my position. I can't punish at random."

A hard-looking man with a pocked face came around the side of a truck. "Major," he said. "The supply trucks are ready to go. We are awaiting your orders to depart."

Adrian had to keep them here somehow. "If I could just have more time, I'm sure..."

"I'm sorry, Doktor," Major Schmidt said, already climbing into his truck. "We have a war to fight."

※ ※ ※

And so Major Schmidt led his ragtag procession into the desert, leaving the hospital behind. He pictured the sad reproachful face of the young doktor. It was as though he could not bring himself to judge anyone, despite the mess Schmidt and his Guardsmen had made of everything. *But maybe I deserve to be judged.* Who did Major Schmidt have with him, after all? He had a rapist, and now... two unidentified murderers.

What would these men do in the battle to come? Perhaps they would be the most efficient. And wasn't he a murderer also? His friend Jürgen might make a distinction between justified and unjustified killing. Major Schmidt did not completely understand Jürgen's philosophical arguments, but he knew when a line had been crossed. In the prison, they had done what was necessary. He regretted none of that. But what he had just allowed and the things he would allow... What had he felt when the doktor failed to identify the culprits? A guilty relief. Not real guilt. That—he assumed, or at least hoped—would come later.

※ ※ ※

There would be a funeral for Doktor Abuawad later that day, Marsela informed Adrian. Her eyes were red from crying. She wiped her face with a handkerchief. "I just can't believe it."

Adrian stabilized himself with a hand on the wall.

"And you?" she asked. "How are you handling it?"

What an amazing person, that she could think of his welfare right now.

"I was there. I saw it... I should have done something."

"Stop thinking like that."

"I don't know..." Adrian said. "It's that..."

"I understand."

She squeezed his hand. Her big palm was warm and comforting.

"You're a good man, Adrian."

"Thank you." He held her hand for another moment. "If it wasn't for you, I might have left that first week."

She released his hand. She leaned back in her chair, taking him in with sympathetic appraisal.

"I don't think so. I don't think you would have."

"Thank you," he said again. He shifted and glanced to the door behind him, thinking of Ariah. "I really should..."

"Go do your job," Marsela said with her usual courage. "It's all we can do at a time like this."

※ ※ ※

Two hours until the funeral. *Two hours until we bury Doktor Abuawad.* He imagined the face of Abuawad, dead and mangled, as he was lowered into the ground. But right now, he had to focus on Ariah's blood-filtration. *She needs me.* (His eye was still twitching and the nerves along his left leg were pure electricity.) He asked an orderly for help moving the blood-filtration machine.

Before they were fully in the supply room, Adrian understood something was very wrong. The machine was tipped over. The tubes were crushed; he checked the centrifuge—useless. He lifted it halfway off the ground, his body still weak from his seizure, and trembling, let it drop to floor. The orderly came forward to help him.

Adrian waved him away. "No."

Major Schmidt. When I get out of this place...

※ ※ ※

There wasn't another karavan for a week. But even then, what good would it do? Without a recent blood-filtration, Ariah would never survive the trip back to Joshua City. No, they would have to fix the blood-filtration machine. Adrian learned that an engineer, a civilian from Major Schmidt's konvoy, had stayed on at the hospital. Adrian took this man, Jürgen Moritz, to the room with the smashed blood-filtration machine.

Jürgen poked around in the fragments, turned a piece of the pump over in his hands, clicked his tongue.

"Can you fix it?" Adrian asked.

"It will be difficult. I'm not familiar with this machine."

"But you can do it?"

"I'll try. I see some possibilities here."

"Can I trust you?"

"I stayed here for a reason."

"It has to work. Her life depends on it."

Jürgen nodded. "Take me to the hospital laundry."

※ ※ ※

"My ad hoc centrifuge should work, but we have another problem," Jürgen said. "We are missing the blood pressure monitor usually included in these devices."

There would be no way to regulate the filtration process mechanically. It would have to be done manually.

"And how will we do that?" Adrian asked.

"It should be easy enough to fashion a hand-pump to get her blood out, into the centrifuge, and back into her. The difficulty will be doing it as evenly as the original machine did and keeping her blood pressure at safe levels. I don't know much about medikal science, but I assume there is an exact amount of blood the body can do without for a certain amount of time."

"Yes, of course," Adrian said. "If blood pressure gets too low . . ." He did not finish his thought.

"So, you're going to have to monitor that and whatever else, as you or someone pumps her blood."

With all the new wounded Guardsmen and civilians, the doktors were stretched thin, but Adrian imposed upon a fellow medikal skolar to help him in the procedure ("You have to help me with this please.") Adrian asked Skolar Karols to monitor Ariah's heart as he pumped her blood out and back into her body.

※ ※ ※

"You're being very brave," Adrian said.

"What choice do I have? And besides, you're here."

Adrian's mind was still somewhat wobbly from his seizure, but he focused through the muddle. He had inserted the needles into each of her arms—one for outflowing blood, one for inflowing. Jürgen stood beside his machine, ready to start it at Adrian's order. Karols had the diaphragm of his stethoscope set on Ariah's chest, listening and prepared to warn Adrian should the pulse dip below safe levels. There was nothing else to do, yet Adrian hesitated, lingered in this moment so plenteous with potential for good and for bad.

"All right, Jürgen," Adrian said and pointed at the machine.

Jürgen flipped a switch, then another one, examined all the moving parts with paternal scrutiny. The tube leading from Ariah's left arm to the machine slowly filled with her deeply red blood. Adrian continued pumping. Karols nodded that her blood pressure was at an acceptable level.

Adrian pumped slowly, watching the tubes. Jürgen flipped another switch and the centrifuge began spinning.

Ariah's eyes closed and her limbs went limp. Adrian checked with Karols; everything was fine. Adrian continued pumping, sweat rising on his palms and back and forehead. He focused himself, ignored the tiredness already in his arms from the pumping.

The centrifuge whirred. "I think it's working," Jürgen said. "Get ready for the other pump."

Adrian moved to the other side of Ariah's bed and awaited Jürgen's signal.

"Now."

Adrian leaned over the pump and pushed with his full weight.

Karols said, "Her heartbeat is getting a bit erratic. Slowing down."

"How bad is it?" Adrian asked.

"Not critical yet," Karols said, "but we need to move faster."

Adrian pressed and pressed. The slow blood made its way into her right arm.

Ariah's eyelids were fluttering now.

"Her blood pressure is falling," Karols said.

Adrian's hands shook as they worked the pump.

"It's not working," Adrian said.

Jürgen came around the foot of the bed and examined the pump. "It should be working fine."

Adrian pressed, pressed, pressed.

"Now we've got it," Karols said. "Her pressure is rising."

"Good," Jürgen said. "Now you'll want to work the other pump." He went back to the centrifuge and checked it again.

More blood flowed out of Ariah's left arm and into Jürgen's machine; the centrifuge whirred and shook.

"Now the other one," Jürgen yelled.

Adrian ran to the other pump.

"Levels are dropping again."

The accordion-like pump went down and up. Unnoticed drops of sweat fell from his forehead onto Ariah's face. Her eyelids quivered open. Her mouth moved silently, saying words he couldn't understand.

"Levels still dropping. They are getting dangerously low now."

Adrian pressed down on the pump as hard as he could. His arms shook and his whole body trembled. It had to work. He would make it work.

Her face went slack.

Karols took his stethoscope off. "There is no pulse."

Adrian leaned his whole body over the pump and threw himself onto it frantically. Karols reached over and stopped Adrian's hand.

"There's nothing to be done."

Adrian stepped back. His hands were shaking uncontrollably. The tubes sprawled alien-red from both her arms. A back part of his brain quivered, an aftershock of his seizure. Karols stared dumbly at his stethoscope. Ariah's moist unseeing eyes had rolled slightly back in their sockets and were staring emptily at the ceiling. With each passing second, her face was less the face of the woman Adrian had loved and more that of a mannequin's made to resemble her. He set his hand on her shoulder—as if to console her, as if to say it would still be all right somehow—and was disturbed to find her flesh was still warm.

※ ※ ※

Now passed a time of disoriented stasis; no ember of rage, no sparkle of hope, no swell of love; nothing. He was dead; he should have died. He did his medikal duties in numbness. When these duties were done, he went straight to bed and slept without dreams. He woke as late as possible. He did not speak except when it was necessary. He offered no comfort to the patients because he had none to give.

Day in and out, he saw that man Jürgen wandering the corridors of the hospital, tinkering complacently on the machines his friend's army had helped ruin. One day, Adrian could take it no more.

"You promised," he said. "You promised it would work."

They were in an unoccupied supply room. Jürgen looked uneasily over Adrian's shoulder, toward the door. No one was coming. No one was listening.

"I'm sorry," Jürgen said, "but you must understand it wasn't supposed to happen this way."

He gestured to the mess of the room, the empty shelves, as if to take it all in.

"You don't feel it, do you?" Adrian said. "You don't feel anything. You have no understanding."

Jürgen hung his silent head, allowing Adrian to castigate it, to weigh it down with his angry blame. After some minutes, Adrian got tired of speaking. He flung up his arms and walked out into the hall, leaving Jürgen alone as before.

※ ※ ※

In this time came Ariah's funeral. Adrian looked at her file, searching for family members, though of course he had looked at it many times before and knew every word it contained. Her husband was dead; and anyone she knew in Joshua City was too far to arrive in time. He recalled what she told him about her life in the work camp before they met. She had not liked the wives of the free workers, but Adrian summoned up what little energy he had and went around to the workers' houses and made a few inquiries. He remembered a woman named Lucette who had been kind to her if nothing else. He found this woman and she agreed to come. She passed the message on to some of the other women who had known Ariah.

All in all, it was a meager turnout. It was his second funeral in just a matter of days, but while Doktor Abuawad's burial had been attended by the majority of the hospital staff, this was just him and those few women, all strangers to him. He thanked them for coming, eyes dry. He did not look in the coffin before the lid was shut (and this was something that he would forever wonder about, and forever regret: if only he'd had that last look). Then it was closed and it was just like any other box. The women pressed his hand one last time and thanked him for looking after Ariah. If they had only known . . . but they knew nothing; none except Lucette had visited Ariah in the months he knew her—and that was just a single token visit, the mildest show of respect. And then they left and he was alone with the priest who said words that Adrian no longer heard or understood. Then the hot desert sun, taunting the nape of his neck. Back to the hospital and back to work.

4.

DRIP, DRIP, *the belly's lip.*

Slug squinted up at the dripping boiler. He scratched his dirty scalp. Why was it dripping?

The belly slips the belly's heat.

No, no. Someone needed to fix it. Why wouldn't they fix it? He touched his finger to the metal surface and drew it back quickly. He looked at his burned finger. Hot. Good. Just a leak.

The belly eats and then it leaks.

With one hand he held up his too loose pants. Nikolas had given them to him. Good Nikolas. The pants didn't fit but they had no holes. New shoes too. Floppy shoes! He flippity-flopped down the hall, opening doors and humming to himself.

The beast it leaks, the belly's ship.

He saw two people doing the moaning thing on top of each other. He knew the moaning thing. Sometimes he did it to his pillow and then the too-good happened. When he was done he felt a little sick in his stomach and once he cried.

Here it is! A closet full of tools. Big-grabbers, the flat-pounders, the twisty-offs. Sticky glue. Gloves for his fingers to work on the hot belly metal. He lifted the bucket as easily as a child might lift a toy figurine. And he carried it down the hall, singing his happy little work song.

※ ※ ※

Nikolas sat on the floor of his room, cross-legged, with his eyes closed. He was trying to clear his mind, trying to meditate as he had been taught by Messenger, but the *I* kept coming back in. He remembered Elias, smugly standing over the bags of money he had stolen. Mouse and the others congratulating him. Jealousy...what a petty useless emotion. But the fact that he recognized it as petty didn't reduce its power over him.

He heard Messenger's voice as vividly as if he were in the room. "*I. Me. Myself. Mine.* The strangest and most useless of human words. The great human weakness. The man who says *I* willingly singularizes his identity, and by doing so shrinks it to all his fears and doubts and ignoble impulses. Say *we* and become humanity. Say *we* and become the greater good. Say *we* and destroy even the fear of death—which is, after all, simply a fear of the obliteration of the *I*."

We, Nikolas thought...*we must consider what is best for The Underground. I must put aside emotion, for my friends and for Katya and even for myself. Yes, me. Nikolas Kovalski. I don't exist. I am a grammatical construct, one part of the plural known as we.*

"Nikolas," a voice said. It was Radjin, an Elias acolyte if there ever was one.

"What?" Nikolas snapped, angry at having been disturbed when he was just beginning to find his concentration.

"You should come see what your pet has done."

Slug. What was it now? *Something that will make me look bad, no doubt.* Slug was not exactly a popular figure around The Underground. There were those who questioned why Nikolas had brought him off the street, as if the perfectly noble impulse to protect a wounded creature were somehow a weakness. True, Slug had his oddities. But what of it?

Nikolas followed Radjin down the hall. As they approached the boiler room, there was a clank of loose metal, a rumbling groan. Slug was sitting on the floor of the room, tools spread all around him. He was holding an L-shaped piece of metal, turning it over and over in his hands. Radjin slipped away, no doubt to tell tales of the destruction Nikolas's *pet* had caused.

"Nikolas," Slug said. "I like my shoes."

"That's good, Slug," Nikolas said. He kneeled before him. "What do you have there?"

Slug flung the piece of metal away casually. It struck against the wall, chipping a brick. "Don't need it."

"Was that from the boiler?"

Slug shrugged. He hopped to his feet. "Don't need it." He put his hand out to pat on the boiler, thought better of it, pulled it back. "Here?" he said, gesturing to a place along the edge of the boiler, where two pipes met. He scratched his head. "Why? You don't need it. I fixed it for you. No more drip-drip."

Nikolas looked up at the big tank of the boiler, happily giving off steam. Fixed? It was true there was no more dripping. But did it work? He held his hand up to the tank. Hot, sure. But it was hot before. He followed the line of the pipes. Nikolas was no engineer, but he understood basic mechanics. It seemed to make sense. And by removing the pipe, Slug had effectively bypassed the leaking section. As Nikolas looked at what Slug had done, he thought back to the map of New Jerusalem he had drawn on the day he found him, and his excitement grew.

He touched Slug's fidgeting fingers, calmed them. At Nikolas's touch, Slug opened up his hand and released a pair of screws he had been holding. They fell onto the floor, rolled away meaninglessly.

"What else can you do, Slug?" Nikolas asked. "Show me."

5.

PRIVATE TANNER, a Guardsman of medium height and average looks, with nothing much to recommend him in terms of original thought or military aptitude, sat at his post at the entrance to the Laborers Kolony. It was nearing six o'eve and his guard duty was almost over. He looked forward to a warm greasy meal at the tavern and a few beers with his fellow enlisted men. Then he would pass out alone and do the same thing tomorrow. His father wanted him to marry—he even had a woman in mind, the daughter of a family friend. She was a nice enough girl, but Tanner had no desire to settle down just now. He liked his life: clean, simple, boring. In that sense, this guard detail suited him fine.

He was preparing to report to his superior officer and go home for the day when a man walked up to the gatehouse. He was thin and wore glasses held together with tape; he had the disheveled look of a battered skolar.

"Visitors' hours are over," Tanner told him.

"I'm not visiting. I plan on staying," the man said. "I'd like to turn myself in."

Tanner groaned inwardly. At least once a week, there was a case like this. There was something in the Joshuan character, Tanner often reflected, that led to excess feelings of guilt. The desire to confess and be punished. He bore no ill will toward religion; in fact, he didn't much think about it one way or the other. But it made for an awful lot of paperwork. And most of the time for crimes that weren't really crimes— infidelity, petty theft, a lie told at a party. Once there was even a mother who wanted to be arrested for not loving her son enough.

"What's the crime?" Tanner said to the man now.

"High treason."

Tanner looked up sharply. The man's face was in dead earnest. Tanner flipped through the papers on his desk. "I'm not sure I have a form for that . . . Let me . . . What's your name?"

"Jürgen Moritz."

"*The* Jürgen Moritz?" The man had leaked classified information and evaded the authorities. Location unknown. For a while before Tanner left Joshua City, it was all the radios were talking about. "I think I should get my superior."

"Maybe you should detain me first? I'm considered highly dangerous, you know." The man extended his wrists. "It would be a shame if I
got away."

"Right. Right."

Tanner grabbed a pair of arm restraints kept under the gatehouse
desk. He snapped one around the man's wrist and another to a metal
bar running along the side of the gatehouse. Then he hurried into the
camp to report to the lieutenant. This one time, Tanner didn't mind
being late for his supper.

6.

AFTER THE FUNERAL, Adrian decided to leave for Joshua City on the
next karavan, despite his internship technically having three more
weeks left. He had already made the decision, in fact, but hadn't artic-
ulated it to himself until now. He stood in his quarters, looking out of
the window. A vast expanse of purgatorial wasteland awaited him. He
recalled the strain of the journey to get here and felt a moment of terror
at experiencing all that again. But there was nothing for him here. He
packed his bags, shut off the lights, and left the room without so much
as looking back.

7.

IN HIS CELL in the work camp, skin smudged black from his first day
in the mine shaft, body sore from swinging a pickaxe at hard stubborn
rock, Jürgen lay on his cot and reflected on the strange shape of his life.
He had worked so hard to get his position in the Ministrie of Technology and had thrown it away on a principle. Then he had ended up in
prison and had worked so hard to escape. Now he turned himself back
in...on a principle. Was that poor doktor right? Did he not properly
feel? What were feelings, though? They came from the same place as
thought. *Properly speaking they are thoughts.*

Somehow, he felt, it all came back to Hilda. They had only been together a matter of weeks, but a day seldom went by that he did not think

about her. About her look of weary contempt as she left. He had failed her. He had failed. *If she had stayed, if I had only found the words to make her stay...Would this all have turned out differently?*

Romantic nonsense. He closed his eyes and turned over on his side, away from the light.

CHAPTER SIX

THE ARCHITECTURE OF HISTORY

1.

From the Journals of Nikolas Kovalski:

THE ROLE OF THE REVOLUTIONARY is a not a static thing, but rather a dynamic being-in-motion. As the situation changes, so must the revolutionary. To ossify into a preset series of tactics or objectives is to ensure defeat at the hands of the better armed forces of the system the revolutionary has made his life's promise to overthrow.

Query: If the revolutionary's mission must be dynamically mutable in this way, what core values must be in place to ensure the ethical superiority of the revolution over the system it seeks to usurp? Are there any such core values, or are they as fluid as the tactics themselves?

Query: The common Joshuan ought to be the primary beneficiary of the revolution, yet we only enjoy twenty percent or less support among the general Joshua City population. How to educate the citizenry so that they understand their own best interests? Should we wait until we have fifty perfect or more support? Or do we need a political vanguard to lead us all forward, working on the assumption that the others will soon enough see the advantages of a system not designed to exploit them at every turn?

Query: What should an ideal society look like? Which freedoms can be curtailed to achieve a better living situation in the aggregate for the population? Which freedoms are utterly inalienable, without which a society cannot even pretend to utopia?

Query: Is utopia achievable, or is it merely an ideal that must be held before us to show us the direction of improvement—a roadmap for an endless journey, not a final destination?

Query: Does the revolution need a single leader or a triumvirate? And if the former, am I worthy of the mantle? Or is Messenger correct? Does the entire idea of leaders run counter to the utopic ideal? But what, then, will the people unite around? Doesn't a leader act as the readily identifiable face of the revolution? As the personification of abstract principles? And don't we, as thinking and feeling beings, identify most closely with other thinking feeling humans? Is there some way to be a leader but also a self-effacing (and I mean that in its most literal sense—*faceless*) part of the we?

2.

AT FIRST, taking the Bataar Military Outpost had seemed a decisive victory for the Baikal Guard. It was situated directly on the main tributary to the Selenga River. Whoever controlled this tributary, the Bataar River, controlled access to a vast supply of fresh water flowing down from the mountains where the Selenga and Uda rivers met. And the walls of the outpost, five meters deep of solid mountain rock, provided an excellent base to defend advances downriver into Joshuan territory or to make attacks upriver against the Ulani Army. It had—over the weeks since General Oster and what was left of the 3rd Battalion, 7th Regiment had taken the outpost—become a strategic hub for Guardsmen on their way into Ulani territory. Supplies passed through the military outpost; kompanies stopped here to replenish their troops and rest themselves before going deeper behind enemy lines.

And for a while, taking the outpost had seemed like a personal coup for General Oster as well. He received a letter of personal congratulations from the mayor's office, instructing him to secure the outpost and maintain the position as a valuable base of operations for further engagements. General Oster found himself fantasizing—in bed with the lights off, in much the way other men fantasize of women—about the stars that would decorate his uniform upon his triumphant return to Joshua City. He might even be made Minister of Defense; no more risking his life out in the battlefield.

But then came the news of an alliance between Ulan-Ude and Al-Khuzir. Aided by this fresh influx of troops, the Ulani Army had moved quickly to take back the key military assets they had lost. And now General Oster and his greatly diminished regiment (down to fewer than one hundred men) were surrounded by not one, but two armies. The Al-Khuziri army was weak on its own, but they were bolstered by Ulani military expertise and Baikyong-doan technology. Give any man, no matter how ill-trained, the right weapon and he can accomplish some killing.

What had at first seemed like General Oster's personal coup now seemed like his personal grave. Walls: they protect, but they also entrap. Day and night now, they shook with the impact of mortars and explosives planted in holes dug under the base of the walls. Vast sections of rock fell and Oster's men repaired them as well as they could. One day soon, they would not repair them fast enough. And then Ulanis and Al-Khuziris would come swarming in. And then...

※ ※ ※

"My father hated rats," General Oster said to Kaptain Susskind on that particular morning.

It was a morning like any other in the past weeks. They were awoken by explosions. The Guardsmen assigned to night duty were on the walls already, firing back at the enemy. They had even taken to dumping their chamberpots—to use the polite term for buckets of piss and shit—over the walls. It wouldn't kill anyone, but it would sure give them an unpleasant surprise. Besides, they had to be emptied somewhere.

"Sorry, sir?" Susskind said.

Susskind was young, with a scraggly mustache and pimples. He was hardly who General Oster would have chosen for his advisor. But his major was dead, and so was the kolonel under him. And several kompanies had been captured, delayed, or diverted before coming to join the regiment. General Oster had radioed to Joshua City many times, requesting more support, but now that he needed help, communications from the mayor's office were not so forthcoming.

"Rats. He had this thing about them," General Oster said. "We were poorer than he would have liked. And he regarded that as a personal failing, I think. And so, he took it out on the rats."

And on me, Oster thought. But he didn't mention that part.

"Sir?"

"He set traps all over the house—in the closets, under the sink, in the stove. It got so you had to watch your step or risk losing a toe." The table shook—another explosion. General Oster winced. "One day, he gathered the traps up and called me outside. He put the traps with the rats—still alive and wriggling, mind you—into this big metal can. Then he doused some newspaper in gasoline. And he handed me a match. I lit it and threw it in the can. What happened next . . . the yelps, the claws scratching at the metal walls . . . "

More explosions, rapid gunfire.

"If we don't do something soon, we'll be like those rats," Oster finished.

"Sir, if I may?" Susskind said.

General Oster nodded.

"Why don't we just mount an all-out attack?"

Predictable. Susskind had balls, Oster had to admit. But he also had youth on his side, the illusion of invincibility. You would think that would vanish with the first taste of battle, but illusions are stubborn things. Sometimes, it takes more than one brush with death for a man to believe he not only *can* but inevitably *will* die. General Oster understood: he used to be like Susskind. And he still admired the Susskinds of the world, in their way. It wasn't that he had become a coward in his old age. It was just that he had become more cautious. He had children now, a wife, a nice home—in short, he had something to lose. *It's easy to be brave when you have nothing to lose.*

"Because they outnumber us three to one," General Oster said patiently. "It would be a slaughter."

"At least we'd take down some of those sheep-fuckers on the way out. And who knows, we might even come out on top."

Maybe he had a point. Every day that they stayed inside this tomb was one day closer to death. If it wasn't a breach in the walls that killed them, it would be their dwindling supplies. They had lived on boiled oats for weeks now. His men were showing signs of malnourishment. With seemingly no relief on the way, their morale was diminishing by the hour. None of them had bathed in weeks. It's amazing what a warm bath can do for a man's morale. But there wasn't water for that. The river flowed through the middle of the outpost, the structure's ground floor arching over it like a bridge, but it was summer—the dry season. They had to use the water judiciously, collecting it in barrels for cooking and drinking and to clean wounds. Baths were a wasteful luxury.

But at least they had water to drink. Take away a man's drinking water and you might as well have shot him in the gut. In fact, gut-shot men often survive longer.

%% %% %%

It was only a few hours later that one of General Oster's lieutenants came running in to the kommand room. He looked like he had seen his own death.

"They're damming the river," he said. "Those bastards are damming the river."

Correction, Oster thought, *he hasn't seen his death. He's seen all our deaths.*

There was no choice but to mount an all-out attack. A suicide mission, surely. But it was his duty to make it a meaningful one.

3.

FROM *Hub and Spoke:*
A Journal of Joshuan Arts, Technology, and Culture
(VOLUME 18, ISSUE 7)

The Architecture of Grief: An Interview with Abraham Kocznik
conducted by Olivia Parnassus-Fairweather

Abraham Kocznik once seemed like a man who had it all: a successful career in the Ministrie of Technology; a marriage to the most beautiful and famous aktress in Joshua City; a daughter and a loving home; the worship of the Joshuan people.

And then in one earth-shattering moment, it was all taken away. On a trip to Khakusi Springs, the Northern Baikal resort popular with Joshua City's elite power couples, tragedy struck. What was supposed to be a romantic getaway ended in a horrific automobile accident that took the life of Vivian Scott, leaving her daughter motherless and her husband bereft. Abraham Kocznik retreated from the public eye, embarking on a masterwork not even his most fervent admirers could have imagined. This time his creative genius took a new form: architecture. But this was no ordinary house. Most famous for its Infinite Hallway, a seemingly unsupported glass structure extending far out over the Baikal Sea, the Kocznik Mansion, as it has come to be called, boasts a menagerie of structural wonders and oddities. It has become somewhat of a tourist attraction. Joshuans and tourists from the Lesser Six are requesting visitation passes for Checkpoint Four just to stand outside the mansion's gates. But Mr. Kocznik, reclusive as ever, does not admit them inside. He did, however, grant me a tour prior to this interview. I could barely take in everything I saw; it truly is a marvel of the human intellect. Afterward, we sat down for a conversation over cakes and tea.

But before I could even ask my first question, Mr. Kocznik got right to the point.

Abraham Kocznik: This is not going to be one of those "pity the poor inventor" pieces, is it?

Olivia Parnassus-Fairwater: No, of course not. The focus of this journal, as you know, is on culture and arts. You are a well-known Joshuan figure. You're also an artist, if I may use that term.

AK: I am a scientist.

OPF: Of course, but I would say that an inventor such as yourself blurs those two professions. May we proceed?

(silence)

OPF: I want to talk to you about the house, the Kocznik Mansion as people are calling it. You started building it soon after your wife's passing.

AK: Her death. You mean her death. She didn't pass anywhere.

OPF: Her death, then.

AK: And I dislike that term, "Kocznik Mansion." If anything, it is an elaborate sarcophagus.

OPF: But the house seems to, on the surface at least—how shall I say this?—to have little to do with her.

AK: There's The Infinite Hallway all you people seem to love.

[Ed. Note: The Infinite Hallway displays a memorial to Vivian Scott's acting career—her awards, her publicity stills, the promotional posters of the films she was in.]

OPF: I was just about to mention that. However, what about the freestanding arches, the stairway to nowhere, the train engine?

AK: It all relates to her in some way. But look, you want a simple truth for your magazine. You want a neat one-to-one correspondence. Inventor's wife dies. He builds a memorial to her. An architecture of grief. You should use that for your title.

OPF: It's a good one.

AK: It's not that simple though. The truth never is. Or maybe it's simpler. I don't know. I just built what I saw. And the thing is I'd been seeing it for a long time.

OPF: Before your wife's . . . ?

AK: Yes, before her death. And then afterward, when I started build-

ing it, when I drew up the blueprints and hired my people, it became about her. I guess in some way it always was . . . We'd talked about it a lot. Having a place that was more ours somehow, you know? So the project became ours, even if the details of it may not make sense to you.

(pause)

I'm sorry if I've been hard on you. You have to find an angle. I get that. But why not let the angle find you? You know, as a scientist, the most dangerous thing is going into an experiment with a desired or expected result. You fail to notice what's right in front of you. You might even find yourself manipulating the results. All you so-called journalists could learn something from science.

OPF: *So why did you agree to speak with me today?*

AK: *It seemed like the right time.*

OPF: *In public life, you and Vivian Scott appeared to be the perfect couple. Your contrasting personalities complemented each other. You were quiet and elusive and she was everybody's favorite starlet. To put it another way, you made Joshua City function while she gave it something to live for. But there were rumors that your marriage was troubled.*

AK: *I am not going to discuss that.*

OPF: *Khakusi Springs is, after all, home to the famous Lover's Maze, designed by the psychoanalyst Doktor Laikan. Many couples go there to repair their marriage.*

AK: *Our marriage was just fine.*

OPF: *So what happened then?*

AK: *An accident.*

OPF: *A simple accident? Is that all? We've obtained records that sug-gest that your wife was pregnant at the time of her death.*

AK: (standing up) *This interview is over.*

4.

MAJOR SCHMIDT and several Guardsmen were dug in behind a copse of trees, surveying what in a few hours would be a bloody battlefield. It was perhaps an hour before dawn. The moon was out and it limned the night-blackened rocks in an ephemeral grayness. The river flowed white-ly in the moonlight, lined with trees on either side; Schmidt thought it almost beautiful. It led all the way down to the military outpost, which was a structure of solid and imposing bulwarks, of parapets jutting with toothy menace into the pale-dark sky. General Oster and his regi-ment were inside, awaiting exactly the kind of improbable rescue Major Schmidt intended to deliver. And in between the copse and the outpost was the enemy camp—a sea of tents, fires, flickering gas lanterns... *and heavy artillery. Hundreds of well-trained enemy combatants. Outnum-bering us two to one. And that's not even taking into account the advan-tages given them by our woeful supplies and the wounds we've suffered.* And who knew what shape General Oster and his men were in?

What was more, the hills to the east would give the enemy a cer-tain advantage over Major Schmidt's men. They could position them-selves there, using their higher field position to bombard the Guards-men with their artillery. Or they could take cover behind the hills. In fact, there might be untold troops there already, just out of sight. Major Schmidt knew the hardest thing was going to be allowing the deaths of his fellow Guardsmen while he waited for the enemy to be fully drawn out and vulnerable to his surprise attack, but softness of purpose would serve no one except the damned Ulanis. If his plan was going to work—and it absolutely had to work—he would have to be hard as Larki steel.

Kharkov approached them. "Sir, there is a slight problem."

"What is it?"

"One of the Guardsmen on artery-bomb duty is blubbering about his beautiful wife and his sweet infant son and so on. He hasn't put the device on, and even if he did, I have no confidence he would have what it takes to detonate it."

"And the longer he goes on, the more the others will begin having second thoughts," Major Schmidt said, finishing the thought.

"Exactly, sir," Kharkov said. "I could take his place, if you like."

Major Schmidt did not hear a note of fear or remorse or hesitation in Kharkov's words. He would happily go to his death on Schmidt's orders. "No, Kharkov, you're much too valuable to me alive. That's why I wanted you to lead the artery-bomb division, to make sure it works, but I need you alive."

A private to Major Schmidt's left said, "Sir, I would like to volunteer."

Major Schmidt had barely noticed the Guardsman was there until now. He had several days of desert growth on his face, but even through the beard, a youthful face could be discerned. *So many young Joshuans going to their deaths.*

"You understand what you're volunteering for, Guardsman?" Major Schmidt asked.

"Yes, sir, I do."

Schmidt nodded to Kharkov. Kharkov saluted and motioned for the private to follow him. Even after Kharkov was gone, a ghostly trace of his impressive presence lingered.

5.

AMBASSADOR KALUKAR handed Mayor Adams the gift he had brought from Ulan-Ude, a regal cape fashioned from the finest pelts and stained wine-purple with true mastery. He chose not to be insulted when Mayor Adams set it aside summarily.

It was early morning and gray clouds hung over Joshua City, the dim light in the mayor's office already casting a pall over the meeting. The ambassadors from Baikalingrad, Al-Khuzir, and Larki Island were all present: one ally of Joshua City, one ally of Ulan-Ude, and a neutral party. Both sides wanted a neutral party to oversee the agreement, if in fact an agreement could be reached. Kalukar needed this to happen, and now, before the news of the Kahn's death reached the other cities. He had thus far kept it secret even from his fellow Ulanis. Once word got out, there would be in-fighting to determine the next Kahn. Kalukar felt confident that would be him, but it would take time, and the Ulani negotiating position would be weakened.

"Here are the Kahn's terms for a peace agreement," Kalukar said, handing a sheath of documents to Mayor Adams's assistant, who in turn handed them to Mayor Adams.

Kalukar waited as Mayor Adams read the terms.

"These are ... interesting terms, Ambassador."

"I think you should find them more than fair, given the current circumstances."

"I think we see the *current circumstances* somewhat differently."

"Please, Mayor, be reasonable," Kalukar began. "Nearly all recent engagements have gone in our favor. We have many of your regiments compromised. And our new alliance with Al-Khuzir has put us in an even stronger position." At this he gave the Al-Khuziri ambassador a nod. "To say nothing of Baikyong-do."

"The use of The Savage Ones should be considered a war crime."

"There are many crimes being committed these days. Which is why we must find a peaceable solution—and today, before more brave Joshuans and Ulanis die."

"Don't forget the sacrifices of Baikalingrad and the other cities," the ambassador to Baikalingrad said.

"I would not dare to, madam."

"Explain your conditions," the ambassador from Larki Island said.

"Simple. We all return to the way things were before this insane war was started. Joshua City removes all troops from lands formerly under Ulan-Ude's control, and we receive all of our previous river-rights. We are asking for nothing to our advantage, merely a return to previous relations. What could be more reasonable?"

6.

A LITTLE over two hours later, Major Schmidt ordered the first attack.

Weak sunlight made a static pulse just beneath deeply gray clouds; the morning seemed an extension of the previous night. Tracer bullets crisscrossed their bright red way toward the rocky hillside where the enemy was burrowed in. The first wave of Major Schmidt's men charged the Ulani encampment. He felt a brief compassion for everyone about to be maimed or killed. He felt detached and wise, and the world made perfect interconnected sense to him. All of these men had to fight, had to kill each other; history demanded it; human nature demanded it. Something caught fire in the enemy camp, sending a pall of yellowish smoke through the valley, and this mood of detached compassion and understanding left Major Schmidt as quickly as it had come.

The first Guardsmen pressed the hill, and Major Schmidt motioned Kharkov to his side.

"Once the Ulanis are fully engaged, that's when you and your ar-tery-bombers make your first move," Major Schmidt said. "Just like we planned. No deviation, no matter what happens. Do you under-stand me?"

Kharkov nodded that he did.

"Go gather them together then. Get their blood and their balls into this. They're going need both, and they'll likely lose both before the day is through."

"Yes, sir," Kharkov said in an affectless tone, and then went off in a crouched jog toward where his unit waited for him to lead them into slaughter.

※　※　※

Their battered brown-and-blue Guardsmen uniforms were dark-ened by the morning dew and by the wet dirt they had been lying on most of the night. The glow from the tracer-fire shone down on them malevolently; their faces floated a devilish red. The barren trees had a jagged beauty, like insects sticking their spindly limbs out in unreasoning disarray. The tracers burnt themselves out and fell to the ground, where they lay lifeless, and the morning's darkness circled around them again.

Major Schmidt ordered his Guardsmen forward, slowly forward. It would not do to be noticed too early. Ulani forces were gathered around the outpost where General Oster and his men were trapped. The Ula-nis were bombarding the structure—and, by the condition of the walls, they had been at it for some days now. Major Schmidt estimated about forty percent were out of their base-camp and in the fray. He lifted his telescopic lenses and saw a troop of Ulani soldiers damming the river that fed into the outpost; on the other side of the outpost, men in Al-Khuziri uniforms were digging at the easterly wall, making another point of attack; he turned his gaze and found Kharkov and his small suicide unit making their way around to the Ulani encampment. Major Schmidt had held one artery-bomber in reserve, instructing him to make his way to the dam and do as much damage as possible. One man should be able to sneak up on the Ulanis unnoticed, where a full unit would be spotted half a kilometer off.

Major Schmidt motioned for the Guardsmen with him to halt. They would wait here for a few minutes. Schmidt made a quick prayer to the Seven Prophets that the Ulanis would send enough of their soldiers out of their base-camp to allow Kharkov the opportunity to fulfill his mission.

Through the telescopic lenses, Major Schmidt saw Kharkov was near the designated spot. Major Schmidt turned his telescopic lenses back toward the Ulani base-camp, where the first wave of his assault had arrived at the designated position and was exchanging rifle-fire with the enemy. But not enough of the Ulani forces were out of base-camp to allow Kharkov's assault. Kharkov put his hand in the air and squeezed it into a fist three times; he waited two minutes and did it again. This was the signal that he could not move forward under current conditions. It was dangerous for Major Schmidt to split his forces so thin, but there was no choice. He motioned several of his men to his side.

"All right, Guardsmen, we need to engage the Ulani forces between here and the outpost where General Oster is holed up. We need to draw more Ulani troops out, so that Kharkov has a chance to lead his men into attack position. We are likely going to die here, so I intend to come with you. I can't ask you to do something I am not willing to do."

He called to Korporal Vidal. The korporal ran over and saluted smartly. Vidal had conducted himself bravely in the prison outbreak.

There was that matter with the murder of the doktor, but that could have been anyone...

"I need you to follow the plan. You'll have fewer troops than we previously thought, but it should still work. You'll have the element of surprise. More so now, even."

When Major Schmidt and the dozen men he had brought with him found a defensible position about halfway between where he had left Korporal Vidal and the outpost, he set them up in six groupings of two. The idea was that one man would fire until he had emptied his clip, and then the other would fire while the first man reloaded. This would mean six different positions constantly firing and never vulnerable to direct assault during reloading. It spread the fire around enough to create the illusion of a larger force, and if one position were overtaken and the men killed, it would not deplete his manpower too severely.

Major Schmidt looked through his lenses again and saw Korporal Vidal making bloody progress into the Ulani ranks. Satisfied, Schmidt joined one group of two himself and chose the highest vantage point for them, so that they could do the most damage and so the others could see his signals more easily. He gave the first signal and the men on the far ends of the formation began firing into the Ulani camp. Then, as the first two Guardsmen on the outer flanks reloaded, their partners took up firing, as did the next men moving toward the center. And so forth, until he had an entire wall of gunfire on either side of him. Then he signaled for one of the two men with him to begin firing, and the others stopped when that man had emptied his clip. This ought to cause a large enough commotion and perhaps even kill a handful of Ulanis. The formation of fire and the pause would allow the enemy ample time to ascertain their location. And that was precisely the point. They needed to know, needed to send as large a number of soldiers Major Schmidt's way as possible.

He put the lenses to his eyes and did a sweep of the camp. They had taken the bait. Some thirty or more soldiers were making their careful way up the embankment to where Major Schmidt and his men were entrenched. He looked to where he had left Korporal Vidal. They were moving slowly toward the Ulani camp. Across the ridge, Kharkov was making his skulking way toward his target.

Major Schmidt gave the second signal and one man in all six positions fired on the advancing Ulani soldiers. A few fell, more made it safely to ground or behind trees and rocks.

The Ulani advancement was slow but steady. They incurred several casualties on the way, but they still outnumbered Major Schmidt and his small troop of men. Now was time for the final signal. The two groups of men on the far sides of the formation broke off and moved to flanking position as all of the other positions opened suppressing fire, then stopped entirely again, hoping to lure the Ulani soldiers farther up the embankment.

Three projectiles with a trail of smoke glowing orange scudded toward them. The closest one landed several meters away from Major Schmidt. One of the men beside him whimpered, and in the confusion of the explosion's aftermath, Major Schmidt could not tell who it was. He chose not to find out. If he did, he would never respect the man again, and the man would never forgive him for knowing he was a coward. And so instead he assessed the damage from the other projectiles. One position decimated. *Two more Guardsmen dead.* The third explosion had been entirely ineffective, exploding a tree a safe distance away.

Major Schmidt gave the final signal and yelled, "Now!" as he ran forward, redoubling his own courage.

The remaining Guardsmen followed Schmidt's order and charged forward, firing and throwing grenades in alternating efforts. As he had predicted, the Ulani soldiers had not expected a frontal assault of this magnitude. They began falling back, but just as they did, Vidal and his Guardsmen caught them in a deadly crossfire, reducing their number by more than half in mere seconds. Major Schmidt pressed on.

7.

MAYOR ADAMS had to admit that some of what the Ulani ambassador had said was true, but he refused to accept that his war was meaningless, that it would not lead to the unification of the Seven Cities. And there was an election next year; the Joshuan people would not re-elect a man who had lost a war. He needed something to sell them. Even if he had to entrench and take drastic actions, the people would prefer a winner. He still had options.

"I cannot accept these terms as you have written them. Joshua City needs access to the Selenga River. We need a new freshwater supply, given our problem with nekrosis. Also, I can't return to my people empty-handed."

"The Kahn's terms are non-negotiable. And, as I already pointed out, our terms are more than reasonable."

Hanna Kaplani leaned over and whispered something to Mayor Adams. He nodded.

"We need peace in the region," said the Larki Islander.

"If you could reduce tariffs on Joshuan imports to Ulan-Ude . . . to zero, perhaps . . . I could bring my people around."

"The terms are non-negotiable."

"Then let us put an end to this farce. I wish you safe travels." Mayor Adams added insincerely: "May your thousand-thousand herds stampede across the sky."

Kalukar stood and offered his hand. "May your days be pure-baikal."

Mayor Adams did not accept the handshake.

8.

As THEY PENETRATED deeper into the enemy's camp, Major Schmidt and his men stumbled over bodies splayed over the ground, still warm but motionless. No way to tell in all the chaos which bodies you were tripping over—Joshuans or Ulanis—and it didn't matter anymore; all that mattered was the pulse and press forward, the forcing through. This extreme limit of experience brought him clarity. He pressed forward and pressed forward and something as solid as stone in him knew he would win the battle. The sputter-crack and hollow boom of heavy artillery was everywhere around them now. He had lost three of his men and another was limping badly, a shard of exploded stone wedged in his thigh.

※ ※ ※

General Oster could not believe his luck. He had prepared to send his men out in one last desperate attack, but with these new Joshuan forces—thank the Seven that Mayor Adams had finally sent them—there was a real chance at victory. He ordered all of his able-bodied men to gear up and ready themselves for an all-out charge.

The front gate of the outpost lowered with a thud and General Oster's troops ran and scattered throughout the battlefield, firing on the Ulanis as rapidly as possible. They were taking heavy casualties but, Oster was pleased to notice, so were the Ulanis.

※ ※ ※

The sulfur and phosphorus of the bombs wafted sickly in Major Schmidt's face. Something hot and airy hit them from the rear; Major Schmidt was thrown to the ground along with a dozen other men. Muffled screams emerged from a wall of heat and confusion. As the world returned to him, he got another faceful of the acrid smell of the bombs both sides were using.

Everything around them was a chemical hell. The smell of his singed hair; he slapped frantically at glowing embers on the sleeves of his uniform. The ground was wobbly and the air was thick with smoke and particulate matter. He wanted to use his telescopic lenses to examine Korporal Vidal's status, but he had to keep moving. And the smoke was likely too thick for visibility. No, he would just have to trust that Vidal had made it to the next agreed-upon position and that they would meet as planned and kill these Ulani herd-fuckers.

Through the chemical fog, Major Schmidt saw Guardsmen pouring from the outpost's gate with loud bursts of rifle-fire and screams of death. He was happy to have been right about General Oster's good tactical sense.

※ ※ ※

The artery-bomber assigned to the dam ran, his back and legs covered in sweat. His heart beat frantically in his chest, from exertion and fear. Darts of pain went through his lungs, yet he ran faster. When he was only a dozen meters away, he slowed and hid behind a tree. He walked slowly toward the Ulani men, his arms raised in a gesture of surrender. One of them looked up from his work.

"You there! Halt!" he said in common Slovnik and made his way to his rifle which rested against a stack of wood planks.

"I surrender," the artery-bomber yelled out. "My unit is dead. I want to surrender."

More Ulanis were now moving toward him, smiles of contempt on their faces. "Another Joshuan coward," one of them said and spit.

All the while, the artery-bomber was making his way closer to their work site.

"Call me what you will, but please just spare me," he begged.

Now he was no more than two meters from the dam, and the Ulanis were all gathered around him. He lowered his head and closed his eyes; he mouthed the words to "The Glory of the Baikal Guard." He pressed the detonator.

※ ※ ※

A shard from Jürgen's false star severed an Ulani's arm at the shoulder, flew on and through the engine block of a digging machine like hot metal through ice, on and through a section of the dam and went on slicing through the water until it came to rest some two hundred meters downstream. Another shard exploded a man's skull and carried on, cutting through another section of the dam (and somewhere off in the distance, unseen by anyone, severed an ox's spine). Another carved a useless ditch in the earth. Another and another, slicing and destroying everything in their paths. There was nothing left of the artery-bomber himself. He had been entirely successful.

Sections of the dam fell into the river; the structure leaned precariously, creaked loudly, collapsed; the pent-up water rushed forth, carrying wooden debris and the mingled body parts of dead men.

%. %. %.

With a wave of his hand, forefinger stabbing forward—such a slight gesture—Kharkov sent two more soldiers equipped with Jürgen's artery-bombs into the fray. With another gesture to the man at his left, he ordered covering fire for these two brave Joshuans who would be transformed into a bloom of meat and bone.

9.

"WAS I TOO HARSH there?" Mayor Adams asked Hanna after the other ambassadors had left.

"Baikalingrad would have preferred a different outcome to this meeting," she said. "But you still have our full support."

Was this a betrayal? He had allowed himself to think of Hanna as an intimate companion. But no, he had to concede he was alone now. He would win this war, and everyone would bow to him, Hanna included.

10.

KHARKOV FOUND THE FIRST of his two forward-Guardsmen lying limp, his neck snapped. Kharkov had not heard a gunshot. He grabbed the dead man's machine-rifle and slung it over his shoulder. He disliked the wastefulness of leaving the man's artery-bomb on him, but he didn't want to be encumbered by carrying it. He went ahead with the plan, as Major Schmidt had ordered. He checked his grenades unnecessarily and continued toward his target.

When he found the second forward-Guardsman, dead in the same manner as the first, he thought one word: *Messenger.* Only Messenger was capable of killing men in so efficient and silent a manner. But Major Schmidt was still counting on him. Kharkov stripped his torso bare, laying his grenade belt, the machine-rifle, and his uniform shirt on the ground beside the corpse. He removed the man's artery-bomb and fastened it snugly to himself. He put his shirt back on and strapped on his grenades and shouldered the machine-rifle.

He went into a dead sprint toward the first designated target. Major Schmidt's plan was working magnificently; the flanking assault had forced the enemy to reduce patrols on this side of their position. The red tracers went up faster and in a more concentrated area. Major Schmidt was drawing the enemy out, leaving their rear unguarded, as planned.

Kharkov reached the top of a shadowed ridge, from which vantage point he could see several structures built from what looked like little more than corrugated tin, wire, and deadwood. He pulled a grenade free, released its pin, and threw with all his strength. The grenade landed true, a meter or so from the nearest structure. The explosion leveled the target deafeningly.

He ran another dozen meters and threw a second grenade. Again, his aim was true and the target went up in a flash-bang of debris and smoke and fire. He ran farther, throwing another grenade, and even before it had exploded he was further along the ridge, releasing another into the enemy camp. It was his last grenade that finally hit what he was after. The explosion was huge and sent a display of light across the enemy camp.

He ran a bit farther and nestled himself against a rocky incline. He pulled his and his fallen man's machine-rifles free. He set the second one across his lap and put his own against his shoulder. He began a random spray-fire, hoping to create a larger presence, as Major Schmidt had ordered him to do. If he could trick the Ulanis into sending a sizable unit to fight off one man, then the others could overtake the camp. He only hoped it would be enough. The other three forward-Guardsmen should have made their way into the camp by now, lying in wait to set off their artery-bombs.

He fired blindly into the Ulani encampment. The jarring kick of the rifle felt good, felt real. When he had emptied his machine-rifle and the extra clip he had for it, he tossed it aside and pulled up the second one he had taken from the dead Guardsman. There was movement several hundred meters in the distance, enemy combatants making their way from the main melee to come answer his assault. He would wait until they were closer. Perhaps he could kill some of the Ulanis, and then take out more when he detonated his artery-bomb. He thought of Major Schmidt's victory, not of his own certain death.

He sat solid as a cast-iron statue, waiting, when he heard a clank and the machine-rifle flew from his grasp. He looked to where it lay on the ground. He sprung to his feet to face the man.

"Messenger."

The man did not respond.

Kharkov pulled his knife and lunged at Messenger, feinting with the knife then kicking sharply into Messenger's lower-leg at the last second. He executed the move deftly and swiftly, but Messenger dodged and the blow glanced off. Still, he had connected and caused some small damage.

The two men stalked each other in a circle for several seconds, neither daring a move.

Kharkov made a few slicing attacks, all of which Messenger evaded without effort. Kharkov knew this was going to end poorly for him; it was a matter of whether he could make it cost Messenger as much.

Then, faster than a fleeting thought, Messenger darted forward and made a sharp downward blow to Kharkov's arm. There was a sick crack like a green branch breaking, and Kharkov saw the knife on the ground between them. Messenger kicked it away.

Kharkov leaned down, let his elbow depress the detonation button on his artery-bomb, masking his action with a grunt at the broken pendulum of his forearm. He rushed Messenger; his hands darted out, not to hit but to grab; Messenger moved fluidly and faster than Kharkov thought possible. But Messenger was dodging a blow that was not coming; Kharkov grabbed Messenger's tunic, and as he was thrown, he held tightly, despite the movement of the bones in his arm. They hit the ground, and even before the jarring thud fully registered in Kharkov's mind, Messenger was already on his way up again, but Kharkov's good arm chained them together, and he came up halfway with Messenger.

"I've won," Kharkov said.

The artery-bomb exploded and the two men disintegrated in a confusion of flesh and bomb-flash.

※ ※ ※

On the other side of the enemy camp, Major Schmidt made his slow yet commanding forward progress. It would be three more hours before the Ulanis surrendered, and many more combatants on both sides would die, but Major Schmidt would secure a victory, one that would prove pivotal for the Joshuan forces.

Very few would ever mourn Kharkov, and none would know of his bravery in battle with Messenger. Major Schmidt would see to it that his name made the Registry of Heroes, but there would be so many names crowded around his, and no one would ever come looking for it.

11.

From the Journals of Nikolas Kovalski:

Later:

There is a cultural mechanism that causes various part of a society to cohere. There is some connection between the laws that both bind us and create new possibilities of freedom, between the language of the poet and the language of the water-baron, between the urge to revolt and dragging inertia that keeps us in stasis. What is that mechanism? I know intuitively that it must exist, since the processes which create every individual are shared across the culture and created in tensions that permeate every aspect of that culture.

I had assumed for many years that science (including medikal science) was somehow outside this web of ideology, because its findings were tested against the realities of the world. And in some sense this is the case. Ideology is somewhat restrained by the blunt facts of chemistry and physics and the decaying corpse. But the directions scientists are allowed to stretch their knowledge is confined by economics and religion and the small-mindedness that confines all other realms of human existence. I learned that only too well in university. It is, in a very real sense, why I am here.

How then to transcend these confines? What is that mechanism that binds all things together and slows human progress so?

※ ※ ※

Later:

An effective and vigorous revolutionary movement is only conceivable if it includes diversity. The forces we oppose, as well as too many allied with us, envision a normalized and predictable populace. I maintain that human conformity should only be found in the cemetery. That said, one cannot tolerate the intolerable. But how to define the intolerable in a meaningful way that is not mere bourgeois sentiment? Just because we recoil from something emotionally does not mean it isn't the best thing for us. One need merely think of the patient who cringes at the thought of the doktor's tools—the very tools which will save him. There must be an underlying principle that separates the surgeon's knife from the thief's. When I have discovered that, I will be able to reshape society into a fair and healthy body politic.

※ ※ ※

Later still:

Why would Messenger have sought me out? They are mercenaries—mysterious, to be sure, and powerful, but just mercenaries. Or that's what I've always heard. To my knowledge they have not profaned their secret bond by taking a personal interest in political affairs. They either accept payment for a task or they don't. That's their way. Some have even thought they were a myth, but of course that is just idle talk, born from ignorance.

But I return to my question: Why me? Does not it contradict their stated goals of the eradication of the singular to choose *me*, a single solitary man, for some special destiny? And what is that destiny? (I use the word in the most metaphorical of senses.)

Possible answer: I am in fact destined to wipe this filthy world clean and to make way for the new society. Let it be so.

I believe myself in (perhaps temporary) disagreement with Messenger. History needs its singular aktors. History needs its avatars. For now, at least, I must adopt the role of leader. Of the *I* exalted. Later, once true equality has been achieved, *I* can dissolve myself back into the *we*.

CHAPTER SEVEN

THE RETURN

1.

T HE RETURN to Joshua City was not merely the reverse of his journey out to the hospital. The landscape played itself in reverse, like
watching a Silverville film fed through its projektor backwards, but the
joy of discovery was replaced with the melancholy of heavy experience.
Everything was... Adrian couldn't quite think of the right way to describe it... *warped*, perhaps, like an image reflected in the funhouse
mirrors you found at karnivals. And when he looked more closely, even
the landscape was not a perfect reversal—there were new additions:
abandoned broken-down military vehicles littered the vistas, and black-
ened craters where bombs had exploded pocked the desert ground.
And the weather was different, with cool air swirling lazily around the
karavan where previously summer swelter lay over everything like a
moist blanket. Even his own emotional state was not as neatly opposite
as he might have liked to think, in large part because he was a different
person feeling those emotions, but also because joy and melancholy
are not exact opposites, and joy and melancholy were just words which
shrank the complexity of what he felt on his way out and what he was
now feeling on his way back to Joshua City.

Adrian did not take the front seat this time. No one out here recognized anything special about a Joshua University student venturing out
on a humanitarian mission. They saw a weary doktor-in-training with

barely enough money to pay his fare and too few belongings to consider robbing. He performed his karavan duties diligently, if absently—digging the trucks out of drybogs when they got stuck, gathering kindling, and keeping a vigilant eye on the desert for potential ambush. But he did not strike up any friendships. He had had enough of that and now knew what friendship could cost.

When he had secured his passage back to Joshua City, he had not selected Heinrich's karavan, as he had promised he would. It had been less than three months, yet lifetimes upon lifetimes had transpired—come into existence and passed into oblivion—in that short span. Sore from his travels and numbed by his melancholy, Adrian barely felt the pang of guilt at having avoided Heinrich. He was a good man, and one Adrian still had a large amount of sympathy and warm regard for, but he simply couldn't bear to face him just now. Adrian felt he was no longer himself; he would not have been the same person who had come to know Heinrich and whom Heinrich had come to know. This fact embarrassed him for reasons he did not understand, and he was too weary and world-worn at this point to try to understand them. Besides, Heinrich had likely forgotten him. He saw hundreds of passengers a month; it was foolish to think he would care to see Adrian again.

※ ※ ※

It is not until you have left a place for a length of time—and have had a wealth of experiences somewhere else—that you can call that place home. Returning to Joshua City, Adrian felt a tugging from the core of his being toward his home, as though an invisible thread, half-umbilical and half-chain, were connected to his heart and tied at the other end to The Train Hub. But even as he handed his papers to the Baikal Guardsmen stationed at the city's eastern entrance, memories from the previous months came back to him, despoiling waves washing over him, eroding the joy of homecoming.

But no, he would not let this moment be entirely destroyed. He looked up from where the Guardsman verified his citizen-number to the skyline of Joshua City. It really was a grand city, wasn't it? After the months out in the desert, the sight was overwhelming. Not that the desert didn't have its own pared-down beauty; it most certainly did; but the edifices in Joshua City seemed as majestic as the mountains he had crossed, perhaps more so. And seeing them now, after his time away, allowed him to see them as if for the first time. He understood suddenly what émigrés to Joshua City must feel upon their arrival. He at once saw his native city as a foreigner would and saw these foreigners in a richer fuller light.

"Here you are, sir," the Guardsman said and handed Adrian his papers.

"Thank you," Adrian said. "Thank you very much."

※ ※ ※

Finding Nikolas's mother's home was simple enough. Adrian had kept the scrap of paper with her address in his wallet and had nearly forgotten he had it during his time in the desert. Perhaps she knew where Nikolas was living. And if that didn't work, he would head to The Nameless Tavern and wait around a few hours each evening until Nikolas showed up, as surely he would if he was still spending time with Elias and the others.

"Oh, Adrian, I have heard so much about you!"

I doubt that, Adrian thought. "That's nice to hear," he said.

(Without realizing it, Adrian had begun losing his earlier innocence. His travels in the desert and the events at the hospital had changed him in subtle ways even he had not noticed. He was, for example, now capable of duplicity with this nice woman; he was also capable of returning falsehood for falsehood, something he had previously detested.)

"Come in," Mrs. Kovalski said. "May I offer you tea?"

"That would be very nice. I've been out in the desert. You can't find decent Joshuan tea out there."

She fussed with the teapot and the water, gathering her thoughts, trying to divine what might have brought this young man into her home. *What has Nikolas done now?*

She set the cup of tea before him. A pleasant mint aroma mixed with something else he couldn't place. He took a long drink and savored the warmth as it spread through his chest.

"This is very nice, Mrs. Kovalski," Adrian said and hesitated. "I was wondering... do you happen to know where I might find Nikolas?"

"Oh, I never know when he is going to visit," Mrs. Kovalski said. "Have you checked with the university? I'm surprised you didn't go there first."

So she doesn't know then. Adrian was shocked by a possibility he hadn't considered: should he be worried about Nikolas? He had always assumed Nikolas could fend for himself, but if his mother still thought he was at university then he might be in real trouble.

"I thought about it," Adrian said, dissembling once more, "but I've just returned from the Outer Provinces and I wasn't quite ready to return to university. There will be so many forms to fill out and tedious duties... I guess I wanted my vacation to last a little longer."

"Well, if you do talk to him, tell him to visit his mother."

2.

AFTER THE BATTLE, after the dead Guardsmen had been buried and the wounded had been treated as best as possible using the supplies Major Schmidt had taken from the hospital, what was left of Schmidt's kompany joined with General Oster's regiment and set to repairing the Bataar Military Outpost. They removed pieces of the exploded dam from the river. They hauled river stones and rebuilt the walls. They cleaned up the wreckage of the enemy camp. They imprisoned and interrogated the few prisoners they were able to take alive; the rest had either managed to escape or, if Ulani, had committed honor-suicide. They extracted what information they could; and Major Schmidt met with General Oster and the remaining officers to exchange the military intelligence each group had managed to gather.

Then this makeshift regiment, under Oster's kommand, waited in the outpost for their new orders.

The orders weren't long in coming. A coded message sent by radio: "Congratulations. Replacement regiment on the way. Please return to Joshua City for debriefing."

"All of us, sir?" Major Schmidt asked when he was summoned into the kommand center and shown the message, transcribed on a scrap of bandage (the closest thing to paper they had) by a private who functioned as the 11th regiment's kryptografer.

"It would seem so."

"And there was no reason why?"

General Oster shrugged. "It would seem now that this operation is a political success, we'll be getting the support we've needed for weeks. I would suggest you accept the reprieve, however long it turns out to be."

Major Schmidt was not exactly eager to return to Joshua City. Out here, he was a major—respected and trusted by his men. He had led them to freedom, he had led them to the hospital, he had led them to victory. In Joshua City, he would be an imposter. And imposters have a way of being discovered.

※ ※ ※

General Oster watched the young major go. He was almost as bad as Kaptain Susskind, that one—brimming with a righteous hatred of the enemy. That was probably for the best. You had to hate the enemy to kill them. But that didn't mean you shouldn't practice a certain restraint. It mattered more to know when to fight than to always want to be doing it.

Oster dimly remembered meeting Major Schmidt just before the war. It had been at an officers' party and he had been one among a dozen faces and names. That was years ago, but war only seemed to have made Major Schmidt younger. Strange. General Oster had never felt older.

He picked up the dispatch from Joshua City. He read the final line. *Please return to Joshua City for debriefing.* The most important words jumped out at him. *Return. Joshua City.*

There it was. Home. He set the dispatch back on the table. Hadn't he done enough? Didn't he deserve some peace? A promotion, a military pension. Some comfortable political appointment perhaps. Not the Minister of Defense, of course. That had been a silly dream. But a subminister...

He stood from his desk and began making arrangements for their return.

3.

THAT FIRST SATURDAY, Adrian waited in The Nameless Tavern well into the evening. But no one he recognized came. The barkeep, not the man from before but a matronly gray-haired woman, kept wiping the bar near where he sat.

"Still don't want anything?" she asked. "Not even water?"

The woman gave him an order-or-get-out look.

"Do you have any tea?"

"I think there's some blackroot back there somewhere."

"Oh, that would keep me up all night."

"Wouldn't want that," she said with flat sarcasm. "I'll see what else we have."

In the end, she brought back a cup of Baikyong-do white tea. Even after five minutes of steeping, it was thin and flavorless. Adrian made a show of sipping it gratefully. His eyes drifted toward the door every time it swung open.

"Waiting for someone?" she asked him.

"Yes," he said. "Maybe. There was a young man, about my age, with a goatee. He used to come here with some friends. Probably four or five of them. One of the friends had very white hair and pale skin."

She shrugged. "Haven't seen anyone like that. But I've only been here since my husband...had to retire for a bit."

Adrian fished around for a name and amazingly came up with it. (Why is it we remember the most trivial things and forget important ones?) "Dmitri?"

For the first time she seemed to warm to him. "Yes. That's him." She squinted, as if seeing him for the first time. "Do I know you?"

"I've been here before. A long time ago," he said. Then improvising, "Your husband seemed like a good man."

"He is. Hard, but good."

Adrian found it hard to imagine the bullish barkeep he remembered being married to this woman.

"What happened to him?"

She looked away. "The usual. What always happens here."

He nodded to show that he understood. "How is it now? I've been away for a while."

She looked around and seeing the tavern was empty save the usual drunks, leaned in close to him. "You aren't one of those government men, are you?"

He smiled. "Will you believe me if I say I'm not?"

She studied him carefully. "I think you're exactly who you say you are. Still, these days . . ."

"It's that bad, is it?"

"When good strong men are going down," she said, "I'd say it is exactly that bad. Maybe worse. We're supposed to be fighting a war to stop it. But I don't see anything changing."

Adrian thought about the desert, what had happened at the hospital, and felt a low impossible anger.

"No, I guess not," he said. "Not for the better, at least."

% *%* *%*

After the young man left The Nameless Tavern, the woman who had been serving him tore of a bit of receipt paper and wrote the following message on it:

Someone was looking for the head. Says his name is Adrian. She slipped it into the middle of a stack of drams and when the liquor shipment came the next day she gave the money to the delivery man. He stuffed it in his pocket without counting it.

"Say," she said. "You don't sell tea, do you?"

"No'm," he said. "We don't. But I could pick some up for you on my next run."

"That's all right," she said. "I'll walk down to the market. Baikal knows I could use the walk."

Later, once he was safe in his truck, the delivery man would flip through the bills and find the piece of paper. He would slip it in a special pocket in his coat. Once back at the liquor distribution warehouse, he would hang the coat on a rack. Another employee would search the pockets of the coat during his break. Most days he found nothing there. Today he would find the message. He put it in his own pocket and went to the water-closet. There, he slipped it into his shoe. It stayed there all day as he worked loading boxes, the paper growing limp and sweaty. After he left work it traveled with him to The Underground, where he handed it to Alarik who read it and nodded.

"Thank you, komrade," he said. "You're a good soldier."

Alarik took the message to Katya. It wasn't worth troubling Nikolas with yet. Besides, this way there was always a shield of protection between Nikolas and any possible threats. Katya read the note and thanked Alarik. He left and thought no more about it.

Some days passed, filled with the more pressing concerns of recruit training and operative debriefing, before Katya had the time to deal with the message. She went to visit the old man. He was still alive and still lived above the tavern.

※ ※ ※

Adrian went to The Nameless Tavern every day after that. The woman, whose name was Petra, began giving him his tea for free. She even bought fresh tea leaves—more of the Baikyong-do white, which Adrian was too polite to tell her he didn't care for. Adrian was nearly ready to give up, when on the second Sunday he saw a familiar face. It wasn't actually a face at all.

Again, Adrian's recollection of names helped him.

"Katyana?" he said as she walked by.

The porcelain-masked woman stopped and looked at him.

"Do I know you?"

"I'm Adrian," he said. "Nikolas's friend."

"Nikolas has a lot of friends."

"So you do still see him? I wasn't sure, but I didn't know where else to go. Petra said she doesn't know him."

"I don't know where he is." She began walking off.

"Wait."

She turned, looking back at him over her shoulder through the mask.

"If you see him," Adrian said, "can you tell him I'll be here?"

"It's like I told you. I haven't seen him."

"If you do . . . "

She nodded once and showed him her back.

※ ※ ※

Katya was getting ready for bed. Propped up by pillows and writing in his journal, Nikolas looked up from time to time, taking in her body as she undressed. She pulled her sweater over her head and eel-slid out of her pants. Last, she removed her mask to reveal her true face. This was, for Nikolas, a greater thrill then seeing her naked body. He knew how much it meant to her to be face-naked this way in front of him.

"I saw your friend today," she said.

"Which friend?"

"The one from the university. Pale, thin."

Nikolas set his journal on the end table. "Where was this? What did he say?"

"At Dmitri's," she said. "He's been asking about you. Hanging around. Making himself known."

"And you didn't bring him here?"

"I thought we agreed. We have to be careful now."

"He's a friend of mine. A good friend. I'd even hoped to bring him into our circle one day. But then we went our separate ways. He's more conservative than I am, sure, but I still think he'd make a good lieutenant. He's smart."

She was taking down her hair now, removing the crossed knitting needles which had held it in place. It cascaded down, shiny and dense.

"Remember what you said at the meeting the other night? *'Trust no one. Not even your own brother.'*"

"I know what I said."

She raised a thin plucked eyebrow, taking advantage of her exposed face to express the full extent of her skepticism. He was often surprised that her facial expressions were so normal—so predictably *human*—after being hidden to almost everyone most of the day. He also wondered why she bothered to pluck her eyebrows—was it for him? Or, despite being raised in the religion of the mask, did she still retain this last portion of ordinary vanity?

"Shouldn't the leader of a revolution follow his own standards? Shouldn't he be harsher on himself, even? To raise the level of those around him?"

"Adrian would never compromise us."

She sat down beside him on the bed. She took his hand.

"Look, I know this is hard to accept. But how long did you know him, really?" She spoke gently now. "A few months? And you weren't the man you are now."

"I set the standards I do so that when they're broken the transgression is tolerable," he said. "You draw a line on the floor ten meters from where the actual line is. When someone crosses it, they are still in safe territory."

"Even if he approves of your ideas, he might not approve of your new tactics. We both know they're necessary, but that's because we recognize what's at stake. Most people are content to let things be, you know."

"That doesn't mean he's turned government agent."

"*'Everyone's a potential informant when privacy itself is deemed subversive,'*" she recited.

More of his words thrown back at him. Her recall was impressive.

She often flattered him by saying that she only remembered *his* words so exactly.

"But where do we draw the line?" he asked. "At some point we have to trust somebody. I trust you absolutely, for example. How is that any different?"

"Well, for one thing we've been to bed together."

He stroked her bare shoulder. Her skin was hot, almost feverish. He touched her lips, felt the welcoming softness there.

"I know you," he said. "I trust you with my life."

"Do you? How do you know this is not all some clever ruse?"

"That's a chance I'll take."

She put her hand between his legs. "How do you know I'm not sleeping with you to extract information? How do you know I won't chain you to the bed in your helpless state?"

"You know I can't withstand such techniques."

She leaned over, blowing her words into his ear. "Then tell me what I want to know. Tell me everything."

"You'll have to break me first."

"With pleasure," she said, climbing on top.

4.

GENERAL OSTER and Major Schmidt entered Joshua City accompanied by pomp and circumstance, a mass of loyal Joshuans cheering and crowding alongside their konvoy, barely held back by the barricades and armed Guardsmen. There were hundreds of placards with the two men's names on them, but there were many more that simply read *Schmidt*. Major Schmidt barely noticed the discrepancy, worried as he was about being discovered, and thinking of the many men who were not returning home, some of whom he had sent to their deaths. He thought of Kharkov. He thought of Jürgen, wondering what he would make of all this, and imagined his face filled with satisfaction and pride. Yes, Jürgen would be happy to see their plans come to fruition.

General Oster, however, did notice the extra attention Schmidt received. He told himself that Schmidt had been brave, but as the ranking officer the accolades ought to be his.

It was not until they had nearly reached the military headquarters that Major Schmidt—who felt a bit of Marcik Kovalski creeping back into his psyche—allowed himself to fully assess the danger he was in. He had no idea what the punishment for impersonating an officer was. Were there any cases in Joshuan history of such a breach of protocol? He consoled himself with the thought that he had won a decisive victory for the city. *They have to take that into account, don't they?* His mind churned round and round in the same pattern of fear. If need be, he would admit fully what he had done and beg amnesty on the grounds that he had done what the situation had required; he had freed many Joshuans from captivity; he had led those Joshuans to victory. *They have to take that into account.*

When they reached the headquarters, several Guardsmen dressed in formal regalia greeted them.

"Sir," one of the men said to General Oster, "I have instructions to bring you to the mayor's office at once. He wants to hear news of the battle from you directly. And of course to congratulate you on your outstanding service to Joshua City."

Major Schmidt looked about, wondering what to do with himself. Where should he go?

"Alone?" General Oster asked, his mood changing swiftly to happiness.

"I was only given orders to bring you," the Guardsman said.

"Very well then," Oster said and motioned to his men that they were free to pursue the joys of returning soldiers. Major Schmidt lost himself in the celebratory crowd, and was everywhere congratulated as a hero, and everywhere felt a hollow dread.

5.

NIKOLAS ENTERED the tavern by a rusty metal side door and stood for a second in the doorway—taking in the late-afternoon light through the soot-streaked window, the familiar smell of spilled drinks and tobacco ash. A radio played low: a folk song with reed-flute and Baikyong-doan zither. Though Nikolas did not spend as much time here as he used to, it still felt like home. What's more, he would always think of it as the birthplace of The Underground, and for that reason if nothing else, he would retain a special fondness for it.

Across the room, Adrian was leaning over the bar looking at something Petra was showing him. He was absorbed by whatever it was and did not look up. Nikolas lingered in the door for a moment, observing his old friend after so many months separation. Petra glanced briefly in Nikolas's direction but gave no indication that she recognized him. She returned her attention to Adrian, leaning her motherly frame across the plain wood of the bar to better explain the object in her hand.

Well done, Nikolas thought. *Just as we discussed.*

Adrian looked older, Nikolas decided. It had been what...eight months at the most? But even from this distance, something in Adrian's demeanor had aged. A certain weary but confident squaring of the shoulders, perhaps. He looked at home in these squalid surroundings in a way he hadn't before. Nikolas had a vivid flash from the one time they had come here together: Adrian's prim posture on his stool, his legs tight together and his hand on his knees, his stiff but polite smile as Nikolas had drunkenly ranted about some sort of nonsense. Nikolas had done a lot of drunken ranting back then; he had even meant some of it.

He approached the bar and sat next to Adrian. "Pure-baikal to you," he said.

As Adrian recognized Nikolas, his features relaxed until finally he grinned. "Nikolas," he said. "You're finally here. Petra was just showing me pictures of her children. They're very charming."

"What can I get for you, sir?"

Perfectly played. Not a hint that she knew him, not a hint that The Underground had been bringing stolen medikal supplies to her husband Dmitri for months—bandages to dress his wounds, good clean water for him to drink, various antibiotics and homeopathic cures. Nothing worked. Nikolas had even examined him several times per-

sonally. A surprising case, that one. Dmitri had been a robust physically powerful man—or at least he appeared to be. Nikolas suspected
the nekrosis was a consequence of some prior illness. One thing he
had learned about nekrosis during his summer internship: it preyed
on the already weak. Dmitri was a smoker and Nikolas had listened to
his lungs for signs of infection there. His hope was to do a radiation
scan, but that required expensive medikal equipment they didn't yet
have access to—not that they could bring here anyway. That was the
next step.

Nikolas glanced down into Adrian's cup. "Is that tea? They have tea
here now?"

"Yes," he said. "Petra makes very good tea. Petra, this is my good
friend Nikolas."

"Pleased to meet you," she said. "Ready to order?"

"I'll have a tea, please."

"What kind?"

"Oh, it doesn't matter. Whatever Adrian's having," he said. And then
to Adrian, "I see you've made yourself at home."

"Yes. I've been looking for you for some time. I have so much to
tell you. I asked Petra if she'd seen you, but she didn't know who I was
talking about. I guess you don't come in here so much these days?"

"Not so often. I've quit drinking, in fact."

"Good for you. Things are going well then?"

"I'll tell you about what I'm doing later," Nikolas said. "Let's start
with you."

※ ※ ※

Adrian told Nikolas about his spring semester at Joshua University, the
strangeness of living in their shared dormitory room without Nikolas.
*It was nice, having more space. But at the same time, I couldn't get used
to it.* He told Nikolas about his studies with Brandt. *At first, I think he
just wanted someone to replace you.* He then talked about his shock at
Brandt's death, the aimless casting about that followed.

"I realized I needed something," Adrian said. "I wanted to clear my head. To remind myself of why I wanted to study the medikal sciences in the first place. I don't know, maybe it's foolish, but I thought that being away from Joshua City for a while might help."

As Adrian spoke, he watched Nikolas closely. He nodded at the right places, asked sensitive and insightful questions, made understanding comments to show he was really listening. But his attention seemed divided. His eyes flicked about the room, measuring everything. He was anxious about something, Adrian could tell. And what was with this reluctance to talk about himself? Nikolas had never been shy on that account.

%% %% %%

As Adrian told his story, they drank cup after cup of white tea. When it ran out, Petra went to the back to boil up more. Nikolas watched her trod stolidly off, admiring her in a kind of sweeping impersonal way—a woman of good working class stock, the very type The Underground hoped to win to its cause. Nikolas, Katya, Elias and the others of his central circle had often debated about how best to accomplish this. Elias was of the opinion that they might do it by propaganda—leaflets, doctrines, slogans, and so forth. And while Nikolas agreed that those methods were useful, necessary, even, he wondered if a people who had been lied to so often—by the radio, by *The Joshua Harbinger*, by the smooth voices and slippery speech of politicians—would be readily convinced by yet more propaganda, no matter how rooted in truth.

(Nikolas did not realize this thought had come directly from Adrian, who had made the same point in this very tavern so long ago.)

"They swallow it whole from their priests," Elias pointed out.

"We won't get anywhere by mocking their religion," Nikolas said.

He hated this particular weakness of poor Joshuans as much anyone, their tendency to cling to outmoded beliefs for the scraps of comfort they provided. But the time had not yet come to fight that battle. There would be plenty of time for that . . . if things went the way he hoped.

"We need to give them something," Katya suggested. "Something practical. Food, water. Not promises."

And so it was that The Underground settled on a strategy. They would first win the love and respect of the people through charitable action; then they would provide the ideological framework for revolution; last, they would show how and when to act.

A man will fight for what he loves, Nikolas said at the next group meeting. *He may also fight for what he fears, but with a heart full of resentment, secretly hoping he is defeated.*

Adrian continued with his story. Nikolas nodded sympathetically at the right places, half his mind on The Underground as always. He had a speech to give tonight, operations to oversee, new recruits to monitor. Adrian described his travels by karavan, a driver he had befriended, the worries about banditii and Ulani troops, his meeting with Messenger. Nikolas became more attentive at this.

"I'd always thought it was a child's tale," Adrian said. "But they exist."

Nikolas wondered if it was the same one. "What did he look like?"

Adrian shrugged. "Like a man who could kill you as easily as breathe. But one who wouldn't take any particular joy in it. I liked him. I think he might have even liked me some. He seemed to want to protect me for some reason."

"I've heard so much about them," Nikolas said. "It must have been fascinating to meet one."

Adrian described his arrival at the hospital, his battles with the staff, his frustration with the inadequate supplies. Then he came to the part where the Baikal Guard stripped the hospital of supplies. "This is hard to talk about. I knew my patients, Nikolas. I'd come to care about them. Some more than others. I guess it's always like that. You come to care about your patients and then you lose some of them. But this is different. They didn't have to die. This was an act of great injustice. And stupidity."

Nikolas made a wild guess. "Was there a girl?"

Adrian nodded. "Ariah." His voice wavered on the edge of cracking as he said her name. "I might have... But without my supplies, there was no hope. I'm just so angry. I'm ashamed of that. I keep telling myself I must forgive. God would want me to. But I don't want to. I want to be angry. I want to hold onto my anger. Some days it feels like all I have. I'll never forget the name of the man who did this to her. Major Schmidt. Sorry, I know you don't like the God talk."

Nikolas waved Adrian's apology aside. "Unbelievable. Just unbelievable what they're doing these days."

He remembered the first time he saw Adrian, standing in front of their dormitory seeming lost, clutching his battered suitcase. Now look at him, slumped under the weight of a more sorrowful baggage. *This is what's aged him*, Nikolas thought. He felt a surge of anger on Adrian's behalf.

The name Major Schmidt meant nothing to Nikolas. But he stored it away, as he did with all potentially useful information these days.

"I am truly sorry for what you've been through."

Adrian described his return to Joshua City, how he looked for Nikolas straight away.

"I visited your mother before I came here," Adrian said. "She still thinks you're enrolled, you know."

"What did she say? Did you tell her anything about me?"

Petra returned with more hot water. Nikolas poured it over his tea leaves, not showing his worry.

"Nothing. I didn't feel it was my place," Adrian said. "What *are* you doing, Nikolas? You've listened to me talk for nearly an hour and said almost nothing about yourself."

Nikolas relaxed. "I think it might be better if I show you."

※ ※ ※

Adrian followed Nikolas down a series of increasingly narrow and filthy alleys, finally stopping in front of a heavy cast-iron grate.

Is he living in the street now? Adrian thought. *Has it gotten that bad?*

Between the bars of grate ran a metal chain. Nikolas jangled it three times in a precise way. The grate opened half an inch. Then it slid back entirely. A man the size of an ox was standing on a wide metal ladder like a fire escape. He nodded at Nikolas and barely looked at Adrian. He stepped aside and let them pass. Adrian descended the slick metal rungs and stepped into a room more immense than he would have believed possible.

"What is this?" Adrian asked. "What am I looking at?"

Nikolas took in Adrian's surprise and awe out of the corner of his eye, his face glowing with a sort of fatherly pride.

"Welcome to The Underground."

※ ※ ※

As Nikolas showed Adrian around this place he called The Underground, Adrian felt ashamed of his initial thought. He should have known Nikolas would not let himself fall into decline. His friend was too brilliant, too resourceful for that. But where was this all leading? He felt himself torn between wonder and a growing trepidation. What was it all for—this vast network of underground rooms, these elaborate if quaint domiciles? They passed a room stockpiled with food and barrels of water, as well as mysteriously marked crates. In another room, a vast map of Joshua City had been pinned to a wall. Areas were circled, others marked with darts. People peeked out from below curtains, from balcony enclosures, from behind loose-hanging doors. Two men played a game of Baikyong-doan checkers. Another sat eating a loaf of bread and drinking directly from a bottle of wine. A radio was on.

"This," Adrian said. "You did this?"

"I like to say we all did it together."

"But what is it for, Nikolas?"

"All that in good time." And he walked on, saying no more.

Whatever its meaning and purpose, Adrian marveled at the intricacy of the society Nikolas had created. He met person after person, a blur of names and faces he made little attempt to remember. What he did take note of, however, was the universal respect and admiration with which they addressed Nikolas. In a way, this did not surprise Adrian—his friend had always been charismatic—but there seemed to be a newfound seriousness in his enterprises. It wasn't just that he didn't smoke and didn't drink. It wasn't just that he looked to be in incredible physical shape. It was the supreme confidence with which he moved through his underground living quarters, patting a shoulder here, giving an encouraging smile there—even stopping at the domicile of a pregnant mother to enquire about her health, to listen with a stethoscope to the baby's heartbeat. That a pregnant woman was willing to live in such conditions for a cause she believed in—and Adrian had guessed there *must* be some grand cause behind all this—that was another thing for Adrian to marvel at.

"Well, if it isn't the young doktor," a voice said from behind them, as Nikolas let the drape fall on the pregnant woman's tent.

Elias looked much the same as he had at university, still dressed in a fashionable leather coat, workman's boots, the casual insouciance of a scarf.

"Elias," Adrian said. "You're here too?"

"Of course," Elias said. "The question is where you've been. The revolution could use you."

"Revolution?"[9]

Elias raised an eyebrow at Nikolas. "I'm sorry. How much does he know?"

"Not much," Nikolas said. "How much he wants to know is up to him."

"What is this all about?" Adrian asked.

"You'll learn more at the meeting tonight," Nikolas said.

---

[9] Author's Note: Here the reader should know that Nikolas had set up this little bit of theatre entirely for Adrian's benefit. Elias would never be so clumsy as to give up information accidentally. The previous evening, Nikolas had told Elias to find the proper moment to pique Adrian's curiosity. He needed to know how far Adrian was willing to go. And no one's instinct for this kind of subterfuge was as keen as Elias's. Nikolas had come to rely on him more and more.

%. %. %.

"Tonight I want to talk to you about The Great Step Forward," Nikolas said.

Adrian was on a small bench behind where Nikolas was now speaking. Katya sat beside him, Elias and Alarik to either side of them. Adrian looked out at Nikolas's admirers. They sat on the floor or stood against the wall at the back of the room. A few even perched on the intricate pipeworks high above the concrete floor.

"Throughout the history of civilization, even in the Before-Time," Nikolas continued, "there have been the oppressors and the oppressed. And too many of us have accepted that this is the natural order of things. The powerful, they tell us, are powerful because they have earned it. Because they are better than us. But who really is better? The son who inherited his father's faktory or the workers who create the wealth that he enjoys? Would he last a day on the assembly line?"

And now he made a calculated pause. The crowd applauded and whistled their approval. Adrian admired Nikolas's seamless showmanship.

"Increments. They tell us that we will change it by increments. Joshuan politicians give us one paltry concession and take away a dozen essential rights. And when we get impatient they tell us change takes time. They tell us society is one long evolution to a better tomorrow. But how many tomorrows have come and gone? And the only change I see is for the worse. The rich are getting richer and poor are getting sicker. It's not evolution that we need . . . It's a Great Step Forward."

He paced back and forth, seeming to consider what to say next.

"It's not the poor who are sick, but civilization itself. And in order to find a cure we must first diagnose all the symptoms. And what are the symptoms that concern us? The material conditions of the present that are preventing a healthier future. But I've been talking in abstractions. Every problem is a specific problem. And we have someone here tonight, a respected and trusted colleague from my days as a medikal skolar, who will tell you about one of these specific problems. About the brutal lengths the Baikal Guard will go for their war agenda."

Nikolas turned to Adrian. "Would you do us the honor of telling my friends here what you shared with me?"

※ ※ ※

After Adrian had finished speaking, several of Nikolas's hangers-on had come up and thanked him, many of them sincerely moved by his words. Later, the meeting truly at an end now, everyone turned to drink and celebration, and Adrian found a quiet corner. From across the room, he watched Elias, Alarik and other important members of The Underground gathered around Nikolas. Katya approached him, her posture asking permission to engage him in conversation. Adrian offered her a welcoming smile.

"I very much enjoyed what you said up there," Katya said.

Adrian's nerves still hadn't settled from Nikolas's ambush. "I'm glad someone did."

Adrian's first instinct had been to flee the room entirely, but he had no choice but to honor Nikolas's request. He trembled his way to Nikolas's side and with a dry mouth told his story. He had fumbled with his words, getting several events out of order. And even when what he had said was true, it did not feel truthful. His words communicated fact but not feeling.

"I see why Nikolas holds you in such high regard," Katya said.

She sat down beside him, her body angled toward his with a familiar closeness. She gave his shoulder a komradely squeeze.

"It's really nice having you here. Nikolas needs someone like you. And anyone so important to Nikolas is important to me."

At that, they fell into a companionable silence.

※ ※ ※

"Thank you for doing that," Nikolas said, setting his hand on Adrian's back with brotherly affection as they walked down one of the tunnels in

The Underground. "I know it was unfair of me to surprise you. But I felt it was important. As you'll see, we all share openly here."

It was a few hours after the meeting, the revelry had ended, and most of the rest of The Underground had gone to sleep. Nikolas was leading Adrian to the room where he would be staying. Nikolas had ordered a nice electric samovar and some good tea leaves be placed there for Adrian's enjoyment.

Painted directly on the pocked grainy walls of the tunnel were images of unexpected care and detail. They were as good as any Adrian had seen at the Joshua University Institute of Fine Arts. One showed three shrouded figures running from an unseen pursuer, a wash of grays and reds looming ominously behind them. The artist had even gone so far as to paint an ornate frame around the image. Another showed a man at a metal-press, muscles standing out and face dripping with the sweat of exertion. His square-jawed boss leaned over his shoulder, inspecting his work with oversized eyes.

"These are impressive," Adrian said, indicating the images.

"That's Oriana," Nikolas said. "Our resident artist."

"That's all one person? They're so different."

"The true artist can find the form to fit his needs, wouldn't you agree?"

They walked on, taking in the other images on the wall. They were made new for Nikolas by seeing them through Adrian's eyes. They didn't speak for several minutes, which might have been uncomfortable among lesser friends.

"It's wonderful to have you here," Nikolas said.

"It's nice to see what you've built here."

"Speaking of that," Nikolas said, "here's where I leave you. Your room's down at the end of the hall."

Nikolas walked back the way they had come. Adrian looked down the empty distance of the hall. As he made his way toward the room Nikolas had set up for him, Adrian felt real warmth for Nikolas and what he had accomplished here. He even forgave him the ambush at the meeting. And Katya was perfect for him. Just perfect.

A dissonant crackle of a radio echoed lightly through the hallway. A door stood open, a thin light stretching across the tunnel's floor. As Adrian passed, he heard a quiet tittering song.

The boom comes soon
in the month of June...

Not wanting to spy, Adrian looked into the room. A small hunched figure crouched over a radio on the floor. Parts from several other radios were scattered around him. He made minute adjustments to the radio dial and voices emerged: "[crackle-crackle]...*the film was panned...But what about the censors?* [crackle]...*sent him a bottle of my finest.*"

The hunched figure turned to Adrian, his eyes shiny and the drool of excitement running down his chin. "You're here!"

"I'm sorry..." Adrian said.

"Listen to my new channel."

"I didn't mean to..."

"Listen to my song!"

He returned to tinkering with his radio, singing the same song as before, more loudly now.

The boom comes soon
in the month of June!

"My name is Slug. That rhymes with Slug!"

"I'm a friend of Nikolas's," Adrian said.

The moon comes soon,
I hear the tune!

The boom in June.

"Do you hear it?" Slug asked.

Adrian, confused, "What are you doing here?"

"Making channels," Slug said. "Come listen."

Adrian stepped fully into the room.

"This one is my favorite," Slug said.

He turned the radio dial again: "[crackle] ...*seventeen tonnes of munitions delivered*...[zzzzhhhh] ...*enemy combatants dispatched...*"

"Isn't that military communication?"

"Machine-words," Slug said matter-of-factly. "I like them. Do you want to listen more?"

"No," Adrian said, "I should go to bed. It was very nice to meet you."

Slug hopped to his feet. "Slug . . . hug? That rhymes! June!"

Slug grabbed Adrian around the waist and lifted him off the floor, spinning him around. The breath went out of Adrian's chest. This little man was stronger than he looked.

※ ※ ※

Nikolas left Katya sleeping in their bed and walked through the main room of The Underground, so recently vibrant with momentous fervor. He grabbed an abandoned half-empty bottle of spirits and climbed the stairs to the street. The anemic light of near-dawn called forth gray shadows, and the cold air roused him to unusual wakefulness. He sucked down a burning gulp from the bottle and pondered on nothing in particular.

Everything had gone exactly as planned—better than planned, in fact. A dedicated member of The Underground had given up his domicile and had moved all of his personal belongings so that Adrian could use his room. Nikolas had wanted Adrian to sleep in this particular room because he would have to pass Slug's workshop. He wanted them to meet, and in particular, for Adrian to see The Underground's capacity for counter-surveillance. What would be his reaction? Was he ready? The desert had changed him. But had it changed him enough?

Nikolas tilted the bottle back. It had been some time since he had allowed himself to drink. *Not since Messenger.*

Nikolas closed his eyes and imagined all the moveable parts of History, the total interconnectedness of the entire system of existence. He had to keep the total system in mind at all times, like a doktor treating a patient. As he had told the members of The Underground, civilization was sick, but a good doktor knows to treat the entire patient, not each symptom separately. The blood affects the muscles which affect the skeleton which depend on the ligaments which depend on the blood to bring them nutrients, and the brain controls it all like an omniscient diktator.

He considered another drink but instead threw the bottle against the brick wall across the alley. The tinkling shatter of glass and the spray of shard and fluid made a strange star for Nikolas and Nikolas alone. He was the center of a series of threads that ran the length of the known world and wove the Seven Cities into one collective destiny. Sunlight sliced over the edge of a small building and stung Nikolas's eyes. *Time for sleep.* Tomorrow he would need to be in his finest shape.

※ ※ ※

"So, what do you think?" Nikolas asked Adrian the following morning as they walked the streets of Joshua City. He had foregone his usual lieutenants' breakfast, leaving the proceedings in Katya's capable hands.

"That Slug fellow is a strange one," Adrian said. "But endearing."

"There is no one like Slug in all the Seven Cities, I imagine," Nikolas said with a loving laugh in his voice. Then, in a serious tone, "And?"

"And what?"

"I'll be blunt," Nikolas said. "Could you see yourself joining us? Your mind and skills would be very useful."

"I can be useful elsewhere too."

"You could. That's true. But I would be personally very happy to have you around. Our collaboration at Joshua University was cut short, I feel."

"You know I was sad to see you leave."

"I had my reasons. And what's past is past."

They walked along in silence a few moments longer.

"Let me think about it," Adrian said.

"Take all the time you like," Nikolas said. "Enough of that kind of talk though. Let's get some breakfast. I know just the place."

※ ※ ※

At an open air stall in the market, Adrian and Nikolas had a breakfast of griddle cakes and duck sausages. They washed it down with good strong black coffee. The summer was ending, but the morning was warm. Nikolas joked with the owner of the stall, a gaunt man with a long drooping mustache and an apron covered in grease. He asked about the man's daughter. Did she still want to study violin?

"It's all she talks about," the man said. "But there's no way I can afford such a thing. The instrument itself, even a poor one, is hundreds of drams. And then the lessons..."

"It might be that I know someone," Nikolas said.

The man brightened considerably. He set down his spatula. "She would still need a violin."

"That, too, could be arranged."

"You are too kind, Mr. Kovalski."

"Please," Nikolas said. "I've told you to call me Nikolas."

"More to eat?" he offered Nikolas. "It is my treat."

"No, thank you."

"Your friend then?"

Adrian patted his full belly. "I can't eat anymore. Thank you, though. It was truly excellent."

"Only the best for Mr. Kovalski's friends."

"You could do one thing for me," Nikolas said to the shopkeep.

"Anything."

"You could come to one of my meetings."

The man grew dour. "I've told you, I am not interested in politics."

"That's fine." Nikolas held up his hands in a placating gesture. "Come, listen. Leave whenever you want. Besides, you can meet little Yelena's violin teacher."

"All right. I'll come. This one time."

"Can you close shop by five o'eve? I'll send someone to show you to the meeting-place."

Nikolas slapped twenty drams on the counter, more than twice as much as their breakfast likely cost, standing and saying goodbye before the shopkeep could protest. Adrian gave an apologetic shrug to the man, who was holding out the money, still trying to give it back, and followed Nikolas, moving fast through the market.

"So," Nikolas said. "What should we do today?"

"That was kind of you back there," Adrian said.

It was a side of Nikolas he hadn't known existed before, this gregarious man of the people. Nikolas had always been charming...but was there a new cunning there? Something darker?

Nikolas brushed the words away. "I've got my motives."

"Recruiting."

"Yes," Nikolas said. "That too. To inspire the people, you must first show them something concrete."

"Where is this all leading?"

Nikolas paused on the corner of the street, looked left, looked right. He frowned. "You know, it's been so long since I've just done something fun, I'm not sure I know how any more. What do you do to relax?"

"I don't know. Read, I guess. But ... "

"In the past, I would have had a drink."

"Listen, Slug said something odd last night."

"He says a lot of odd things."

"You're not planning something...dangerous, are you?"

Nikolas stopped so suddenly Adrian nearly bumped into him. He spoke with emphatic earnestness, "I merely want to show the people another way. Something outside of their circumscribed lives. It doesn't have to be like this, Adrian. We can change the world. Remember how we used to talk about that?"

"I remember," Adrian said. "I do."

"So ... ?"

"Maybe I'm simply not like you."

Nikolas gave a resigned shake of his head. "No," he said. "Maybe not.

※ ※ ※

Later that night, Adrian lay on his strange bed, staring at the strange ceiling, hearing the strange clanking of pipes and a distant festive laughter. He had gone to bed early, wanting to be away from all the unfamiliar faces. But he couldn't sleep. He sat up, planted his feet on the floor. Then he slipped on his shoes and picked up the one small bag he had with him. He pulled out of the room, down the hall, and toward the stairs leading up from The Underground. No one stopped him. No one questioned him. He did not know where he was going, only that he didn't belong here.

6.

THERE WAS A KNOCK at Major Schmidt's door, and his stomach sank. *They've come.* He wanted to ignore it, but he forced himself from the bed where he had been lying since being planted here by his escort. The floor was carpeted and he felt each sink of his boots into that soft material. He opened the door with dignity, ready for the punishment he knew awaited him.

"Major Schmidt, sir." So the escort would continue to play the role. So be it. He was ready. "Mayor Adams seeks an audience with you." Such official language. You could hide anything behind official language, even a court martial or a death sentence.

"Let us go then," Major Schmidt said, grabbing his hat from the table. *Major Schmidt.* He still thought of himself that way. Marcik Kovalski no longer existed, even if it was Marcik Kovalski they would indict and arraign and imprison again.

In the long car ride to The Hub, Major Schmidt gazed lazily out of the window. This city and its people fascinated him as though he had never seen them before. The streets and the Joshuans walking them were more worn-down than when he had left, yet there was something exuberant about them that had not been there before. *I brought that to them,* he thought. *I am part of the air, even if they cast me out.*

As they entered The Hub, he looked around for Guardsmen ready to take him into custody, but none were present.

In the anteroom to Mayor Adams's office, a man named Pierre he had seen fotografs of over the years greeted him. "A pleasure, Major Schmidt. Mayor Adams is excited to make your acquaintance."

Was all this an elaborate ruse? But why go to such lengths?

※ ※ ※

When Mayor Adams had spoken with General Oster, a particularly drab and uninspiring man, he had been told some disturbing news.

"Do you have any proof of this?" Mayor Adams asked.

"That would be easy enough to find in the Baikal Guard record archives," General Oster said. "There would be fingerprints, birth certificates, and we could find any number of men who served with the *real* Major Schmidt."

"But you say he saved the outpost?"

"Yes, sir. I have to admit he played an integral role in our success."

"So what action would you suggest, General?"

"The punishment should not be too severe, considering his service."

※ ※ ※

"Please, take a seat." Mayor Adams gestured toward a chair in front of his desk, a chair which seemed ominously empty to Major Schmidt. The emptiness he had just been asked to fill would swallow him, his entire shabby self, would swallow Major Schmidt and vomit forth the shell of Marcik Kovalski who no longer existed. Major Schmidt wondered vaguely whether he could resurrect Marcik for the trial and prison sentence (execution?) that would follow. Or would he have to venture into his fate still pretending to be the man he had become?

Mayor Adams sat down behind his desk and motioned again toward the empty chair. Major Schmidt reminded himself to breathe and sat stiffly down.

"Even though the words already ring false in my mind, I must say how much this city owes you," Mayor Adams said.

"I just did what any loyal member of the Baikal Guard would do, Mr. Mayor."

"You are too modest. I daresay very few men would be as bold as you have proven capable of."

A cowardly pit opened up in Major Schmidt's gut. He decided not to respond. Mayor Adams opened a drawer and pulled out a gold-plated box and sat it on his desk. The mystery of what was in the box frightened Major Schmidt immensely and without reason. Mayor Adams opened the box and offered a cigarette. *Classic interrogation.* Olgar's face arose in a foggy corner of Major Schmidt's mind. He took a cigarette anyway. Something to do with his hands, an excuse not to talk. The two men sat smoking and looking at each other for long seconds.

"My administration could use a man like you."

Major Schmidt sucked in and puffed out smoke, waiting for whatever was coming next.

"Would you like a drink?" Mayor Adams asked. "I'm going to have a drink." He crossed the room and opened a large elegant cabinet. "Let's have a drink."

Mayor Adams handed him a drink and stood there before him, glass half-raised. Major Schmidt felt suddenly small and inappropriate in his seated position. He stood and raised his glass. Waited. Mayor Adams looked him in the eye, yet said nothing. His gaze was one of bemused interest. And something else . . . the look of a man considering a major purchase. Again Major Schmidt felt inappropriate, standing there in silence, though there was nothing to do or say.

"May all your days be pure-baikal," Mayor Adams finally said and touched his glass to Major Schmidt's almost daintily.

"And may yours as well."

The two men drank in further silence.

"What are we to do with you, Major Schmidt?"

"What do you mean, sir?"

"A hero can be useful, *Major Schmidt.*" It was unsettling the way he lingered on those last two words.

"I hope we might find some way for me to be of further service to Joshua City, sir."

"That is my hope as well, Major Schmidt," Mayor Adams said. "That is my sincerest hope as well."

"Anything, sir. I am at your disposal."

"Indeed you are." He went back to the cabinet and refreshed his drink, not offering any to his guest. "What is your real name?"

Major Schmidt's knees nearly buckled beneath him.

※ ※ ※

General Oster had described the intense loyalty of Schmidt's men and his unorthodox but effective tactics.

"And the people seem to love him," Mayor Adams said.

Oster frowned and said, "Yes, that's apparent."

"And besides you, who else knows about this?"

※ ※ ※

"I'm sorry...what, sir?" Major Schmidt said and blew nervous smoke toward the high ceiling of Mayor Adams's office.

"If we are going to work together, and I think we can, I will need to know everything. I have been able to piece together scraps here and there, but I must trust you before I can make use of you. And the only way for me to trust you is if I know the entire story—especially anything that might be damaging should the truth ever come out."

Major Schmidt wanted to sit down, but he tapped reserved funds of courage and remained on his feet. Swirled the murky fluid around in its cup and emptied it.

"How rude of me. Would you like another?"

Major Schmidt nodded that yes, he would. Mayor Adams took his time in the preparation.

"Here."

Major Schmidt took a light sip, just enough to wet his mouth. It would not do to have his voice crack. "My real name is Marcik Kovalski. I joined the Baikal Guard voluntarily and served as best I could."

Mayor Adams motioned for him to continue.

"My kompany was ambushed and those of us who survived were taken captive. While in the prison, I organized and led a revolt. There was a certain Major Schmidt who died in captivity, under torture. To my knowledge, he did not give up any useful information to the enemy. He was a good Guardsman as best I know." He took another sip. "In order to get the men to follow me, I assumed his identity. And you know the rest."

"Yes, I do. You went on to sway the tide in a decisive battle, for which I do thank you."

Major Schmidt looked out the window, toward the sprawl of the city he loved, now more than ever.

"What happens now?"

"First, a promotion. A decorated war veteran deserves a promotion, wouldn't you say? How would you like to be a general?"

General Schmidt—just when he had become accustomed to his new identity, an identity that he had in effect stolen off a dead man. What did this amount to but another theft? But at the same time he wanted this, very much.

Major Schmidt nodded. "And after that?"

"We throw a parade," Mayor Adams said. "One worthy of a true Joshuan hero. And then we will discuss how you might be of further use to me."

※ ※ ※

"And I understand you have applied several times for a position in the Ministrie of Defense."

"Yes, sir," General Oster had said.

"I predict there will be an opening for a man of your talents," Mayor Adams said. "One with a considerably higher salary than your current position. And you would be stationed here in Joshua City with your family."

"That would be ideal, sir."

"But I'm going to need something from you as well."

"Anything."

"You will give a full-throated endorsement of our new general, General Schmidt. You will go on the radio and give testament to his bravery. And if anyone questions his identity, you will swear that he is the true Malcolm Schmidt."

CHAPTER EIGHT

A TRUE JOSHUAN HERO

I T WAS TIME for a big move. Their small acts of sabotage and subterfuge were causing widespread unrest, perhaps even drawing attention to many of the problems Joshua City faced, and Nikolas occasionally dared to hope that they were forcing Mayor Adams into a corner. Debate was constant in The Underground. What was the next move? They had avoided damaging the lives of civilians when possible, but he was still worried about losing the common Joshuans' support. Some had suggested that they should recruit politicians, or would-be politicians, to run for office and change the system from within. This was, of course, absurd. The elections were rigged to the point that less than forty percent of Joshuans bothered to vote anymore. It was an open secret that only pre-approved businessmen and party bosses had any chance of being elected, or even making it on the ballot.

Nikolas spent many hours walking the streets of Joshua City, getting a feel for the mood of the people. Though he knew his methods were not exactly scientific, he felt he knew the pulse and thrum of the citizenry, where their anxieties lay and where their hopes looked to. But were they ready for something truly revolutionary?

"We have to make a mark on the consciousness of our time," Elias insisted. A wave of excited murmurs rose up among The Underground.

Elias was standing and gesticulating with a pamphlet he had been handing out earlier that day. Nikolas had to agree with him but wondered if their pamphlets were going to make that mark. Nikolas was also annoyed that he did not know what might.

"And the only way to impress an idea on a populace," Elias continued, "is for it to first disturb the consciousness—and the conscience even more so—of the populace. How did any of us first come to consider ourselves members of The Underground except due to the ideas of those in power and how much they disturbed us?"

More noises of approval from the crowd.

Just look at all of them. Look at this room. Look at where they had come, after such a short amount of time. The city must be ripe for action, or else Nikolas never would have succeeded in amassing such a following. Now they had to bring history to its moment of crisis.

"Elias is right," Nikolas said and stood. He looked to Alarik and Katya for strength. "The time has come, komrades. In fact, it has been upon us for some time. But our move must be both decisive and precise. We have the people's trust sufficiently to make a bold attack, but it needs to cripple the government, so we can take control. Even if there are those Joshuans who dislike the tactic, I feel enough will follow us until we can improve their conditions."

"With all due respect, Nikolas," Elias said, "I fear you are overestimating our resources. Cripple the government? In one move? I would be fascinated to hear what such a move might look like."

Nikolas swallowed the urge to cross the room and throttle Elias. It would be simple enough, but its very simplicity is what allowed him to resist.

"I confess, Komrade Elias, that I do not know yet what this move might be. But that is no reason for rash and premature action. We are making headway and when we increase the scope of our efforts, we must be baikal-right."

A few nods, a few unenthusiastic murmurs.

Elias had for some time now been the main author of The Underground's pamphlets. Nikolas approved each one before printing and distribution, but usually there was very little to alter. He reflected briefly on Elias—or rather on two Eliases, the one he had met and the one who stood before him now. What a marvelous change he had undergone. He had started as a flippant would-be dissident, a witty but ultimately toothless provocateur, an attractive university boy who enjoyed leftist circles mostly for their transgressions in the realms of intoxicants and sex. Now, Nikolas acknowledged with some mild chagrin, Elias was an eloquent theoretician of history and human psychology and was dedicated to the revolution in ways that matched anyone's commitment, even his own.

Presently Elias was unfolding one of his pamphlets and straightening his spine and filling his lungs with stentorian air.

"What do we say in our very own educational pamphlets?" The question was not addressed to anyone in particular and did not have the tone of conflict or polemics. He was not challenging Nikolas's authority, his tone said; he was innocent of ambition and wanted only to investigate the matter clearly and honestly. "What message have we brought to the overworked citizens of Joshua City whose government represents water-barons and train manufacturers, yet ignores their most basic needs? Here, I will read to you what we have asked them to read in our own pamphlets."

Nikolas noticed with something like admiration that Elias did not mention that he had written these very words, but rather represented them as the collective message of The Underground, composed collaboratively and in a spirit of komrades-at-arms.

Elias began: "'With each daily compromise, with each blind eye turned to the suffering of our fellow citizens, we are sliding into a totalitarian state. With each new fence built to cloister the politicians and Silverville stars from the masses and with each reinforcement of our Outer Wall, Joshua City becomes a stratified and alienated society.

"'And what are the mechanisms of this stratification, this alienation? They are economic and militaristic. Without the control of currency and means of production, the elite class would not be able to ensure the precarity of average Joshuans. They would not be able to keep us in such a state of need that we cannot afford to stand up to them, for risk of losing what little we have."

Here he stopped and stood silent, allowing the room to take in his words. No one spoke, eager for what he might say next. Still he let them wait a few seconds longer. Again Nikolas admired Elias despite himself.

"Economic and military institutions," Elias said, not exactly a question, yet not quite a statement. "These are the two means of control. They must therefore be the targets of our sabotage."

A quiet wave of affirmation went through the room. His reasoning was valid and, more importantly, simple and understandable. Even Nikolas could not help but agree. He had been mistaken not to watch Elias more carefully. He was so taken up in his own growth as a thinker and a fighter under the tutelage of Messenger that he had neglected to consider how others might be maturing. He had assumed everyone else remained unchanged as he improved. This was basest hubris and had he not caught himself now, had Elias not so skillfully shown his prowess by this display, Nikolas might have gone on in that state of self-delusion.

※ ※ ※

That night in bed, Katya reading beside him and echoes from the festivities of The Underground tunneling into their domicile, Nikolas attempted to study a faktory manifest that Alarik had managed to copy for him, but his mind wandered and he found himself reading over the same numbers and inventories several times. Finally, he set his work aside and picked up a recently released collection of essays by Anwym Laikan titled *The Being of Our Time*. Katya had purchased the book from a rack of dilapidated volumes a peddler in the marketplace had on offer. Doktor Laikan was an author Nikolas felt ambivalent about— clearly brilliant but sometimes frivolous—but this was widely considered her most important book to date. And she was Katya's favorite author; he should make more of an effort to understand her thought.

Nikolas opened to the table of contents and scanned the essays' titles. "The Vanishing Mediator; or Silverville's Construction of Human Identity" seemed particularly interesting, yet Nikolas could not work up any attention for reading just now.

"It was only one evening," Katya said, setting her book aside.

"But one of potentially grave consequence."

"All evenings are of potentially grave consequence for people in our position, Nikolas."

"You know what I mean."

She did.

"You will just have to take the best parts of his ideas and make them your own," Katya said. "And then leave him stained with the worst parts."

"One thing he certainly had right was that the target must be either economic or military."

"A barracks? A bank?"

"You know I would love nothing more than to see the whole Financiers Distrikt burn to the ground," Nikolas said, "but is there a way to do real damage without harming common Joshuans?"

Nikolas lay down and stared at the ceiling. He cleared his mind, let thoughts drift in and out of his consciousness without any special attempt to shepherd them. He kept returning to this possibility of military targets... There was something to it, but he couldn't quite make the connection. They needed a target that would attract public attention. Furthermore, it should be at once symbolic and practical. The people would respond to the symbolism, the government to the "salient damage," as the Baikal Guard called it... suddenly he remembered the story Adrian had told about what Major Schmidt had done to the work camp hospital. This was the man they had just raised to general, the youngest in Joshuan history.

"No, I've got it," Nikolas said. "The military parade they've been talking about incessantly on the radio. It shows that we are not weak, but it shouldn't harm many Joshuan civilians, perhaps none if we're careful. And this new general is the centerpiece of the whole thing."

"And given Adrian's speech the other night, The Underground will be primed to accept that," Katya said, echoing his own unspoken thoughts.

Nikolas looked her over with a heady mixture of awe and love. How had he come by such a companion? He reviewed the past several months of their relationship, their first meeting (so embarrassing for him to recall) to their first real discussion about the future of Joshua City to their first love-making. This, like so much else, seemed...not destined to happen exactly...but historically necessary.

"I love you, you know."

"Yes, of course I do."

Nikolas got out of bed and began dressing. "It has to be the parade," he said. "I'll go tell the others."

"I wouldn't."

Nikolas waited for her to explain.

"Summon Alarik. His input will be invaluable. We'll tell the others tomorrow."

Of course she was right. To run out now announcing this new idea would seem desperate, weak, as though he had been in here brooding for hours—which of course he had been, but there was no reason to announce that. He finished dressing and went to find Alarik.

※　※　※

The next day, Nikolas and his lieutenants gathered around the breakfast table. Nikolas stood and said he had a major announcement. Nikolas had arranged kommunal breakfasts to bring the lieutenants together as a family and to ensure that everyone knew that day's agenda. With such a sense of kamaraderie in the air, what better place to ask that they embark on a venture that could raise their mission to the level of reality?

※　※　※

There is something asunder in Joshua City. Oh, there is something asunder in Joshua City.

Slug sang as his stub-fingers arranged filaments of wire and explosive kartridges.

And things are about to break in the funniest of ways!

He performed a neat spin, turning himself around two times, and curtseyed with more grace than his twisted form would have suggested was possible.

Boom! BOOM!

Boom! BOOM!

He bent back to his trimming and threading together of wires; he took a soldering iron and, with a surgeon's precision, connected various parts from several gutted radios whose hollow plastic husks lay scattered around his work station. Nikolas and Elias watched as he performed his duties with alacrity and loving attention.

And things are about to break in the funniest of ways!

Boom! BOOM!

"Are you sure it is wise to put so much stock in this odd creature's abilities, Nikolas?"

"He has proven his skill and his loyalty. I trust him."

※ ※ ※

Technicians in the Municipal Waterworks entered the under-city labyrinth of passageways and pipes. They had been sent in on the monthly maintenance detail to ensure regular and safe delivery of water supplies. It was a tedious process—checking pipe pressure every one hundred meters, recalibrating flow gauges, and testing water samples in each sub-grid for bacterial or chemical contaminants. Since the nekrosis outbreak, these inspektions had been instated, with special attention shown to governmental sectors and wealthy neighborhoods.

The technicians would be down here all day and might have to come back tomorrow. On the best days, they had a thankless job, and it was even worse when you were assigned maintenance detail. Some of the technicians requested the detail or would take another man's place, because you were paid a ten-percent hazard bonus. The pressure might be too much and the pipe could explode in your face; if there was a chemical pollutant, you might be exposed; and once, several years ago, a technician had been boiled alive when an industrial boiler cracked open and super-heated steam spewed forth; other technicians present that day still told stories about the way his screams rose over the volcano of steam and how he lay writhing for nearly an hour after they turned the steam off, his skin a mass of seething bubbles. The ten-percent hazard bonus was a cruel joke, but enough of the workers were desperate for the extra money that they volunteered and were even thankful for the opportunity.

Nikolas of course knew this and had members of The Underground infiltrate their workforce.

He instructed Slug to build several small bombs, ones that could be fitted into a secret compartment of the toolboxes the technicians would be carrying with them. Slug was ecstatic with possibilities.

"Hiding boom?"

"Yes, Slug," Nikolas said, "hiding boom."

Slug stamped his feet and spun his arms in tight little circles, building up energy, then releasing it in a gesture toward the heavens. "Boom!" he screeched and stood there with his arms stretched upward, as though welcoming his angel of reckoning.

"You can do this?" Nikolas asked. "It is essential that it be exactly right."

Slug grew earnest. "I can do. I can do it perfect." He considered the gravity of the task his beloved Nikolas had charged him with. "Essential to be right. Slug will be right, Nikolas. Promise-promise!"

He would rather die than disappoint me. The thought made Nikolas feel both proud and guilty.

%% %% %%

And so the technicians went down into those dark and fetid tunnels to gain their hazard pay and to keep the city's water flowing safely.

Nikolas's men—whom I cannot name because there is no record of which technicians were in his employ—carried their toolboxes calmly, innocuous as a breeze off the Baikal Sea. They had volunteered in large numbers, but they did not make up the entire crew. They therefore had to be stealthy when they innocently forgot their tools in the prescribed locations. The plan was ingenious, really, though I am loathe to call something that brings about the demise of Joshuans (or any humans) *ingenious*. But from a tactical standpoint, it has to be admired.

The parade itself would be heavily guarded. No way to plant bombs on the floats or at street-level. By planting them beneath the streets, not only did they allow for maximum effect—the pavement rushing up and forming deadly shrapnel—the plan also allowed for Nikolas to pick his target with precision.

And by using the maintenance detail, which was meant to keep Joshua City safe, as a cover to plant the bombs for his attack, he not only ensured the success of his plan, he allowed for a dark irony as well, something my readers no doubt can appreciate, albeit reluctantly, given the consequences.

※ ※ ※

General Schmidt, now playing the role of General Schmidt, endured the prettifying attentions of three of Mayor Adams's public relations officers.

"Can't we make these medals shinier?" one of them said and buffed the insignia on the epaulets of General Schmidt's uniform. "They need to glint for the kameras."

General Schmidt looked down at his starched Guardsman's uniform. His arms felt alien in these crisp new sleeves, nothing like the worn and dirtied one he had walked into the city wearing. He had received his promotion in a private ceremony; there had been debate among Mayor Adams's advisors about whether to do this in public or private. It was decided that it would be more effective this way.

Nearby, last-minute adjustments were made to General Schmidt's float. He, several other decorated officers, a dozen heads of ministries, and prominent Joshuan citizens would be riding on this float, which would head the parade.

Someone straightened the shoulders of his uniform. "Come with us, sir."

A young man with blue intelligent eyes led him up the steps of the float. "There's where you'll stand. We've marked it for you," he said.

"Thank you."

General Schmidt wondered if he should take his place right now or wait until everyone was on the float and the parade had begun.

"I know this must all seem insignificant to you," the young man said, "given what you did in the Outer Provinces."

"Not at all. I just don't know what to do with myself right now."

"Don't worry. They're all going to love you."

%% %% %%

The people pushed and crowded against the barricades, craning their necks to be the first to see the spectacle. Shopkeeps had shuttered their windows; lawyers had postponed court appearances; Joshua University skolars took full advantage of their summer break; mothers brought their children; workers were given leave—the whole of Joshua City was brought together by the Patriots Parade. A priest had set up a booth on a prime corner and was handing out marriage certificates to those young Joshuan couples who wanted to forever bind their love with the glory of this day.

The first float came around the corner. Two oversized mock-rifles constructed from wood and paper, painted to look like the real thing, jutted from its prow. They squinted and there he was—*General Schmidt!* Other important personages stood in V-formation behind him, but the people barely noticed. They had heard stories of how the great General Schmidt had killed one hundred Ulanis singlehandedly. He had even killed one of the Messengers, who were rumored to be invincible. But as the float went by, they were struck by his small stature; they told themselves he must surely look more impressive up close.

As the next float passed, there was much cheering. This float depicted the defeated Ulanis. At the back of the float, there was a gallows. From it hung a thick-haired effigy swaying in a flimsy noose. The float drivers lowered the stuffed Ulani figure for the pleasure of the crowd. A small boy ran forward and hit the legs with a stick. It lurched sideways and swung back to him. He hit it again.

The crowd roared.

※ ※ ※

The boy's name was Timofey. He was nine years old. His mother did not know he was at the parade. She had forbidden him from going—he was sickly and she imagined him being trampled by the crowds. But who could listen to his mother on such a day! He hit the Ulani like General Schmidt would. As the float moved along, he chased after it, brandishing his stick.

※ ※ ※

Nikolas had lodged himself in the crowd, waiting to give the signal. He had placed his men in a line down the path of the parade at strategic intervals. The newspapers and radios had said there would be a Heroes Float and that several ministers and military figures would be riding on it. Most importantly, the Joshuan war hero, General Schmidt—whose war crimes everyone could not stop glorifying as the greatest acts of courage in Joshuan history—would be also be on the float. This was the man who had destroyed Adrian's hospital and killed the woman he loved. Nikolas could not wait to kill him.

There would only be one chance to get this right. The bombs had been placed precisely to inflict maximum damage. The radio detonators Slug had designed only had a twenty-meter range. This meant that the people who detonated the bombs had to be dangerously close to the explosion. Nikolas had wanted to detonate one of the bombs himself. Wasn't he trained for this, after all? And shouldn't it be his responsibility? But Katya and his lieutenants had argued that he was too valuable to lose. And he needed to learn to trust others if the revolution was to succeed.

The signals came down the line and Nikolas saw the Heroes Float a hundred meters off. He had set up this first signal to verify that the lead float was in fact carrying their intended targets. There was no way to trust what the papers said; Nikolas wanted to be absolutely certain. Nikolas was pleased to receive the go-ahead.

As the float drew closer, the people threw flowers and cheered more loudly. A military figure stood at the head of the float, waving to the crowd. *That must be him.* Nikolas knew he must be patient.

%% %% %%

The flowers arced the way the flares had in the battle where he lost Vidal and Kharkov. General Schmidt forced himself to continue playing his role. He smiled widely and waved to one side of the float and the other. The cheering Joshuans knew nothing of the sacrifices his men had made. They thought they were celebrating General Schmidt, but there would be no General Schmidt without those men. And others.

He waved some more, knowing he was doing it for them.

%% %% %%

In a small apartment on the second floor of an undistinguished building, Samir Hosani sat at his kitchen table, a freshly purchased bottle of vodka and an unclean drinking glass before him. He refilled the glass and drank it down without desire, without reaction to the burn as it went through him. In the depressed economy of his mind, desire and distaste were no longer available. He had thought briefly about attending the Patriots Parade, though he knew even as he entertained the possibility that he would not go. Mayor Adams had set him up with a nice little pension and this functional apartment "as payment for such grand service to Joshua City." He had not protested and had managed some measure of honest gratitude.

He was unable to work. All he knew was soldiering, and he'd had more than enough of that. He slept fitfully and spent his days dowsing his senses in vodka.

He put his hand over his eyes and squeezed his face in concentration. He saw the girl and saw Yoyo holding her squirming form. (*"Why, Samir?"* his dead friend asked again.) Samir felt the flesh of her, felt his hardness inside her. In the prison, after his beating, he had thought that his genitals would never work again. He had been wrong but also right: he could still get aroused, only now it produced as much pain as pleasure. He poured another vodka, gulped it, poured another. He carried his drink to the bedroom where on a bookshelf he had a copy of the *Book of the Before-Time*. He flipped through its pages, seeking the wisdom so many people claimed was contained here. He happened upon "The Fable of the Lonely Carpenter." The carpenter worked and worked on a ship meant to save all the people of his village, even though he had no friends among them. An angel of God had told him to put his entire storehouse of love into the making of this ship and that one day he would save the people of his village and they would reward him with admiration and praise. Samir tossed the book carelessly on his bed without finishing the fable. "Sand-rot," he said to no one. He had never seen an angel or a demon.

As a child, his mother had told him about the religion of Kazhstan—about rebirth, about how he might return as a worm or goitered gazelle or even a king. But the myths of his homeland bored him too. His own all-too-human heart had been enough to guide him to this place.

He went back to the kitchen and drank several more glasses of vodka, forcing the face of the girl from his mind unsuccessfully. His stomach churned from the vodka he had drunk too quickly. He made it to the sink in time and wretched and wretched until there was nothing left in him, and yet he continued to wretch painfully. When he was finally done, he stumbled back to his bedroom and fell limply on the bed, beside the *Book of the Before-Time*.

It was a little over an hour later, when he was deeply immersed in unconsciousness, that one of Mayor Adams's most trusted agents entered the apartment through the unlocked front door and walked stealthily around until he found Samir lying vulnerable. The agent stood over Samir and nearly pitied this man he had been following for a week. He pulled his long-knife out of its sheath. As he slid it steadily into Samir's heart, his hand over Samir's mouth to muffle the confused waking cries, he had the sense that he was doing this man a favor.

※ ※ ※

On the float behind Schmidt's, there were a dozen low-level Guardsmen. They had been selected at random and ordered to man this float. The Ministrie of Information had decided it would look good to see common Guardsmen in the parade, to show that Joshua City did not just honor its military leaders but all Guardsmen and the many sacrifices they made.

Armory Sergeant Tenzin tried to stand at attention as he searched for his wife in the crowd. As Armory Sergeant, he had never seen battle. He arranged and kept the weapons clean for those who did fight. He had done his part as best he could. Many of his friends could come home and brag to their wives about their exploits. But what woman gets baikal-wet over a man who polishes other men's guns? Tonight would be different, though. His wife and entire family would see him up here.

※ ※ ※

The float was closing in. Nikolas wanted to see the face of the man who had done so much damage to his friend. Sara and the others with the detonators signaled they were ready for Nikolas's order. To ward off his anxiety, Nikolas went to his situational mantra; Messenger had instructed him in the uses of these mantras; they kept your mind focused when chaos threatened to unseat it. As he mentally recited his mantra, Nikolas unconsciously rubbed his forearm, where the Messenger Tattoo blackly marked him.

Wait. Wait. Wait. It has to be perfect.

Wait. Wait.

※ ※ ※

On a deserted street corner some ten blocks distant, Private Omri Petrenko and Private Gustav Atak had been assigned to a two-man security detail. They stood in the heat of late summer, bored. Well, at least Omri was bored. With Gustav it was impossible to tell. The man wouldn't shut up.

Omri disliked chatter for chatter's sake. In fact, there were days were he hardly said a word to anybody. But some people have to fill every second with the sound of their own voice. It is like they are worried that if they stop talking their brain will start working.

"...a really fine Joshuan woman. You know the type? You almost want to fall down and worship at the feet of women like that. Only she knew it. And she used it to her advantage."

Or maybe she just didn't like you that much. Maybe she wanted a little fucking silence.

It was bad enough that he was stationed at this useless location, far from the main action of the Patriots Parade. It was bad enough that he had to miss the coronation of his friend and fellow Guardsman, Major Schmidt...*No, General Schmidt.* True, he knew who Schmidt really was. A lowly private like himself. But did that matter? No, Schmidt had led Omri and Gustav and all the others to freedom from the Ulani prison. Then he had led them to victory in battle. What was more, Omri liked the man personally. He had been his driver for a while; they had many good conversations out there on the desert roads. Yes, General Schmidt deserved everything he got.

Missing the parade for a man he admired was bad enough. But if Omri had been by himself, this security detail might have been a nice break from his usual Guardsman duties. He could have read a book; Omri loved a good war story. Actually, it didn't even have to be good. He had stacks and stacks of the things, cheap editions written by authors with made-up names who penned half a dozen books a year. He knew which of these authors were better than others, but he read them all, taking comfort in the predictable turns of phrase and plot mechanisms. Soon he would have exhausted the supply of these books at the Baikal Guard librarie. Then he would have to find some new type of story.

But his latest book sat untouched in his jacket pocket. Twice he had taken it out and twice he had put it away. *An Honorable Death* it was called, by someone named Alexi Tovic.[10] It was a piece of trash, surely, but Omri was eager to return to it. The main character, a lieutenant who rises through the ranks thanks to bravery in combat, reminded him of Schmidt. Omri didn't know whose *honorable death* the title referred to, but he hoped it wasn't the brave lieutenant.

Now Gustav was talking about war. "You know, I volunteered to strap one of those artery bombs to my chest and blow those sheep-fuckers back to hell. Boom! But it turns out someone else already had the job."

Sure you did. I seem to remember a certain private about to piss his pants at the thought. That wasn't you, was it?

Gustav suddenly shut up. A car was approaching. Omri had been leaning against the wall, but now he stood up straight and put his hands on his rifle. The car wasn't slowing, though it was impossible to miss the barricade blocking the street. Omri raised one hand, gesturing for the car to stop.

"Fucker isn't stopping. What should we do, Omri?"

"Easy."

"Doesn't he see us?"

"Easy."

The car was only twenty meters off now. Omri waved his hands. *Turn around.* The car slammed on the gas, tires squealing. It struck the side of the barricade and sent it flying. *He's aiming for us.* The car struck Gustav, rolled forward, backed up. Then it sat gunning its engine. Omri backed up against the wall. *Please oh please just let me . . .*

---

[10] Translators' Note: It would seem that in his early years, Aleksandr Tuvim authored several such books as a means of quick income. The similarity between the names has led to us to speculate this might be one; we were unable to verify this during our research.

The car struck Private Omri Petrenko head on, pinning him against the wall of a building, mashing his legs to pulp and severing them from his torso. He slumped over the hood, blood bubbling from his mouth. For a moment, everything was still. Then the driver's-side door opened and Mayor Adams's agent stepped out. He moved around to the hood and put his fingers to Private Petrenko's neck. Satisfied, he walked calmly down the street and disappeared around the corner. This was hardly the death Omri would have envisioned for himself, but it was the one he got.

※　※　※

Nikolas stepped a bit closer to the street, still a safe distance from the bomb. He trusted Slug's ingenuity, but makeshift devices were prone to failure. Beside him, a teenage couple was handing telescopic lenses back and forth, giggling at the spectacle.

"May I borrow those for a moment?" Nikolas asked.

The boy clearly did not want to hand over his prized possession, and he likely did not want to seem weak in front of his sweetheart.

"I'll give you ten drams for just one minute with them," Nikolas said. "How does that sound?"

"Let me see the money."

Nikolas produced a ten-dram note and the exchange was made, though the boy stared at him untrustingly. Nikolas felt almost bad for having ruined the romantic mood the two had been enjoying. *But I was about to do that much more violently anyway.* He scanned the crowd for his men and saw they were all in place. He turned his attention to the head float. There was a high-ranking military man waving like a puppet at the front of the float. *That must be the bastard General Schmidt.* His back was turned to Nikolas; he was saying something to the Joshuan officials lined up behind him. There were various subministers and aides, military officials and water-barons—a veritable who's-who of Joshua City's power elite. Nikolas felt the swell of excitement and revolutionary righteousness. *This is going to cripple them.*

Just as he was about to give the signal to depress the detonator, the man he supposed was General Schmidt turned 180 degrees to offer his cheerful waving to the Joshuans on the other side of the float. It was then that Nikolas saw his face. *It can't be.* Nikolas did not give the signal, even though the slow-moving float was just above the strike point. He took a few steps toward the street and adjusted the telescopic lenses. The boy grabbed his arm, worried he was trying to make away with the lenses. Nikolas shrugged him off without a word. He stared at General Schmidt's face. But it wasn't General Schmidt's face; it was Marcik's. The float was nearly past the strike point now, yet Nikolas stood stunned and indecisive. He was certain now that it was his brother.

The float was now well past the strike point. Nikolas cursed under his breath, then saw the float behind his brother's. He scanned it quickly and saw it was covered with Guardsmen, no civilians. He couldn't let this moment go to waste. He waited until the second float was directly over the explosives and signaled.

There was a slight rumble in the pavement and then a deafening explosion of concrete and metal and human screams.

※ ※ ※

Armory Sergeant Tenzin watched the lower half of his left leg shoot from its knee joint and fall over the edge of the shattered float. The grisly stump poured a dark red stream. To either side of him, Guardsmen lay charred and broken, eyes staring lightlessly into the panicked crowd. He reached for the wound and saw that his left hand was also missing. He thought of his wife, and just before the pain rushed in through the shock, he was disappointed with the absurd thought that now he would not be able to enjoy sex with his wife tonight due to his injuries. He screamed and screamed; as he passed out from blood loss, he heard his own screams as the distant wails of a dying animal.

※ ※ ※

General Schmidt's float was hit by large shards of concrete, one piece shattering the face of the Subminister of Internal Defense with a sickly wet crunch. The man lay screaming and writhing on the float's floor. General Schmidt looked back to where the explosion came from and saw bodies strewn haphazardly on the ground. He climbed down and ran to where a boy lay on the street and picked him up, carried him away from the flames and rubble. When he had the boy safely in the arms of the military mediks they had stationed on-site, General Schmidt ran back to free other others from the debris. He only barely noticed the flash of the kameras' bulbs as the newspaper reporters gathered near.

%% %% %%

The following day *The Joshuan Harbinger* and several smaller newspapers, even those not overly warm to the Adams administration, ran fotografs of General Schmidt carrying the small boy away from the flaming debris. The boy had a gash on his forehead that sent a thin rivulet of blood down his face, and General Schmidt's uniform was smudged with charcoal-colored filth. In short, it was a better foto than the entirety of the Ministrie of Information could have dreamed up with all their propagandistic fervor. Now the war hero who had fought to defeat the Ulanis in the Outer Provinces had proven himself a hero at home as well. Mayor Adams thanked the Seven Prophets—even though he did not believe in them—for the good fortune of the attack. What were a dozen Guardsmen and a few civilians compared with the usefulness of that one foto?

It also gave him the perfect opportunity to blame The Underground for the deaths of Schmidt's men from the desert. Mayor Adams summoned General Schmidt to his office to tell him the sad news that he was not the only target of yesterday's attacks.

"There's our hero," Mayor Adams said, unable to keep his joy at this fortunate turn of events out of his voice.

"You can call me that when I've found the cowards who would stage such an attack."

"You're going to want them even more after you hear what I have to say."

General Schmidt sat silently as Mayor Adams explained that Samir, Omri, Gustav, and several other Guardsmen he had fought with had been killed, and he remained silent as Mayor Adams speculated that he, General Schmidt, had likely been the real target of the parade bombing and that there must be some double-agent in the Ministrie of Defense who had given away the addresses of these brave Guardsmen. An investigation was underway, Mayor Adams assured General Schmidt, that would determine who this double-agent was and why the revolutionaries had targeted him and his men.

"And though I don't want to burden you further on this day, I fear I have no choice," Mayor Adams said. "I would like to promote you to head of the Subministrie of Internal Defense. You have proven yourself in combat, and now you have proven you can protect Joshuans here at home."

"I don't know what to say."

"Say yes. The city needs you. And you can make avenging your fellow Guardsmen your first task in office."

"Yes," General Schmidt said, "I'll do it."

General Schmidt thanked Mayor Adams and left in a conflicted state—enraged at the loss of men he had served with, yet grateful that he now had the means to right that wrong. He vowed to himself that he would catch and kill every one of those revolutionary bastards.

※ ※ ※

Back in The Underground, Nikolas contrived a story of the detonator's malfunction and held his tongue as his heart wrenched in his chest when Slug began slapping himself in the face over and over and then ran to his laboratory saying "wrong, wrong, wrong . . . " and letting out little whimpers of self-hatred. Elias pointed out that he had warned against trusting Slug with such an important task.

"It's not his fault," Nikolas said. "It could have been any number of things. We knew there were risks going in."

"As Komrade Sara learned all too well."

Mouse's face clenched at the mention of Sara's name. She hadn't said a word since her death. Sara had died in the explosion and they had been forced to leave her body behind.

"What are we going to do?" Endre asked.

"We're going to burn The Hub to the ground," Mouse spat out. "That's what we're going to do."

For the rest of the evening, they drank heavily and joylessly.

CHAPTER NINE

WE ARE MESSENGER

M ESSENGER CAME from near and far. From the sparkling sea-shores of Baikalingrad, from the grassy plains of Baikyong-do, from the mountainous passes of Ulan-Ude, from the valley below where the Selenga River forks, from the rocky northern cliffs of Larki Island, from the limestone flats of Kazhstan, from the sand-colored temples of Al-Khuzir, Messenger came. By foot, by horse, by karavan, by rail or truck, alone, in pairs, as the hired escorts for rich men and valu-able cargo, accompanied by vast armies, Messenger came. By sunrise, by moonlight, in broad day, under forest cover where not even stars got through, along lonely dirt roads, over vast paved highways, through unmarked fields, with haste, Messenger came. Messenger came bloody and wounded, with unfinished business, flush with bounty, carrying gold or human heads or nothing at all. Messenger came down the river's course to the Proval Delta, where the Selenga forks in eight branches, spilling into the Baikal Sea, to the ruins of the Eighth City, the city of Messenger, where the many became one.

This always: many paths, one destination.

※ ※ ※

In the cavern beneath the abandoned temple, Messenger gathered. There were ten arched openings around the elegantly carved cavern wall. One small torch lit each opening. Nine figures emerged and stood at the edge of nine openings, the small light from the torches casting their robed shadows across the length of the room. Small splashing echoes came from the baikal-clear pool at the bottom of the cavern. One of the openings was empty. None of the nine figures looked in the direction of the unoccupied space.

"We are Messenger," nine voices said in unison. They stepped forward, walked slowly down their steep staircases, and converged on the shallow pool in the center of the room.

One waded through the water and stopped at the rock altar in the center of the pool. He pushed the hood of his robe back, showing his face clearly. His red hair was slicked back against his head; his faced was leathered from much desert travel; there was a thick raised scar along his left cheek.

"Messenger is here to join his brothers," he said. "We offer testimony. On Larki Island, this Messenger's efforts have been fruitful. The Second Calamity is nigh."

"We are Messenger," eight voices said in unison.

The second one waded through the water and stopped at the rock altar. He pushed his hood back, showing his face to all. "Messenger is here to join his brothers," he said. "We offer our testimony. In Baikyong-do, The Tongue is rising among his people, as we planned. This Messenger helped him in his functions as ambassador, learning much useful information at a meeting with the ambassadors of the Seven Cities. The New Era is coming."

"We are Messenger," seven voices said in unison.

The third waded in, pulled back his hood, showed his face. "Messenger is here to join his brothers," he said. "We offer our testimony. Among the Joshuans, this Messenger found and trained a man he believes to be the Harbinger."

There was no reaction from the others. In the silence after his proclamation, the shimmering water echoed thinly on the walls of the cavern.

"The weight of this news is massive. But he took to the Messenger training as no outsider ever has."

"We are Messenger," six voices said in unison.

The fourth waded forward. He turned back his hood. "Messenger is here to join his brothers," he said. "We offer our testimony. In the Outer Provinces, on a lowly karavan, this Messenger found a man he believes to be the Harbinger. The weight of this news is massive." Silence again. "He was not trained in the ways of Messenger. He possesses the qualities of the Harbinger without need for instruction. He will usher in the New Era."

"We are Messenger," five voices said in unison.

The Messenger ceremony continued until the last one waded through the pool and stepped up to the altar. He pushed back his hood. "Messenger is here to join his brothers," he said. "We offer our testimony. Al-Khuzir is developing as planned. May the Second Calamity call forth the New Era, brothers. And may we find the Harbinger. We have heard of two possible Harbingers. We should recall that our tradition hints at the possibility of more than one."

"We are Messenger," nine voices said.

%. %. %.

They gathered in close. They set their left hands on the small altar. They looked at each other's faces as they pulled out their knives. They splayed their fingers wide, their shoulders now touching. They set their knives at the top knuckle of their smallest finger. Still looking at each other, they pressed slowly yet firmly until the blade's edge severed the finger and met the stone beneath.

"We have lost a member of Messenger. We are still One, but less by one."

CHAPTER ONE

THE WAY THINGS WERE

1.

I HAVE BEEN CHARGED with writing a history of Joshua City—to tell the stories of the people, to preserve an image of the way things were—and as explained much earlier in this ever-growing document, I have chosen what I call a *novel-history* as the form for our story. I have attempted, to the best of my limited abilities, to stay true to recorded facts and my own memories from the time in question. Looking over this ponderous stack of pages, I suddenly doubt my choices and my ability to carry the task to its conclusion. It seems unconscionable that one man should create the definitive narrative of an era. Just think of the impossibility of such an endeavor.

We tend to confuse history, memory, and the past. Allow me to offer a provisional way of distinguishing these three notions. History is the accumulation of cultural documents that record, however accurately or inaccurately, certain aspects of the past. These documents, even when devoid of outright falsities, include facts and events selectively, leaving out exponentially more than they include. History is as much the expurgated story a culture tells itself about itself as it is a recording of actual past events. And this story differs at various times in a culture's development. One might say that history is always changing.

Memory, however, is a more personal version of history. As our skolars at Joshua University tell us, memory is likewise selective and ever-changing—and, to my great chagrin, ever-fading as we age. But memory has the virtue of including myriad events that would seem trivial to the historian—the way a certain pastry tasted, the despairing clutter of the alleyways that housed the nekrotic homeless, the sweet-chemical perfume of a particular teacher I had as a boy (a teacher who first sparked in me the rudiments of romantic interest as well as a love for literature and learning in all its iterations). We have false memories; we have fragmented memories; we have faded memories. But they are ours, personal and charged with the drives of life.

Then we have the past. It is important to note that neither history nor memory can ever fully access the past, but rather only approximate it with varying degrees of success and failure. The past is truly what happened, exactly as it happened, observed from all angles simultaneously. Sadly, all of our careful archiving and attentive memorization will only give us a fraction of the past, and what little we do get will be distorted by the biases inherent in all human knowledge, to say nothing of the intentional falsities printed in a great majority of history books.

Think also of the *Book of the Before-Time*. Many Joshuans take it as literal truth, but really, how much of it is even remotely verifiable? But then again, why should we care about its accuracy? It has thoroughly shaped our history and our personal lives whether it is true or not. This, too, I have to contend with: the myths that entangle themselves with events and charge them with extra meaning or grotesquely distort them.

And yet I accepted and continue to accept my task. I have dutifully told you what I know about the friendship of Adrian Talbot and Nikolas Kovalski, how they came together and went their separate ways. I have told you how Nikolas left Joshua University to pursue something more urgent. I have told you about Marcik Kovalski. I have told you about Adrian and Marcik's respective journeys beyond the Outer Wall, and how they both returned as new men, Marcik quite literally. I have told you how Nikolas was there waiting for him and how his last-second decision—some would call it a weakness—not to kill his brother altered the course of Joshuan history for decades to come. Had he acted differently, I might not have been sent to a work camp and this strange chronicle would never have been written.

History skolars speculate that there is something called a *hub-moment* which leverages history in a radically new direction. There is a clear *before* and a clear *after* in regard to a hub-moment. The Great Calamity described in the *Book of the Before-Time* is the prime example of this theory of history, but I maintain that such events need not be massive in scope. They often are, of course, but they are not necessarily so. I do not have time here, nor would it be the place, to develop a full systematic philosophy of history; suffice it to say that I wonder if there might not be thousands of hub-moments—not merely the grand historical events usually discussed under this rubric. I have tried as much as possible to focus on those hub-moments within the domains of recorded history and accessible memory, as well as the connective tissue that forms them. I do not make any claims on the objective past. If there are any gods, they would be the only entities with access to that opaque region of Being known as the past. My job is to tell the story that Joshuan culture tells itself about itself through its history, literature, and memory.

In the months that followed the failed attack on the Patriots Parade, Nikolas and the other members of The Underground scrambled to find other targets and to undo the damage to their movement caused by the botched attempt. They never took credit for the attack, as they had planned to do. They even engaged in a campaign of misinformation, spreading rumors that it had been an inside job, something the Adams administration orchestrated in order to gain a firmer grip on the populace. They redoubled their efforts feeding the homeless and offering minor medikal care for nekrotics and others in need. Nikolas made greater demands on his operatives to recruit new members. They organized public protests against the new conscription law which allowed Mayor Adams to "recruit" any able-bodied male in the city. But most of all, The

Underground engaged in several raids on munitions holdings to arm themselves for the coming battle.

But I have gotten ahead of myself. I had meant to speak of Abraham Kocznik, who has not factored into my narrative overmuch of late. Let us consider this man from a distance for a moment.

Abraham was an engineer, first of train technology, then of surveillance devices, and later of that strange mansion on the cliffs of Baikal. He made the devices that move history but made few appearances in history itself. It was not until Adrian, needing money to continue his studies in the absence of Doktor Brandt, was hired to be Lydia Kocznik's pedagogue that Abraham truly became a historical figure.

Nevertheless, Abraham strikes me as the perfect microcosm of history and memory. We almost have to conceive of him as a historical hub-moment unto himself—if such a moment can be said to span a life— yet he ended as a man who lost himself in memory. And so it is, with so much behind us, that I choose to open Part III of this novel-history with Abraham Kocznik, that citizen of his own private realm of history.

2.

LIKE EVERY new visitor to the Kocznik mansion, the first thing Adrian noticed was The Infinite Hallway. It was not, of course, actually infinite. But it did jut out some seventy or eighty meters unsupported, tapering to a needle point over the Baikal Sea. That it had not fallen into the water was an architectural marvel. In the process of his research on his new employer, Adrian had read an interview where Abraham described the physics of the hallway. It had something to do with the intricate angles of steel crossbeams, the thickness of the glass, the fact that the hallway sloped every so slightly upward. But even Adrian, with his scientific acumen, had not fully understood the explanation. He hoped he would not be required to use the hallway much. The thought of walking out over the cliff's edge with nothing but transparent support beneath him was unnerving.

And it wasn't just the hallway that was bizarre. The entire house had been described as a "tumorous growth of a diseased psyche twisted with grief." (The phrase was so odd and overblown that Adrian had remembered it verbatim.) Still, reading about the mansion was one thing; seeing it firsthand was a different matter. Half of the foundation rested on the expansive grounds of the estate, while the other half perched on a sheer cliff face. The lower level of the house was built into the cliff itself; the upper levels were piled on top of each other like haphazardly stacked puzzle pieces. The third floor stuck out farther over the grounds than the second; and the fourth floor was little more than a turret, like a strange skullcap. A half-arch extended out of the wall of the house onto a stone patio, touching down in the midst of benches and garden chairs. The garden itself was a patchwork of exotic plants, tall furry trees and birdbaths, tiny ponds and greenhouses.

Adrian took as much of this in as he could while the car made the long curve up the driveway to the mansion. The driver hopped out and ran nimbly around the back of the car to fetch Adrian's bags. Adrian looked up at the looming upper stories of the house, with their windows of various sizes and shapes—some round, some triangular, some bulging concavely. This was to be not just his new place of work, but his place of residence as well. He would continue his studies at Joshua University, but living here would save him the trouble of a new roommate and the expenses of making his own food. Besides, he only had to be on campus two days a week this semester, so the added travel time would not be overly tedious.

"You'll get used to it," the driver said, seeing Adrian's apprehension at the spectacle of the house.

An old servant-woman greeted them at the door and gave some quick instructions to the driver about the bags. The interior of the house was as odd as the outside. In the middle of the foyer was a staircase leading nowhere; it went up a wall and stopped; on the opposite wall was a door five meters off the ground with no stairs leading to it.

"You come this way," the old woman said, in a mottled common Slovnik. "He waits for you."

She walked quickly for her age. Adrian wanted to ask her about some of the odd things they passed but decided against it. It might seem rude on his first day. He followed her up an actually functional set of stairs.

"What is your name?" Adrian asked the servant-woman.

She looked surprised and flattered that he wanted to know. "Agnieszka, sir."

They came to a door. Agnieszka knocked lightly. Adrian heard nothing from the other side of the door before she opened it and motioned for him to enter.

Abraham Kocznik was looking out the window in a posture of contemplation.

"You can come over here if you'd like," he said in a soft voice. "Agnieszka, bring us some tea. And maybe some teacakes. Would you like some teacakes?" This last was directed at Adrian, but without waiting for him to answer, he spoke to Agnieszka again. "Yes, a plateful of teacakes. The good ones."

The woman left. Adrian approached the window, making his way across the strangest room he had ever seen. It was low and long and the walls and ceiling were made of smooth metal, curving in and down as you approached the end of the room. The windows themselves were at head height, two small portals of thick glass. *It's the inside of a train engine,* he realized. *One of the old ones, before the Kocznik trains.* The Kocznik engine had made this sort of engine obsolete, and it struck him as curious that Kocznik would make a shrine to the thing he had helped to kill. There was a desk cluttered with blueprints and grafs and other papers with scribbled math. He walked around the other side of the desk and stood beside Mr. Kocznik. The windows, small as they were, nevertheless offered a surprisingly good view of the garden.

"I like to look out these windows," Mr. Kocznik said with quiet pleasure.

In the garden, a child entertained herself. She removed various props from boxes and set them up in an elaborate display. It was hard to see what all of the items were, but there were life-sized figurines and clothing involved.

"My daughter Lydia," Mr. Kocznik said. "Your pupil. Should you accept the job."

"I'd like to meet her," Adrian said.

"You will," Mr. Kocznik said. "But first let's drink some tea. I think you'll find that Agnieszka, or Agnes as Lydia calls her, makes the perfect teacake. Not too dry or crumbly."

"That sounds nice," Adrian said, not knowing what to say.

They sat down and Mr. Kocznik asked Adrian various questions about himself, though he didn't seem overly interested in the answers. Adrian didn't get the impression that the man was callous, only that he was very much distracted.

"As you know from the advertisement," Mr. Kocznik said, and paused to look around, as though trying to locate it, "you would have to be here for a few hours in the morning and then a few more in the evening. We would feed you and you can use all of our facilities. There's a private room we've set up. It's nothing princely, but it's got a good desk." Here he looked around again, at nothing in particular, and went silent long enough that Adrian wondered if he should interject. Finally, Mr. Kocznik continued, "And I imagine it will be nicer than what you had at university, at least if it's the way I remember it." He barked out a strained laugh. "So what do you think? Will you take it?"

"This all seems very generous," Adrian said.

"Why don't you meet Lydia before you give me a final answer?" Mr. Kocznik said.

※ ※ ※

The nice man came out into the garden with slow cautious steps. Lydia could tell the man was nice just by the way he walked—a little confused, like he wasn't sure of his right to be there. She continued arranging the mannequins and pretended not to notice him. She consulted the foto again. Something was missing. Abraham was in a reclining sun-chair with his shirt unbuttoned. Vivian was standing, squinting into the sun, wearing a big-brimmed hat that shadowed most of her face. There. One of Abraham's sandals was hanging half off his foot. She adjusted the sandal and went back to work. Every detail had to be perfect or her motion-foto would be ruined. Maybe the nice man could be part of the motion-foto too!

THE SCREENPLAY OF THE SCREENPLAY
a Screenplay
by Lydia Kocznik
(as imagined by your dear author)

EXT. KOCZNIK MANSION—DAY

Lydia Kocznik, a very witty and talented eleven-year-old girl, is in the garden arranging a pair of mannequins, one male and one female. She dresses them with clothes from a box, gives them accessories, and positions them carefully. She consults a fotograf, adjusts one of the mannequins, and satisfied, walks over to a kamera a few feet off. The kamera is one of those old-fashioned ones with a bulb on a string.

A NICE MAN enters the garden. She motions for him to wait. She squeezes the bulb on the kamera and it takes a fotograf. She shakes her head in frustration.

LYDIA
(to self)

No, stupid. That's still not right.

The nice man comes around her side of the kamera, to see what she is seeing.

NICE MAN

What are you doing?

LYDIA

Making a film.

NICE MAN

Isn't that just a regular kamera? How can you make a motion-image
film without the proper kamera?

Lydia gives him a tell-me-something-I-don't-know look.

LYDIA

A film is just a bunch of fotografs, silly. You just show them real fast.

NICE MAN

What is the film about?

LYDIA

Abraham and Vivian. The trip they took to the desert spa. Here.

*She hands him the fotograf. He studies it. Then he compares it to the
mannequins.*

NICE MAN

It looks exactly the same.

LYDIA

That's the problem. Hold this.

*She hands him the squeezebulb for the kamera. She walks over to the
mannequins and positions herself between them.*

LYDIA

Do it.

The nice man squeezes the bulb.

LYDIA

Now it will be like I was there.

(suddenly grave)

That was the last time she was alive, you know. They were very much
in love. They didn't take me because I had school. Sister Nadya's.
I hated it there. Only now Abraham says I don't have to go anymore.

(more brightly)

I guess that's why you're here. Come on. One more.

She rummages through the box and produces another fotograf.

LYDIA

Help me.

They look for props to match the fotograf.

LYDIA

This one was taken before I was born. See how young they were? Don't
you think it's funny how we don't fear the time before we were born?
I mean, everybody's so afraid of death. What's the difference?

NICE MAN

Well . . . I suppose we can't fear what's already happened to us.
Only what might happen.

Lydia frowns, unconvinced.

LYDIA

Only... one other thing. If you take a fotograf and it's exactly like the other one, how do you know which one was real? It's like the story about the ship. There was a big beautiful ship and every night a thief came and took a board. And then every morning, the shipowner replaced that board. Eventually, the entire ship was different. Which one was the real ship?

NICE MAN

But your fotografs aren't exactly the same.

LYDIA

I know. Mine are better.

⁄⁄ ⁄⁄ ⁄⁄

Abraham watched Lydia and the new pedagogue do whatever it was they were doing in the garden. They seemed to be getting along well, thank the Seven. He liked this Adrian; something about him. A sadness he recognized. He no longer trusted people without some obvious wound. Adrian would make a good companion for Lydia. He reflected not for the first time that Lydia could have used a sibling—a little brother or sister might have helped her adjust. She had spent too much of her childhood playing alone. And she rarely enjoyed the company of other children her own age. Perhaps this young pedagogue was precisely what she needed.

⁄⁄ ⁄⁄ ⁄⁄

There had been a time when things might have been different.

"Would you like to know the sex?" the koroner had asked him. Vivian lay dead on a metal slab in the other room.

Abraham didn't understand the question.

"The sex of your child, sir."

"I have a daughter. At home."

The koroner glanced at his paper work.

"I see that. I'm referring to the child your wife was carrying. Some people like to know. That way, if they've picked out any names..."

Pregnant. Abraham struggled to process this new information while the koroner waited for him to respond. Finally, he shook his head in the negative. What could matter less than the sex of an unborn fetus that might not even be his?

He or she—*it*—might have made a good friend for Lydia.

How had it all gone so wrong? Even now it made no sense. A dream. They had left for the desert with a sense of renewal. The drive north, along the coast of the Baikal Sea, through the desert night and into the morning. They had been warned by the Guardsmen at the Joshua City Customs and Regulations checkpoint not to stop for anyone or anything. While the war had not reached up here—and except for a few small fishing villages, the land was largely uninhabited—banditii were still a problem.

Abraham and Vivian had a driver, Cesar, who had been with them for years, but for this trip Abraham had insisted on driving them himself. It would be more private that way; besides, Cesar could use a vacation of his own. Midway through the trip, they passed a truck stopped in the road, smoke curling from its hood. The driver of the truck looked at them in dismay and perhaps hostility as their headlights washed over him and passed by.

"You aren't going to stop?" Vivian asked. "He needs help."

"And get us robbed or worse?" Abraham said. "You heard what the Guardsmen said."

Vivian gave him a look of scornful pity.

"Do you want me to turn around?" he asked. "Because I will, if you insist."

Vivian didn't answer, and so they kept driving north.

It was late winter and the drive up was cold. But as they pulled into the resort, it grew warmer, everything heated from below by a vast network of hot springs. The air reeked of sulfur, but apparently you grew accustomed to that. A concierge greeted them and the other new arrivals—mostly well-dressed couples with Joshuan accents. The concierge took their bags, and escorted them to their room, pointing out various attractions and amenities. There was an aviary, a stable with thoroughbreds, riding paths, a pavilion with a dance floor, two bars and a restaurant, men's and women's bathhouses, a sauna of hot rocks and cedar chips, and of course the hot springs themselves. There were pools of varying sizes, some as small as private baths, some as large as small ponds. You could feel the lagoon-like heat; it was like nothing he had ever experienced.

In the distance was a vast network of hedges. Unseen birds chirped and twittered in the branches.

"Is that . . . ?" Abraham ventured.

"Yes, that is our infamous Lovers Maze," the concierge said. "It was designed by the famous Doktor Anwym Laikan, whom I am sure you know all about. She thought that by going into the Lovers Maze together, couples could get to the bottom of their relationship. The process relies on her theory of hub-mind, which develops in all close human relations, particularly among soldiers who have fought together in battle and romantics lovers—any relationships that form under extreme emotional and physical situations. Some of you have likely heard of hub-thought, the phenomenon of an entire society or culture sharing quasi-unconscious assumptions or beliefs; in order to understand hub-mind, just take that concept and apply it to a smaller group, usually two or three, and give it more personal and emotional charge. That these two groups—soldiers and lovers, which seem so disparate—should most commonly exhibit hub-mind confuses many people at first, but I assure you, after reading her case studies—and especially after you have walked the Lovers Maze—you will understand exactly what she means. I cannot recommend the maze highly enough . . . though it's not without its perils. Many relationships have not survived it. Hidden pathologies of the psyche can be exposed, and sometimes these revelations are too much to handle. Sometimes it's best not to know the truth." The concierge stopped speaking abruptly, sensing he might have said too much in his enthusiasm for Doktor Laikan's work.

"Sounds like a bunch of herd-shit," Vivian whispered to Abraham.

It was this kind of willingness to cut to the essence of an issue that first made him love her. And just look at her—as all Joshuans did every day on the Silverville screen. How many men wanted to be with her? Thousands, of course. *Why should I be offended to be only one of the two?*

%. %. %.

That first night, they ate dinner in the resort's lavish restaurant. There were a few others scattered through the place: a young couple held hands in the candlelight; an older couple swayed on the dance floor of the adjoining pavilion; and, oddly, a lone man in a three-piece suit drank in easy solitude at the bar. But Abraham and Vivian had the patio to themselves. The peak season was still a few months off, and war had cut down on unnecessary travel to the Outer Provinces.

They had Baikal grouse in lemon butter, asparagus spears and wild rice, duck-fat dumplings with a fiery sauce. Vivian only picked at her food, opting instead to drink most of a bottle of wine. Abraham ordered a vodka martini and sipped it slowly during dinner. Vivian gave her wine a graceful swirl and watched it with a curiosity that landed somewhere between feline and scientific. When Abraham gave no indication of wanting a second drink, she ordered for him.

After a few more drinks and talk of how Lydia might be doing and how nice the restaurant was, Abraham suggested they dance. Abraham stood and extended his hand romantically, wearing the expression of a loving puppy. The pavilion had a raised dance floor and a pianist who supposedly could play any request you could think of. Vivian went over to the man and whispered her request.

"What did you ask for?" Abraham said when Vivian joined him on the dance floor, draping her arms over his shoulders, putting forth a show if affection. She pinched her lips in an I'm-not-saying expression.

The pianist began "The Single Bed," a song that had been popular in the early days of their marriage. Abraham nearly said something, but she kissed him and began their slow dancing. Abraham knew the words of the song so well he heard them despite the absence of a singer.

> *I'd sleep in the center of a king-sized bed,*
> *Just to be closer to you*
> *I'd lose all my mind and live in your head,*
> *Just to be closer to you*
> *I'd buy up the heavens and leave you for dead,*
> *Just to be closer to you*
>
> *But I wake up alone in my single bed,*
> *and I've never been farther from you.*
>
> *Yes, I've never been further from you.*

The smell of her. Abraham had read a study that said human attraction had as much to do with smell as anything else. There was lilac and honey, the smell of whatever she used to wash her hair. There was the smell of the powder she used in her underarms. There was cigarette smoke and sweat and wine, too, but even those were good smells. Her arms on his shoulders had barely any weight at all. He could feel her wonderful heat. He had never danced better.

At the end of the song, Abraham suggested to Vivian that they go back to the room. But she had another idea. They had yet to try the hot springs. Night swimming, wouldn't that be romantic?

She led Abraham by the hand, rejecting some of the bigger and more visible pools along the path. They came upon a small pool hidden by palm leaves. The steam rose off of it in great translucent clouds. The water, illuminated by torches on poles of wicker, was a deep green.

"What are you doing?" Abraham asked, when she began peeling off her bath-suit.

"What do you think?"

Topless, she lowered herself into the pool, wincing lightly at the water's temperature. Once fully immersed, she pulled off her bath-suit bottoms. With one foot, she kicked them up on to the side of the pool.

"There are people around," Abraham said.

"That's exactly the point," she said and scissored her legs, propelling herself backwards to the other side of the pool. Abraham stood there dumbly. "Your turn," Vivian said, a sexy challenge in her voice.

And she *had* done it precisely to challenge him, of course—to see if he would do something reckless, potentially embarrassing. He stood with his hands on the waistband of his swimming shorts.

"It's all right," she said. "You don't have to."

He slid into the pool with his swimming shorts still on.

※ ※ ※

Looking out of his window, Abraham wondered if Vivian would have approved of his hiring Adrian instead of insisting that Lydia matriculate at Sister Nadya's. Below, Lydia was putting the props back into their box and Adrian was helping her. Lydia said something and Adrian shook his head. Lydia waved her finger at him mock-scornfully, and Adrian laughed. Together, Adrian carrying the mannequins and Lydia struggling with the cumbersome bulk of the box, they went inside.

※ ※ ※

Following that first day at the resort, Abraham and Vivian established the routines that make vacationing its own life-in-miniature. They slept in most mornings, something they never did back home. After they woke and breakfasted, they went out to the enclosed gardens with their steam-heating. Abraham sat in the sun and did some light reading while Vivian hit a few balls around with the exercise instructor. She was still light on her feet from her years on stage. Her hair, pulled back, bounced in the sun. Abraham watched her between reading pages of a monograf on architectural mechanics. He hadn't told her yet but he wanted to build a house for her. For them. Something special.

Then it was usually time for a late lunch. They dined at the restaurant in that strange late afternoon silence. Perhaps Abraham would have a drink, which would leave him a little sleepy but full of goodwill. Vivian generally didn't drink until later in the evening, but she managed not only to catch up with Abraham but to surpass his level of drunkenness.

They went on leisurely promenades around the grounds. The paths were lined with cherry trees, their white petals falling like snow on the red clay walkways. A cool breeze seemed always to be blowing.

"I wish we could stay here forever," Abraham declared on their third day, as they walked down one of these paths. "Let's never go back."

※ ※ ※

Some days they went to the stables. Vivian was good with the horses. They liked to nuzzle against her hand as she fed them sugar cubes. The stablehand was an old grizzled man, half-deaf; Abraham would try to strike up a conversation with him while Vivian decided which horse to take out. She usually settled on a dappled grey, a wild-maned stallion that seemed to bear a special resentment of Abraham. Maybe it sensed that he had no interest in horses. He picked the same horse every time; a slump-backed old gelding that reminded him of one of Lydia's stuffed animals she had recently outgrown. While Vivian galloped across fields of sunflower and poppy, Abraham trotted in cautious circles in the dirt near the stable.

After that, they went back to their room. Abraham napped while Vivian read. When he woke up, it was time for dinner. More drinks, a late dip in the pools. She did not repeat her stunt of the first night, though he wished every evening that she would. They made love a few times, not with the fire of new lovers but rather the tenderness of long-time friends. If things were unexciting, at least they were peaceful.

※ ※ ※

Why did we wait until the last day to explore the maze? Abraham wondered now. It flooded over him again; Vivian was dead; and his every heartbeat struck her dead again.

※ ※ ※

The day before they left the resort, Vivian reclined on the bed and read aloud to Abraham from the pamphlet that had brought them here.

"The thing about the maze is that there is not a maze," she said, taking on a stentorian voice. "Or rather, the maze is your maze. You project everything into it. There is no maze as such." Here she threw the covers back, hopped out of bed, and, with professorial seriousness, paced the room in her underwear. Abraham smiled admiringly at her play-acting. *She can become anything.* "You will find nothing there that is not already in you. The maze will gaze back at you, of course, but it will be you who put the gaze in the maze." Peering over the edge of the pamphlet, she raised an incredulous eyebrow at Abraham. She continued: "It will be you gazing back at yourself, or if you are fortunate, *into* yourself. Everything at Khakusi Springs is about you coming back to the place you always were. You know, though you do not want to know. You hide your most essential self in symbolic trappings, and though we cannot hope to fully escape such trappings, it can be therapeutic and emotionally productive to begin to see the contours of this prison-house." And now she broke character entirely: "What is this stuff? Who thinks or talks like this?"

Abraham shrugged his shoulders dumbly, agreeing with her, but he wasn't entirely sure Doktor Laikan didn't have some wisdom in her charlatanism. Some of what she said Abraham had felt when he was younger and smoked blackroot. He sensed that all the meaning there was in the world was projected there by himself, that all he ever saw was his own psyche staring back at him. And Doktor Laikan got results. How many couples in Silverville swore by the Laikanian methods?

"We don't have to do it if you don't want to," he said.

"No, we came here to do this," Vivian said. "And it might even be fun. I always loved mazes when I was a little girl."

"You never told me that, I don't think."

"I might not have told anyone that. I just recalled it myself. Haven't thought of it in years."

She is mine right now. And she was beautiful. He could feel the jealousy creeping in at the edges of his mind, but he forced it away.

"Why don't you put that down and come back to bed?"

She gave him a knowing look. "Maybe I will."

As Vivian crawled tigress-like from the foot of the bed, something in him recoiled, and the image of her with Neil filled his mind. When she kissed him warmly, allowing her tongue to just barely breach his lips, he closed his eyes and made himself think of how many men would die to be here right now.

※ ※ ※

After the maze, Vivian told him everything he already knew. Well, not quite. She refused to name the man. She insisted it didn't matter and he couldn't exactly shake it out of her. Of course he knew it was Neil, but he wanted her to say it. Why was she protecting that water-bug? Did she worry Abraham could use his government connections to bring him harm?

Or was she protecting me? She didn't tell me about the child she was carrying either. Did she know it was Neil's? He had heard that women simply knew who the father of a child was, but he doubted that. That was likely another superstitious belief.

The maze was truly was incredible, an architectural wonder that Abraham couldn't help but appreciate. Vast hedges had been trimmed into the shape of the Seven Cities, with a maze of high shrubbery connecting them. Near the entrance was Joshua City, represented by a train running down some tracks. Beside it was Ulan-Ude, a pair of mountains and a forked river. At various points along the outside of the maze were the other cities, though all they could see from the entrance was a bit of the domed sun-temples of Al-Khuzir. The entire maze was about five thousand meters squared, the concierge had told them, or about the size of a modest estate in Joshua City.

"Look at that," Vivian said, giggling.

There was a sign hung over the entrance to the maze. It was hand-painted, with crude but effectively dramatic lettering:

<u>LOVERS MAZE</u>

LOVERS BE WARNED:

- This maze is not for the faint of heart
- It is for those lovers who truly wish to know the TRUTH about their love
- You might learn things you don't wish to know
- You may get LOST
- If you fear for your safety or are unable to complete the maze, push one of the RED BUTTONS placed regularly throughout the maze
- Someone will come get you straight away

Despite the histrionics of the sign, it did give Abraham pause. *But really*, he thought, *how complicated can it be?*

Very complicated, it turned out. About ten feet in, they came to their first split in the path. You could go straight; you could go left or right. All directions were the same—perfectly uniform green hedgerow extending about fifty meters before making an abrupt turn.

"Which way?" Vivian asked.

"Right," Abraham offered, for no special reason. He wanted to appear decisive.

"I was thinking left."

"Left then," Abraham said.

She looked at him skeptically. "Don't defer. You're always deferring."

"Fine then," he said. "Right. Does it really matter?"

Of course it did. "Let's go straight," Vivian said.

They continued, straight ahead. Along the way, they saw two of the red buttons. They turned right, then left, each thinking with petty satisfaction of how they had gotten their way after all, before they reached a dead end.

"Damn," Vivian said.

"We'll turn around, that's all," Abraham said.

They followed the path back to the original split. Vivian seemed annoyed at having to backtrack, but Abraham felt reassured. An entrance is also an exit, after all.

Vivian began walking right, and he followed. The path turned left and the entrance disappeared from sight.

Soon they had to choose a direction again. This time it was easier: by going straight they would continue along the outer edge of the maze; by turning through an archway to the left, they would head toward the maze's center. They turned left.

Maybe thirty meters later they encountered a more difficult choice. *Choices* would be more accurate. Three gaps in the hedge were lined up at three meter intervals. The two on the right would take them deeper into the maze, while the one on the left headed toward the maze's edge again.

"The middle one," Vivian said.

They went down the middle path, toward the maze's center. After about forty meters it dead-ended.

"I never realized it was so big," Vivian said. "What do we do now?"

Press the red button, Abraham thought. There was one just a few feet away. But that was a ridiculous thought. They had been in the maze perhaps twenty minutes. And besides, he did not want to be the one to do it.

"Turn around," he said.

They retraced their steps and came back to the gaps in the hedge. "You choose," Vivian said.

"You know this would go a lot faster if we had some kind of system," Abraham said.

"You're the engineer," she said. "Suggest something."

"We can't just keep heading toward the center."

"Maybe if we split up."

"Even if one of us found the way out," Abraham said, "how would that help the other one?"

"It was just a suggestion," Vivian said.

Let's just get out of this, he told himself. *Together.*

% % %

Twenty minutes later, they were still wandering lost. There were the twin kameleon heads of Baikyong-do. Again. Were they closer to the end or just going in circles? The sun was setting. With sudden childish panic, he imagined himself in here after dark. They turned left. They turned right. Another wall of endless green after another.

% % %

It did not take long for someone to come after he pushed the button. It must have been wired to the front office, because it was the concierge who came to their rescue.

He smiled sympathetically.

"It's all very silly, isn't it?" Vivian said.

They walked back to their room in stiff silence. She started to un-lock the door, but instead turned and leaned back against it, her hands crossed behind her.

"I've got to tell you something."

% % %

They passed their last night at the resort in bleak silence. There was a tasteless dinner. They both drank too much. Then there was the awk-ward moment back in the room when they tried to decide who would get the bed and who would sleep on the floor, or whether they should sleep side by side as if nothing had happened. In the end, they both took the bed, but slept as far apart as possible.

They did not know it would be their last night together. *What would we have done differently if we had known?* Of course, the question was nonsensical. Abraham, with his scientific mind, understood this. Knowledge of the impending disaster would have allowed him to avoid it. Still, nonsensical or no, it was a question he couldn't stop asking. The heart has its own urgent logic.

The drive was as morose as the night that preceded it. Vivian blew cigarette smoke out the window and it swept back into the car, making Abraham nauseous. He gripped the steering wheel. He imagined a faceless man, his enormous perfect phallus pounding into Vivian with machine-like efficiency. He imagined Neil.

"You're driving too fast," Vivian said.

The road was straight and flat, no trees or other impediments to their view for miles in any direction. The land around here made a glacial-white crust like the surface of the moon. It was cracked in a million places—the world's most boring jigsaw puzzle. He stepped down harder on the gas, thinking of all the times she had come home late from parties, kissing him with a mouth that had just been kissing Neil. He thought of the nude scene she had done in a recent film, how quick he had been to give his blessing. Together, they had practiced explaining it to Lydia. *It's part of Mommy's job. She's just pretending.* Now he didn't know which part was pretending and which was real.

"Slow down," she said. "You're scaring me."

He would never be able to say for sure whether there really was a man in the road. It didn't seem likely. Where would he have come from? Where did he go? Maybe it was an animal. Later, as he wandered in dazed circles in the desert heat, waiting for rescue that was a long time coming, he would see an enormous bird with great black wings perched on the wheel of the overturned car. He would see many things as the sun went down, a burning ball of recrimination and nightmarish import. The air was dry but his forehead was wet. *Get away from her*, he yelled or maybe just thought, picking up a rock and flinging it at the bird. The rock vanished and the bird did not move. Vivian's bloodied hand was still pressed against the window in a gesture of fatal goodbye.

3.

AFTER ADRIAN ACCEPTED the job, as he had been certain he would, Agnieszka led him to his new room. It was in a back wing of the house, on the third floor, a pleasant and private space.

"I will call you for dinner."

"Thank you," Adrian said.

Agnieszka nodded and left.

Adrian eased the door to the room open. He stood in the doorway and took stock of his new life. So many times he had started over—Saint Ignatius's when just a boy, Joshua University, the Laborers Hospital, his aborted attempt to join The Underground, and now here. In each case, there had been a new room and he had called it *his*. But he had little hand in the decoration or selection of the furniture; it was not his, but something borrowed.

The room was small and clean. As promised, there was a good desk of polished teak, a single window, a small clean bed with an ornate headboard. Despite its spars furnishings, it was nicer than any of his previous "fresh starts."

His bags were on the floor by the bed. He unzipped the smaller bag, took out a few books and a notebook. He arranged them on the desk. He sat down in the plush red chair. He leaned back luxuriously. The chair moved in perfect tandem with his body. The softness was perhaps too much, Adrian thought. It was as likely to put him to sleep as inspire real work. He leaned forward and placed his palms on the desk, running them along the smooth grain. He repositioned the books so that the stack was perfectly squared with the desk's edge. He took the notebook off the top of the stack. He opened it and, pen in hand, stared out the crescent-shaped window. The view was mostly obstructed by oaks in an explosion of late-summer foliage, but through a gap in the trees he saw a sliver of the Baikal Sea. It shimmered in the last of the afternoon's light.

He looked down. His pen hovered forgotten above the page. He closed the notebook and walked across the room to the bed. He sat down on its edge, testing its give. It was the best mattress he had ever felt. Falling back against it, he absorbed the coolness of the sheets. He let his eyes close momentarily, cocooned by a perfect white sail of bed linen.

Done with his self-indulgence, he began unpacking his clothes. He examined the shabby fare folded in his suitcase. The items were far too worn and modest for such a house. He was reminded of when he had arrived at Joshua University for his first semester. How Nikolas had stared at him as he unpacked; how self-conscious it had made him, aware of every little movement, of how it must look to this cynical and brooding stranger. Later, he learned that Nikolas was not like that; or rather, he was, but he was not *only* like that. *People are never as simple as they seem.* Like his current employer, who seemed kindly and a bit lost. Or Lydia, whom he did not know what to make of yet. He would have to learn to understand their world.

4.

ADRIAN HAD NEVER taught before. He picked the subjects he knew best to start with—the sciences, mathematics, and of course, theology. He would have to brush up on his Now-Time history and literature in the coming weeks. Actually, he might have to re-read some of the theological texts he had read before. He thought briefly of Alyosha, not really a thought, just a fleeting sense of that holy man.

Lydia had chosen a sort of parlor as their place of study. She was such a willful child, but her willfulness endeared her to him. It was not the demands of privilege he had expected from a spoiled girl, but a sign of a fiercely individual intelligence. There was a nice view of the grounds out the window, but Adrian closed the blinds; he wanted nothing to distract his pupil.

A few minutes later, precisely at nine o'morn, Lydia entered. She was freshly showered, her hair in a neat braid. She wore a school uniform. Adrian remembered what she had said about her former school that morning they had first met in the garden. What was it called? . . . Sister something. Someplace elite and expensive. He hoped he could come close to matching that level of education.

"I wanted to make it more like going to school," she said.

"I thought you hated that place," Adrian said.

"That's why I tore this part off, see?" She pinched part of the blouse and thrust it forward. There was a lighter patch and a circle of loose threads where some sort of emblem had been.

"It's our uniform now," she said.

"Do I have to wear one, too?" he joked.

She frowned. "Of course not. You're the teacher."

"Pedagogue."

She nodded. "I like that. It's more serious."

She skipped over to her chair and flung herself down in it. She primly crossed her legs and set her hands on her knee, in imitation of a high society lady. Adrian recalled reading in an article by the famous psychiatrist Doktor Laikan, titled in her playful way "Look at Me!: On the Public Development of the Ego in Precocious Children." Laikan argued that all children, but especially those of above-average intelligence or talent, must always test their worth and the validity of their powers against the friendly judging gaze of their adult supervisors. Adrian couldn't quite recall the entirety of Laikan's theory—he had read it for a class he wasn't much invested in, given its lack of connection to his direct field of study—and Laikan was as famously dense in her prose as she was playfully irreverent, so Adrian wasn't sure he had even understood it all. But the part of the theory that had stuck with him, the part that had struck him as immediately true, was the idea that children constantly put themselves on display, saying in effect, *Look at me!*, in order to test the boundaries of their abilities. And wasn't Lydia a nearly textbook example of this? Even her precociousness as an inciting factor for such behavior fit Laikan's theory. Recognizing his sudden interest in the subject, Adrian thought he might find that article and reread it as well; it might improve him as a pedagogue. And then just as suddenly, the thought came: *Perhaps I will change my focus at university to psychiatry.* But he let the thought disappear as quickly as it had appeared.

"Let's work," Lydia said.

"What do you want to start with?"

"I told you," she said. "You're the pedagogue."

"I'm not much of one, really. You're my first pupil. So I'm learning with you."

"You shouldn't tell me that."

"Tell you what?"

"Vivian said that in order to be successful you have to act successful. I heard her tell Abraham that once. 'You have to project *authority*,' Vivian said. They were fighting, though. They used to fight a lot." Here she paused, and she was all little girl. "But you know what's strange? I miss it. It's too quiet at night now."

Adrian didn't know what to say to that. He thought again that he should read more of Laikan's work. Should he console Lydia over the loss of her mother? She had no doubt heard it all before.

"Well, let's get started then," Adrian said, having come up with nothing to say about her mother's death or her parents' previous relationship. "I thought we might begin with mathematics."

He reached over and grabbed the book, from where he had so carefully placed it.

"What's that?" she said, pointing to Adrian's ancient worn copy of the *Book of the Before-Time*. Its cover was red cloth stitched with an intricate lattice-like design; much of the stitching had come loose.

He set the mathematics book back down. "That's the *Book of the Before-Time*," he told her.

"I know *that*. What I'm asking is, do we have to learn that?"

"It's an important part of Joshuan culture," Adrian said, lamely echoing his reasoning from earlier. "Many people believe in its teachings."

"Do you?"

"For me it's a source of solace," he said, strangely awkward in the presence of this inquisitive eleven-year-old girl.

"Abraham says it's superstition," she said. "He doesn't like what-do-you-call-them . . . *ideologues*. Are you an ideologue?"

"I'm a pedagogue, remember?" Adrian said, trying again at humor.

"A *gogue* not a *logue*," Lydia observed.

"And besides, that is not what I said we were learning today. We are doing mathematics today. And I'll talk to your father about what other materials he wants or doesn't want you to learn later."

Lydia ran her fingers along the worn threads of the book's cover.

"No," she said. "Let's do this. I want to know."

※ ※ ※

For the next hour or so, they read from the *Book of the Before-Time*, beginning with the creation story. Adrian paused occasionally to explain a difficult passage or to answer Lydia's questions.

"If this god created the world," Lydia asked at one point, "who created him?"

"That's a very good question," Adrian said. "That's an issue that has troubled theologians for as long as there have been theologians, and to be honest, I don't know the answer. I think some would say that God doesn't have a root cause. He just is. The unmoved mover, as some say. I've even heard some say that God is the Cosmos with all the planets and stars in it. When He created the Cosmos, He created himself. I still find myself thinking of Him as something outside of it, though."

"Then if He can just *be* without anybody creating Him, why can't the world just be, too? How do we know there's a creator?"

"We don't," Adrian said. "That's the thing about faith. Some would say that's the beauty of it. If you had proof, it wouldn't be faith."

The sophistication of her arguments reminded him of nights with the old Nikolas, back when they were roommates.

"So then…" she said. She had a habit of chewing her lip when thinking hard. "What makes you choose to believe in this one thing you can't prove and not a million others?"

Adrian had asked himself the same question many times. He didn't want to be one of those unquestioning believers who knelt in pews and poured money in coffers and thought they had done their duty to God.

"You don't choose it," he said. "It chooses you."

"When did it choose you?"

"I'll tell you about it later," he said, feeling that he had failed in his duties as a pedagogue. "Here, let's read the next story."

5.

LATER THAT EVENING Abraham, Adrian, and Lydia had their first dinner together. It was not clear who had arranged the dinner; Adrian suspected it had been Agnieszka, who seemed to be in charge of all the practical elements of the house in addition to keeping a tender eye on Abraham and Lydia's wellbeing.

If you had asked Adrian, he would have guessed the dining room had never been used before. But he would have been wrong. He would not, however, have been far off. It had been used only once since the construction of the house. There were many rooms that had never been used at all. There was The Water Room: you opened a door and were confronted with a wall of glass, behind which were hundreds of liters of inaccessible water, baikal-clear. There was The Crystal Prison: the first thing you saw when you opened the door was yourself. This was an effect created by the geometric arrangement of crystalline surfaces around the room. But it was not a mere reflection. A three-dimensional image floated in the center of the room, and unlike in a mirror, left and right were not reversed. In Abraham's previous existence, he had theorized about the reflective properties of certain crystals. But only now in his desperate obsession did he bother to explore those properties. To no use at all, some would argue.

Adrian sat down at one end of the lengthy table, a dozen seats between him and Abraham who sat at the other end. Lydia sat on one side of the table, halfway between them.

※ ※ ※

The one other time this room had been used was for Lydia's birthday just a few weeks earlier. Lydia had still been enrolled in Sister Nadya's, with the school year just about to start. Agnieszka had planned the party. She sent out invitations to all of Lydia's classmates. Agnieszka knew

Mr. Kocznik had important things to think about, especially now. This was why he had hired her.

Because Abraham Kocznik was still an important person—though he had, the affluent Joshuan mothers whispered among themselves, become a little strange after his poor wife's death . . . such a tragic accident . . . —almost all of the girls attended. Mamie, Danila, Josephine—the popular girls. They were all right, Lydia supposed. And Claudette was here. She wore a red bow in her hair and handed Lydia her present without a word. Lydia stacked it with all the other presents in a high pile on a side table.

Agnieszka brought out a strawberry cake, and Lydia did her best to be the gracious host in her frilly summer dress. The cake was many-layered and the paraffin candles flickered brightly.

"Eleven years old," Agnieszka said. "You are almost a woman now."

Lydia dreaded the idea of being an adult. Their lives were so unhappy.

"I should make a wish, right?" She wanted this to be perfect for Agnes.

"Anything you want."

Lydia held her silence for a long while. She considered what she should wish for. She gathered in her breath and swept it across the cake. The candles all went out. She had made her birthday wish, the contents of which no one will ever know.

Agnieszka nodded at Lydia, a motherly smile on her face. Lydia cut the cake and served it to each of her classmates. The girls formed a polite line to receive their slices, and, ladylike, waited until everyone was served to begin eating. Lydia served herself last. With dainty careful bites, the girls ate their cake, pretending, as they had been taught in their etiquette class at Sister Nadya's, to be amply satisfied with one small slice.

"Lydia, dear, this is the best cake I have ever eaten!" one girl said.

They dabbed their lips with silk napkins.

"Your father's house is just magnificent!"

The party fell silent. Lydia tried to say something. What was she supposed to do now? She looked to Agnes. Her father poked his nervous head around the corner. Agnes motioned him in, but he skulked back.

"Lydia," Agnieszka said, "don't you want to open all your wonderful presents?"

Lydia looked at the pile of ribboned boxes. Now the girls reverted to their natural state of squabbling childhood.

Danila shoved her present in Lydia's face. "Open mine first."

"No. Open mine."

Lydia was jostled as Mamie elbowed Josephine in an attempt to get to the center of the action.

"Mine's best. You'll see."

In the end, she chose the present from Claudette. Claudette blushed to be picked first. Her present was flat and rectangular and light as air. Lydia peeled back the tape and worked apart the tiny hard knot of the ribbon, careful not to tear the wrapping paper. Inside were several thin translucent sheets covered with lines and musical notes.

"It's a song my father wrote," Claudette said. "I thought you might learn to play it. It's for piano."

(Claudette's father was a composer. He had even written a concerto for Mayor Adams's inauguration ceremony. The Mayor had seemed visibly moved by the performance, though later, in a column about the ceremony for *The Joshua Harbinger*, a society critic had voiced objections to the decadent nature of the piece. *A statelier, less bombastic melody might have better suited the occasion*, he wrote in a tone of gentle condemnation.)

Lydia held the piece of music up to the light of the dining room's chandelier, and studied the busy bunches of notes, their elegant rise and fall on the lined staves.

"He wrote it for my mother," Claudette explained.

All the girls looked at Lydia. She continued holding the pages delicately. The girls were motionless, awaiting Lydia's reaction to the mention of mothers.

"What a stupid present," Danila said finally.

"You really should learn to be more tactful," Mamie added.

"I'm sorry," Claudette said. "I didn't think..."

"Clearly not."

"You forgot her mother is dead."

"It's beautiful," Lydia assured Claudette. "I can almost hear it."

She set the music down on the table.

Agnieszka picked up a bright red box. "Who is this one from, Lydia?"

"That's mine! Open that one next. I just know you're going to love it."

Agnieszka handed Lydia the present and urged her on. What followed was a parade of presents that said more about the giver than the receiver. Shoes from the finest department stores of Printz-Påhlsson. Gloves better suited for tea parties than protecting the hands. A pocketbook (this one from Danila, who despite being upset at having to wait to have her present opened, now gamely instructed Lydia on the proper placement of makeup and wallet and personnel affects in the pocketbook's many pouches). Lastly, Lydia opened the biggest box of them all. It was from Mamie, who as the daughter of a powerful weapons merchant, was perhaps the wealthiest girl at the party.

Lydia removed the lid of the enormous box and pulled out a long white dress with a cinched waist and flowing train. The fabric sparkled mysteriously, as if jewels were hidden within its very thread. The other girls awaited Mamie's explanation. She was their unspoken leader, older by a few months in age but more than that in composure, and they all looked to her for how they should behave.

"It's for your first society gala," she said. "I'm having mine this spring. You're invited, naturally."

"There will be boys there," someone said.

"You are very pretty, you know," Mamie said. "If only you took more effort."

She reached out and brushed Lydia's hair back.

Lydia put the dress back in the box and set it on the table.

"All the presents are wonderful," Lydia said. "Thank you. Thank you all."

Moments later, Lydia took Agnieszka aside and said, "Agnes, I would like the party to be over now."

※ ※ ※

But as I was telling you, Esteemed Reader, the dining room had not been used since that unfortunate party.

The air was stale, unturned. Adrian straightened his silverware and fidgeted with his napkin. Should he tuck it into his shirt? He sat with his hands folded in front of him on the table. His mind wandered to the lessons he might teach Lydia the next day and then to his own university studies, then to a series of trivial memories not worth recounting here.

Lydia idly braided the gold-and-dove-gray tassels hanging from the tablecloth, her left eye slightly squinted in concentration. Adrian wanted to join her in her game, for something to do with his hands if nothing else.

"Well," Mr. Kocznik observed, "here we are. Our first dinner."

Adrian fumbled for something to say. He unfolded the napkin and put it in his lap, smoothed it neatly with both hands.

"I think you will be impressed with Agnieszka's talents," Abraham added after a few elongated seconds.

"If it tastes as good as it smells," Adrian said, indicating the appetizers Agnieszka had set before them, "then I am certain I will be."

"Agnieszka is an excellent cook," Mr. Kocznik said, having nothing new to add.

"Why are we using *this* room?" Lydia said.

"This is a special occasion. It's Mr. Talbot's first night with us."

"We never use this room," Lydia told Adrian.

"Lydia," Mr. Kocznik admonished. "Pour our guest some wine. Mr. Talbot, would you like some wine?"

Abraham finished his own glass and motioned for Lydia to refill his as well. "Thank you. Very kind of you." He made a small bow of his head in playful deference.

Adrian took a small sip. "I don't usually drink. But, as you say, this is a special occasion." Adrian raised his glass to Mr. Kocznik and then to Lydia. He hadn't had a drink since his night with Leni. So strange to think of that now; unfathomable the changes that had occurred since that pleasant yet unfortunate encounter.

"So," Abraham said, "you're a doktor."

"Not yet," he said. "I am still studying."

"And what will your specialty be?"

"I must confess," Adrian said, "that's less certain than it used to be."

Mr. Kocznik took another drink of his wine, and with some effort, conjured up further interest. "What has your research consisted of thus far?"

"During my first year, I worked with the renowned Dr. Brandt on experimental kardiology."

"A major loss for Joshua City when that man died."

"I agree, sir."

"And have they found his murderers?"

"I don't think so," Adrian said, "but I was not in Joshua City most of the summer."

"That's right. I recall some sort of internship in the Outer Provinces?"

"I worked at the hospital in New Kolyma."

"That must have been so rewarding to a doktor like yourself."

Adrian did not bother to correct his new employer a second time. "Yes, very rewarding," he lied and drank more deeply from his cup.

"What I love most about your field," Mr. Kocznik said, "is that you get to mix the mechanical with the biological. My own work too often ignores the human element." He paused. "But that is also the pleasure of my work. It is so . . . neat . . . "

"And mine is often too messy."

Agnieszka brought in the first course of their meal. Desert-gazelle steak with a creamy roe-sauce. Adrian picked up his cutlery—which fork do you use for the first course?—and began cutting the meat.

Lydia let out a high-pitched laugh. "Not that one, dummy!"

Adrian blushed.

"Lydia, be nice," Mr. Kocznik said. "Use whichever fork you prefer, Mr. Talbot." Abraham considered this young brilliant man before him. "Let's do away with all formality, in fact. Would you please call me 'Abraham' from now on? I would consider it an honor."

"As would I, sir," Adrian said, switching his forks. "And, of course, call me Adrian."

"So, tell me more about your research."

"As I mentioned earlier, the only real research I conducted was as part of Doktor Brandt's experimental kardiology team," Adrian said, and then added with a hint of excitement, "We even successfully conducted corpse-to-corpse heart transplants. We were making real progress, I guess you could say, but . . . "

"But Doktor Brandt's untimely death put an end to all that."

"Yes."

"Something you learn after many years in the scientific field is that progress is never linear and is often impeded or makes a great leap forward due to historical accident. A wealthy patron finds a sudden interest in some technology and funds its development. Or a laboratory mishap turns out to reveal a radical new discovery. Or, in this case, a man is killed in cold blood and, ironically, kardiology is set back several years. In my own work, in fact, I would never have developed my 'Kocznik trains' without municipal funds. Had there been more political opposition to that funding—and though you would never think it now, there was political opposition at the time—I would never have been able to make the advances I did."

"Yes, precisely," Adrian said. "A former colleague of mine at Joshua University, my roommate in fact, had worked with nekrosis as a research project before being moved to experimental kardiology. He considered this a setback of course, but Doktor Brandt pointed out that the things he had discovered about human blood while working on nekrosis could be transferred to kardiology." Adrian took a bite of his food. "And vice versa, I guess."

"This is boring," Lydia said. "Have you ever treated a rotter?"

"The medikal term is *a nekrotic*," Adrian said, frowning. "But the answer to your question is yes. The colleague I was just telling you about and I once visited an infirmary with a nekrosis ward. It's quite sad, the conditions they are in. Not enough doktors. Not enough medikaments. Unsanitary living quarters."

"Maybe I'll be a nurse," Lydia mused.

"There's always need," Adrian said. "I'm sure your father would be very proud."

"Abraham has money. He could help fix up the hospitals. Couldn't you, Daddy?" Lydia said, loading her voice up with little-girl sweetness.

Abraham was spared the need to answer by Agnieszka's arrival with a tray of various pastries and cakes. "Who is ready for dessert?"

"I am!" Lydia said.

6.

"I've been thinking," Lydia said a few days later. "This god of yours. I don't like him."

Adrian and Lydia were walking the grounds of the estate. Their path had taken them through the gardens and then through a small woods and finally out along the bare cliffs looking over the Baikal Sea. The wind beat stiff and choppy out here and Adrian shivered while Lydia ran around him in giddy circles. He had found it was good to get her outside, to burn off some of the excessive energy common to all children. This was just a part of his developing pedagogy technique. Every day he added some new refinement to his instruction methods. One day, if this kept up, he might become a decent instructor. If, that is, he could keep her focused on the matter at hand. Right now that was supposed to be biological taxonomy, another reason for being outside.

"Let's get back to your lesson," he said.

"Kingdom, phylum, class, order, genus, species," she said. "I told you, I know it all."

"And what tree is that? How would it be classified?"

"I don't know. Did you hear what I said?"

"That you dislike God." Adrian half-expected some thundering rebuke from the clear autumn sky. It was not difficult to imagine God's real physical, acting presence out here, on the edge of the world, above so much water.

"Not *God. Your* god."

"Most people would say he's everybody's God," Adrian said. "Why do you say you don't like him?"

"Because he doesn't make any sense. Because he killed my mother."

"I know. I'm very sorry."

"But is he sorry?"

"I couldn't say. I doubt his intention was to make you suffer."

"Then why did he do it?"

Adrian had no answer for that. "We should get back to today's lessons," he said and launched into the taxonomical differences between various plants in the garden.

Lydia was resistant at first but finally relented and named each plant by its scientific name along with Adrian. They often consulted the botany text Adrian had brought with him. After half an hour or so, Adrian was pleased to see Lydia's attention entirely focused on the genus and species of each plant, utterly taken with the organization of God's plenitude in the world instead of His unknowable characteristics.

CHAPTER TWO

REUNIONS

1.

From the Journals of Nikolas Kovalski:

I WAS ON A SIMPLE supplies run, dry goods and water purification tablets, when it happened. One of our contacts in the Baikal Guard's Municipal Reserves, a man recently swept up by Mayor Adams's conscription policy, had given me the lock combination to a storage warehouse. When possible, we prefer not to steal from Joshuan citizens. The revolution is meant to ameliorate their situation, not worsen it. (And after my failure at the Patriots Parade and its fallout, we can't afford to do anything that might shine an unflattering light on us.) Mayor Adams has been stockpiling goods, which he uses to feed his war machine. We are merely redistributing supplies which already belong to the people of the city.

I took two new recruits with me. Our man on the inside had done well. The combination worked perfectly; we were in and out swiftly. Back on the street, we each began our separate routes back to The Underground as planned. If they caught one of us, it would be unfortunate, but if they caught all three of us, it would be catastrophic.

I had only traveled a few blocks when I saw Leni, or a person I thought was her, except this woman was hugely pregnant and lacked all of Leni's stylishness. I had chosen a path through a run-down part of town, hoping to attract less attention. Why would she be in this sort of neighborhood? When last I spoke with her—when was it? a year ago now?—she had seemed, if not exactly well-to-do, at least on the path toward a modicum of privilege—a student in the Institute of Fine Arts, attractive and well-kempt, from a stable family (or so I had assumed). But look at her now. Her clothes had clearly not been laundered in weeks; furtively looking over her shoulder, she took pains not to make eye-contact with anyone; her hair that had so enthralled me was now chopped off into ragged knots. (That was probably a smart move on her part. These days, Ulani braids could cause employers to "misplace" your application or might be the excuse for Guardsmen to harass you as an enemy sympathizer.)

I found myself following her. She went deeper into the neighborhood, picking her way down the trash-lined streets, stooping now and then with great effort, due to her bulging stomach, to test the value of a discarded object. Most of these things she dismissed, but she pocketed something that might have been a scrap of fabric or leather. I told myself I should let her go on her way, should make my way back to The Underground with the supplies I had in my rucksack. But I couldn't make myself turn away from this woman who looked so much like Leni. I had not thought of her in months, something which filled me with a kind of guilt. Had she mattered to me at all? Yes, she had. Not like Katya. No one was like Katya. But Leni had mattered.

Finally, she arrived at a door. A marked door—two violent red slashes in the shape of an X or a sloppy cross. Why would Leni's door be marked?, I wondered and doubted all over again that it was her. But then she turned and gave another of her scared-rodent glances at her surroundings, and I got a clear view of her face just before she scampered inside. It was definitely Leni.

I stood before her door. Should I knock? There was a rustle behind me. A rat. I felt the weight of the supplies in my rucksack. I knocked. Further rustling from the inside. The door opened a few cautious centimeters.

"Hello?" she asked. "What do you want?"

She didn't recognize me at first. Why should she? I had changed too. "Leni?"

"Nikolas?"

"Yes. Can I come in?" I needed to get off the street.

"Why are you here? How did you find me?"

And here, I misspoke idiotically. "I saw you and followed you."

"Why are you following me? Are you with them?"

There was no way she could mean The Underground. That was not the *them* she was worried about.

"Who do you think I am with?"

"The bastards who took my brother."

I never knew she had a brother. We hadn't talked about that during our brief time together. Another wave of guilt. I had told her all about Marcik at the time, about our mother, but I had exhibited a total lack of curiosity about her life. I had felt it was my job to entertain her with speech. Isn't that often the male's position? Prove you are worthy by proving you are smart and interesting, funny and lovable. The female is reduced to what she is; she is merely her beauty so often. Katya would rightly scold me for my masculine small-mindedness at the time. But now things were different. I had changed in more ways than one.

"The Guardsmen?"

"Yes," she said. She let herself fully recognize me now. "Nikolas? Is that really you?"

The door squeaked open on its hinges. Behind Leni, I saw the remains of meager meals, a few books on the floor, clothing strewn in absurd places.

"What happened to you?"

"Nikolas," she said, her voice a moist desperate whisper, "do you have any money?"

We had taken so much from the Municipal Reserves, and wasn't our point that it belonged rightly to the people? That was a rationalization, of course. And yet it was also true.

"I have this."

I opened my rucksack and handed her two small packages of grain and a handful of water purification tablets, then, looking at her swollen frame, I handed her a slab of butter as well.

That's when I heard General Schmidt's men.

What happened next happened fast. Messenger would be embarrassed that I had allowed myself to be so stupidly distracted, that I didn't realize General Schmidt's military thugs had gathered around me. At first, I considered fighting my way free. It would not have been easy, but I felt certain I was capable of it; I was capable of a great many things now.

Then I saw a man of mine among them; the revolution has someone everywhere these days. He looked at me, wondering if he should help in some way. I nodded *no*. I allowed them to grab me, and maneuvered them away from Leni's door. This felt familiar. A baton hit my arm; the Guardsman who had hit me did not really want to hurt anyone, though he no doubt thought he did. Then the next man. His baton put me to the ground, and I almost did it, almost unleashed brutal hell upon them— but a wild idea occurred to me: I would allow myself to be arrested in order to get a glimpse at the inside of their holding facilities and perhaps to speak to my brother, now a general, in his own environment. My man kicked me without conviction.

"Is that all you've got, you piece of nekrotic shit?" I said, looking at him only.

He hesitated, but then his kick half-lifted me off the ground. I had taught him well.

The Guardsmen dragged me away. They threw me in the back of their wagon. My man would not meet my eyes, which was also as I had taught him. Instead, he focused his brutality on the other prisoners in the wagon. Some were nekrotics, so sick they could barely move. His baton smacked them wetly. I admired and pitied him: he played his unenviable role to perfection.

We pulled up before the holding facility. Despite everything, I wasn't worried (though later I realized I should have been). My infraction was minor. All they knew was that I had contraband, not that I had broken into their warehouse to get it. Black-market materials were common enough. They would not hold me indefinitely. And, if the need arose, I could test the limits of what Messenger had taught me by breaking out—though I assumed it would not come to that.

The Guardsmen led me through the holding facility, my arms behind my back. I took in everything: the loose chain of keys around a guard's belt; the locking mechanism of the doors; the number and types of prisoners. I used the methods of observation Messenger had taught me. Many of the prisoners appeared healthy and strong. One even looked at me hopefully, as if asking me to free him so he could join our cause. I added him to my mental inventory. I was learning much of use for later.

They pushed me into a holding cell. The door slammed shut. High-wattage bulbs were trained at my eyes. The Guardsmen moved in on me, their implied violence a precursor to their questions.

Half an hour later, I was numb to the pain. No, that's not quite right. I had retreated into that deep place, the place that Messenger had shown me. Pain was a mere theory, something someone was feeling somewhere, not me here and now. As they struck me with stones wrapped in wet cloth, I repeated my situational mantra.

"Schmidt," I said. This was the mantra I had chosen for the occasion. It would keep me on my task.

They approached with the live wires. I decided again to let them do it, finding a yet deeper place. How far would I let them go? How much could I endure? Part of me was curious where my limits lay. I knew I was not anywhere near the level of Messenger, but I felt a pervasive calm, did not fear these men in the least. I went even deeper.

"Schm-idt," I managed, as my body convulsed.

"Why won't he stop saying that?" one of them said to the other.

I did not dare tell them that the good general was my brother, the lowly Private Marcik Kovalski. They would not have believed me anyway.

"All right, you pathetic sand-flea," one of the interrogators said, "what do you know?"

"I know something General Schmidt needs to hear. Tell him it is about his brother. Tell him I will only speak with him."

The men tensed, and I thought they were going to return to their torture-work. One of them left the room, presumably to gather my brother, while the others stood in a circle around me, a few looking at me with something approaching respect. Most of their victims are not so resilient, I imagine.

An hour later, "General Schmidt" came striding in with an imperial air (he had changed, indeed, from the Marcik I had known; this world was changing everyone in remarkable ways). He saw my battered face. He pretended not to recognize me. Even the long wait was likely part of his show. And now it was my turn for reluctant respect. Marcik knew how to conduct himself in his new persona.

"Why have you been calling for me?" He motioned the Guardsmen away. "Leave me with him."

The Guardsmen left without question, demonstrating their absolute trust in my brother. I was almost happy for him.

"Nikolas?" he said. "So you're a common criminal now?"

"I was stupid to do it."

"You should know that if you need food you can always ask me."

"I know I can count on you, brother."

He enjoyed my deference. I let him enjoy it. Marcik—no, I must begin to think of him as General Schmidt—relaxed and walked about the room regally. He knew his current power.

"We've all made mistakes," he said. "Someday I will tell you about what I had to do to get out of prison."

He paced the room in further silence. I waited.

"You were always the smart one, Nikolas."

"That's what Mother told us anyway."

"No, it is true. But smart is not as important as you think," he said. "Just look at you. Last time I visited with Mother she told me your studies were going well. She couldn't shut up about how you're going to be this famous doktor. I take it she doesn't know about this?" He made a sweeping gesture, indicating all he thought I had become.

"I have made nothing of myself," I lied.

"Well," he said, his tone softening a little. "I heard about your famous professor. What was his name?"

"Doktor Brandt," I said and lowered my face again.

"That must have been hard."

"Yes," I said. "Very hard. He was a mentor to me, you know. And when he died, I don't know how to explain it... It just all seemed so... pointless."

"We all make mistakes, brother. I've made my share, as you know. But we can be redeemed. With effort. It is time to put away childish things. We have to find something larger than ourselves."

He sat in the chair opposite me and leaned warmly forward, the very image of understanding.

"How's Mother?" I asked.

"She wishes you'd come visit her. I won't tell her what you've become."

My brother's face became a curious blank stare as he processed (I assume) the massive sea changes in our lives, the wild reversal of our roles.

"Nor will I tell her about you, Marcik."

He stood sharply.

"You're a brilliant man, Nikolas, the real genius of the family. We could use you on our side." He put his hand on my shoulder. "I just worry about you, Nikolas," he said. "You continue like this..."

I knew then he would release me. My gamble had paid off. I had gained much useful information about the enemy's operations, and it had only cost me one rucksack of supplies and a few bruises.

2.

NIKOLAS HAD INSTITUTED daily training sessions in The Underground. They worked in rotations of six core members at a time, meaning every lieutenant received one hour of direct training from Nikolas each week. It was a strain on Nikolas to take a precious hour out of each day for the sessions, but he couldn't have any member of The Underground inept at combat, even those whose primary duties in the coming revolution were not combat-oriented. Anyone and everyone might be called on to fight, and they needed to be ready. Also, as Messenger had taught him, training was as much for sharpening the mind as it was for hardening the body.

"Alarik," Nikolas said, and Alarik stepped forward dutifully. "You've done heavy labor and lived in some unsavory areas of our grand city, haven't you?"

"I have," Alarik said without pride or shame.

"And I imagine you've seen your fair share of violence?"

"I have."

"And what, if you reflect back on these episodes, was the decisive point that determined the victor?"

Alarik pondered this, wanting to get the answer right—to please Nikolas but also because it seemed like an important question, and one he had never asked himself. Size and strength had certainly helped him both as a schoolboy and later, in more serious situations. But he had seen smaller men beat bigger men, and he had once hidden in the corner of the kitchen in his childhood home as his mother beat his father into a cowering pulp with a large metal pot because he had gotten drunk again and slapped her.

"Wanting to win. You have to want nothing more at that moment."

"That's right," Nikolas said and looked over the group before him. "Or, as I would phrase it—*focus*. You have to be focused utterly on the task at hand, not scared of what might happen in ten minutes or what you might have done ten minutes earlier to avoid the situation. You have to be there fully and give yourself fully to the fight. And that focus takes the form of confidence that you will win. This is the secret of the revolutionary's psyche. That focused confidence will dull the pain your enemy inflicts and will amplify your own blows. We gain this focused confidence only if we deserve to win, and if we don't have the focused confidence that we will win, then we don't deserve to."

Alarik nodded and stepped back into line with the others. *He's a born soldier*, Nikolas thought, *but not all of them are.* Among the six members training today, perhaps only Alarik and Mouse had the revolutionary constitution required to kill an enemy in close combat. The others might pull a trigger from a distance or detonate a bomb from a safe hiding place, but only these two would twist a knife in a Guardsman's guts and watch the light leave his eyes.

"But focus, while the most important element, is by no means the only one. And if you meet an equally determined enemy, it will be your superior ability that wins the day. This morning, we are going to learn a key grappling maneuver that can be of use in many situations. We will simulate a knife attack scenario, but it can be helpful in strict hand-to-hand combat as well."

He motioned Alarik forward again and stepped forward himself to demonstrate the maneuver, favoring his left leg where one of his brother's men had struck him several times with a metal pipe, bruising deeply into the muscle. Alarik stabbed with the wooden knife. Nikolas pivoted on his front heel, grabbed Alarik, and with a tight twist of his hip, tossed the massive bulk of his komrade to the floor where he had placed a mattress to create a soft landing during this exercise. A shot of pain went through his leg as he heaved Alarik over his shoulder, but he made no show of it. (Why had he chosen Alarik, the largest and heaviest of them, to demonstrate the maneuver on? Was it some form of masochism? Only the likes of Doktor Laikan can pretend to know the answer to such questions.)

Nikolas paired the group in various ways, making sure everyone executed the throw several times, with a different partner each time. This gave them the opportunity to repeat the maneuver, but it also forced them to feel the difference between throwing assailants of different heights and weights. When the training hour was over, Nikolas instructed them to practice what he had taught them over the course of the next week. They would review this maneuver in their next training session and learn a series of joint-locks, he said before dismissing them. Alarik and Mouse remained to practice the throw. Just like the skolars he had known at Joshua University, Nikolas recalled: it was always those who needed the extra practice least who did it most, out of some personally imposed obligation to the material. If only he could find a way of instilling that kind of motivation in all of his komrades, the outcome of the impending battle would already be certain. As it stood now, there were days he felt foolhardy to attempt a revolution with so many of his soldiers only half-prepared. What could they hope to do against trained and battle-hardened Guardsmen?

※ ※ ※

After the training session, Nikolas took a hot bath to soothe his pain and to prepare for an excursion. He shaved and dressed in a clean formal shirt and jacket, better than anything he had owned as a skolar in fact. Among the various acquisitions of The Underground were clothes that could be worn to disguise operatives in nicer areas of the city. Going past Checkpoint 4 looking like a street urchin simply would not do; he needed to go unnoticed, there more than anywhere perhaps.

3.

ELIAS FOLLOWED Nikolas up the stairs to the train platform. He kept a safe distance. Nikolas walked with a casual air, giving no indication he thought he was being followed. Of course, that was exactly how he would act even if he knew for certain Mayor Adams's best agent was on him. All the members of The Underground had training in how to avoid being followed: the first rule was not to let on that you knew were being followed. And Nikolas himself had taught them the rule.

If he knows I'm following him, Elias thought, *he'll probably try to lose me at the next stop. Get off the train and get right back on.* Of course, if he knew it was Elias, he might simply confront him. And then what?

I'll just tell him, that's all. I'll ask him where he's been slipping off to lately.

Nikolas had been disappearing more and more often in recent weeks. And the last time, just a few days ago, he returned with his eye swollen and his lip split. Whatever he was doing, it was dangerous. It wasn't tactically prudent for the so-called leader of their organization to compromise himself—and indeed all of them—this way.

On the train platform, Elias was surprised to see Nikolas waiting for the Silverville train. On the other side of the platform was the stop for the train to the Seven Points neighborhood. He knew this was where Nikolas had grown up. Nikolas liked to remind him of this, as if the fact that he had been raised poor made him better than Elias. More committed to the revolution. He lorded it over Elias in all sorts of subtle ways.

But doesn't giving up a life of bourgeois decadence, as Elias had, demonstrate more commitment? While Nikolas had made sacrifices for the revolution—he could have been a doktor, after all—there were others in their ever-growing circle who were simply there because they had no better alternative. The homeless, out-of-work laborers... Maybe they were just doing it to have a roof over their heads, humble though that roof was.

He criticizes me for my bourgeois origins and yet he would have me continue at university, studying the law. The truth is, I'm useful to him the way I am. I know how to deal with people. But he seeks out any excuse to diminish me. He can never forget that I was the one who started all of this.

The Silverville train arrived and Nikolas got on. Elias waited and then slid through the doors as they closed. Standing in the car directly behind Nikolas's, he positioned himself so that he could see Nikolas but Nikolas could not see him.

Who do you know in Silverville? There was that old professor of his, but Nikolas had taken care of that, hadn't he? In one dumb lucky stroke, Nikolas asserted his dominance while binding everyone's fate to his with a blood secret. Never mind that it had been an accident—the poor sap just happened to come home at the wrong time, that was all.

At Checkpoint 1, a ticket-inspektor came around to see their identification. The ticket-inspektor wasn't Endre, but that shouldn't matter. Elias still had his residency card listing his parents' address in Jardin Prospekt, a moneyed neighborhood just beyond Checkpoint 4; he was to all appearances an upstanding Joshuan. Elias handed his card to the inspektor and flashed a white-toothed smile, showing he had been to the dentist recently—what kind of threat could he be if went to the dentist? All the while, Elias looked through the door to the other car. This would be the perfect time for Nikolas to lose him; he had already shown his identification (a false one made by a counterfeiter in The Underground), and so it would not seem untoward if he were to exit at this stop. And Elias would be helpless to follow without arousing suspicion.

Satisfied, the inspektor handed Elias's identification back to him and moved on. Elias gave a quick glance to where Nikolas had been sitting. He was still there. *He hasn't seen me. Good.* They pulled out of the station, and Elias allowed himself to relax against the car's wall.

The second checkpoint was more of the same, but at Checkpoint 3 a different inspektor came to Elias's car before Nikolas's. Elias once again produced his residency card. The inspektor, a portly bushy-eyebrowed man of medium age, scowled at the fotograf on the card and looked up at Elias. Behind his crude features, his eyes were unexpectedly sharp. He took in every detail of Elias's appearance in one glance—the blond-white hair, the nice-enough gray-lined jacket with two casual buttons worn by most juristic skolars, the dress trousers, the polished leather shoes. Nikolas insisted that Elias dress in the unspoken uniform of the juristic student when he was at university. ("You have to fit in perfectly. No grandstanding or calling attention to yourself.") Elias would have preferred his work boots and a heavy overcoat. But it was fortuitous that he had just come from class when he started following Nikolas. A man in a suit was welcome everywhere: the poor looked up to him while the rich saw him as one of their own.

And wasn't he in his element . . . this same element of bourgeois decadence that Nikolas so derided? ("Your background has given you certain skills. Use them.")

"Is there a problem here?" Elias said. "I think you'll find my papers are in perfect order."

The inspektor ignored that. "And what is it that you do, Mr. Kreutzer?"

"For a living, you mean? I'm a litigator."

"You mean a lawyer," the inspector spat out. "Shouldn't you be able to afford a nicer suit?"

He took a deep breath. "I am a juristic skolar at Joshua University," he said. "I mostly help licensed practitioners with research and briefs."

"If I recall, you've been on this train since the New Jerusalem stop," the inspektor said. "What were you doing in that part of the city? A little rough around edges for someone like you."

"I wasn't aware that I had to have a reason. When I was going in the other direction, no one asked me why."

"It's procedure."

"Fine," Elias said with a sigh. He was aware his tone had grown somewhat imperious. His reaction came from genuine annoyance, but it was also a calculated tactic. The rich do not take kindly to being questioned by those beneath them. *What would my father do if he were here? He certainly wouldn't be even this patient.* And after Elias's father was home, he would probably call up the man's superiors and have him fired. Elias did not miss his father. At all.

"If you must know, I was meeting with a steelworker whose leg was crushed in an accident. His employer refuses to compensate."

"A bleeding heart, huh?"

"My heart only bleeds for money," Elias said. "If we win this settlement, we'll make hundreds of thousands of drams. And as lead clerk on the case, I will receive a bonus."

The inspektor paused briefly, as if considering something. "At the expense of industry. I know people who have lost jobs because of such cases. People I worked with, in fact."

"I am sorry to hear that," Elias said with real concern.

The man, encouraged, continued, "Remember that rail accident of a few years back? They tried to claim the train hadn't been properly maintained. But I knew the man doing the inspektion. A good fellow. He did his job well, and was rewarded by being shown the door."

"Tell your friend the firm I work for also handles wrongful termination suits," Elias said. "I am sure they would be happy to represent him, and others like him in fact." He looked over the inspektor's shoulder to make sure Nikolas was still in the car ahead. He was. Elias returned his attention fully to the man before him. He knew this was not the time or place for a disquisition on the nature of the legal system, but he was unable to quash the urge. "Litigators are not your enemy. The only way to make these men of industry change their tactics is to make them pay when they ruin people's lives."

"But I thought you said your heart only bleeds for money?" the inspektor asked.

Elias gathered himself and said, "Well, we all have more than one motivation. And right now, my motivation is to get home. It has been nice talking with you, and I wish you and yours well, but I fear we are holding up the other passengers." Elias nodded over his shoulder at the other passengers and looked coolly at the inspektor.

The inspektor looked at Elias's identification one more time, then back into his face. There was a moment when Elias was not sure what he would do. He stared back at the man calmly and levelly. This was a trick he had learned in his law classes; most people can't maintain eye contact for more than a few seconds, and so they naturally trust and fear someone who can.

The inspektor handed him back the residency card. "I appreciate your patience, Mr. Kreutzer. Sorry to have troubled you. Have a good day."

He checked a few more identifications. One man was escorted from the train by armed guards. The inspektor moved on to the next car. When he got to Nikolas, Nikolas flashed his card. Though Nikolas was dressed no better than Elias and had the added offense of facial hair, the inspektor gave his card a cursory glanced and continued down the length of the car. Unbelievable. He had to hand it to Nikolas. He really did have the baikal-touch.

Or was it that the inspektor recognized Nikolas from his previous excursions?

※ ※ ※

The inspektor having already accepted Elias's residency card, there were no further problems at Checkpoint 4. Now they were in Jardin Prospekt, but still Nikolas did not get off. They were in the neighborhood Elias had once called home. He could visit his family. Wouldn't that be a surprise? Elias and his father were no longer on speaking terms since Elias had turned down a prestigious internship at a law firm run by one of his father's friends. His father continued to pay for Elias's studies and general living expenses, which Elias reluctantly allowed; the revolution needed the excess money that Elias did not spend.

Elias had to admit that he did miss his little sister, Elizabeth—or Bunny as he called her—sometimes. He had been tempted to bring her into the movement somehow, to save her from the perils of high society. *The Underground is no place for a girl of her age, though.* Hard as it was for Elias to accept, she was probably better off with his father.

The train kept rolling on toward The Hills, which marked the end of the line. There were only a few more stops now, and they were getting into territory where the truly wealthy lived. Few people were still on the train—the people who lived in these palaces had their own autos and drivers. There was a woman with a small child; by the look of her clothing she was probably the child's nanny. Elias had been raised by such a woman, while his mother gave society dinners and his father was always busy with one high-profile case after another. There were others like his nanny on the train—gardeners, maids, and servicemen for the rich.

"Last stop, last stop," the ticket-inspektor came through the train calling. "Three Sisters' Point. End of the Line."

The train stopped and the doors slid open. He waited for Nikolas to clear the train platform. The platform was pristine: well-watered plants in elaborately decorated pots; smooth-swept granite; a waiting area of light-blue colored glass to shelter passengers from the weather; there was even a lifting-box for those passengers too lazy or encumbered by bags to use the stairs. Ahead of him, Nikolas bounded down the stairs, quickly disappearing from view.

The whole neighborhood seemed like one giant park, nestled in rolling hills, traversed by slow-winding roads. It was autumn and not as green as it would have been a few months back. Some of the trees had shed their leaves, but as Elias followed Nikolas down a stately avenue, he was washed in a splash of oranges and purples and reds. Leaves crunched underfoot. It had been so long since Elias had set foot in a neighborhood such as this one—and even *his* family had not been quite this rich—that he had forgotten how clean, how perfect everything was. How quiet. He loved the squalor, the noise, the *realness* of New Jerusalem. But he had to admit everything there was a bit...shabby. Fraying at the edges. *If the people there could see how the rich truly live*, he thought, *they would rise up and smash their machines without any of us having to lift a finger.*

Now ahead, Elias could see the profile of Three Sisters' Point: the saw-toothed rocky cliff, the totem-like shapes of the eponymous sisters—three tall wind-carved projections of rock that vaguely resembled the heads of old women. Beyond that, some fifty meters down, was the water. You couldn't see that yet, though. That view was the provenance of the person who lived in the house at the end of the point. And everyone knew who that was.

As Elias walked up a steep road toward the mansion, The Infinite Hallway came into view. Like everyone else who saw it, no matter how jaded by the wonders of human industry, Elias was impressed. He nearly forgot he was supposed to be following Nikolas. He stared, drunk on the glittering knife of glass that projected into the nowhere, suspended by nothing. Then he resumed following Nikolas up the hill, right up to the gates of the Kocznik mansion.

At the gate, Nikolas pushed a button and spoke into the intercommunications system. After a minute, the gate swung open and Nikolas stepped inside. Elias watched him disappear up the path to the house.

He's been here before, Elias thought, his suspicions confirmed.

※ ※ ※

It was Nikolas's third visit to the Kocznik Mansion. If he was not quite a welcome visitor, at least he was an expected one. He didn't know why he came here, yet he continued visiting Adrian. Had he made any progress? What sort of progress was he even hoping for? And yet surely Adrian's attitude toward him had changed.

On his first visit, Nikolas was made to wait for ten minutes at the gate before some old woman came down and told him that "Mr. Talbot" was busy.

"Please," he said, "tell him it's urgent."

The woman went puffing and grumbling back up to the house. He stood stoically for a few minutes, wondering whether Adrian would receive him. Nikolas worried about security. Was he being recorded? There was more and more surveillance these days. Perhaps even now the old woman was calling Guardsmen to haul him away. But no, Adrian would not allow that, no matter how much he had distanced himself. Nikolas pulled a book from his rucksack and read a few pages, taking in almost nothing. Had it been a mistake to come here?

Ten minutes or more passed, an eternity to wait so exposed, before Adrian finally came down the path. He looked like a proper gentleman in his new shirt and black coat, tailored perfectly to his shape.

"Nikolas? What are doing here?" Adrian said, neither displeased nor inviting.

"I was hoping to talk to you. You slipped away without saying goodbye."

Adrian set his hand on the gate between them. "It's complicated."

"Everyone says things are complicated when they are scared to act. It is the most useful excuse I have ever heard."

"I am in the middle of a lesson with my pupil," Adrian said. "Could we meet later? Someplace else." Adrian sighed. He rubbed his forehead. He was his usual haggard self, yes, but more confident. In his element.

Nikolas offered a conciliatory smile. "I've got something you will want to hear. About your time at the Laborers Hospital."

Adrian blanched. "I really have to get back to my lesson," he said, "but I want to know what you have to say. How can I contact you?"

"You can't. I'll contact you."

Nikolas offered his hand through the gate, and after a worried pause, Adrian accepted it with something like fraternal warmth.

※ ※ ※

"I can't have you coming here, Nikolas. It looks bad for me," Adrian said the next time Nikolas showed up at the gates.

"Just hear what I have to say. You owe me that much."

"I've moved on, Nikolas. I still have affection for you and warm thoughts about our time together. But you have to realize I have a new life now and new obligations."

"Just let me in."

"I shouldn't," Adrian said, his voice faltering.

"Adrian, please."

Adrian pushed a button and stood back as the gates opened. Nikolas stepped inside, onto the paved driveway which curved along a gentle slope up to the house.

Adrian gave Nikolas a tour. At first it was a polite concession, but he soon found himself exhibiting an unexpected pride of place. He walked him through the botanical garden. Every plant was set in neat rows. They were planted in a tiered system. Adrian knew Nikolas would recognize this as a means of allowing for maximum sunlight.

"You have to have to admire the engineering," Adrian said and pointed to a complex structure. "Those slanted panes of glass redirect sunlight between themselves, more than tripling the concentration."

"Thereby tripling the plants' fotosynthetic intake. Wonderfully constructed," Nikolas agreed. "Yes, your new boss is obviously a genius."

"Yes," Adrian said, with genuine admiration. "He really is."

It was pleasant to be in the presence of Nikolas's mind—to have a conversation with a peer, not an aloof genius or precocious child.

"And is that The Infinite Hallway?" Nikolas asked.

"Notice how there is no rock support."

"Yes," Nikolas said, "I read about that."

"Impressive, isn't it?"

Adrian got the sense that most of what he said fell on deaf ears. Nikolas had always been more interested in ideas than his surroundings. Adrian led him around the side of the mansion, under the half-arch, and into the garden. Several wrought-iron chairs were arranged on a flagstone patio. They sat here, in the shadow of an enormous sundial. Like much of the house, the sundial served no practical function. Instead of numbers on its face, there were various glyphs.

As if at some hidden cue, Agnieszka came out with a samovar of tea and various cakes. Nikolas and Adrian sipped from their tea saucers in silence. A bird with a bright scarlet bill landed on the bird bath and took dainty sips from the rainwater pooled there.

"This is nice," Nikolas observed. "Much better than our dormitory."

"I like it."

"It's not so bad, I guess," Nikolas said, "to live like an ordinary person. I wish I could do it."

"This started as a means to pay for my coursework, you know. Ever since Brandt . . . "

"Yes," Nikolas said. "That was unfortunate." He took a bite of one of the cakes and emptied his tea.

"I plan to focus more on my medikal studies," Adrian said. "But now I've discovered I quite enjoy pedagogy. I would have thought that you'd be the teacher. And I guess you are in a way, with your group." Adrian refilled Nikolas's cup. "What was it you wanted to talk about? I've told you I'm not coming back."

"Not even if I told you I knew Schmidt's secret?"

Adrian set down his cup with a shaky hand, barely containing the force of his memory. He saw the battered corpse of Doktor Abuawad; he felt the anguish of watching Ariah deteriorate in what Schmidt and his men had left of the hospital.

"Don't play games, Nikolas. Tell me now."

‰ ‰ ‰

"I've been thinking about it," Adrian said the next time Nikolas visited. "It changes nothing."

They sat on the patio as usual. The weather had grown chill, and the plants in Kocznik's elaborate garden were wilted.

"His actions caused the death of the woman you profess to have loved. You know that, don't you? You said as much yourself."

"I know what he did," Adrian said. "And of course I'm angry. I've wanted to kill him. But what would that make me?"

"Normal."

"And what about you? He's your brother. That doesn't change anything for you?"

Nikolas thought of his moment of hesitation at the parade. He thought of General Schmidt letting him go after the interrogation.

"He's a puppet for Adams's regime. An enforcer of his repressive policies."

A door opened and Lydia Kocznik stepped out onto the patio. She was carrying a book.

Adrian stood. "Is something wrong? What are you doing out here?"

"I know you said not to interrupt you when you were visiting with your friend," she said. "But I don't understand this part. And I need to understand it to finish the assignment." She turned to Nikolas, "Hello, friend. I'm Lydia, by the way."

"Yes," Adrian said hurriedly. "This is Nikolas. We went to university together. What was the part you needed help with?"

She held the book out to Adrian, open-faced. She pointed to something on the page. While Adrian read the passage, Lydia studied Nikolas with a frank curiosity. Finally, having made some mysterious decision about him, she grinned.

"I don't see what's so bad about you," she said.

Nikolas laughed. "Did Adrian say that? That I was bad?"

Adrian shook his head at Nikolas.

"No," Lydia replied. "He just said not to come out here. When Agnes says not to do something it usually means it's bad. Agnes is our house-keep, by the way."

"You should listen to her," Nikolas said.

Adrian closed the book. "Just skip to the next section," he said. "I'll explain this part later. Go back inside now. I'll be in shortly."

Lydia took her book and went back into the house.

"She's a very bright girl," Nikolas said. "I can see why you like her."

Adrian was still standing. "You should go," he said. "And I don't think you should come back, Nikolas."

Nikolas was shocked by the change in Adrian's demeanor.

"Please," Adrian said. "If you are still my friend, if you have any affection for me at all, leave me to my life."

※ ※ ※

From the bushes outside the gate, a pair of telescopic lenses held up to his eyes, Elias watched as Nikolas left. He did not shake Adrian's hand. From this distance, Elias couldn't hear what they had said, but they seemed to have had some kind of break. He tried to make sense of what he had seen. The Kocznik girl reminded him of Bunny. About the same age. But it was more than that. It was in the adult way she carried herself, not afraid to look her elders directly in the eye. To stand her ground. Yes, she was very much like Bunny. *Don't be senti-mental now.*

As Nikolas left, Elias waited in the bushes and began to formulate a plan.

4.

ADRIAN CLEANED HIS SCALPELS and arranged the various bandages, staples, and ointments as he waited for the day's assignment in the Medikal Practices course all medikal skolars were now required to take. He saw the utility of such a course. Shouldn't every medikal skolar know how to treat basic wounds—broken bones, infected cuts, and so forth? But after the excitement of Experimental Kardiology last year, and after his stint at the Laborers Hospital, he found the course both boring and redundant. And Doktor Malmud seemed uninterested in the loftier possibilities of the subject he taught.

Adrian's new lab partner, Bertrand, arrived—a few minutes late as usual. He always seemed harried and put-upon, always forgetting his notes or misplacing some instrument. But Adrian found him endearing and enjoyed helping him with the laboratory work.

"Hello, Adrian," Bertrand said. "We haven't started yet, have we?"

"We're just about to."

Bertrand set his rucksack down and tucked in a corner of his shirt. "I was caught up in the radio report."

The other skolars settled in as Doktor Malmud put a slide on the board. It showed a Baikal Guardsman lying in the sand with his right arm roughly severed at the elbow. The wound was likely from an explosive device. A jagged edge of bone protruded; burnt strings of meat dangled; his eyes were rolled back in his head in an ecstasy of pain. Bertrand stared at the image, awestruck by its gruesomeness. Doktor Malmud put another slide on the board. A gut wound—white sausage-like entrails hung between the man's fingers as he clutched at his abdomen.

"In this situation, a medik will have to make a decision," Doktor Malmud said. "Imagine you have these two patients before you, and you have the time to treat one of them. Which do you choose?"

Adrian raised his hand.

"Yes, Adrian?"

"The first one."

"That is correct, Adrian. Good. But why? Enlighten the rest of the room."

"A wound like the one in the second slide is ultimately fatal, no matter how much attention you spend on the patient. The bile from the intestines will have already spilled into the chest cavity, poisoning the other organs. Even if you successfully close the wound, it will not matter. The first man, while in danger of eventually dying, can be saved if you stop the bleeding and stanch the wound. A clean surgical amputation of the remaining lower arm would likely be necessary as well."

Adrian would never have answered so confidently before his time at the Laborers Hospital.

"A thorough answer," Doktor Malmud said. "Your fellow skolars would do well to learn from your clear assessment."

Doktor Malmud set up several more sets of slides, asking for the same comparison. Adrian resisted the urge to answer each time; it would seem presumptuous to pretend he knew more than the other skolars, and many times when he sat silently and listened to the others speak, he was exposed to ideas he wouldn't have otherwise had. Even when the responses were incorrect, they sparked new insights in him.

Bertrand leaned in and whispered, "I don't think I can go out there."

"Join your partners and come up with ten possible scenarios like the ones I've put before you. Describe the injuries, the instruments you have at your disposal, and the decisions you would make."

It was exercises like this Adrian found most tedious. He had made these decisions, in real situations. What could this course teach him? It is easy to simply imagine two choices. But there are times when you have no choice, or the only options you have are forced on you and therefore are choiceless choices. When Ariah was dying, he had no alternative but to trust Jürgen's engineering expertise and his own medikal abilities. And in the end that was not enough. She died. Then he had no choice but to return to Joshua City.

Bertrand wasn't focused on their task. He was more nervous than usual. "How did you survive out there? I don't think I could."

"Don't worry," Adrian said. "This is just an exercise."

"But with the conscription now..."

"What are you talking about?"

"Didn't you hear the radio?"

"No, I guess not," Adrian said, slightly annoyed.

"They're conscripting skolars now as well."

Adrian set down his pen.

"They say we'll get officer status, and we'll even get credit toward our degrees for going out there. They want engineers and medikal skolars mostly, of course. We're useful. To repair things and help the wounded, I guess. But you don't have to worry. You already volunteered. I wish I had thought of that."

But Adrian hadn't "thought of that." He had volunteered for his own reasons.

"Let's get back to work," Adrian said. "And don't worry. There's no way to guess who they will select for conscription, so worrying about it will do you no good."

5.

GENERAL SCHMIDT TOOK only a small detail of Guardsmen with him on his visit to his mother. She offered him a slice of berry pie he did not particularly want but accepted anyway. She would be in a foul mood the entire visit if he refused.

"How have you been, Mother?" His crisp uniform and the medals on his shoulders felt out of place here where he had been a scrawny child fighting his way out of his brother's superior shadow. But he needed his mother now, perhaps more than ever, if he was going to help Nikolas. A small thrill of pride went through him at the thought that he should be looking after Nikolas, not the other way around.

"Eat your pie, General," she said and fussed about the kitchen, barely suppressing a smile.

"Have you heard from Nikolas lately?"

She washed the pie cutter, dried it, and put in the drawer; she could never let a single dish sit in the sink unwashed.

General Schmidt ate a dutiful bite.

"He comes to see me occasionally."

"And how is he doing these days?" He took another bite to make his question seem more natural.

"He was by just last month, in fact." She sat beside him and took a forkful of his pie. She chewed it slowly. "That is really good, if I may say so."

"You may, Mother. You're the finest cook in all of Joshua City."

She kissed him on the cheek. She patted him on the shoulder. "Such nice medals. I am so proud of you."

Proud. That's what she had said the first time he visited her after his return, after his face was in all the newspapers. He had been worried whether she could keep the secret. Mayor Adams had made it abundantly clear that there could be no loose ends.

"You can tell no one, Mother," General Schmidt had said. "And I mean no one."

"You've made me so proud. I would never do anything to hurt you," she said. "Was it very bad? In the prison?"

"No, Mother," General Schmidt lied. "Don't worry about that."

Now, General Schmidt set down his fork, the pie half-finished. "Here," he said, "you finish it." He knew he needed to get back to work. "And what did you and Nikolas talk about when he was here?"

"Oh, the usual. His medikal studies. I never understand any of it."

"Did you notice anything unusual?"

"No, he was very kind. He even gave me five hundred drams to pay my rent."

Five hundred. That was a lot for a petty thief. Perhaps his activities were tending toward the more ambitious. Where did he get that kind of money?

"Did he say where he got that money?"

"Why are you suddenly so interested in Nikolas's finances?"

"I've been gone for a while. I just want to know how my brother is living these days."

"He said it was from a new—what do you call them?—*grant*—yes, that's it—a new grant he got for his research."

Schmidt subtly pressed her for more information but received only vague unknowing responses. He did not want to think too much about how Nikolas had gotten the money. Even if his brother was now a common criminal, at least he was giving something to Mother.

"Mother," General Schmidt said and stood, kissed her with a young boy's affection, "I really have to get back. But I am glad you are doing well and that Nikolas visited you."

She forced the rest of the pie on him. "For your men," she said, beaming. "How lucky I am to have two such successful sons."

CHAPTER THREE

POTLATCH AND DIALECTIC

*E*VEN IN THE BRIGHT *heart of Silverville*, Neil thought, *a sickness.* He stood on the balcony of his Silver Avenue hotel room, smoking and watching the busy goings-on at street level—the flashing neon of the nightclubs, the new fully automated trains controlled via circuit board (which Abraham had designed), the people shoving past on the crowded sidewalk. He took another drag. *Yes, even here.* Ladies stepped into furriers and came out draped in pelts; men went down basement stairs and emerged wearing their shame. Or they came to hotels like this one, where they paid for the illusion of glamour—the well-stocked bar, the satin sheets, the great city view—but mostly they paid for discretion.

He was sick, too, and behind him on the bed was proof—Mina-ki, a pretty Baikyong-do lily of a thing with doll's eyes and a face that reminded him so much of Vivian. Vivian, who had been dead for months now. He sank his face in his hands and hated himself for the affectation of the gesture (*I can't even feel this properly*). Though truth be told, because of Mina-ki's age, she resembled Lydia, Vivian's daughter, as much as Vivian herself. He closed the window.

On the damp twisted sheets, Mina-ki—if that was her name, and of course it wasn't—shifted restlessly. Her tiny pink nipples and the pleasingly dark hair between her legs glared at him. They could go again. He had enough money for anything. She would let him do unspeakable things if he gave her enough—anything could be bought—but, without warning, he was disgusted.

"Get out," he said.

She blinked at him slowly, questioningly. On the telefone, the madame had told him she was an aktress, that she could play any role—no doubt, assuming that what he wanted was simple enough.

He threw her blouse at her, then lifted her underwear with one finger, and with a flick of the wrist sent it to the foot of the bed. She bent down to pick it up and when she straightened, he was surprised to see that she looked almost sad. She wasn't crying, nothing so awful, but there was a slack defeated quality to her features that made him question his assumptions about her. Her real age—sixteen? eighteen?—showed on her saddened features.

"Here," he said, softening. "A little extra for your sick grandmother."

"Sick grandmother?" she asked.

"Just take it."

She stuffed the hundred drams in her purse.

"Maybe we could do it again sometime," she said.

"Maybe I'll put you in one of my films," he said, and for a moment actually considered it.

"Really?" the girl beamed.

Neil opened the door and stepped aside like a loyal servant.

When the girl was gone and he was free for a moment from the ghosts she had brought with her, he walked over to the bed and reached under it and pulled out a leather briefcase. He undid the clasps. He looked inside. An old service revolver with an authentic ivory handle lay on a bed of money. Big bills, hundreds, fresh from the bank and bound together in thick stacks.

He closed the briefcase and buttoned his shirt. He pulled on his jacket and made his way to the lift-box, took it to the ground floor, and stepped out onto the street with a neat clack of his heel. Maybe he would see Mina-ki again and they could go back to what they had been doing in that sordid hotel room—her kneeling before him, hair in pigtails, lips pursed in an innocent pout.

"What do you want, little girl?" he had asked, feeling sick and aroused at the same time.

Neil looked around the crowded street, but Mina-ki was nowhere in sight, likely already with her madame, giving her all but a few coins of what Neil had paid. He hoped she held out on that last bit he had given her. Maybe she would use it to buy vodka, maybe waste it on crystal-black—he didn't care. Just so long as she kept it for herself.

Lost in his reverie, he nearly stumbled over an old man slumped in a gutter. His face was covered and his arms were bandaged in rags, perhaps to conceal nekrosis sores that would have him snatched up and *quarantined*, as they were calling it.

"A dram for a bite, kind sir?" the old man asked him.

Neil patted his pockets in a gesture that said he would love to help, only times were tight. *If he only knew what's in this briefcase.*

"I've got to go in there," he said, nodding at a casino, The Devil's Quarters, where a neon devil poked with a phallic pitchfork at the bare buttocks of a curvaceous angel. Even as he said it, he realized it wasn't a very good excuse: if he had money to gamble, he had money to help an old man eat.

He entered the smoky mirrored foyer of the casino, blinking in the high-ceilinged glare.

"Sir?" said the cashier.

"Fifty thousand," Neil said, handing him a stack of drams. The cashier counted out an enormous tray of chips—blues, whites, reds. If he was at all disconcerted by the amount of money the chips represented he gave no indication. Nor did he appear to recognize Neil. Like the employees of the hotel, the men in these places were paid not to recognize faces. They saw small fortunes won and lost on a daily basis, and by men who would rather it not end up in the morning edition of *The Joshua Harbinger*.

"Put this somewhere safe, would you?" Neil said, giving him the briefcase.

"Of course, sir," the clerk replied. He gave Neil a claim ticket and carried the briefcase to the back room, where presumably there was a vault of some kind.

※ ※ ※

An agent from the Ministrie of Aesthetics—another man in another gray suit, like that man at his party so long ago—had visited Neil several months earlier. They wanted him to make a film about The Great War. It should pay tribute to the Guardsmen of the past; it should remind Joshuans that the Guardsmen of today were just as heroic; and it should, without making the point too obvious, draw a parallel between the heroic statesmen of that time and ours.

"I make entertainments, not political pieces," Neil said.

The funding would be more than adequate, the gray man assured him, and indicated that this was not precisely a request. If he wanted to restore his good name with the Adams administration, if he wanted to see any of his future films cleared by the review board of the Ministrie of Aesthetics, he would make the film they wanted.

※ ※ ※

Hating himself, Neil hired the most complacent screenwriter he knew, the author of such mediocrities as *Flowers on a Guardsman's Grave* and *Baikal-Love*. And the studios were only too happy to supply their best technicians. With polite excuses he turned away the skilled aktors he had worked with in the past. But there was a bevy of third-rate aktors and aktresses who would do anything, no matter how demeaning, to be in one of his films. And demean them, he did. During the auditions, he was constantly drunk. Many of the hopeful aktresses he took back to his bedroom. But mostly he drank. He missed production meetings, put off every deadline, and only rarely answered calls from his financiers at the Ministrie of Aesthetics. When he did answer, they asked how the production was coming along.

"You hired me," he said. "Trust my process."

After one of these calls, he went into his study. He pulled a revolver from his desk drawer. He released the chamber and let the bullets spill onto his desk. The empty gun looked strange in his hand. He inserted one of the bullets back into the chamber. He took a drink. He spun the chamber, marveling at the randomness of everything. He pointed the gun at the ceiling. A hollow click. A title for a film he would never make came to him: *The Gentleman in White.*

The following afternoon he went to the bank and drew out what was left of his production budget in hundred-dram notes, which he put in a briefcase along with the gun.

※ ※ ※

Now, standing at the dice table, Neil counted out five thousand in chips and put them on the Pass Line. He flung the dice into the center of the felt-covered table. They came up six and five.

"Natural roll. Shooter wins," the dealer said and swept half of the other players' chips Neil's way. He pushed Neil the dice again. This time Neil bet on Don't Pass and rolled a one and a two.

"Shooter wins again."

The other players, some of whom had superstitiously switched to the Pass Line, groaned. A few players gathered up their chips and moved on. They knew a hot hand when they saw one. Neil rolled the dice.

Hot, indeed; his hand seemed to be on fire. Or maybe it was the dice. They radiated a pale orange light through the bones of his hand. As he stared at the table, all sounds—the false titters of girls-for-hire, the clink of coins fed into slots, the groans of yet more money lost—fell away, leaving only him, Neil Martin, Joshua City's most beloved direktor, and the two glowing dice, their six sides, their permutations nearly as varied as fate itself.

He threw the dice, and was unsurprised to see he had won again. In interviews he had done for celebrity magazines, the most common question asked was: "What is the secret of your success?" Or, "How do you always know what the public wants?" His inevitable answer: "I have no idea. I'm just lucky I guess." As answers went, it was as good as any. But it was a lie. The truth was, he didn't give a damn about any of it—and it was for this reason that he got what he wanted.

He had watched direktors pour their lifeblood into their latest project, hoping to make a film that was both critically acclaimed and commercially successful, a work of art so transcendent even the brainless Joshua public would have to sit up and take note. But they inevitably failed—failed on both ends. They produced neither time-less masterpieces nor successful entertainments. Poor dressmakers, their ambition showed through at every seam. There was brilliance, too—but this brilliance was its own type of flaw. It called attention to itself. It didn't care about the audience or the story, but only about itself. It did not love; it only wanted to *be loved*. What was it Bello Marvinski, Neil's favorite silent film direktor, had said? *All things to those who want them least.* When a waitress came by and offered him a drink, he tossed it back in one swallow and grabbed another from her shiny tray.

And time passed. And time passed.

※ ※ ※

When he first started losing, two hours into his hot streak, he couldn't quite believe it. That his luck should fail as randomly as it had begun—impossible, unfair. One minute he was rolling for five-hundred thou-sand drams, ten times what he had bought in with, and the next he was sending the cashier to retrieve his case. Another bundle of fifty-thou-sand. And another, until more than half was gone. Still, he couldn't give up, though he saw the pity on the dealer's face, and the disgust of the patrons, who, well-off as some of them were, couldn't stand seeing such a vast fortune squandered.

At some point much later, a waitress came around. She walked right by him and took the drink orders of the other players. He grabbed her arm. "What's your name?" he asked.

The waitress glanced across the room, where a security guard stood. Neil tightened his grip.

"Don't lie to me." He squeezed even harder, but she still did not respond. "Fine, I'll call you Vivian. Vivian," he said in a courtly tone, "might I have another drink?"

Security guards approached, professionally ominous. Neil let the waitress go, straightening himself on his stool. He held his hands up, showing they held no violence. The security began to ease off. Even dead drunk, he was too important to treat lightly. *An undead importance, lumbering past its time.*

"Well, Vivian," he said, with a final stab at dignity, "How about that drink?"

"I've been told not to serve you another." She rubbed her arm, where he had grabbed her.

"My money's no good?"

"Sorry, sir," she said. "Orders of the house."

Neil turned to the dealer, who had watched the scene in silence.

"Will you be placing another bet?" the dealer asked.

"And be cheated again? No, thank you."

"No one's cheating anyone."

"Of course not," Neil said. He sank back into his seat. "One million, then on Don't Pass."

"I'd have to advise strongly against that," said one of the other players, a mustachioed man who seemed to have inherited—stolen?—Neil's good luck.

"Who asked you?"

The dealer pushed over the dice and Neil scooped them up. The table was silent as he blew into his closed hand and flung the dice against the table's far wall. Double sixes. He exhaled slowly, straightened his damp collar.

"Boxcars. House splits."

Neil's wager came back his way—but none extra. The other players watched. The room tilted just a fraction of a degree and he felt himself falling into a wonderfully black realm where nothing mattered, where there were no consequences. He threw the dice. One and one—snake eyes. He stared blankly, unable to move.

"Give me those dice," Neil said to the dealer.

"I'm afraid it's my roll now," said the mustachioed man. He picked up the dice and rubbed them together between his fingers. He threw the dice into the center of the table. Neil reached out and grabbed them before they could settle.

"I knew it," he said. "One's heavier. Feel them. "

He offered the dice to a lady beside him. She jumped back as though he were brandishing a pistol.

"This is absurd," said the man whose roll Neil had ruined.

"You switched the dice," Neil said. "Everybody knows it."

"Now listen . . ." the man began, coloring slightly.

But Neil was already reaching across the table. He grabbed the man. "He's coming for you, too," Neil said.

Neil laughed and pulled tighter. The man turned purple and Neil was in that black realm again, but this time he could see an oily light just around the corner, and in that light, a familiar face he could almost make out. He felt the weight of the revolver in his jacket pocket. He had taken it from the suitcase earlier on a whim, to feel the power of carrying a gun. He could end this all right now. He wanted to, more than anything, he wanted to kill this lying perverse thief of luck. Who would steal a man's luck? Only the lowliest and meanest spirit, one deserving of death.

Then hands were grabbing him and locking his arms behind his back, and with trained efficiency he was pulled outside and unceremoniously tossed on the street. His briefcase was thrown on his chest with force enough to knock the air from his lungs. The door banged shut and he was alone. He sat there, trying to clear his head. He had to go somewhere, but he didn't know where. Finally, he made his drunk-rubber legs stand beneath him.

Most of the reputable establishments were closed, and he hurried past a few bars and sex-dens, knowing there was only more ruination inside. He turned down an alley and was overwhelmed by the smell of alcohol and piss. Bags of trash were stacked and spilling onto the ground. In the gutter were a crumpled copy of the periodical *Hub and Spoke*, a discarded necktie, and a sleek yet simple black leaflet reading *Day-R* in bright red letters.

He leaned against the wall and heaved nothing into the hot night air. He bent into a half-crouch, heaving and heaving, finally managing a gush of thin acidic fluid.

"Pathetic," the Gentleman in White said, smiling merrily and leaning on the handle an obsidian cane.

"You again," Neil said and leaned over to wretch again.

"The pleasure's all mine, I assure you."

"What do you want?"

"Me? Nothing at all," the Gentleman in White said. "What do you want? That's the question."

"I don't want anything."

"But I think you do want something. Very much." The gentleman poked him with his cane. Neil kicked it away. "And what if I could give it to you?"

"I told you I don't want anything. Now leave me alone."

"Leave you *alone*?" He put a biting emphasis on the last word, smiling at an irony Neil didn't grasp. "That's rich, considering . . ." The Gentleman in White tilted his head back, searching the Joshua City sky bemusedly. "Would you like to hear a story?"

I'm not your chickadee, Neil thought absurdly. He laughed. The gentleman laughed along with him—a pleasant sparkling laugh. He tapped his cane against the wall rhythmically, a tune vaguely familiar to Neil. On the tip of the cane, there was a many-headed lion made of purest gold.

"Once there was a young *artist*," the gentleman said, with all the contempt he could summon for the word. "Full of hope for the future. But also full of the fear that there might be nothing inside him."

Neil knew where this was going.

"He wasn't just a dreamer, a gambler on idle fancies. He wanted to prove others wrong about him, but most of all, he wanted to prove himself wrong. Prove the secret wrong. Do you know what the secret was? Do you know what it said to him? What it whispered in his dreaming ear at night?"

"I imagine you'll tell me."

"That there was nothing—and I mean absolutely nothing—inside. It wasn't that this particular young man was a bad man. Nor was he good. It was just that ever since the first moment he could remember, he knew there was something essential missing. He was a room with no furniture and no light."

Neil started to object, but the Gentleman in White put a finger to his lips and shushed him like one would a bothersome child.

"He thought if maybe he could be an artist and make something great...that he might fill in the missing piece. And so, he enrolled in the Film Institute at Joshua University and there his head was stuffed with techniques and tricks of the trade. And he met great minds who saw the world whole, undivided, and whose purpose was clear. And he watched them. He studied them. He learned to put on the right faces in the right circumstances, use the right aktors and the best writers, find funding from the right sources. He won and he won. And no one suspected the room was empty and lightless."

Neil tried to stand, stumbled drunkenly.

"But he still knew," the Gentleman in White continued, "in that part of ourselves that cannot lie. Worse than all that, however, is that he was also suspected by the only woman he ever loved."

"But if he loved her," Neil said, "how could there be nothing inside?"

"Therein, my boy, lies the paradox. And because he knew himself to be empty he doubted the—how shall we say it?—veracity of his love, never quite acknowledging it for what it was until too late. She died. Though he hadn't actually lifted the knife, he had killed her. And then he knew the truth behind the earlier truth he thought he had known."

"What? What was the truth?" Neil was standing now.

"He had never been empty. Merely *afraid*."

Neil stared at the tip of the gentleman's cane. He tried to count the number of lion's heads, but they seemed to shift positions. Was he that drunk? He shook his head. The gentleman noticed the object of his attention and lifted the black cane with its golden tip. He turned it in his hands, examining it as though he were seeing it for the first time. He stroked one of the lion's golden manes.

"Where did you get that?" Neil asked.

"A man must have his secrets," the Gentleman in White said. "Now, if you'll excuse me, I have other business to attend. I wish you the best of luck."

The gentleman walked down the alley, twirling his cane. He seemed to glide along, his feet not quite touching the ground. As he entered the traffic of Silver Avenue, he dissolved in the glare of a dozen streetlights and storefronts.

Neil leaned against the wall until he felt strong enough to move on.

"A dram for a bite, kind sir?"

It was the same old man from earlier, and Neil saw that he was again across the street from the Devil's Quarters. How could that be? He could have sworn he had been heading in the other direction.

"Your friend," the old man said, lifting a bony finger and pointing in the direction from which Neil had come, "he went *that* way."

"What did you say?" He leaned in closer, trying to overcome his disgust.

"You'd better follow him."

The cheesecloth had come unwound about the lower part of the man's face, revealing a toothless mouth. He grinned and his wet pink tongue darted lasciviously about. "He's waiting."

Neil grabbed the old man by the shoulders and shook him. "How do you know about him? Can you see him?"

The old man put up his hands, terrified and confused. "A dram for a bite?"

Neil let him go. "You know nothing."

"It's cold out."

"Here," Neil said, handing him the briefcase.

When he looked back the old man had the briefcase on his lap, and was staring inside with a foolish grin. He stood and bowed to Neil, spilling a small fortune onto the pavement in the process. He snatched it up hastily and bowed again.

※ ※ ※

Around the next corner, there was a motion-image theatre marquee. The theatre was one of the small privately owned kinds that played *classics*—which often meant those films that had not yet been deemed objectionable by the Adams administration. One of Neil's old films was playing in just fifteen minutes. He stepped up to the ticket window. "One for *A Love Undying*, please."

The teller eyed him laconically. "That'll be six-fifty."

He took out his wallet and fished inside. He laughed. "You're not going to believe this, but I just gave my last three hundred thousand to a complete stranger."

The teller didn't blink. "Six-fifty, sir."

Neil felt the option of the pistol in his jacket—he could just shove the barrel in this boy's face and demand admission—but instead dug into his pockets, finally piecing together enough for the ticket. The teller gave him a flimsy yellow stub and looked past him to the next customer.

Neil entered the theatre. As his eyes adjusted to the dark, he saw the seats were mostly empty. A few disheveled old ladies and a half dozen men, sipping from paper bags and cackling at jokes no else could hear—that was it. *No one appreciates the classics*, he thought wryly. He took a seat as far from the others as possible and slouched down in the shadows. The credits began, deliberately grainy and ponderous, meant to give the effect of the silent films of Silverville's youth—an homage to Bello Marvinski and the other direktors Neil had grown up admiring.

A Love Undying, the screen read, *directed by Neil Martin. Starring Vivian Scott.*

A courtyard full of palms. Sunlight. A high gate opens and an unmarked vehicle pulls out. We follow the car down eerily quiet city streets until it pulls up to a government building.

Neil was swept up in the double vision of viewing his own work through the telescope of so many years. He felt dislocated, disoriented, like a broken compass. The work was at once his and not. He could remember having made it—the process of pitching the script to the studio's board, the endless revisions he had gone through with that lunkhead screenwriter—but he couldn't conjure to the present what he felt back then. He could even remember the reviews, the most positive of his career. "Has Neil Martin finally come of age?" one reviewer asked, adding that "the marriage of his usual slick storytelling with the hint of something deeper would suggest so." But how had he felt about those reviews? Had he felt anything? A cheap pride, no doubt.

Then she came on screen: Vivian Scott, as Ginger Mondrake, the unhappy housewife.

She moves from room to room with a languid grace, reflected in the many mirrors of her lonely palace. Her husband is the Minister of Health. (And here was where the film benefited from its current neglect, as well as the relatively permissive time in which it was made. Nowadays, he would never have been able to show a minister in such a light.) When the minister is not ignoring his wife, he berates her for some imaginary fault. He grabs her wrist at the dinner table, bruising her. He tugs at his sinister mustache and plots how to save the ministrie a few more drams at the expense of ordinary citizens. The money would go back into the minister's own pocket, the audience is led to suspect.

Neil knew it was limp insipid stuff—had known it at the time—and yet the image of Ginger staring into the bathroom mirror, wiping the mascara stains from her teary eyes, made Neil believe in the quiet suffering of this woman. And when the hero, Robert, spies her in a private balcony of the opera house, where her husband has come to discuss business with a powerful but disreputable Ulani, Neil's heart swelled with something a different man might have called hope.

Robert and Ginger meet on bridges and at discrete hotel bars. They kiss. He undresses her in an unspecified bedroom. Afterwards they smoke cigarettes and tell stories of their childhood. From a window across the street, unseen by our lovers, a pair of telescopic lenses nudges aside a curtain.

"We've got to stop this," she says. "My husband will find out."

"Let him," Robert says, grabbing her in his strong arms.

(Oh, it was insipid trash, but Neil watched on).

Ginger pushes him away. "Where is this going?"

Still naked, Robert goes to window. He looks down on the white winter street. A couple walks happily arm in arm, laughing. A drunk with a paper bag crouches, shivering in front of a street lamp. The couple passes him heedlessly by.

"All I know is I love you," Robert says. And with those words, the question is put aside.

The couple meets for the last time on Saint Nevsky's Bridge, where they have met so many times before. Except this time it's snowing; the bridge is different than in previous scenes. The flakes are fat and wet and they fall with a lazy grace in stark contrast with the fierceness of our lovers.

"I think he knows," she says.

"Were you followed?"

She looks around. "I don't think so. But if you could have seen his face when I left . . . "

He embraces her again. He lifts her chin and makes her look into his eyes.

"Everything will be fine," he says. "I promise."

What were my last words to Vivian? Neil wondered. *Did I tell her the same calm and necessary lie? Or did I say something cruel? Come on, you remember. Or if you don't, it's because you don't want to. Don't be afraid. The worst it can do is kill you.* He laughed bitterly at his little joke.

※ ※ ※

It was just a few weeks before Vivian died. He had thrown a party—not for any specific reason, but to show the world that he might have been knocked back by the business with *Potlatch* but that he was not defeated. Pleading illness, Abraham hadn't attended this party. Looking back, Neil suspected Vivian was right: Abraham knew. When and how he had found out, Neil had no idea—and it certainly didn't matter now.

When all the guests had finally gone, Vivian leaned against the door and stared at him. He touched her cheek. It was cold, he noticed, in spite of all the alcohol and the fire blazing in the hearth.

"You've been odd all evening," he said.

She poured herself another glass of wine, though she was already wobbling in her high heels.

"Forget about it," she said. "Don't worry your beautiful brilliant little head one bit."

"Don't speak to me like I'm him."

She gripped the stem of her wineglass hard, and he was afraid she might fling the glass at him, but then she slumped, her anger gone as suddenly as it had come on.

"That's just it," she said. "You're not."

"Aren't you glad?" he said, doing his best impression of a boyish smile.

"Sometimes."

She smiled, too, also with an effort, and he had a flash of intuition. "You missed it, didn't you?"

"How did you know?"

"You must hate me now," she said, not exactly a question.

"Don't say that."

"I can see it in your face."

"That's concern you're seeing," he said. "I'm concerned."

Again she smiled feebly. "It does complicate things, doesn't it?"

He looked around at the debris of the party—lipstick-stained glasses, plates of half-finished food. A woman's shoe, blue with a diamond-studded strap, rested in the center of the room. He wondered who would have left such a valuable item behind. He imagined some fairy-tale princess, forced to flee before she turned back into her real self—a housemaid in a brown bonnet. There was always a sadness to the end of parties, a nostalgic ache that seemed to him a metaphor for death but was not entirely unpleasant. He went over and picked up the shoe. He set it on the mantle, like an avant art piece. He surveyed the improvement of the room.

"There's one thing we could do," he said.

She held her neck stiff the way she did when some unpleasantness confronted her. "I was afraid you'd say that."

"You can't leave him," he said. "It would be disastrous to both of us."

"I don't care."

"Think about Lydia, then."

"You don't give a damn about Lydia," she said. "Or me. So long as you're not dragged down with us."

"Don't say things you'll regret."

"I know what I'm saying." But she made a visible effort to calm herself. She poured another glass.

"It couldn't be his?" He gestured at her belly.

She laughed without humor. "The odds certainly aren't in favor of that."

Now *he* needed wine. He poured a glass and took a big swallow, feeling its dryness coat his tongue. He thought and thought, and kept running into the same wall. "It's really not so terrible a procedure, you know."

"How would you know?"

"I know a doktor. It's all perfectly safe."

"Is that what you do? Get other men's wives pregnant and pay one of your friends to fix it for you?"

He refused to respond to that.

"Well, I won't do it," Vivian said.

She looked down at her belly, still flat in her evening gown. She touched it with one hand. They could make it happen if they really wanted it, couldn't they?

"This is ridiculous," he said. "You're talking about a couple of cells, a smear of fluids, not a life."

"I'm aware of all the scientific arguments. In fact..."

There was such a long pause that he almost gave up on her speaking again at all. Finally, she cleared her throat.

"When I was pregnant with Lydia," she said, "things were complicated. Not as complicated as now, but there wasn't much money. I'd only had a few jobs, commercials mostly. Abraham was still working for the Ministrie of Transport, trying to get them to listen to his plan to *revolutionize Joshua City's rail system* and so on."

"This was right before I found you, I guess."

"We both wanted a child, or Abe wanted a child and I wanted what he wanted because I was young and in love with him." She trailed off, and he could see she was remembering those years.

"That must have been nice," he said.

"But because I wasn't quite as set on the idea of a child, I was more clear-sighted than he was." She paused. "I almost didn't tell him. I took the test, and when it came back positive, I didn't want to believe it. I went to the doktor, and he finally managed to convince me that, yes, it was true. The doktor said he would do something for me, set up an appointment—that Abraham didn't have to know."

"You actually considered it?"

"I was like you. If it was necessary... But I told the doktor to wait. I needed to think about it. I drove home and I cooked dinner. I still cooked in those days. We couldn't afford Agnieszka yet."

"You really were poor," he said, trying to lighten the mood.

"But really, I'm a decent cook. I should make dinner for you sometime."

"I'd like that," he replied, and they considered the impossibility of such a thing.

"We sat at the dinner table, and Abraham asked me about my day. I made up something about a magazine fashion spread, and then told him about going to the market, and how I wanted a corned beef, but all they had was this brisket—because as every liar knows, a half-truth is more convincing than a total lie—and by that time he wasn't even listening. He chewed his food and remarked on how good it tasted . . . "

"Again with the cooking," Neil said. "You really are a braggart, you know." But she didn't take his bait to playfulness.

" . . . and I couldn't look him in the eye. I couldn't betray his innocence. Because that was what I loved most about him."

"How much has changed," Neil said, hoping to wound but not draw blood.

"So I told him. He took it all in calmly, and when I was finished he said something that surprised me."

"What?"

"He said, 'If that's what you think is best.' And just like that I saw how wrong I'd been. How thoroughly I'd deceived myself. Because it wasn't what I thought was best. It wasn't what I'd wanted at all. Right then and there, I decided we'd have the child."

"Lydia."

"Yes. Lydia. And no matter how terrible things have gotten between Abraham and me," she said, and now she took Neil's hand, "and they have gotten terrible, I haven't regretted my decision to have her."

She gathered up her coat and purse. He called his driver to take her home.

%% %% %%

That was the last time he had heard her voice. He told himself it wouldn't be right to go her funeral. He mourned her at home, drinking a bottle of wine they had bought together and listening to the radio until he couldn't take it anymore—the endless speculation, the impersonal police report. The truth was he couldn't stand the thought of seeing her body—her lightless eyes, the set lips without the power to frown or smile. Or kiss. And of course, their dead thing inside her.

※ ※ ※

Onscreen, in this dingy theatre where Neil now found himself, Robert awakes in the musty damp of a windowless room...and as he tries to move his arms only to find himself strapped to a table, as he lifts his head as far he can, looking around for someone, anyone, to appeal to for help, and as, realizing he is all alone, he cries out *Let me go, I don't belong here*, screaming himself hoarse, the kamera pulls back to reveal a vast dungeon opening onto a long lightless hallway, and then it takes us up a flight of spiraling steps, into another hallway, and another flight of steps and another hallway, past an impenetrable iron door. Then the kamera makes its final pull-back to reveal the side of a cliff over a wild and a dark sea; we are left with nothing but water and waves and moonless night stretching toward a black horizon.

"How prophetic," a voice behind Neil said. It was the Gentleman in White again. Without seeming to move at all, he was in the seat beside Neil. "Now *that's* ridiculous. After all..." and he winked delightedly.

"I know one way to get rid of you," Neil said, reaching into his pocket.

"There is that."

Chuckling, the gentleman reached into his own vest pocket. He took out a gold lighter with the same engraving of the seven-headed lion as on his cane. With one smooth motion, he produced a cigar, lit it.

He blew smoke in Neil's direction. It hovered for an unnaturally long time, finally shaping itself into a suited devil resembling the gentleman himself. Another puff formed an angel. They locked arms in an embattled embrace. The gentleman stabbed at them with the point of the cigar and they dissolved.

"You *could* do that," the gentleman said. "And frankly, I would be relieved. I'm getting quite tired of following you around. Watching you wallow like some filthy animal. It's embarrassing."

"Go away then."

"I've been charged with a duty and I intend to see it through."

"Who are you? Why are doing this?"

"I've already told you."

"Fine. Don't answer."

Neil turned again to the screen.

The torture is too much for Robert's starved and grief-wracked body. He is strapped to a table in the dungeon. But not for long. His torturers, cloaked in the hoods of inquisitors, gather around the table. One of them produces a long gleaming syringe. He plunges it between Robert's ribs and Robert throws his head back in a soundless howl. He slumps against the table, lifeless again. But the kamera pulls in close to his eyes to reveal a light—empty, passionless, oily even, but light nonetheless.

"Good film, don't you think?" said the gentleman, munching from a bag of caramel candies.

Ginger Mondrake is in a convent now. Her husband has sent her there after he learned about the affair—to "protect you from yourself," he told her. She wanders the dark stone hallways, her expression listless. The other nuns view her with tight-lipped suspicion. In her bedroom, devoid of all furniture save a simple cot, is one small high-set window. She pushes the cot over to the window, and standing on it, gazes out at the sun setting over the sea. It is her only pleasure. One time when she is doing this, a nun comes to her with a tray of toast and tea; Ginger hops down from the cot, as if caught trying to escape.

"How are you feeling today?" she asks.

Ginger sighs.

"Give it time, dear," she says. "You'll adjust."

Meanwhile, the torturers' experiment has gone horribly awry. Robert, or what used to be Robert, has broken his straps. The torturers back away as he throws medikal instruments. He strikes one of the torturers, who falls to the floor. As he moves ponderously toward the fallen man, the kamera pulls in close on the man's face, revealing the terror in his eyes. Across the room, another torturer, the one who performed the injection, fumbles with the keys that will let him out into the hall. He finally succeeds in getting the key in the lock, and slips out into the hall, leaving the others to their own defenses.

Cut to: a small washroom. The torturer stands in front of a mirror, and slowly removes his mask. The kamera shows only the back of his head as he lowers his face to the sink. But then he raises his face and looks into the mirror. It is Ginger's husband, the minister. His eyes are haunted; he grins mysteriously.

"Remind you of someone?" the Gentleman in White asked. Now he was sipping from a saucer of tea, his finger extended daintily. The teacup empty, he threw it over his shoulder. Neil waited for the sound of shattering china. It didn't come.

Then the voice took on a deeper tone, all-powerful, commanding. "Look me in the eye. Good. Now take out what you brought with you."

Neil removed the gun from his pocket, fumbling a bit with the oddity of its shape. Except for that one time, he had never fired a gun.

"Don't worry," the Gentleman in White said. "I'm going to help you through this. Put the gun to your head."

The metal was cold against Neil's temple.

"I don't want to," he said.

"I know, I know," the Gentleman in White said. "But it really is for the best. Now I'm going to count to five. And you're going to pull the trigger."

One.

Robert has escaped his underground prison. He marches down the halls, followed by legions of newly undead. When they reach a locked door, Robert rips it off its hinges. Two guards round a corner with their guns drawn. They fire at Robert, but he keeps coming. A scream. A crunch. After a minute, the two guards stand up. But they are not the two guards anymore. Their faces are deathly pale, their eyes hungry.

Two.

In the convent, two men in monk's robes drag Ginger through the halls, one of them whispering in her ear. As his tongue flicks sibilantly about her earlobe, she squirms and breaks free. She dashes down the corridor but is snatched by a waiting hand.

Three.

Neil released the gun's safety.

Now Ginger is in a courtyard, the full moon illuminating a sinister scene. Motionless nuns, their faces granite and scowling. Monks move about like the shadows of forgotten ghosts. Ginger is pushed onto a platform. In its center is a table like a sacrificial altar. The monks begin chanting, a hypnotic hum.

Four.

Moonlight slides across the platform. Two monks force Ginger to kneel. The Mother Superior moves forward, something concealed in her hand. Just before she reveals the object, a noise makes her turn. In the archway leading into courtyard is Robert. He moves forward and the other zombies follow. The monks scatter, but to no avail. More screams, people pulled to the ground—the Mother Superior among them. A moment later, she springs to her feet, her eyes burning and her teeth dripping blood.

"Funny," the Gentleman in White said, and for a moment he sounded almost sad. "I don't remember this part."

Meanwhile, Robert approaches. Ginger inches backwards and bumps into a wall. She picks up a rock and turns to confront Robert.

"It's Ginger," she pleads.

Robert pauses, a dim recognition making his face almost human again. Ginger lifts the rock and smashes Robert's head in. When the kamera pulls in, there are tears in her eyes.

Five.

CHAPTER FOUR

NEW VELOCITIES

1.

A DRIAN ADJUSTED the angle of the inclined plane he had set up for Lydia's physics lesson. To start the lesson, he had gathered iron balls of various weights and sizes and instructed her to roll them down a wooden plank to compare their speed. Of course, they all rolled at the same rate.

"But why don't the heavier ones go faster?" Lydia asked.

"The pull of gravity is equal no matter the weight."

"But gravity's about falling," she said.

Adrian felt the enjoyment all teachers feel when a student begins stumbling down the right path.

"That's true. Very good," he said. "Now, what might the connection here be? Why did I bring up gravity?"

Lydia chewed her lower lip and stared at her white shoes, wondering through the possibilities.

"Roll it again," he said, indicating the iron ball in her hand. "And really observe it."

She did as he instructed. When the ball had completed its path, she left it on the ground. Concentration twisted her brow, then—after a few seconds—her face brightened. "When it's rolling, it's really just falling!"

"That's correct. Only it's slowed down by the plank. And the steeper we make the incline, the less it is slowed down."

"And when something just falls, it's like rolling down a straight-up-and-down plank."

Adrian would not have thought of it like that, but in a way she was right. "Yes. And therefore it has no resistance—except for the air, of course."

Excited by all of this, she ran to her rucksack and pulled out a sheaf of papers with a red bow tied around it. She thrust it at him with a shy smile.

"I wrote them for you."

He undid the bow. The first page read *For my favorite pedagogue*. He flipped through the pages and saw that they were poems with unstudied-yet-elegant pen illustrations. The first poem was titled "The Moon Over Baikal" and the first lines read: "We walk along the soaring view / The water is alive with you." He flipped through a few more quickly.

These were love poems, Adrian recognized with dismay.

"I'll read these later," Adrian said. "But for now, let's get back to your physics lesson."

※　※　※

Adrian knocked lightly on the open door of Abraham's study. Abraham was bent over his desk, hard at work. Adrian considered coming back later; he disliked interrupting Mr. Kocznik when he was working.

Abraham looked up with a benign smile. "Adrian, how nice to see you."

"I hope I'm not bothering you."

"No, no, not at all. I was just remembering what you said the other day. About the medikal uses of the desert-aloe that grows in my botanical garden. I've been considering growing more. Maybe I could supply it to the medikal skolars at Joshua University? I think Vivian would have wanted some good to come of this house of mine."

"I can certainly enquire, if you like," Adrian said.

"That would be excellent. Very kind of you," Abraham said and wandered off a bit in some reverie, at last bringing himself back to attention.

"But I don't imagine you came here to talk about plants. What did you want to ask me?"

"Well, sir, it's about Lydia . . . "

Abraham sat up a little straighter. "Nothing's wrong, I hope?"

"Don't worry. Nothing serious. She's an excellent student. And clearly very intelligent. My concern is not with her skolastics, but rather with her social development. Having a private pedagogue has many advantages, as studies have shown, but there's also something lost—the social element. Which I think is just as important. I worry she identifies too much with the adults around her."

"So what do you suggest?"

"Something very simple. Some group activity with girls and boys her own age."

"I trust your judgment," Abraham said. "That's why I hired you. And it's clear she adores you."

Adrian blushed at how unwittingly close to the mark his employer had come.

※ ※ ※

It was a bit early in the season to go ice-skating at the most popular locations, but there was a small pond in one of the parks in The Hills, shallow enough to be frozen now. Adrian had signed Lydia up for an introductory class for children her age. Agnieszka gave him twenty drams from the house allowance to buy Lydia a pair of ice skates. Mr. Kocznik's driver, Cesar, took them to a department store where skates were sold. Lydia insisted on a dark-blue pair with lightning bolts running along the sides, ignoring the shopkeep's suggestion of a pink pair with wisps of clouds.

On the way to the pond, Adrian and Lydia sitting in the back of the auto, Lydia asked, "Can I put them on now?"

"I don't see why not."

She tied them up to the top and leaned back, kicking her feet and making swooshing noises.

"Look how fast I'm going!"

When they arrived at the pond, there were several children with the instructor. On the ice, adults and more skilled children skated in gliding circles. Adrian handed the instructor the ticket for Lydia and retreated to the benches where parents sat watching.

Lydia put on her skates and joined the group on the ice. She stood wobblingly. She slipped, swung her arms to catch her balance, and fell on her back. Adrian half-stood, concerned, but she let out a squeal of laughter.

The instructor gathered the children and showed them how to stand, leaning slightly forward to balance their weight. He pushed off with one leg and demonstrated the lean-and-pump motion that they would employ to propel themselves forward.

There was a deep chill in the air, but Adrian's new coat, courtesy of Mr. Kocznik's generosity, kept him warm. He kicked at the old autumn leaves on the ground. The park really was beautiful and Adrian felt lucky to be there. Nikolas would be critical of all of this, but why couldn't he just appreciate such simple pleasures? He was always thinking of the world as it ought to be, not taking in the beauty that was already there.

"Isn't it a joy to see them play together like this?" a woman beside him said.

"It is, isn't it?" he said, still with a watchful eye on Lydia.

"You're too young to be her father. Older brother? Uncle?"

The woman was probably in her late thirties, with an easy aristocratic beauty. Her clothes matched perfectly, white fur lining her hat as well as the cuffs and collar of her jacket.

"I'm her pedagogue, actually."

"Oh, whose service do you work for? We use Asarov's Pedagogical Institute for our little Timofey. We're very pleased with the results. I can't imagine sending him to a municipal school or one of those religious akademies."

Adrian nodded politely.

On the ice, the children imitated the instructor's lean-and-pump motion with varying degrees of success. Some of the children who had come together paired off to practice. Lydia stabbed down with her skates ineffectually, her previously bright mood graying. Her face was a mixture of focus and frustration. A boy with more skill than the other children skated a sneering circle around her and scraped to a stop.

"Are those your brother's skates?" he said.

Lydia's eyes raked across the boy's face. "What's that supposed to mean?"

He gave her a contemptuous little laugh and skated off gracefully. Adrian had wondered if he should intervene, but the boy seemed satisfied now to show off in front of the other children.

"I'm sorry," Adrian said, "what were you saying?"

"They can be so cruel at that age," the woman said.

Lydia pushed forward, made some small progress, nearly fell, but caught her balance. Encouraged by this, she ventured forward and fell again, hard onto her tailbone. This time she did not laugh.

Adrian made his way over to her, walk-sliding awkwardly along on the ice.

"Are you all right?" he asked, holding out his hand to help her up.

She sat on the ice, her shoulders slumped. "This is stupid," she said. "I want to leave."

Without bothering to remove her skates, she stomped toward the car, slicing small wounds into the semi-frozen earth on her way. The woman in white fur smiled pityingly at Adrian as he walked by her.

%. %. %

In the auto on the way home, Lydia yanked at the laces of her skates, trying to work them off. But the knots were small and tight. She dug the toe of one skate into the heel of the other, managing to push it half off her foot before kicking it against the back of the driver's seat. She slumped back, blowing air out through her mouth.

"Here," Adrian said. "Let me."

"I can do it," she said.

She hunkered down to the task. Eventually, she picked the knot loose and slid the skate off. A similar struggle followed with the other skate. The two skates now lay in a sad tangle on the floor of the auto. She burrowed her face in Adrian's shirt.

"I'm sorry," she said.

He felt the heat of her tears, the sleeve of his shirt getting wet. Up front, Cesar made the smooth subtle calculations of changing lanes. His eyes passed over Adrian's in the mirror, expressionless.

"You have nothing to be sorry about," Adrian said.

"You wanted to help me . . . but I . . . I ruined . . . "

He couldn't make out the rest.

"Maybe this was a bad idea," he said.

She lifted her face. Mucus ran out of her nose and she wiped it with the back of her sleeve.

"Why can't I be like everyone else?"

On an impulse, and though still aware of Cesar's presence, Adrian took her hand in his.

"Listen, Lydia. I'm *glad* that you're not like everyone else. And you don't ever have to do anything you don't want to do. All right?"

She nodded timidly, still unsure. "All right."

"Good," he said. "Now let's get rid of those stupid skates."

They pulled over at the first available waste bin and Adrian instructed Lydia to throw the skates on top of the stacks of rotten food and broken bottles ("where they belong"). It would have been more practical to return them, but Adrian felt Lydia should have this moment.

When they finished this ritual disposal, he asked, "What do you want to do today? It seems we have the afternoon free."

She deliberated, mimicking what she must have imagined adults considered seriousness. "Can we do more of the inclined planes?"

Adrian was unable to hide his pleasure at this answer. He had expected her to ask to play some children's game. Her enthusiasm for science and her awe at the workings of physical laws reminded him so much of himself as a boy. He promised himself he would never again try to shape Lydia to the mold of others; he would let her become who she was at the rate and in the ways that were most comfortable for her. During the remainder of the drive home and during their experiments with the inclined planes, Adrian thought more about the field of psychology, particularly developmental psychology, and pondered the practicalities of switching his area of study.

2.

"MAYOR ADAMS'S OFFICE released a report today on the recent spate of sabotage around Joshua City. Yesterday's ransacking of a military food supply truck—a truck destined for our troops in the Outer Provinces— was just one more in a series of subversive acts that have plagued our city over the last several months."

Radios were on across the city. Citizens everywhere heard the same reports at the same time. The goal of these reports was to bind them together, to give them a collective identity. Those citizens who wanted hear a different message tuned in to Radio Free Joshua, but even its broadcast had begun parroting the main stations, though in slightly different terms and with somewhat more creative formats—that is, it created the illusion of an alternative and little more.

In Silverville, they wore shiny dresses and listened. In Baikyong-shi, they gathered around a single transistor in a merchant's booth and listened. In the dormitories of Joshua University, they looked up from their textbooks and listened. In the barracks, Guardsmen polished their rifles and listened. Mayor Adams sat in his office at the heart of the city, muttering to his unseen advisors, and listened.

In The Underground, Nikolas Kovalski and his komrades listened as well—cheering when they heard the consequences of their insurgencies, shouting profanities at the blatant misinformation. From his perch on the wrought-iron stairwell, Nikolas observed with pleasure how the revolution was taking on a life of its own.

※ ※ ※

"Workers took the manager of a meat-packing plant hostage today in Seven Points. There have been no demands as of yet. The manager's family has been notified, but his name is currently being withheld to protect their identities."

Alarik looked up from his work table littered with scraps of metal and fine cloth. "Good boy, Maurice," he mouthed silently. Alarik had trained those workers and hand-picked Maurice as their cell-leader.

※ ※ ※

"In their boldest move since the attack on the Patriots Parade, the subversives wreaking havoc across our city set off a bomb in the Lower Municipal Courthouse this morning. The group known as The Underground took credit for the bombing, claiming that the prisoners and nekrotics on trial in the Lower Municipal Courthouse had been unjustly incarcerated."

※ ※ ※

"Mayor Adams's chief aide, Pierre Kabot, had this message for all Joshuans: 'Remember, beloved citizens, remain ever-vigilant.'"

Nikolas turned the radio off. In the resulting silence, he summoned the attention of the members of The Underground. It was pleasant to revel in their accomplishments, but there was work to do. These small acts of defiance were just the first step.

3.

"HAVE YOU HEARD what the radio's saying?" Mayor Adams thundered.

Pierre cringed. Mayor Adams was in one his moods. They were happening more and more frequently. Just this morning, Pierre brought him his coffee and Adams nearly flung it back in his face after the first sip. ("You know how important it is for me to focus right now. Why bring me this watered-down filth?") The coffee was the same as always, of course.

"I have, sir," Pierre said now.

"So has everyone else. What in Baikal's name am I supposed to do?" Pierre fumbled for an answer.

Fortunately, at just that moment, there was a knock on the door. Pierre hurried to answer it.

"What now?" Mayor Adams complained.

Pierre opened the door to reveal General Schmidt standing in strict military posture.

"You!" Mayor Adams said. "What new failure do you have for me today?"

Pierre quietly left now that Mayor Adams's attention was no longer focused on him.

"It's Friday, sir," General Schmidt stammered.

Mayor Adams looked at him with blank disgust.

"My weekly report?" Schmidt offered.

General Schmidt had heard others complain about Adams's tyrannical demands. But wasn't his demandingness precisely how he brought you to his level of greatness? General Schmidt did not want to disappoint him. Mayor Adams deserved better than that.

"What are you doing about this so-called Underground?"

"Well," Schmidt started, "We have some promising leads on the parade bombing. And we've doubled the Guardsmen at each checkpoint."

"Clearly your efforts are not enough."

General Schmidt absorbed this like a blow to the face. He looked down briefly, gathered himself, and looked back up.

"You're right, sir," he said. "I take full responsibility. Joshua City deserves better. I promise you I will get you results."

"You're going to have to," Mayor Adams said. "Remember who made you. Remember that I know who you really are. I could have exposed you, but I didn't. You owe everything to me. So give me what I want or you'll go back where you belong."

"Yes, sir," General Schmidt said. "You won't be disappointed."

Adams waved his hand, letting him know their meeting was over. General Schmidt executed a crisp half-bow, regaining some of his military composure. Thus dismissed, he left the room, closing the door softly behind him.

Finally alone, Mayor Adams looked at his desk. It was a mess. He would have to do something about that.

※ ※ ※

General Schmidt left the mayoral office in such a strident march, absorbed so utterly in his thoughts, that he did not notice Pierre's small gesture of farewell. Outside, on the bustling streets, the good citizens of Joshua City brushed by him, a few pausing to take notice of the famous hero he could not, just now, feel himself to be.

General Schmidt had to prove to Mayor Adams he had not made a mistake by appointing him as a Subminister of Internal Defense. *There has to be a solution.* His mind ran over an image of Joshua City. Over the last few months, he had stared at strategic maps so many hours each day he had every street, every alleyway, every Silverville mansion's location memorized. How many hours had he spent identifying possible targets? If he were The Underground, where would he strike? But it didn't seem as though they were trying to maximize damage precisely. They could have chosen high-population areas. Aside from the bombing at the Patriots Parade, civilian causalities had been negligible. Their motivations had to be tactical. *There has to be a pattern.* He visualized the sites of their attacks: a faktory, a military supply truck, a courthouse. Industry, military, and government.

But there was still the parade bombing. It didn't fit. They hadn't attacked another public event since then.

He stepped into his limousine.

"Home, sir?"

General Schmidt didn't answer at first. He looked around the limousine, at the nice upholstery. He thought for a moment where else he could go, what useful thing he could possibly do.

"Yes, home. I suppose."

※ ※ ※

Inside his apartment, General Schmidt went to the kitchen. He stood with the door to the cooling-cabinet open, selecting nothing. He looked around the apartment; the high ceilings made the room feel even emptier. There were no decorations on the walls. A simple desk of unvarnished Larki oak stood in the corner, nothing on it. He shut the cooling-cabinet door and walked toward the bedroom. The light from the living room cast his long shadow down the hallway. In his bedroom, he did not turn on the light. He unbuttoned his jacket from the top down, pausing between each button. When he was done, he set his jacket on the bed, precisely folded. He stood motionless in the dark.

※ ※ ※

Back in the kitchen, standing at the counter, he ate a modest steak and two potatoes. He turned a card over and over. It was not one of the usual ones. *Day-R Is Nigh*, it promised. He was washing his plate when the telefone rang. He dried the plate and set it in the rack. The telefone kept ringing. The knife was still sitting in the sink unwashed. He washed it quickly. He walked across the room and answered the fone.

"General Schmidt," he said.

"Sorry to bother you, sir," a voice said. "This is Undersekretary Litvak. We spoke before? I'm from the Ministrie of Water Resources?"

"Go on."

"Your offices had asked all Ministries to report any anomalies immediately, and I was here late . . . "

"Go on."

"The municipal water reserves are ten percent lower than expected, sir."

"For all of Joshua City? That can't be."

"No, sorry. Just for the governmental buildings."

"What does this mean?"

"It's, well, an anomaly. And I thought I should report it." There was silence. "It's probably just a cracked container."

"If it's probably just a cracked container, then why call me?"

"Well, the thing is, sir, we just checked those containers last week."

General Schmidt rested the fone against his chest.

"Sir?" the muted tinny voice came from the receiver.

He returned the fone to his ear.

"Thank you for your vigilance," General Schmidt said.

"Thank you," Litvak said. "I hope this helps."

※ ※ ※

General Schmidt sat at his desk. He pulled his map of Joshua City from the drawer. He unfolded the paper rectangles, revealing each neat quadrant. But was this the way to understand Joshua City? He stood up. Looked at it all. It told him nothing.

He went back to the kitchen and put away the dishes. This he could do. There was a *drip drip drip* from the faucet. He turned the handle tight, sealing off the flow of water. He gave one last fastidious scan of the kitchen, making sure everything was in its proper place. Before entering the Baikal Guard, he had not been interested in cleanliness and order, but since assuming the mantle of major and then general, Schmidt had become almost fixated; everything had to be exactly right, exactly where it should be. Satisfied, he turned the light off in the kitchen.

Back at the map, he stared blankly. *There is a pattern. There has to be.* What if he ignored the parade? It was their first large-scale attack, after all. Maybe they hadn't developed their technique yet, or maybe something just went wrong.

He looked around his apartment. He looked into the dark of his kitchen. He felt the absence of the dripping water. He heard it without hearing it. It would have been preferable to have the actual dripping instead of this phantom drip echoing through his mind.

He walked over to the fone. He called the man back.

"Undersekretary Litvak," the man said, formally and professionally. Schmidt decided he liked him.

"This is General Schmidt."

"Sir?"

"Those anomalies you mentioned?"

"Yes?"

"You have documentation?"

"Yes," Litvak said. "Yes, sir, I do."

"Bring them to me right now."

※ ※ ※

General Schmidt spent several days studying the documents Litvak had sent him. The amount of data was overwhelming. He consulted at length with a clerk Litvak had put at his disposal. They poured over the documents and cross-referenced them with the pattern of attacks to determine the most likely path of the water redistribution. Even then he was only able to narrow their search down to an area spanning several neighborhoods—a huge amount of ground to cover. But this was enough to start with. He made another call, this time to the Ministrie of Technology; he requested all the kamera and audio footage from their archives that had been recorded near sewer entrances.

"Sir," the technician protested. "There are sewer entrances all over the city. In fact, we don't even have data on where they are all located. We would need to consult with Water Resources."

"So do that," Schmidt said. "If it helps, you can focus on these particular areas." Schmidt rattled off several locations from his map. "But I want everything."

He hung up. He surveyed the too-small room. He bounced restlessly up and down on the balls of his feet and then, tired of that, flung himself down on the floor and began a series of kalisthenics—like he had been forced to do when he was first in Baikal Guard, like he had forced himself to do every day as a prisoner. Tendrils of pain filled his mangled fingers, but he ignored that. He relished the taut strength of his muscles, the animal feeling of being alive. He imagined the praise Mayor Adams would shower on him, how indispensible this would make him to the future of the Adams administration. One day, maybe, when Mayor Adams was weary of the burdens of authority, he would pass them on to Schmidt himself, in a bloodless transfer of power. The people would approve, of course; they would recognize all he had done for Joshua City and all he would do in the years to come. Schmidt thought about a bottle of cherry liqueur he had in his cooling-cabinet at home. He had been saving it for a special occasion.

Later, he told himself. *When I've truly earned it.*

% % %

When General Schmidt received the surveillance footage, he immediately understood that he would need help to view all of it. He put in a call to the mayor's aide and asked for an urgent meeting with Mayor Adams.

General Schmidt sat in the anteroom to Adams's office, anxious at the prospect of speaking with him, given their last conversation. At least he had good news this time, or possible good news.

The door opened and Mayor Adams emerged alongside a man in an expensive suit, someone important no doubt. Adams's face was ruddy and he was laughing.

"Well, Lauris," Mayor Adams said to the man, "I'll see you next Thursday?"

"Indeed," the man said, his voice laden with secret importance. Adams patted the man warmly on the shoulder as he left.

Turning his attention to Schmidt, "Come on in, General!"

Inside, Adams poured them both drinks. As Schmidt took his, he smelled a strong waft of liquor from Mayor Adams.

"So, have you solved all my problems yet?" Mayor Adams said with expansive good humor.

"Sir, I think I might be on track to."

"Very good then. Tell me all about it." Adams set his drink heavily on his desk.

Schmidt told him about the water shortages and about his suspicion that The Underground was responsible. "I have requested surveillance footage from sewer entrances in an area where I think the water is being redirected, the area I believe the revolutionaries are likely located."

"Excellent! I was right after all. When people told me I had made a mistake to give you this position, I assured them they were wrong. I knew you had promise none of them could see."

"Thank you," General Schmidt said. "I do not intend to disappoint you. But I need men. Quite a few of them, in fact. First to view the surveillance footage and then to conduct a search of the underground sewer system based on what we find."

"Whatever you need, General. Make it happen."

General Schmidt left happy but befuddled. For the next few days, as he organized a team to execute his new plan to find The Underground, he would be unable to forget the oddity of the meeting. He had gotten the resources he needed, and much more easily than he had expected, but he remained unsettled by Mayor Adams's change in demeanor.

% % %

This might be an enormous waste of all our time, General Schmidt thought. The dozen low-level Guardsmen he had assembled to help him view the video-kartridges were at individual video-projektor stations, awaiting instructions. It had taken hours to drag the stations to this one room.

"General Schmidt invited me here today to make sure things run smoothly," a technician from the Ministrie of Technology said. "Now, it is not my intent to insult you, but I know that unless you studied at Joshua University or have worked in the Ministrie of Technology, you might have never operated a video-projektor. But General Schmidt has impressed upon me the importance of this mission, so I am going to be as clear and thorough as possible."

The man went on to explain, point by point, how to use the machines and how to log and save salient data. He showed them how to insert the video-kartridges into the player, how to adjust the focus on the projektor-screen, how to speed up or replay the recording, and how to pause on a particular frame.

"And of course, I'll be right over there if you have any technical difficulties, watching video just like the rest of you."

"Thank you, Jaspers," General Schmidt said when the man had returned to his own video-projektor station.

To the Guardsmen, he said, "If you find anything of interest, no matter how insignificant, I want to be alerted immediately. I don't care if it looks like 'nothing.' I will be the judge of that. Understood? Then let's get started. As you can see, we have a lot of material to cover."

On a table in the center of the room were crates filled with gray video-kartridges, distinguishable only by a label identifying them by date, a range of hours, and their source kamera. There had been dozens of sewer entrances with nearby surveillance equipment in the areas Schmidt had requested. And for each of those entrances, there were hundreds of hours of footage; Schmidt had instructed the Ministrie of Technology to go back two weeks in their archives.

"We have to go through all of this?" one Guardsman asked.

"And there are three more crates on the way," General Schmidt said.

He could only hope two weeks of footage was going back far enough. He also had to trust that he was right about the areas he had identified. And of course, his whole theory could be wrong to begin with. But there were no other options; and if he was right...

※ ※ ※

For the first few hours, the excitement of such an important task carried them through. But soon enough, as happens with all repetitive activities, tedium set in. In order to maintain the morale of his men, and to show that he was not above such menial labor, General Schmidt manned his own video-projektor station. It took all his effort to focus through the glut of meaningless footage—an alley cat rummaging in a waste bin, a homeless man rummaging in the same bin, crystal-black fiends exchanging sexual favors for more of their drug, and hours of absolutely no activity which blurred together in one long montage of boredom. Several times he was called to other video-projektor stations to view more of the same type of footage. When his eyes began to ache from the glare of the projektor-screen, he decided to take a short break. He had instructed his men to do the same whenever they began to feel tired, but of course no one wanted to be the first person to do so. He hoped that his taking a break would make the men feel they had permission to do the same.

In the staff kitchen, he poured himself a large cup of coffee from the pot a sekretary had brewed. There were glazed almond cakes, but the idea of eating made him nauseous. He sipped at the black steaming fluid and enjoyed its almost scalding heat. He refilled the cup and carried it back to the video-projektor to continue his search, already imagining the acidic churning in his stomach that would come after his third or fourth cup.

He watched video-kartridge after video-kartridge. He refilled his coffee several times. His men were refilling their own cups more and more often, and taking frequent trips to the water-closet, wanting any excuse to get away from their stations for even a minute or two. He offered them words of encouragement where he could; it was Guardsmen like these, who bent unshirkingly to even the humblest of tasks, that made this city what it was.

"Sir, I think I've found something," a Guardsman named Deschai said some eight hours into their search.

General Schmidt stood stiffly. His leg had all but healed from where it had been broken by a Savage One so long ago—was it really only nine months?—but it still hurt when he sat in one position for too long. He went to the Guardsman's video-projektor, fully expecting some incidental crime: a drunken fight or someone pissing in a doorway.

Deschai fumbled a bit while backing the footage up to the proper place, his fingers trembling with nervousness or excitement. The technician started to come over to help, but Deschai got the footage to play.

A hooded figure moved down an alleyway, keeping mostly to the shadows; then, without warning, he leapt and planted his right foot against the brick wall, pushed off and planted his left foot against the wall on the opposite side of the alley; then he was back to the other wall and pushing off again; the figure was moving up the walls, toward the kamera. His movements were agile and lightning-quick, unlike Schmidt had ever seen anyone move, even the most seasoned of Guardsmen. The figure leaned back, and the hood slid slightly away from his face. In the split second before a hand came crashing down, disabling the kamera, Schmidt saw the face clearly.

Nikolas.

Now all the rest of the Guardsmen had gathered around the table, observing this footage as Deschai played it over and over. Like Schmidt, what most impressed them was Nikolas's physical prowess.

"He's not a Guardsman, that's for sure," one of them remarked.

"But where could he get that kind of training?" another responded.

Schmidt was silent for a long moment, taking in what he had seen. He waited until his emotions were under control and then he spoke slowly and deliberately.

"Very good, Private Deschai. I will make sure your direct superior officers know about the excellent work you've done here."

"What do we do now, sir?" another Guardsman asked.

Several crates of video-kartridges remained unwatched on the table. They might of course contain even more useful footage; they would have to be viewed soon enough. But for right now, General Schmidt needed to think about what to do with this new knowledge.

"That's it for the day," General Schmidt said. "We'll pick up again tomorrow when we've all got fresh eyes. I want to thank everyone for your hard work."

"And the footage I found, sir?" Deschai asked, oddly protective about the fate of his discovery.

"I will inform Mayor Adams's office."

4.

ADRIAN STOOD in line at the university dining hall. Metal warming-trays held boiled whitefish, wilted carrots, and stale bread. He went back and forth between these equally unappealing options. Perhaps he was spoiled now: all those meals of truffles and pheasant and Al-Khuziri honeyed pecans at the Kocznik mansion. He spooned a few mounds of dry unseasoned potatoes onto his plate—just enough to sustain him until supper. He filled the one small glass of water they were allowed with each meal ("war rations") and went in search of a table.

It was midday, lunchtime, and yet whole sections of the dining hall were deserted. There was no one he recognized. Where was Bertrand right now? Had he already left Joshua City? Or was there some basic training that went along with conscription? When Bertrand's conscription number was called, he spent three days drunk in his dormitory room. Adrian had visited, bringing food and tea, but Bertrand was inconsolable.

Taking the first bite of his flavorless meal, Adrian tried to imagine Bertrand loading a gun or participating in any of the grueling drills Baikal Guardsmen had to master. This was the first time conscription had taken someone he knew.

And it wasn't just the dining hall; the effects were everywhere. The classrooms were emptying out bit by bit every day. And reports of mass conscription were whispered all over the city.

Adrian was forking a lump of potato into his mouth when he heard shouts outside the dining hall, an echoing clamor of feet and voices down the stairwells and through the hallways. Adrian went to the window. Skolars were pouring into the commons from the surrounding buildings and streets. The few skolars in the dining hall abandoned their tables to join the crowd outside. Several of them carried trays and knives and large metal ladles taken from the kitchen.

Outside, Adrian asked someone at random, "What's happening?"

"Mayor Adams has gone too far," the skolar said. "We have to do something."

On the steps of the librarie, ten skolars stood in a row with their arms linked. Adrian made his way to the edge of the crowd. There were Guardsmen at the perimeters. Someone was passing out leaflets with the phrase *Day-R* written on them in big red letters; Adrian had seen this term around campus more and more lately. He brushed the leaflet aside.

A skolar joined the other ten on the steps and paced back and forth in front of them with a megafone.

"Skolars and all Joshuans," he said. "The ten young men you see before you have been conscripted to go to a war you no longer believe in. How many sons, brothers, fathers have already been stolen from our beloved city? How many?"

Adrian watched the Guardsmen move into position. They kneeled with their rifles raised. More skolars gathered noisily all around Adrian, bumping him roughly and taking up all the free space on the commons. He felt the tingles along his scalp and was taken up in the benumbed perception that usually signaled an oncoming seizure. He pushed back against the wave of skolars entering the commons, trying to get himself free, and came face-to-face with a female skolar who looked uncannily like Lydia. But no, this was an adult. *And Lydia is safe at home.*

"We are not going to sit idly by," the skolar with the megafone said, "while—"

A loud crack, and the first of the ten skolars collapsed. Then more bullets and the other nine were dead too. Their arms lay uselessly across each other. The megafone fell and the skolar ran to the bodies. The crowd rushed the Guardsmen, hitting them with anything they could—trays, bricks, books; they threw food in their faces. More shots. The protestors fell in numbers.[11]

---

[11] Author's Note: The ten skolars killed on this day would come to be known as The Joshua Ten, a moniker that became a symbol of resistance, a rallying cry for revolutionaries and sympathizers alike. Any mention of them aroused suspicion, yet still their names were whispered at the back tables of The Samovar, in The Nameless Tavern, or anywhere that likeminded people met and spoke freely.

Adrian stumbled and ran without thought, guided by an unconscious panic, leaving the roar of havoc behind him.

5.

PIERRE LOCKED UP the office, the last to leave as usual, and took the lift-box down to the ground floor of the Ministrie of Ministries. On the way down, the lift-box operator—a kindly elderly man named Saulic—made small talk about the weather ("unusually cold for this time of year, isn't it?") and other harmless subjects. Pierre nodded at the right places and made vague noises of agreement, but his mind was elsewhere. All he could think about was his impending meeting and the object he carried with him in his small black briefcase.

As recently as a few months ago, he never would have imagined himself headed to a meeting like this one. Even then, he had disagreed with some of the administration's policies—particularly those concerning what Mayor Adams described as Pierre's "proclivities." (Mayor Adams was quite aware of Pierre's preferences, but he had chosen to overlook them because Pierre was useful. Pierre knew this, but he wondered how long Mayor Adams's would condescend to ignore his activities.) But this was about more than self-interest. Mayor Adams had changed. And Pierre, who had always considered himself loyal, had been forced to make some hard decisions. He had to think about what was best for Joshua City as a whole. Mayor Adams had grown erratic, dislodged from reality at times, even. Often, while Pierre was asking him about some important issue, Adams would stare off in the direction of that closet of his. One day, against his better judgment, Pierre had taken Mayor Adams's keys while he was out of the room. He unlocked the closet and found it completely empty, just a wall of smooth black wood.

But that wasn't what decided Pierre. No, it had been Denis. Sweet idealistic Denis, who always had everyone's best interests at heart. *Naïve* Denis, Pierre might have called him when they met. But that was before the raid on a club called The Sub Rosa. The Sub Rosa was one of Denis's favorite places to spend a weekend night; he continued going there after he and Pierre had met, though Pierre begged him not to. Denis hadn't been there on the night of the raid, fortunately. But many of his friends had, and two had even been killed by Guardsmen in the ensuing violence. Denis had grown increasingly bitter after that.

"You want to have it both ways," he accused Pierre. "You wear one face in public and another in private."

"It's not ideal," Pierre said. "We both know that. But what choice do I have?"

"You're *working for* the people who did this. Don't pretend that doesn't mean something."

"So I should quit my job? And do what? I'd never get hired in this city again."

"Well, there are other options. You know, it's not just party-boys who spent time at The Sub Rosa. There are people. There's a movement."

"I don't want to hear of it," Pierre said angrily, shutting his book. They were in bed for the night. "You're putting me in a compromising position. I've always tolerated your more questionable activities. But you need to keep them away from me."

"*Tolerated my activities?* That's a laugh. What do you think I do for you? What do you think my friends say about you? 'How can you be with him?' they ask me. 'He's an agent of the enemy.' I tell them you're not like that. But sometimes I'm not so sure."

"Stop being so dramatic." Pierre rolled over in bed and turned out the light. But in the dark, and in a dozen other similar conversations that followed, some part of him, deep down, knew that Denis was right.

Pierre left his municipal-issued vehicle in the Ministrie parking lot. There was a small risk in that: the parking lot was mostly empty; someone might wonder why his car was parked there so late. But it was less risky than driving to the meeting.

He boarded a train—something he had not done in years—and sat stiffly among the passengers, clutching his briefcase, hoping that no one recognized him and that he wouldn't have to answer any questions. It was mostly government clerks at this hour, a few office secretaries. He had readymade excuses should he have to speak to anyone (drinks with an old friend, easier and safer not to drive), but he preferred not to use them.

The ride passed without incident, though the passengers did become of a more questionable type as he drew toward his destination. An old drunk sat next to him, holding his head and moaning. Pierre scooted down his bench; the man reeked. And then there were the train-dogs. Wasn't that problem supposed to be taken care of? Pierre had attended speech after speech where someone had asked about them. Mayor Adams always assured his interlocutor that steps were being taken.

Who is the naïve one here? he thought, in a voice that was not quite his and not quite Denis's. *You knew this city was a wreck. You just didn't want to see it.*

He exited the train at the New Jerusalem stop. Prostitutes from the Lesser Six, garbage everywhere. On the wall of the train platform someone had scrawled the words *Day-R* in blood red. He hurried down a series of streets and alleys, following the directions he had memorized so as not to write them down.

He stopped before a storefront matching the description he had been given: a tin awning on wooden poles. No name on the door. *The Nameless Tavern.* The door was locked, but that too was expected. He knocked four times, two quick taps and then two slow ones, as instructed. Silence. Then a series of locks being turned; the door opened a cautious crack.

"Pierre Kabot."

The door opened just wide enough for him to step inside.

※ ※ ※

Inside the tavern, Pierre scanned the room as casually as he could manage. On his second sweep, a hunched man at the bar nodded at him, stood fully upright on the stool's crossbar and nimbly hopped to the ground with something almost resembling a bow. The man was clear-

ly enjoying the situation. He motioned—now all subtlety and subterfuge—toward a table in the back of the tavern, and Pierre joined him
there. The corner was heavily shadowed and blocked by a thick wooden
support pillar.

"Pierre, I assume?" the man said in a quiet voice devoid of his previous showiness.

"Yes. Nikolas?"

"That is correct. Would you like a drink?"

"No, let's get to business," Pierre said. "I am risking everything to
meet you. The less time I am here, the better."

"Agreed," this Nikolas character said with an ambiguity of meaning
Pierre did not appreciate.

"Did you bring what you promised?"

The arrangement was for Pierre to bring a Kocznik circuit board,
which had been installed in every train—part of the new initiative to
automate Joshua City's rail system[12]—along with the blueprints for the
circuit board for this Underground that Denis spoke so highly of. But
Pierre had underestimated Mayor Adams's ever-increasing paranoia. It
was easy enough to get his hands on one of the circuit boards, since they
were being mass-produced for immediate installation in all the trains
(over half were already equipped), but the blueprints had been split up
between three Ministries—the Ministrie of Transport, the Ministrie of
Technology, and the Ministrie of Ministries. Pierre had access to the
Ministrie of Ministries, but he had been unable to obtain the blueprints
from the other ministries without drawing suspicion.

"As best I could," Pierre said, and from his briefcase removed a pack-

---

[12] Author's Note: The reader will, of course, remember glimpsing this circuit board on the night
that Jürgen Moritz paid Abraham an unexpected and disturbing visit. At that time, the circuit
board was little more than a prototype. It was, however, developed enough that Abraham—
needing something to preserve his good standing with the Adams administration—was able to
hand it off to another skilled engineer, along with detailed instructions for its completion and
implementation. That engineer, of course, has a story and a name. But that, as they say, is best
left for another time.

age that might have held nothing more threatening than a university textbook. He slid it across the table.

"What does that mean?"

"It means you have your circuit board, as agreed, but I could only retrieve one third of the blueprint."

The man across from Pierre stared at him with the fierce eyes of a soldier but also the careful scrutiny of a scientist. *He's trying to determine if I am lying.*

"I assure you," Pierre said, "they will hang me just the same for this amount of treason. Mayor Adams is not known for his forgiveness or benevolence."

"And what I am supposed to do with this then?"

"You have the full circuit board and a third of the explanation of how it was designed. Surely you can deduce the rest?"

Nikolas slid the package into his rucksack. "If you've made some kind of deal... if any of my people are hurt because something you've arranged, I promise you, your death will be spectacular."

Pierre did not doubt for a second that this reptilian beast of a man would follow through on his promise where Pierre had failed in his. But he had dealt with ambassadors and water-barons, men of great power and cruelty, and was not going to be cowed by this man. "Then I sincerely hope some accident does not befall your people. I would hate to die because you misinterpreted such an event."

Nikolas rose and walked out of the tavern without another word. Pierre wanted to do the same, but he found that he had a need for a drink he couldn't ignore. He ordered one shot of almost passable vodka (the best this desert cave of an establishment had), drank it slowly, and left. He would meet Denis and tell him it was done.

※ ※ ※

Nikolas was all but certain that Stefan's connection had given him the means to get everything The Underground would need. Between Slug's savant capabilities and a few of the advanced engineering skolars at

Joshua University he now had contacts with, the circuit board and the incomplete blueprint should be more than enough. But he couldn't let Pierre know that. Never let an outsider know your plan and never let them think they've given you enough.

The pleasant heft of the package in his rucksack already felt like victory.

When he entered The Underground, there was commotion everywhere. *Something has happened.* Mouse ran up to him, barely able to enunciate her words.

"Oh Nikolas," she began. "You have to, just have to see what Elias has done."

He followed her down the hall to a room with a large cage with bars of interlocking steel. They used this cage to store valuable goods, but also to house someone they did not want leaving The Underground. It had happened only twice before—once a suspected informant, and another time a low-level government agent who had caught them robbing a municipal building. They had kept the government agent for three days, hoping to extract useful information. Eventually they released him, driving him to a distant part of the city and dropping him off battered and disoriented. He had been blindfolded when they took him into custody and so there was little he could tell anyone that would be harmful.

The informant had not been so lucky.

Huddled in the back corner of the cage, in a torn and dirty dress, was Lydia Kocznik. Recognizing Nikolas, her face registered relief. She ran to the door of the cage.

"I know you," she said. "Are you going to let me out now?"

"What's the meaning of this?" Nikolas asked.

Elias shrugged. "She might prove valuable."

Now the circuit board felt like so much dead weight in his rucksack.

"We don't use such tactics, Elias. I didn't not authorize this."

"Why? Because innocents might get hurt?" Elias spat back. "You're one to talk."

Of course he was referencing the botched bombing of the Patriots Parade, and of course he was right.

"That was different. An accident. This is premeditated."

"Don't worry your tender little heart, Nikolas. The girl will come to no harm. But we need leverage."

Nikolas set his rucksack on the floor, unzipped it, and pulled out the circuit board.

"Isn't this enough?" he said. "This will allow us to control a train. Isn't that enough?"

"And what if it doesn't work? What if your precious creature can't make it work? This way we have access to the man who invented the thing. If something goes wrong, he'll be only too willing to help."

Again, Elias was right. Nikolas considered the girl, who was now back in her corner of the cage. Though clearly frightened, she was doing her best to appear brave. He understood why Adrian had become attached to her.

"Well, there's nothing we can do about it now. Keep her here until the attack is complete. We'll return her to her rightful place when everything is done."

6.

ADRIAN ENTERED the Kocznik mansion and hung up his coat in a closet in the foyer. The dark cloth swayed in front of him. He closed his eyes against the headache that had begun on the train home. He needed to lie down in his bed—needed not to think of those Joshuan skolars shot down so brutally, needed not to see their falling bodies, not to hear the resonating echo of gunshots off the librarie steps.

Agnieszka was standing on the stairwell. "Mr. Talbot," she said. "We heard the radio. You are not hurt are you?"

"No," he said. "I'm fine."

"They said some Guardsmen were attacked. And some students...We were worried...I don't understand it," Agnieszka said. "All the violence these days."

"Lydia and I have a lesson in half an hour. I really should rest, though. If you see her, could you tell her we might start a little late?"

He pressed his knuckles into his temple. He imagined a throbbing blue vein on his forehead.

"Last time I saw her she was out in the garden," Agnieszka said. "Your friends? Any of them were hurt?"

"No, none of my friends," Adrian said.

"Why do they want to upset things? I like Joshua City very much. I just don't understand such things."

"Neither do I," Adrian said. "Thanks you, Agnieszka. I'll be down in a bit."

※ ※ ※

Adrian's eyes slowly opened; his mouth was dry and he was momentarily confused about where he was. In the Kocznik mansion, where he lived now. He checked the clock; two hours had passed.

He dressed and made his sleepy way downstairs. Agnieszka was in the kitchen.

"Has Lydia been waiting?"

"You know her, Adrian. She can amuse herself without you."

Lydia wasn't in her room either. Adrian rubbed his still-aching head. He checked the garden. He called her name a few times. Was she hiding? She had done that before. It was late afternoon, and at this time of year the sun was already getting low. The estate was vast and there were any number of places she could disappear to. Once he had found her in the highest branches of a tree, another time in the gardener's shed. When he couldn't find her, he returned to Agnieszka's kitchen.

"I called for her and she didn't come."

Agnieszka turned the temperature down on the soup she was making, expecting to be gone only a few minutes, and not wanting their dinner to burn. "I should help you find her."

They went out to the garden together.

"She is always worrying me," Agnieszka said, "Such a willful child."

"I'm sure she's fine," Adrian said.

She wasn't in any of the outbuildings—not the greenhouses, not the pool house, not the garage. She wasn't on the path by the water where they sometimes did their lessons. It was growing dark now. Adrian blamed himself for being preoccupied with his own concerns—his laboratory partner, his headache, his fear of having another seizure. Agnieszka blamed herself as well. Hadn't she given the young girl too wide a berth, especially after her mother's death?

"Maybe she's back inside?" Adrian asked.

"I would have heard," Agnieszka said. "She always comes in through the same door. Near the kitchen. Where I was."

"Well, it's worth looking anyway."

"Yes," Agnieszka said. "I will look inside."

"Maybe she's with Mr. Kocznik?"

Agnieszka frowned. "Maybe."

※ ※ ※

Agnieszka and Adrian knocked. After a moment, Abraham opened the door of his study. He stood there, a mess of wires in his hand, a vague smile at some private thought on his face, assuming he was being called to dinner. Agnieszka and Adrian deferred to each other in silence. One of them finally informed him of the troublesome news, the other filling in the details. He set the wires on a table.

Behind him, the belly of the faux train engine curved down.

※ ※ ※

By nine o'eve they had to admit the obvious: Lydia was missing. They had gone through the house three times, from the wine cellar to The Infinite Hallway. They had gone back outside with a battery-powered lantern, calling her name over and over. Agnieszka and Adrian were impatient with this search, having done it already, but they went through the motions with Abraham again.

"She probably just ran away," Abraham had said to Adrian early in the search. "Children do it all the time. Why, I did it once myself." He looked for Lydia behind a row of bushes and, seeing nothing, continued, "I don't even remember what I was upset about. I packed two sandwiches and walked down to the train yard. My father always used to take me there on Saturday afternoons, so we could watch the trains come and go. Did I tell you he was a ticket-inspektor? Anyway, he wanted to be an engineer. And I guess this was his way of instilling his love of trains in me." He frowned. "It worked, obviously. So I ran down there for whatever reason. I think I planned to steal away on a train. But then it got dark and the shadows started to scare me. I couldn't have been more than eight at the time. I went back home. They hadn't even noticed I was gone."

And thinking of this story, and of his father and how these weekly visits to the train yard had shaped his interest in trains and determined, to a large extent, the rest of his life, Abraham chastised himself for not paying more attention to Lydia over the last few months. For using grief as an excuse to neglect his responsibilities. He resolved to be a better father starting as soon as they found her, which would surely be any moment now.

※ ※ ※

Later, Abraham was yelling into the telefone. Agnieszka and Adrian stood in the open door.

"No," he said. "It's *you* who don't understand. This is my daughter we're talking about. An eleven-year-old girl . . . Yes, I know that. You've told me that five times already . . . No, don't think about it. Just do it . . . All right, fine. I'll expect someone up here in, what, half an hour? Fine. But *soon* better mean just that."

He slammed down the telefone receiver. He stalked back and forth on his long thin legs.

"They said a person has to be missing for twenty-four hours before they can file a report. Can you believe that? As if there's some magical grace period where nothing bad can happen to her."

"I'm sure nothing like that has happened," Adrian said.

"They're sending someone up here. It turns out my name still counts for something."

Abraham collapsed in a chair, all his energy suddenly depleted. But just as soon, he leaned forward, staring at the heavy emptiness of his hands.

"She talks to you," he said to Adrian. "Where would she have gone?"

Adrian had asked himself that many times already. He went over every piece of data she had given him, no matter how trivial. She disliked her classmates at her old school. Except for one. What was her name? Claudette. He suggested that name to Abraham now. Abraham lit up with hope at this new possibility. Agnieszka managed to find her parents' telefone number.

Claudette's father, the famous composer, answered. Adrian listened in on Abraham's half of the conversation.

"Hello, Abraham Kocznik here. Fine, how are you? Yes, they seem to be running smoothly enough. I gave them the new circuit board. So listen, you don't happen to have my daughter there with you, do you? All right. I'll wait."

Abraham cupped the mouthpiece. "He's going to ask his wife. He's been upstairs composing and he thinks there might have been a visitor or two."

After a minute, Claudette's father returned and Abraham listened somberly. His face fell in darkening degrees. "Well, thank you for looking. What? No, I'm sure it's nothing to worry about. Thank you again."

He hung up the fone with gentle distaste, wanting nothing more to do with the uncooperative apparatus. "Nothing."

"Don't worry," Adrian said. "She'll turn up."

Agnieszka twisted and picked at the cloth of her skirt, thinking not at all of the soup that was burning downstairs.

7.

THIS TIME when General Schmidt visited his mother, he brought a dozen of his most trusted men. He would have preferred to go by himself, but there was a chance, however small, that he would find Nikolas there. Based on what General Schmidt had seen on the kamera footage, he knew arresting Nikolas would be no easy task. He did not want any physical harm to come to his brother, despite everything. He had not put out a municipal information-flyer seeking Nikolas's arrest, and he had not told the Guardsmen he brought with him what their purpose might be. There was nothing suspicious about a man in his position demanding a heavy guard, especially given the increase in violence of late.

General Schmidt ordered his men to wait outside. He entered the house without knocking. His mother was in the front room, stuffing needles, thread, and fabric into a wicker basket.

"Marcik!" she said. She set down her sewing supplies. "Sorry . . . *General*. I wasn't expecting you."

"Are you alone?"

"Alone?" She seemed not to understand the word. "Why, yes. I am always alone these days. I was just going to the market. I go there on Saturdays to sell a few things."

His mother had a booth at the market where she mended clothes for a few extra drams. General Schmidt had forgotten about that. He felt oddly ashamed to have interrupted her at so humble a task.

Nikolas wasn't in the house; she would have no reason to lie about that. Schmidt went to the window and pulled back the drapes—handsewn by his mother, of course. The material was rough and cheap, but the pattern was attractive; she was quite good at this, General Schmidt thought. Through the window, he signaled to his men to continue waiting.

"What's going on, Marcik?" his mother asked. "Is something wrong?"

"Has Nikolas been by recently?"

"You asked me that last time. Is something going on between you?"

"I don't know. Maybe." He hadn't considered this part. How much should he tell her? By protecting her innocence, wasn't he also protecting Nikolas? "I'm afraid he may be involved in something."

"Well, these days he only comes by here to give me money."

"How much money? Have you spent it?"

"Just a bit," she said, almost ashamed, "on odds and ends. He said it was for me. But mostly, I save it in case he needs it."

"Where is it?"

She waved vaguely at her bedroom. "In my jewelry box on top of the bureau. What is this all about?"

The jewelry box was so full of money that it started spilling out when he opened the lid. Wadded dram-notes, hundreds of them. He grabbed a handful and ran into the from room. He waved them at his mother.

"He gave all this to you?"

"It's like I told you, I've been saving it up."

"And where do you suppose he got it?"

"From his research grants."

"Do you have any idea how much is here?"

"I haven't counted."

"You don't need to count it," Schmidt said. How could she be so...*willfully stupid*? "This is tainted money. Look at it."

He shoved the money in her face. She turned her head and made quick little defiant shakes in the negative. She had never seen Marcik like this, so angry. She had never physically feared him as a man, the way she had sometimes feared her husband. "No, no. Not Nikolas. No."

"Yes, Mother."

He took the money between the fingers of each hand and tore downward. But it is harder than you would think to tear a stack of drams. After shredding just a few of the notes, he flung the bills away. They drifted to the floor. Neither of them picked the money up. His mother still had her head tucked protectively against one shoulder. General Schmidt touched her cheek.

"I'm sorry," he said. "But this is very important. I need you to tell me next time Nikolas comes to visit."

She lifted his hand away, pushed it gently to his side.

"Don't ask me to choose between my sons," she said. "I can't. I won't."

Schmidt saw then how it was. She would go on defending Nikolas no matter what—no matter how indefensible his actions—simply because he was her son. There was nothing Schmidt could tell her—not even the truth, that Nikolas was in some way, however peripherally, involved with The Underground, and that the security of the city might depend on Schmidt speaking with him—that would convince her to act against him. He wondered if all mothers were like this, traitors on a social level, fierce patriots of the home and hearth. But that wasn't important right now. He would find Nikolas, no matter what he had to do.

He did not kiss his mother on the cheek as he left.

CHAPTER FIVE

THE TIGHTENING THREADS

1.

"WHY DID YOU do it?"

"I don't know why I'm here."

"You know why you're here."

"All I know is you snatched me up from work."

"Is that your story?"

⫿ ⫿ ⫿

"I don't have a story," the second prisoner said.

"Where is the water going?"

⫿ ⫿ ⫿

"I don't know what you mean."

General Schmidt nodded to the interrogator. The interrogator poured some water for the prisoner.

"Thank you," the prisoner said.

"I've done you a kindness," the interrogator said. "Tell me what you know."

The prisoner took his glasses off and wiped the sweat from his forehead.

※ ※ ※

"Does that hurt?"

※ ※ ※

The blond-haired prisoner looked up from the floor, blood dripping from the split on his lip.

※ ※ ※

"Where is the water going?"

※ ※ ※

The interrogator grabbed the man's arm and twisted it brutally. "Do you understand what I can do to you?"

※ ※ ※

"Where are they?"

※ ※ ※

General Schmidt stepped forward. "Do you recognize me?"

"Yes," the first prisoner said. "You're the war hero, General Schmidt."

"Do you understand why I brought you back here?"

"I'm sorry. I don't."

"You know Joshua City is at war, don't you?"

"Yes, of course."

General Schmidt put his hand on the man's shoulder. The man shrank from his touch. "We all have to do our part in these desperate times."

※ ※ ※

"I haven't done anything."

※ ※ ※

"It's all right, citizen," the interrogator said, "you can tell me."

The interrogator loomed in, thumbing his baton.

2.

THEY LEFT the man curled on the floor, his left eye swollen shut and a large gash along his forehead. His glasses lay crushed, bits of the lenses scattered in front of him. General Schmidt and the interrogator locked the door behind them with a solid metal clunk. The man breathed heavily and dragged himself into the chair.

Back in his office, General Schmidt stood silently, his fist planted squarely on a stack of papers on his desk. The interrogator sat in a different kind of silence, awaiting orders. General Schmidt punched the desk and let out a low animal grunt.

Another failure. He had brought in over a dozen municipal water-workers, everyone who had access and the knowledge to redirect the water supply. But none of them had offered any useful intelligence. Many of them, such as this man he had just left, had been subjected to the harshest interrogation techniques he was willing to use.

"Sir?" the interrogator began, "I could always let him sweat for a while longer and then take the coffin-maker in."

General Schmidt stared at the man.

"I might not even have to use it," the interrogator said. "Just seeing that thing turns most men to jellied meat."

"What? And continue this farce?"

He dismissed the interrogator and called Miklós. "Come to my office at once."

Miklós ducked slightly as he came through the door. He stood nearly two meters tall, and his neatly pressed suit strained against his broad shoulders and thick musculature. His blunt broad face was expressionless, and many people assumed he was unintelligent. But General Schmidt knew how quick-witted he could be when it counted the most.

"Sir?"

"We're going to have to send all of them home. They're useless to us here."

"But you figure if one of them is guilty, the interrogator's little sessions would have rattled him?"

"Exactly."

"What course of action do you want to take, sir?"

"Have all of them followed."

% % %

But Nikolas had trained his operatives well. Pavel took a circuitous route from the Ministrie of Defense where they had interrogated him. He went into a small street kitchen that served greasy sandwiches and lumpy stews. He ate slowly, taking his time, hoping to spot the municipal agent he assumed was following him. He looked casually through the open doorway, but without his glasses and with his left eye swollen as it was, he saw only blurred figures. He finished his meal and paid. The owner stared at his wrecked face as he counted out his change. Pavel ignored him and walked back onto the street. He would have to lose the agent somehow.

He walked aimlessly, took a train for a few stops, and exited at random. He was unfamiliar with this part of town, but that was the point. He entered a brightly lit tavern and took a seat at the bar. The loud conversations and music hurt his aching head.

"You look like you need a strong one, friend," the barkeep said.

Pavel emptied the first drink in a gulp and pretended to enjoy it. He motioned for another. More customers were filing in and the noise was nearly unbearable. He took a breath, steeling himself, emptied the glass again, and again motioned for another.

"Friend, you need to pace yourself."

"I'm fine. Thank you for your concern," Pavel said tersely.

He ordered and drank several more. A queasy warmth rose through his chest. He reminded himself to stay focused. He had seen so many members of The Underground lose all discipline on nights of celebration. There were habits of mind Nikolas had taught all of his higher-level operatives. Pavel found what Nikolas called the *sunken center*. The noise of the room and the conflicting bodily sensations—the pain from the beatings and the seductive wash of the alcohol—became mere data.

"What happened to you?"

Pavel looked at the barkeep. It occurred to him what he had to do.

"Look at what they did to my glasses." Pavel fished the mangled frames out of his pocket and offered them as evidence.

"The streets are more violent every day," the barkeep said, commiserating.

"This didn't happen on the streets," Pavel said. "It was a much more dangerous class of criminal that did this to me. And after how many years of showing up to work and being a good citizen? Not one blemish on my record."

"Here, friend, let me stand you a drink."

Pavel held the glass precariously, swayed in his seat. "Glad to see there are still good Joshuans out there." He tilted the drink back, as much of it pouring down his chin as into his mouth.

"Those bastards at the Ministrie..." He slumped heavily, losing all animation. The barkeep leaned forward to make sure he was all right. Then suddenly collecting himself, Pavel demanded, "One more drink, *friend*."

The barkeep reluctantly poured the drink. "You take it easy here. I have to go help these other good patrons."

※ ※ ※

Miklós watched Pavel from a back corner. He sipped a beer and read a newspaper. He had ordered his men to follow the other targets. But he wanted to take this one himself. There was something about him. Miklós had learned to trust his instincts. He was, however, beginning to wonder. The man seemed not only harmless, but pathetic. He would watch a bit longer. Miklós wanted to be certain; General Schmidt's program was edging toward success; it would not do to be careless at this precarious juncture.

※ ※ ※

The barkeep handed another patron a glass. He had made the drink weak; the train-dog bastard wouldn't notice anyway. He came in every night, offered nothing as a tip, and offended all the ladies. At the other end of the bar, the bruised man was well drunk now. The poor man. You hated to refuse such a person a drink.

"Me? Me?" Pavel shouted, swiveling in his seat, addressing the entire room. "Why me? I have nothing but love for this city."

The barkeep put his hand on Pavel's shoulder. "Hey, friend, I like you. But you need to calm yourself."

"Fine, fine..." Pavel said, and put up both of his hands in acquiescence. "I'm sorry. I'm sorry. Just one more."

Normally, this was the point he would kick a patron out... but just look at him. And he had been generous with the tips. It was sad to see a man like this, but the barkeep also knew to respect his patrons' right to whatever self-destruction they were engaged in for whatever private reasons they might have.

※ ※ ※

Pavel choked the drink down. The warm queasiness was back, but he wasn't there yet.

"Please, look at my face..."

The barkeep paused.

"Just one more..." Pavel pleaded. He turned to the rest of the room. "Do you know what happened to me today? I was taken from work. A place I have worked for years. Best worker there. I was just taken. Look at my face! This is what they did to me. For no reason. Those municipal agents..." He steadied himself against the bar, looking at his hand, now alien and distant. "Those... they beat me for no reason. Look at my face..."

Several patrons were looking toward the bruised man and then to the barkeep, expecting him to put an end to this inappropriate speech.

"Friend, here, have your drink," the barkeep said, "but keep that kind of talk away from here."

The barkeep poured Pavel a drink.

Pavel looked at the half-full glass. "More," he slurred.

"All right," the barkeep said. "But you have to promise me you'll be quiet."

"On my mother's grave."

The barkeep filled the glass up to the brim. Pavel looked down into the brown fluid, hating what would happen next. This would be enough. Then he could leave.

Halfway through the drink, he gagged, spitting the liquid back into the glass. He drank it again. *Now.*

He slid off his stool and onto the floor, making little quick retching sounds. His mouth opened, his whole head trembling, as he squeezed up from the stomach and throat. He clenched his jaw. The room circled. He pushed upward and clenched. *Now. Do it.* He tightened his stomach, pushing the poison up. His bruised ribs screamed out.

‰ ‰ ‰

Miklós watched as the man he had followed all evening heaved and spasmed on the floor, a stream of bile-whitened liquor issuing from his mouth. He hoped the other men he had ordered his agents to follow were more fruitful prospects. This one, Pavel Neustadt, had been made somewhat too talkative and disrespectful by his experience of interrogation, but Miklós could hardly blame him. He would overlook some of the licentious things he had said. The man would suffer for his lack of moderation enough tomorrow morning.

Miklós grabbed his hat and left the tavern. A few patrons noticed him now and glanced his way as he left, but none dared let their eyes linger overlong on him. They did not know his real rank and circumstance, but they knew he did not belong in this place. Outside, he paused and took in the city night. This truly was the most glorious of the Seven Cities.

He hailed a taxi and told the driver to take him home. He would renew the search tomorrow.

※ ※ ※

Pavel woke to the barkeep washing his face with a cold wet towel.

"Feeling better, now, friend?"

"Huh? Where am I?"

"No longer on the floor where you collapsed, if that's what you're asking," the barkeep said.

Pavel raised himself to one elbow and looked around. He was on a cot in what must be a backroom or upstairs loft.

"What time is it?"

"I closed the tavern about an hour ago." He checked his timepiece. "Twenty past midnight."

"I must go," Pavel said. Then, as if an afterthought, "Is anyone here but us?"

"Just you and me, friend."

"Do I owe you anything?"

The barkeep seemed to consider lying. "No, you paid in full."

"I apologize sincerely for any trouble I caused you."

As Pavel made to stand up, he nearly keeled over. He was still drunk, very drunk indeed.

"You're welcome to wait it out here tonight."

"That is very kind of you," Pavel said, "but I must be on my way."

Despite the barkeep's assurance that no one else was there, and despite his relative certainty he had ditched whoever had been following him—if in fact anyone had been—Pavel took an indirect route to The Underground. He would not have anyone finding its location, especially not after all he had just gone through to make sure of its safety.

As he reached the entrance to The Underground, he checked over each shoulder to make sure the alleyway was empty. When he was certain it was, he grabbed the metal chain leading from the surface to the first guard station below. He jangled it three times in the precise way Nikolas had shown him. He shivered lightly in the night's cold and from a nervous sweat all over his body. His stomach quivered and growled. Finally, the metal grate slid aside, revealing Alarik's face.

"I must see Nikolas," Pavel whispered urgently.

Alarik looked him over, returning to his bloodshot eyes and vomit-encrusted collar.

"What is wrong?"

"Nothing, maybe," Pavel said. "But maybe everything." He began down the stairs, but Alarik did not move. "Please, I must see Nikolas immediately."

"Let him by," Nikolas's voice commanded from below.

Pavel rushed forward, taking two steps at a time on his way down. Midway, he stumbled and fell, catching himself painfully on the metal railing. He leaned, bent double and panting. Nikolas hoisted him to a standing position and guided him to a mattress in the corner. He cradled Pavel's head in his lap.

"I'm sorry," Pavel said. "I didn't want to be like this. But I had to because they were following me..."

"Who was?"

Pavel rubbed his head, confused. "I..."

"It's all right." Nikolas stroked Pavel's sweat-plastered head.

"The man," Pavel blurted out, "from the interrogation."

Nikolas's eyes went to his lieutenants, communicating his concern, before he asked, "You were interrogated? Do we have anything to worry about?"

"Not from me, Nikolas," Pavel whimpered. "I gave them nothing."

"Of course you didn't, Pavel, but what do you think they know? What did they ask you exactly?"

Pavel recounted as best he could the questions he had been asked, and when he had gone through it all once, Nikolas coaxed him through it all again several times more.

"Good," Nikolas said. "You've done exactly the right thing."

"I did?"

"Yes," Nikolas said. "Rest now. I'll bring you some water."

⁂ ⁂ ⁂

But after Pavel was asleep, Nikolas conferred with his lieutenants about what to do.

"He poses a danger to us," Elias said. "They've already interrogated him once.[13] They've seen his face. It's very possible he was followed despite all his countermeasures."

"If he was followed, we'd know about it already," Nikolas argued.

"Not necessarily. They wouldn't have one man storm in here alone. They could be preparing a raid as we speak."

"So what would you suggest we do?" Nikolas said.

"What's necessary."

"I think Elias is right," Mouse said. "We've all had to make sacrifices here."

Nikolas said, "He's done exactly as I instructed. Besides, what does it gain us? Either they know where we are or they don't."

"It prevents another interrogation," Elias said.

"He was beaten and they released him. What would another interrogation accomplish? He gave them nothing."

"So he claims," Mouse said.

"And I believe him." But even as Nikolas said the words, and though he believed them, he knew Pavel was a liability now. His face was known, and he might be vulnerable to any number of coercive ploys—they knew where his family lived, where he worked, and

---

[13] Author's Note: Careful readers will notice a discrepancy here. But before they feel a smug superiority, I would like to stress that the discrepancy is not mine but Pavel's. Even the most loyal of soldiers cannot help representing their actions in a favorable light. Pavel, despite his drunkenness, understood that being interrogated twice was a cause of greater concern than an isolated incident. And so, he omitted that detail. If a lie of omission is still a lie, charitable readers will forgive him, especially given the conversation that followed.

likely much more given the new levels of surveillance everywhere. Pavel was a capable man, but with the city's kameras appearing in more and more distrikts each day, Nikolas could not risk letting him roam the streets freely. Katyana stood in the door, offering no assistance, though Nikolas knew what she was thinking. There was no way she would allow a loyal member to be so casually disposed of.

"We won't use Pavel anymore, not publicly anyway." Nikolas said. "You are right that he has been compromised. It's too dangerous to have him in circulation. He'll stay here. Safe. Until Day-R. And he might still prove useful then."

"Our margin for error is small," Elias said. "Especially now. No one questions your motives, Nikolas, but sometimes I wonder if you possess the proper resolve."

So it had come to that then? Mouse stood beside Elias, her arms crossed defiantly. Alarik wore only a silent frown, impossible to read.

I lack resolve? Nikolas wanted to say. *Who was it that killed Brandt? Who was it that brought us all together? Who was it that trained with Messenger? Who was it that found Slug and saw his uses before anyone else? Who was it that met with the mayor's aide and got us the essential component for our plan? Whose plan is it, anyway?*

"Capturing an innocent little girl doesn't make you ready to lead a revolution," Nikolas said to Elias, for the benefit of all in the room and for anyone in the corridor who might be listening. "I know exactly what has to be done and I aim to do it."

Elias took the rebuke silently; the revolution was more important than any disagreement between him and Nikolas.

3.

THE LITTLE GIRL had no one to play with. Slug remembered when he was little and had no one to play with. The other children pushed him and laughed and he fell in the mud. He ran home and his mother took him on her lap and rocked him and made bird noises. "My little Slug," she said and he fell asleep. He had a different name then but that was what she called him.

He had a present for the girl. Found it on the street. It was all dirty, but he brushed it clean and took it down to her cage. No one saw him. She was sitting sad. When she saw him, she got smaller at the back of the cage.

He held out the doll. It was a girl-doll, with a dress like hers. "See?" he said. "For you."

He waved the doll back and forth, made it dance. Its hair was long and red. The girl took a step forward, another, stopped. He waved the doll. Another step. She came to the door of the cage. He squeezed his hand through the bars. She touched the doll.

"Friend," he said.

He let go of the doll and it dropped on the floor of the cage. She snatched it up and hopped back. She looked at the doll and then to him with her wet sad face. She came closer again.

"Thank you," she said.

"Welcome," he said. Then leaning closer, his mouth nearly touching the metal of the cage, he whispered, "Don't tell Nikolas."

She shook her head. "I won't. I promise."

Slug spun around once happily. "My name is Slug! My mother called me Slug. My other name is Robert. No one knows that but you. Call me Slug."

"My name is Lydia. Very nice to meet you, Slug."

"Goodbye!" he said.

And Slug-Robert disappeared down the hallway in lunging hops.

4.

GENERAL SCHMIDT'S MEN crawled through the sewers of Joshua City, looking for something—none of them knew precisely what—"any evidence of suspicious persons or activities," they had been told. They waded through muck and murk, through twists and turns, through tunnels coated in slime and algae blooms, their legs sunk in filth and human waste, their protective uniforms growing heavy and wet. They saw rats and lizards and other slinking shadows. They cursed their luck, being on this detail; and under their breath, never to each other, never out loud, they cursed Mayor Adams and General Schmidt and the city itself, its teeming walls that produced so much subterranean grime and shit. They took back these curses as soon as they were uttered. They were good Guardsmen. (Though there were also men among them with different loyalties to a different leader.) They did their duty. They rooted, they burrowed, they sniffed. They waved their battery-powered lanterns down tighter and tighter passages. They opened metal grates, turned the latches on pressure-operated doors. They noted evidence of human life: cheap wine bottles, scraps of newspaper, old blankets, boxes erected like tents. They logged the data and at the end of the day, reported it dutifully, imagining it amounted to nothing. They each told themselves that they would be the one, that they would find these traitors in their low dirty hiding place, and that they would receive the glory, the promotion, all the attendant rewards. It would be a story to tell their children, their wives, their girlfriends, their jealous drinking companions. Until then, they searched. The sewers were extensive but didn't go on forever.

Each day, as they came back to General Schmidt empty-handed, he instructed them to widen their search. He had to be getting close now. Logic dictated it, but it was more than that: he could feel it in some elemental place that connected him to this Underground he had been chasing for so many months. It was odd, but he had come to think of these traitors—these men and women he loathed, who represented everything he hated—almost like an old friend. He both wanted desperately to catch them and feared that day. He hoped Nikolas would not be among them, that the surveillance footage showing him punching the kamera had been about something else entirely. He had told no one about the footage, deciding it was inconsequential to his final goal. (The Guardsmen had searched the area near where Nikolas had punched the kamera and had found nothing. This was not surprising. Nikolas would never have allowed himself to be caught on film so near the location of the The Underground—a fact which had occurred to Schmidt, and which, though he did not consciously admit it to himself, on some level made him proud of his brother.) And yet, he knew from that same elemental place that Nikolas was one of them. He only hoped that when he arrested them all, Nikolas would be elsewhere. Or that his crimes would turn out to be minor. If not for his own sake, then for that of their shared history. And for their mother, who surely deserved to be spared such heartbreak.

But being a loyal Guardsman and Joshuan citizen, General Schmidt put all these feelings aside and ordered an ever-widening search. And Mayor Adams, desperately needing this victory, supplied him with yet more men.

%% %% %%

Mayor Adams's new policy of conscription had lowered his approval ratings drastically. Parents did not like having their sons torn from their homes; skolars did not want their studies interrupted; workers did not like the prospect of losing their jobs while away, and their employers looked with distaste at the cost of training replacements. But Mayor Adams believed that when the war was won, he would have the adoration of the entire city, as was his rightful destiny. He could not, however, have predicted that among the few who supported conscription was Nikolas Kovalski. When members of The Underground or fellow travelers with The Underground received orders to report to the Baikal Guard for their compulsory service, Nikolas told them to accept happily and quickly. He would have men among the Guard, perhaps his most valuable asset in the coming battle. Mayor Adams was unaware of the gift he had given his greatest enemy and went about his plans blissfully ignorant of being the architect of his own undoing.

At precisely this moment—on the other side of the city, beneath its streets—Nikolas and his lieutenants were receiving a report from a recently conscripted private in the Baikal Guard.

"Our search is still a safe distance away from The Underground, sir. Your plan to shunt the water through a complex series of pipes has led the search teams down many false tunnels. So there is still time, but they will find us eventually."

"How long?" Nikolas demanded.

"Impossible to say, sir. For now they are spread out in the wrong directions. But I should say it's a matter of weeks. Less even."

"Thank you, komrade," Nikolas said, frowning at these new developments. He had known that General Schmidt's men were closing in, but he had hoped they would have more time.

"What does this do for our plans?" Elias said.

"Should we prepare to evacuate our domiciles?" Alarik asked.

Katya was the only one who heard the note of sadness in Alarik's voice. He had put so much into his home.

Nikolas asked, "Elias, are all the pieces in place?"

"They will be."

"And, Alarik, your men?"

"Awaiting the order."

"So we'll simply have to act faster, then," Nikolas said. "Day-R has never had a specific date. We deliberately planned it that way."

Katya interjected, "Actually, this could work out perfectly. The anniversary of the declaration of war with Ulan-Ude will be soon."

Nikolas motioned her to go on.

"You know Mayor Adams, with his flare for public events, will have to do something to commemorate that. And I imagine he will want it at The Hub, for practical and symbolic reasons."

"Excellent. That's when we'll strike," Nikolas said, "and I'll start finding escape routes." Nikolas wrapped his arms around Katya and Alarik and pulled them into a reassuring embrace. "General Schmidt hasn't hindered anything, komrades. We're still going forward exactly as we planned. He's simply made our action all the more urgent."

※ ※ ※

The following day, Nikolas scouted secondary locations for The Underground. They would not be able to replace the infrastructure they had so laboriously and lovingly created, but there would be no need for new domiciles if everything went according to plan. They simply needed a provisional space to hide if General Schmidt's troops got too close. And many of the members of The Underground still had homes aboveground where they could stay temporarily. The slick whoosh of fluids (he did not allow himself to think what they were) in the pipes overhead had a calming effect as he went tunnel to tunnel, seeking out a suitable location for those who had nowhere else to go. He turned a corner and encountered a reckless geometry of spider webs. As he brushed them aside, he felt some sympathy for the creatures whose work he had dismantled so effortlessly.

Nearly a kilometer away from The Underground, Nikolas found several grates covering holes in the wall. What the original designer had meant these for, he had no idea. He kicked one forcefully and it flew free from its concrete casing. He stepped inside what he now realized had once been a control center for the flow of sewage, but which must have been decommissioned many years (decades?) ago. What was more, this control room opened on other smaller rooms beyond it, even less visible and accessible from the main tunnel. This was perfect, he decided. Like some flawlessly constructed machine, everything was tightening and ratcheting into place. It was hard to believe: after so many months of planning, of training, of rigid self-discipline and abnegation, Day-R was becoming a reality.

5.

From the Journals of Nikolas Kovalski:

THE DAY has nearly arrived; I thought I should document it somehow. It's hard to believe that it's been months since my last journal entry. But I've had more important things to do than to scribble down my every waking thought. In fact, looking back over some of my earlier entries, I am somewhat embarrassed—not just by the floridness of my prose, but by what I thought worth preserving. Ah, youth! (I say that only somewhat ironically...Many of my words and sentiments do seem penned by the hand of an alien creature now.)

I feel I ought to say something meaningful here. But won't the true meaning be revealed by our actions, whether they succeed or fail? On an intellectual level, I know that everything is in place. We are ready. Joshua City is ready. And yet I can't help feeling that I've forgotten some crucial detail...

CHAPTER SIX

DAY-R

1.

MAYOR ADAMS entered his office early that morning. It was the anniversary of the official declaration of war—an unpopular war, a war some people were even calling a *failed war*. But Mayor Adams would not let such traitorous talk carry the day. He was going to make a speech—and it would be his most rousing speech yet. Like all great leaders, he had been blessed with the gift of oratory and would use it to lift the populace to a patriotic fervor. Once he had done that, it would be easy enough to root out and crush the dissidents.

But Mayor Adams was also prudent. He had decided not to risk the embarrassment of a paltry crowd and so had decided to address his city by radio. (Here again, Mayor Adams had unwittingly aided Nikolas, as the reader will soon find out.) He had stayed up into the middle of the night perfecting the language of what might be the most pivotal speech of his career. He must offer a solid presence, a reassuring voice Joshuans could rally around, a vision of the future that would shine an obscuring light on the present. Of course he had a staff of writers for such occasions, and he had commissioned several drafts from them, though he couldn't trust his fate to the talent of others. *You must do this / You must do this / You must do this alone*, and he knew they were right.

He read over the pages, mouthing the words, hearing them intoned with historical import in his mind. He imagined listeners across the city—in New Jerusalem hovels, in Silverville mansions (Abraham Kocznik flashed quickly through his mind), in university dormitories, everywhere—at first not listening with much care, but slowly, as his rhetoric built and his argument came together like a complex machine (again Kocznik), they became rapt, could not pull themselves away from that magnetic voice speaking so reasonably, so steadily. He flipped back to the first page and started again, focusing on the words this time, not some fantasy of adoring masses. He was the epicenter, the hub; history flowed through him, and the opinion of others be damned.

There was a knock at his door and several broadcasters with portable equipment set up around his office. He needed all of the stations at once, and it must be a live broadcast if it were to be felt as an important and singular event. And it also would not have been right for him to travel to any of the stations, even though the others could channel the same broadcast. No, they must all come to him. And, though he did not admit it to himself, the familiar surroundings of power his office provided were a comfort to Mayor Adams just now, when he needed so badly for the tide of events to turn in his favor.

2.

ACROSS THE CITY, on the bluffs overlooking the water, an important wedding was underway. The son of a minister was marrying the daughter of a water-baron. In itself, this was not an uncommon event; power weds power, and thus power is perpetuated. But the Groom's father was not just any minister: he was the Minister of Defense, the most powerful man in the city after Mayor Adams. Under Mayor Adams's direction, he kommanded the entire Baikal Guard. Once his son was united with the water-baron's daughter, his family would possess a significant portion of the most valuable resource in Baikal. And in return, the water-baron would receive the protection of the most powerful army in the Seven Cities.

For all the obvious symbolic reasons, they had chosen the anniversary of the war as the wedding day. The war had made both their families richer and more powerful than ever. This was simply the next step.

The Groom was handsome and nervous in his broad-shouldered suit, his boyish face shaved of what little hair it could grow. The Bride was tall and elegant, a beautiful baikal-white swan. They were everything a modern Joshuan couple should be. The parents looked on proudly, venially, dreaming of their mutually assured futures. The sun was glistening on the water, which seemed to everyone there an auspicious sign. Rain might have been even more auspicious, given the presence of the water-baron, but it would have been decidedly less convenient for this outdoor wedding. A canopy covered the altar where the couple would be married; its white edges flapped like the sail of a swift-moving boat. The guests sat in rows of white chairs in the sun. It was early in the morning and still a bit cold and the women shivered in their dresses.

The priest spoke. "Marriage is like water," he said. "It is pure, natural, necessary to life. And a married couple should be joined as thoroughly as water is joined to itself, as thoroughly as rain dissolves itself in a lake, as thoroughly as the Selenga River merges with the Baikal Sea. And so it should be for these two young people here before us today. They should merge their lives, souls, and hearts into one, until it impossible to say where one begins and the other ends."

Standing across from the Bride on the altar, the Groom did not feel that he was a body of water joining another. He felt that he was drowning in circumstances beyond his control. His wife was beautiful, of that there could be no doubt. But she was also cold, and he did not love her. Over the last few years, since he had come of age, the Groom had developed the reputation as something of a rake. His father had, if not exactly encouraged this behavior, at least not prevented it. He believed it was good for a young man to get the lust out of his system. In the process, though, the Groom had fallen in love. Quite accidentally, and with a woman of unacceptable background. He had been to visit this woman just the night before, and she had made it quite clear that she wouldn't continue seeing him once he was married. And no amount of wheedling or lavish gifts would change her mind.

The Bride was not in fact cold, as the Groom believed. She was more nervous than he was, only concealing it better. She was still a virgin. Her father had been very strict in his efforts to keep her away from temptations; this marriage had been arranged for years and he did not want any hint of impropriety disrupting his plans. She had not been permitted to join the Dames of Joshua City or go to any society galas. She was schooled at home, by an array of female tutors. Her soon-to-be husband seemed polite enough, but she had no idea what to expect. She had heard her parents' servant girls giggling of their sexual escapades. It all sounded so violent and frightening. Did she, could she, love this man across from her? She did not know what love was. Her heart felt empty of everything but fear.

Their lives were closing in around them. It was just moments until they would be sealed in forever. The priest asked them the questions, and they said *I do I do*, and the water-bearer stepped forward with the vial of sacred water and poured a few drops on each of their heads. It ran down the Bride's veil and beaded in its lace. It ran through the Groom's hair and onto his smooth cheeks.

"May your days be pure-baikal," the priest said.

"May your days be pure-baikal," the guests said from their rows of chairs.

"You may join your lips as water joins the sea," the priest said.

And they stepped forward, into each other, and kissed. *That wasn't so bad*, he thought. *That wasn't so bad*, she thought. They stepped back, still strangers, but maybe, now that it was done, a little more determined to make the best of it.

They left the wedding together, followed by their friends and family. At the edge of the crowd was a circular drive. A limousine was waiting. As they neared it, unseen by them or anyone else in the gathering, one of the ushers kneeled as if to tie his shoe. Instead, he grabbed something from the underside of an empty seat.

He raised the gun and fired twice, both bullets meeting the Groom's chest expertly, sending him to the ground in a lifeless slump, crimson growing down the white of his expensive suit.

The Bride stared mutely at the man she would never know, never grow to love as she had just moments ago been hoping she might. The usher pulled the trigger twice more, sending the baffled Bride to the ground beside her husband, where they lay with an uncanny serenity in the perverse tableau created by this opening move in Nikolas's gambit.

3.

NIKOLAS HAD SENT Yu and Yi into the Baikyong-shi distrikt to incite the members of that community. The Baikyong-do émigrés would be unhappy, Nikolas reasoned, because many Joshuans saw them now as the enemy. And there were entire communities whose way of life had been made illegal. Stefan was reluctant to organize his fellow switchers at first, but Nikolas convinced him that since people "of his orientation" had been routed out of all official offices, and since those businesses which catered to "them" had all been raided, what else did he have to lose? And then there was Nawaz, who had been stationed in Silverville for months, building a network of beloved aktors who might be sympathetic to the cause. Yes, Nikolas's gambit spanned the entire city.

4.

THE WORKER had not wanted to get out of bed that morning. It was cold in his small apartment and blankets embraced him. But as always, he rose on sore muscles, heated up a kettle for tea, and dressed. He needed his job, such as it was. His wife worked as well, but between them they barely made enough to feed their three children. And now the littlest one was sick and there were doktor's bills. Not that the doktor had done anything useful for them. Still, you had to try.

From the bed, his wife mumbled. He thought of kissing her forehead but did not, for fear of waking her; she did not have to be up just yet. He looked in on his sleeping children, testing the cheek of the little one to make sure she was not too feverish. Then he slipped out the front door into the morning.

He rode the train to the steelworks. At the gates of the building, he looked up at its smudged façade. He was lucky to have this job. That was what his wife said. But was he? The manager worked them hard, denying them breaks and discouraging idle talk. Some of the men became so tired they dozed off and made dangerous errors. Just a few months ago, a man named Jonah had his leg crushed when the headstock fell off a lathe. It took three men to lift the headstock, and when they finally got it free there was nothing left of the leg but pulverized gore. The machine had been poorly maintained; its inspektion was months overdue. However, the whole thing might have been prevented with a lighter workload or better failsafe mechanisms.

The injured man was dismissed, unable to work any longer. He was given no compensation, nor were his medikal bills paid.

Not long after, there was the strike. The Worker had nearly walked out with the rest of them. But in the end he had stayed, cursing his cowardice. As always, they brought in outside workers—immigrants from the other cities. They had not been experienced in steelwork; and they lacked the raw physical strength for the job. That didn't matter. They were only there to scare the men into returning. And many of them did. Those who did not were fired. The immigrant workers were shipped off to break some other strike. Predictably, many of the workers blamed the immigrant labor force, not the bosses who had used them in such cynical fashion.

After that day, Guardsmen were installed in the steelworks to "prevent acts of sabotage."

The Worker entered the faktory under the careful scrutiny of these Guardsmen. He grabbed his helmet and protective goggles and went down to the faktory floor. Some of the men were already there—making casts by pouring molten steel into various molds; welding and soldering; shearing, cutting, grinding, and bending metal into the desired shape. A few of the men nodded to him as he took his place in line. His task this morning was to rivet short pieces of steel into L-shaped joints. They had been working on this project for most of the last week.

Something was different today, though. The men seemed less focused on their work. As often as they dared, they glanced at each other or at the walkway above them. Up there, behind glass doors, the manager sat in the relative cool of his office; down here the men sweated and suffered. The manager poked his head out from time to time to yell at them, to remind them of who was in charge. Then he returned to paring his nails or whatever he did all day. For this, he earned ten times their pay.

The Worker told himself to stop thinking about how he hated the manager. He focused on his work; hours passed in hypnotic repetition. He had a gun that shot rivets into thin steel beams. The steel slid smoothly along a motorized track; it was the collective responsibility of the men on the line to keep the process moving. Any hesitation threw off the rhythm. That would bring the manager.

But a few hours into their work, the beams stopped coming so fast.

"What is wrong with you?" he hissed at the man beside him.

"Nothing at all, komrade," the man said. (He used that strange new form of address—*komrade*—that the Worker had been hearing everywhere recently.) "The question is, are you ready?"

"Ready for what? Send down the next plank, damn you. You want to get our pay docked?"

But production had ceased all over the faktory. One of the other workers stood on top of a milling machine. The Worker recognized him as the man who had led a strike a few months earlier. His name was Alarik. The men in the faktory admired him; they listened to him.

"Komrades," Alarik roared. "Day-R has arrived. Join me."

Day-R. The Worker had seen that phrase plastered all over the city, had wondered what it meant. It had the flavor of prophecy, of doom and salvation. He felt a thrill go through him. He picked up his riveting gun and stepped forward into riotous confrontation with the Baikal Guard.

※ ※ ※

Alarik's men, at his signal, took up their heavy rods, their shaping hammers, sharp metal scraps that could work as blades. The workers bunched together and surrounded the Guardsmen. The Guardsmen, outnumbered, fumbled for their guns; they grabbed their radios. It was too late. A man swung a pipe and a Guardsman's head was cleaved. This was all as Alarik and Nikolas had planned, but Alarik had not been sure until this moment that it would work. It depended on the other workers, those not yet with The Underground—they had to follow the lead of him and his men. And they had: as Alarik watched, one man with a riveting gun dashed up the stairs, toward the manager's office.

Meanwhile, other workers relieved the unconscious or dead Guardsmen of their firearms, gathered more materials as weapons. Alarik went upstairs and found the manager crouching behind his desk, the Worker holding the riveting gun to his head.

"Please," the manager said. "I have children."

The Worker's eyes begged Alarik's permission. As Alarik turned away, he saw the Worker squeeze the trigger of the gun and heard the rivet enter the manager's skull. The sound was unlike any he had ever heard. He was not sorry.

Alarik exited the steelworks and joined the other workers, who had taken to the street. He breathed in the rank chemicals of the smelting process, which suddenly smelled like a strange flower he did not know the name of. All across the city, in the hell-hot foundries, in tanneries and refineries, in the mills and shipping yards and auto plants, in classrooms and mail rooms, in any place citizens toiled in large numbers for little reward, a similar moment was taking place. It had all been coordinated, down to the day, to the hour, to the minute. Men died for the cause of Day-R, shot down by Guardsmen, trampled in the chaos, but many more lived, and those who did took to the streets, to celebrate their freedom, to take what they could while they could in the name of something new.

With the invigorating fragrance of his labor in his nostrils, Alarik went forth to perform his next task.

5.

THE TIME HAD COME: The Underground was leaving The Underground. Nikolas's informants had warned him that the Guardsmen in the sewers were nearing their location, and Nikolas had given the order to relocate.

Many of the permanent residents had already left, having important business to set in motion on this day. The rest gathered their few belongings, stripped their domiciles, and said goodbye to this place that had become home. A few allowed themselves a moment of sentiment; here they had made fast friends, taken lovers, and learned to start hoping again.

A woman stood in front of the murals she had painted, admiring them one last time. Nikolas had hinted that she might receive a position in the Ministrie of Aesthetics—if he retained the various ministries as they currently existed, a subject of much vigorous debate in The Underground. How could they change society if they kept its old structures? But the hint was enough for Oriana Janusk. How else would a woman of her background rise to such a position? When she had attended the Joshua University Institute of Fine Arts, her works had been praised by the most respected professors. She had even won the Douglas Szymanski Prize for most outstanding final portfolio. But her career as an artist had never taken off as it might have. Gallery showings always came with a fee, which the privileged of Joshua City could afford without effort, but which was well beyond her means. How often had she seen the most rudimentary paintings and sculptures displayed for all to venerate, while she begged her father for a loan to enter contests? And who cared what Nikolas called it when he was in power; he would need someone to control the shape and feel of the propaganda; he would need *her*. As he had needed her before, to design the various leaflets they handed out in the city and to paint the murals here in The Underground. In fact, it was she who had designed the Day-R iconografy circulating throughout the city. Everyone (not just Nikolas) had praised her design—its sleek elegance, its marriage of artistry and utility.

Oriana stood in front her murals, knowing that, if everything went according to Nikolas's plan, this would be the last time she would ever see them. She was not a person given to self-admiration. She knew her talents and her weaknesses. Many of her fellow artists at the Institute had bought their way in, while others were skolarship apprentices like herself. One thing nearly all of them had in common was what was called *the imposter's dilemma*—the sense that they did not belong where they were and were unworthy of the calling to high art. She had seen them vacillate between emptiest arrogance and drunken self-hatred, lingering mostly nearer the latter. Her own position, she thought, was much more modest. Oriana had never expected to achieve the heights of the great painter Celan Crenshaw (who could?), but she knew she had a talent broader and richer than most of her fellow apprentices. She knew she belonged at the Institute and was meant to be doing precisely what she had always wanted to do—create. And when she had to take a job teaching the children of the privileged at Sister Nadya's Preparatory School for Girls, she did not mind it so much. It was a way to pay rent and to continue her real work.

And hadn't Nikolas given her an even better outlet for her work than any gallery could? She grew sad at the thought of never seeing these murals of hers again. In part because they were no longer merely hers. Of course she had painted them, but Nikolas had proposed themes; Alarik (more an artist than he knew) occasionally suggested an addition or an alteration (always politely and without criticism); and then, most important, was Katyana. An equal in every way to Nikolas. She had even wondered what might happen if Nikolas were killed on one of his outings and relished the thought of Katyana assuming leadership of The Underground. Not that she didn't admire and even, after a fashion, love Nikolas, but to see Katyana in full blossom would be magnificent to behold.

The murals were really quite good, Oriana thought, with no sense of arrogance or shame. There, that curvature of color. There, that exacting look of a worker. There, an homage to Katyana, though so veiled no one had remarked on it (a testament to her skill!). Yes, she would miss these works and the hours spent producing them, but she was certain there were more important works to be done in the future, a future Nikolas and Katyana would bring into existence. Oriana set her hand against the wall and ran a finger across a particularly well-rendered image of a train.

It was time to go.

When Lydia called out to her, Oriana was so taken with thoughts of the future, having sloughed off all past grievances from a life that was about to end, that she did not at first hear the child's plaintive voice.

"Teacher Janusk!" Lydia said. "Teacher Janusk!" she said again, a bit more desperately.

Oriana had known that Lydia Kocznik, a former student of hers, was being held here. She had even consulted Katyana about the matter, and was reassured that no harm would come to the girl.

"Lydia," she said, taking steps toward her former pupil despite herself. "Is everything all right? Do you need something?"

"Please, let me out of here, Teacher Janusk. Do you have the keys?"

Lydia tapped the door of her cage.

Oriana took a step back now.

"I can't do that, Lydia."

Before the incredulous slackness of the girl's face could soften her purpose, Oriana turned and walked down the corridor, heading toward the assignment she had been given for Day-R.

Behind her, Lydia collapsed to the floor of her cage and began crying silently.

※ ※ ※

One man did not leave with the rest of The Underground. His glasses had been repaired, but his face was still battered from the beating he had taken from General Schmidt's thugs. Though he had been removed from active duty for security concerns, Pavel Neustadt's loyalty had not wavered. When Nikolas had offered him this final assignment, he had accepted gladly. The chance to deal such a mortal blow to the enemy could not be ignored. If he felt any fear, Pavel did not show it. He sat on the floor of a darkened hallway, listening to the clanking of pipes. He thought about his life before The Underground; it seemed a pale imitation of his life since. He thought about his friends in The Underground and thumbed the device in his pocket.

He prayed it would work.

6.

ALL ACROSS the city, Joshuans turned on their radios to hear Mayor Adams's speech. Some remained patriots; they believed in the war. Others were merely curious. But more were angry. They no longer trusted Mayor Adams. For so long they had equated the truth of his words with his precise turns of phrase, with their emotional heft and lift. If it felt true, it must be true. Now they listened to hear his lies, and they took pride in their ability to identify those lies.

"Citizens of Joshua City," Mayor Adams began. *"This is your mayor…"*

7.

NIKOLAS AND HIS entourage arrived at the broadcast station of Radio Free Joshua—a small building of rustic brick on the edge of Joshua University's campus—and knocked on the side door. Nikolas's man ushered them in nervously. He said nothing as he led Nikolas and his men down a dingy carpeted hall and up a series of stairs. They entered the office where they would broadcast.

Softly, in the background, Mayor Adams's speech was audible. Adams's public relations team had announced that he would give this speech just a few days ago. When Nikolas heard, he grabbed Katya, kissed her on the mouth of her mask, and called her a genius.

"… have questioned the necessity of this war. Well, I call those doubt-

ers naïve or hopelessly idealistic. Our enemies depend precisely on this strain of idealism . . . "

Nikolas examined the array of instrument panels, pretending to know more about their function than he in fact did; it was important for a leader to project total competence.

"We have considered you a fellow traveler," Nikolas said to the man. "We know the constraints your broadcasts have been under in recent months. You spoke to my komrade, Elias, correct?"

"That is correct," the man said.

"And so you know what is required of you today?"

"I do."

"Then let us begin," Nikolas said.

The man set about patching wires and attaching the generator Nikolas and his men had brought with them. The station would need extra power to override the other frequencies.

"How long will this take?" Nikolas asked, made impatient by his nervousness.

"Difficult to say. Not long."

"It's important I start before Adams finishes."

The man resumed his preparations and Nikolas listened to Mayor Adams drone on.

"*. . . be fooled by their facile and fictive arguments. What is required is pragmatism, the ability to make difficult and necessary decisions. I have done this and I will continue to do this for one reason and one reason only: the strength and security of Joshua City.*"

(*He sounds weak,* Nikolas thought with satisfaction. *He shouldn't be on the radio justifying himself. Not today.*)

The man connected the last few cables and checked the microfone levels. "It should work just fine," he said.

"And it will override the broadcasts of Joshua City Radio as well?"

"If your equipment functions as you say it does."

Nikolas sat in the chair in front of the microfone. He put his finger above the button and inhaled. He knew exactly what to say.

※ ※ ※

"Citizens of Joshua City," Nikolas's voice crackled.[14] "Friends, komrades. This is Nikolas Kovalski. You do not know me, but you will have surely heard of The Underground. You know of our deeds on behalf of the people of Joshua City. You have seen how we work to bring you clean water and medikal supplies, to cure your nekrotics, to alleviate in any way we can the suffering caused by the cruel and callous policies of the Adams administration.

"Komrades, I am here to tell you it is a momentous day. No, I do not speak of the anniversary of this costly and unjust war. Yes, we should always remember this war, as a symbol of the betrayals of a corrupt administration. But let us never commemorate it. I speak instead of a phrase you may have seen plastered on walls and written on leaflets, a phrase you may have heard whispered on the streets and at your worksites. I am speaking of Day-R.

"What is Day-R? Quite simply it is the day we rise up. It is the day we take back what is rightfully ours. Too long have our doors been marked. Too long have we stood idly by. We have even aided our oppressors. It is an uncomfortable thing to admit, but you know what I say is true. Too long. But not anymore. Day-R has arrived, fellow Joshuans, komrades."

(One has to admire the possibilities of technology for liberating the bodies and minds of humankind. Without the Kocznik trains and the new circuit boards, without this radio broadcast, would Nikolas's revolution have been possible?)

"By now," Nikolas continued, "industries across the city will have been seized. Many of you have already taken to the street; many more have thrown off their shackles, have cast down their chains and said, *No*

---

[14] Author's Note: You will recall I told you Mayor Adams had yet again inadvertently aided Nikolas in his schemes. Adams's radio address caused nearly every shopkeep and municipal office to have their radios on, out of obligation if not always authentic interest in what the mayor had to say. Nikolas's message was, therefore, heard by an audience I can only estimate at twice or thrice what it would have been, had Adams not primed the airwaves for him.

more. But this is just the beginning. No longer will we allow our sons to be conscripted for a war we did not choose and do not believe in. No longer will we allow our sick and dying to be quarantined and left to die. No longer will we suffer the indignity of tainted water and hungry bellies while the rich of Silverville gorge themselves and swim in their backyard pools.

"As for Mayor Adams, his punishment will greet him soon enough. Day-R is upon us, I tell you. Leave your fear behind you and join in the future. Take to the streets—as so many already have—and usher in new age of equality and freedom and peace!"

⁂ ⁂ ⁂

All across the city, Nikolas's message resonated as Mayor Adams's had not. It resonated with the force of a truth long denied, with the thunder of moral epiphany. All across the city, skolars and young workers left their classrooms and labor stations to populate the streets. At first they went outside out of curiosity, as spectators drawn to the spectacle. But slowly, their attitudes changed; they converged at the subtle suggestion of many among them, anonymous voices who said, *This way, komrades; this way.*

8.

THE GUARDSMAN who found The Underground had only a moment to savor his victory. *Empty,* he thought, looking around the room in dismay. But it was obvious that this was the right place. This was what General Schmidt had been looking for. There was evidence of a vast community everywhere: food and blankets left behind, empty crates identified by their government markings as stolen merchandise. On the walls of a tunnel were several intricate murals, more than one of a subversive subject matter. He alerted the other the Guardsmen that their days of trudging through human shit were over.

A worried thought went through the Guardsman's head: *if they took such pains to evacuate, why did they leave all these clues behind?* He was about to mention these concerns to his kommanding officer when a man stepped out of the mouth of a darkened hall. He held one hand in the pocket of his jacket.

"Greetings," the man said. "The Underground thanks you for joining us. But I'm afraid you are too late."

"Arrest him," the kommanding officer ordered.

Half a dozen Guardsmen encircled him with guns drawn. The man removed his hand from his pocket. In it was a detonator.

Shit, the Guardsman thought.

(Sometimes our last thoughts are no more eloquent than that, but what is eloquence compared to the destructive power of sixty kilograms of explosives?)

9.

IN THE KOCZNIK MANSION, at the precise moment of the explosion, Adrian was working in his room distractedly. How could he focus on the tensile resilience of ligaments (the topic of an exam scheduled for next week) when Lydia was still missing? He read another passage (*. . . the healing process is slowed by tightening . . .*) and lost his place, started over from the beginning again.

"Mr. Talbot?" It was Agnieszka. She stood embarrassed and scared in his doorway.

"What is it?"

"The radio, Mr. Talbot," she said. "You should come hear."

※ ※ ※

The shock of recognition hit him like an electrified fist. *I invited him into this home. I am responsible.* Nikolas's voice on the radio made promises; it soared with possibilities. But Adrian knew it had to be he who kidnapped Lydia. This couldn't be a mere coincidence.

"Agnieszka, I must leave immediately."

"Where are you going?" Her voice trembled, and she stepped closer to him, as though to detain him, to prevent him from leaving her alone. "It is too dangerous!"

Adrian waved off her warning and ran upstairs to get his jacket. When he came back downstairs, Agnieszka was at the door. She pleaded with him not to go.

"Agnieszka," Adrian said, "I think I know where Lydia is."

"The person on the radio?"

"Yes, I believe so."

Agnieszka stepped aside silently.

%% %% %%

Luckily, the train into the heart of Joshua City was still running. It was packed, and everyone chattered excitedly: *Have you heard the radio? Yes, but what does it mean? I heard there are riots everywhere. Well, I'm going to see what it's all about. Are you crazy? I heard it's not safe.* Outside the window, as they drew closer to Adrian's destination, the chaos increased. There were traffic accidents; people wandered the streets, poured out the doors of faktories, clambered over the hoods of stalled autos. Guardsmen were everywhere.

He knew something was very wrong a few blocks from The Underground. A wall of smoke and ash rose from between two buildings. He forced his way through. The road was barricaded, a dozen Guardsmen holding the onlookers back.

A crater had opened in the center of the street. Ice-like floes of asphalt slanted into the ground. Above this, a building somehow still stood, half its façade gone. There was shattered glass, exposed drainpipes, an auto on fire. Guardsmen walked through the wreckage, covering their mouths. A ladder had been lowered into the crater. Two men loaded a gurney into an emergency hospital vehicle.

Adrian squeezed between the barricades. A Guardsman blocked his path.

"Sir," the Guardsman said, "this area is restricted."

"Please," Adrian said, trying to see around the Guardsman's wide body, "I have to . . . "

"This area is restricted."

Another gurney was loaded into the hospital vehicle. The victim was covered. Adrian stepped forward. The Guardsman wrenched his arm.

"Sir, if you don't leave now I'll be forced to arrest you."

"Have you seen her? A little girl?"

The Guardsman reacted with a mixture of sympathy and suspicion. He slackened his grip. "A girl, you say?"

"She's eleven years old."

"What was she doing here?"

"I . . . I'm not sure she was here."

"What are *you* doing here? Do you know something about the bombing?"

"Please," Adrian said. "I need to look."

The Guardsman shook his head. "It's too dangerous. Now I'll have to ask you to leave."

Adrian clenched his fists impotently. Even if he could break past this first Guardsman, what good would it do? There were dozens of other Guardsmen nearby. Besides, he had no reason to believe that Lydia was being kept in The Underground at the time it exploded. In fact, he needed to *not* believe that. He had to believe she was still alive. And if she was, he must find someone who could lead him to her. It was clear that none of the members of The Underground were here. And if they has been, they were already dead.

He turned his back on the uncooperative Guardsman and headed to the only other place he knew he might find Nikolas.

10.

KATYA HAD her assignment and she intended to complete it. But first there was something she needed to do. She entered The Nameless Tavern and went up the back stairs without stopping to talk. She knocked on the old man's door. No answer.

She pushed the door slowly, felt some resistance. A pile of clothes on the floor. She shoved them aside.

The stench in the room was overpowering. Her eyes took some time adjusting to the dull light coming through the soot-covered window. He was in the bed, a shriveled phantom of the man he used to be. She hated that man, but she almost pitied this one.

"Katyana?" he said. "Is that you?"

So he recognized her. That gave her pause: there was still something of him inside. But what did that change? Nothing.

"I think..." he said. He tried to sit up, fell back in frustration. "I think..."

"Hush."

"I think I've soiled myself."

She inspected the yellow and brown discoloration of the sheets. So that was the smell. Holding her breath, she leaned across the bed and opened the window. The late November air rushed in. She went to the communal washroom in the hall to wet a rag.

"Cold," he complained when she returned.

"Do you want me to help you or not?"

He flushed, as much as his colorless face would allow. She recognized how it pained him to be this helpless. She touched his forehead. *Why do I feel pity for him?* The things he had done... She turned him on his side. She lifted his fragile body and slid his pants from his legs. For a moment, she examined the naked sunken flesh there, both pale and loose, marveling that it should come to this. That the blight of time could inflict such horrors. With the wet cloth, she cleaned his genitals and backside, smearing waste from his slack skin. She considered changing the sheets, but there were no clean ones. And besides, did it matter? She had provided him his little bit of dignity, that was all.

She cupped his head and slid the pillow from under it.

He gazed up at her with unexpected lucidity. "Thank you."

"Close your eyes, Papa."

She pressed the pillow into his face. He struggled with his feeble strength, insectile legs kicking the dirty sheets. She pressed harder. Through the pillow came a muted gasp. His feet twitched and were still.

She kneeled and listened for breathing. Then she stood and straightened her clothes. On her way out she left the door open for someone to find him.

11.

AT THE NAMELESS TAVERN, none of Nikolas's hangers-on were drinking, only the regular run-down customers, but Dmitri was bartending. He seemed haggard, little remaining of his former brawny strength. Adrian recalled his wife mentioning an illness (nekrosis?). That didn't matter now.

"Where is he?" Adrian demanded.

"And who might you be asking after, boy?"

"He's taken a little girl!"

Dmitri considered this, considered Adrian's face.

"I will call the Baikal Guard," Adrian said. "I work for Abraham Kocznik, and it's his daughter they've taken."

A few customers looked up at Adrian's threat.

Dmitri considered further. "And what might you tell the Guard, if you did call?"

Adrian knew Dmitri was right. He already had his chance to tell the Guardsmen and had said nothing. Anything he could tell them would either sound ridiculous or would cast suspicion back on him. And with all the commotion in the city, it seemed unlikely—even if he could make them believe him—that any Guardsmen would abandon their current problems to find one little girl, no matter whose daughter she was.

"We have to do something," Adrian said. "I know your wife. Is she here? She'll want to help me."

"Petra is not here." [15]

But there was someone very nearby who could have helped Adrian. Dmitri knew she was there, having seen her go upstairs. Adrian did not. At that moment, she was preparing to smother her stepfather with a pillow. By the time she was finished, Adrian had already left the tavern, and so their paths never crossed. As a novelist, it is interesting to speculate about what might have happened had this meeting taken place. Would Katyana have helped Adrian by escorting him to the hiding place where Lydia was being held captive? We know, given Katyana's character, that she was likely not comfortable with Lydia's kidnapping. However, she had already delayed her Day-R assignment with this personal mission. Would she have done it again when she had reason to believe that Lydia was safe? Or would she simply have explained to Adrian how to get to the hiding place? Would she have volunteered any information at all?

But that meeting never happened, and so this is all conjecture. The reader may recall an earlier disquisition I made on the nature of coincidence. In that instance, it related to the way Leni Castorp had changed the lives of Adrian Talbot and Nikolas Kovalski without either of them realizing it. That was a coincidence that *did* occur. What about a coincidence that does not occur? Or a near-coincidence? There ought to be a term for that. The reader might protest that a near-coincidence is in fact a coincidence itself. Whatever the case, there were very real consequences of this non-meeting, which will become apparent upon further reading.

℀ ℀ ℀

Dmitri knew that Katyana was upstairs, but he did not feel it was his place to share that information. He did, however, want to help Adrian. He knew nothing about this little girl, but it sounded like a nasty piece of business—not the kind of thing he wanted to do endorse through

---

[15] Author's Note: Petra had left early that morning to play her role in the events of Day-R. She and Dmitri had agreed; they owed it to Nikolas after all he had done for them. Dmitri, not being able-bodied enough to participate, stayed behind to mind the tavern.

What Dmitri did not know was that only a few minutes earlier, Petra had been gunned down by a stray bullet. It is not clear whether the shot was fired by a Guardsman or if it was komradely fire, so to speak, from a member of The Underground. Dmitri did later learn of his wife's death, and so at least he got the satisfaction of closure. He was able to tell himself she had done some good, that they both had.

his participation in The Underground. He and Petra had wanted children, but had never been able to conceive. Now, of course, they had larger problems, but Petra still cried at nights about it, and the helpless rage he felt at those times was almost too much. It was possibly this mothering instinct that had caused her to take such a shine to Adrian. While Dmitri had lain in bed, sweating and shivering, she would check in on him and regale him with stories of what the tea-drinking young man had done or said. Adrian had even remembered Dmitri's name and asked after him, she reported. He had shown a genuine sympathy and concern over Dmitri's illness. For all these reasons, Dmitri wanted to help. But how?

He did have one piece of information. He knew that after Petra completed her part in the events of Day-R she was supposed to go to The Hub. Something large and unspecified was happening there. Nikolas Kovalski and the rest of The Underground would be there. It wasn't much to go on, but maybe it would help. Besides, the more people at The Hub the better.

‰ ‰ ‰

"And you're sure Nikolas will be there?" Adrian asked once Dmitri had told him.

"I've told you everything I know," Dmitri said. "I'm sorry there's not more I can do."

Perhaps Adrian wanted to argue, but concluded it would be useless, just as he had with the Guardsman at the sight of the explosion. Perhaps he was simply too desperate to find Lydia to spend more time pursuing a dead end. Whatever the case, he thanked Dmitri (the habits of a lifetime of politeness being ingrained) and hurried out the door. He joined the crowds heading toward The Hub. Had he stayed just moments longer, he would have seen Katyana come down the stairs and into the tavern. She crossed the room and went out into the street, heading in a different direction from Adrian, neither of them the wiser.

12.

JUST A FEW BLOCKS away, Lydia stared up at a grate in the ceiling. Through it she saw a small section of the world at street level: the day was sunny and there were loud crashes and explosions and shouting. Something was happening, but she couldn't get to it.

It was so close but so far away. The walls were smooth and slick with old moisture and there was nothing to grab. Even if she could climb up there, she would have to remove the grate. It looked heavy.

There was no other way out. Outside of her little hole, in the main room off the tunnel, were two men with guns. She couldn't see them now, but that didn't mean they weren't there.

When they had first come to move her, she had felt a surge of hope. Maybe they were taking her home? Maybe her teacher had said something to Nikolas? Even when she realized that they were simply relocating her, she continued to hope. She allowed herself to be pushed through the tunnel, rubbing her eyes and crying. Yes, she was sad. But it was also an act: she was watching, calculating.

But the men stayed close. *Protect her,* she heard a pale-haired man about Adrian's age say to the men with guns. *She's our insurance.*

A shadow moved over the grate; hands lifted the grate free. She did not know whether to shrink back or run forward.

A face, scarred and mostly toothless, stared down. It was him.

"Hello, Lydia," he said. "Where is doll?"

She rubbed her face dry. "I'm sorry. I lost it."

"It is all right. Come with me?"

He reached his hand down and she jumped to catch it. With incredible strength, he pulled her to freedom. He hugged her and clapped his hands.

"Lydia," he said. "My friend. Don't tell Nikolas."

"Where are we going?" she said.

"A ride."

13.

THE PASSENGER BOARDED. The Minister boarded. The Accountant boarded. They bumped each other and apologized at their non-offense. The train was crowded, as it always was on a Tuesday afternoon. The pneumatic doors sealed them in; the train had never so resembled a prison, never so resembled a missile rocketing down the tracks.

The Passenger took his seat, as did other passengers. The Passenger rode this same train five days a week, twice each day, completing the to-and-fro pendulum of his quotidian existence. He rode and he rode, the city's lovely lights and lovely darknesses whisking by beyond the windows he stared out mutely. Once he thought he had witnessed a murder on a train going the opposite direction, but it was moving too fast for him to be sure. He checked the papers in the following days, but no news of a murder on the train was forthcoming. The Passenger did not wish to admit it, but this came as a disappointment.

The Minister thought only of the ivory thighs of his mistress, the bai-kal-blue of her eyes, and expert movements of her tongue when she had him in her mouth. Her name, if it was her real name, was the same as a beautiful warbling bird that populated the southern cities in large num-bers. High-society women flaunted jaunty hats lined with the feathers of this poor beautiful bird. The Minister did not mind that his mistress used a false name, did not mind the money he gifted her on occasion (not in exchange for sex, of course, but out of affection for his bird-lady). He did not even mind riding the train on Tuesdays—every Tuesday—to visit her; it gave him an opportunity to see how common Joshuans traveled and made him feel more connected to the city which he truly loved as much as his wife and children, as much as he loved his mistress.

The Accountant fretted over a wealthy client's recent gambling loss-es. She would have to find a way for her client to remain solvent while her firm consolidated what money he had left and reinvested it in ways that might return him to his previous status. The Accountant was next in line for promotion to the executive board, something she had been working toward and dreaming of for over a decade. She would be the youngest woman ever to receive such an honor—and one of only three women in the history of the firm, one of the oldest in Joshua City. She fretted and fretted, chewing her lower lip until it was a ragged series of blood-swollen flaps of skin; she bit down unconsciously and cut a flap of skin free, bit down again, bringing a small dot of blood to the surface.

The Passenger was the first to notice the men with the rifles.

The Accountant saw the men next. She thought of her mother at home, safe at home. She regretted she would never receive her promotion; she regretted working so hard for it.

The Minister wondered what his wife would think. There was no reason for a Minister to be on this train; all of his earlier thoughts about being among common Joshuans and feeling connected to them were suddenly absent from his bewildered and frightened mind. After his death, she would know. She would know he was just like his father, a philanderer.

"All of you!" the first man with a rifle shouted. "Get out at the next stop!"

The second man with a rifle stood at the back of the train-car and fired two shots into the ceiling. The Passenger ducked his head and prayed he might survive this; he made many empty promises to a god he did not much believe in, bargaining for his life.

"If you want to live," the first man said, "you will all get off of this train at the next stop. And don't think of being a hero. Hero is just another word for dead today. You understand me?"

Several people nodded that, yes, they understood the man with the rifle. In the train-cars ahead and behind them, shots could be heard, and screams, and the muffled commanding voices of more men with rifles.

14.

GENERAL SCHMIDT LISTENED to the radio, a sick feeling in his gut. Nikolas had said his name several times during his speech, but even if he hadn't, General Schmidt would have recognized his voice anywhere. He had grown up in the shadow of it: that taunting superior voice. That he was the older brother, that he was the one who should feel superior, only made it worse.

How could he have underestimated Nikolas so badly? To think that Nikolas was merely a low-level member of The Underground. He had always been first in his class at everything, the best at every sport; there was no way he would relegate himself to a position of taking orders from lesser man. Had it been a kind of wishful thinking to believe his brother was not so centrally involved? The clues were all there—the money Nikolas had left for his mother, his dropping out of university and then lying about it, his thieving from the Municipal Reserves, little things he had said during his interrogation. Schmidt had made himself stop there, unwilling to think that Nikolas could have ... But wait, did this mean ... The Patriots Parade? Nikolas must have been responsible for that too.

He tried to kill me, General Schmidt realized. *And here I was, pitying him. I had him, and I let him go.*

He had been given one job, to protect the city, and he had let Nikolas—his own brother—destroy everything. It was like they were children again, and Nikolas was beating him at a game. Except this time there were human lives at stake.

General Schmidt grabbed the telefone off his desk. He wasn't going to let Nikolas win. Not this time. A man with a gravely voice, hoarse from screaming, answered.

"Major Volfgang here," the voice said.

Volfgang? Could it be? But when did he become a major?

"This is General Schmidt," Schmidt said, shaking off his momentary confusion and surprise. "I want you to—"

"Sir, thank Baikal you called," Volfgang interrupted. "It's terrible down here."

"Why? What happened?"

Volfgang informed him of new acts of sabotage. Ten military vehicles had been destroyed in a series of explosions. Luckily, there were only two casualties: a pair of Guardsmen who happened to be inspecting one of the vehicles at the time. General Schmidt listened with growing dread: without transport, it would take hours for the emergency Guardsmen to get from the training base, located near the Outer Wall, into the heart of the city. And, Volfgang informed him, an armory had been raided. Hundreds of weapons had been stolen and the perpetrators of the theft had escaped while the Guardsmen were distracted by the explosion.

"What should we do, sir?" Volfgang asked dutifully.

"How many vehicles are left?"

"Five, sir. Most are being used in the war effort."

Five. Transport for at most one hundred men. Not nearly enough.

"Bring who you can by vehicle. Send the rest by foot. Have them requisition citizen vehicles where available."

"That will take some time, sir."

"See that it doesn't."

General Schmidt hung up without waiting for a reply. He turned around and saw a Guardsman standing in the door, a grave look on his face.

"Sir?"

General Schmidt motioned for the Guardsman to enter, already preparing himself for whatever the next disaster would be.

15.

THE PASSENGERS now safely off the train, and the new circuit board installed, the hijackers gathered on the vacated station platform. Endre was among them. It had been his train, in a manner of speaking. The New Jerusalem-Silverville line—the same train where he had collected tickets for the last several years. And now... he was going to miss it, but he had no regrets. He had been a part of The Underground since its inception, and in that time he had seen and done many things he never imagined.

Today, he had held a gun for the first time in his life. He participated in the violent hijacking of government property. And that was just the start. He felt good. Brave. Alive. His former friends from university, those shut-ins who spent Saturday nights playing games of Seven

Cities, afraid of women, ignorant and defensively hostile to the larger world, wouldn't recognize him. He had changed. There had been a revolution within him to mirror the revolution growing all around him.

A revolution within me, he thought, as the train left the station at its usual pace. Its empty windows slid by. He liked the sound of the phrase. He would have to share it with his friends in The Underground when this day was done. He tried to imagine what life would be like after they had accomplished their goal. He knew this much; there would be a place for him.

No more meek little Endre Talisin Pinyak III, son and grandson of two men with the same name, undistinguished engineering skolar at Joshua University, undistinguished ticket-inspektor on the New Jerusalem-Silverville line. That man was dead; killed by the revolution.

A flickering shadow within the train. Two faces passed in one of the rear cars. What was this? As they passed, they turned and he saw: Slug and the little girl, the kidnapped daughter of Abraham Kocznik. Hadn't they cleared the train of passengers?

"We've got to stop it," he said.

The men with him looked at him without comprehension.

"Stop the train!" he yelled.

But the last car had already left the station. It was too late now. Too late to stop it this way, at least. Endre took off sprinting to tell Elias.

CHAPTER SEVEN

HUB-MOMENT

1.

THE TRAIN LEFT the station at its usual pace, and at first Lydia did not suspect that anything was wrong. She was going home. She was going to see her father and Agnieszka... and Adrian! Except, why were there no people on the train?

"Slug?" she asked. "Where are we going?"

He did not answer. She followed him through the empty cars, toward the front of the train. He was humming softly to himself, a half-audible melody of eerie joy.

"I want to go home."

"Home," he said, his voice emptied of all emotion.

He moved forward, in his own strange dream. They arrived at the front car, and Slug slid the door back. The car was stacked from floor to ceiling with long gray cylinders of thick glass. They were bound together with dull copper wires. Lydia had seen enough Silverville films—some of them her mother's—to recognize what these devices were.

"Slug?"

He walked past the stacks of explosives, uninterested in them. At the head of the car was some sort of electric panel, glowing with activity. He kneeled in front of its complex grid of wires and fuses and, face illuminated by electrical pulses, he smiled an ancient rapturous smile.

Lydia turned and ran.

2.

THE SUN was going down on Joshua City, and still the train moved at its usual pace. Endre dashed through the crowded streets, ignoring the smoke and the gunfire and the breaking of glass. Some ten minutes later, he arrived at the edge of Joshua University's campus, where Radio Free Joshua's broadcast station was located. He knew Elias and Mouse would already be there. They had been rallying skolars to join in the cause of Day-R.

The university was in a state of foment, and so it hadn't taken much, just a gentle push and the right words. Elias and Mouse had gone from building to building, interrupting classes, turning on radios to Nikolas's speech, addressing the masses gathered in the commons. Mouse wore a revealing low-cut shirt. It was not something she would have chosen; she had done it for the revolution. Men were foolish creatures, and they listened more closely to words dressed up in a pretty package. As soon as her assignment was done, she slipped into a man's work-shirt of rough flannel.

Their mission completed, they had come to the broadcast station to meet Nikolas. Together, they would go to The Hub to see the culmination of their plans. Seeing Endre arrive unexpectedly and in such a state, Elias thought, *Something's happened with the train.*

"What? What is it, Endre?" Mouse urged him on.

"The train . . ."

"What is the problem?" Elias said, already suspecting him of having mishandled the operation.

"We have to stop it. Lydia's on the train."

"Why would she be on the train?" Mouse asked.

"I don't know. I only saw her after we set the train in motion. She was with Slug."

"And you didn't check the cars first?" Elias said.

"No," Endre said. "We weren't instructed to. Besides, the men had ordered everyone off."

"Well, you clearly didn't do a good enough job."

"It's not his fault," Mouse said.

"No," Elias said soberly. "I suppose not. But this is . . . unfortunate. She's a valuable asset."

"She's a little girl!" Endre yelled.

"Yes, that too," Elias said. "All right. Thank you for telling us. I think the best course of action would be for you to go on to the last stop before The Hub. We'll need you there to get Lydia off the train."

"What are you going to do?"

"Mouse and I will wait for Nikolas."

Mouse and Elias exchanged a quick glance. Something was wrong, but Endre didn't quite know what.

"You'll stop the train?"

"I'll tell Nikolas. What he does is up to him."

"But . . ."

"Go to the last stop, Endre," Mouse said.

Endre left them there, troubled but trusting that Nikolas would stop the train. Meanwhile, the train continued at its usual pace, and the people of Joshua City moved toward The Hub as if drawn there by a magnetic force—the force of Nikolas's words or the force of the rails, or for those of my Esteemed Readers who subscribe to the theories of Doktor Laikan, the force of hub-thought. Whatever it was, the people came and kept coming.

※ ※ ※

Nikolas exited the broadcast station with two other members of The Underground. A third man had stayed behind to make sure Nikolas's radio broadcast continued to play on a loop.

Seeing Elias and Mouse there already, Nikolas felt further confidence that everything was going according to plan.

"All went well, I assume?"

"Better than we had hoped even," Elias reported.

"Komrades," he said. "This is it. This is everything we've been work-ing toward. Tomorrow, we will wake up in a new city. Are you ready?"

Yes, they assured him, they were ready to bring Day-R to completion.

3.

THERE WERE RIOTS in all quarters now—in manufacturing, in finance, in the municipal sector, in the fashion distrikts of Silverville. Guards-men were out in force; there had been countless casualties. Windows were smashed, vehicles overturned. Buildings were burning. The whole city was collapsing.

Let it burn, Abraham thought. He was in his study, listening to the radio, a drink held loosely in his hand. With each sip, he descended deeper into his drunken stupor. *Let it burn.* That same phrase kept go-ing through his head, until it no longer had meaning.

"Mr. Kocznik," a woman's voice said.

It was Agnieszka. He had always liked Agnieszka. He should tell her that.

"Mr. Kocznik," Agnieszka said. "We must lock all the doors. There are bad people in the neighborhood. They are going from house to house, breaking things and hurting people."

"Let it burn," he said aloud, but the words sounded false beyond the melancholy confines of his mind.

"Mr. Kocznik, we would be safe in your vault."

It was true. He had built a steel vault in the basement just for this purpose. You could lock yourself inside and live for a month on the food and water there. There was even a generator so you wouldn't be in the dark. He had intended it to protect Lydia in case of emergency. What use did he have for it now that she was gone?

He stood woozily. "To hell with the vault," he said. He snatched the half-full bottle off the table and lurched downstairs. Agnieszka followed him, protesting. "I need some air," he said.

"Mr. Kocznik, it is not safe out there."

But what could be safer than the chill of the early evening, than the soil of his own backyard? The grass was dead at this time of year. Barefoot, he wiggled his toes in the dirt and the raspy-dry yellow snatches of grass.

It's a strange thing, he thought. *To be alive.*

For a beautiful moment, he felt nothing but his immediate experience: the purple and peach sunset, the lengthening shadows of the lamps in his garden, the uncanny music of a solitary bird—these strange phenomena of existence. Then there were new shadows, moving over the hills, carrying clubs and bringing menace and destruction.

It was getting dark now. The train he had designed moved at its usual pace, but with a new sinister purpose. Abraham Kocznik waved a jolly hello to the men who had come to kill him.

4.

ALYOSHA'S FLOCK—many of them nekrotics he had hidden away when their doors were marked—huddled together in the back room of the small dank church he had called his temple since leaving St. Ignatius's Home for Boys. A small transistor radio played the voice of a man who claimed to be taking over the city. Alyosha wondered if this were possible, though he knew it was. The way things had been going in recent months, this outcome felt inevitable.

What role should he play in this drama? Taking the side of Mayor Adams was impossible, even if Adams represented order; it was a terrifying order that crushed the will of the people. Yet siding with a revolutionary force seemed equally immoral. How many would they kill to reach their goals? And he had read some of the pamphlets people were handing out and knew this group called The Underground was no friend of churches. But he couldn't simply do nothing. He prayed deeply, digging into the recesses of his psyche for an answer. *Human life, in all its myriad nocturnal aspects, will continue.*

Yes, that was it. Whatever happened, spiritual leaders would be needed. There was no need to trouble himself with the insignificant goings-on of governments and revolutionaries; his was the realm of the Eternal, and that was where he would put his energies.

In the corner, three nekrotics leaned together, the pustular mess of their cheeks sticking together. Alyosha kneeled before them with a small clay basin of water and a clean white rag. He dabbed at their open sores.

"You do not know it, brothers," Alyosha said, "but you are blessed."

He washed the yellow suppuration of their faces, squeezing puss and brown blood into the water, thinking how lucky he was.

5.

STANDING IN the open door of his military vehicle, General Schmidt surveyed the blockaded road. Guardsmen with riot shields and steel helmets crouched behind a wall of sandbags. There were fifty men in total—all he could spare for this particular street. Would it be enough?

He had one goal and one only: to protect The Hub. Chaos reigned in Joshua City and there were not enough Guardsmen to bring it under control—especially after losing so many men to the explosion in the sewer tunnels. He would have to ignore the outskirts of the city for now; The Hub and the ministries surrounding it had to take precedence.

A crackling came through his radio. He took it off his belt and listened.

"And we're sure that they're all shut down?" he asked when the korporal on the other end had finished speaking.

"Yes, sir," the korporal said. "We used the master circuit board to shut down the entire train system. That's the nice thing about these new circuit-boarded trains, sir. You can control them from a central location. In the old days . . . "

He cut the man off. "Very good, Korporal. Nevertheless, I'd like you and a few men of your choosing to personally account for each train."

He had assigned this particular korporal to oversee the shutdown because he had training in basic engineering. He would understand what the technician at the Ministrie of Transport was doing and would make sure it was done properly. It did worry Schmidt that this korporal was a conscripted man; if anyone was responsible for the recent acts of sabotage in the Baikal Guard, it was likely the conscripted soldiers. However, General Schmidt had no choice but to trust someone to the task. And this man had proven himself loyal and competent in his short time in the Guard.

General Schmidt returned his radio to his belt and said to the three Guardsmen with him, "It looks secure here. Let's move."

※ ※ ※

They drove from barricaded street to barricaded street, making sure the proper defenses were in place. Each time, General Schmidt grimaced at the thinness of the Guardsmen's ranks. Yet each time, he had no choice but to move on. He felt as though he was in charge of inspecting dams on the eve of a great flood. Some of the dams would surely break. He only hoped they didn't all break at once. He hoped the important ones would hold.

"Sir," one of his men said to him as they left one of the barricades and returned to their vehicle around the corner. "We have reports of fighting. A massive crowd has gathered near Checkpoint 2. They are headed this way."

"How many?"

"Hundreds, sir. Too many to count."

"Have they broken through the Checkpoint?" Schmidt asked.

"Not yet, sir. But they will."

"Tell Kaptain Hugo to—"

There was a sharp pop and the Guardsman fell to his knees. He clutched his neck where the blood spasmed out.

General Schmidt looked wildly up and down the street. He didn't see anything. "Get to cover, now!" he yelled.

He ran to the vehicle, the two remaining Guardsman flanking him. Another shot. Another man down. Out of an alley stepped a masked woman, gun raised. General Schmidt's hand slid to his side, toward his service revolver.

"Don't try it," the woman said.

The remaining Guardsman had his own gun drawn.

"Private Hysjulien," General Schmidt ordered. "Shoot to kill."

But the Guardsman pointed his gun at Schmidt. "Be careful what you demand, General."

Schmidt raised his hands in reluctant surrender. "Make it quick."

"I come on behalf of Nikolas Kovalski," the masked woman said. "We have a proposition for you."

"Who is we?"

"The Underground."

"Is that what you're calling this mass of lawless scum? You know you'll fail, don't you?"

"Brave words for a man who is outnumbered," the woman said. "In case you hadn't noticed, the people are somewhat on our side."

"What does Nikolas want?"

"He wants you to join him."

General Schmidt snorted his disgust. "Join him? Under what conditions?"

"That depends on you."

"He must know I can't possibly accept."

"Can't? Or won't?"

"Both, I suppose."

"Where has all this gotten you?" She gestured with her gun barrel at the streets around them.

Schmidt heard the shouts of an angry mob. *Not long now.*

"So you refuse?" she asked.

"Yes."

She raised her gun and took aim. "Nikolas will be sorry to hear that."

Schmidt eyes darted back and forth, looking for any way out. But Private Hysjulien kept his gun pointed at General Schmidt's temple. Schmidt felt a slackening in all his muscles and a tingling along his face and scalp. A terrified curiosity took hold of him; *so this is what it's like to die.*

The woman's attention shifted from him, to something over his shoulder. Before Schmidt could turn to see what it was, the woman had broken into a dead sprint, heading for cover behind a large portion of concrete debris about the size of two grown men. Schmidt threw himself to the ground, still not knowing what was happening.

A massive explosion shook the street. Clouds of dust and debris smothered him in a gray churning wall. He climbed to his feet—stumbled and coughed. There was smoke everywhere, leaps of orange flame. He covered his eyes with his arm and tried to find his way out. He tripped over something—a wrenched and twisted piece of metal; he felt the heat rising off it through the leg of his uniform. He saw a doorway where he might be able to take shelter.

The smoke cleared. The woman and the traitorous Guardsman were gone. So was his vehicle. Or most of it. All that remained was a smoldering metal hulk.

※ ※ ※

Katya made her hurried way from the scene of her failure. It was not integral to today's events, but either converting or eliminating Schmidt was key to Nikolas's long-term plans. And to have the plan ruined by one of their own komrades from The Underground made it even worse. At least she had seen the rocket in time to save her own life. She almost allowed herself to hope that Schmidt had been killed in the explosion, but given the distance between the exploding truck and where he stood, she thought it highly unlikely.

Disappointed in herself and the turn of events, she did the only thing left to do. She headed toward The Hub.

6.

THE TRAIN MOVED at its usual pace, closer now to its final destination. Its self-appointed konduktor stood in the front car, his shirt removed and wrapped around his head, his bare chest sweating and an absent gleam in his eye as he peered down at the circuit board. Everything was going smoothly for now, but he wanted to make absolutely sure. The last boom, he made a mistake. Bad Slug! But he wouldn't let it happen again. No-no.

The lights lit up and the train changed tracks as it was supposed to. Happy Slug! He had his train and the boom and Lydia was with him to see it. Where was Lydia? She ran away. He should get her so she didn't miss it. He had time before the train changed tracks again.

He started off down the cars.

"Lydia?" he called out. "Lydia-Lydia? You're going to miss it!"

No answer. Where was she?

※ ※ ※

Lydia was in the rearmost car, trying to open a window wide enough to squeeze through. The tracks blurred by underneath. Still, she would jump if she could just get the window open wide enough. What choice did she have?

The door slid open, and Slug's voice echoed through the car. She pressed herself against the wall of the car, behind a dirty and dark-blue seat. At her feet, the floor was smeared with the mud and soot of Joshuans' shoes; a crumbled page of *The Joshua Harbinger* was matted into a corner with the filth of the city; Slug's voice echoed on in its sad-menacing nonsense, and Lydia began to cry quietly.

"Lydia-Lydia?"

She saw his shadow on the floor. She didn't believe he wanted to hurt her. Could she make him understand what he was doing?

"You're going to miss it!"

The footsteps receded and the door slid shut. Then she was alone and she went back to pushing at the window, trying desperately to dislodge it from its frame to make space for her to crawl through. The train wobbled on a loose bit of track, and Lydia's face slapped against the cold glass of the window, bloodying her nose and making her cry even more, but she refused to give up. Blood-laced snot ran from her nose and tears streamed from her eyes, but still she pushed and pulled at the window with all the spindly strength she could muster.

7.

MAYOR ADAMS had locked his office and would admit no one. He sat at his desk with his face in his hands; his head felt like it was going to rip open. He heard the pounding on the door and ignored it. They were all against him now.

Not everyone.

We are still with you.

We love you.

Yes, *they* were still here. They shimmered above his desk. Their three faces merged as one, separated, merged again. He clutched his head and moaned.

"You," he said. "Go away."

Away? Where?

There is no away. There is only here.

And now.

Here and now.

"Leave me alone," he told them. "What have you ever done for me?"

We made you mayor.

We gave you power.

We gave you everything you wanted.

"And look at me now!" he yelled.

The knocking on the door stopped. Footsteps moved away.

Abruptly, he stood. He went to the window, attempting to take in the chaos and ruin. But from this height it looked almost peaceful, some smoke in the distance, but largely an unperturbed vista of buildings. The view, once so precious to him, was bitter poison now.

8.

ENDRE ARRIVED at the platform where Elias had sent him. He waited, sweating and quivering despite the changes his time with The Underground had wrought on him. He felt he must save Lydia; somehow it had become his true mission for the revolution. He knew many others would die during the course of Day-R, but he could not accept this death. He would be the one to stop it.

The platform was elevated, and in the distance he saw the frenzy and the tumult. Up here it was almost peaceful. There were others gathered, some hoping the trains had not all been stopped, hoping the revolution was a mere oddity for the day, not something that would change their lives permanently. Others had sensed the gravity of the day's events and wanted to be a part of them.

A bird, black and sleek, alighted on a lamp post. It cawed softly. That seemed an omen somehow. The bird ruffled its wings, gave a short circular hop, and landed on the post again.

"Go away," Endre told it.

The other people on the platform stared at him, but said nothing, likely thinking him one of the crazy people drawn out by the events of the day.

Down the track came the train's black snout. Endre approached the edge of the platform, ready for the doors to open so that he could help Lydia off. Endre liked children, though he never felt entirely comfortable around them. He would take her home himself, he decided, Nikolas be damned. He smiled at this small blasphemy.

// // //

Her hands bruised and lacerated from struggling with the window, Lydia had given up and decided she should try to convince Slug to stop the train. She made her way through the cars to the front of the train, passing once again the cylinders of explosives.

"Mr. Slug?

"Lydia-Lydia! There you are! You'll see it all now!"

Lydia wiped her face with her shirt-sleeve and forced a happy smile. "Thank you for showing me," she said, "but I don't need to see anymore."

"Do you know velocity?" Slug asked. "What it is?"

Adrian had taught her the term in one of their lessons. (She so wished Adrian was here now.) It had something to do with speed and direction.

"I think so..."

"Here. See?" Slug said and cranked a lever round. The train lurched more swiftly forward, causing Lydia to stumble against the rack of explosives lining the walls of the engine car.

The train's speed increased to seventy kilometers per hour, much faster than its usual pace.

※ ※ ※

The train whipped through the station deafeningly. Some cheered its swift going, some despaired; Endre was one who despaired. Elias must not have been able to convince Nikolas, or some other error had occurred; he guessed at what it might have been and slumped to the station's floor, feeling the revolution—which he had sacrificed so much for—was now sullied beyond cleansing.

A pack of train-dogs had gathered on the platform. They howled forlornly at the train's rattling passage, ignoring Endre for now.

※ ※ ※

On a quiet back street some five blocks away, a boy perched on a bicycle too big for him. He could not ride it yet; he was only five years old. But his father said he would teach him. His father was an important man who worked in The Hub. He worked late. He was probably there right now.

The familiar rumble of a train. The boy's mother complained about the noise; why did they have to live so close to The Hub? Why couldn't they get a proper house like the families of other ministrie workers? *We can't afford it*, the boy's father said, *not until I'm promoted.* So they lived in a ministrie apartment building near The Hub. But the boy loved the noise. He liked to play on the streets until after dark, until his mother finally found him and called him in.

The train rumbled down the tracks. It was loud. As it passed, the whole street shook. The boy laughed, delighted. Look at how fast it was going! He had never seen a train so fast. Then it was gone and silent and the boy went back to wiggling the handlebars of the bicycle, one foot on the pedal and one on the ground, pretending that he was a train flying along the tracks.

9.

AS NIKOLAS, Elias, and Mouse made their final approach toward The Hub, a small troop of Baikal Guardsmen burst from an alleyway, running nowhere in particular. Mouse fired and the first Guardsman slumped to the ground, transformed from human body to cadaverous weight on the street.

Nikolas took two deft steps, jumped, planted his a foot on the hood of a smoldering car, and launched himself into the middle of the Guardsmen. For one second that stretched to timelessness, Elias and Mouse watched as two, then three, Guardsmen were disarmed and rendered unconscious. But as Nikolas gathered their weapons and tossed two rifles to his komrades, a larger group of Guardsmen approached from a different alleyway. Elias and Mouse began firing as they ran.

Nikolas brought the butt of his rifle down on a blond Guardsman's exposed forehead, crushing the arched bone of his brow, sending fragments of skull into the man's brain. He wrapped an arm around another's helmeted head and twisted; the sickly sound of cartilage separating from vertebrae could be heard over the commotion, evaporating much of what remained of the other Guardsmen's courage. One fired at Nikolas, but in this close and crowded brawl, a quick side-step made one of the Guardsman's fellows the victim of his bullet.

Mouse and Elias split up, positioning themselves about ten meters apart in order to divide the Guardsmen's efforts. Mouse was taken up with the joy of battle, while Elias efficiently did what he must. (Whatever Elias's failings, bloodlust was not one of them.)

Several minutes later—minutes blurred by mayhem and fear and adrenaline and the desperate struggle to stay alive—Mouse saw Elias was pinned down, giving off defensive fire, taking out one of the numerous guards surrounding him. She herself was likewise pinned down, could not run to his aid, as she wanted to. Nikolas was dispatching Guardsman after Guardsman, but he didn't give a glance in Elias's direction. (Nikolas had seen Elias's situation, but he focused on the Guardsmen before him instead of running to his komrade's aid. Later he would ask himself if he could have done more. He would assure himself that he could not have, and in time he would come to believe it.)

Then Elias fell, a bullet destroying his hip. Dangerous as it was to her, Mouse exposed herself to send a burst of fire at Elias's attackers, but it served no purpose. Another bullet entered his gut; another, his right arm; another, his skull. Screaming loudly, almost like an Ulani warrior, Mouse ran at her own attackers, startling them. Her bullets landed true as Nikolas had trained her. When she looked over her shoulder, Nikolas had likewise killed his portion.

Now they heard the caterwaul of the train.

"Come on!" Nikolas yelled. "We're running out of time."

They left Elias dead and alone on an unfamiliar street. Mouse told herself they would come back for him.

※ ※ ※

"He died nobly and for the cause," Nikolas said as they ran. "I know how close you two have become..."

"None of that now," Mouse said. "Let's finish this."

The black dome of The Hub crested into view.

10.

ADRIAN HAD NOT spent much time in downtown, and even more rarely had he entered the Ministrie Distrikt. He felt more helpless now that he had arrived. At least on his way here, he had a false sense of doing something. Now, standing impotently amidst the growing chaos, his full uselessness flooded in. Without any idea what he might do with it,

Adrian picked up a stray length of pipe. It had a solid heft to it; it could sink a man's skull with a single swing.

It came to him then: he could kill Nikolas for what he had done. He could do it easily and with no regret. He squinted through the crowd— Nikolas would be here, Dmitri had told him. But where? When he found him, Adrian would go up to him with the pipe behind his back. Nikolas would greet him with his same disarming false smile. And Adrian would raise the pipe and end him. Simple as that.

A growing murmur at the edge of the crowd. Something was happening. "A train!" someone shouted. "There's a train coming!"

※ ※ ※

Pandemonium everywhere, like a vision from the *Book of the Before-Time* of demons scattering and skittering, screeching and screaming. No one knows what he or she will do under such circumstances, in extremis. You think you do, but you do not. As someone who survived the work camps, let me tell you in no uncertain terms: you do not know yourself well enough to imagine what you are capable of, what untoward hidden agendas would direct your actions, what depths of psychopathy stalk the sewers of your psyche, what angelic lifts of compassion your better elements might call forth. You do not know what you would do, just as none of these people you are about to see knew how they would react—even minute by minute on Day-R, they did not know what they would do. I beg you therefore not to judge them too harshly; remember that you might be capable of any of the following actions, no matter what kind of person you think yourself to be.

One man—whose daughter wanted to be a chemist, and for whom he had just purchased an elaborate set of beakers and harmless chemicals in the Young-Skolars series (popular among the well-to-do because it gave their children an advantage when applying for skolarships to Joshua University)—left this expensive gift unattended and ran across the station platform to where his supervisor cowered. They had both stayed late at the office, a lesser branch of a lesser ministrie, the supervisor because he wanted a promotion and his employee because his supervisor had ordered him to. When their building was evacuated, they had nowhere to go. There were no trains running (none for them anyway), and the streets were impassable. The supervisor took in the frenzied crowd, the masses that had broken through General Schmidt's blockades, with growing fear. His employee (who had no thoughts of his daughter or her future at Joshua University just now) felt fear as well, but he also felt something else. Something new.

When the supervisor looked up with recognition and hope that he might be safe now, being with someone he knew, the man began kicking him, hard, and did not stop until the supervisor was comatose (he would die a few hours later, having gone ignored in the pandemonium). This supervisor had been, previous to finding his corner to cower in, an unbending and brutal individual. He enjoyed petty power; he took one of his few pleasures in making his underlings miserable; he imagined he was strong, which was why he was in charge (or so he imagined); but he was wrong; he was weak and had gained his position of authority by chance. The man whose daughter wanted to be a chemist, left the bloodied body of his supervisor and the expensive chemistry set on the station platform, and, with a greater sense of freedom and elation than he had ever felt, went to join the revolutionary forces. He suddenly knew, with a knowledge as certain as he knew his own name, that this was what his entire life had been meant for; he would dedicate himself to the betterment of humankind by joining the revolution; he would give up his family and his job; everything was clear as pure-baikal water now.

And let us look at one more, which should prove my point sufficiently, before we move on with the main thrust of our narrative:

A teenaged boy—a young man about to become older at a moment's beckoning—saw a yet younger boy knocked to the ground and stepped on ruthlessly by the rushing feet. He tackled and shoved his way through the wall of stampeding flesh, lifted the boy by hooking one arm under him and pulling with strength he never supposed he had. He carried the younger boy to an abandoned ticket booth and sat there with him to wait out the revolution. He had no opinion about the government, as the young often do not. He did not think to blame or praise the revolution or Mayor Adams; he simply saw another Joshuan in need and did what he thought was right. No, that's not entirely correct; he did not think of it in those terms; it was pure reflex, an impulse toward kindness he had never known he possessed—he had mostly squandered his time thus far in life on frivolous entertainments—but which would now grow throughout his life. He would later join the Ministrie of Health (which would be reformed and reorganized under the new administration), hoping to help others in any way he could, his unknown impulse having grown to a conscious aspect of his personality, this moment having defined him in ways nothing in his life had previously done. But that is a story best left for another time. Now back to main plot, which I assume interests you more than my philosophical musings...

〃 〃 〃

Mayor Adams stood before his window, where he had stood hundreds of times before to take in the glory of his beloved city. It *was* glorious, wasn't it? And he had brought it to the pinnacle of greatness. Him. Mayor Adams. Jagged pain went through his head again, but he ignored it. In the distance, in the faktory distrikt, the oranges and greens of chemical fires lighted the darkening horizon with a sinister flicker.

This beautiful city had betrayed him utterly. Even Pierre was gone, having failed to show up to work today for the first time in his many years of service. Everyone had abandoned him.

Not everyone, three voices said as one.

The trains lay stalled on their tracks like the carcasses of ancient animals. See? What worth did Abraham Kocznik's vaunted genius have when a simple order from Mayor Adams's office could shut down his most prized invention? There they lay, useless, their segmented spines broken by a word.

A riotous murmur vibrated its way through the glass of Adams's perchful window. He would survive this. Nothing could prevent his destiny which had begun so many years ago.

It is all yours.   All of it.   All.

Those three voices he had carried with him since childhood, as real as his own, more real at times.

Adams walked calmly to his liquor cabinet and poured himself a drink and drank it with a further show of calm. He poured another and returned to the deteriorating vista outside his window. His attention was drawn again to the motionless trains strewn about the city; now they seemed to him like the discarded toys of a toddler grown bored with his playthings. The thought amused him.

As he looked the trains over, one of them seemed to be moving. He squinted. It was still far off and difficult to make out, but he was almost certain it was headed straight toward The Hub.

Toward him.

All of it.   All.   Still yours.

⁝ ⁝ ⁝

A high-pitched screech of metal on metal bounced between the ministrie buildings. The train came into view, going much too fast. What was it doing? The crowd around the track scattered in all directions, pushing, screaming, fighting to be clear of that barreling force of destruction.

It's going to kill us all, Adrian thought.

⁝ ⁝ ⁝

The pain in Mayor Adams's stopped. Clarity. Against the backdrop of his city, the Oracles glowed saintly and beatific. They lit up the night sky. Their smiling faces assured him of his safety, of his special providence.

Do not worry.

A massive impact shook the building from bottom to top. A piece of the ceiling fell but missed him.

We will protect you.

The building trembled, groaned. He braced himself against the desk, and stepped forward with a delighted laugh. He opened his arms, ready to be embraced. The floor fell away and Mayor Adams was weightless, arms outstretched, clutching nothing.

We will protect you

We will . . .

    . . . protect

        . . . you

           . . . We will

               . . . pro

                  t

                  e

                  c

                  t

⁂

Adrian watched as the train barreled into The Hub. The cars flew off the track, whipping around like a great tail and crashing into the walls of the building. A chain of rapid explosions, louder than any thunder, tore through the night air. The flames swept up the side of the building. The vast spiderlike dome folded in on itself, concrete piling on brick. The sound of wrenching steel and cracking concrete merged into one enormity. Vast constellations of glass shattered with brittle slicing music. Gray plumes of dust and smoke rose in the air and spread outward, roiling over the gathered crowd. The wall of dust came at him like a tidal wave, like the mouth of a giant creature, Adrian helpless to do anything but watch. And then everything was gray and choked and screaming and he could not breathe.

He knelt to the ground in prayer, and perhaps his god heard him or perhaps he was merely lucky, for he survived.

⁂

Others were not so fortunate. A pregnant woman was impaled by a flying scrap of metal. An old man was trampled by the stampeding crowds. Many others suffocated, their lungs clogged with smoke and debris. Those still in The Hub—maintenance workers, Guardsmen on security detail, a few lingering governmental employees—were killed instantly, crushed by a mountain of falling concrete and glass and steel. One entire wing of the building went toppling sideways, slicing into the onion dome of the Ministrie of Justice and decimating three courtrooms. A judge in his chambers, unable to return home in all the chaos, had his entire skeleton pulverized by an anonymous chunk of debris. The most successful female lawyer in Joshuan history was killed on a collapsing marble staircase. The list could go on indefinitely, but eventually the smoke clears and someone comes out of the ashes, mercurial and risen, to claim victory— to say, *look what I have wrought; now hear my words.*

11.

TWO MEN, united as one, stood on the ledge of a nearby building.

They watched the crowd assemble in the ruins below. The men's robed silhouettes were haloed in the sepulchral flame. A black bird landed on the shoulder of one of the men and he petted it familiarly.

"It seems this Nikolas Kovalski was the Harbinger, after all," Messenger said.

"Perhaps," Messenger said.

"Hasn't he proven it with all this?"

Messenger thought separately of Adrian Talbot, whom he had journeyed with in the Outer Provinces. Whom he, separately, had come to trust and admire.

"If he is the Harbinger, we created him," he said.

Because Messenger had started this all. It was Messenger who had poisoned the reservoirs and aquifers of Joshua City, of Baikalingrad, of Al-Khuzir. It was Messenger who had planted the seeds of dissent that led to war. It was Messenger who would bring about The Second Calamity that would usher in The New Era.

"He has risen admirably to the needs of the moment," the man with the bird said. "No man exists alone."

"Yes," Messenger had to agree. "Did I tell you I had a bird as a child?"

Of course the other man did not know this. They were not supposed to talk about their past. They were not supposed to use the word *I* in idle conversation; Messenger used the word only rarely and never referring to himself; it barely made sense and sounded strange on his lips. *Something is changing*, thought the man with the bird, his eyes reflecting the grenadine horizon. The drunken white moon was dulled by clouds of ash.

What was this new thought? *I.*

TO BE CONTINUED . . .

EPILOGUE

B UT THAT IS NOT the end of our story. No, stories do not ever end; they merely move into a new phase. It is an inherent falsehood in the work of novelists, this neat wrapping-up of all events and problems in the lives our characters. It is no different for the historian. Time does not end; Before-Time becomes After-Time becomes Now-Time; and the future will have many names as well but will merely be more unending time.

As I sit here at my desk, reflecting on the absurdly mammoth document stacked beside my typewriter, I wonder if General Schmidt knew what he was getting into when he asked me to write this novel-history. Will it please him? Or is it too long, too shapeless, too digressive? He asked me to include everything. But the moment I write THE END, I begin the process of omission. No book is infinite. It would take the rest of my lifetime and more simply to describe to you this drab little room I occupy, the grain of my desk, and the gap between the boards where I dare not set a drink lest it spill and contaminate my precious work. And so, Esteemed Reader, I choose to write TO BE CONTINUED... There is another story yet to tell, one of Nikolas Kovalski as the new mayor of Joshua City, of Adrian Talbot and the surprises and challenges awaiting him, of the Church of the Dead Girl, of a rift within Messenger, of General Schmidt himself, and many important personages you have not yet met.

But there is one more detail I must share in our current narrative. If the reader will indulge me a moment longer, I will return briefly to my personal story:

It was some weeks later that the news of the revolution finally reached ███████ [16] Laborers Kolony, where I was currently an inmate. As much as could be expected, I had adjusted to life under my new conditions. It wasn't easy for me, harder than it was for some, though perhaps easier than for others; let us say I received a normal portion of human suffering.

The reader will realize that I had made my living in letters. It had therefore been some time since I had done physical labor. We worked in a quarry some fifty meters deep, scraping the salt deposits from the walls at the bottom. The descent into the quarry was made in a rickety wooden cage lowered by hand. Here I should confess a quirk of my personality: I am morbidly afraid of heights. I did my best to accept the fact of my death with each ride up or down in this infernal contraption. Even in winter, the sun was hot, glinting off the bright white salt. The pickaxe rubbed my hands raw, chafing away the skin until they bled. At the end of the day, I was so tired and stiff I could barely move. And for dinner come evening? A thin soup, a heel of stale bread. If we were lucky the soup would have a gristly pig's joint in it. Fortunately, there was plenty of salt to season it with.

One particular evening, we had finished our day's labor and I had been lifted to the safety of ground level without incident. The sun was setting over the quarry's opposite ridge and the trucks loaded with salt were pulling away with their shipments—off to be refined, bottled, and sold in the stores of Joshua City. Odd to think—and isn't thinking itself odd?—that all our labor was demanded in order that strangers might

---

[16] Translators' Note: We are unsure why the name of this particular Laborers Kolony has been redacted. Based on Tuvim's description of salt extraction, we believe it to be located to the south of Joshua City, toward the salt flats of Kazhstan, but that description could apply to any one of a dozen such locations.

enjoy a bit more flavor in their meal. I had never thought of where salt comes from until my time in the mines. Esteemed Reader, has this question ever crossed your mind?

In this one moment, despite my circumstances, I was almost happy. I do not know why. Maybe it was the multi-hued sunset glinting on the concertina wire at the top of the prison's wall; maybe it was simply knowing that the time when I could rest was near. It occurs to me once again that perhaps the *Book of the Before-Time* is correct: perhaps the single defining trait of human beings—that which truly sets us apart from beasts—is our ability to adapt.

A prisoner came jogging back from one of the trucks. He had been helping the driver to get the tailgate closed. He whispered something to one of the other prisoners and he in turn whispered it to someone else. The murmurs spread. I stood to one side, not inquiring about the commotion. I did not have many allies here. I was viewed as something of an *intellectual*, that most distrusted person among workers.

"Tuvim," said a man I barely knew. His name was Viktor; they all seemed to be named Viktor. "Did you hear? Something's happened in Joshua City."

"What do you mean?"

"The Hub has been exploded. There's a new mayor. He's pardoned all the political prisoners within Joshua City. Some of us out here might be next."

This man, to my knowledge, was not a political prisoner. But that did not stop the naked joy from spreading across his face. I looked from him to the other prisoners, back to him, and what I saw there was like a mirror of what I felt.

I know only one horrible word to describe it: *hope.*

ABOUT THE AUTHOR

ALEKSANDR TUVIM is widely recognized as the foremost Joshua City author. Winner of the prestigious Baikal Book Prize and the Titus Short Fiction Award, he is the author of *The Doors You Mark Are Your Own* and its sequel, *The Engineer of Souls*, as well as the poetry collection *From the Dread Gospel*. Imprisoned for crimes of opinion under the Mayor Adams administration, he now enjoys his former freedom and status as a major literary figure.

ABOUT THE TRANSLATORS

OKLA ELLIOTT is currently an Illinois Distinguished Fellow at the University of Illinois, where he works in the fields of comparative literature and trauma studies. He also holds an MFA from Ohio State University. His nonfiction, poetry, short fiction, and translations have appeared in *Another Chicago Magazine*, *Harvard Review*, *Indiana Review*, *The Literary Review*, *The Los Angeles Review*, *Prairie Schooner*, *A Public Space*, and *Subtropics*, among others. He is the author *From the Crooked Timber* (short fiction, 2011), *The Cartographer's Ink* (poetry, 2014), and *Blackbirds in September: Selected Shorter Poems of Jürgen Becker* (translation, 2015).

RAUL CLEMENT lives in Urbana, IL. His fiction, nonfiction, and poetry have been published in *Blue Mesa Review*, *Coe Review*, *As It Ought to Be*, and the *Surreal South '09* anthology. He is an editor at New American Press and *Mayday Magazine*.

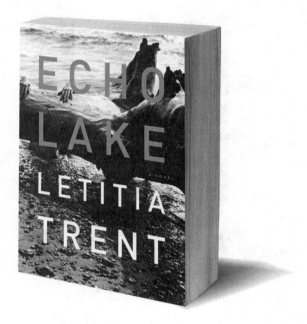

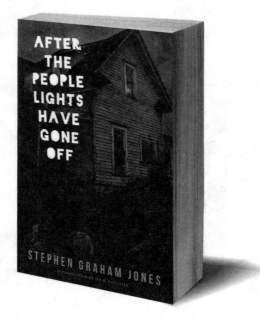